THE LIFE OF CRIME

The Life of Crime

*Detecting the History of Mysteries
and Their Creators*

MARTIN EDWARDS

COLLINS
CRIME
CLUB

COLLINS CRIME CLUB
An imprint of HarperCollins*Publishers*
1 London Bridge Street
London SE1 9GF
www.harpercollins.co.uk

HarperCollins*Publishers*
1st Floor, Watermarque Building, Ringsend Road
Dublin 4, Ireland

Published by Collins Crime Club 2022
23 24 25 26 27 LBC 8 7 6 5 4

A catalogue record for this book
is available from the British Library.

ISBN 978-0-00-819242-6

Typeset by Palimpsest Book Production Ltd, Falkirk, Stirlingshire.

Printed and bound in the United States of America
by LSC Communications

For more information visit: www.harpercollins.co.uk/green

Contents

To Helena, Jonathan and Catherine

Introduction

The Life of Crime tells the story of fiction's most popular genre. There are clues in the title. This book traces the development of the crime story from its origins to the present day and also explores events that shaped the lives of crime writers and their work. In addition, I've tried to convey a sense of crime writing's sheer vitality.

The literary value of crime fiction was consistently under-estimated throughout the twentieth century. Ground has been gained in the battle for critical respectability, but it will not be possible to declare victory until nobody blinks an eye when the best crime novels are ranked alongside outstanding examples of mainstream fiction.

Even then, pockets of resistance will remain. As recently as 2004, the commentator Ben Yagoda claimed that: 'The American detective novel may be commercially viable, but it is devoid of creative or artistic interest.' I don't agree; nor do I agree with many other critical rants about detective fiction. But at least Yagoda had warm words for Raymond Chandler and Dashiell Hammett, if not their modern successors. Of course, bad crime novels are published and always have been; but this is equally true of 'literary fiction', and there are enough high-calibre crime stories, of the past as well as of the present, to sate even the most voracious appetite.

Half a century has passed since Julian Symons first published his ground-breaking history, *Bloody Murder*, known in the US as

Mortal Consequences. Three editions appeared over a twenty-one-year span. No rival study published subsequently has come close to matching its quality. My own attempts to detect the history of mystery owe more to Symons than to anyone else. But the time is ripe to take a fresh look at how the crime story has evolved.

What explains the absence of a satisfactory successor to *Bloody Murder*? Symons' insights were acute, but no historian or critic can ever be allowed the very last word. The most daunting challenge is the scale of the subject. Any attempt to write a single-volume survey of crime writing that purports to be both comprehensive and definitive is doomed to fail, even if the book is the size of a breeze block. By necessity, one must be *extremely* selective, and this means I've not been able to discuss many authors and books I admire.

I console myself with the reflection that, in the age of the internet, vast quantities of information are a click or two away. As will be readily apparent, this is not an academic study or an encyclopaedia. For me, the key question is: why bother to write a non-fiction book unless it has a distinct personality of its own? So, as with my previous titles, *The Golden Age of Murder* and *The Story of Classic Crime in 100 Books*, I've employed novelistic techniques in the hope of making the story come alive.

Questions fly around at the start of any investigation, criminal or literary. Where do the boundaries of crime fiction lie? Where do spy stories fit in? Does it make sense to draw a firm line between detective novelists and thriller writers? For decades, the quest for concise yet meaningful definitions of the genre and its offshoots has generated more heat than light. Raymond Chandler once said that the 'form . . . is too various for easy classification'. Some people see the broad term 'mystery' as trivialising, but it *is* convenient, even if vague. A crime story has as its main focus the revelation of the truth about a crime. That truth concerns, typically, whodunit, howdunit, whydunit, or whowasdunin. Beyond that, pedantry seems pointless. Most people recognise a crime story when they see one, and many writers flit between different branches of fiction.

Readers seldom think of *Crime and Punishment* and *The Trial* as crime fiction, although the spirits of both Dostoevsky and Kafka pervade many crime novels. Even Francis Iles, who once favoured strict definitions, later reviewed both Harper Lee's *To Kill a Mockingbird* and John Fowles' *The Collector* in his crime column. A. S. Byatt's *Possession* is in one sense a detective story, while Eleanor Catton took inspiration from authors as diverse as Agatha Christie, James M. Cain, Wilkie Collins and Graham Greene when writing the Man Booker Prize-winning *The Luminaries*. Today, it hardly matters whether or not books by writers such as John le Carré and Georges Simenon are marketed as spy or detective stories, or as mainstream novels.

Libraries and bookshops often organise separate sections for crime fiction, however, and this dismays some writers. Categorisation can be helpful (as can that handy word 'genre'), provided the effect is not to relegate crime fiction to a literary ghetto. The risk is that segmenting different types of crime writing can create artificial distinctions and prejudices, and there are already too many of those in the world. Even fans and the writers themselves sometimes harbour jaundiced views about types of mystery outside their usual beat. In *The Life of Crime*, I've tried to weave different strands together, so as to highlight connections between one branch of crime writing or one particular group of writers and others. Those connections are often much closer than they seem at first sight. As with so many connections in life, they are more interesting and instructive than the obvious but shallow divisions.

I haven't confined myself to examining the usual suspects, although many of them are lined up for inspection. The mere fact that a novel suffers critical or commercial neglect doesn't mean it is worthless. And if a book written decades ago evinces attitudes that we now deplore, that isn't a reason to airbrush it from history. If we ignore the follies of the past (sexism, antisemitism and other forms of racism, homophobia or anything else), we'll fail to understand what caused them, and what *continues* to cause them – and so risk finding new ways to repeat old mistakes.

Gems lurk in dusty corners, and the recent revival of classic crime fiction has seen books scaling the bestseller charts after being out of print for up to three-quarters of a century, while many new novels pay tribute, with varying degrees of awareness, to their Golden Age predecessors. How many commentators (or publishers) had the vision to foresee that? Neglected crime authors have long written fiction as worthwhile as that produced by their better-known colleagues. Even deeply flawed books often possess interest and merit.

The main narrative of *The Life of Crime* follows broadly, but not slavishly, a chronological path. Typically, a chapter opens with an incident or a sequence of events in an author's life that had a bearing, however oblique, on his or her crime writing; the discussion then explores a particular subject or theme connected with that writer. I've adopted a flexible structure, so as to accommodate books and topics that I find worthy of discussion, but which don't fit in with a straightforward linear account.

These introductory vignettes cast light on literary lives. Symons feared that too much biographical detail would disrupt the balance of *Bloody Murder*; I understand his anxiety, and also the impossibility of presenting authors' lives in their full, rich detail in a book of this kind. However, Symons' reticence meant that he disregarded events in the lives of authors, such as his *bête noire* Dorothy L. Sayers, which – properly understood – put their writings in a proper context, and answer some of the lazy criticisms about their work. Unreliable biographical information is ubiquitous, however, and attempting to make sense of the innumerable contradictions is a challenge to any literary detective. Disentangling fact from fiction (did Arthur Upfield really base his cop Bony on a tracker of mixed parentage, or did he make the story up?) isn't always feasible; but that, too, reflects life.

Authors often draw on their own experiences, and on other people's lives, in fleshing out their characters. Apparent parallels are often fascinating, but it is unwise to read *too* much into influences and inspirations, actual or inferred. Red herrings abound. Even when real-life crimes supply the raw material for plots, the facts are apt to be reinvented. The craft of writing fiction is a form of imaginative alchemy.

Detecting the genre's history helps to uncover similarities between the experiences of authors working in different periods of time, different parts of the world and different branches of literature. It also casts light on the creative ways in which writers and publishers promote their wares. It often seems necessary to devote as much ingenuity to selling books as to writing them. This is not simply a modern development, even though, once upon a time, some authors would decline to supply a photograph for publicity purposes or a biographical note for the jacket copy. These days publishers' perceptions of an author's 'promotability' or 'platform' count for a great deal, sometimes far too much. Self-respecting writers prefer to be judged on the merit of their work, rather than on their photogenic appeal or the strength of their (or their publicists') marketing and social media skills, but it is futile to bewail the commercial pressures associated with producing and selling books. They are blunt realities. Murder, as Dorothy L. Sayers well knew, must advertise.

A broader aim lies behind my discussion of individual authors. Whenever I talk to readers, wherever they are in the world, it's striking how fascinated they are by insights into the writing life. My aim is to give a flavour of the ups and downs, the strokes of luck and the unexpected misfortunes that make or break literary reputations. The aim is not to invade privacy or seek out the sensational for its own sake, but to try to understand.

There's nothing new about the division of authors between a tiny, richly remunerated elite and a silent majority, who, having striven to fulfil the dream of seeing their first book published, find it a desperate struggle to stay in the game. Even the most apparently successful authors can face mental health challenges, as can writers (and there are many of them) who are abandoned by their publishers because their sales fail to satisfy the accountants. A better understanding of those stresses may encourage others to temper their judgements on writers, their books and their failings with a touch of compassion.

I've also kept in mind reaction from readers and reviewers to *The Golden Age of Murder*, my study of the Detection Club, its members' lives and their achievements. Crime fans, like detectives, love to make fresh discoveries, and Symons' 'curiosities and singletons' formed an invaluable ingredient of *Bloody Murder*. Therefore the chapter endnotes to this book give pointers to further reading, watching and listening, together with a wealth of detail for trivia buffs.

*

A key question when writing *The Life of Crime* was whether to include spoilers that reveal the endings of books. Symons had little compunction about this. The conventional argument goes that it's impossible to discuss the stories in a meaningful way if one does not examine how they end. Such defeatism strikes me as unattractive and unconvincing.

My overriding aim is to encourage people to share my enjoyment of and enthusiasm for crime fiction. Despite avoiding spoilers so far as possible, I don't accept the joyless view that one can't take pleasure in a mystery if one already knows how it ends. The better crime stories often benefit from more than one reading.

Raymond Chandler, who wrote incisively about how writers practised 'the simple art of murder', expressed relief that the 'dead hand of the academicians' had not strangled the genre. He'd be shocked to discover that crime fiction is now taught in universities, while erudite studies of the subject proliferate; as with novels, they vary widely in quality, but I have personally benefited from the encouragement and wisdom of scholars across the world, as well as from the researches of those whose books are mentioned in the Select Bibliography at the back of this book.

Over the years, I've contributed to all manner of volumes about crime fiction: encyclopaedias (*British Crime Writing: An Encyclopedia*), reference volumes (*The Oxford Companion to Crime and Mystery Writing* and *Twentieth Century Crime Writers*), academic doorstops (*The Routledge Companion to Crime Fiction*), essay collections (*101 Detectives*), introductions to novels, anthologies and non-fiction books, and so on. My endeavour here is different. *The Life of Crime* is one person's journey through the genre's past, with all the limitations and idiosyncrasies that implies. I'm a fan as well as a writer.

Symons struggled to reconcile a devout faith in objective standards of literary judgement with awareness that his pronouncements reflected his own tastes. As time passed, he emphasised that his views were open to 'reasoned contradiction'. In an age where people sometimes display a frightening intolerance of views that conflict with their own, civilised debate is to be encouraged. None of us has a monopoly of wisdom, whether about crime fiction or anything else. I make no secret of my own opinions, but they continue to evolve, and I've referenced a wide range of literary judgements, including some with which I disagree profoundly. In keeping with my focus on the realities of the crime-writing life, I've quoted fellow crime novelists often, academic authors rarely. With any luck, people will read the stories for themselves, and make up their own minds.

The Life of Crime covers a much wider territory than *Bloody Murder*, and not simply because biographical material is included or because so many more novels now exist. I've mentioned many writers and books Symons overlooked, including plenty of curiosities that appeal to me, even if they are hardly masterpieces. I was determined not to ignore altogether crime writing for the theatre, radio, television and film, or the field of true crime. I've also talked about fiction originally written in languages other than English.

Yet space is limited and something has to give. Like Symons, I've dispensed with the clutter of footnotes. Unlike Symons, I've included a bibliography, together with extensive references in the endnotes to each chapter. Many living authors are mentioned, but I've striven to avoid recency bias. My main focus is on how crime fiction has reached its present stage of evolution, rather than on surveying the contemporary scene, which is already widely discussed.

Stylistically, I've opted for flexibility rather than consistency, for instance in making selective references to film and TV adaptations of novels. Books often have alternative titles, some of them almost identical; many, but by no means all, are mentioned. Dates of first publication are usually given for genre novels mentioned in the main text, to help set the books in their historic context, but, given that *The Life of Crime* isn't an encyclopaedia, I've tried to avoid swamping the reader with dates and other minutiae that can easily be Googled. In the case of books first published in other languages, I've used the English titles in all but a few cases. Where authors use pen-names, I've referred to them by their pseudonym if it's more familiar than their real name; examples are John Rhode, Milward Kennedy, J. J. Connington and S. S. Van Dine. Exceptions include Anthony Berkeley and Francis Iles, two equally significant pseudonyms of A. B. Cox; I've used whichever one suits the context, whereas I've usually referred to Ross Macdonald by his less well-known real name, Ken Millar, because of my focus on the Millar family story.

Above all, I hope this book encourages people to explore and enjoy books and authors they haven't previously encountered. If readers are prompted to gain fresh pleasure from the treasure trove of mystery fiction, *The Life of Crime* will have achieved its goal.

Martin Edwards
www.martinedwardsbooks.com

ONE

Revolution

Origins

'Terror was the order of the day; and it was feared that even the humble novelist might be shown to be constructively a traitor.'

William Godwin wrote the above words in 1795, a year after publishing what today we would call his 'breakthrough novel'. His story explored the unravelling of a crime.

Despite what he claimed, Godwin was far from humble. Contrary by nature, he'd spent four years as a dissenting minister before his thirst for argument led him into radical politics. A friend of Thomas Paine, one of the US's founding fathers, he was an anarchist inspired by the French Revolution, although even he had begun to wonder by this point if the enthusiastic guillotining of the rich and powerful was getting out of hand.

Ten years as an author had left Godwin disillusioned: 'Everything I wrote fell dead-born from the press.' He craved 'the undoubted stamp of originality', and so came up with the idea of 'a book . . . that should in some way be distinguished by a very powerful interest . . . a series of adventures of flight and pursuit; the fugitive in perpetual apprehension of being overwhelmed by the worst

calamities'. The result was the first thriller about a manhunt, and
the literary ancestor of chase novels from John Buchan's *The
Thirty-Nine Steps*, published during the First World War, to
Frederick Forsyth's *The Day of the Jackal* (1971) and Lee Child
thrillers such as *A Wanted Man* (2012).

To make readers care about his protagonist's fate, Godwin made
him play for high stakes. He devised 'a secret murder, to the
investigation of which the innocent victim should be impelled by
an unconquerable spirit of curiosity. The murderer would thus
have a sufficient motive to persecute the unhappy discoverer, that
he might deprive him of peace, character, and credit, and have
him for ever in his power.'

Godwin had invented a storytelling method that many detective
novelists would later adopt. He constructed his plot by working
backwards. Recalling the process in 1832, he said that he only
wrote 'when the afflatus was upon me'. This is seldom a recipe
for success. Most writers find the afflatus, or divine inspiration,
as elusive as any fugitive on the run. He finished the book in a
year, mostly writing in 'a state of high excitement'.

Godwin paid close attention to point of view, abandoning early
pages written in the third person in favour of the immediacy of
first-person narration. Some authors, fearful of subconscious influences and accusations of plagiarism, avoid reading books relevant
to their own work while they are writing. Godwin had no such
qualms.

He pored over the *Newgate Calendar*,[1] with its vivid and highly
popular if lavishly embellished accounts of actual crimes. The gaol
breaks and use of disguise in his story drew on the criminal career
of Jack Sheppard, while Dick Turpin's gang of highwaymen
provided a template for Godwin's band of outlaws. Another influence was the folk tale of Bluebeard, which had roots in stories
about murderers such as the fifteenth-century Breton serial killer
Gilles de Rais. For Godwin: 'Falkland was my Bluebeard . . . Caleb
Williams . . . persisted in his attempt to discover the forbidden
secret.'

In April 1794, he completed work on his 'mighty trifle', but
doubts of a kind familiar to most authors assailed him: 'How
terribly unequal does it appear to me . . . What had I done? Written

a book to amuse boys and girls in their vacant hours, a story to be hastily gobbled up by them, swallowed in a pusillanimous and unanimated mood.'

Godwin gave his book the soporific title *Things As They Are*, but almost forty years after first publication, it had become known by the subtitle *The Adventures of Caleb Williams*. He'd finally realised that the appeal of his novel lay in his hero's quest for truth, rather than in the political prejudices that drove him to write it.

Godwin set out to present 'a general review of the modes of domestic and unrecorded despotism by which man becomes the destroyer of man', and his explanatory preface so alarmed booksellers that it was withdrawn. Publication coincided with the suspension of habeas corpus by William Pitt the Younger's government, allowing arrest or imprisonment on 'suspicion', without charges or a trial. A reviewer in the pro-establishment *British Critic* said that Godwin's book provided 'a striking example of the evil use that can be made of considerable talents'.[2]

In Godwin's story, young Caleb Williams becomes secretary to an amiable country squire, Falkland, who had previously been acquitted of the murder of an obnoxious neighbour called Barnabas Tyrell. Two other men were hanged for the crime, but Caleb suspects that Falkland has something to hide. As a result of his amateur sleuthing, he is dismissed, thrown into prison, and then pursued by Falkland and his brutal henchman, Gines. Having framed others for his crime, Falkland is belatedly assailed by a guilty conscience. For Godwin, the real culprit is the society that bred his behaviour.

Falkland's virtues make him a forerunner of the 'least likely suspect', so often revealed as the murderer in later whodunits. Godwin had stumbled on the question asked by writers of detective fiction and psychological suspense ever since: *whom can I trust?*

Caleb Williams sold well. The playwright Richard Brinsley Sheridan oversaw a stage-musical version, written by George Colman and with songs by Stephen Storace, retitled *The Iron Chest* in an attempt to evade censorship. A generation after the book's first appearance, William Hazlitt, essayist and critic, claimed that 'no one that ever read it could possibly forget it', but present-day crime fans may struggle to wade through Godwin's muddy prose. P. D. James described the book in her memoirs as 'unreadable'.

Julian Symons argued plausibly that the book was the first to strike 'the characteristic note of crime literature', but was on shakier ground when he claimed that the book's 'particular importance . . . is that it denies all the assertions to be made later through the detective story. In the detective story, the rule of law is justified as an absolute good, in Godwin's book it is seen as wholly evil.' If one reads between the lines of the best detective stories, their attitudes towards law and justice are often more subversive than Symons and other critics realised.

William Godwin was an unlikely crime novelist. Born in 1756 in Wisbech, Cambridgeshire, scarcely a hot-bed of murder and mayhem, or indeed revolutionary fervour, he was educated in London prior to becoming a minister. An armchair revolutionary, his attitudes and behaviour were mired in contradictions. Godwin was a religious man who became an atheist, a preacher about economics who was hopeless with money, and an advocate of female independence who was enraged when his daughter ran off with a poet.

Godwin met Mary Wollstonecraft at a dinner given by his publisher for Thomas Paine. She departed for France, and had a relationship with an American businessman by whom she had a daughter. After the father of her child deserted her, she returned to England, and renewed her acquaintance with Godwin. The couple married and Mary gave birth to a second daughter, also called Mary, on 30 August 1797, but died ten days later.

Grief-stricken, Godwin wrote *Memoirs of the Author of a Vindication of the Rights of Woman* (Mary had published her early polemic of feminist theory five years before her death), but his honesty was counter-productive. Too many people saw Mary as a fallen woman, rather than a shining example of intellectual feminism. In 1801, he married again. His second wife was a publisher of juvenile fiction, and before long the couple were bringing up five children, and battling to stave off financial disaster.

Help arrived in the improbable form of young Percy Bysshe

Shelley. He introduced himself to Godwin, and, despite his own lack of money, borrowed on the strength of an expected inheritance to help pay off the older man's debts. Shelley was married, but became infatuated with young Mary; when she was sixteen, they eloped to France. Godwin disapproved, although the death of Shelley's wife enabled the couple to marry. But Mary later dedicated her novel *Frankenstein* to her father; and Godwin also became her literary agent, though declined to help with her novella *Matilda*, perhaps because its subject was father–daughter incest. It remained unpublished until 1959.

A few years on from publication, *Caleb Williams* inspired the American magazine editor and novelist Charles Brockden Brown[3] to write *Arthur Mervyn*, published in two parts in 1799 and 1800. Again the story concerned a young man's misadventures as he tries to discover the truth about a concealed murder; the emphasis is on suspense rather than detection.

An English melodrama, *Pelham* (1828), by Edward Bulwer-Lytton,[4] also contains elements reminiscent of *Caleb Williams*, but stripped of the political agenda. A real-life murderer, John Thurtell,[5] influenced the portrayal of Thornton, the fictional killer. And Bulwer-Lytton's best-known novel, *Eugene Aram* (1832), centred on an eighteenth-century murder that Godwin had once contemplated fictionalising.

Godwin kept writing, but became an early example of publishing's eternal realities: today's hot property is tomorrow's has-been. By the time he died in 1836, according to his biographer Peter Marshall, 'he was virtually unknown except to a small coterie of intellectuals'. His finances remained in a parlous state. And three years before his death, this scourge of society's parasites solicited the sinecure of Office Keeper and Yeoman-Usher of the Receipt of the Exchequer. A proposal to abolish the post prompted the old anarchist to beg the new Tory Prime Minister, Robert Peel,[6] to allow him to stay on the gravy train. Peel agreed, citing a 'grateful Recollection of the Pleasure' he'd taken in Godwin's writings.

In his strengths and weaknesses, his passions and his hypocrisies, Godwin was all too human. His career, as with so many later crime novelists, had more troughs than peaks. But, with *Caleb Williams*, he sparked a literary revolution.

How deep are the roots of the mystery story? Literature about crime dates back to the tale of Cain and Abel, while *Oedipus Rex* is a dark domestic psychodrama. Some believe that, if William Shakespeare were alive today, he'd be earning a crust as a crime writer, and *Macbeth* is indeed occasionally described as a 'psychological thriller'. Modern crime fiction, however, is far removed from the ancient riddles and accounts of murder and mayhem, whether in the West or in the venerable Chinese court-case (*gong'an*) stories, which are occasionally seen as prefiguring the modern genre.

Dorothy L. Sayers, whose critical insights were as influential in the first half of the twentieth century as Julian Symons' in the second half, made a valiant effort to identify the first four detective stories as ancient classics, two from the Apocrypha of the early Christian Church, one Greek, and one Roman. She argued that the biblical tale of Susanna and the Elders dealt with 'analysis of testimony', while, in Bel and the Dragon, also part of the extended Book of Daniel, 'the science of deduction from material clues, in the popular Scotland Yard manner, is reduced to its simplest expression'. The story of Egyptian King Rhampsinitus,[7] meanwhile, as told in Herodotus, concerned 'psychological detection', and that of Hercules and Cacus in the *Aeneid* 'fabrication of false clues'. But as Symons pointed out, these four stories focus on 'natural cunning rather than detective skill'. The various tricks in *The Arabian Nights*, and in Chaucer's 'The Nun's Priest's Tale', are equally remote from the detective story.

In the first half of the seventeenth century, John Reynolds' *The Triumph of God's Revenge against the Crying and Execrable Sinne of (Willful and Premeditated) Murther* enjoyed enormous popularity. As the American scholar Douglas G. Greene has pointed out, it comprised 'stories of murder that in later times would have been investigated by detectives and tried in the courts, but the theme . . . was that God will punish murderers'.

Change came with the Enlightenment. Daniel Defoe, best remembered for *Robinson Crusoe* (1719), wrote what would now be called 'true crime', including a pamphlet about the infamous aforementioned Jack Sheppard, thief and prison escapee,[8] as well as fiction. *Roxana* (1724), with elements of pursuit and the threat of murder, anticipates the crime novel, although Defoe's main concern is to make a moral point. Reginald Hill, a leading British detective novelist, argued that 'Defoe is not a crime writer in the modern sense, but as a writer on criminal matters, his importance and influence cannot be overstressed.'

In Voltaire's *Zadig* (1747), the title character makes brilliant deductions from physical evidence, almost in the manner of a Great Detective. This reflects, Greene argues, 'the assumption of the Enlightenment that humans can find answers through reason.' It was no longer enough to wait for God.

Published in the same year as *Caleb Williams*, Ann Radcliffe's[9] *The Mysteries of Udolpho* is a Gothic tale in which the villainous Montoni seeks to deprive Emily St Aubert of her inheritance. Thirty years earlier, Horace Walpole had produced *The Castle of Otranto: A Gothic Story*, set in medieval Sicily, and his lurid thriller prompted Radcliffe and others to pursue the Gothic tradition. A ruined castle or abbey makes an atmospheric backdrop in these stories for the menacing of a lovely young heroine by a malevolent older man.

Gothic tales with a supernatural resolution are forerunners of ghost and horror fiction. Radcliffe developed the form by supplying a rational explanation for the baffling events she described. This anticipated the focus of detective stories, although her priority was to arouse fear of dark and unseen forces. Samuel Taylor Coleridge[10] was among those gripped by *The Mysteries of Udolpho*: 'Mysterious terrors are continually exciting in the mind the idea of a supernatural appearance . . . and yet are ingeniously explained by familiar causes; curiosity is kept upon the stretch from page to page.'

The American critic Michele Slung claims that: 'the gothic is women's fiction.[11] Women read it, write it and, most importantly, identify with it . . . Jane Austen knew that gothic belonged to her sex and had great fun fleshing out this notion in *Northanger Abbey*.' Austen's novel, published in 1817, pokes fun at 'horrid' Gothic fiction, above all at *The Mysteries of Udolpho*. And yet P. D. James has suggested that *Emma* (1815) can be read as a detective story in which 'Austen deceives us with cleverly constructed clues'.[12]

Male Gothic writers included Matthew Gregory Lewis, responsible for the sensational *The Monk: A Romance* (1796), and Charles Maturin, who wrote *Melmoth the Wanderer* (1820), a story that rambles as much as the title character. There was also a Gothic tinge to a book originally published anonymously but later credited to James Hogg: *The Private Memoirs and Confessions of a Justified Sinner* (1824).

Hogg's extraordinary book is an ancestor of the suspense fiction of Patricia Highsmith as well as the dark contemporary mysteries labelled Tartan Noir. The complex story, presented as a 'found document', concerns a Calvinist minister's son who embarks on a crime spree in eighteenth-century Scotland. As Ian Rankin puts it, it's an example of 'psychological grand guignol', with an emphasis on moral ambiguity and doppelgängers representing the natures at war within a human being.[13]

Just as British and American writers were using elements of crime and detection in forms recognisable to modern readers, so too were their counterparts on the continent of Europe. E. T. A. Hoffmann's novella *Mademoiselle de Scudéri*, published in 1819, is a precursor of the 'impossible crime' story, and the British novelist and critic Gilbert Adair has argued that it is the very first detective story.[14]

A more credible but less well-known candidate for that description also came from a German writer. Adolf Müllner's *Der Kaliber*, which concerns an apparent fratricide, is an early example of a mystery involving ballistics, and appeared in 1828. Müllner was a lawyer, and his legal knowledge gave the story a touch of authenticity, but his death the year after it was published meant that he never developed as an author of crime fiction.[15]

And long before the era of Scandi noir, the Norwegian teacher and poet Mauritz Hansen published stories about crime, including 'The Troll Mountain' in 1836, which has a courtroom revelation of the culprit's identity anticipating Erle Stanley Gardner's stories about Perry Mason. Three years later, in *The Murder of Machine-Builder Roolfsen*, Hansen offered a criminal puzzle, a detective and a solution to a mystery.[16]

Sweden's Carl Jonas Love Almqvist, an ordained priest, published

The Mill of Skallnora, a crime story with a Gothic flavour, in 1838. Thirteen years later, suspected of attempted murder and fraud, he fled to the USA, where he married bigamously and stayed for fourteen years.[17]

The conventional view, however, is that the first detective story was Edgar Allan Poe's 'The Murders in the Rue Morgue', published in 1841. But should the credit go to Hoffmann, Müllner or Hansen, or an even more obscure candidate? The answer depends on slippery issues of definition. As Reginald Hill has said, there is no more a single starting point for the modern crime story than there is for modern society.[18] Whatever the strength of rival claims in terms of strict chronology, by far the greatest influence on the development of the detective story was exerted by Poe. Unquestionably he created the first *major* fictional detective, the Chevalier C. Auguste Dupin.

Notes

The main sources for this chapter include Peter Marshall's biography of Godwin, P. D. James' *Time to Be in Earnest* and *Talking about Detective Fiction*, Symons' *Bloody Murder*, Doug Greene's biography of John Dickson Carr, and Reginald Hill's 'A Pre-History' in H. R. F. Keating's *Whodunit?* Here and throughout this book, I have drawn on books mentioned in the Select Bibliography, especially those by Symons, Sayers, Haycraft, Murch, Barzun and Taylor, Knight, Panek, Murphy, Rzepka, Greene, and Priestman, *Twentieth Century Crime and Mystery Writers*, and the OUP and Routledge Companions.

1 *the Newgate Calendar*: This series of anonymous compilations of crime first appeared in 1773; earlier, the French advocate François Gayot de Pitaval had published similar accounts of *causes célèbres*, which became known as 'Pitavals'. The *Calendar*'s popularity spawned a vogue for 'Newgate Novels', melodramatic fictions celebrating or romanticising criminals such as Dick Turpin. In *The History of the Life of the Late Mr Jonathan Wild the Great* (1743), Henry Fielding flavours his account of the thief-taker with satire. The protagonists were remote literary ancestors of A. J. Raffles, Tom Ripley and Jeff Lindsay's Dexter Morgan.

2 *a striking example of the evil use that can be made of considerable talents*: A pioneer in the critical study of the emergence of the detective story in modern fiction, LeRoy Lad Panek considers that Godwin's political prejudices result in 'self-righteous whining'. The Marxist critic Ernest Mandel made a different complaint: the book 'exhibits a *radical* petty-bourgeois . . . ideology. The author longs for a small community composed of honest, amicable and basically equal individuals, in other words, small property owners'.

3 *Charles Brockden Brown*: Brown's *Wieland* explores homicidal psychology.

Edgar Huntly, or The Memoirs of a Sleepwalker, in which the eponymous hero seeks to discover who killed his friend Waldegrave, is sometimes called 'the first American detective novel', but Brown's main focus is on the prime suspect's disturbed psyche rather than detection. He also took an interest in the Native American skill in following trails, an investigative technique prominent in James Fenimore Cooper's popular 'Leatherstocking Tales', notably *The Last of the Mohicans* and *The Deerslayer*. These featured Nathaniel 'Natty' Bumppo, the child of white parents, who grew up among Native Americans, and whose companion in many adventures was the Mohican chief Chingachgook.

4   *Edward Bulwer-Lytton*: Bulwer-Lytton became an establishment man, a Member of Parliament, and was eventually raised to the peerage. It would be a stretch to call him a crime novelist, but crime plays a significant part in several of his books, including *Paul Clifford* (1830), about a gentlemanly highwayman, which famously opens: 'It was a dark and stormy night.'

5   *John Thurtell*: Thurtell disposed of his victim in a pond in Elstree, long before it became home to a film studio. *Thurtell's Crime* by Dick Donovan, the pen-name for J. E. Preston Muddock, is a loose fictionalisation of the case. *Murder at Elstree* is more closely based on the facts; the author, Thomas Burke, also wrote a chilling story about a serial killer in the mould of Jack the Ripper, 'The Hands of Mr Ottermole'.

6   *Robert Peel*: In 1829, as Home Secretary, Peel introduced the Metropolitan Police Force based at Scotland Yard. The 'Peelian principles' set standards for policing by consent, and officers became known as 'Peelers' or 'bobbies'.

7   *King Rhampsinitus . . . 'psychological detection'*: In John Dickson Carr's whodunit *To Wake the Dead*, Dr Gideon Fell gives a nod to the precedent of Rhampsinitus when unravelling the mystery.

8   *Jack Sheppard*: William Harrison Ainsworth's novel about the notorious thief sparked a moral panic (discussed in Claire Harman's *Murder by the Book*) when the killer of Lord William Russell claimed that reading it had driven him to commit his crime. Thus began the enduring tradition of scapegoating authors for the misdemeanours of others.

9   *Ann Radcliffe*: Radcliffe specialised in strong female characters, and produced four novels culminating in *The Mysteries of Udolpho* by the time she was thirty. After publishing one more novel, and at the height of her fame, she vanished from public view, prompting rumours that she was insane and confined to an asylum. Much of her life remains shrouded in mystery, but her biographer Rictor Norton concludes in *Mistress of Udolpho* that she suffered from clinical depression and had a mental breakdown. Her style of writing was susceptible to mockery, but her admirers included Dostoevsky, Byron and Thomas De Quincey, who described her as 'the greatest enchantress of that generation' in *Confessions of an English Opium-Eater*.

10   *Samuel Taylor Coleridge*: Coleridge's *Christabel* was a Gothic narrative in verse which he never finished. As a young man, the future private-eye novelist Ken Millar, aka Ross Macdonald, had the 'wild ambition' of completing the poem before opting instead to write a dissertation on Coleridge's philosophic origins. Millar argued in *Self-Portrait* that: 'The early Gothic writers learned in its modern sense the fear of death . . . the urge towards literary detection must arise from a need for meaning in lives which have been stripped of some prior meaning. The solution of a crime like

murder seems to reinject into our lives a saving grace, a more human and tragic knowledge.'

11 *the gothic is women's fiction*: Among the exceptions to this principle was the work of P. M. Hubbard, starting with *Flush as May* in 1963. His low-key novels of suspense, typically with backgrounds in rural Britain, which prove to be menacing rather than idyllic, were never bestsellers but Philip Hubbard's elegant prose attracted admirers including Anthony Boucher and H. R. F. Keating.

12 *Jane Austen*: P. D. James' *Death Comes to Pemberley* is a murder mystery written in a pastiche of Austen's style, opening six years after the events of *Pride and Prejudice*. There are faint echoes of Austen in *Darkness at Pemberley*, a quirky stew of whodunit and thriller by T. H. White, author of *The Once and Future King*. Val McDermid's *Northanger Abbey* gives Austen's novel a contemporary makeover, with the satire targeted at vampire stories. Reginald Hill's novella *Poor Emma* imagines Emma's life after her marriage to Mr Knightley, while his *A Cure for all Diseases* projects Austen's unfinished novel *Sanditon* into modern times and adds a murder mystery. Alexander McCall Smith's *Emma* is an update published in 2014. Austen's great-great-niece Lois Austen-Leigh began a brief career as a detective novelist with *The Incredible Crime*, which combines light comedy with a sketchy plot about drug smuggling. Her final novel, memorably titled *The Gobblecock Mystery*, appeared in 1938.

13 *Ian Rankin*: In 'Why Crime Fiction is Good For You' in *Howdunit*, Rankin explains Hogg's influence on his writing, not least in *Knots and Crosses*, which pits DI Rebus against his evil alter ego.

14 *E. T. A. Hoffmann*: Ernst Theodor Wilhelm Hoffmann (who adopted 'Amadeus' as a forename in tribute to Mozart) was a leading figure in the Romantic movement. *Mademoiselle de Scudéri* is a seventeenth-century historical mystery, set in Paris in the aftermath of the Brinvilliers poisoning trial, a case on which John Dickson Carr drew for his unorthodox 'impossible crime' mystery *The Burning Court*. Introducing a reprint of *Mademoiselle de Scudéri*, Gilbert Adair cited it as an example of a serial-killer story, while suggesting that Scudéri is a 'genteel elderly spinster not a thousand miles away from Agatha Christie's Miss Marple'. Hoffmann's story 'The Marquise de la Pivardiere' drew on a real-life case recounted by de Pitaval.

15 *Adolf Müllner*: Müllner's career is discussed by Tannert and Kratz in *Early German and Austrian Detective Fiction: an Anthology*.

16 *Mauritz Hansen*: Nils Nordberg says in 'Murder in the Midnight Sun: Crime Fiction in Norway 1825–2005' that Hansen wrote over twenty stories 'that in a broad sense could be classified as crime fiction. The earliest one was published in 1821 . . . "The Mad Christian" . . . a psychological thriller.'

17 *Carl Jonas Love Almqvist*: Early Swedish mysteries are discussed in Bertil Falk's introduction to *Locked Rooms and Open Spaces*. Sweden's first significant female detective writer was Aurora Ljungstedt.

18 *Reginald Hill has said*: In 'Looking for a Programme' in *Colloquium on Crime*, ed. Robin W. Winks.

TWO

Mystery and Imagination

Edgar Allan Poe and the first detective stories

The death of detective fiction's founding father was as strange and baffling as any of his tales of mystery and imagination. Edgar Allan Poe even left an enigmatic 'dying message' clue to his fate. Over the years, sleuthing biographers have come up with enough explanations of his death to fill a convoluted whodunit. And as with so many cold cases, the puzzle remains officially unsolved.

On 27 September 1849, Poe said goodbye to Elmira Shelton, the woman he hoped to marry. The couple were old flames, reunited after years apart. Growing up in Richmond, Virginia, Poe and Elmira Royster had been sweethearts, but her father destroyed letters Poe sent to Elmira from university, believing that at fifteen she was too young for a serious relationship. Two years later she married a businessman, who died in 1844. When the widow and Poe met again, their old romance was rekindled.

Poe's plan was to take a steamer from Richmond to Baltimore, and then catch a train home to New York, stopping en route at Philadelphia. Elmira expected a letter from him, but the next news came on 9 October, in a brief press report. Poe had died in Baltimore 'after an illness of four or five days', and had already been buried.

It seems Poe had vanished prior to turning up in Baltimore,

and, on arrival, had appeared in a wretched state. Sodden with drink, he wore shabby clothes that apparently belonged to someone else. He couldn't explain what had happened to him, and kept lapsing into delirium before the end came, repeating the cry: 'Reynolds! Reynolds!'

But who was Reynolds?

'Inflammation of the brain', the given cause of Poe's death, is a term that prompts more questions than answers. Some say that he died of natural causes, such as alcohol poisoning, carbon monoxide poisoning (from coal gas used for indoor lighting), or mercury poisoning, as a result of taking mercury after being exposed to an epidemic of cholera. The novelist Matthew Pearl[1] has suggested that Poe was killed by a brain tumour. Or perhaps he caught rabies? One possibility, so disappointingly anticlimactic as to be entirely credible, is that he succumbed to influenza which developed into pneumonia.

But for decades it was widely believed that Poe had been a victim of 'cooping', a crude form of electoral fraud. Gangs supporting a particular candidate would kidnap victims, disguise them and force them to vote multiple times under different names for their candidate. Elections had indeed been taking place in Baltimore at the time. If Poe had been 'cooped', plied with alcohol and dressed in someone else's clothes, that might explain his dishevelled state and delirium. He was found outside Ryan's Tavern, a notorious haunt of 'coopers'. But he may simply have drunk himself into a stupor of his own free will, and then been roughed up by thugs.

The most sinister theory is that Poe was murdered. John Evangelist Walsh argues in *Midnight Dreary* (1998) that Poe was attacked in Philadelphia by Elmira's three brothers because they regarded him as unfit to marry their lonely – and wealthy – widowed sister. Walsh suggests that Poe then proceeded to Baltimore, only to be ambushed again by the Roysters. They forced him to drink a large amount of whisky, beat him and left him to die. Perhaps they put about the 'cooping' story to divert suspicion.

Why would anyone go to such extremes to prevent the marriage? According to Walsh, the brothers regarded Poe as a debauched fortune hunter, whose literary gifts counted for nothing in comparison to his shockingly dissolute lifestyle. Walsh regards the Reynolds 'clue' as a red herring, and points out that one Henry B. Reynolds was among the judges presiding over the Baltimore elections. It is also conceivable that Poe was obsessing about Jeremiah Reynolds, a key influence on his novel *The Narrative of Arthur Gordon Pym of Nantucket* (1838).

The murder theory is intriguing, but the case against Elmira's brothers has never been proven. *Midnight Dreary* was, nevertheless, nominated for one of the prestigious awards given by the Mystery Writers of America. Those awards are called the Edgars, in Poe's honour.

Poe was born in Boston in 1809 to two members of a travelling theatrical company. From first to last, his life was plagued by misfortune. His father vanished shortly after his birth, a disappearance so puzzling that it has excited wild speculation that he too was possibly murdered. Then, before Poe reached his second birthday, his mother died of consumption, and he was taken in by a childless couple, John and Frances Allan of Richmond, Virginia. Allan was a businessman whose firm opened a branch in Britain, and so Poe attended school in England[2] for five years before returning to the United States.

Poe, however, habitually compounded his bad luck with self-destructive behaviour. For example, he dropped out of university after running up gambling debts, and then enlisted with the army, taking an assumed name, Edgar A. Perry, and lying about his age. An inglorious career in the military ended with a court martial for gross neglect of duty. Chronically short of money, he turned to journalism to supplement his income as a poet and writer of short stories.

In 1836, Poe married his cousin Virginia Clemm, who was only thirteen years old at the time. Their relationship has raised questions about Poe's sexual tastes, and whether the marriage was ever consummated, but it seems clear that the couple were devoted to each other. Poe found an outlet for the darker side of his personality in writing macabre fiction.

*

In 1839, Poe began to write for *Burton's Gentleman's Magazine*.
The magazine was owned by William Evans Burton, an English-
born actor, playwright and author who had moved to the United
States five years earlier. Burton dabbled in fiction, and in 1837
he'd contributed 'The Secret Cell' to the magazine. This story, set
in England, is recounted by an unnamed detective who describes
the case teasingly as 'a jumble of real life; a conspiracy, an abduction, a nunnery and a lunatic asylum are mixed up with constables,
hackney-coaches and an old washerwoman'. The narrator solves
a mystery about a missing woman, relying on persistence and the
use of disguise rather than deductive reasoning; the story anticipates the sensation novel rather than classical detective fiction.

Poe's relationship with Burton collapsed, and he either resigned
or was fired. Burton then sold the magazine, which was merged
with another magazine to form *Graham's Magazine*, and shortly
after the change of ownership, Poe became editor. Here – whether
or not influenced by 'The Secret Cell' is unknown – he published
his first detective story, 'The Murders in the Rue Morgue', in 1841.

His most famous poem, 'The Raven',[3] appeared four years later.
By then his young wife was suffering from tuberculosis. Poe was
drinking heavily and probably experimenting with opium. He
indulged in a series of ill-judged flirtations, narrowly escaping a
pistol duel with the brother of one disgruntled admirer. Virginia's
death at the age of twenty-four was a shattering blow. His last
poem, 'Annabel Lee', inspired by the loss of his wife, concerns a
theme that obsessed him: 'the death . . . of a beautiful woman is
unquestionably the most poetical topic in the world, and equally
is it beyond doubt that the lips best suited for such topic are those
of a bereaved lover.'

He consoled himself with a series of rash emotional entangle-
ments, described by Julian Symons[4] as 'the stuff of French farce.
He proposed to marry Helen Whitman, he would certainly have
wished to marry Annie Richmond had she been free, he also
wanted to marry . . . Mrs Shelton . . . Yet although Poe's conduct
was ridiculous, there was nothing comic about his misery.'

Therefore, nobody could blame the Royster brothers for
regarding Poe as an unsuitable husband for Elmira. His chaotic
lifestyle obscured his genius, and he made an unhealthy number

of enemies. A brutal obituary[5] in the *New York Daily Tribune* said: 'Edgar Allan Poe is dead . . . This announcement will startle many, but few will be grieved by it.' Today, few critics harbour any doubts that he was one of America's greatest men of letters.

Poe admired Byron, and other literary influences included E. T. A. Hoffmann, to whose romanticism he added a distinctive American flavour. Two contrasting aspects of his personality shine through his detective fiction. He was, like so many later crime writers, both a gifted poet and an enthusiastic puzzle-maker.[6] The visionary side of his nature and his love of the grotesque unite with his passion for logic in 'The Murders in the Rue Morgue', which presents a bizarre murder-mystery puzzle. Only a Great Detective could solve it.

Poe created the Chevalier C. Auguste Dupin as an exercise in wish fulfilment. Throughout the history of detective fiction, according to the private-eye novelist Ross Macdonald, 'the detective hero has represented his creator and carried his values into action in society . . . Poe's detective stories give the writer . . . a means of exorcising or controlling guilt and horror . . . The guilt was doubled by Poe's anguished insight into the unconscious mind. It had to be controlled by some rational pattern, and the detective story, "the tale of ratiocination", provided such a pattern.'

Dupin comes from an illustrious family that has fallen on hard times. His gift for deductive reasoning is matched by a romantic streak that causes him to close the shutters of his Parisian apartment at dawn and wander outside only when he can relish 'the advent of true darkness'. An unnamed friend records Dupin's three cases, a clever device that enables the narrator – like the reader – to be humbled by the detective's genius.[7]

In 'The Murders in the Rue Morgue', the body of Camille L'Espanaye is stuffed up the chimney of her locked apartment, while the savagely mutilated corpse of her mother lies in the yard outside. As the *Gazette des Tribunaux* reports, 'A murder so mysterious and perplexing . . . was never before committed in Paris . . . There is not . . . the shadow of a clew apparent.' Dupin scoffs at the police's lack of acumen, and dismisses Vidocq, the rogue-turned-criminal who founded the Sûreté, as 'a good guesser'.

'An inquiry will afford us some amusement,' Dupin says, anticipating the game-playing approach to crime detection adopted by
successive generations of 'Great Detectives'. The police are baffled,
but Dupin's gift for deduction enables him to come up with an
ingenious solution[8] to the macabre 'locked-room mystery',[9] a type
of detective story that would become a staple of the genre.

Dupin returned in 'The Mystery of Marie Rogêt', described by
Charles Baudelaire,[10] an early translator of Poe, as a 'masterpiece'.
The story was based on a real-life case,[11] the death of 'the beautiful cigar girl', Mary Rogers, which Poe transposed from the United
States to France. From careful study of newspaper reports, Dupin
deduces what has happened to Marie Rogêt, whose body has been
found in the Seine.

The story introduced the 'armchair detective',[12] but it also did
something more. Here was a crime writer setting out to solve an
actual crime. Poe claimed that, 'under the pretense of showing
how Dupin . . . unravelled the mystery of Marie's assassination,
I, in fact, entered into a very rigorous analysis of the real tragedy
in New York.' Whether his deductions were valid is debatable,
but his lead in behaving thus was followed by crime writers as
prominent as Arthur Conan Doyle[13] and Erle Stanley Gardner,
both of whom involved themselves in high-profile criminal investigations.

Dupin's final case, 'The Purloined Letter', set the template for
detective stories in which the solution to the puzzle is so obvious
that everyone overlooks it. Dupin this time acts as a professional
detective, accepting payment for his services, but this was his last
bow. Neither Poe nor any of his contemporaries realised the scale
of the breakthrough represented by the three tales, but their long-
term influence was so profound that Dupin deserves his exalted
rank in the pantheon of fictional detectives.[14]

Poe wrote two other stories of crime and detection. 'The Gold-Bug'
won a competition run by Philadelphia's *Dollar Newspaper*, and
features a cipher concerning the whereabouts of buried treasure.
Poe was fascinated by cryptography, and popularised it by inviting
readers of *Graham's Magazine* to submit ciphers for solution. 'The
Gold-Bug' features a 'substitution cipher', similar to the puzzle

that later confronted Sherlock Holmes in Arthur Conan Doyle's 'The Adventure of the Dancing Men'.

As substitution ciphers are relatively straightforward, detective writers searching for variety began to create increasingly fiendish codes and ciphers[15] to challenge their readers' intellects. The drawback is that explaining a complex scheme of encryption can occupy many pages, and test the reader's patience to breaking point. Poe and Conan Doyle were wise enough not to allow the complications to become tedious.

'Thou Art the Man' concerns the disappearance and presumed murder of Barnabas Shuttleworthy, the wealthiest resident of Rattleborough. The culprit proves to be the person who seemed least likely to be guilty. This light-hearted story lacks subtlety, but the villain's laying of false clues, and the notion of 'the least likely suspect' both became staples of the genre in the whodunits written by Agatha Christie, Ellery Queen and others after the First World War.

Poe's quintet of ground-breaking crime stories illustrates what Edward Shanks[16] called his flair for 'the mechanics of the short story'. The five tales were sensational and paid little heed to police work, but they supplied blueprints for thousands of mysteries.

Notes

The main sources for this chapter are the biographies by Edward Shanks and Julian Symons, *Midnight Dreary* and Natasha Geiling's 'The (Still) Mysterious Death of Edgar Allan Poe', 7 October 2014, www.smithsonianmag.com

1   *The novelist Matthew Pearl*: Pearl's *The Poe Shadow* concerns a Baltimore lawyer's quest to learn the truth about Poe's fate.
2   *Poe attended school in England*: *The American Boy* by Andrew Taylor is a Gothic tale set at the time of Poe's schooldays in Stoke Newington. The story's genesis was an idea for a play that Taylor ultimately decided not to write, *Missing Edgar*. One of his historical sources was the journals of Clarissa Trant, which also supplied material for John Dickson Carr's 'impossible crime' story *Fire, Burn!*, in which a twentieth-century policeman is transported back in time. Carr's 'The Gentleman from Paris' reflects his enthusiasm for Poe, and was filmed as *The Man with a Cloak*.
3   *'The Raven'*: William Hjortsberg's *Nevermore*, like *Midnight Dreary*, takes its title from a phrase in the poem. In *Nevermore*, Arthur Conan Doyle investigates a series of copycat murders patterned on tales by Poe with the assistance of Harry Houdini. The action is set in New York in 1923, and the cast of characters includes Damon Runyon.

4   *Julian Symons*: His mystery novel *The Name of Annabel Lee* makes inventive use of his knowledge of Poe's work, and his insight into Poe's obsessive nature.

5   *A brutal obituary*: Its author was Rufus Wilmot Griswold, who succeeded Poe as editor of *Graham's Magazine*. Remarkably, this character assassin was also Poe's literary executor.

6   *like so many later crime writers, both a gifted poet and an enthusiastic puzzle-maker*: Ellery Queen's *Poetic Justice* is an anthology of crime stories by poets. Poetry and detective fiction typically share, among other things, a focus on form and structure. Stephen Dobyns is an example of a talented poet who has achieved success both with his private-eye series about Charlie Bradshaw and stand-alone suspense novels such as *The Church of Dead Girls*.

7   *a clever device that enables the narrator – like the reader – to be humbled by the detective's genius*: This method, perfected by Arthur Conan Doyle in the relationship between Sherlock Holmes and Dr Watson, became a staple of detective fiction. A. E. W. Mason's Hanaud and Ricardo, Ernest Bramah's Carrados and Carlyle, Agatha Christie's Poirot and Hastings, and R. Austin Freeman's Thorndyke and Jervis are celebrated examples, but there were many less renowned pairings, such as Rupert Penny's Chief Inspector Beale and his stockbroker chum Tony Purdon. The popularity of the 'Watson' device persisted until the Second World War, by which time it had been subverted in one of Christie's finest novels. Colin Dexter revitalised it with his books about Morse and Lewis, and more recently, the role of Watson to Anthony Horowitz's brilliant detective Hawthorne has been taken by Horowitz himself.

8   *an ingenious solution*: As Symons has pointed out, its credibility is questionable: 'If the reasoning is faulty the merit of the stories is reduced.' This is a recurrent failing in the genre, but the best books offer compensation in the stylish way that the writers skate over thin ice.

9   *the macabre 'locked-room mystery'*: This story was not, however, the first 'locked-room mystery'. Quite apart from Hoffmann's *Mademoiselle de Scudéri*, Sheridan Le Fanu published 'Passage in the Secret History of an Irish Countess' in 1838, but it lacks a detective in the Dupin mould.

10 *Charles Baudelaire*: Ross Macdonald said: 'I once made a case for the theory (and Anthony Boucher didn't disagree) that much of the modern development of the detective story stems from Baudelaire, his "dandyism" and his vision of the city as inferno.'

11 *The story was based on a real-life case*: The murder in 1841 of Mary Rogers is examined by Daniel Stashower in *The Beautiful Cigar Girl*. Mary worked in a tobacco shop patronised by such literary luminaries as James Fenimore Cooper and Washington Irving. The puzzle of her death was never officially solved, but was the first of countless 'true crimes' to inspire works of detective fiction.

12 *'armchair detective'*: Fictional 'armchair detectives' included Prince Zaleski, a reclusive Russian exile who solves crimes from his couch; his creator was M. P. Shiel, a writer with mixed-race origins who declared himself King of Redonda. Baroness Orczy's The Old Man in the Corner, meanwhile, is a regular at an ABC teashop in London; his 'Watson' is a young journalist, Polly Burton. Harry Kemelman's Nicky Welt is a rigorously logical detective,

an academic who plays chess with a pupil who acts as his 'Watson'. Nicky's most famous case was 'the Nine Mile Walk'. An unorthodox example of the form, where the author takes the role of armchair detective, is Julian Symons' *Death's Darkest Face*.

13 *his lead . . . was followed by crime writers as prominent as Arthur Conan Doyle*: Peter Costello's *The Real World of Sherlock Holmes*, revised as *Conan Doyle, Detective*, examines the author's true-crime investigations. The most celebrated was the Edalji case, fictionalised in *Arthur & George* by the literary novelist Julian Barnes; under the pen-name Dan Kavanagh, Barnes wrote four breezy novels about the bisexual private eye Duffy.

14 *Dupin deserves his exalted rank in the pantheon of fictional detectives*: Later writers who have resurrected Dupin include Michael Harrison, also an exponent of the Sherlockian pastiche.

15 *codes and ciphers*: Examples in Golden Age detective fiction include John Rhode's *Peril at Cranbury Hall*, Dorothy L. Sayers' *Have His Carcase* and Rupert Penny's *Policeman's Evidence*. J. J. Connington employed codes and ciphers in *The Case with Nine Solutions* and *The Castleford Conundrum*, while *A Minor Operation* features love letters in cipher created by a Braille-writing machine. Any belief that cryptology had lost its appeal in the modern age has been dispelled by the multi-million selling *The Da Vinci Code*, a thriller by Dan Brown that features his series character, Harvard professor Robert Langdon.

16 *Edward Shanks*: Edward Richard Buxton Shanks was another poet and critic with a taste for detective stories, which he reviewed for the *Evening Standard*. Among his own novels, *Old King Cole*, an eerie story of rural England, lurks in the crime genre's outfield.

THREE

Guilty Secrets

Sensation novels

Mary Anne Maxwell died of natural causes on 5 September 1874 at the home of her brother, John Crowley, near Dublin. News of her death was broken by telegram to Mary Anne's husband, a prominent magazine publisher based in London. Whatever grief John Maxwell may have felt at his loss was swamped by panic.

Maxwell wired Crowley, promising money for the funeral, but warning: 'Neither advertise nor telegraph anybody.' He said he would attend the funeral, only to change his mind four hours later. A second telegram pleaded ill health and urged: 'Do things quietly, funeral should be strictly private.' An hour later he despatched yet another message, begging Crowley to request his sister 'not to advertise death, as I shall do whatever is necessary'.

These demands for secrecy infuriated Crowley. The death of Maxwell's wife was therefore announced in several national newspapers. This provoked the publisher into a wild and hopelessly dishonest response. He circulated a message to members of his social circle in which 'Mr and Mrs Maxwell . . . beg to disclaim any knowledge of the maliciously-intentioned announcement of a death on the 5th inst.'

Maxwell's frantic attempts to keep the news secret were explained by the craving for respectability.[1] As far as the world at large was concerned, Maxwell was not married to Mary Anne at all. His wife was widely believed to be the best-selling novelist Mary Elizabeth Braddon. The couple had been living together for more than a decade, and she'd borne him five children. When their servants discovered that their employers were 'living in sin', they were so horrified that all but one of them resigned.

Maxwell, on good terms with many journalists, strove to hush up the story in the British press, but his influence didn't extend overseas. The *New York Times* broke the scandal on its front page under the headline *Miss Braddon as a Bigamist*. This was a nineteenth-century form of 'clickbait', since the report itself made clear that Braddon and Maxwell were simply pretending to be married. But the London correspondent was scathing: 'Having, like so many of her heroines, committed a species of bigamy, she has at last been found out . . . far from becoming the wife of two husbands, all Miss Braddon did was to go through some facetious form of marriage with a man who was already married. She thus became, not indeed a bigamist, but at least an accomplice in bigamy.'

The condemnation was cruel, but the irony inescapable. A woman who had made her reputation with stories about secrets and lies, mysteries crammed with adultery, bigamy, deceit and impersonation, had herself been leading a double life.

Mary Elizabeth Braddon cherished few illusions about the challenges of matrimony; her own parents separated when she was four years old. Born in Soho in 1835, she was the daughter of a solicitor whose taste for gambling, drink and women proved incompatible with family life. Eventually Fanny Braddon could no longer tolerate him. Life as a single mother in Victorian England presented financial and social challenges, but Fanny's strength of character enabled her to cope.

Mary inherited Fanny's independence of mind. Tall, with curly auburn hair and a musical voice, Mary realised early on that there was more to life than finding a husband. But a young woman who needed to earn a living had few options. Not wishing to follow Jane Eyre's example and work as a governess, she decided to go on the stage. In later life she described this mockingly as 'the lapse of a lost soul'. In deference to the conventions, she adopted a stage name, Mary Seyton, blending the virginal with a hint of the satanic. The closeness of her bond with Fanny is illustrated by the fact that her mother also took to using the name Seyton.

Braddon spent the next few years touring provincial theatres from Aberdeen to Winchester, but she also nurtured literary ambitions. She met Edward Bulwer-Lytton in 1854, and he – like Fanny – encouraged her to keep writing. She began to publish poetry and acquired a patron. A wealthy Yorkshireman, John Gilby, offered her a wage, which meant she could leave the stage to write full-time.

Gilby commissioned her to write an epic poem about the Italian nationalist Garibaldi, but her life changed course when she met the owner of the *Welcome Guest*, a hearty Irishman called John Maxwell. After Maxwell began to publish her work – including an early ghost story, 'The Cold Embrace' – Gilby began to suspect his motives. Maxwell was married, but his wife lived in Ireland and their six children remained in his care; he gave the impression that she was mentally deranged, and confined to an asylum. Occasionally he described her as 'defunct'.

In his final letter to Braddon, Gilby ranted: 'Gratitude! Why you hardly know the meaning of the word . . . You have become such an actress that you cannot speak without acting.' He stopped supporting her, but she no longer needed him. Her first novel, drawing on the life and crimes of the swindler and Sligo MP John Sadleir,[2] was already being serialised. *Three Times Dead*, aka *The Secret of the Heath* (1860), failed to make an immediate impression, but enjoyed greater success after Maxwell encouraged Braddon to revise it and try a fresh title, *The Trail of the Serpent*.

Tangled and concealed relationships abound in *The Trail of the Serpent*: Jabez North engages in blackmail, impersonation and murder in his quest to acquire a fortune, while the dissolute Richard Marwood battles to prove that he did not murder his wealthy uncle. The mute Joseph Peters – first in a long line of fictional detectives with disabilities[3] – helps to ensure that justice is done, but it is too much of a stretch to claim that Braddon's debut was the first detective novel.

*

Maxwell and Braddon became lovers, and she gave birth to their first child in March 1862, when she was twenty-six. That year also saw her break through as a writer. Maxwell began to serialise *Lady Audley's Secret* in his magazine *Robin Goodfellow*, but the publication folded before the story reached its climax. Enthusiastic readers were desperate to find out what happened, and Maxwell's new venture, *The Sixpenny Magazine*, provided a home for the completed story prior to its publication as a novel.

The book's power derived from its revelation of the true nature of a woman who is small and sweet, blonde and beautiful, and prepared to go to any lengths to preserve her position in society. Anticipating Wilkie Collins' *The Moonstone*, the storyline draws on aspects of the real-life Constance Kent case, which turned upside down the sentimental Victorian notion of 'the angel in the house'.[4]

Lady Audley's sociopathic criminality[5] is eventually explained away as the product of hereditary madness. The briefless barrister Robert Audley, 'a generous-hearted fellow, rather a curious fellow, too, with a fund of sly wit . . . under his listless, dawdling . . . manner', who investigates the disappearance of his friend George Talboys, is a forerunner of the gentlemanly amateur detective[6] who became a familiar figure after the First World War.

Lady Audley's Secret remained Braddon's masterpiece, but she was prolific as well as popular. When *Aurora Floyd* was published in 1863, the year in which she gave birth to a second son in January and a daughter in December, Braddon was paid handsomely: one thousand pounds for a copyright licence lasting just two years. She took care not to pretend to be married when it came to business activities. A wife's earnings could be sequestered to pay her husband's debts, and Maxwell's commercial acumen didn't match his ambition. He mortgaged all his magazines and had a habit of teetering on the brink of bankruptcy.

She remained devoted to Maxwell, and they married soon after his first wife died. Braddon gave his publishing empire financial backing and edited one of his magazines, *Belgravia*. Her mother edited another, the *Halfpenny Journal*, but Fanny's death led to her daughter suffering a breakdown that restricted her writing for almost a year.

Braddon had a flair for the sensation novel, which reached a peak of popularity in the 1860s. The public's obsession with thrill-seeking was satirised in *Punch* with a jokey advertisement for a new journal, *The Sensation Times, and Chronicle of Excitement*, devoted to: 'Harrowing the Mind, Making the Flesh Creep, Causing the Hair to Stand on End, Giving Shocks to the Nervous System, Destroying Conventional Moralities, and generally Unfitting the Public for the Prosaic Avocations of Life'. People loved having their nerves jangled, for instance by the exploits of the tightrope-walker Charles Blondin and acrobatic Jules Léotard, who popularised the one-piece exercise costume, giving his name to the leotard, and inspired the song 'The Daring Young Man on the Flying Trapeze'. Readers delighted equally in stories about bigamy, lust, fraud and murder, embellished with disguises, poisonings and clifftop struggles to the death.

Braddon became known as 'The Queen of the Circulating Libraries'. If there was something patronising about that accolade, there was a touch of envy as well as admiration in William Makepeace Thackeray's claim that 'If I could plot like Miss Braddon, I should be the greatest novelist that ever lived.'

Even before Braddon's emergence, crime and mystery played a part in the work of female writers as different as Elizabeth Cleghorn Gaskell, a novelist and biographer of distinction, and the much more obscure Caroline Clive.[7]

The storyline of Gaskell's first novel, *Mary Barton* (1848), hinges on the murder of wealthy Harry Carson, and Mary Barton's attempts to save the man accused of the crime from the gallows. In building her plot, Gaskell made use of a real-life precedent: the murder of Edward Culshaw by John Toms in Lancashire, in 1794. Toms' guilt was established when paper used as wadding to pack a bullet in a gun was found to match a torn sheet in the culprit's pocket.

This was an early example of a storyline hinging on forensic ballistics, although Gaskell's main focus was on industrial strife in the north-west of England. 'The Squire's Story', published by her friend Charles Dickens in *Household Words* in 1854, is a forerunner of the historical mystery.

Like Gaskell, Caroline Clive was married to a minister of religion, and published her first novel relatively late in life, in 1855. The opening words of *Paul Ferroll* are 'Nothing looks more peaceful and secure than a country house seen at early morning', but by the end of the first chapter the tranquil vision has dissolved into nightmare. The lady of the house has been stabbed to death while asleep in her bed.

Paul Ferroll not only kills his wife, he proceeds to enjoy happiness and prosperity – complete with a passionate second marriage – for seventeen years, until fate catches up with him. Even then, he manages to evade justice, escaping abroad with his devoted daughter. The book enjoyed a brief vogue, although its moral ambiguity alarmed some critics. Only in the third published edition of the book did Clive bow to pressure by adding a passage at the end to show that crime did not pay.

The narrative is interspersed with extracts from the diaries of Ferroll and his wife. This structural device[8] is to this day a popular means of giving readers an insight into the psychology of key characters. Clive also published a prequel, *Why Paul Ferroll Killed His Wife*, whose very title was a spoiler, but her earlier book is a more interesting example of sensational fiction. And yet, prior to a recent revival of interest, her work had languished in obscurity.

Braddon called Wilkie Collins 'my literary father', and acknowledged *The Woman in White* as the prime influence on her own fiction. She had been a professional actress, while Collins enjoyed acting. Their novels reflected their taste for drama and were adapted for the stage. Braddon even lived long enough to see a silent film version of *Aurora Floyd*.

Equally successful, on the strength of *East Lynne*, was Ellen Wood – better known at that time as Mrs Henry Wood. Wood's dark short story 'St Martin's Eve', published in 1858 and expanded into a novel eight years later, told the story of a homicidal woman and displayed a fascination with the morbid. The ingredients of *East Lynne* include murder, seduction, impersonation and infidelity, but detective work in the novel is incidental to the action.

Theatrical legend has it that a staged version of *East Lynne* was performed somewhere in the English-speaking world every Saturday night for forty years. The most famous line from the play is the bereaved Isobel Vane's fevered cry, 'Dead! Dead! Dead! And he never knew me, never called me mother!' These words do not appear in the novel, but were written by a hack playwright, T. A. Palmer. Seized on by music hall comedians, they became a mocking catchphrase that conveyed the overblown sentimentality of Victorian melodrama.[9] In unskilled hands, tragedy teeters into farce.

An American counterpart to Braddon and Wood as a novelist of sensation was Louisa May Alcott, who became famous as 'the children's friend' following the publication of *Little Women* in 1868. Among her early thrillers, neglected for more than a century, *Behind a Mask* (like *East Lynne*) is a Victorian 'governess novel'. The notion of the governess as someone with an unknown and mysterious past was perfect for sensation fiction. The book's alternative title, *A Woman's Power*, is significant. Alcott was a feminist with a pragmatic view about writing commercial fiction. She wrote in her diary that 'rubbishy tales . . . pay best, and I can't afford to starve on praise.'

V. V. , or Plots and Counterplots was published anonymously in 1865 in instalments. Five years later it re-emerged under Alcott's regular pseudonym, A. M. Barnard. The setting is Scotland, which perhaps seemed as strange and exotic to Alcott as central Europe did to Mrs Radcliffe. A confection of secret marriage, jealousy, murder and impersonation, the story was the first by an American woman to feature a detective. Like Braddon, Alcott didn't focus primarily on detection, but her Parisian private investigator Antoine Dupres, who likes 'to fathom a secret, trace a lie, discover a disguise', was in the mould of Poe's Dupin.

Seeley Regester's[10] *The Dead Letter* (1866) is often cited as the first American detective novel. A young attorney called Richard Redfield helps New York City detective Burton to solve the stabbing of Henry Moreland. Burton's daughter Lenore has psychic gifts, and he puts her into a trance to reveal information that complements material evidence and logical deduction. Regester wrote a second detective story, *The Figure Eight* (1869), but despite her status as a pioneer, the accolade of 'Mother of Detective Fiction' was bestowed not on her, but on another American novelist, Anna Katharine Green.

Notes

The main sources include Jennifer Carnell's *The Literary Lives of M. E. Braddon*, R. F. Stewart's *And Always a Detective*, and *The Cambridge Companion to Sensation Fiction*.

1   *the craving for respectability*: Reviewing Alan Brock's *Further Evidence* in 1934, Dorothy L. Sayers said: 'of all motives for crime, respectability – the least emphasised in fiction – is one of the most powerful in fact.' This timeless motive plays a part in such different books as Seishi Yokomizo's *The Honjin Murders*, from 1946, and Ann Cleeves' *The Long Call*, in 2019.

2   *the swindler and Sligo MP John Sadleir*: Sadleir, whose corpse was found at Hampstead Heath next to a jug of prussic acid, also inspired Charles Dickens' portrayal of the financier Mr Merdle in *Little Dorrit*.

3   *first in a long line of detectives with disabilities*: See Susannah B. Mintz's *The Disabled Detective*. Among deaf detectives, for instance, the stone-deaf former actor Drury Lane starred in four novels written by Ellery Queen's alter ego Barnaby Ross, while Samson Trehune investigates in Dwight Steward's *The Acupuncture Murders* and Caleb Zelic in Emma Viskic's *Resurrection Bay*. Today's disabled detectives include Jeffery Deaver's Lincoln Rhyme, the former head of NYPD forensics, who is quadriplegic, and J. K. Rowling's Cormoran Strike, who lost a leg during the war in Afghanistan.

4   *the sentimental Victorian notion of 'the angel in the house'*: Coventry Patmore's 1854 poem 'The Angel in the House' idealised the self-sacrificing devotion and purity of a woman such as his wife Emily. The concept made such a lasting impression that, as late as 1931, Virginia Woolf insisted that 'killing the Angel in the House was part of the occupation of a woman writer'.

5   *Lady Audley's sociopathic criminality*: A. B. Emrys compares the mystery about Lady Audley's psychology to that of the title character in Vera Caspary's *Bedelia*.

6   *a forerunner of the gentlemanly amateur detective*: R. F. Stewart sees Audley as a literary ancestor of A. A. Milne's Anthony Gillingham, Philip MacDonald's Colonel Anthony Gethryn and especially H. C. Bailey's Reggie Fortune. He argues that Bailey and Braddon were gifted writers who became victims of their own success, unable to develop because of the pressure to keep writing what their readers wanted.

7   *Caroline Clive*: Born in 1801, Clive was plagued throughout her life by disability. She contracted polio in childhood, and when, in 1873, after a period of deteriorating health, a spark from a fire caught her dress, her restricted mobility meant that she could not save herself from burning to death.

8   *This structural device*: Amelia B. Edwards' *My Brother's Wife*, published in the same year as *Paul Ferroll*, is even more inventive, including letters, a passage presented in the form of a play complete with stage directions, and a transcript from a court trial.

9   *the overblown sentimentality of Victorian melodrama*: As early as 1867, the American satirist Bret Harte was making fun of Wood and Braddon among others in *Condensed Novels*.

10 *Seeley Regester*: This was one of many pen-names adopted by Metta Victoria Fuller Victor, a prolific author of 'dime novels', cheap thrillers popular from the time of the American Civil War.

FOUR

Detective Fever

Wilkie Collins, Charles Dickens and early detective fiction

One moonlit summer night in the 1850s, three men were walking through the dimly lit and semi-rural lanes in the vicinity of Regent's Park, London. They had spent the evening at a party in Hanover Terrace, hosted by Wilkie Collins'[1] mother. Wilkie and his brother Charles were accompanying the artist John Everett Millais on his way home.

A woman's scream ripped through their conversation. The cry came from the garden of a large villa. Suddenly, its iron gate was flung open. A beautiful woman dressed in flowing white robes emerged from the garden, seeming not to run but rather to float through the air. As she saw the three men, she paused for an instant, as if frozen by terror, before vanishing into the shadows cast on the road.

'I must see who she is, and what is the matter!' Wilkie Collins announced to his startled companions.

Without another word, he dashed after her into the darkness. The two other men waited in vain for him to return, and eventually went on their way back to Gower Street. The following day, Wilkie was back at home, and although he was coy about discussing what had happened after his abrupt departure, they gathered that he'd caught up with the fugitive, and listened to her story.

A young woman of good birth and position, she'd fallen into the hands of the villa's owner. For months he'd kept her as his prisoner, threatening her life if she tried to escape. When a chance to get away presented itself, she'd seized it, but her captor was in hot pursuit, brandishing a poker and threatening to dash out her brains.

Was this strange encounter the inspiration for the first major sensation novel, Wilkie Collins' *The Woman in White*?[2]

The answer, alas, is that this story is unlikely to be true. It was only recorded (by Millais' son) forty years after its supposed occurrence. Wilkie Collins himself never mentioned the incident. Was the reason for his reticence that 'the woman in white' was Caroline Graves, who became his mistress? Perhaps, but perhaps not. Their relationship was an open secret among Collins' friends, even though he usually introduced Caroline as his 'housekeeper'. Collins was an unconventional man with a lifestyle to match, and yet he became the most influential British crime novelist of the nineteenth century.

Wilkie Collins' birth in January 1824 was as complicated as the rest of his life. Rough handling during his delivery probably caused the startling bump on the right side of his forehead. His father was an artist, and J. M. W. Turner was said to have dandled the infant Wilkie on his knee. Short, with prominent eyes and tiny hands and feet, Collins had high shoulders and that disproportionately large, bulging head. Self-conscious about his appearance, he accentuated its oddity with endless fidgeting and a flamboyant dress sense. Poor health plagued him, but he had a gift for friendship.

His closest friend was Charles Dickens, twelve years his senior. They met in 1851 when Collins played a servant in a production of a stage comedy by Edward Bulwer-Lytton in which Dickens took a leading role. The two men shared a concern for social justice as well as amateur theatrics, and regularly travelled together around England and to the Continent.

Like many writers, Collins regarded himself as one of life's outsiders. Called to the Bar, he never practised, although his fiction often demonstrated insight into the law's failings. He regarded the 'scope and purpose' of marriage as 'miserably narrow', and his contempt for Victorian laws about matrimonial property, illegitimacy and divorce often surfaced in his writings. As he said, some 'would rather see murder committed under their own eyes' than approve of a fair distribution of assets on the ending of a marriage.

In 1858, he set up home with Caroline Graves, a widow whose daughter he treated as his own. While he was writing *The Moonstone*, Caroline left him and married someone else, only to return to Collins shortly afterwards. Meanwhile, he had met the nineteen-year-old Martha Rudd, who was to give birth to his three children. For the rest of his life he maintained two households, a luxury made possible by his literary success.

In 1856 Dickens published in *Household Words* Collins' story 'The Diary of Anne Rodway'. Structured in the form of a sequence of diary entries, the story is notable for introducing an amateur female detective.[3] A 'plain needlewoman', Anne investigates the murder of her friend Mary Mallinson. Collins' short crime fiction also included a comedy, 'The Biter Bit'. This was one of the first of thousands of mystery stories with 'biter-bit' twists of varying quality, typically involving would-be criminals who receive their comeuppance in a final reversal of fortune, often at the hands of their intended victim. He wrote an arsenic-poisoning story too, 'The Poisoned Meal', and an early example of the 'impossible crime' mystery, 'A Terribly Strange Bed'.[4]

Secrets fascinated Collins, perhaps because his personal life was as convoluted as his plots. *The Dead Secret* (1856) reflects the Gothic tradition, concerning a mystery about parentage rather than murder. Collins was learning narrative craft, and that it was a mistake to think it 'desirable to let the effect of the story depend on expectation rather than surprise.'

On a trip to France, he acquired Maurice Méjan's *Recueil des Causes Célèbres*, a 'Pitaval' similar to the *Newgate Calendar*. Méjan's account of an eighteenth-century abduction supplied material for *The Woman in White*. Recent scandals also fired Collins' imagination. Bulwer-Lytton, now a Tory cabinet minister, had confined his estranged wife Rosina to a lunatic asylum,[5] only for her to be released following a public outcry. Louisa Nottidge, meanwhile, who had joined a mystical sect known as the Agapemone, or 'Abode of Love', in Somerset, was abducted by her family and incarcerated. After being freed, she returned to the Agapemone and sued successfully for false imprisonment. A witness in the case was Bryan Proctor, who multi-tasked as a poet, solicitor and Commissioner of Lunacy. His report had led to her release, and in 1860 Collins dedicated *The Woman in White* to him.

Collins' first big hit began life as a cliff-hanging serial in Dickens' *All the Year Round*. In it, Walter Hartright has a brief encounter with a distressed young woman in white prior to taking up a teaching appointment at Limmeridge House in Cumberland. There he meets Laura Fairlie, who bears a striking resemblance to the woman in white, and falls in love with her. Unfortunately, Laura has already promised to marry ruthless Sir Percival Glyde. After the marriage, Laura's devoted half-sister Marian Halcombe and Walter find themselves pitted against Glyde's puppet-master, Count Fosco. Grotesquely obese but superficially charming, Fosco is one of fiction's most memorable villains. Marian is an equally charismatic and resourceful heroine, a New Woman ahead of her time.

Readers had now discovered the addictive pleasures of crime writing and entrepreneurs leapt on the bandwagon. According to Kenneth Robinson,[6] 'Manufacturers were producing *Woman in White* perfume, *Woman in White* cloaks and bonnets, and the music-shops displayed *Woman in White* waltzes and quadrilles . . . Thackeray sat up all night reading it. Edward Fitzgerald named a herring-lugger he owned *Marian Halcombe*, while the Prince Consort was another admirer.' One dissenting voice belonged to Bulwer-Lytton, who described *The Woman in White* as 'trash'.

Armadale (1866) followed the success of *The Woman in White*, a gallimaufry of confused identities, murder and inheritance. The alluring but dangerous Lydia Gwilt is reminiscent of the real-life Madeleine Smith[7], who was tried in Scotland in 1857 for poisoning her husband with arsenic. The jury returned a verdict of 'Not Proven', but many people thought Madeleine had got away with murder.

The popularity of mystery fiction soon provoked a backlash. As early as 1864, James Fitzjames Stephen was moaning[8] that 'this detective-worship appears one of the silliest superstitions that ever were concocted by ingenious writers'. This put him in the vanguard of a long line of commentators who have scoffed at detective stories for a century and a half, only to see their popularity continue to climb.

Collins was quick to spot the potential of detective characters. He sent his mother a copy of Andrew Forrester Jr's *The Female Detective*[9] (1864), featuring the first professional female detective.[10] Under his real name, James Redding Ware,[11] Forrester had published *The Road Murder* (1865), fictionalising the murder of a small boy, Francis Saville Kent, at Road House, Wiltshire: the boy's half-sister Constance was found guilty of the crime. The case has fascinated generations of crime writers and criminologists.[12]

The Road Murder was investigated by Inspector Jonathan Whicher, and Collins borrowed details from the case for *The Moonstone*[13] (1868). A sacred diamond stolen from Rachel Verinder's room was originally looted from an Indian shrine, and Collins treated his Indian characters, and their religious attachment to the jewel, with a sensitivity uncommon for its time. Sergeant Cuff, modelled on Whicher, is a formidable investigator who dreams of retiring to grow roses, but the riddle is eventually solved through amateur detective work.

The Moonstone's excellence derives in part from Collins' diligent research and attention to detail, but above all from a change of approach described in his preface: 'In some of my former novels, the object proposed has been to trace the influence of circumstances upon character. In the present story I have reversed the process.' Tormented by gout while writing the book, he needed heavy doses of laudanum to keep going. Good writers don't waste experiences, and laudanum plays a crucial part in the storyline.

Collins' publishers called him 'the King of Inventors' and the book brims with ingredients destined to become tropes of detective fiction: a country-house mystery, physical and psychological clues, red herrings, a Great Detective with a touch of eccentricity, a reconstruction of the crime and a 'least likely person' culprit. The idea of an apparent 'closed circle' of suspects has a timeless appeal. Enclosed communities, and the tensions fomenting within them, have long been a crucial backdrop for all manner of crime stories.

The Moonstone is a masterpiece of domestic suspense. This was no Gothic tale but a pioneering blend of sensation and realism. As Henry James said,[14] Collins 'introduced into fiction that most mysterious of mysteries, the mysteries that are at our own doors . . . Instead of the terrors of Udolpho, we were treated to the terrors of the cheerful country house, or the busy London lodgings. And there is no doubt that these were infinitely the more terrible.'

Setting plays a key role in crime fiction. In the words of P. D. James,[15] it 'establishes atmosphere, creates the appropriate mood of menace, excitement, horror, or loneliness, influences character-isation and plot, and helps root the sometimes bizarre events of the story . . .' Collins intensifies the drama by contrasting the apparent stability of the Verinder household with the dangers of the Shivering Sands, 'the most horrible quicksand on the shores of Yorkshire'.

The Moonstone's narrative structure was crucial to the book's success and reflected Collins' experience of witness testimony in court cases. He elaborated on an approach used in *The Woman in White*, telling the story from five nicely contrasted viewpoints. The changes of voice and tempo enhance the story's credibility and depth. Readers can identify with each narrator in turn and learn more than can be gleaned from a single version of events. The central plot twist enables Collins to dodge the usual challenge of adopting multiple viewpoints in a detective story: how to avoid misleading the reader by concealing the culprit's thoughts?

Anthony Trollope[16] damned Collins' methods with faint praise: 'The construction is most minute and most wonderful. But I can never lose the taste of the construction.' Yet it's a taste to savour, just as film connoisseurs relish the *Rashomon* effect.[17]

Above all, Collins gave readers what they wanted. The Verinders' garrulous house steward, Gabriel Betteredge, asks the hero, Franklin Blake: 'Do you feel an uncomfortable heat at the pit of your stomach . . . and a nasty thumping at the top of your head? . . . I call it the detective-fever; and I first caught it in the company of Sergeant Cuff.' Betteredge was speaking for the new generation of detective fiction fans.

At the peak of his powers, as when satirising the hypocrisy of the evangelist Drusilla Clack in *The Moonstone*, Collins subordinated social comment to the demands of his story. *The Law and the Lady*

(1875) attacks the Scottish justice system, but is most memorable for a resolute female protagonist. Valeria Woodville discovers her husband Eustace's dark secret – that he was tried for the murder of his first wife. The verdict was 'Not Proven', and Valeria's desperation to find out what actually happened, and remove the stain on Eustace's reputation, gives her the impetus to turn detective.

Collins denounced the law's harsh treatment of women and illegitimate children, but as the years passed, his desire to write novels 'with a purpose' became self-defeating. As with so many authors who try to weaponise their fiction, he fired too many blanks. The preachiness of his weaker books was mocked by Algernon Swinburne:[18] 'What brought good Wilkie's genius nigh perdition? / Some demon whispered — "Wilkie! have a mission."'

Charles Dickens shared Collins' enthusiasm for crime, detection and mystery. Dickens had been a teenager when the Metropolitan Police Act 1829 paved the way for a paid professional police force. Then, after the Detective Department – staffed by two inspectors and six sergeants – was established at Scotland Yard in 1842, he wrote laudatory articles about early police officers in *Household Words*. Whereas William Godwin romanticised criminality, Dickens was acutely aware of the misery crime caused, especially to those least able to defend themselves. An encounter with the artist, forger and poisoner Thomas Wainewright[19] seems to have been the inspiration for the villainous Julius Slinkton in his story 'Hunted Down'.

The softly-spoken Nadgett in *Martin Chuzzlewit* (1842–4) is a private investigator who exposes a murderer, while *Bleak House* (1852–3) featured the first major fictional police detective, Inspector Bucket. Based on Inspector Field, a Scotland Yard man Dickens held in high esteem, Bucket is shrewd and credible, a model for many of the genre's police detectives.

Jonathan Coe has characterised Esther Summerson[20] in *Bleak House*, like Arthur Clennam in *Little Dorrit* and Franklin Blake in *The Moonstone*, as a reluctant detective. Their investigations 'function as thrilling metaphors for the processes by which we all acquire our knowledge of the world'.

Dickens' final, unfinished novel, *The Mystery of Edwin Drood*[21] (1870), falls within the crime genre more obviously than its predecessors. As in *Bleak House*, Dickens experimented with story-telling technique, combining chapters in the present tense with others told in the past tense.[22] Like Collins, he was an influential innovator as well as an entertainer.

The book was cut short by Dickens' death. Debate has raged ever since about how he intended to resolve the puzzles in the storyline, which halts abruptly at a point where Drood has vanished, and the enigmatic Datchery is watching the movements of creepy choirmaster John Jasper. Was Drood murdered? If so, by whom? Dickens left no notes explaining what he had in mind, thus creating one of the genre's most enduring puzzles.[23]

The Irishman Sheridan Le Fanu,[24] great-nephew of the playwright Richard Brinsley Sheridan, reworked the central idea of his 'locked-room' story 'Passage in the Secret History of an Irish Countess', aka 'The Murdered Cousin', to form a plot strand in *Uncle Silas* (1864), a Gothic thriller with a sinister villain.

Le Fanu's output included ghost stories, sensation novels and mysteries such as *Wylder's Hand* (1864). The story lacks both a detective and the analysis of clues, but as Julian Symons says, 'it poses a puzzle entirely in the manner of a detective story, and the solution of this puzzle is expertly disguised'; Symons points out that the key plot twist recurs in Dashiell Hammett's *The Thin Man*. Even more improbably, Le Fanu's *The House by the Churchyard* (1863) was a significant influence on James Joyce, who makes numerous allusions to his fellow Dubliner in *Finnegans Wake*.

What was the first *detective* novel written in English? *The Notting Hill Mystery* is a strong candidate. Originally published as a serial in *Once a Week* magazine in 1862–3, it appeared as a novel in 1865, attributed to Charles Felix, a pen-name for the publisher Charles Warren Adams.[25]

The story records the efforts of Ralph Henderson, an insurance investigator, to look into a suspicious death, and comprises documents such as letters, diary entries, business reports and maps. Adams was a pioneer who developed the concept of the 'casebook' novel[26] and demonstrated its flexibility and potential.

*

Crime writers fall in and out of favour. As they grow older, attention usually shifts to younger, fresher talents. When a small Bristol press published Hugh Conway's *Called Back* as a 'Christmas annual' in 1883, the exciting (if coincidence-heavy) story about a blind man who stumbles upon a murder rapidly sold more than a quarter of a million copies.

'Many prophesied the displacement of Wilkie Collins by the new star,' according to an obituary of Collins in the *Palace Journal* six years later, 'but professional jealousy so little affected the older man, that he took great pains to assist the rising writer in elaborating his plots.'

Conway, whose real name was Frederick John Fargus, succumbed to tuberculosis, and after travelling to the French Riviera to recuperate, he was diagnosed with typhoid fever, and died at Monte Carlo aged thirty-seven. Conway's publishers asked Collins to produce their Christmas annual for 1886. He obliged with *The Guilty River*, a hastily written novella that confirmed that his powers were waning.

But there is never a shortage of hopeful new writers. A Christmas annual published by Beeton's the following year introduced another young novelist and a new detective character. Neither made an instant impact, but soon they changed crime fiction for ever. The author was Arthur Conan Doyle, and his detective Sherlock Holmes.

Notes

The main sources are the biographies of Collins by Robinson, Clarke, Pykett, Lycett, Ackroyd, and Catherine Peters (the step-daughter of Francis Iles), and Andrew Gasson's *Wilkie Collins: An Illustrated Guide*.

1   *Wilkie Collins*: Collins features in John Dickson Carr's *The Hungry Goblin*, while a supposedly unpublished Collins novel also supplies the title and a plot strand for Carr's *The Dead Man's Knock*.
2   *The Woman in White*: The novel has been filmed, televised, and adapted for a stage musical by Andrew Lloyd Webber and David Zippel, with a book by Charlotte Jones. A 'woman in white' features in Gillian Flynn's *Sharp Objects*, while Flynn's *The Grownup* explicitly references the novel: see Emily Foster's article in *Politics/Letters*, 20 December 2018. Flynn's *Gone Girl* utilises Collins' casebook storytelling technique to fashion a twenty-first-century novel of sensation. James Wilson's *The Dark Clue* offers a sequel to Collins' novel, while Sarah Waters' *Fingersmith* has a twist similar to

Collins', which was 'the engine both of the text and of my own excitement at constructing it' (*The Guardian*, 17 June 2006). Douglas Preston and Lincoln Child give a hat-tip to Collins in their Special Agent Prendergast novel *Brimstone* by naming one of their villains Count Fosco.

3   *amateur female detective*: The title character in Catherine Crowe's 1841 bestseller *Susan Hopley* is a working-class proto-detective, a maid-servant with a nose for crime.

4   *the 'impossible crime' mystery, 'A Terribly Strange Bed'*: Joseph Conrad's 'The Inn of the Two Witches', published in 1913, features an identical plot. Conrad claimed not to have read Collins' story.

5   *Bulwer-Lytton . . . , had confined his estranged wife Rosina to a lunatic asylum*: Elaine Showalter, author of *The Female Malady: Women, Madness, and English Culture, 1830–1980*, has pointed out that Charles Reade's *Hard Cash* and Le Fanu's *The Rose and the Key* both concern wrongful incarceration in asylums.

6   *Kenneth Robinson*: Robinson was a minister in Harold Wilson's government during the 1960s. He attributes to Collins the dictum 'Make 'em weep, make 'em laugh, make 'em wait', but although this is sound advice for any author who wishes to keep readers on the edge of their chairs, the phrase was probably coined by Collins' friend Charles Reade.

7   *Madeleine Smith*: Smith lived for seventy-one years after her trial, and, following two further marriages and emigration to the United States, was buried there under the name Lena Sheehy. Her independence and sexual confidence informed Mary Elizabeth Braddon's presentation of Lucy Graham in *Lady Audley's Secret*. Other novels to draw on the Smith case include *Letty Lynton* by Marie Belloc Lowndes. *Madeleine* was David Lean's film version of the case.

8   *James Fitzjames Stephen was moaning*: In 'Detectives in Fiction and in Real Life', *Saturday Review* 17, 1864. Stephen, a barrister, was concerned that fictional detectives of the time did not approach questions about evidence with the rigour appropriate to a court of law. A prominent campaigner for law reform, he became a High Court judge. Unfortunately, his mind failed, and his bias against Florence Maybrick when summing up in her trial for murder in 1889 resulted in a legendary miscarriage of justice. Ironically, the Maybrick case has itself been fictionalised in detective novels, notably Anthony Berkeley's *The Wychford Poisoning Case*.

9   *The Female Detective*: The protagonist operates undercover using the alias Miss Gladden; she is also known as 'G'. Not until after the First World War did the British police have women officers.

10 *the first professional female detective*: Fictional female detectives remained uncommon until the late nineteenth century; even then their creators were usually male. A notable exception was Catherine Louisa Pirkis, an animal rights activist and creator of Loveday Brooke.

11 *Under his real name, James Redding Ware*: Ware's authorship was discussed by Mike Ashley in a twenty-first-century reprint of *The Female Detective* by the British Library. Ashley also introduced a reissue of *Revelations of a Lady Detective*, published anonymously a few months after *The Female Detective*, and featuring Mrs Paschal. Like Miss Gladden, she acts as an agent for the police and also investigates cases in a private capacity. Ashley identifies her creators as Samuel Bracebridge Hemyng and William Stephens Hayward.

12 *The case has fascinated generations of crime writers and criminologists*:
Kate Summerscale's account of the case, *The Suspicions of Mr Whicher*,
spawned a TV series with Whicher investigating fictional crimes. John
Rhode edited *The Trial of Constance Kent*, and later wrote an account
of Constance's hitherto unknown adult life, included in the Detection
Club's *The Anatomy of Murder*. Dorothy L. Sayers played armchair
detective, making copious notes about the case in her copy of Rhode's
book.

13 *The Moonstone*: The book has been adapted for film, television and radio,
while Collins himself wrote a version for the stage.

14 *Henry James said*: In 'Miss Braddon', *The Nation*, 9 November 1865. James
corresponded with the criminologist William Roughead about the Madeleine
Smith case, and his little-regarded novel *The Other House* deals with child-
murder and its concealment.

15 *In the words of P. D. James*: When introducing an Oxford University Press
edition of the book in 1999.

16 *Anthony Trollope*: The remark is from his autobiography. Trollope's fiction
often deals with crime, as in *The Last Chronicle of Barset* and *The Eustace
Diamonds*, but he was hardly a 'crime writer'.

17 *the Rashomon effect*: A term derived from Akira Kurosawa's 1950 psychological thriller film *Rashomon*, in which the characters give divergent,
self-serving accounts of the same incident. The film noir *Crossfire* employed
flashbacks in a comparable way in 1947. In *Vantage Point* (2008), an
attempted political assassination is seen from multiple perspectives.
*Rashomo*n was adapted from 'In a Grove', a short story by Ryonosuke
Akutagawa, often described as father of the Japanese short story.

18 *mocked by Algernon Swinburne*: In *Fortnightly Review*, November 1889.

19 *Thomas Wainewright*: Fictional versions of Wainewright surface in books
as different as Bulwer-Lytton's *Lucretia* and Andrew Motion's intriguing
'experimental biography' *Wainewright the Poisoner*.

20 *Jonathan Coe has characterised Esther Summerson*: In 'Shuddering
Organisms', *London Review of Books*, 12 May 1994.

21 *The Mystery of Edwin Drood*: In 2009 alone, three books illustrated what
D. J. Taylor calls the principle of 'morphic resonance' in literature: Dan
Simmons' *Drood*, Matthew Pearl's *The Last Dickens* and Jean-Pierre Ohl's
Mr Dick are 'three independently conceived but uncannily similar versions
of the final years of Charles Dickens', 'Who Did It – and Why?', *Guardian*,
21 March 2009.

22 *combining chapters in the present tense with others told in the past tense*:
Collins' use of the diary in *The Woman in White* is an example of a similar
technique. In 'Dickens's Tricks', John Mullan argues that: 'the present tense
strand of *The Mystery of Edwin Drood* is where mania, obsession, and
fantasy are released. These are not just the novel's themes – they are the
forces that ripple through it.'

23 *one of the genre's most enduring puzzles*: *The D Case* by Carlo Fruttero and
Franco Lucentini is a postmodern metafiction inspired by the mystery,
featuring assorted Great Detectives and a chapter called 'Waiting for Poirot'.
So many writers have completed Dickens' novel that R. F. Stewart devoted
a book, *End Game*, to their efforts. In Bruce Graeme's *Epilogue*, two investigators go back in time to solve the puzzle. In 1914, the Dickens Fellowship

organised a trial of Jasper for Drood's murder, with G. K. Chesterton as judge; the jury returned a verdict of manslaughter.

24 *Sheridan Le Fanu*: In Dorothy L. Sayers' *Gaudy Night*, Harriet Vane is researching Le Fanu. Sayers worked on a biography of Wilkie Collins but never completed it. She argued, 'if the detective story was to live and develop, it must get back to where it began in the hands of Collins and Le Fanu, and become once more a novel of manners instead of a pure crossword puzzle'.

25 *Charles Warren Adams*: Mike Ashley's introduction to the British Library edition of the book reveals Felix's identity. Adams later became Secretary of the Anti-Vivisection Society.

26 *the 'casebook' novel*: This form of crime fiction is discussed further in Chapter 31. Multiple viewpoints also feature in Victorian horror novels such as Bram Stoker's *Dracula* and Richard Marsh's *The Beetle* (which at first far outsold *Dracula*). Marsh was a pen-name for Richard Bernard Heldmann. Gaoled for issuing forged cheques in 1883, he became a successful writer under his pseudonym. His detectives include Judith Lee, a skilled lip-reader. Marsh's grandson, Robert Aickman, was a gifted author of 'strange stories', which are in many ways the antithesis of rational detective fiction.

FIVE

Poacher Turned Gamekeeper

The French Revolution: Vidocq, Gaboriau and their worldwide influence

'Amongst the delicate monsters and other curiosities which are now exhibiting in London,' declared the *Morning Post* in 1845, 'Vidocq is pre-eminent.' The newspaper was reporting on the latest treat at the Regent Street Cosmorama, exhibition rooms originally designed to house a sophisticated version of the traditional peep show. The star attraction, on a visit to England from his native France, was the criminal-turned-detective Eugène-François Vidocq. Vidocq was no ordinary celebrity. He was a Jekyll and Hyde of crime.

People queued for the chance to pay five shillings to enter Vidocq's exhibition. Once inside, they were treated to a bizarre mixture of paintings, wax fruit (sixty varieties selected from a collection originally bought for the palace of King Louis Philippe I) and a Chamber of Horrors. This assortment of macabre memorabilia featured a knife belonging to Louis Philippe's would-be assassin, the Corsican Giuseppe Marco Fieschi;[1] the pen with which the double-murderer Pierre François Lacenaire wrote his memoirs while awaiting his encounter with the guillotine; and miscellaneous instruments of torture. Spectators could also marvel at the type of manacles and weighted boots worn by Vidocq himself at a time when, as *The Times* put it, 'he fell under the displeasure of the French government', prior to going straight.

Presiding over it all was the bluff, extrovert Vidocq. He took part in a production designed to show off his mastery of disguise. His knack of concealing his true size took the fancy of a reporter from *The Times*: 'by some strange process connected with physical formation he has the faculty of contracting his height several inches and in this diminished state to walk about, jump etc. . . . .' In every other respect, Vidocq was larger than life. *The Times* was certainly impressed: 'He is extremely intelligent, communicative and good-humoured . . . he would make an excellent actor . . . [and] possesses all the strength, vigour and buoyancy of a man 25 years his junior.'

Vidocq's theatrical skills matched his flair for public relations. He was a great pretender.

In Vidocq's life story, fact and fiction are hopelessly blurred. At the age of fourteen, he ran away from his home in Arras, taking with him money stolen from the family bakery; his plan was to sail for the Americas. After losing his ill-gotten gains, he joined a band of travelling entertainers before returning home to seek forgiveness. His continuing exploits included enlisting in the army, deserting, and ultimately being sentenced to eight years in gaol with hard labour for forgery. He broke out of gaol repeatedly, only to be recaptured time and again. A dashing swordsman, he claimed to have fought fifteen duels in six months.

Audacious to a fault, he offered his services to the police as an informant in 1809. His spying proved so successful that he was allowed to form his own band of agents, the Brigade de la Sûreté. Supposedly, he helped to recover a necklace stolen from the Empress Josephine. What is certain is that when Napoleon Bonaparte formalised the brigade as the Sûreté Nationale in 1813, Vidocq was put in charge.

As with Scotland Yard's Detective Department, the Sûreté began modestly but grew fast, and Vidocq claimed credit for significantly reducing crime. His questionable methods (including his habit of hiring ex-convicts with a penchant for acting as *agents provocateurs*) meant that he antagonised police officers jealous of his popularity and outraged by the state's reliance on a shameless rogue. He was also at odds with his superior, Marc Duplessis.

Vidocq eventually tired of battling for power within the police, and resigned in 1827. He published his memoirs, founded a paper factory and went bankrupt before being reappointed as chief of the Sûreté following the July Revolution of 1830. His belief that, in detective work, the end justified the means continued to attract controversy. After a couple of years he left again.

This time, he founded the world's first private detective agency, Le Bureau des Renseignements, anticipating by twenty years Allan Pinkerton's famous agency in the United States. Again he drew most of his staff from the ranks of former convicts. His brushes with the law, usually in connection with alleged fraud and corruption, continued until shortly before his death at the age of eighty-one. He left eleven wills, each giving what remained of his fortune to a different woman.

His contributions to police work included innovations in crime-scene investigation and record keeping. As recently as 1990, when a group of retired FBI officers and other experts seeking to solve cold cases was formed in Philadelphia, they called themselves the Vidocq Society.

Vidocq served as a model for several characters created by his friend Honoré de Balzac, notably the arch-villain Vautrin, an escaped convict and criminal mastermind; Vautrin, meaning 'wild boar' in the local patois, had been a nickname given to Vidocq in his youth. Victor Hugo's portrayals of both police Inspector Javert and the reformed criminal Valjean in *Les Misérables* (1862) were also inspired by Vidocq. So were the police officers Rodolphe de Gerolstein, from Eugène Sue's *Les Mystères de Paris*[2] (1842–3) and Jackal, who appears in Alexandre Dumas'[3] *Les Mohicans de Paris* (1854–9).

Vidocq's *Memoires*, padded out by ghostwriters, and published in 1828–9, were translated into English,[4] and two plays based on them reached the London stage. Vidocq's memoirs arguably fell within the tradition of the 'Newgate novel' and the British reading public hungered for colourful accounts of heroic detective work.[5]

Bulwer-Lytton's *Night and Morning* featured a Vidocqesque detective, Favart, 'a man of the most vigilant acuteness', while 'I am Vidocq!', the phrase with which the great man regularly greeted captured criminals, had its echo in 'I am Hawkshaw, the detective', a recurrent phrase in Tom Taylor's stage melodrama of 1863, *The Ticket-of-Leave Man.*

'Vidocq' was a term used by American newspapermen as a synonym for 'detective'. His *Memoires* fired Poe's imagination, although in 'The Murders in the Rue Morgue', Dupin snipes that 'Vidocq . . . was a good guesser and a persevering man. But, without educated thought, he erred continually . . .' And Vidocq was a direct inspiration for a French detective created by Émile Gaboriau, Monsieur Lecoq.

Émile Gaboriau worked for Paul Féval[6] before deciding to write on his own account. Like his contemporaries Sue and Dumas *père*, Féval wrote against the clock for *feuilletons*, supplements inserted in newspapers. The stories were melodramatic and suspenseful thrillers, each instalment ending with a cliffhanger. Excitement was everything. There was no time for the order and method of a cerebral detective like Poe's Dupin.

Gaboriau's prose wasn't as breathless. *The Widow Lerouge* was serialised by a newspaper called *Le Pays* in 1865, but attracted little attention until it was reprinted the following year by *Le Soleil*, which was saved from oblivion by the story's popularity. The main detective is Père Tabaret, a retired pawnbroker. He surveys the crime scene before announcing that the culprit 'is a young man, below average height, elegantly dressed and wearing a top hat. He carried an umbrella and was smoking a Havana cigar in a holder.'

Although Tabaret takes centre stage, more significant in the long run was a minor character to whom he explains his methods. Like Vidocq, the detective Lecoq was 'an old offender reconciled with the law'. Gaboriau realised that he had created a character too interesting to waste, and Lecoq returned in *The Mystery of Orcival* (1867). Readers warmed to this master of disguise, the first major detective character to feature in a series of novels, by modern standards, but Gaboriau's attempts to maintain reader interest for the span of a full-length book seem laboured.

File No. 113 (1867) illustrates both his strengths and his shortcomings. The story opens with a bank robbery, which gives rise to a puzzle: only two men had a key to the safe, so is one of them responsible for the crime? However, a protracted flashback kills the pace of the narrative, and Lecoq's contribution is subdued. The original novel ran to 145,000 words; a revised English translation, called *The Blackmailers*, halved the length of the book, but even this abridged version is verbose and meandering.

In *Monsieur Lecoq* (1869), the detective breaks a simple cipher in a manner similar to that in the Sherlock Holmes novel *The Valley of Fear* (1915): the numbers in the code indicate words on the pages of a book. Gaboriau's work was influential and its commercial success prompted an early example of the 'continuation novel',[7] to this day a lucrative outgrowth of the publishing ecosystem. After Gaboriau's early death, his principal disciple, Fortuné du Boisgobey,[8] wrote *The Old Age of Lecoq, the Detective* (1878). As with many continuation novels, it was a pale shadow of the original.

Gaboriau's influence extended across the globe.[9] In Australia, a legal clerk called Fergus Hume[10] tried writing plays without success. He 'inquired of a leading Melbourne bookseller what style of book he sold most of. He replied that the detective stories of Gaboriau had a large sale, and as I had never even heard of this author I bought all his works – eleven or thereabouts – and read them carefully. The style of these attracted me, and I determined to write a book of the same class, containing a mystery, a murder and a description of low life in Melbourne.'

The result was *The Mystery of a Hansom Cab* (1886), a fake-identity story that (if one suspends natural disbelief about hype over book sales) became the first crime novel to sell half a million copies. It was no instant success, however. A leading Australian publisher, George Robertson, turned it down, on the basis that 'no colonial could write anything worth reading': Hume had, in fact, been born in England, but emigrated to New Zealand before moving to Melbourne. Undaunted, he self-published the book and sold five thousand copies in three weeks. He parted with the copyright for fifty pounds, and had the bittersweet experience of seeing copies fly off the shelves without receiving another penny in royalties.

The novel opens with a newspaper report – referencing Gaboriau and Lecoq – about the discovery in the back of a hansom cab of a man's corpse, reeking of alcohol and chloroform. Hume's detectives, Gorby and Kilsip, make a contrasting pair, respectively incompetent and dishonest.

'Bestseller' is a slippery term that can mean all things to all publicists, but there is no denying that Hume's book sold in large numbers. Back in Britain, Arthur Conan Doyle was not impressed,[11] describing it as 'One of the weakest tales that I have read, and simply sold by puffing.' He'd just published *A Study in Scarlet*, but the first appearance of Sherlock Holmes made much less of a splash than Hume's novel.

Hume was one of many crime writers to discover that beginning with a bang is no guarantee of long-term success.[12] He returned to England, where he churned out potboilers for more than forty years before dying in a rented room in an Essex bungalow.

Gaboriau was the literary model for Anna Katharine Green, a New York attorney's daughter who published *The Leavenworth Case*, subtitled *A Lawyer's Story*, in 1878. She shared Gaboriau's interest in forensic science and her police detective, Ebenezer Gryce, has something in common with Tabaret and Lecoq.

He investigates the shooting of Horatio Leavenworth, and Green's single-minded focus on mystification set her apart from less skilled contemporaries.[13] The novel features many ingredients that soon became familiar in detective fiction: a rich victim who was about to change his will, floor plans, a clue in the form of an initialled handkerchief, a numbered list of significant points in the investigation and the shifting of suspicion from one potential culprit to another.

Gryce, 'a portly, comfortable personage' is – despite foibles such as a habit of not looking straight at the person he is questioning – much less vividly characterised than Sherlock Holmes, who came along almost a decade later, but the book's admirers included Wilkie Collins, who extolled Green's 'fertility of invention', Arthur Conan Doyle and Agatha Christie.[14]

Her detective became a long-running series character and Green became known as the 'Mother of Detective Fiction'. In 1897, she introduced Amelia Butterworth, who narrates *That Affair Next*

Door, and becomes Gryce's unofficial collaborator. Butterworth, who appeared in two subsequent novels, is an inquisitive elderly spinster with a flair for detection, a forerunner of Christie's Jane Marple.

Violet Strange, Green's third major sleuth, was driven to work as a private investigator more than half a century before P. D. James' Cordelia Gray followed the same path. Violet appears in *The Golden Slipper*, a linked set of short stories, but once she finds true love she no longer needs to 'meddle with matters so repugnant to a woman's natural instincts' as crime.

Green's career lasted into the Roaring Twenties, although she had little time for feminism or campaigns for votes for women. Her storytelling remained as decorously Victorian as covered piano legs, but she demonstrated that writing detective fiction was a highly suitable job for a woman. In the early twentieth century, she became a role model for younger writers, including Carolyn Wells,[15] who was inspired to become a crime novelist after hearing *That Affair Next Door* read aloud.

Green's success encouraged another woman to supplement the family income through writing. From the first, Mary Roberts Rinehart displayed a flair for melodrama coupled with a prose style livelier than Green's. She became the most successful female American crime novelist of her time.

Notes

The main sources are James Morton's *The First Detective: The Life and Revolutionary Times of Vidocq*, Haia Shpayer-Makov's *The Ascent of the Detective*, T. J. Hale's introduction to *Great French Detective Stories*, Lucy Sussex's *Blockbuster!* and 'The Queer Story of Fergus Hume' in *Murder in the Closet*, Stephen Knight's essay in *Criminal Moves*, and Patricia D. Maida's book about Green.

1   *the Corsican Giuseppe Marco Fieschi*: Fieschi's principal murder weapon was his 'infernal machine', a gun with twenty-five barrels, which killed eighteen people, but not Louis Philippe, in 1835. Fieschi himself suffered severe facial injuries; traces of them can be seen on his death mask, which is held at Norwich Castle Museum; the public taste for grisly sightseeing is not confined to the mid-nineteenth century.

2   *Les Mystères de Paris*: Published in no fewer than ninety parts in *Journal des Débats* between June 1842 and October 1843, this massive, rambling

thriller drew inspiration from Vidocq and also from James Fenimore Cooper's Natty Bumppo tales; its popularity prompted many imitations.

3   *Alexandre Dumas*: Dumas, although best remembered for his swashbuckling historical stories, often worked on the edge of crime fiction. Among many books that take inspiration from Dumas' classic revenge thriller *The Count of Monte Cristo*, Reginald Hill's *The Woodcutter* is outstanding. *Les Mohicans de Paris* introduced the phrase '*cherchez la femme*'. In Ross Macdonald's *The Chill*, Lew Archer gives the alternative perspective: 'When a woman is murdered, you ask her estranged husband where he was at the time. It's the corollary of *cherchez la femme.*'

4   *Vidocq's Memoires . . . were translated into English*: George Borrow is said to have been the translator; this may not be true, but he admired the 'fertility of invention, knowledge of human nature, and easy style' of the *Memoires*.

5   *The British reading public hungered for colourful accounts of heroic detective work*: 1827 saw the publication of *Richmond; or, Scenes in the Life of a Bow Street Officer*, an anonymous account that purported to be factual. 'Richmond' was another poacher turned gamekeeper, a criminal who became one of the Bow Street Runners who policed London at the time. Haia Shpayer-Makov has chronicled the growth of interest in 'pseudo-memoirs' of police work, 'fictional autobiographical texts' such as the very popular *Recollections of a Detective Police-Officer* by 'Waters', a pen-name for William Russell. The Edinburgh police officer James McLevy also published books about his cases, and in the twenty-first century his career inspired a long-running radio series and novels written by David Ashton.

6   *Paul Féval*: Féval turned from law to thriller writing, prompted by Sue's success to publish *Les Mystères de Londres* in 1844, featuring Robin Cross, an English private detective who (unlike many a trusting gumshoe of later years) insists on being paid in advance for his services. The story concerns Irishman Fergus O'Breane, who plots revenge against England for the wrongs done to his countrymen; in a hat-tip to Féval, Anthony Boucher created a Golden Age detective called Fergus O'Breen. In *Les Couteaux d'Or*, Féval took a leaf out of Fenimore Cooper's book by transplanting the Native American Towah and his faithful dog Mohican to the streets of Paris. *Jean Diable* pits Scotland Yard's Gregory Temple against a mysterious criminal mastermind, and the novel sequence *Les Habits Noirs* earned Féval a fortune. He lost it in a financial scandal, and abandoned crime writing for religion.

7   '*continuation novel*': A key question for anyone writing such a book, or completing an unfinished manuscript, typically after an author's death, is whether to adhere scrupulously (so far as possible) to the original writer's style and approach. Jill Paton Walsh rose to the challenge of completing Dorothy L. Sayers' *Thrones, Dominations*, with one of the genre's finest examples of literary ventriloquism. Authors who prefer to impose their own vision on their predecessors' work are often better suited to writing their own books.

8   *Fortuné du Boisgobey*: The pen-name of Fortuné Hippolyte Auguste Abraham-Dubois. He also created Saintonge, an early example of the newspaperman who plays amateur detective; A. E. Murch suggests that he borrowed the idea from *Great Porter Square* by B. L. Farjeon, father of the crime writer J. Jefferson Farjeon.

9   *Gaboriau's influence extended across the globe*: The Irish novelist George

Moore even described *Crime and Punishment* as 'Gaboriau with psychological sauce', but Dostoevsky's biographer Leoníd Grossman was nearer the mark, calling the book 'a philosophical novel with a criminal setting'. Dostoevsky's own influence on crime fiction is explored by Muireann Maguire in 'Crime and Publishing: How Dostoevskii Changed the British Murder'; she notes that Robert Louis Stevenson's story 'Markheim' is a 'cameo version' of Dostoevsky's novel. Riga-born David Magarshack consciously channelled Dostoevsky in *Big Ben Strikes Eleven* (a mystery praised by Dorothy L Sayers) and two more Golden Age detective novels before finding his true vocation as a translator.

10 *Fergus Hume*: Fergusson 'Fergus' Wright Hume was born in a pauper's lunatic asylum in Worcestershire where his father worked. The family emigrated to New Zealand and Hume subsequently moved to Melbourne. His quoted remarks come from a preface added to a revised edition of *The Mystery of a Hansom Cab*. The chloral poisoning of John Fletcher, a Lancashire merchant, during a cab journey in 1889 was allegedly a copycat crime inspired by Hume's book. As usual with such claims, the suggestion that fiction inspired the criminal was fanciful.

11 *Arthur Conan Doyle was not impressed*: Nor were many critics. Howard Haycraft, for instance, found the book 'scarcely readable', although Julian Symons considered it 'a reasonably good imitation of Gaboriau, containing some convincing scenes of low life.' Clare Clarke has argued that the book supplies 'a fascinating foreshadowing of the hard-boiled detective genre and the growing number of respectable murderers and corrupt detectives', and that its failure to secure an enduring reputation is due to its 'transgressive' nature.

12 *no guarantee of long-term success*: Hume's most interesting character was Hagar Stanley, a 'gypsy detective' who runs a pawnshop. Lucy Sussex suggests in 'The Queer Story of Fergus Hume' that he was gay and was blackmailed because of his sexual orientation.

13 *Green's single-minded focus . . . set her apart from less skilled contemporaries*: A. E. Murch contrasts Green's professionalism with the elementary errors made by early British detective writers: Helen Mathers' *The Land o' the Leal* was flawed by ignorance of the legal system, while E. S. Drewry's *A Death Ring* gave too much away in the title, preface and early chapters.

14 *the book's admirers included . . . . Agatha Christie*: As late as 1963, in *The Clocks*, Hercule Poirot describes *The Leavenworth Case* as 'admirable', and praises Green's 'excellent psychological study' of the murderer. Julian Symons, however, dismissed the book as 'drearily sentimental'.

15 *Carolyn Wells*: Wells introduced her bookish detective Fleming Stone in *The Clue*, published shortly after Rinehart's *The Circular Staircase*, and he appeared in a further sixty mysteries. In 1913, she published *The Technique of the Mystery Story*, the first in a never-ending sequence of books dispensing advice to would-be crime writers. She observed, for instance, that 'it is always unpleasant to contemplate the hanging or the electrocuting of the . . . criminal. For this reason he not infrequently takes poison (which he has ready in his pocket), as soon as he is discovered, and dies peacefully, close upon the last words of his confession. This is one of the conventions adopted to spare the reader's feelings.'

SIX

The Great Detective

Sherlock Holmes

The young clerk at Edinburgh University's medical school showed another patient in for diagnosis. Waiting for them in a large room was the surgeon, accompanied by the students he was training in his methods. He was thin and wiry, with angular shoulders, and a jerky way of walking, and his dark hair stood up from his head like bristles on a brush. When he spoke to the patient, his voice was high and discordant.

'Well, my man, you've served in the army.'

'Aye, sir.'

'Not long discharged?'

'No, sir.'

'A Highland regiment?'

'Aye, sir.'

'A non-com. officer?'

'Aye, sir.'

'Stationed at Barbados?'

'Aye, sir.'

Satisfied, the surgeon turned to his bewildered audience. 'You see, gentlemen, the man was a respectful man but did not remove his hat. They do not in the army, but he would have learned civilian ways had he been long discharged. He has an air of authority and he is obviously Scottish. As to Barbados, his complaint is elephantiasis, which is West Indian and not British.'

There was a moral to this deductive *tour de force*. The surgeon, whose name was Dr Joseph Bell,[1] wanted his students to understand that they should use all their senses when conducting an examination. They were impressed. So was the young outpatients' clerk, Arthur Conan Doyle.

Arthur Ignatius Conan Doyle, born in Edinburgh to a Catholic family, began writing stories as a student. After setting up a medical practice in Southsea, he continued to produce fiction, but with such lack of success that, in a fit of the gloom familiar to authors since time immemorial, he contemplated penning *The Autobiography of a Failure*. Instead, he wrote a detective story.

Joseph Bell had taught him the value of trained observation. 'If he were a detective,' Conan Doyle mused, 'he would surely reduce this fascinating but unorganised business to something nearer to an exact science.' Why not create a sleuth who cut an even more striking figure than the Edinburgh surgeon, and who put his powers to the service of solving crime?[2]

Conan Doyle conceived a detective called Sherrinford Holmes whose investigation would be narrated – much like Dupin's cases – by a friend named Ormond Sacker. His original title was *A Tangled Skein*, but the story became *A Study in Scarlet*, and the narrator Dr John H. Watson. The detective's name changed to Sherlock Holmes.

Detective work at this time lacked sophistication. Hans Gross's legendary textbook *Criminal Investigation*[3] did not appear until 1893. But in the first chapter of *A Study in Scarlet*, Watson, in search of lodgings in London, learns about Holmes and his enthusiasm for science from his friend Stamford: 'I believe he is well up in anatomy, and he is a first-class chemist.' When Stamford introduces the pair, Holmes has just discovered 'a reagent which is precipitated by haemoglobin, and by nothing else . . . it gives us an infallible test for bloodstains.' So begins a beautiful friendship: within forty-eight hours, Holmes and Watson move into 221b Baker Street.

A Study in Scarlet is a lively entertainment. Conan Doyle amuses himself by having Holmes dismiss Dupin as 'a very inferior fellow' and Gaboriau's Lecoq as 'a miserable bungler'. The story structure, however, is flawed, with an over-long flashback explaining the murder of Enoch J. Drebber. The book was rejected by several publishers, including Arrowsmith's, who had done so well out of Hugh Conway's *Called Back*, but finally appeared in 1887. Conan Doyle sold the copyright for twenty-five pounds, and never earned another penny from it. He adapted elements of the story (including Watson, but *not* Holmes) into a play, *Angels of Darkness*, but it was not performed, and remained unpublished until 2001.

In August 1889, Conan Doyle was invited to dinner at Langham's Hotel by Joseph Marshall Stoddart, editor of *Lippincott's Monthly Magazine*. Stoddart was visiting London from Philadelphia, and his other guests included Oscar Wilde. Wilde praised Conan Doyle's historical novel *Micah Clarke*; the doctor, who valued his historical fiction more highly than his ventures into crime, was duly flattered. Wilde and Conan Doyle agreed to write stories for Stoddart, and the eventual results were *The Picture of Dorian Gray* (a story with crime at its heart) and *The Sign of Four*.

The Sign of Four (1890) marked an advance on *A Study in Scarlet*, and not merely because of its pace, smoother construction and more intricate plotting. There are echoes of *The Moonstone* in the tale of a gang's pursuit of stolen Agra treasure, and Holmes' dark side becomes apparent: in the opening scene, he injects himself with a seven per cent solution of cocaine. Reproached by Watson, he explains that he abhors 'the dull routine of existence. I crave for mental exaltation . . . I am the last and highest court of appeal in detection.'

He also rebukes Watson for the 'romanticism' of *A Study in Scarlet*, but, for the doctor, love is about to blossom. The book's finale, which sees the doctor announcing his engagement and Holmes reaching for the cocaine bottle, captures the contrast between the two men. Their duality echoes that in Robert Louis Stevenson's[4] *The Strange Case of Dr Jekyll and Mr Hyde*[5] (1886).

Conan Doyle acquired a literary agent, A. P. Watt, and moved to London with his wife and young daughter. He was thirty-two, and his life was about to change for ever. At this point, he was still practising medicine, but patients were in short supply. It struck him that the serial was out of date; a new market for writers was emerging: the magazines that supplied exciting stories for readers who liked to read them while commuting to and from work. Conan Doyle reckoned that 'a single character running through a series, if it only engaged the attention of the reader, would bind the reader to that particular magazine.' His instinct was timely and also timeless. The magazine market for crime stories has faded away, but publishers still love series characters in crime stories – because readers do.

Holmes was the obvious choice for a series character. Conan Doyle's first short story about him, 'A Scandal in Bohemia', opens with a memorable line about the opera singer Irene Adler: 'To Sherlock Holmes she is always *the* woman.' Watt sold the story to Herbert Greenhough Smith, editor of the recently established *Strand Magazine*, and in a feverish burst of energy, Conan Doyle produced another five stories before turning his attention elsewhere.

The immediate and massive popularity of the stories (the *Strand* was soon selling half a million copies of each issue, with Holmes their star attraction) meant that Greenhough Smith was desperate to publish more, and willing to pay handsomely for the privilege. Conan Doyle dashed off six more tales while complaining to his mother that detective stories kept him from 'better things'.

The first twelve stories comprised *The Adventures of Sherlock Holmes* (1892), which Conan Doyle dedicated to Joseph Bell. A cliché of crime fiction criticism is that the detective story appeals because it shows order being restored within a disturbed community. Yet criminals elude Holmes in one quarter of the cases in the book. He contemplates breaking the law more than once, and twice he lets the culprit go free. In 'The Five Orange Pips', he even fails to prevent his client from falling victim to murder.

What readers loved (and still love) was the resolution of uncertainty, the Great Detective's ability to discern rational explanations for baffling mysteries. The clamour for Holmes stories[6] became deafening, but Conan Doyle saw them 'as a lower stratum of literary achievement'.[7] He decided to escape from well-paid bondage by killing the public's darling. During a trip to Switzerland, he visited the Reichenbach Falls, and decided they would make a suitably dramatic location for Holmes' demise. In 'The Final Problem', he pitted his detective against a worthy adversary, Professor James Moriarty, 'the Napoleon of crime', before plunging both of them into the abyss. Watson's closing remarks were heavy with sorrow: 'deep down in that dreadful cauldron of swirling water and seething foam, will lie for all time the most dangerous criminal and the foremost champion of the law of their generation.'

The short story form suited Conan Doyle's gifts to perfection; only Wilkie Collins had mastered the art of writing a full-length detective novel of high quality and sustained interest. The knack of juggling clues and red herrings, of shifting suspicion from one potential culprit to another, was yet to be refined.

Conan Doyle believed early mysteries that failed to explain how the detective solved the puzzle were unfair. He sought to emphasise Holmes' chain of reasoning. The cases were not, however, 'fair play' whodunits giving the *reader* a chance to solve the mystery; that kind of game-playing came later. The reader's role was not to compete with Holmes, but to fall under the spell of his extraordinary personality.

Although Holmes investigates murders, his cases often concern less serious crimes. Puzzles about a jewel theft or the desertion of a bridegroom on his wedding day were enough to absorb readers if resolved within a short span. A typical storyline sees a client present Holmes with a strange and tantalising problem; the joy comes from seeing the detective make sense of the riddle.

Conan Doyle didn't explore the psychology of his characters in depth, and didn't need to. He painted Holmes and Watson, Irene Adler, Professor Moriarty and Sherlock's brother Mycroft, with bold, indelible brushstrokes. Adler and Moriarty appeared in one story each, Mycroft in two, but they have an enduring fascination for readers. Conan Doyle had the complementary knack of coming up with names for his people that were offbeat – Thaddeus Sholto, Dr Grimesby Roylott, Jephro Rucastle – yet splendidly memorable.

'The Red-Headed League', his second Holmes short story, is an enduring masterpiece. A rich mix of flavoursome ingredients is enhanced by a title calculated to pique curiosity. Holmes conveys the charm of his cases when he says, 'I know, my dear Watson, that you share my love of all that is bizarre and outside the conventions and humdrum routine of everyday life.' Readers identified with the doctor. They craved escapism too.

After casting an eye over Jabez Wilson, whom Watson regards as a commonplace British tradesman, notable only for a head of fiery red hair and a mood of chagrin, Holmes remarks: 'Beyond the obvious facts that he has at some time done manual labour, that he takes snuff, that he is a Freemason, that he has been in China, and that he has done a considerable amount of writing lately, I can deduce nothing else.'

The last deduction bears directly on the plot: Wilson has accepted a handsomely paid sinecure supposedly funded by the late Ezekiah Hopkins, an American millionaire. The position, reserved for a red-headed Londoner, involves being confined to the offices of the Red-Headed League and copying out the *Encyclopaedia Britannica*. When the League disbands suddenly, and the man who hires him vanishes, Jabez Wilson seeks advice from Holmes.

The consulting detective duly retires to smoke and reflect, commenting: 'It is quite a three-pipe problem.' This demonstrates another of Conan Doyle's gifts: time and again, he conjures up a phrase so picturesque yet telling that it has entered the lexicon.[8] The riddle proves to have a straightforward explanation, but the presentation is so entertaining and assured from start to finish that the reader cannot help but feel exhilarated.

Conan Doyle employed other tricks to amuse and tantalise his readers, including occasional references to Holmes' unrecorded cases. In 'The Five Orange Pips' (another irresistible title), Watson mentions 'the adventure of the Paradol Chamber, of the Amateur Mendicant Society, who held a luxurious club in the lower vault of a furniture warehouse, of the facts connected with the loss of the British barque *Sophy Anderson*, of the singular adventures of the Grice Patersons in the island of Uffa, and finally of the Camberwell poisoning case.'

Several touches verge on the postmodern; Holmes discusses Watson's accounts of his cases, and, in 'The Veiled Lodger', Watson threatens that if those seeking to destroy unpublished records do not desist 'the whole story concerning the politician, the lighthouse, and the trained cormorant will be given to the public'. As he says darkly, 'There is at least one reader who will understand.'

The gimmicks seasoned stories of substance. Conan Doyle's ideas were fresh and his observations on human behaviour insightful. In 'The Copper Beeches', a train journey takes sleuth and sidekick through the rolling hills around Aldershot, prompting Watson to remark on their beauty. Holmes, in contrast, is struck by their isolation: 'the lowest and vilest alleys of London do not present a more dreadful record of sin than the smiling and beautiful countryside.' He sees the skull beneath the skin: 'Think of the deeds of hellish cruelty, the hidden wickedness which may go on, year in, year out, in such places, and none the wiser.'

This sense of the macabre, coupled with atmospheric description and dialogue, was Conan Doyle's hallmark. In his finest work, sensational effects that would seem ludicrous in less accomplished hands seize the imagination and compel the suspension of disbelief. 'The Speckled Band' is an 'impossible crime' story boasting a 'dying message' clue of the kind later associated with the American Ellery Queen. Writhing in terror moments before her death in a room she'd kept locked, Julia Stoner cries out to her sister: 'Oh my God! Helen! It was the band! The speckled band!' The case takes Holmes and Watson to sinister Stoke Moran, where old, malevolent Dr Grimesby Roylott allows a cheetah and a baboon to roam in the unkempt grounds and mysterious whistling is heard at night.

Anomalies abound in the Holmes stories. There is no such creature as the 'swamp adder' described in 'The Speckled Band'; Watson's first name switches from John to James; and his wife, having died, miraculously reappears. Such cavalier disregard for facts and consistency sits oddly with an emphasis on meticulous detective work, but most crime readers (although less easily satisfied than some critics suggest) are not pedants. They want to care about the characters, and what happens to them. The mistakes amounted to an added bonus. Aficionados derive endless pleasure from debating whether Watson had two wives, and what really happened to Holmes at the Reichenbach Falls and in the aftermath of his encounter with Moriarty, during 'the Great Hiatus'.[9]

*

Holmes' death caused such mourning, according to popular legend, that clerks in the City of London wore black armbands. His departure created a vacuum that other writers raced to fill, but neither Sexton Blake[10] nor any of the other innumerable rivals of Sherlock Holmes[11] was a match for the original. Conan Doyle continued to produce a wide range of fiction, notably 'The Man with the Watches' and 'The Lost Special', two stories in the Sherlockian mould.

In 1901, a journalist friend, Bertram Fletcher Robinson,[12] told Conan Doyle the legend of a gigantic and terrifying hound that roamed Dartmoor. Conan Doyle thought it would make a good story – a 'creeper' – which he called *The Hound of the Baskervilles*, and he told Greenhough Smith that Fletcher Robinson should be named as his co-author. After he decided that the story would work best with Holmes as the protagonist, cold commercial reality meant that it made sense for him to write the whole story. The book appeared under his name alone, although he paid Fletcher Robinson for contributing the idea and background colour. The first instalment appeared shortly before William Gillette starred as Holmes at the Lyceum Theatre; both book and play enjoyed a rapturous reception.

The Hound of the Baskervilles, although supremely enjoyable and packed with distinctive touches, was again clumsily structured, with Holmes off-stage for too long. Conan Doyle set the book in the period prior to the deadly encounter at the Reichenbach Falls, but eventually yielded to financial inducements to revive Holmes. 'The Empty House', published in the *Strand* in 1894, saw Holmes reappear. He told Watson that he'd killed Moriarty, employing his skills at the martial art of *baritsu* (presumably Conan Doyle meant *bartitsu*), and then travelled for a couple of years before returning to London to investigate the murder of Ronald Adair by Moriarty's henchman, Colonel Sebastian Moran.

Conan Doyle, who was knighted for services rendered in the South African war, wrote more Holmes stories following his attempt to kill his hero off than before, and 'Shoscombe Old Place' appeared as late as 1927. By then, a new generation of writers were publishing ingenious detective novels very different from Conan Doyle's. Some of his later tales are thin, and occasionally he repeated himself; 'The Three Garridebs', for instance, reworks the plot of 'The Red-Headed League'. Yet the old magic is often present, as in 'The Bruce-Partington Plans', in which Mycroft makes his second appearance.

Conan Doyle occasionally modelled his villains on real-life criminals and his plots on actual cases. John Clay in 'The Red-Headed League' was probably based on the Chicago bank robber John Clare. The blackmailer Charles Augustus Milverton was a version of Charles Augustus Howell (who was found dead in 1890, with his throat slit and a coin in his mouth); and Moriarty was to an extent modelled on Adam Worth, the high-living criminal mastermind described by Scotland Yard's Robert Anderson as 'the Napoleon of the criminal world'. Aspects of the unsolved murder of Caroline Luard in 1908 inform the plot of 'Thor Bridge'.[13]

More remarkable was Conan Doyle's personal involvement with crime and detection.[14] His contributions to the *Strand* included 'Strange Studies from Life', retelling real-life cases from thirty years earlier, and he took up unpopular causes with characteristic determination. In 1907, he played a leading role in the campaign to secure justice for George Edalji, a solicitor of Parsee heritage convicted of mutilating a pony. His diligent investigations led to Edalji being pardoned. Conan Doyle believed he had identified the real culprit, but the suspect was never prosecuted. The furore about the case contributed to the creation of the Court of Criminal Appeal.[15]

Conan Doyle opposed capital punishment – except in 'extreme cases' – and took up the cudgels on behalf of another member of an ethnic minority whom he saw as a victim of a miscarriage of justice. Oscar Slater, a German Jew, had been convicted of beating a woman to death, but appeared to be a victim of mistaken identity. Ultimately, Slater was pardoned, released from prison and – after Conan Doyle underwrote his appeal – compensated.

These achievements, coupled with the fact that he was a former Deputy Lieutenant of Surrey, caused the county's chief constable to consult him when Agatha Christie went missing in 1926. He took a glove owned by Christie to a medium, Horace Leaf, who maintained that she was still alive, 'half dazed, half purposeful'. Once she was discovered in Harrogate, Conan Doyle argued that the case 'offered an excellent example of the uses of psychometry as an aid to the detective'. For her part, Christie parodied Conan Doyle's 'The Disappearance of Lady Frances Carfax' in 'The Case of the Missing Lady', collected in *Partners in Crime* (1929). The solution to the puzzle of the vanished woman is deliberately anti-climactic.

Conan Doyle had abandoned Catholicism for spiritualism shortly after creating Holmes, but did not see the contrast as ironic, since he regarded spiritualism as a branch of science. Most crime writers are more sceptical. Phoney mediums and fake séances crop up in detective novels by Christie, Sayers and a host of others. But Conan Doyle never relinquished his spiritualist views, even when he was ridiculed for his belief in the 'Cottingley fairies', photographs taken by two teenage girls that he regarded as supplying visual evidence of psychic phenomena. More than fifty years after his death, it was finally established that the fairies were a hoax.

There is so much to admire in the Holmes stories that the scientific ingredients are easily overlooked. But by taking science seriously, Conan Doyle paved the way for succeeding generations of crime writers who understood that crimes cannot simply be solved by intuition or flashes of inspiration, and even influenced the actual practice of scientific detection.

At the dawn of the twenty-first century, the forensic entomologist Dr Zakaria Erzinçlioğlu cited in his memoirs a dozen of Conan Doyle's stories that highlighted the value of his contribution:[16] 'It was he who introduced the idea of taking plaster casts of footprints. His Sherlock Holmes stories, which emphasise the central importance of physical evidence in criminal investigations, were actually used as instruction manuals by the Chinese and Egyptian police forces for many years, and the French *Sûreté* named their great forensic laboratory at Lyon after him. He transformed the very way criminal investigators thought about their work.'

Notes

The literature concerning Sherlock Holmes, let alone Arthur Conan Doyle and his world, is so voluminous that its bibliography is itself a chunky volume. The account of Bell's diagnostic technique comes from Conan Doyle's autobiography.

The principal texts to which I've referred in addition are the biographies by Andrew Lycett and John Dickson Carr, Michael Dirda's *On Conan Doyle* and Leslie Klinger's *The New Annotated Sherlock Holmes*.

1   *Dr Joseph Bell*: Bell was a prosecution witness in the trial of Alfred Monson for the murder of Cecil Hambrough. Monson was Hambrough's tutor, and his wife was a beneficiary of two life insurance policies taken out on the life of the young man, who was killed while out shooting with Monson. Bell thought Monson was guilty, but the jury's verdict was 'Not Proven'. J. J. Connington fictionalised the story in *The Ha-Ha Case*, aka *The Brandon Case*. 'Open Season', a TV dramatisation of the case in 1984, was scripted by Peter May. A quarter of a century later May's *The Blackhouse* was rejected by British publishers, only to become a word of mouth hit in France which launched the bestselling Lewis Trilogy.

2   *Why not create a sleuth who cut an even more striking figure . . . ?*: Conan Doyle told *The Bookman* that Sherlock Holmes was 'the literary embodi-ment' of his old teacher, but that was an over-simplification. The author's son, Adrian, claimed that 'the first great truth' was that 'Holmes was to a large extent Conan Doyle himself'. A possible fictional inspiration was Maximilian Heller, who appeared in Henry Cauvain's *The Killing Needle*, an 'impossible crime' story set in 1845 and published in 1871. Heller was a neurotic, drug-taking misanthrope, a master of disguise and deductive reasoning with a doctor for a confidant. The novel was translated into English in 2014 by John Pugmire, who points out that Conan Doyle could read French.

3   *Hans Gross's legendary textbook Criminal Investigation*: In S. S. Van Dine's *The Greene Murder Case*, cases in Gross's study parallel the bizarre crimes in the story.

4   *Robert Louis Stevenson*: Stevenson's work includes some material familiar in crime fiction. *Kidnapped*, a historical romance involving a manhunt, makes fictional use of the Appin Murder of 1752. *The Wrong Box*, co-written with his stepson Lloyd Osbourne, concerns a tontine survivor-takes-all invest-ment scheme that supplies a catalyst for murder in several detective stories. The story was filmed as a wacky black comedy in 1966.

5   *The Strange Case of Doctor Jekyll and Mr Hyde*: Dissociative identity disorder, formerly known as multiple personality disorder, is a recurring ingredient in crime fiction. Stevenson's story is perhaps the first example. The idea at the heart of the story, that human beings have warring natures within them, was clearly in Ian Rankin's mind when he was working on his first DI Rebus novel. He originally intended to call the second Rebus book *Hyde and Seek*; it was published as *Hide and Seek*.

6   *The clamour for Holmes stories*: This led to an ongoing demand for Sherlockian parodies and pastiches, as well as Sherlockian scholarship. An early parodist of the stories was Conan Doyle's smoking companion, the Scottish-born, Canadian-raised Robert Barr. His major contribution to the genre was the satirically titled *The Triumphs of Eugène Valmont*, featuring a French private detective based in London and including one of the most highly regarded short mysteries of the era, 'The Absent-Minded Coterie'. Conan Doyle's son Adrian collaborated with John Dickson Carr on *The Exploits of Sherlock Holmes*, a dozen stories about cases tantalisingly

mentioned in the Holmes canon. Accomplished modern exponents of the Sherlockian story include Britain's June Thomson and Anthony Horowitz and the Americans Nicholas Meyer and Laurie R. King. Holmes' renown has been reinforced by innumerable adaptations of the stories for film, television and radio. In the twenty-first century, the global success of two television series, *Sherlock* and *Elementary*, both transplanting Holmes and Watson to the present day, illustrates the continuing appeal of the characters and their mysterious world.

7   *Conan Doyle saw them 'as a lower stratum of literary achievement'*: Crime writers complain about literary critics who patronise their work, but sometimes under-value their own contributions to the genre. Agatha Christie, for instance, casually discloses the solutions to four of her earlier novels in *Cards on the Table*, presumably because she thought hardly anyone would read them in future.

8   *a phrase so picturesque yet telling that it has entered the lexicon*: A famous example is the passage in 'Silver Blaze' discussing 'the curious incident of the dog in the night-time', which became the title of Mark Haddon's best-selling novel of 2003.

9   *'the Great Hiatus'*: This term, describing the period of Holmes absence from London, seems to have originated in an article by Edgar W. Smith for *The Baker Street Journal* in 1946.

10   *Sexton Blake*: Originally created in 1893 by Harry Blyth, Blake has featured in innumerable stories written by a couple of hundred different authors, as well as on radio and film. On television he was played from 1968 to 1971 by Laurence Payne, himself an occasional crime writer whose *The Nose on My Face* was filmed as *Girl in the Headlines*.

11   *rivals of Sherlock Holmes*: Hugh Greene, brother of Graham, edited four seminal anthologies of stories featuring those rivals, which spawned two 1970s television series. He and Graham compiled *The Spy's Bedside Book* and also *Victorian Villainies*, comprising Hawley Smart's *The Great Tontine*, Arthur Griffiths' *The Rome Express*, Richard Marsh's *The Beetle*, and the American Richard Harding Davis's crafty *In the Fog*. Davis was as anxious about his publisher's marketing efforts (or lack of them) as generations of later authors, nagging Robert H. Russell: 'I trust your sudden flight south is not going to halt your efforts to push "In the Fog". I believe . . . it has sufficient strength to carry it over the Christmas slump and I hope you will take it up on your return and pound at it.'

12   *Bertram Fletcher Robinson*: Fletcher Robinson contributed the notion of a fingerprint clue to another Holmes story, 'The Norwood Builder'. His own crime stories included *The Chronicles of Addington Peace*, featuring a Scotland Yard inspector rather than a brilliant amateur. *Bertram Fletcher Robinson: A Footnote to The Hound of the Baskervilles*, by Brian W. Pugh and Paul R. Spiring, discusses this unjustly neglected writer.

13   *'Thor Bridge'*: Published in 1922, this is among the finest of the later Holmes stories, although arguably Conan Doyle borrowed from 'The Red-Haired Pickpocket', published by Frank Froest and George Dilnot seven years earlier. In turn, there are echoes of 'Thor Bridge' in Margery Allingham's *Police at the Funeral*. The Luard case was also fictionalised by Alan Brock in *After the Fact* and as a 'quick read' novella, *A Dreadful Murder*, by Minette Walters.

14 *Conan Doyle's personal involvement with crime and detection*: Peter
   Costello's *The Real World of Sherlock Holmes* discusses many examples,
   some peripheral, a few highly significant.

15 *The furore . . . contributed to the creation of the Court of Criminal Appeal*:
   Also significant was the work of George Robert Sims, a journalist, playwright
   and crime writer, who helped to secure justice for Adolf Beck. Sims was
   briefly one of that large band of luckless Victorians who were suspected of
   being Jack the Ripper; he also claimed to know the Ripper's identity. Study
   of his unpublished papers led his cousin's grandson, the television presenter,
   former MP and crime novelist Gyles Brandreth, to write a book optimistically
   titled *Jack the Ripper: Case Closed*. Sims' principal detective character was
   Dorcas Dene, an actress with a gift for impersonation. His *The Case of
   George Candlemas* is a stand-alone story hinging on the amateur detective's
   strong resemblance to the criminal. Sims also wrote the much-parodied
   monologue that begins 'It is Christmas Day in the Workhouse . . .', but his
   strangest claim to fame was as proud inventor of 'the George R. Sims hair
   restorer, *Tatcho*'. Advertisements for the trademarked product sometimes
   included Sims' photograph. Unfortunately, in time his own hairline began
   to recede.

16 *Dr Zakaria Erzinçlioğlu cited in his memoirs . . .* : See *Maggots, Murder,
   and Men*. Ronald R. Thomas's *Detective Fiction and the Rise of Forensic
   Science* explores the use made by Conan Doyle and other early crime writers
   of aspects of forensic detection.

SEVEN

Rogues' Gallery

Raffles and other villains

'You must not make the criminal a hero,' Arthur Conan Doyle insisted.

Conan Doyle was shocked when his brother-in-law, Willie Hornung,[1] confided an intention to do precisely that. The dark side of life fascinated Conan Doyle, but he thought it irresponsible for writers to glamorise law-breaking.[2] William Godwin's radicalism belonged to a bygone era, and so did admiration for the likes of the highwayman Dick Turpin. Vidocq was long dead, but as the nineteenth century drew to a close, readers of detective fiction longed for a new character with a touch of his edginess and flair. They wanted something different.

Hornung's previous fiction had enjoyed modest success. Now he'd devised a fresh approach to the detective story, and Conan Doyle's reservations failed to deter him. In 1898 *Cassell's Magazine* published 'The Ides of March', introducing handsome, debonair A. J. Raffles, who was a cricketer by day and burglar by night.[3]

Conan Doyle, a cricket lover,[4] was dismayed that Raffles, although 'a dangerous bat, brilliant in the field, and perhaps the very finest slow bowler of the decade', preferred stealing to playing the game. Raffles wasn't even in the same sympathetic mould as the outlaw Robin Hood: he didn't rob from the rich simply to give to the poor.

As he told his friend Harold 'Bunny' Manders: 'What's the satisfaction of taking a man's wicket, when you want his spoons?'

Cricket, with its elaborate rules and ingrained ethos of sports-
manship and fair play, seemed a counter-intuitive pastime for a
criminal. Hornung, short-sighted and severely affected by asthma,
was an enthusiastic but indifferent cricketer,[5] so Raffles' sporting
prowess offered the pleasure of wish fulfilment. The esteem in
which Raffles was held in upper-class society provided 'glorious
protection' for his nefarious activities,[6] and he reckoned that 'if
you can bowl a bit, your low cunning won't get rusty.'

The stories – 'the Confessions of a Late Prisoner of the Crown,
and sometime accomplice of the more notorious A. J. Raffles,
Cricketer and Criminal, whose fate is unknown' – were collected
in *The Amateur Cracksman* (1899). Hornung dedicated the book
to Conan Doyle, as a 'form of flattery'.

Raffles' exploits are narrated by the devoted Bunny, who
attended the same public school. When they meet again, Bunny
faces disgrace, and is about to kill himself. To enable him to pay
off his gambling debts, Raffles enlists his help in a jewellery theft.
Their relationship is a skewed version of the Holmes–Watson
pairing. In their snobbish moral universe, it is 'not cricket' to
betray a friend or steal from a host, but perfectly acceptable to
rob a fellow house guest. Raffles is prepared to kill if need be, but
regards the use of violence as a sign of failure. In the long run,
though, crime could not be seen to pay. In the final story, 'The
Gift of the Emperor', Raffles jumps into the sea to escape arrest;
Bunny is caught and sent to prison.

Just as Conan Doyle succumbed to pressure to rescue his hero
from the watery depths, so did Hornung. Raffles returned in 'No
Sinecure', living in London under the name Maturin.[7] He explains
to Bunny – now an ex-convict struggling to earn a crust with journalism – that he managed to swim to safety. Inevitably a cricketing
metaphor quashes the notion that he might have ended it all: 'I'd
rather be dropped by the hangman than throw my own wicket away.'

Raffles' patriotism is emphasised in the stories, collected in *The
Black Mask* in 1901. He marks the Diamond Jubilee in 'A Jubilee
Present' by sending a gold cup he has stolen from the British
Museum to Queen Victoria, 'infinitely the finest monarch the world

has ever seen'. Finally, Raffles and Bunny set off for South Africa to fight against the Boers. Raffles duly unmasks a spy in the camp before being shot by a sniper.

The law of diminishing returns applies with particular rigour to series about anti-heroes.[8] Hornung's third set of Raffles stories, *A Thief in the Night* (1905), explained by Bunny as filling in 'the blanks left by discretion in existing annals', suggested that the game had run its course. Regrettably, Hornung was tempted to revive Raffles yet again in a novel. *Mr Justice Raffles* (1909), which, quite apart from an unpleasant whiff of antisemitism, represented the feeblest of farewell bows.[9]

For all Conan Doyle's reservations about the morality of the Raffles stories, even he found their influence impossible to resist. In 'Charles Augustus Milverton', after the Great Hiatus, Holmes says: 'You know, Watson, I don't mind confessing to you that I have always had an idea that I would have made a highly efficient criminal. This is the chance of my lifetime in that direction. See here! . . . This is a first-class, up-to-date burgling kit, with nickel-plated jemmy, diamond-tipped glass-cutter, adaptable keys, and every modern improvement which the march of civilisation demands. Here, too, is my dark lantern. Everything is in order. Have you a pair of silent shoes?'

Raffles wasn't the only *fin de siècle* roguish hero, or even the first. Two years before 'The Ides of March' appeared, the Oxford-educated Canadian Grant Allen[10] created Colonel Clay, an Anglo-French swindler and master of disguise with the useful knack of moulding his 'india rubber face . . . like clay in the hands of the potter'. His schemes were recorded in *An African Millionaire* (1897).

Raffles was also pre-dated by Simon Carne, an audacious master of disguise who appears in half a dozen stories written by Guy Boothby[11] in 1897 and collected in *A Prince of Swindlers*. In a pleasing twist on the concept of the Great Detective, Carne masquerades as Klimo, 'the now famous private detective who has won for himself the right to be considered as great as Lecoq, or even the late lamented Sherlock Holmes'. Klimo investigates and 'solves' crimes committed by Carne, duly pocketing the reward.

Arthur Morrison gave an even bolder twist to the idea of the detective who is not all he seems. Previously, he'd tried to fill the gap left by Sherlock Holmes by creating Martin Hewitt, an amiable private investigator whose unique selling point was his sheer ordinariness. Because Morrison was a writer of calibre, the Hewitt stories were enjoyable. But Hewitt was rather dull; there is a reason why the great fictional detectives are so often quirky mavericks. Morrison soon came up with a more compelling character. Horace Dorrington, apparently a suave inquiry agent, is in reality a ruthless sociopath, for whom blackmail, fraud and murder are all in a day's work.

The structure of *The Dorrington Deed-Box* (1897) is as unorthodox as its content. In the first story, James Rigby describes how Dorrington goes on the run after having tried to drown him in an iron tank in the hope of securing his inheritance. Rigby and the police discover Dorrington's casebook and files, which supply material enabling Rigby to narrate the remaining stories about Dorrington's deeds – and misdeeds – and also reveal his backstory. The result is a highly original book, but Dorrington's talent of making crime pay was too much for the moralists, and H. G. Wells, who admired Morrison's writing, bemoaned his habit of indulging in 'despicable detective stories'.

Mary Elizabeth Braddon had shown in *Lady Audley's Secret* the dramatic potential of the female villain, especially if her looks were deceptively angelic. L. T. Meade and Robert Eustace created two wicked ladies in rapid succession.[12] Madame Kalouchy, who headed a gang of criminals in the lurid melodrama *The Brotherhood of the Seven Kings* (1899) was superseded by Madame Sara, whose escapades were gathered in *The Sorceress of the Strand* (1902). Quite apart from the protagonists' gender, the stories intrigued because of their ingenious, if often far-fetched, use of scientific know-how.

Meade had made her name as a writer of stories for girls before turning to crime fiction, often in collaboration. Eustace was a doctor who came up with clever plot devices. In 'Madame Sara', Dixon Druce, a private investigator, hears about a 'professional beautifier . . . very clever . . . a most lovely woman herself, with blue eyes, an innocent child-like manner, and quantities of rippling gold hair'. When she sings, her voice is 'sweet and low, with an extraordinary pathos'. But Madame Sara is a fraudster who does not scruple at murder.

Druce pursues her, assisted in 'the great hunt' for Madame Sara by Eric Vandeleur, a police surgeon who is also a skilled toxicologist. In 'The Talk of the Town', Vandeleur's scientific expertise enables him to foil a plot to kill a professor in order to secure a valuable patent, and to explain to Druce the cunning means by which an artificial palm was used to shower the unsuspecting victim with odourless and colourless carbon monoxide gas. But Madame Sara continues to evade justice, until in the final story she suffers a suitably grisly fate.

Fiction's rogues often masqueraded as pillars of respectability: cricketers or charming ladies. Arnold Bennett's Cecil Thorold[13] is a gentleman of leisure who involves himself with crime to stave off boredom. Uniquely, Romney Pringle was a con man who adopted the (arguably) respectable profession of literary agent as a cover for his swindles. Pringle appeared in two series of stories by Clifford Ashdown, a name concealing the identities of two doctors. John James Pitcairn was medical officer at Holloway Prison, while Richard Austin Freeman[14] worked there briefly as his assistant.

'The highest crimes, even murder, may be committed in such a manner that although the criminal is known and the law holds him in custody, yet it cannot punish him.' So said Melville Davisson Post,[15] an attorney in a small West Virginia law firm, when introducing *The Strange Schemes of Randolph Mason* (1896). Mason is both a misanthropic 'knave' and a brilliant lawyer.

In his first and most famous case, 'The Corpus Delicti', Mason shows a client how to commit a murder and get away with it. Richard Warren murders his blackmailing lover and dissolves her dismembered corpse in acid. In the absence of a body, the circumstantial evidence is not enough under New York law (as it then stood), and Mason secures his acquittal. Post argued that his stories were based on existing legal principles, and that rather than encouraging criminality, he was performing a public service by warning 'the friends of law and order' about the loopholes that existed.

Sensationally, two real-life murder cases – in Chicago and New York respectively – gave the impression of being inspired by 'The Corpus Delicti', although in each case the culprit was convicted. Legislators in several states are said to have raced to close loopholes that Post's story revealed. The attendant publicity, coupled with the disapproval of puritanical critics, made Post's name.

The success of the early Mason stories led to a demand for more, but – like Hornung – Post found that the shine wore off his original concept. In *The Corrector of Destinies* (1908), at his publisher's suggestion, he transformed Mason into 'the champion of right instead of the tutor of criminals'. The aim now was to 'find within the law a means by which to even up and correct every manner of injustice'. But once he joined the side of the angels, the crafty lawyer lost his appeal.

Frederick Irving Anderson's[16] short stories attracted less attention than Post's, but his mysteries concerning the villainous Godahl and the author Oliver Armiston display originality with a dash of metafiction. Armiston's plots are so ingenious that criminals copy them and the police plead with him to stop writing. Armiston collaborates with Deputy Parr, 'the Man-Hunter' of the NYPD; Parr also investigates 'the notorious Sophie Lang', Anderson's contribution to the ranks of female rogues. She was supposedly inspired by a New York thief who was so delighted that she purchased many copies of the book containing Sophie's adventures.

In the early twentieth century, a hack journalist called Maurice Leblanc created France's answer to Raffles, with a dash of Vidocq thrown into the mix. Arsène Lupin[17] leads a gang of villains and is a master of disguise. He often does battle with a plagiarised version of Sherlock Holmes, variously called Herlock Sholmès and Holmlock Shears.

Derivative as Leblanc's stories were, the best of them, such as 'The Red Silk Scarf', have a vim that compensates for the silliness. In *813* (1910), Lupin poses as Lenormand, the Chef de la Sûreté, for four years, and even conducts a search for himself. He often behaved like a Gallic Robin Hood. Similar characteristics were evident in Leslie Charteris's Simon Templar,[18] whose career began in 1928 and continued in various media for the rest of the century.

Just as Raffles was a response to Sherlock Holmes' departure from the scene, so writers took inspiration from Holmes' greatest adversary, creating criminal masterminds so ruthless that even Professor Moriarty might disapprove. Hell-bent on destruction, these supervillains also played on *fin de siècle* fears about threats to the established order and xenophobia. The most exotic was Sax Rohmer's Fu Manchu,[19] an evil genius with a taste for torture who wants to rule the world. This ambition pits him against an upstanding Englishman, Sir Denis Nayland-Smith. Yet after the Second World War, even 'the Devil Doctor' mellowed. Rohmer reported that he was 'flat out against the Communists and trying to help democracy'.

The most extraordinary early crime novel about a rogue is Roy Horniman's[20] *Israel Rank* (1907), subtitled *The Autobiography of a Criminal*. This black comedy about serial killing traces the narrator's scheme to inherit a fortune by eliminating those members of the Gascoyne family who stand in his way. Horniman was a member of Oscar Wilde's circle, and there is a Wildean tang to Rank's preface: 'I am convinced that many a delightful member of society has found it necessary at some time or other to remove a human obstacle.' Rank's pragmatism about murder anticipates the amorality of Patricia Highsmith's Tom Ripley by almost half a century.

The story's power derives from Horniman's personal identification with an outsider such as Israel Rank, a man at odds with convention and the establishment. An actor and theatre manager, Horniman was a vegetarian, animal rights activist, a campaigner against profiteering by the railways and against censorship. Israel Rank is the son of a Jewish commercial traveller and his first victim is an obnoxious antisemite. The name Israel Rank itself hints at the main targets of Horniman's satire: antisemitism and the British class system.

After the Second World War, the novel was transformed into a classic film, *Kind Hearts and Coronets*, and in the twenty-first century it became a Tony-winning musical, *A Gentleman's Guide to Love and Murder*. In fiction, there is something timeless about a charming sociopath. Reading (or writing) about daring law-breakers without risking the misery of falling victim to real-life fraud or murder offers vicarious thrills.

But is delighting in crime fiction a guilty pleasure? The first major detective writer and critic to address moral concerns about the risks of glamorising crime was G. K. Chesterton. As his detective Father Brown said in 'The Secret of Flambeau': 'You may think a crime horrible because you could never commit it. I think it horrible because I could commit it.'

Notes

The main sources are Peter Rowland's biography of Hornung, and the books about Conan Doyle and Victorian crime fiction previously mentioned.

1　*his brother-in-law, Willie Hornung*: After leaving school, Ernest William Hornung spent time in New South Wales, and was inspired to create the bushranger Stingaree, an Oxford-educated thief who pre-dates Raffles, first appearing in Hornung's *Irralie's Bushman* in 1896. Hornung later revived him in a series of stories collected in *Stingaree*, which George Orwell praised. In 1914 Hornung published *The Crime Doctor*, stories about one of the first 'psychological detectives', Dr John Dollar, a character who has been overshadowed by Raffles but is interesting in his own right.

2　*he thought it irresponsible for writers to glamorise law-breaking*: Conan Doyle wasn't the first to fret about this. In 'Sensation Novels', published in *Blackwood's Magazine* in 1862, the Scottish novelist Margaret Oliphant described Count Fosco as a 'new type of the perennial enemy of goodness', and expressed the fear that Wilkie Collins had 'given a new impulse to a kind of literature which must, more or less . . . make the criminal its hero'. Conan Doyle's biographer John Dickson Carr shared his reservations. In *The Gilded Man*, Sir Henry Merrivale said that Raffles 'put my back up every time I tried to read about him. What beat me was why we were supposed to regard the feller as a gentleman.'

3　*handsome, debonair A. J. Raffles, who was a cricketer by day and burglar by night*: In 'Raffles and Miss Blandish', published in *Horizon* in 1944, George Orwell said that 'Raffles . . . has no real moral code, no religion, certainly no social consciousness. All he has is a set of reflexes – the nervous system, as it were, of a gentleman.' Orwell compared Hornung's stories with James Hadley Chase's violent thriller *No Orchids for Miss Blandish*, the plot of which he said bore 'a very marked resemblance' to William Faulkner's *Sanctuary*. In Chase's book, 'there are no gentlemen, and no taboos', but Orwell was left wondering whether snobbishness 'is a check upon behaviour whose value from a social point of view has been underrated.'

4　*Conan Doyle, a cricket lover*: Conan Doyle may have drawn the first names of Holmes and his brother from two fast bowlers who played for Derbyshire, Shacklock and Mycroft. Conan Doyle was a good enough player to appear in first-class cricket; his solitary victim at that exalted level was the legendary Dr W. G. Grace. Conan Doyle celebrated by writing a poem about his feat; it ran to nineteen stanzas.

5　*Hornung . . . was an enthusiastic but indifferent cricketer*: He and Conan

Doyle played for a team of authors put together by J. M. Barrie, and whimsically named the Allahakbarries (or 'Heaven help us!'), whose exploits are recorded in *Peter Pan's First XI* by Kevin Telfer. Their ranks included A. A. Milne and A. E. W. Mason, as well as George Cecil Ives. Andrew Lycett suggests that Ives' exotic lifestyle contributed to Hornung's portrayal of Raffles. Ives, the illegitimate son of an English army officer and a Spanish baroness, was fascinated by crime and criminal psychology. A former lover of Lord Alfred Douglas, he founded the Order of Chaeronea, a secret society with a homosexual ethos. Bunny adores Raffles, and it is easy to read a gay subtext into their relationship.

6   *'glorious protection' for his nefarious activities*: Almost half a century later, Raffles' ploy was adopted by Ernest Bisham, in the enjoyable yet neglected *The Announcer*, aka *A Voice Like Velvet,* by Donald Henderson, published in 1946. By night Bisham is a cat burglar. By day he is an announcer for the BBC.

7   *living in London under the name Maturin*: This is a clue, Hornung's biographer Peter Rowland suggests, to the fact that Raffles was in part based on Oscar Wilde, whose great-uncle, Charles Maturin, wrote *Melmoth the Wanderer*. When Wilde went into hiding, he adopted the name Melmoth. Hornung liked Wilde; he called his son Arthur Oscar, and there is a Wildean whiff of decadence about Raffles.

8   *The law of diminishing returns applies with particular rigour to series about anti-heroes*: An intriguing exception arose with Kenneth Royce's *The XYY Man*, published in 1970. His premise (at the time scientifically respectable, but now discredited) was that the cat burglar William 'Spider' Scott had an extra 'Y' chromosome which predisposed him towards crime. The novel was televised, and two spin-off series, *Strangers* and *Bulman*, dispensed with Scott but also enjoyed success. Royce continued to write about Scott for the rest of his life.

9   *the feeblest of farewell bows*: Raffles' appeal has proved irresistible to other writers. Philip Atkey, writing as Barry Perowne, produced more stories about the character than Hornung did, and, since his death, Peter Tremayne has taken up the baton. In 1977, David Fletcher (under which name Dulan Barber wrote thoughtful psychological crime novels) published *Raffles* to accompany a television series starring Anthony Valentine. Graham Greene brought Raffles back from the Boer War in *The Return of A. J. Raffles*, a play first performed in 1975.

10 *the Oxford-educated Canadian Grant Allen*: Charles Grant Blairfindie Allen also wrote science fiction. He succumbed to liver cancer, leaving *Hilda Wade* incomplete; the final part was written by his friend Arthur Conan Doyle. Hugh Greene described *An African Millionaire* as 'one of the most amusing collections of crime stories ever written'.

11 *Guy Boothby*: Guy Newell Boothby was a prolific Australian writer best known for his thrillers about Doctor Nikola, yet another of those ambitious villains who seek world domination.

12 *L. T. Meade and Robert Eustace created two wicked ladies in rapid succession*: Elizabeth Thomasina Meade Smith produced over three hundred books. In collaboration with Dr Clifford Halifax (pen-name of Dr Edgar Beaumont), she wrote half a dozen books, including stories in which apparently supernatural incidents are given a rational explanation. Her partnership with

Eustace Robert Barton encompassed the creation of a female detective, Florence Cusack, and *The Gold Star Line*, a collection of mysteries featuring a ship's purser. Eustace also combined with Edgar Jepson on the famous 'impossible crime' story 'The Tea Leaf', and with Dorothy L. Sayers on *The Documents in the Case*.

13 *Arnold Bennett's Cecil Thorold*: He appears in *The Loot of Cities*. Bennett's fiction occasionally touched on crime and he reviewed detective novels, expressing the startling opinion that Francis Everton's debut *The Dalehouse Murder* was 'at least as good as any detective-story I have read since Conan Doyle'.

14 *John James Pitcairn . . . Richard Austin Freeman*: Their collaboration proved short-lived, but the Pringle stories represent an important step in Austin Freeman's development into a major crime writer. His *The Exploits of Danby Croker* is a minor work featuring a scoundrel in the Raffles tradition.

15 *Melville Davisson Post*: Publishers believe that their readers prize novelty, and the jacket of *The Sleuth of St James's Square*, featuring Sir Henry Marquis of Scotland Yard, hailed Post as creating 'a new formula for the mystery story . . . The Plan used by Poe, Gaboriau and their later followers has been to build up first a mystery and then explain it. This naturally caused repetition. Mr Post's method is to develop the mystery and its solution together, which results in immense gain in movement and suspense.' Post's other detectives included Uncle Abner, a God-fearing scourge of roguery in pre-Civil War Western Virginia.

16 *Frederick Irving Anderson*: Anderson gave up fiction to concentrate on his farm in Vermont. Julian Symons identified a 'Borgesian' flavour in *The Infallible Godahl* – written long before Borges came along.

17 *Arsène Lupin*: The stories have been adapted in various forms. The most recent screen version inspired by the stories is *Lupin*, which became a popular binge-watch on Netflix in 2021. Lupin also resembles Rocambole, an exuberant Parisian rogue created by Ponson du Terrail, who was a sensationalist rather than a detective writer. More ruthless than Lupin was Fantômas, a popular criminal genius created by Marcel Allain and Pierre Souvestre.

18 *Leslie Charteris's Simon Templar*: Leslie Charles Bowyer-Yin was born in Singapore, educated in England and spent much of his life in the US. The stories about Templar, known as 'the Saint', were equally popular when adapted for radio, television and film. His 1941 novel 'The Saint's Second Front', which dealt with a Japanese invasion of America, was rejected as inflammatory shortly before the attack on Pearl Harbor. At the time of writing, it remains unpublished.

19 *Sax Rohmer's Fu Manchu*: Julian Symons dismissed the stories as 'absolute rubbish, penny dreadfuls in hard covers'. He acknowledged that the stories in *The Dream Detective* about Moris Klaw, who utilises his dreams and a sleep-walking daughter to solve crimes, 'have a sort of ludicrous logic about them which is amusing in small doses'.

20 *Roy Horniman*: Horniman's other work includes *The Viper*, another novel about a sociopath, this time a confidence trickster who resorts to murder.

EIGHT

The Nature of Evil

G. K. Chesterton and faith and sin in detective fiction

On a bright March morning in 1904, two friends went walking across the moors of west Yorkshire. One was a diminutive Irish priest called John O'Connor. His companion, six feet four and heavily built, was towering in reputation as well as in physique. A poet and philosopher, a critic and controversialist, he liked to wear a cape and carry a swordstick. He was Gilbert Keith Chesterton, the only detective novelist (so far) to have been seriously considered as a candidate for sainthood.[1]

As they strode across the moorland, the two men talked about anything and everything: madness, vagrancy, the burning of heretics, confession and Zola. Their destination was a house in Ilkley where Chesterton and his wife were staying with a Jewish family called Steinthal.[2] Among the visitors were two Cambridge undergraduates, who displayed an amused contempt for the 'cloistered virtue' of the little priest. But Chesterton was in no doubt that, compared to O'Connor, a man prepared to confront 'solid Satanism', the naive students knew as much about 'real evil as two babies in the same perambulator'.

The priest's understanding of the nature of evil led Chesterton to transform him into one of fiction's most famous detectives, 'knocking him about, beating his hat and umbrella shapeless, untidying his clothes, punching his intelligent countenance into a condition of pudding-faced fatuity, and generally disguising Father O'Connor as Father Brown'.

Chesterton was educated at St Paul's School, where he met E. C. Bentley – whose clerihew verses he illustrated – and the Slade School of Art. Turning to journalism, he became a highly opinion-ated columnist. Eventually he produced a hundred books, hundreds of poems, five plays, five novels, two hundred short stories and thousands of articles. He even founded and edited his own news-paper, *G.K.'s Weekly*.

Chesterton's pungently expressed views commanded respect and exerted influence. He detested the way that the governing class of his day condescended to the underprivileged, and was sceptical about capitalism. His unrelenting hostility towards the notion of controlled and selective breeding of the human race was captured in the title of *Eugenics and Other Evils*, while 'A Denunciation of Patriotism' mocked 'deaf and raucous jingoism' that confused lust for territory with ancient love of country.

The Napoleon of Notting Hill, set in 1984, was an inspiration for both the Irish freedom fighter Michael Collins and George Orwell. A book of Christian apologetics, *The Everlasting Man*, played a significant part in C. S. Lewis's abandonment of atheism; he said it baptised his intellect. In 1914, Chesterton began writing for the *Daily Herald* 'regular weekly articles of a high merit and great political significance', according to the one-time Marxist and occasional crime writer Raymond Postgate,[3] who claimed that if Chesterton had remained with the *Herald*, 'the course of history might have changed'.

The Man Who Was Thursday, subtitled *A Nightmare* and often described as 'a metaphysical thriller', is prefaced by a poem addressed to E. C. Bentley, recalling early challenges to their faith. A Christian poet, Gabriel Syme, is recruited by Scotland Yard to infiltrate a gang of anarchists, but Chesterton's prime concern was to explore questions of evil and freedom of will.

C. S. Lewis compared the book to the work of Kafka, but Ronald Knox was nearer the mark when he said it was 'rather like the

Pilgrim's Progress in the style of the *Pickwick Papers*'. Amory Blaine, the protagonist of F. Scott Fitzgerald's *This Side of Paradise*, liked the story, but didn't understand it. Chesterton joked that he'd forgotten why he'd written it, other than to please himself and Bentley, and to try something fresh – by unmasking villains as decent citizens.

Chesterton was crime fiction's first important commentator.[4] As early as 1901, he argued that it is 'the earliest and only form of popular literature in which is expressed some sense of the poetry of modern life' and that the detective is 'the agent of social justice . . . the whole noiseless and unnoticeable police management by which we are ruled and protected is only a successful knight-errantry.' His observations teem with insights: the 'abrupt and staggering substitution or reversal . . . is the very essence of the success of a detective story', he said, highlighting Gaboriau's *The Widow Lerouge* as an example of clever foreshadowing that makes the plot twist artistically effective.

The good detective story, according to Chesterton, made the mysterious comprehensible: 'A footprint, a strange flower, a cipher telegram, and a smashed top-hat – these do not excite us because they are disconnected, but because the author is under an implied contract to connect them. It is not the inexplicable that thrills us; it is the explanation we have not heard.' Thus, for him, *Jane Eyre* was not only 'a human document written in blood, [but] also one of the best blood-and-thunder detective stories in the world'. He had no time for writers who peopled their stories with stock characters because they thought real characterisation was wasted on an unreal form of literature.

Gleefully provocative, he claimed that 'The Christian Church can best be defined as an enormous private detective, correcting that official detective – the State.' His faith led him to express scepticism about scientific detection and devices such as lie detectors. What mattered most was 'knowledge of man and society'.

By the time Father Brown appeared in 'The Blue Cross', published in the *Story-Teller* in September 1910, Chesterton had thought deeply about how to express his beliefs through the medium of the short detective story. The priest was crisply and memorably characterised: 'he had a face as round and dull as a Norfolk dumpling; he had eyes as empty as the North Sea; he had several brown paper parcels, which he was quite incapable of collecting . . . He had a large, shabby umbrella, which constantly fell on the floor. He did not seem to know which was the right end of his return ticket.'

For all his diffidence, Father Brown can outwit a criminal who is a master of disguise. 'Has it never struck you that a man who does next to nothing but hear men's real sins is not likely to be wholly unaware of human evil?' he demanded, after deducing that a thief was masquerading as a priest. 'You attacked reason,' he explained. 'It's bad theology.'

The early stories, collected in *The Innocence of Father Brown* (1911), are especially effective. Chesterton's love of paradox led him to favour stories about seemingly impossible crimes, while clever plotting enabled him to make powerful points. The question in 'The Hammer of God' is how a strong man could have been bludgeoned to death by a tiny hammer; Father Brown finds the answer and highlights the murderer's lack of humility. In 'The Three Tools of Death', in which a death proves to have been the result of a mistake, the priest emphasises that 'even the most murderous blunders don't poison life like sins.'

Everyone sins; for Chesterton, what counts is acknowledgement of the sin, and repentance. In 'The Flying Stars', Father Brown warns that: 'Men may keep a sort of level of good, but no man has ever been able to keep on one level of evil. That road goes down and down . . . Many a man I've known started like you to be an honest outlaw, a merry robber of the rich, and ended stamped into slime.'

Chesterton converted to Catholicism in 1922. Among those who encouraged him were Father O'Connor and Ronald Knox. Knox came from a formidable family of intellectuals, and earned distinction as a classicist at Eton and Balliol. One of his schoolmasters, C. A. Alington,[5] became head of Shrewsbury School, and recruited Knox to the staff. A popular teacher, Knox was ordained as an Anglican priest, only to resign, convert to Catholicism, and become a Catholic priest.

Knox amused himself by making up acrostics as he shaved or travelled on the train, and he cashed in on the post-war craze for puzzles by publishing a book of them in 1924. The same year saw the appearance of *Sanctions: A Frivolity*, a mainstream novel strangely overlooked by historians of the crime genre. At that time, Knox had yet to write a detective novel, but in this book his character John Lydiard[6] outlines the 'ten rules of detective fiction'.

At a time when the detective novel had become a game in which readers pitted their wits against those of author and detective, A. A. Milne, T. S. Eliot and the American S. S. Van Dine all tried, with varying degrees of seriousness, to set out a framework for playing the game fairly. G. K. Chesterton had set the ball rolling[7] in an article published in 1921, and Knox's 'Ten Commandments' – the Detective's Decalogue – became famous once he adapted Lydiard's rules and wrapped them up in a religious metaphor.

Knox's Ten Commandments were summarised sixty years later by the American crime writer Ross Thomas:[8]

1. Mention the criminal early on.
2. No supernatural stuff.
3. Only one secret passage per story.
4. No arcane poisons or long scientific explanations.
5. No Chinamen.
6. No marvellous intuition or miraculous accidents.
7. The detective never does it.
8. No clues that aren't immediately revealed to the reader.
9. The detective's dumb friend can't conceal his thoughts, nor can he be noticeably dumber than the detective.
10. No twins or doubles.

Knox's rules satirised incompetent crime writing. The ban on Chinamen, for instance, was a dig at racist and stereotypical portrayals of Asian villains such as Fu Manchu: 'if you come across some mention of "the slit-like eyes of Chin Loo", you had best put it down at once; it is bad.' His own detective novels[9] boasted ingenious touches, but unlike Chesterton he made no serious attempt to explore questions of faith through the medium of a murder mystery.

His 'Studies in the Literature of Sherlock Holmes' installed him as a pioneer of Sherlockian scholarship. The essay prompted Arthur Conan Doyle to drop Knox a line, saying he was amused and amazed that 'anyone should spend such pains on such material'. More than a century later, Sherlockian fandom spans the globe,[10] a light-hearted cult rather than a religion.

Chesterton became President of the Detection Club on its foundation in 1930. This was the first social network for crime writers, a small, elitist group that aimed to raise the literary standards of the genre. Membership was by election and thriller writers were excluded. Snippets from Knox's 'rules' were incorporated in the Club's jokey ritual for the initiation of new members.[11] Club stalwarts amused themselves (and bamboozled critics) by paying lip service to the rules, while finding fresh and engaging ways to break them.[12]

The Club's ranks included members of the clergy – Canon Victor L. Whitechurch,[13] as well as Knox – and authors whose Christian faith was threaded through their fiction. Among them was H. C. Bailey, who turned to detective fiction after the First World War, and whose short stories are morality plays in miniature. Within a decade he was regarded as one of the 'Big Five' crime writers.[14]

A journalist, Bailey created Reggie Fortune, a doctor with close ties to Scotland Yard. Science often plays a part in Bailey's stories, but their distinctive tang comes from his acute sense of sin.[15] A reserved family man, Bailey had a world view much darker than Chesterton's. Long before Patricia Highsmith and Ruth Rendell, he examined the anthropology of evil through the medium of detective fiction. Perhaps one day his stories will be repackaged under that label beloved by publicists: *noir*.

In time, Bailey's reputation declined because his oblique, mannered style obscured the power of his writing. Reggie is forever mumblin' and moanin', and even the most sympathetic modern reader is likely to find this irritatin',[16] but those willing to hack their way through the thickets of Bailey's prose will uncover psychologically complex studies of child abuse, domestic dysfunction and suburban malice. In the first Fortune novel, *Shadows on the Wall* (1934), the cancer that destroys a hate-filled murderer symbolises the disease of cruelty.

Bailey was preoccupied, as were many other Golden Age writers, with the nature of justice. In his moral universe, unrepentant sinners rarely found mercy. Fortune articulates Bailey's outlook in the characteristically unorthodox *No Murder*, aka *The Apprehensive Dog* (1942): 'The wages of sin is death . . . Don't trouble whether it's the real sinner that gets the wages.'

A generation younger than Chesterton, Dorothy L. Sayers admired the great man and attended a lecture he gave while she was a student at Oxford. As a detective novelist, she shared his view that the central challenge was 'to make the solution neither too obscure nor too obvious', and although originally she believed that 'love interest' got in the way of the action, she conceded that, as Chesterton thought, it made a useful red herring.

Her Great Detective, Lord Peter Wimsey, solves an unusual puzzle in *The Nine Tailors*[17] (1934), in which the Reverend Theodore Venables, rector of Fenchurch St Paul, is essentially a fictional portrait of her clergyman father. She engaged an architect to design the parish church for an illustration in the book. The building is lovingly described, as are the church bells, which play a crucial part in a clever and original plot. She made sixty-three pages of notes about bells and campanology, soaking herself in the minutiae, so that although she never pulled a bell rope, her imaginative grasp of change-ringing ensured a sense of authenticity. This fussiness about accuracy in detail set her apart from most of her peers.

The novel's religious symbolism is not to everyone's taste, and Sayers' work continues to divide opinion, perhaps mainly because her writing, like her opinions, was usually so *definite*. When one realises that this deeply religious woman spent most of her adult life tormented by the belief that she had sinned by giving birth to an illegitimate child whose existence she never dared to acknowledge in public, one understands her better.

When she tired of writing about Wimsey, Sayers turned her attention to writing religious plays and translating Dante. At heart, she was a conservative Anglo-Catholic. She didn't care to describe herself as a feminist, but her work and her life showed what a woman might achieve.

*

Freeman Wills Crofts' religious faith coloured his fiction. Money-grubbing capitalists get their comeuppance[18] time and again thanks to the remorseless detective work of Chief Inspector French, but Crofts went further in *Antidote to Venom* (1938), a bold 'effort to tell a story of crime positively'.

George Surridge, a likeable but weak-willed zoo director, commits murder only to find, following a series of twists of fate, that 'he had exchanged financial worry for a moral burden'. His sins find him out, but the book culminates in redemption, and even his unpleasant wife improbably benefits from 'a contact with the Divine'. The plot combines a cat-and-mouse tussle between Surridge and French with a 'howdunit' mystery involving a Russell's Viper, but Crofts also uses the phrase 'antidote to venom' to refer to the love of God. His ambition was laudable, but the book was compromised by his inability to portray his characters in depth. He described *Antidote to Venom* as an experiment, and never repeated it.

A supporter of Moral Rearmament, Crofts tried in vain to enlist Sayers' support for the Oxford Group's vision of 'world rebuilding', before Hitler put paid to such aspirations. His faith was unwavering, and in 1949 he produced *The Four Gospels in One Story*, an attempt to rewrite the Gospels in simple language.

'Is it an accident?' W. H. Auden enquired in 'The Guilty Vicarage',[19] 'that the detective story has flourished most in predominantly Protestant countries?' Like almost all British crime fans of his generation, he wasn't aware of the extent of crime writing in other languages, because translations were rarely available. The detective story, Auden claimed, was the mirror image of the Quest for the Grail, and its milieu should reflect its inhabitants and be the Great Good Place: 'for the more Eden-like it is, the greater the contradiction of murder.'

Auden reckoned that the typical detective fan suffered from a sense of sin. He didn't regard detective stories as works of art, but simply as a form of escapism. They offered a magical satisfaction, the illusion of being dissociated from the murderer. Detective stories offer 'the fantasy of being restored to the Garden of Eden, to a state of innocence . . . The driving force behind this daydream is a feeling of guilt . . . The fantasy of escape is the same, whether one explains the guilt in Christian, Freudian, or any other terms. One's way of trying to face the reality . . . will . . . depend very much on one's creed.'[20]

Notes

The main sources include Chesterton's autobiography, biographies of Chesterton by Maisie Ward and Michael Ffinch, Francesca Knox's *Ronald Knox: A Man for all Seasons*, notably Sheridan Gilley's chapter, William David Spencer's *Mysterium and Mystery*, Erik Routley's *The Puritanical Pleasures of the Detective Story*, and Barbara Reynolds' biography of Sayers.

1 *a candidate for sainthood*: See www. chesterton.org/cause/ for the statement by Dale Ahlquist, 5 August 2019.
2 *a Jewish family called Steinthal*: Despite having Jewish friends and being quick to condemn Nazi antisemitism, Chesterton frequently expressed views that can be interpreted as antisemitic. His admirers defend him with vigour, but some of his writings provide his critics with ammunition.
3 *Raymond Postgate*: Postgate, brother of detective novelist Margaret Cole and at one time a Marxist, wrote an outstanding courtroom-based crime novel, *Verdict of Twelve*. He shows how the life histories of members of a jury may affect their attitude to justice. *Somebody at the Door* varies that pattern, utilising biographical sketches to show how a diverse group of individuals might all have a motive to murder the same man.
4 *crime fiction's first important commentator*: G. K. Chesterton on Detective Fiction, compiled and edited by John Peterson, gathers his writings on the genre, and records the *Oxford English Dictionary*'s statement that Chesterton was the first person to use the term 'mystery story' in reference to detective fiction, in the *Illustrated London News* in 1907. Chesterton's introduction to Bernard Capes' posthumously published novel *The Skeleton Key* suggests that: 'A detective story might well be in a special sense a spiritual story, since it is a story in which even the moral sympathies may be in doubt . . . the hero may turn out to be a villain, or the villain to be the hero.'
5 *C. A. Alington*: Cyril Argentine Alington was another all-rounder who dabbled in detection, starting with *Mr Evans, a Cricketo-Detective Story* in 1922. After spending sixteen years as headmaster of Eton, he became Dean of Durham; he also served as chaplain to the King. He was a member of a 'panel of experts' who advised on potential titles for the Collins Crime Club imprint. *Archdeacons Afloat* and *Archdeacons Ashore* are examples of the clerical mystery, although his crime writing lacked Chesterton's panache.
6 *John Lydiard*: Lydiard was to an extent modelled on Knox's brother Dillwyn, a cryptographer who worked for British Intelligence during both world wars.
7 *G. K. Chesterton had set the ball rolling*: In 'How To Write a Detective Story', in *Hearst's International*. His starting point was that 'the aim of a mystery story . . . is not darkness but light.'

8   *summarised . . . by the American crime writer Ross Thomas*: In the *Los Angeles Times* of 26 February 1989, in the course of a brutal review of *Sins for Father Knox*. This collection of stories featuring a female sleuth who happened to be a blues singer from Prague was designed to illustrate each of Knox's Ten Commandments being broken, but Thomas didn't get the joke. The author was Josef Skvorecky, a distinguished Czech-born writer who was nominated for the Nobel Prize in 1982 despite his temerity in venturing occasionally into detective fiction.

9   *His own detective novels*: *The Three Taps* is a locked-bedroom mystery; as with 'Solved by Inspection', a short story about an inexplicable death by starvation, it features the pleasant but forgettable insurance investigator Miles Bredon. Knox's last detective story, 'The Adventure of the First Class Carriage', was a return to Sherlockiana and another 'impossible crime' mystery.

10 *Sherlockian fandom spans the globe*: Foremost among Sherlockian groups are the Baker Street Irregulars, who celebrate Holmes' birthday in New York City on 6 January each year. The Irregulars were formed by Christopher Morley, and held their first annual dinner in 1934; invested members have included Isaac Asimov, Rex Stout and Neil Gaiman. The BSI archives are held at Harvard.

11 *the Club's jokey ritual for the initiation of new members*: Writing in 1942, Howard Haycraft said that the Detection Club's existence was an 'inestimable advantage denied to their American brethren'. The Club continues to thrive and to preserve a modified version of the ritual.

12 *fresh and engaging ways to break them*: Anthony Berkeley's prefatory note to Milward Kennedy in *Panic Party* said: 'I . . . take the greatest pleasure in dedicating to you a book . . . which breaks every rule of the austere Club to which we both belong, and which will probably earn my expulsion from its membership.'

13 *Canon Victor L. Whitechurch*: Whitechurch created two 'railway detectives', Godfrey Page and Thorpe Hazell, who appeared in short stories. His novels include *Murder at College*, aka *Murder at Exbridge*, set in a fictionalised Oxford. He was supposedly one of the first crime writers to ask Scotland Yard to check his accounts of police procedure for accuracy.

14 *the 'Big Five' crime writers*: The others were Christie, Sayers, Austin Freeman and Crofts.

15 *his acute sense of sin*: Dictionaries of quotations attribute to Bailey the phrase 'faith is a higher faculty than reason'. In 'The Business Minister', Superintendent Bell and Fortune share the view that the odious villain must be lacking in religious faith. In the masterly 'The Yellow Slugs', the perverted religiosity of a 'pious brute' leads to psychological torture, child abuse and murder.

16 *even the most sympathetic modern reader is likely to find this irritatin'*: John Dickson Carr described Reggie as 'an animated cream-puff'.

17 *The Nine Tailors*: Sayers was influenced by J. Meade Falkner's *The Nebuly Coat*, at the heart of which is another magnificent church. Her admirers included Charles Williams, a notable Christian writer, and a member of 'the Inklings' (he is not to be confused with the American author of the same name who wrote high-calibre paperback originals, several of which were filmed, including *Dead Calm*). Williams' own metaphysical thrillers tiptoed

along the boundaries of detective fiction, but his major contribution to the genre was as a critic; Jared Lobdell's collection of his reviews reveals his love of the traditional mystery.

18 *Money-grubbing capitalists get their comeuppance*: In *Masters of the 'Humdrum' Mystery*, Curtis Evans discusses examples such as *Fatal Venture*, set on board a luxurious floating casino.

19 *'Is it an accident?' W. H. Auden enquired in 'The Guilty Vicarage'*: Auden wrote a poem called 'Detective Story' and was the physical model for Nicholas Blake's detective Nigel Strangeways. Auden and P. D. James discussed the possibility of his writing poetry which she might present in her novels as the work of her poet-cop Adam Dalgliesh, but he died before this pleasing notion could be progressed.

20 *One's way of trying to face the reality . . . will . . . depend very much on one's creed*: Harry Kemelman's books about Rabbi David Small, for instance, were grounded in conservative Judaism; the Rabbi solves crimes by applying Talmudic logic. Kemelman, an Orthodox Jew, told *People* magazine that he 'got more insight into Catholicism from Father Brown than I got from most of my studies in comparative religion'. He performed a similar service for the Jewish faith. His successors include Faye Kellerman, member of a family of bestselling crime writers, whose series about cop Peter Decker and Rina Lazarus, beginning with *The Ritual Bath*, gives insights into Jewish culture. Kenneth Wishnia's anthology *Jewish Noir* illustrates the range of stories with Jewish themes, and includes a translation of Yente Serdatsky's 'A Simkhe', first published in Yiddish in 1912.

NINE

Plot Minds

Marie Belloc Lowndes and Edwardian-era detective fiction

Over dinner at Lord Glenconner's home in November 1912, the Prime Minister was chatting about murder. Herbert Henry Asquith took refuge from the cares of office by studying the latest sensational cases, as well as notorious mysteries of the past. Sitting next to him was a small, vivacious woman, a charming conversationalist who spoke with a faint French accent and was entirely at ease among London's social elite. Marie Belloc Lowndes was an author who used mysterious real-life crimes as source material for her fiction.

'My heart warmed to [Asquith] very much,' she confided to her diary, 'when I discovered that busy and worried as he now is, he yet finds time to follow the extraordinary and mysterious disappearance of Mrs Nowill.'

Six days earlier, the young wife of an elderly Sheffield businessman had gone missing. Marian Nowill[1] had been staying at the Atlantic Hotel in Newquay; a fellow guest was her golfing partner Arthur Delay, a retired solicitor who had made a fortune in Singapore. She believed Delay to be a bachelor, and when she discovered that he had a wife in London, she became distraught and vanished from the hotel. A frantic Delay joined local coastguards in trying to find her. When the search came to nothing, he tried to throw himself off the cliff. Subsequently, a witness claimed to have seen Delay and Marian Nowill arguing while on the cliff, and a couple of days after her disappearance, Delay was discovered in his room. He'd hanged himself.

After the Prime Minister and the writer had speculated about Marian Nowill's fate, the conversation turned to a puzzle from seventeenth-century French history. Asquith explained why he believed that Madame Henriette (also known as Henrietta of England) had been poisoned, and the pair proceeded to debate the unsolved Balham mystery[2] of 1876, enjoying a lively disagreement about the Prime Minister's theory that Mrs Bravo murdered her husband Charles.

'What to me is very startling and terrible,' Marie Belloc Lowndes said, 'is that the intelligent criminal has nothing in his appearance, manner or I fear nature, making him any different from those about him. To me, with regard to murder, the word that should be used is not "Who?" but "Why?"'

Marie Belloc Lowndes was born in 1868, the daughter of a French lawyer and a prominent English feminist called Bessie Parkes; her brother, the polymath Hilaire Belloc,[3] became a close friend of Chesterton. The difference between the outlook of the French and the British fascinated her, and she liked to point out that there was no French equivalent for the term 'wishful thinking'. A prolific author and leading member of the literary establishment, she encouraged a host of younger writers, including Hugh Walpole, James Hilton and Graham Greene. Walpole fictionalised her as Mrs Launce in *Fortitude*.[4]

In 1912 she was given a ticket by the Public Prosecutor to attend the Old Bailey. She watched the trial of the Seddons, a couple accused of committing murder by arsenic. Characteristically, she was more interested in the psychology of the husband and wife than the technicalities of the poisoning.

'Watching the prisoners was to me intensely interesting,' she wrote in her diary. 'They were the most respectable, commonplace-looking people imaginable . . . What I found strange and unnatural in their behaviour was the way in which they constantly talked to one another, and his laughter at anything in the proceedings which could be considered as comic.'[5]

Her circle included Lord Moulton, a distinguished judge, with whom she debated the Lamson murder case[6] of 1882; 'he is convinced that Dr Lamson did not give his brother-in-law the poison in the capsule which he brought and administered to the lad for a cold. He thinks he put it in the currants of a cake.'

A 'trunk murder'[7] committed in Monte Carlo inspired her to write *The Chink in the Armour*[8] (1912). A former Irish tennis champion, Vere St Leger Goold, had conspired with his wife to murder a wealthy Swedish widow, whose remains were found in a large trunk left at the railway station in Marseilles. In the novel, tension mounts as Madame Wachner and her husband target naive Sylvia Bailey, who only realises the peril she faces when she spots in the Wachners' kitchen 'a large trunk, corded and even labelled . . . Close to the trunk was a large piece of sacking – and by it another coil of thick rope.'

In 1913, the *Daily Telegraph* began to serialise the novel for which Belloc Lowndes is now remembered. The idea for *The Lodger*[9] came from yet another dinner party, at which someone said that 'his mother had had a butler and a cook who married and kept lodgers. They were convinced that Jack the Ripper had spent a night under their roof.' She wrote this anecdote up as a short story, subsequently expanded into a novel that 'did not receive a single favourable review . . . Then, to my surprise, when *The Lodger* had been out for two or three years, reviewers began to rebuke me for not writing another *Lodger*.'

Belloc Lowndes' inherited feminism is evident in her portrayal of Ellen Bunting, who wonders whether her lodger, who calls himself Mr Sleuth, may be 'the Avenger', a puritanical serial killer who has brought terror to the streets of London, preying on women who commit the sin of drinking in public. Ellen's housekeeping duties make it easy for her to play the detective, snooping around her tenant's room whenever she gets the chance. For once in a story derived from the Ripper murders, a strong woman plays a central role without becoming a victim. Yet when Ellen's suspicions are aroused, she does not behave as one might expect.

The moral ambiguities of this masterpiece of domestic suspense anticipate those in Patricia Highsmith's novels after the Second World War. Long after the book first appeared, Gertrude Stein advised Ernest Hemingway to read Belloc Lowndes.[10] He found *The Lodger* and *The Chink in the Armour* 'splendid . . . the people credible and the action and the terror never false.'

Belloc Lowndes continued writing until her death in 1947, but her heyday was before the First World War. The coming of the Golden Age of detective fiction marked a major shift in literary fashion, and her focus on criminal motivation – one of her books was *Motive* (1938), retitled in the US as *Why it Happened* – rather than puzzles of whodunit or howdunit meant she was out of step.

She introduced a French investigator called Hercules Popeau in *The Lonely House* (1920) at about the same time as the first appearance of Agatha Christie's Hercule Poirot. Believing (wrongly; this seems to have been a simple case of synchronicity) that Christie was guilty of plagiarising her,[11] Belloc Lowndes complained to the Society of Authors, only to find she had no right of redress.

She claimed that, like Wilkie Collins, Dumas *père* and Fergus Hume, she had 'what is called a "plot mind"', which she said was 'curiously rare . . . [but] does secure for its owner a kind of immortality'. Her plot mind was not a match for Christie's brand of ingenuity but her merits as a crime novelist have been obscured for too long by the mists of literary fashion.

The Edwardian era represented, in crime fiction as well as in British society, a period of transition between the bluff confidence of the Victorian age and a post-war hunger for escapist fun. The tectonic plates were shifting, but the short story continued to dominate the genre, as crime novelists, from talented amateurs[12] to grizzled professionals,[13] groped for a satisfying way of combining plot with pace in a full-length mystery.

The leading rivals to Sherlock Holmes and Father Brown were Baroness Orczy's Old Man in the Corner, and Ernest Bramah's Max Carrados.[14] Carrados, blinded in an accident,[15] turns his disability to advantage. As he tells Louis Carlyle, a discredited solicitor turned inquiry agent who acts as his Watson, he has no 'blundering, self-confident eyes to be hoodwinked'. He appeared in one novel, the late and inferior *The Bravo of London* (1934), while Father Brown and The Old Man in the Corner only featured in short stories.

The most prolific crime novelist was J. S. Fletcher,[16] whose tally of over two hundred and forty books made even Marie Belloc Lowndes seem an under-achiever. *The Middle Temple Murder* (1919), brisk and incident-packed if far from ground-breaking, was expanded from a short story, 'The Contents of the Coffin', but secured Fletcher's reputation after benefiting from praise from President Woodrow Wilson.

Godfrey Benson, who became Lord Charnwood, and wrote an admired biography of Abraham Lincoln, typified a cohort of authors who amused themselves by dabbling in detection. The stately pace of his solitary crime novel, *Tracks in the Snow* (1906), and his lack of interest in concealing the culprit's identity were characteristic of a leisured age – leisured if one belonged to the upper echelons of society, that is. The same is true of the two detective novels written by the unrelated E. F. Benson,[17] which are pleasantly readable but lack the macabre flair of his stories of the supernatural.

S. R. Crockett, whose novels of Scottish life had enjoyed a vogue in the late nineteenth century, sought to reinvent himself in the twentieth as a detective novelist. *The Azure Hand* introduced an unusual policeman, Luiz Perez Grant, with a Portuguese mother and connections to 'the Orient'.

Crockett's interest in human behaviour is evident in discussion of the criminal who takes to breaking the law 'like dram drinking – for the stimulus it gives his system'. Towards the end, the murderer tells the detective that he realised he was at risk 'as soon as you began to study character and take your time, instead of bothering about footprints and dropped tobacco ash'. Crockett was reacting against the forensic brilliance of Sherlock Holmes, but his ornate style was dated while the emphasis on criminal psychology was ahead of its time. His book was not published until 1917, after his death.

A younger novelist, Alfred Edward Woodley Mason,[18] also set out to create a Great Detective quite different from Holmes except for his ability to solve baffling mysteries. Inspector Gabriel Hanaud of the Sûreté was an urbane policeman, whose cases are narrated by a wealthy financier, Julius Ricardo.

Hanaud made his debut in *At the Villa Rose* (1910), a novel inspired by the murder of Eugénie Fougère at Aix-les-Bains. As if to emphasise the difference between his approach and Conan Doyle's, Mason made clear his disdain for spiritualism; a fake séance forms a central part of the villains' plan to murder rich and credulous Madame Dauvray. Mason aimed 'to make the story of what actually happened more intriguing and more dramatic than the unravelling of the mystery and the detection of the criminal', and consequently indulged in an extended flashback after the revelation of whodunit. He'd fallen into the same trap as Conan Doyle in *A Study in Scarlet* and *The Valley of Fear*, dissipating the tension so carefully built.

The most influential detective novel of this period published in a language other than English was Gaston Leroux's[19] locked-room puzzle *The Mystery of the Yellow Room* (1908). The young hero Joseph Josephine, always known by his nickname of Rouletabille because his round head resembles a bullet, is a journalist. At the tender age of eighteen, he is the youngest of all the Great Detectives, with boundless self-confidence and a Watson in the shape of the lawyer Sainclair.

The reader is told that 'the entire world hung for months' over the puzzle of the Yellow Room, a problem described (Leroux was not a man for understatement) as 'the most obscure . . . that has ever challenged the perspicacity of our police or taxed the conscience of our judges'. The crime occurred in a pavilion owned by a scientist working on a new theory 'destined to overthrow from its base the whole of official science'. Mathilde Stangerson is found lying 'in the agonies of death' in the locked and barred Yellow Room. The question that defeats everyone is not simply 'whodunit' but how the culprit managed to vanish from the Yellow Room. In his quest for the truth, Rouletabille pits his wits against those of the legendary policeman Frédéric Larsan, 'the great Fred'.

A ground-floor plan of the pavilion clarifies details of the puzzle. Plans and maps were becoming popular adornments to detective stories, helping readers to grapple with convoluted plots. Leroux hurls into the melting pot extracts from newspaper reports, transcripts of interviews, and enigmatic remarks such as 'the presbytery has lost nothing of its charm, nor the garden its bright-ness'. The reader is constantly challenged to work out what has happened and why.

Rouletabille identifies the culprit during a dramatic murder trial, but that is not the end of the story. The groundwork is laid for a sequel, just as in the final episodes of so many modern television series, when Sainclair asks his friend to explain why the phrase 'the perfume of the lady in black' troubles him. Rouletabille's cryptic response is: 'Perhaps – some day, some day.'

The Perfume of the Lady in Black, another locked-room mystery featuring Rouletabille, duly followed. Leroux kept the series going until shortly before his death, and the franchise was continued by Noré Brunet, who wrote two authorised Rouletabille novels in the 1940s. As so often, the first novel remained the most memorable.

The sinking of the supposedly unsinkable RMS *Titanic* in 1912 is often seen as marking a historical turning point, a disaster that destroyed confidence and fostered insecurity and fear. Among those who died was Jacques Futrelle, an American first-class passenger who was travelling home from Europe.

Futrelle, whose real name was John Heath Futrell, wrote short stories and a single novel about an idiosyncratic Great Detective, Professor S. F. X. Van Dusen, a scientist known as 'the Thinking Machine'. Van Dusen has an appropriately huge head to accom-modate his formidable brain, but is short, near-sighted and arrogant. Van Dusen's most famous case, 'The Problem of Cell 13', established Futrelle's reputation for ingenuity, and the stories often featured seemingly impossible crimes.

Futrelle was only thirty-seven when an iceberg holed the *Titanic*. He made sure his wife escaped in a lifeboat, but refused to join her, and was last seen smoking a cigar in the company of John Jacob Astor. The personal tragedy of his death seems, with hind-sight, to have coincided with the end of an era in detective fiction, at a time when the wider world was about to change for ever.

Two years before Futrelle's death, Chesterton's friend Edmund Clerihew Bentley[20] decided 'to write a detective story of a new sort' with an investigator who was 'recognisable as a human being' rather than infallible. To poke fun at the clichés of the genre, he would make 'the hero's hard-won and obviously correct solution of the mystery turn out to be completely wrong. Why not show up the infallibility of the Holmesian method?'

The result, dedicated to Chesterton and published in 1913, was *Trent's Last Case*, aka *The Woman in Black*. Philip Trent, gentlemanly artist and occasional sleuth, investigates the murder of an odious American financier, falls in love with the dead man's widow, and works out whodunit, only to be shocked when the true culprit is at last revealed. Bentley was equally confounded by his readers' reaction. Rather than sharing the joke at the expense of Sherlock's followers, they loved the country house setting, and above all the plot twists.

The book's devotees included two young women, Agatha Christie and Dorothy L. Sayers. *Trent's Last Case* was the harbinger of a new era in crime fiction, with readers no longer content merely to sit back and admire demonstrations of deductive brilliance. As the First World War came to an end, they were ready to take up the challenge of trying to solve ingenious mysteries themselves. They wanted to play what John Dickson Carr called 'the grandest game in the world'.

Notes

The main sources include Susan Lowndes' edition of Marie Belloc Lowndes' diaries and letters, Elyssa Warkentin's introduction to the Cambridge Scholars' edition of *The Lodger,* Joseph A. Kestner's *The Edwardian Detective, 1901–1915*, and Bentley's *Those Days*.

1   *Marian Nowill*: Her body was discovered in the sea. Delay had left her £30,000 in his will. Whether he caused her death was never established.
2   *the unsolved Balham mystery*: Belloc Lowndes talked to Edward Clarke, last surviving counsel in the Balham case, and eventually fictionalised the case in *What Really Happened. Murder at the Priory* by Bernard Taylor and Kate Clarke, and James Ruddick's *Death at the Priory* are non-fiction studies of the case, which supplied plot elements for *So Evil My Love* by Joseph Shearing (the pen-name under which Marjorie Bowen wrote crime novels that, like Belloc Lowndes', were frequently based on actual cases) and John Dickson Carr's *Below Suspicion*.
3   *her brother . . . Hilaire Belloc*: Belloc dabbled in light-hearted detective fiction, sometimes collaborating with Chesterton.
4   *Mrs Launce in Fortitude*: She is vividly described: 'There was no crime black

enough, no desertion, no cruelty horrible enough to outspeed her pity. She hated and understood the sin and loved and comforted the sinner . . . Everything, however horrible, interested her . . . she adored life.'

5   *his laughter at anything in the proceedings which could be considered as comic*: Seddon was hanged just over seven weeks later but his wife had the last laugh. She was acquitted, remarried before the end of the year, and subsequently emigrated to the United States with her new husband and her five children.

6   *the Lamson murder case*: Dr George Henry Lamson, an American-born war hero who practised medicine in Bournemouth and became a drug addict, was convicted of murder and hanged. He was nicknamed 'the Wimbledon poisoner', a phrase borrowed by Nigel Williams for the title of a black comedy about a solicitor whose homicidal career does not go to plan. The novel was the first in a trilogy; Williams' other forays into crime fiction include *Charlie*, a private-eye story, novelised from his own television scripts. His sons Harry and Jack have written TV crime serials such as *The Missing* and *Rellik*.

7   *a 'trunk murder'*: Murderers needing to dispose of an inconvenient corpse have sometimes stowed body parts in a railway trunk. The 'Brighton Trunk murders' of 1934 feature in Peter Guttridge's *City of Dreadful Night*. R. Austin Freeman's *Dr Thorndyke Intervenes* begins with the discovery of a human head in a case at Fenchurch Street Station. The story of America's 'Trunk Murderess', Winnie May Judd, who dismembered two women in Phoenix in 1931, was reimagined by Megan Abbott in 2009 in *Bury Me Deep*.

8   *The Chink in the Armour*: The novel became a play, *The House of Peril*, adapted by Horace Annesley Vachell, and a silent film under that title.

9   *The Lodger*: Vachell adapted the book for the stage as *Who Is He?* Alfred Hitchcock saw the play in New York and turned it into a silent film starring Ivor Novello. Later film versions included *The Man in the Attic*, starring Jack Palance; in 1960 the story became an opera, written by Phyllis Tate with a libretto by David Franklin. Lowndes' *The Story of Ivy* became the film noir *Ivy*.

10   *Gertrude Stein advised Ernest Hemingway to read Belloc Lowndes*: Stein's fascination with the genre is evident from her essay 'Why I Like Detective Stories'. Her solitary, predictably bizarre, detective novel, *Blood on the Dining Room Floor*, was written in 1933, but not inflicted on the public until 1948.

11   *Believing . . . that Christie was guilty of plagiarising her*: An even more remarkable coincidence of names involves Frank Howel Evans' Jules Poiret, who from 1909 investigated dozens of cases. Poiret's sidekick is Captain Haven, Hercule Poirot's is Captain Hastings.

12   *talented amateurs*: Such as big-game hunter, explorer, cricketer and sniper Major Hesketh Vernon Hesketh-Prichard, whose *November Joe: The Detective of the Woods* introduced a Canadian backwoodsman in the Fenimore Cooper tradition. Writing with his mother as E. and H. Heron, he created the bandit Don Q and perhaps the first 'psychic detective', Flaxman Low.

13   *grizzled professionals*: An example is the prolific Francis Edward Grainger, who produced more than one hundred books under the name Headon Hill. Many are potboilers, but some showed touches of flair. His Sebastian Zambra enjoyed a career lasting thirty years and was using photography in his

detective work long before Holmes mentioned it in 'The Lion's Mane'. He also created Kala Persad, a Hindu seer who assists the British investigator Mark Poignard and is a very early example of a non-white 'detective' of genius.

14 *Ernest Bramah's Max Carrados*: The American crime fiction commentator Art Scott has pointed out to me in correspondence the striking similarities between the Carrados story 'The Holloway Flat Tragedy' and Rex Stout's novella 'Instead of Evidence', notable for a scene where Nero Wolfe flees in panic from an eccentric inventor hoping to record Wolfe's voice for a novelty talking flower pot.

15 *blinded in an accident*: Crime writers have often explored the challenges faced by blind people, as either detectives or potential victims. Carrados' American counterpart, Thornley Colton, was known variously as 'the Problemist' and 'the blind reader of hearts', but his career was cut short by the death of his creator, Clinton H. Stagg, in a car crash while still in his twenties. The blind Damon Gaunt features in *At One-Thirty* by Isabel Ostrander, who also wrote under various male pseudonyms. Baynard Kendrick's Captain Duncan Maclain, a blind private investigator aided by two German shepherd dogs, made his debut in 1937 and enjoyed a lengthy career, appearing in more than a dozen novels before metamorphosing into the blind insurance investigator Sam Longstreet, hero of the 1970s television series *Longstreet*.

Blind people are menaced in works as diverse as Frederick Knott's play *Wait until Dark* and Jean Redon's chilling novel *Eyes without a Face*, both of which were filmed, while a serial killer targets blind women in Bruce Robinson's movie *Jennifer 8*. The protagonist of Philip MacDonald's Golden Age mystery *The Nursemaid Who Disappeared* was transformed into a blind man in Nigel Balchin's screenplay, renamed *23 Paces to Baker Street*; the tense climax has echoes of the Max Carrados story, 'The Game Played in the Dark'.

16 *J. S. Fletcher*: Joseph Smith Fletcher was a journalist, as was the protagonist of *The Middle Temple Murder*. His principal series character was the private investigator Ronald Camberwell, who made his final appearance in *Todmanhawe Grange*, left unfinished at Fletcher's death. The novel was completed by E. P. Mathers, aka the crossword compiler 'Torquemada'.

17 *two detective novels written by the unrelated E. F. Benson*: Introducing a reprint of Benson's *The Blotting Book*, Stephen Knight argued that it may have influenced Christie, and that it also prefigured the work of Francis Iles.

18 *Alfred Edward Woodley Mason*: A Renaissance man if ever there was one, Mason was an actor, cricketer, M P, spy and playwright. His novels included the frequently filmed *The Four Feathers*. Mason was so busy that fourteen years passed before Inspector Hanaud reappeared in *The House of the Arrow*, a novel combining the strengths of its predecessor with a more elegant structure. Three more Hanaud novels appeared, the last in 1946.

19 *Gaston Leroux*: Leroux inherited and squandered a fortune before settling down to literary life. His other major series character was Jean Mascart, alias Chéri-Bibi, who was (like the husband of Orczy's Lady Molly of Scotland Yard) wrongly convicted of murder. Leroux's admirers included Christie and John Dickson Carr, whose debut novel *It Walks by Night* shares a plot

element with *The Mystery of the Yellow Room*. Today, Leroux is best remembered for *The Phantom of the Opera*, thanks to Andrew Lloyd Webber's
musical. Even more improbably, *The Mystery of the Yellow Room* has been
adapted into a YouTube stop-motion animated video, using pieces of Lego.

20 *Edmund Clerihew Bentley*: Philip Trent reappeared in short stories, including
several gems. 'The Clever Cockatoo' has a storyline similar to that of Sayers'
subsequent 'The Incredible Elopement of Lord Peter Wimsey'. In 1936,
Bentley published *Trent's Own Case*, co-written with H. Warner Allen, a
wine expert and occasional crime writer. He also devised and gave his
middle name to a comic verse form, the clerihew. Late in life, he wrote a
forgettable amnesia thriller, *Elephant's Work*. His son Nicolas, an artist, also
dabbled in mystery fiction.

TEN

The Science of Detection

R. Austin Freeman and scientific mysteries

In the dank cellar of a house in Gravesend, a doctor was rehearsing a murder. A man in his mid-forties, he was charming and handsome, but instinctively secretive;[1] female admirers called his dark eyes mesmeric.

His plan seemed foolproof, but he had to make sure it worked in practice. A friend had lent him a long-barrelled revolver, now lashed to a saw bench in the cellar. He'd picked up a makeshift aluminium dagger. A local garage had fashioned the weapon from a carpenter's chisel. They'd botched the job, but for the purpose of his experiment, it would do. He fitted the dagger into the barrel of the gun.

A small storage room opened off the main part of the basement, and the doctor pointed the gun towards the entrance. He then tied a piece of string to the trigger, and carefully fed it through the keyhole of the main cellar door. Standing well clear, the doctor pulled the string. The dagger fired through the doorway, and into the small room. The recoil knocked over the saw bench.

Hurrying into the smaller room, the doctor examined the result of his experiment. The dagger, he discovered, had cut deep into the brickwork. The impact had damaged the point of the blade.

'It struck so hard,' he reflected, 'that it could have passed straight through a man's body.'

This was unexpected, but it didn't matter. He'd proved to himself how to commit a murder that seemed impossible.

The doctor was Richard Austin Freeman, the friend who supplied the gun an engineer called Frank Standfield. Freeman was working on a set of short detective stories for *Pearson's Magazine*, and asked Standfield to take photographs of visual clues to the stories:[2] three types of human hair for 'The Anthropologist at Large', and sand for 'A Message from the Deep Sea'.

Freeman constructed his stories with meticulous attention to detail,[3] and the experiment with the gun (witnessed by his son John) was crucial to his research for 'The Aluminium Dagger', featuring Dr John Evelyn Thorndyke,[4] the handsome expert in medical jurisprudence seldom to be found without his trusty green bag of forensic kit.

Unlike many British writers of his time, Freeman came from humble origins. Born in Soho in 1862, the son of a journeyman tailor, he refused to follow his father into the business. Science was his passion, and he qualified as an apothecary prior to studying medicine at Middlesex Hospital. His first published works, an article racily titled 'The Phenomena of Exuviation in the Brachyura' (about the molting of crabs) and an essay about moles, revealed a fascination with natural history that resurfaced in his detective stories.

Joining the Colonial Service, he worked as a surgeon on the Gold Coast before succumbing to blackwater fever. Back in England, poor health and lack of money led to ten years of struggle as he drifted from job to job, and wrote magazine stories to keep the wolf from the door. But he was lucky in his friends, including Dr John James Pitcairn and Alice and Bernard Bishop.[5] Pitcairn found him a short-term post as an assistant medical officer at Holloway Prison, and the Bishops allowed Freeman and his family to live rent-free in Gravesend in return for his tutoring their children.

Pitcairn and Freeman began a writing partnership under the name Clifford Ashdown; as well as creating the engagingly villainous Romney Pringle, they co-wrote stories combining science with detection, posthumously collected in *From a Surgeon's Diary*. But having reached the age of forty-three and failed to achieve financial security, Freeman resolved to create a Great Detective of his own.

Dr Thorndyke's life wasn't complicated by a cocaine habit or other Sherlockian eccentricities. He had an unshakeable devotion to scientific reasoning.[6] His real-life model was the nineteenth-century toxicologist Alfred Swaine Taylor, sometimes described as 'the father of British forensic science', whose textbooks Freeman pored over as a student. Taylor was an expert witness[7] in famous murder trials, including those of two homicidal doctors, William Palmer, the Rugeley poisoner, and Thomas Smethurst.

The 'Thumbograph' – a book with blank pages, supplied with an inking pad, for collecting people's thumbprints – inspired Freeman's first Thorndyke novel, *The Red Thumb Mark* (1907). Thumbographs enjoyed a vogue in Edwardian Britain, but Freeman believed that these apparently harmless toys could be misused to forge prints. He tested his 'thesis that fingerprints could be fabricated[8] by making a set of gelatine stamps from my own fingertips . . . with these I was able to produce quite good prints.'

Freeman remained a major figure in crime fiction throughout the interwar years, but he'd established his methods before the Golden Age of detective fiction and wasn't as playful as younger writers. His stories, like those about Sherlock Holmes, were essentially demonstrations of expertise, and he took trouble to ensure the accuracy of Thorndyke's science. For example, when researching 'A Wastrel's Romance', he left microscope slides, moistened with glycerine, on the walls of a factory to verify the nature and quality of dust in Docklands, south of the Thames.

Few readers could hope to beat Thorndyke to the solution of a mystery. As Dorothy L. Sayers said:[9] 'Thorndyke can cheerfully show you all the facts. You will be none the wiser, unless you happen to have an intimate acquaintance with the fauna of local ponds, the effect of belladonna on rabbits, the physical and chemical properties of blood; optics; topical diseases; metallurgy, hieroglyphics, and a few other trifles.'

Freeman took risks as a crime writer, and some of his literary experiments misfired. *The Uttermost Farthing*, aka *A Savant's Vendetta* (1914), a revenge thriller about a homicidal professor who keeps adding to his private museum of skeletons, was rejected by his usual publishers as 'horrible'. *The Mystery of Angelina Frood* (1924) was meant to offer playful commentary on Dickens' unfinished book and a poem by Oliver Goldsmith, but the joke fell flat.

A true innovator, Freeman popularised the 'inverted mystery'.[10] Dispensing with the seductive uncertainty of asking whodunit, he focused on the question of whether the criminal would be caught, and if so, how. He showed the perpetrator in action before describing Thorndyke's methods for achieving justice. Four of the five stories in *The Singing Bone* followed this pattern; his preface explained that: 'Here, the usual conditions are reversed; the reader knows everything, the detective knows nothing, and the interest focuses on the unexpected significance of trivial circumstances.'

The Singing Bone appeared in 1912 and Freeman developed the inverted mystery eighteen years later with a full-length book, *Mr Pottermack's Oversight*. As the potential of the inverted mystery became clear, several of his fellow Detection Club members embraced and adapted the concept.[11] In one variation, the 'false inverted mystery', the presumed murderer proves not to be the actual culprit.

Roy Vickers' ingenious short story 'The Rubber Trumpet', meanwhile, began the long-running series of short stories about Scotland Yard's Department of Dead Ends. Vickers sacrificed Freeman's scientific rigour for quirkiness: 'Judged by the standards of reason and common sense [the Department's] files were mines of misinformation. It proceeded largely by guesswork. On one occasion, it hanged a murderer by accidentally punning on his name.' The scrupulous Thorndyke would have blushed.

American detective writers of the late nineteenth and early twentieth centuries also recognised the potential of science and technology for dazzling readers. Rodrigues Ottolengui,[12] an expert in orthodontics, touched on aspects of forensic dentistry in his detective fiction. 'The Phoenix of Crime' even included a dental chart.

Astrogen Kerby, known as Astro, straddles pseudo-science and the real thing in a cycle of stories collected in *The Master of Mysteries* (1912). A psychic and a charlatan, Astro uses scientific expertise to solve crimes. Published anonymously, the book contained a cipher revealing the author as Gelett Burgess.[13]

William MacHarg and Edwin Balmer created Luther Trant, a 'psychological detective'[14] familiar with a mind-boggling array of gadgetry: the chronoscope, automatograph, sphygmograph, plethysmograph, kymograph and electric psychometer (nicknamed the 'soul machine'). Trant's faith in the supposedly infallible 'galvanometer', a form of lie detector, as the servant of justice now seems over-optimistic.

Trant's career was brief in comparison to that of Arthur B. Reeve's[15] Craig Kennedy, a professor of chemistry dubbed 'the American Sherlock Holmes'. Kennedy's awestruck Watson, journalist Walter Jameson, recorded the experiments and deductions of the 'scientific detective' in breathless style.

Reeve's publishers claimed that his account of tyre treads in detection prompted the FBI and the Department of Justice to set up an 'astounding file of the treads of all the tires manufactured'. A preface to the wartime novel *The Adventuress* (1917) insisted that for all his 'strange ciphers, diabolical machines, subtle poisons and a hundred and one new weapons', Reeve 'never becomes cheaply sensational'.

The Adventuress opens with the suspicious death of a yacht-owning munitions tycoon who has secured the rights to 'a wonderful new war invention, the telautomaton – wireless control of submarines, torpedoes, ships, vehicles, aeroplanes, everything – the last word in the new science of telautomatics'. Spectroscopic analysis reveals that the victim was killed by poison gas contained in a thin-shelled bomb thrown through the window of his stateroom. The storyline is crammed with gizmos ranging from a 'burglar's microphone' to a 'detectaphone', whose operation is explained in jargon-heavy gobbledegook. When Jameson is attacked, Kennedy rescues him with the help of a pulmotor (a mechanical respiration device), and the sobering observation that 'you can be thankful we had that thing and that the gas in this asphyxiating pistol was not chlorine.'

Soon the great man was solving cases in silent movies and on the stage, in syndicated comic strips and on the wireless. In 1930, four years after writing the film serial *Craig Kennedy, Radio*

Detective, Reeve himself became a radio sleuth, collaborating with the police to host *Crime Prevention Program* for NBC. He also wrote a non-fiction study of racketeering and other consequences of Prohibition, *The Golden Age of Crime*.

Reeve paid scant attention to characterisation or credibility. His publishers called *The Stars Scream Murder*[16] 'probably the first astrological detective novel ever published'. By the time it appeared in 1936, he had sold over one million books in the US alone and had been 'translated into practically every language including . . . ancient Korean', but he died four months after publication. The American Sherlock Holmes soon followed him into oblivion.

Reeve plundered the latest scientific journals for topical material. But, in time, even enthusiasts for forensic minutiae weary of stories which overdo the technicalities. When T. S. Eliot reported to his colleagues at Faber on the manuscript of Stacey Bishop's *Death in the Dark*, he said tartly that 'the scientific patter could be reduced'.

Rudolph Fisher was an American doctor whose detective fiction made use of his medical knowledge without overindulging in jargon, obscure technicalities or gimmicks. Unlike his British counterparts and the overwhelming majority of his American peers, he was black.[17]

So were Dr John Archer and Perry Dart,[18] the amateur sleuth and cop who collaborate in *The Conjure-Man Dies: A Mystery tale of Dark Harlem* (1932). The novel is memorable for Fisher's portrayal of life among the black community in Harlem, and the complex and atmospheric storyline displayed rich promise. Fisher's early death[19] meant that it remained unfulfilled.

Frederica de Laguna[20] was unique among female writers of the Golden Age, a distinguished American anthropologist with a passion for ethnology and archaeology. She wrote detective fiction mainly to help finance her research, and published only two novels. In *The Arrow Points to Murder* (1937), essentially a 'workplace mystery' set in the New York Academy of Natural Sciences, an archaeologist suspects that the murderer's choice of weapon un-wittingly reveals an ignorance of ethnology. The book contains everything readers wanted to know about anthropological forensic science and sources of arrow poison; in case they were afraid to ask, de Laguna even supplied a recipe for making curare, notorious as a poison used by certain South American tribes on the tips of hunting arrows.

Outlandish scientific mysteries were investigated by Will Levinrew's[21] Dr Brierly, a specialist in poisonings and multiple murders who is described in *Death Points a Finger* (1933) as 'one of the four foremost scientists in the world today . . . He's nearly eighty years old . . . little more than five feet tall, but built like a miniature Apollo; bushy white hair; deeply sunken blue eyes that seem to dissect one with sharp knives, and bushy black eyebrows.'

Murder on the Palisades, aka *The Wheelchair Corpse* (1930), was remarkable, as Bill Pronzini put it, for 'the sheer number of exotic methods of murder and attempted murder – certainly more than in any other mystery novel in the genre's history', plus a solution of breathtaking absurdity. Levinrew's British publisher, Victor Gollancz[22], described Brierly on the cover of the dust jacket as 'Dr Thorndyke's rival', which was rather like comparing the Keystone Cops to the FBI.

A year earlier, Gollancz had published *Blind Circle*, a translation of an extraordinary novel by French science fiction author Maurice Renard[23] and novelist and playwright Albert-Jean, a blend of mystery and the macabre concerning the discovery of four separate bodies. The trouble is that each corpse is of the same man.

Austin Freeman's scientific approach was emulated by younger writers (invariably men) who strove to make up for any lack of literary prowess with technical expertise and an infinite capacity for taking pains with plot, if not with prose style. The precision-tooled puzzle exerted a magnetic attraction on professional engineers.

Freeman Wills Crofts, for example, worked as a railway engineer in his native Ireland for more than thirty years. He wrote a detective novel as a relief from boredom during a lengthy illness, and the result was *The Cask*, published in 1920, which became a bestseller. Seven years later, the scrupulously detailed construction of his stories led T. S. Eliot to rank him alongside Austin Freeman, and ahead of Christie and Sayers, as one of 'our two most accomplished detective writers'.

Cecil Street,[24] a former chief engineer for the Lyme Regis Electric Light & Power Co. Ltd, often demonstrated his formidable practical know-how during a crime-writing career that only began when he was in his forties, but ultimately yielded no fewer than 143 novels. He published under various names, notably John Rhode, whose Great Detective was a grumpy old boffin, Dr Lancelot Priestley.

The Murders in Praed Street (1928) featured a murder motive later copied so frequently as to become hackneyed, and a serial killer whose eclectic choice of m.o. included the use of 'a remarkably virulent synthetic alkaloid', poisoning by prussic acid, and a metallic potassium bullet with a tip made from a broken hypodermic needle. *Shot at Dawn* (1934) includes a graph illustrating 'probable velocities at spring tides' as an aid to solving the mystery. When his Detection Club colleague Christianna Brand bemoaned a lack of fresh ideas, Rhode kindly offered to let her make use of some of his.

Equally ingenious, but much less prolific, was Francis Everton.[25] An engineer and inventor, he rose to become managing director of the family business, the Sheepbridge Stokes Centrifugal Castings Co. Ltd. In *The Hammer of Doom* (1929), an engineer discovers a new process for manufacturing steel, only to be crushed to death in the jaws of a hydraulic hammer.

Adept at marketing, Everton cheekily publicised his firm in *The Young Vanish* (1932), in which Detective Inspector Allport seeks assistance during the course of a complex investigation involving a burnt-out car.[26] The company's technical director contributes his wisdom on metallurgical and spectrographic analysis, and boasts: 'no other manufacturing company in England – no, I may say, in the world – could place figures more regular and reliable before you . . . you are holding in your hands something new in the annals of crime – a metallurgical fingerprint.'

What hope was there for detective novelists who lacked medical, scientific or engineering know-how? Even Agatha Christie possessed an in-depth knowledge of poisons. Others followed the example of L. T. Meade, who had co-written stories with two doctors, Clifford

Halifax and Robert Eustace, and enlisted collaborators with technical expertise.

Robert Eustace became acquainted with Dorothy L. Sayers and they considered creating a 'scientific character of a new type' as a detective, but abandoned that plan once Eustace came up with an ambitious idea about 'the subtle difference between what is produced by life and that artificially produced by man'. This formed the heart of *The Documents in the Case* (1930), the only Sayers novel not to feature Lord Peter Wimsey.

The scientific premise was challenged,[27] however, much to Sayers' dismay, and although it was ultimately vindicated, this (as with the criticism of her imaginative murder method in her 1927 novel *Unnatural Death*) illustrates the limitations of 'following the science'. What if expert opinions conflict, or lead to a dead end?

While undergoing major surgery, Ngaio Marsh became acutely aware of the vulnerability of a patient on the operating table and this suggested a story in which a helpless Home Secretary is murdered. In writing *The Nursing Home Murder* (1935), she collaborated with a doctor, Henry Jellett. The book became a play, *Exit Sir Derek*, but this crime-writing partnership, like that of Sayers and Eustace, did not last.

Others consulted experts whose identities remained hidden – perhaps for the sake of their reputations. C. E. Bechhofer Roberts[28] created the scientific detective A. B. C. Hawkes 'in collaboration with a well-known Professor of Science, so the reader may rest assured that nothing is related that could not actually have happened'. This was a bold claim, given that A. B. C.'s debut, 'The Island under the Sea', involved an exotic woman preserved in 'a huge slab of solid glass and crystal' and originating from Atlantis.

That story appeared in the *Strand* in 1925. In the same year, in a letter to *Black Mask*, Dashiell Hammett pinpointed the limits of scientific devices of detection: 'excellent when kept to their places, but when pushed forward as infallible methods, they become forms of quackery'.

Alfred Walter Stewart was, like Craig Kennedy, a formidable professor of chemistry with a taste for detection, but the similarities ended there. Under the pen-name J. J. Connington, Stewart flirted with dystopian fiction before creating his Great Detective. Sir Clinton Driffield was a chief constable capable of startling ruthlessness. To achieve justice in one case, he commits murder.

Like Reeve, Connington created a radio detective.[29] Mark Brand, who calls himself 'the Counsellor', operates from Oxford Street, assisted by loyal sidekicks who help him to answer his listeners' questions. In *The Four Defences* (1940), Brand solves a 'blazing car' puzzle with the help of chemical analysis of oil samples, but this, his second recorded investigation, was his swansong.

Up-to-date techniques of science and technology – faked photographic evidence, blood analysis and ballistics – are central to Connington's mysteries. Today their cutting edge has blunted, but Connington's commitment to fair plotting ensured the popularity of his mysteries. He gave readers lacking his professional expertise a sporting chance to play the game and solve the puzzle.

There was nothing cosy about Connington's fiction, the work of a cynic with a bone-dry sense of humour who made few concessions to sentimentality. The cold-bloodedness of his characters is evident in one of his darkest books, *The Case with Nine Solutions* (1928), when a scientist says: 'Still got the notion that human life's valuable? The war knocked that on the head . . . Human life's the cheapest thing there is.'

Notes

My main sources are J. K. Van Dover's *You Know My Method*, the studies of Austin Freeman by Norman Donaldson, Oliver Mayo and David Ian Chapman, *From Ghouls to Gangster: The Career of Arthur B. Reeve*, edited by John Locke, Ronald Thomas's *Detective Fiction and the Rise of Forensic Science*, and Bill Pronzini's *Gun in Cheek*.

1   *instinctively secretive*: Austin Freeman's coded private journal, discussed in *The Golden Age of Murder*, has yet to be deciphered.
2   *photographs of visual clues to the stories*: This was a popular novelty. In Francis Beeding's *The Norwich Victims* and *No Fury*, aka *Murdered: One by One*, photographs of the characters appear at the start of the book. Snapshot clues featured in Rex Stout's Nero Wolfe novella *Easter Parade* and *Where There's a Will* (a story set in July; alas, the leafless trees were photographed in February). In *The President Vanishes*, Stout uses photos to give his thriller a documentary feel.

3 *Freeman constructed his stories with meticulous attention to detail*: Julian Symons compared reading Freeman to 'chewing dry straw', but for Raymond Chandler, Austin Freeman was 'a wonderful performer. He has no equal in his genre and he is also a much better writer than you might think, if you were superficially inclined, because in spite of the immense leisure of his writing he accomplishes an even suspense which is quite unexpected. The apparatus of his writing makes for dullness, but he is not dull.'

4 *Dr John Evelyn Thorndyke*: David Chapman has suggested to me that Thorndyke was based on Freeman's friend Dr Arthur Hensman, Demonstrator of Anatomy at Middlesex Hospital prior to his death in 1893.

5 *Alice and Bernard Bishop*: In her one hundredth year, their daughter Dorothy published a memoir saying that women regarded Austin Freeman as 'quite hypnotic . . . Just looks at you and you feel he knows everything.' Austin Freeman dedicated *The Eye of Osiris* to Alice, as well as *Social Decay and Regeneration*, a treatise on eugenics that, depressingly, he regarded as his best book.

6 *an unshakeable devotion to scientific reasoning*: In *Aspects of the Modern Short Story*, Alfred C. Ward compared deductions made by Thorndyke and Holmes in 'The Anthropologist at Large' and 'The Adventure of the Blue Carbuncle' respectively in which the main clue is a shabby felt hat. For Ward: 'Thorndyke's main deductions are fewer . . . but they are sounder, less capricious, and more practical.'

7 *Taylor was an expert witness*: Despite his expertise, he was rather more fallible under cross-examination than Thorndyke, and his evidence in the Palmer and Smethurst cases came under withering scrutiny.

8 *his 'thesis that fingerprints could be fabricated'*: Fingerprinting was used by Scotland Yard from 1901, but Sherlock Holmes examined for a thumbprint eleven years earlier, in *The Sign of Four*. In the US, fingerprint identification was central to the plot of *Pudd'nhead Wilson* by Mark Twain (Samuel Langhorne Clemens). But Freeman feared that reliance on uncorroborated fingerprint evidence could lead to miscarriages of justice. Hammett's story 'Slippery Fingers' reflects a similar concern, and some experts share it to this day.

9 *As Dorothy L. Sayers said*: When introducing *Great Short Stories of Detection, Mystery, and Horror*. Freeman is referenced in three of her eleven Lord Peter Wimsey novels.

10 *the 'inverted mystery'*: Or 'back to front' mystery. A prime example is the *Columbo* television series. Created by William Link and Richard Levinson, it began life as a play, *Enough Rope*, later retitled *Prescription: Murder*; this became the pilot episode for the TV show in 1968. Lt Columbo was an 'everyman' character whose lasting appeal was illustrated by the publication of *The Columbo Collection*, a book of short stories written by Link alone, almost half a century after Columbo's first appearance on the stage.

11 *Detection Club members embraced and adapted the concept*: Freeman Wills Crofts' inverted mysteries include *The 12.30 from Croydon*. G. D. H. and Margaret Cole's *End of an Ancient Mariner* and Lucy Malleson's *Portrait of a Murderer* (a bleak, sub-Dostoevskyan story published as by Anne Meredith) are among their best novels.

12 *Rodrigues Ottolengui*: His non-fiction included *Methods of Filling Teeth* and *Table Talks on Dentistry*. A pioneer in root canal surgery, he was also an enthusiastic taxidermist.

13 *Gelett Burgess*: Burgess (who is credited with coining the term 'blurb') told
a correspondent in 1930 that the book contained two more ciphers; one
formed by the last letter of each story, while the third was 'a little more
personal' and seems never to have been solved. Burgess said the ciphers
were 'put in mainly for advertising value' but complained that 'the then
Advertising Manager quite failed to use an original scheme for publicity in
the way I intended.'

14 *Luther Trant, a 'psychological detective'*: His cases were collected in *The
Compleat Achievements of Luther Trant*, introduced by Douglas G. Greene.
Trant's creators were brothers-in-law and Balmer went on to make a name
in science fiction, co-authoring *When Worlds Collide*. Trant's crime-solving
career was as brief as that of E. W. Hornung's psychologist Dr John Dollar.
Psychology featured in C. Daly King's eccentric whodunits, but it wasn't until
Helen McCloy introduced Dr Basil Willing in *Dance of Death* in 1938 that
the promise of the psychologist-detective was truly fulfilled.

15 *Arthur B. Reeve*: Arthur Benjamin Reeve's less celebrated creations included
Constance Dunlap ('Woman Detective') and Guy Garrick ('a Scientific
Gunman').

16 *The Stars Scream Murder*: This book appeared in a series of adventure and
mystery novels published in the US by Appleton-Century in 'The Tired
Business Man's Library'. The imprint proved short-lived; perhaps its intended
readers were too exhausted to buy books.

17 *he was black*: Walter Adolphe Roberts is often described as the first African
American author of crime fiction, starting with a story of weird menace set
in the film world, *The Haunting Hand*. In fact, he was born in Jamaica.

18 *So were Dr John Archer and Perry Dart*: Ed Lacy's Toussaint Marcus Moore
has been described as the first truly credible African American private eye.
Moore first appeared in *Room to Swing,* which won the 1958 Edgar award.
Lacy was a pen-name of Leonard S. Zinberg, who was white and Jewish.
Better known still was Virgil Tibbs, created by John Ball, also white. Tibbs
was introduced in *In the Heat of the Night*, successfully filmed in 1967 with
Sidney Poitier and Rod Steiger.

19 *Fisher's early death*: He died in 1934, aged thirty-seven. 'John Archer's
Nose', featuring Archer and Perry Dart, was published posthumously.

20 *Frederica de Laguna*: Known as 'Freddy', she researched the culture of
little-known Arctic civilisations; her second crime novel, *Fog on the Mountain*,
drew on her knowledge of Alaskan prehistory.

21 *Will Levinrew*: The pseudonym of William Levine. *Death Points a Finger*
concerns a tontine dating back to the American Civil War, anticipating Ellery
Queen's 'The Gettysburg Bugle'. In *Murder from the Grave*, a family
descended from the Borgias is rapidly depleted by multiple poisonings.

22 *Victor Gollancz*: A publisher with a flair for marketing as well as for spotting
talented writers, he favoured eye-catching book designs with vibrant typog-
raphy and yellow jackets. When he published *The Visitor* in 1945, the front
cover carried the characteristically bold words: 'It is our opinion that this
is an **exceptional detective story**. What is a matter not of opinion but of
fact is that it is **exceptionally short**. We mention this because, with the
present paper shortage, we do not want to sell too many copies – and the
public is alleged to be so stupid as to dislike short books.' History does not
relate how many copies he did sell, but the American husband and wife

team Carl Randau and Leane Zugsmith never wrote another crime story together, although *The Visitor* was adapted for radio and the stage.

23 *Maurice Renard*: Renard is best known as the author of the much-filmed horror story *The Hands of Orlac*.

24 *Cecil Street*: He also wrote detective fiction as Miles Burton and Cecil Waye.

25 *Francis Everton*: His real name was Francis William Stokes.

26 *a complex investigation involving a burnt-out car*: 'Blazing cars' containing charred and conveniently unrecognisable corpses became a staple of detective fiction following the trial in 1931 of Alfred Arthur Rouse, who attempted to escape to a new life by killing someone and then burning him to death in his (Rouse's) car. Rouse was hanged, but his victim remains unidentified at the time of writing.

27 *The scientific premise was challenged*: A reader claimed that organic muscarine was not optically active, but, after much agonising, Eustace concluded that this criticism was unfounded. The murder method in Sayers' *Unnatural Death* was more dubious. She'd picked up the idea from an impoverished motorcycle enthusiast who, having got her pregnant, promptly disappeared from her life.

28 *C. E. Bechhofer Roberts*: Roberts' principal detective novels – including a fictionalisation of the Wallace case, *The Jury Disagree* – were produced in tandem with George Goodchild, best known as creator of Inspector McLean of Scotland Yard. In *We Shot an Arrow*, the authors feature themselves as characters trying to solve the murders of two politicians.

29 *a radio detective*: Radio detectives later appeared in films such as *Mystery Broadcast*, and in the popular British TV series of the 1970s, *Shoestring*.

ELEVEN

Had-I-But-Known

Mary Roberts Rinehart and 'women in jeopardy' novels

Few authors earn enough from crime writing to employ a butler. Even fewer are victims of attempted murder. Mary Roberts Rinehart had the unique if unwanted distinction of being shot at *because* she had recruited a butler.

At the time of the shooting, Mary Roberts Rinehart was the most successful female crime writer in the United States. It was 1947 and her long career was drawing to a close. In addition to an eighteen-room apartment on Park Avenue, she owned a sprawling mansion at Bar Harbor, Maine. She was spending the summer there, and had hired a butler. This decision offended her cook, a Filipino called Blas Reyes, who had worked for Mary and her doctor husband for twenty-five years. During that time, Reyes had married an Irishwoman called Peggy, who worked as a parlourmaid in the house.

Reyes regarded Mary's husband as his real employer, and, after Stanley Rinehart died, considered himself the senior man of the household. If Mary wanted a butler, she should promote him. When he complained, she said that, since he was an excellent chef, he was better suited to his work in the kitchen. A few weeks later, he said he intended to resign, but since he'd threatened to walk out before, Rinehart presumed this was a bluff.

The next day was Saturday. That morning, Rinehart found Peggy in tears. When she asked what was the matter, Peggy explained that Reyes had been drinking, and that they'd quarrelled when she refused to leave her job with him. Later, Rinehart was reading in the library when Reyes marched in.

The chef was in his shirtsleeves, a breach of the staff uniform code. Looking up, Rinehart asked where his coat was.

'Here's my coat!' he retorted, and whipped a pistol out of his pocket.

From a distance of only four feet, he pulled the trigger.

The gun misfired.

Rinehart scrambled to her feet in panic, and rushed out of the room as Reyes fiddled with his pistol. He followed her as she headed for the servants' quarters. Ted Falkenstrom, her chauffeur, pinned Reyes to the ground so that Peggy could snatch the gun from his hand. Falkenstrom threw the gun into the bushes outside, while Peggy ran to find the nitroglycerine tablets that Rinehart took for her heart trouble.

As Rinehart phoned the police, Reyes broke free from the chauffeur's grasp. He grabbed two carving knives, brandishing them at Rinehart, who fled again, calling for help. Her cries were heard by the gardener, who came running in, and helped Falkenstrom to wrestle Reyes to the floor again. Peggy sat on his chest.

When the police arrived, they were still holding him captive. Reyes had slashed Falkenstrom with the knives, and was screaming wildly. That night in his prison cell, the cook fashioned a noose from his clothing and hanged himself. His priest allowed him to be buried in consecrated ground because he was 'plainly of unsound mind'. Rinehart paid for the funeral.

The irony is that Rinehart is popularly associated with the genre's hoariest cliché, 'the butler did it'.[1] She'd had a narrow escape, but the would-be butler *didn't* manage to do it. Nor was there a body in the library.

Mary Ella Roberts' father was a naive dreamer who invented and patented a rotary shuttle for sewing machines, only to turn down an offer of ten thousand dollars for the rights. When the patent expired, he couldn't afford to renew it, and so never made a penny from a device that became an industry standard. As a result, the family was always short of money, and eventually, in a hotel room in Buffalo, Tom Roberts shot himself.

Mary was also a dreamer, but she managed to make so much money through her writing that her extravagance and poor financial judgement didn't prove as catastrophic. If her background was ordinary, her achievements were anything but.

She hoped to become a doctor, but lack of money and academic qualifications meant she had no chance of going to medical school. Instead, she started work as a nurse, and proceeded to marry a doctor, Stanley Rinehart. The couple had three children, and she wrote poetry and fiction for magazines.

Disaster struck in 1903. A stock market crash wiped out the Rineharts' savings and left them twelve thousand dollars in debt. Spurred on by financial need, Mary began to write serials. Anna Katharine Green's mysteries influenced her approach to storytelling, and she submitted her manuscript to Green's publishers. They accepted *The Circular Staircase* (1908) and it became an instant hit.

Rachel Innes, middle-aged and unmarried, rents a house (misleadingly called Sunnyside) for the summer. A sequence of unsettling events culminates in murder, and Rachel's determination to solve the mystery places her life in jeopardy. She sets the characteristic tone of a Rinehart mystery: 'And so we sat there until morning, wondering if the candle would last until dawn, and arranging what trains we could take back to town. If we had only stuck to that decision and gone back before it was too late!'

The Man in Lower Ten (1909), a train mystery, enjoyed similar success. Coming back from a rest cure after publication, Rinehart tried to book a Pullman berth, but was told that nothing was available unless she was willing to take Lower Ten: someone, they told her, had written a novel in which an occupant of that particular berth was murdered, and now nobody wanted to take it.

The suburban housewife had broken through. The Rinehart recipe was for an intelligent, resourceful, unmarried woman to solve a domestic mystery. Rinehart liked to portray herself as a homemaker who wrote to support her family, but the reality was more complicated. She spent money as fast as she could make it, buying expensive properties and investing unwisely in get-rich-quick schemes and even a non-existent gold mine, so could never afford to rest on her laurels. In 1915, her life took an extra-ordinary turn when she sailed to Europe to become a war corre-spondent. She reported from the Belgian front, and interviewed the King of Belgium, Winston Churchill and Mary of Teck, wife of King George V.

Following the Armistice, she collaborated with the prominent playwright Avery Hopwood to adapt *The Circular Staircase* for the theatre. The book had already been filmed, but the stage version was a complete reimagining of the story, with a new villain in the shape of a flamboyant and mysterious criminal known as 'the Bat'. The blend of mystery, humour and a spooky 'old, dark house' setting was perfect for audiences weary of war and desperate for amusement. Originally called *A Thief in the Night*, the play was renamed *The Bat*, and was a hit on Broadway and in London's West End.

Other writers jumped on the bandwagon, and John Willard's *The Cat and the Canary*, a play in a similar vein, was turned into a silent movie in the German expressionist style. *The Bat* was novelised[2] and spawned a sequence of films. One of them, *The Bat Whispers*, was cited by Bob Kane, the comic-book writer and artist, as the inspiration for the crime-fighter he co-created in 1939. This was Batman,[3] the Caped Crusader, a superhero otherwise known as playboy Bruce Wayne, and now an American cultural icon.

Rinehart also created Hilda Adams, a nurse whose penchant for detection earned her the nickname 'Miss Pinkerton'. In *The Buckled Bag* (1914), it's suggested that 'a trained nurse sees under the skin of the soul'. Hilda's relationship with a cop called George Patton was an updated version of the partnership between Anna Katharine Green's Ebenezer Gryce and Amelia Butterworth. Romance blossomed, despite Patton's inability to understand Hilda's commitment to her work: 'Are you going to spend the rest of your life changing pillowslips and shaking down a thermometer?' Hilda never lost sight of her priorities: 'I was a nurse first and a police agent second. If it was a question between turpentine compresses . . . and seeing what letters came in or went out of the house, the compress went on first and cracking hot, too.'

Rinehart's prose style was straightforward, the embroidery of her plots elaborate. Her detectives were often female, and so were many of her murderers: she was never starry-eyed about her own sex. Telling stories in the first person enabled her to engage readers' emotions. People identified with her characters, just as they empathised with her homeliness and her values. The relentless foreshadowing of calamity as a means of building suspense became a Rinehart trademark.

Overindulgence in this device prompted Ogden Nash to make fun of it in his poem 'Don't Guess, Let Me Tell You', published in the *New Yorker*. The 'Had-I-But-Known' school of writing, as he called it, became a target for mockery[4], as well as critical disdain.[5]

Rinehart was dogged by health problems, ranging from depression to breast cancer; she wrote frankly about her mastectomy, determined that the subject should not be taboo. The frantic pace at which she worked meant that her stories were often slapdash. Her output included romances and mainstream fiction, and she resented attempts to label her, whether as a mystery writer or a women's writer.

The After House (1914), set on board a schooner converted into a yacht, is an early, minor work which made an unexpected contribution to the cause of justice. The plot was drawn from a real-life triple axe-killing on board a schooner named the *Herbert Fuller* and, at the time of publication, the first mate had served more than sixteen years of a life sentence for murder. A fellow crew member had also been a suspect, and publicity about Rinehart's novel led to the case being reopened. When it emerged that the alternative suspect, a patient in a Swedish hospital, had attacked his nurse with a knife, the first mate was pardoned.

In 1929, she supported two of her sons in co-founding a publishing business, Farrar and Rinehart. The new firm's arrival coincided with the Wall Street Crash – which she dismissed as 'a temporary setback' – but she returned to crime fiction with *The Door* (1930), and its sales enabled the company to survive.

For *The Album* (1933), she refashioned the raw material of the Borden axe murders[6] into a complex whodunit with yet another spinster-narrator, Louisa Hall. The story explored the intertwined fates of five families who live in a cluster of mansions known as

The Crescent. Sexual repression plays a central part in the storyline, which concerns the axe-killing of an elderly invalid.

Louisa tells her mother she's learned that she has the 'right to live while I can. To live my own life, not yours.' This yearning for independence struck a chord with Dorothy L. Sayers, who lavished praise on the book:[7] 'This is not the first time that the theories of modern psychology have been used to provide a motive for crime, but they have seldom been used so well . . . Each warped and thwarted personality . . . stands out individual and distinct, acting and reacting upon the rest.' For Sayers, the novel fell within the tradition of the Victorian sensation novels of Wilkie Collins and Sheridan Le Fanu.

Rinehart blazed a trail for other women writers. Mignon Good Eberhart's early short stories sometimes featured nurse protagonists in the mould of Hilda Adams. Eberhart's first novel, *The Patient in Room 18* (1929), introduced Sarah Keate, a nurse who sets out to discover the reasons for the deaths of patients in a hospital with a disconcerting resemblance to a Gothic mansion.

Sarah returned to attend a bedridden elderly stroke victim in *While the Patient Slept* (1930), a spooky-house story which won the $5,000 Scotland Yard Prize,[8] and confirmed Eberhart as Rinehart's leading disciple.[9] By the mid-1930s, she was said to be earning more than $50,000 per year from short stories alone; those were the days. During a career lasting sixty years,[10] she created detectives, including a banker and even a crime-solving butler,[11] but the most noteworthy was Susan Dare, a mystery writer and amateur sleuth, forerunner of a popular television detective of the late twentieth century, Jessica Fletcher.[12]

Abergavenny-born Ethel Lina White threw up a job with the Ministry of Pensions 'on the strength of a ten-pound offer for a short story' and, after a flirtation with romantic fiction, she became Britain's leading exponent of domestic suspense. Two of her finest short stories, later expanded into novels,[13] illustrate her flair for melodrama. 'Waxworks' features an intrepid female newspaper reporter bent on spending a night in a wax museum, while in 'An Unlocked Window', a nurse in an eerie old country house is

confronted by a serial killer who specialises in murdering . . .
trained nurses.

White's first crime novel, *Put Out the Light*, aka *Sinister Light*,
didn't appear until 1931, when she was in her mid-fifties; she
then produced a dozen more. There is a touch of Had-I-But-Known
in *The First Time He Died* (1935), about a man who fakes his
death to claim on an insurance policy. The first chapter ends: 'Had
Dr Dubarry . . . not taken too much for granted, he would never
have written a Certificate of Death for Charles Baxter.'

Her vivid storytelling appealed to film-makers, and three of her
books were adapted for the screen. *The Wheel Spins* (1936) is
the most famous, thanks to Alfred Hitchcock's version, *The Lady
Vanishes*.[14] White builds emotional tension and suspense in the
confined setting of a train journey from eastern Europe. Young
Iris Carr[15] makes the acquaintance of an elderly governess, Miss
Froy, but after taking a nap, she finds that Miss Froy has disappeared, and her fellow passengers deny all knowledge of the
woman's existence.

Hitchcock also directed a masterly film version of Daphne du
Maurier's *Rebecca* (1938),[16] the twentieth century's closest approx-
imation to *Jane Eyre*. A naive young woman is swept off her feet
by a handsome widower, Maxim de Winter. She marries him, but
when he takes her home to Cornwall, she is intimidated by the
housekeeper, Mrs Danvers, who was obsessively devoted to
Rebecca, the first Mrs de Winter, and begins to doubt her husband's
love for her.

The Gothic trimmings of an old mansion in the country, a sinister
adversary and a mysterious death, coupled with a strong plot and
crisp, evocative prose exemplified by the now legendary opening
– 'Last night I dreamt I went to Manderley again' – ensured that
Rebecca achieved classic status. Between them, du Maurier and
Hitchcock made suspense critically respectable,[17] in fiction and in
film.

The American Elisabeth Sanxay Holding was much less well known
than du Maurier, but according to Anthony Boucher: 'For subtlety,
realistic conviction, incredible economy, she's in a class by herself.'

In a private letter, Raymond Chandler gave her an encomium to die for:[18] 'For my money she's the top suspense writer of them all. She doesn't pour it on and make you feel irritated. Her characters are wonderful; and she has a sort of inner calm which I find very attractive.'

Like Marie Belloc Lowndes, Holding was fascinated by the psychology of murder, but her approach was distinctive. When Dodd, Mead published *The Unfinished Crime* (1935) under their prestigious Red Badge imprint,[19] they bragged that it 'makes the usual array of fingerprints, weapons, alibis etc. look like claptrap'.

The story traces the impact on character of an unreasoning act of violence. Andrew Branscombe, priggish and respectable, attacks the former husband of the woman he wants to marry, and finds his life spiralling out of control as he makes desperate attempts to avoid exposure. Crime changes him: "I'm alive!" he thought . . . "I've planned the most complicated and difficult crime imaginable, and I can carry it through without a hitch."'

Unhappy marriages lie at the heart of *The Death Wish* (1934). Artist Robert Whitestone and his friend Shawe Delancey are both discontented with their wives, and when a young woman called Elsie falls for Robert, tragic consequences follow. Holding's apprenticeship in romantic fiction is evident, but aspects of the storyline foreshadow a darker novel published sixteen years later, Patricia Highsmith's *Strangers on a Train*.

Notes

The main sources are the biography of Rinehart by Charlotte MacLeod (herself a mystery writer who cited Rinehart as an early influence), and Catherine Ross Nickerson's *The Web of Iniquity*.

1   *Rinehart is popularly associated with the genre's hoariest cliché, 'the butler did it'*: That phrase does not, however, appear in her books. Butlers were being unmasked as criminals or accessories to crime, for instance in Conan Doyle's 'The Musgrave Ritual' and in one of Herbert Jenkins' Malcolm Sage stories, years before S. S. Van Dine argued that servants were not sufficiently worthwhile to be culprits. Rinehart's response to Van Dine was to write a novel in which a butler did turn out to be the murderer. Although her book sold well, it was hastily written, contributing to a perception that her work had become hackneyed. In 1933, Damon Runyon published a humorous story, 'What, No Butler?'; a quarter of a century later, P. G. Wodehouse's

novel *Something Fishy* was re-titled *The Butler Did It* in the US. Agatha Christie displayed characteristic ingenuity when playing with the cliché in *Three Act Tragedy*. Decades later, the butler did it in a novel by Catherine Aird (a pen-name for Kinn Hamilton McIntosh) that pokes fun at the conventions of the country-house mystery.

2   *The Bat was novelised*: The novelisation, credited to Rinehart and Hopwood, was ghostwritten by Stephen Vincent Benét, a Pulitzer Prize-winning poet and author. Benét's recommendation led to the American publication of S.-A. Steeman's *Six Dead Men*, translated by his (Benet's) wife Rosemary.

3   *Batman*: Kane also credited Leonardo da Vinci's diagram of the ornithopter and Douglas Fairbanks' film portrayal of Zorro (the masked vigilante created by pulp-magazine writer Johnston McCulley) as contributory ingredients. Batman's co-creator was Bill Finger, and in his memoir *Batman & Me*, Kane said: 'I made Batman a superhero-vigilante when I first created him. Bill turned him into a scientific detective.'

4   *a target for mockery*: As in the opening line of C. H. B. Kitchin's *Death of His Uncle*: 'Had it not been for my inability to mash potatoes on Thursday, June 10th, I think it quite possible that I might never have embarked on this third case of mine.'

5   *critical disdain*: Male critics are often unsympathetic. Julian Symons derided 'the formula of needless confusion and mock terror', and felt that 'the mystery is prolonged only by the obstinate refusal of the characters to reveal essential facts'.

6   *the Borden axe murders*: Lizzie Borden was tried and acquitted of using an axe to murder her father and stepmother in Fall River, Massachusetts, in 1892. Nobody was ever charged. Marie Belloc Lowndes' novel *Lizzie Borden: A Study in Conjecture* appeared in 1939, six years after *The Album*. A different axe-killing, of John Hossack in 1900, was covered by a journalist with the *Des Moines Daily News*, Susan Glaspell. In 1916 she fashioned the case into a play, *Trifles*, before reworking it as 'A Jury of Her Peers', one of the most admired American short stories of the twentieth century. Glaspell was a playwright and feminist; she and Rinehart were very different, but both wrote about women resisting the pressure to accept the roles assigned to them by convention.

7   *Dorothy L. Sayers, who lavished praise on the book*: In *The Sunday Times* of 1 October 1933.

8   *the $5,000 Scotland Yard Prize*: This was offered not by the Metropolitan Police, but by an American publisher.

9   *Rinehart's leading disciple*: Others included Dorothy Cameron Disney, whose *Strawstack*, aka *The Strawstack Murders*, opens with Margaret Tilbury's Had-I-But-Known anguish: 'it seems to me now . . . that I could have prevented the dreadful series of crimes which so hideously involved us all.' Disney co-wrote, with her husband Milton MacKaye, a book about Rinehart. Howard Haycraft bracketed Disney with other writers such as Constance and Gwenyth Little, Anita Blackmon and Medora Field, but reserved special praise for Mabel Seeley. He argued that she'd given the Rinehart formula a much-needed 'transfusion', and that her techniques of building suspense were comparable to Alfred Hitchcock's. After meeting her second husband while promoting what proved to be the last of her novels, Seeley abandoned crime writing.

10 *a career lasting sixty years*: Eberhart's productivity slowed during the 1940s
    when she divorced her husband to marry someone else, only to divorce
    again and remarry the original husband. She lived to the age of ninety-six,
    serving as President of the Mystery Writers of America, and becoming an
    MWA Grand Master.

11 *she created detectives, including a banker and even a crime-solving butler*:
    James Wickwire, a New York banker, appeared in short stories in the 1950s;
    elderly and unmarried, he resembled a more celebrated successor, Emma
    Lathen's John Putnam Thatcher. Bland, the butler, appeared in three novellas;
    his Watson was his employer, a refined society lady.

12 *Jessica Fletcher*: Fletcher, played by Angela Lansbury, first appeared in
    1984 in *Murder, She Wrote*, which ran for 264 episodes. Its creators were
    Richard Levinson and William Link, in collaboration with Peter S. Fischer;
    the title was a riff on *Murder, She Said*, a film version of Agatha Christie's
    4. 50 from Paddington. After the show ended in 1996, four television movies
    followed, as well as a point-and-click video game and spin-off novels by
    Donald Bain.

13 *expanded into novels*: These were *Wax* and *Some Must Watch*, which was
    filmed as *The Spiral Staircase*.

14 *The Lady Vanishes*: The screenplay by Sidney Gilliat and Frank Launder
    made significant changes to the original story. Gilliat co-wrote the screenplay
    for Christianna Brand's *Green for Danger* (an unusually successful film of a
    whodunit novel) and also wrote the libretto for Malcolm Williamson's opera
    based on Graham Greene's *Our Man in Havana*. His final screenplay was
    of Agatha Christie's *Endless Night*. Launder's early solo work included a
    co-credit for the screenplay of *The W Plan*, based on Graham Seton's spy
    novel; his collaborators included the actor and writer Miles Malleson, cousin
    of Lucy Malleson.

15 *Iris Carr*: The contemporary American mystery writer K. K. Beck, widow
    of the British crime novelist Michael Dibdin, cited Carr as the inspiration
    for her detective, Iris Cooper.

16 *a masterly film version of Daphne du Maurier's Rebecca*: The original
    screenplay was written by the screenwriter and producer Joan Harrison in
    collaboration with Robert E. Sherwood, a playwright whose work included
    The Petrified Forest. Harrison, whose work on movies such as *Phantom
    Lady* helped to shape film noir, later married Eric Ambler. The script also
    had input from Golden Age novelist Philip MacDonald, whose other film
    work included *Circle of Danger*, co-produced by Harrison. Du Maurier's 'The
    Birds' was also filmed by Hitchcock, with a screenplay by Evan Hunter, aka
    Ed McBain.

17 *made suspense critically respectable*: David Bordwell's *Reinventing
    Hollywood* shows how Hollywood writers and directors of the 1940s deployed
    devices (e.g. flashbacks, dreams and amnesia) from suspense fiction, with
    'tricky plotting, and narrational subterfuges. . . justified not as realism,
    despite offhand appeals to the science of psychoanalysis, but as ways of
    arousing an audience immersed in Murder Culture'. The result was 'a varied
    body of films that changed world cinema'.

18 *Raymond Chandler gave her . . .* : In a letter to Hamish Hamilton of 13
    October 1950.

19 *their prestigious Red Badge imprint*: The imprint survived until the 1970s,

featuring authors from Agatha Christie to Cornell Woolrich. Winners of the Red Badge Prize, first awarded in 1937 for 'the best mystery-detective novel by an author who has not previously has a book published under the Red Badge imprint', included Christianna Brand for *Heads You Lose*, as well as several writers whose work is now forgotten. An interesting example is Ruth Sawtell Wallis, an academic anthropologist and forerunner of Kathy Reichs, who won with *Too Many Bones* in 1943.

The Mary Roberts Reinhart Mystery Novel Prize was awarded to the winner of a contest for new writers. Judged by Rinehart herself in its early days, the contest gave an early boost the careers of talented writers such as Elizabeth Daly, Frank Gruber and, C. W. Grafton. In 1950 the winner was a student aged twenty-one, William Wiegand, for *At Last, Mr Tolliver*, a mystery about motive so ambitious and unorthodox that it is regrettable that Wiegand's career as a novelist proved short-lived.

TWELVE

War and Peace

The First World War and detective fiction

The Somme, 1916. A quietly spoken man, a writer for a humorous magazine, had spent eighteen months training as a signalling officer prior to arriving in France. He was about to 'add some practical knowledge to all the theory which I had assimilated' – even though 'of bombs and rifles and the ordinary routine of the platoon officer I had forgotten what little I had known.'

The attack was timed for midnight. Early that morning, the writer had gone out through the communication trench to lay a telephone line, 'elaborately laddered according to the textbooks and guaranteed to withstand any bombardment'. At 11 p.m., the writer sat in the dugout, smoking with his fellow officers in the candlelight. He chatted with a lance corporal, a Welsh miner who loved books; they discovered a shared passion for Jane Austen while waiting for the British barrage to begin.

But the Germans started firing first. They'd discovered the plan, and had destroyed the line laid earlier. A sergeant major climbed the steps to find out what was happening. Before he reached the top, he was blown to bits.

The dugout was so deep as to muffle the noise of the guns. A shell burst set the candles dancing before blotting them out. At two in the morning, a runner arrived with bad news. The attack had failed, and many men were dead. A major strapped on his revolver. So did the writer. The time had come to run out a replacement line.

The writer had recently completed his first play, a piece of nonsense called *Wurzel-Flummery*. Might it, he wondered, be staged after his death? With three colleagues, he made a dash for it. No time for textbook stuff; the line was just dropped anywhere. They passed a signal station that was now 'a pancake of earth on top of a spread-eagled body'. The writer had spoken to the dead man earlier that evening, saying, 'Well, you'll be comfortable here.'

'More rushes, more breathers, more bodies,' he later recalled. Finally he made the front line.

The battalion moved to Bully-Grenay, and the troops hoped they might spend the winter there. But 'the "blood-bath of the Somme" was not quite full'; the generals decided to launch another attack, this time on a place called Beauregard-Dovecote. The writer was horrified: 'If ever any place looked like a death trap on a military map this did.'

Torrential rain meant the attack was postponed, and the soldiers marched westwards, singing loudly. At Doullens, the writer fell sick. As his temperature soared, the battalion was ordered to move in readiness for the attack. An ambulance was summoned, and the sergeant came to say goodbye. The writer handed over his maps and fell asleep. A few days later, he awoke in hospital in Oxford to find his wife Daphne at the end of his bed, crying. At least he was alive and in one piece. The sergeant, he later learned, 'was lucky. He only lost a leg.'

The writer's name was Alan Alexander Milne, and prior to joining up he'd served as assistant editor at *Punch*.[1] A staunch pacifist, he'd come round to the view that the war was a just cause. Hadn't his former schoolteacher H. G. Wells described it as 'The War that Will End War'? The horrors he experienced as a soldier during the so-called Great War confirmed his belief that war was 'a degradation which would soil the beasts, a lunacy which would shame the madhouse'.

After recovering his health, Milne wrote propaganda for Military Intelligence. He relinquished his commission in 1920, desperate to rid himself of the nightmares of slaughter on the Western Front. Like everyone else, he was ready for some fun. He threw himself into writing for the stage, and flirted with the embryonic film industry, but found – like so many other authors – that the glitter of movieland soon rubs off. He joined the board of Leslie Howard's Minerva Films, but the business collapsed within a year.

Writing a detective novel brought – for once – overnight success. A devotee of crime fiction, he'd begun his career as a freelance writer with a burlesque of Sherlock Holmes' encounter with Moriarty at the Reichenbach Falls.[2] *The Red House Murder* was serialised in an American magazine, *Everybody's*, in 1921; the following spring, the story was published as *The Red House Mystery* in Britain and the US, and translated into languages ranging from Serbo-Croat to Japanese.

The novel, a locked-room mystery, is set in a country house, like E. C. Bentley's *Trent's Last Case*, but Milne aimed to amuse rather than to satirise the notion of the infallible Great Detective. Anthony Gillingham, a suave man-about-town, plays the amateur sleuth, supported by an affable Watson called Bill Beverley. Among the readers who relished the puzzle was an eighteen-year-old schoolboy at Repton who collaborated with a friend in dramatising the story; his name was Christopher Isherwood.[3]

The American critic Alexander Woollcott[4] said that Milne had produced 'one of the three best mystery stories of all time', although Raymond Chandler wryly noted that Woollcott was 'rather a fast man with a superlative'. Chandler acknowledged that the novel was 'agreeable . . . light, amusing in the *Punch* style, written with a deceptive smoothness that is not as easy as it looks', but argued that a story concerned with logical deduction was nothing if the logic was flawed, and proceeded to pinpoint all the plot holes.

Chandler was throwing stones from a glass house. His premise that 'fiction in any form has always intended to be realistic' was questionable, while his own plotting was sometimes erratic. He also missed the point. *The Red House Mystery* offered what readers were yearning for – pleasurable escapism.[5]

Milne started writing to amuse his young son and soon achieved even greater popularity with *Winnie-the-Pooh*. His failure to continue writing detective novels created a vacuum. One of the writers who filled it was another regular contributor to *Punch* whose smooth prose and light touch fitted the times to perfection.

Anthony Berkeley Cox, eleven years younger than Milne, suffered grievously during the war. He was gassed while serving in France as a lieutenant with the 7th Northamptonshire Regiment, leaving his health permanently damaged. When peace came, he wrote sketches for magazines, including another Sherlockian burlesque, 'Holmes and the Dasher', written in the style of P. G. Wodehouse.

He decided to concoct a detective story 'for the sheer fun of it'. *The Layton Court Mystery* (1925) was, like Milne's novel, another light-hearted locked-room puzzle set in a country house. Berkeley shared E. C. Bentley's scepticism about supposedly omniscient detectives, and created in Roger Sheringham an amateur sleuth who was not merely fallible but downright offensive. Naturally, Sheringham's ingenious solution to the mystery proves to be mistaken. The true explanation foreshadows the trick in Agatha Christie's *The Murder of Roger Ackroyd*.

Milne and Cox were very different men. Milne's gentle sense of humour veered towards whimsy, while Cox was profoundly cynical. Whereas Milne was a well-known public figure, Cox was a secretive Jekyll and Hyde, by turns witty and generous or sour and misanthropic. He preserved his privacy with a zeal obsessive even by the standards of an age where publishers permitted authorial modesty to an extent unimaginable today. His first novel was published anonymously, with a question mark substituted for his name, but before long he was publishing as Anthony Berkeley.

Inventive game-playing with the detective story became his trademark. Berkeley made no secret of his ambition as a novelist, and a preface to the second Sheringham novel, *The Wychford Poisoning Case* (1926), which fictionalised the Maybrick case of 1889,[6] announced an intention 'to substitute for the materialism of the usual crime-puzzle of fiction those psychological values which are . . . the basis of the universal interest in the far more absorbing criminological dramas of real life'. A similar claim is made in the preface to a later Sheringham novel, *The Second Shot* (1930), but Berkeley's mission to transform the genre came closer to fulfilment with the crime novels he published under the name of Francis Iles.

As Anthony Berkeley, he demonstrated a restless determination to confound his readers. The police rather than Sheringham sometimes solved the case and the solution to the puzzle was sometimes so obvious as to defy the emerging convention that the culprit should be the last person one would suspect. His culprits were often far more attractive than his victims.

Time after time, he tried something fresh. Even when his experiments failed, they failed in an interesting way. Sheringham hunts a serial killer in *The Silk Stocking Murders* (1928), while *Panic Party*, published six years later, conjures up a scenario anticipating that in William Golding's *Lord of the Flies*. In *Jumping Jenny*, aka *Dead Mrs Stratton* (1933), the victim's unpleasantness prompts Sheringham to defy conventional justice and decide to play God. What could possibly go wrong?

The most celebrated Anthony Berkeley novel was *The Poisoned Chocolates Case*, published in 1929. The previous year, he'd begun to host dinner parties for detective novelists, which led to the formation of the Detection Club. The novel features a group of amateur criminologists, the Crimes Circle, founded and run by Sheringham, and evidently a fictional forerunner of the Club. With Scotland Yard baffled by the poisoning of Joan Bendix, Inspector Moresby puts the facts to the Club's six members, each of whom in turn comes up with a different yet apparently compelling solution to the problem.[7] Sheringham is among those whose triumphant solution is comprehensively debunked.

Julian Symons called the book 'one of the most stunning trick stories in the history of detective fiction'. The blend of wit and ingenuity was worthy of a literary liaison between Agatha Christie and P. G. Wodehouse. And Berkeley's implicit question was whether we should trust apparently neat and convincing answers to life's puzzles.

Long after the Armistice, wartime shadows lingered. The new generation of detective novelists included Henry Lancelot Aubrey-Fletcher, who had joined the Grenadier Guards in 1908. He served with distinction in France, earning the DSO and the Croix de Guerre, and was wounded twice.

Towards the end of the war, he attended – of all things – a talk on detective stories, given at Namur in Belgium during the march to Cologne. The speaker was Valentine Williams,[8] a war corre-spondent who had been seriously injured at the Somme and awarded the Military Cross. When Aubrey-Fletcher finally came to publish his first detective novel, under the name Henry Wade, he presented Williams with an inscribed copy of *The Verdict of You All* (1926). The alibi plot was engineered with the care of Freeman Wills Crofts, while the ironic finale was worthy of Berkeley.

As Wade's confidence grew, so did his literary ambition.[9] His output included police stories, inverted mysteries and stand-alone novels. A scion of a wealthy landowning family, he didn't need to earn a living from his pen, and this gave him the luxury of pleasing himself about what he wrote. As a result, he avoided the traps of over-productivity and formulaic writing at a time when many of his contemporaries scribbled too frantically to ensure consistency of quality.

Wade worried about social change, but didn't shrink from exam-ining it. The consequences of the war affect his characters, just as they shaped real lives. In *Mist on the Saltings* (1933), the conflict has destroyed John Pansel's health, and also his career as a highly regarded painter; the results are tragic. Memories of the Somme flood back during a chance encounter in a police station which opens *Constable Guard Thyself!* (1934). In this 'impossible crime' mystery, what happened during the war is crucial to the plot.

Horrors of the battlefield are evoked in a prologue to *The High Sheriff* (1937), when Robert D'Arcy's nerves snap following a bombardment, and he feels that 'even the sleep of death would be better than this terrible waiting'. In peacetime, while D'Arcy is serving as High Sheriff of Brackenshire, the past comes back to haunt him. D'Arcy's personality is defined by his experiences as a soldier, and Wade shows the corrosive effect of his secret sense of shame, which makes him intolerant of weakness in others, especially his son Peter. Wade, who himself served as a High Sheriff of Buckinghamshire, understood that feeling of terror under fire better than most, but he did not allow empathy to blur his portrayal of D'Arcy's personal failings.

Cecil John Street was the son of a general. Like Wade, he took up soldiering before the First World War; during the conflict he was wounded in action three times, receiving the Military Cross before transferring to Military Intelligence and devoting himself to prop-aganda. He wrote about his experiences in *With the Guns* and *The Making of a Gunner*, prior to launching a long and remarkably industrious career as a detective novelist under the name John Rhode. Using the pseudonym Miles Burton, he created Desmond Merrion,[10] who after being wounded in the war had joined Naval Intelligence; Merrion, a 'living encyclopaedia', became an expert in criminology and amateur detective.

Rhode's literary priorities were different from Wade's. Ingenious methods of committing murder appealed to his practical turn of mind, but he rarely bothered to portray characters in depth. His detective stories were, in keeping with the mood of the Roaring Twenties, purely escapist.

Those who avoided serious physical harm during the war also made sacrifices. The outbreak of hostilities cost Richard Sampson the chance to go up to Cambridge. Almost half a century later, he mourned this as 'a great loss . . . [it] would have done me a power of good'.[11] On his eighteenth birthday, he was given a commission in Queen Victoria's Rifles and later said that: 'In some ways I never really liked soldiering – especially drill, dress and discipline – but I liked the administrative side, and I also liked being one of a side. I also developed a very strong feeling for that particular battalion which has lasted all my life.' But his military experience did not surface in the ironic crime novels he wrote under the name Richard Hull (see pp. 252–253).

Major Lewis Robinson, in contrast, made highly effective use of his time as an army medical officer in his first detective novel, *The Medbury Fort Murder* (1929), a locked-room mystery that appeared under his occasional pseudonym, George Limnelius. The atmospheric setting, an isolated fort in the Thames, and the con-vincing characterisation of military personnel, including the odious victim, are blended with an unusual plot in a surprisingly neglected book. Robinson's army background informed his fiction, which is under-estimated mainly because he published infrequently. *The General Goes Too Far* (1936) is an intriguing but little-known crime novel, filmed by Thorold Dickinson as *The High Command*.

As an ordained priest, Ronald Knox was forbidden to fight. Instead, he worked in the War Office. The slaughter undermined his faith, and his increasing discomfort with the Anglican Church was attributed by some of his friends and family to 'war nerves'. 'History', he wrote, 'began in 1914'; three years after that came his conversion to Catholicism. Knox was more than ready to combine priestly duties with indulgence in light entertainment, but for him detective fiction was never more than a game. Pushing the genre's boundaries was left to the likes of Berkeley, Wade, Agatha Christie and Dorothy L. Sayers.

For women as well as men, the war brought pain and grief. Agatha Christie's brother Monty, wounded in a skirmish with the German army, became increasingly unstable and died in 1929. Josephine Tey lost the man she loved, and so did Ngaio Marsh. The health and temper of Dorothy L. Sayers' husband, 'Mac' Fleming, suffered as a result of his war service, to the detriment of their marital happiness.

The war's legacy forms the heart of Sayers' *The Unpleasantness at the Bellona Club* (1928). The story opens with the death of General Fentiman, on Armistice Day, and a Flanders poppy and the two minutes' silence are skilfully woven into the plot. One of the suspects, the victim's grandson, has suffered the effects of poison gas and shell shock, and the book explores the disconnect between the experience of survivors of 'the war to end wars', and the veterans of earlier conflicts who while away their time at the Bellona Club.

Lord Peter Wimsey himself had suffered a breakdown after being blown up and buried in a shell hole near Caudry. As his mother tells his new wife almost twenty years later in *Busman's Honeymoon* (1937), 'He doesn't like responsibility, you know . . . and the War . . . was bad for people that way . . . There were eighteen months . . . I don't mean he went out of his mind or anything . . . only he was dreadfully afraid to go to sleep . . . and he couldn't give an order, not even to the servants . . . I suppose if you've been giving orders for nearly four years to people to go and get blown to pieces it gives you . . . an inhibition . . .' By this time, Sayers had seen in her husband the lasting harm that war can do.

*

Worried about becoming typecast as a children's author, Milne decided to work on 'a Detective Play which is fun to do'. The result was *The Fourth Wall* (1928), which enjoyed success in the West End, and, renamed *The Perfect Alibi*, on Broadway.

The country-house-party setting was familiar, but audiences were treated to an inverted mystery rather than a whodunit. Milne broke fresh ground as well as the fourth wall: this was the first time that Austin Freeman's method of telling a crime story had been transferred to the theatre. The host, Arthur Ludgrove, falls victim to a murderous conspiracy as two criminals bent on vengeance contrive his apparent suicide in a locked room.

The play was filmed as *Birds of Prey*, and its success encouraged others to follow Milne's lead. Among them was Anthony Armstrong,[12] a *Punch* contributor and former soldier whose bravery had earned him the Military Cross. Armstrong's novels about Jimmy Rezaire, a cocaine trafficker turned crime-solver, enjoyed modest success, but he broke through by writing for the stage. *Ten Minute Alibi* (1933) ran for more than eight hundred performances and offered a fresh kind of inverted mystery. Armstrong's trick was to ensure the audience kept rooting for the killer, hoping that he'd get away with murdering the dastardly Philip Sevilla, despite Scotland Yard's relentless detective work.

Milne became a founder member of the Detection Club[13] on the strength of his single foray into detection. He also wrote a humorous novel spoofing the genre, *Four Days' Wonder* (1933), but was annoyed by a lack of marketing (an eternal complaint of authors)[14] and wrote to demand that his publishers 'make a bit of a fuss' about it. He inscribed a copy to Wodehouse[15] with a verse thanking his friend and fellow detective fiction fan for his appreciation of this 'Four Days' folly'.

Milne then published *Peace with Honour*, a passionate argument against militarism. He believed it was '*absolutely* certain that another European war would mean the complete collapse of civilisation', and his view was widely shared. At a time of economic misery, people had little appetite for investing vast sums in weapons. Yet eventually he changed his mind. As he wrote to one correspondent: 'war is a lesser evil than Hitlerism'.[16] Another conflict had become inevitable.

Notes

The main sources are Ann Thwaite's biography of Milne and Milne's autobiography.

1 *Punch*: E. V. 'Evoe' Knox, brother of Ronald, later became editor of the magazine. An accomplished parodist, he wrote a witty spoof detective story, 'The Murder at the Towers'.

2 *a burlesque of Sherlock Holmes' encounter with Moriarty at the Reichenbach Falls*: This was written shortly after Conan Doyle apparently killed off his hero. *Punch* rejected Milne's effort, but *Vanity Fair* accepted it.

3 *his name was Christopher Isherwood*: Isherwood argued that a novel should be like a detective story in that 'every single word ideally ought to be a kind of clue, leading to a discovery of some sort.' Isherwood became famous for his stories of decadence in Berlin. His character Sally Bowles was partly modelled on Jean Ross, mother of Sarah Cockburn, who wrote detective fiction as Sarah Caudwell. Isherwood's memoir *Lions and Shadows* features his university friend Roger d'Este Burford, who appears under his crime-writing alias, Roger East. East's occasional detective novels display a distinct talent and he wrote collaborative mysteries with Oswell Blakeston under the name 'Simon'; he was also a screenwriter for film and television.

4 *The American critic Alexander Woollcott*: Woollcott, a prominent member of the Algonquin Round Table, claimed he was the model for the armchair detective Nero Wolfe, although Wolfe's creator Rex Stout denied this.

5 *pleasurable escapism*: A century later, during another global pandemic, a 'feel-good' debut mystery achieved similar success. *The Thursday Murder Club*, by television personality Richard Osman, benefited from a resurgent enthusiasm for puzzle-making in the Golden Age vein and (despite being described by Joan Smith in *The Sunday Times* as 'toe-curling') became a worldwide bestseller.

6 *the Maybrick case of 1889*: Florence Maybrick was convicted of poisoning her husband James, but her death sentence was commuted to life imprisonment. Released in 1904, she published her life story before returning to her native United States, where she died in 1941. The case has perplexed criminologists, and Raymond Chandler described it as 'unbeatable'. A diary which came to light in 1992 purported to reveal James Maybrick as Jack the Ripper, but its authenticity has been challenged. The film-maker Bruce Robinson contributed a fresh twist in 2015 in *They All Love Jack*, claiming that the Ripper was James' brother, the composer Michael Maybrick.

7 *each of whom in turn comes up with a different yet apparently compelling solution to the problem*: In Berkeley's story 'The Avenging Chance', apparently written before the novel but published subsequently, Sheringham's solution is correct. Fifty years after the book was published, Christianna Brand devised a seventh solution, and in 2016 Martin Edwards was responsible for an eighth.

8 *Valentine Williams*: Williams, an admirer of Gaboriau as well as Conan Doyle, created a master criminal rejoicing in the name Dr Adolph Grundt, but more commonly known as Clubfoot. Less well known are his stories

about an amateur detective who happens to be a Savile Row tailor, and who shares his surname, Treadgold, with the Scotland Yard inspector in a series by Anthony Weymouth (a pseudonym of the physician Ivo Geikie-Cobb). Williams contributed to the round-robin novel *Double Death*, which is sometimes mistakenly attributed to the Detection Club, perhaps because Sayers and Crofts participated.

9   *As Wade's confidence grew, so did his literary ambition*: *Heir Presumptive*, for instance, wittily updates Horniman's *Israel Rank*. Even an early novel, *No Friendly Drop*, shows Wade's attitude towards crime as more nuanced, and less simplistic, than that of many Golden Age writers: Poole reflects at the end that 'though it was impossible not to feel horror at the callous cruelty that had destroyed two human lives, it was also difficult not to feel some sympathetic understanding of the provocation that had led to it.'

10 *Desmond Merrion*: Among the former military men who became popular series detectives were Philip MacDonald's Colonel Anthony Gethryn and Lynn Brock's Colonel Wickham Gore.

11 *he mourned this as 'a great loss . . .'*: The quotations come from an unpublished letter to his nephew Nic Goodwin, 6 September 1965.

12 *Anthony Armstrong*: This was the pen-name of George Anthony Armstrong Willis. He novelised *Ten Minute Alibi* in collaboration with Herbert Shaw; the play was also filmed. His plays included *In the Dentist's Chair*, where a patient who has been anaesthetised reveals himself to be a killer, and *Mile Away Murder*, an example of a popular murder method (at least in vintage crime fiction): poison on the back of a postage stamp. Armstrong contributed to the screenplay of Hitchcock's *Young and Innocent*, distantly based on Josephine Tey's *A Shilling for Candles*, while his novel *The Strange Case of Mr Pelham* was filmed as *The Man Who Haunted Himself*, starring Roger Moore.

13 *Milne became a founder member of the Detection Club*: Members were meant to have written a minimum of two detective novels to qualify for membership, but the Club's interpretation of its own rules has always been haphazard. Milne wrote an introduction for the Club's anthology, *Detection Medley*.

14 *an eternal complaint of authors*: Savvy writers have long used their own initiative when it comes to marketing their books. David Whitelaw, a prolific novelist, not only invented the popular card game 'Lexicon' in 1932 but cunningly advertised it twelve years later in *The Lexicon Murders*, in which the game is used for a secret code.

15 *He inscribed a copy to Wodehouse*: During the war, however, Wodehouse naively made broadcasts on German radio, which Milne attacked as a betrayal. His stinging comments distressed Wodehouse's step-daughter Leonora. She was the author of a single excellent detective short story, 'Inquest', published under the name Loel Yeo, but died during a routine operation in 1944. Her husband Peter Cazalet became a racehorse trainer; among the horses he trained was Devon Loch, which mysteriously failed to win the Grand National while being ridden by Dick Francis.

16 *'war is a lesser evil than Hitlerism'*: In 1940, six years after *Peace with Honour* appeared, he published *War with Honour*.

THIRTEEN

Treacherous Impulses

Early spy fiction

On a November morning in 1922, a small, bespectacled man with a sciatic limp was led from his cell in Beggars Bush Barracks in Dublin to face a firing squad. It was cold and dark; too dark for his execution to take place with the required efficiency. He waited patiently for the light to improve,[1] smoking and chatting to the men assigned to kill him.

It was a surreal and macabre end to a life packed with extraordinary contradictions. Erskine Childers was a Mayfair-born Englishman who became an accidental spy during the course of fifteen years spent working as a clerk in the House of Commons. He'd published a legendary thriller based on his own yachting exploits, alerting the government to the threat of invasion and earning praise for his patriotism, not least from Winston Churchill.

In the febrile summer of 1914, Churchill's secretary encouraged Childers to become an intelligence officer in the Royal Navy Volunteer Reserve. By that time, he'd become a passionate convert to Irish Home Rule, using his yacht *Asgard*[2] to smuggle guns from Germany for use by Irish nationalists. Yet, as he had during the Boer War, he served his country with courage.

After being demobbed, Childers travelled to Ireland and joined Sinn Fein. When conflict followed, he found himself in an invidious position. The British regarded him as a traitor, while some of his Irish colleagues suspected him of being a spy.[3] The recently created Irish Free State was determined to crack down on dissidents, and he was caught in possession of an unauthorized firearm and arrested. His former admirer Churchill said, on hearing the news: 'No man has done more harm or done more genuine malice or endeavoured to bring a greater curse upon the common people of Ireland than this strange being, actuated by a deadly and malignant hatred for the land of his birth.'

Childers was tried by a military court, found guilty and sentenced to death. A public outcry failed to save him. Prior to his execution, Childers saw his son in his cell,[4] and asked him to shake the hand of every minister in the government who was responsible for his death.

The firing squad party comprised former British soldiers; only five had live ammunition. Once the light improved, Childers shook each of them by the hand, and said: 'Take a step or two forward, lads. It will be easier that way.'

In 1902, Childers wrote to his friend Basil Williams, later an eminent historian, saying that he was working on 'a yachting story, with a purpose, suggested by a cruise I once took in German waters. I discovered a scheme of invasion directed against England. I'm finding it terribly difficult as being in the nature of a detective story. There is no sensation, only what is meant to be a convincing fact. I was weak enough to "spatchcock" a girl into it and now find her a horrible nuisance.' These remarks illustrate the fog of gloom that envelops most novelists at some point during their labours. The solution is to keep going. Childers' painstaking rewrite resulted in a literary landmark.

In *The Riddle of the Sands* (1903),[5] two young Englishmen go sailing on a boat called the *Dulcibella*, after Childers' sister. The unsociable, talented, perfectionist Davies and the worldly but impractical Carruthers embody contrasting aspects of Childers' own complex personality. Members of the supporting cast, less memorably characterised, include a British spy in the pay of the Germans who is described as 'the vilest creature on God's earth'; his daughter provides the love interest. Davies and Carruthers chance upon a German plot to use the bleak and mysterious Frisian Islands as a base for an invasion of England. Maps and charts are included. The story unfolds at a leisurely pace, slowed by vast quantities of minutiae derived from Childers' own sailing exploits, but the detail is convincing.

In an epilogue, Childers warns about the inadequacy of Britain's defences. A cautious postscript records some progress: 'A North Sea fleet has also been created – another good measure; but it should be remembered that its ships are not modern, or in the least capable of meeting the principal German squadrons under the circumstances supposed above.'

Childers' novel earned acclaim because of its plausibility, topicality and literary merit, and the cheap edition sold hundreds of thousands of copies. The defence establishment strove, with mixed results, to address the threat[6] Childers had highlighted. In 1910, two British naval officers were sent to the German coast on a surveillance mission, only to find that Childers' maps (which took into account detail from German charts) were more accurate than those of the Admiralty. The duo enjoyed less good fortune than Carruthers and Davies. Caught by the Germans, they were sent to prison, prompting a belated reorganisation of Naval Intelligence.

This was by no means the first fictional warning that Britain was at risk of invasion by a foreign power. The Napoleonic era, for instance, saw the publication of an anonymous three-act farce, *The Invasion of England*, followed by William Burke's play *The Armed Briton*. In the wake of the Franco-Prussian War, George Tomkyns Chesney, a captain in the Royal Engineers, published *The Battle of Dorking* (1871), a novella that describes a Prussia-like enemy vanquishing an unready Britain.

William Le Queux,[7] whose life was as colourful as that of his characters, and whose accounts of his own exploits were often equally imaginary, carved a niche in 'invasion fiction'.[8] *The Great War in England in 1897* (1894) had an overt agenda: 'to promote public interest in the idea of a larger Navy'. The story concerned a joint attack upon home shores by the forces of France and Russia, and in a preface Le Queux thundered that 'the Day of Reckoning is hourly approaching.'

The year 1897 came and went without Armageddon, however, and in *England's Peril* (1899), war with France was narrowly averted, but Le Queux became concerned that Germany posed a more formidable threat. The success of *The Riddle of the Sands* encouraged him to invest heavily in research in the hope of lending a veneer of realism to his lively, lurid prose.

He engaged a naval expert to advise him and travelled around Britain, spending the vast sum of three thousand pounds as he mapped out the Germans' potential invasion route. The funds came from the newspaper baron Lord Northcliffe, who planned to serialise the story in the *Daily Mail*, and he adjusted the account of the Germans' plans to reflect areas of England in which circulation might be boosted. The stunt worked. The *Daily Mail* gained eighty thousand new readers, and *The Invasion of 1910* (1906) sold over a million copies and was widely translated. In the German edition, however, the British no longer came out on top.

Le Queux created a gallery of professional spies, including Cuthbert Croom, who is 'constantly compelled to pose as a ladies' man', but has 'many queer and startling adventures'. Le Queux's claim to have worked for British Intelligence is probably untrue, but the boast illustrates his foresight. The secret services began to make a habit of recruiting crime writers to their ranks.

Espionage fiction has a long history. As early as 1821, James Fenimore Cooper published *The Spy*, set during the American War of Independence, in which a pedlar is suspected of spying on American revolutionaries, but the genre's leading exponents were predominantly British. Julian Symons explains this in terms of the impact of the Industrial Revolution, since secret plans concerning newly invented weapons of war were of incalculable value, and constantly at risk of being stolen by an enemy ambitious to expand its power, and perhaps its frontiers.

In the early years of the twentieth century, two gifted writers dipped toes into the murky waters of espionage. Rudyard Kipling's *Kim* (1901), set in India at the time of the British Raj, popularised the term 'the Great Game', describing the nineteenth-century rivalry between Britain and Russia in central Asia. In contrast, Joseph Conrad's *The Secret Agent*[9] (1907) addresses the challenge of 'the enemy within' domestic British society. Conrad's portrayal of the double agent Verloc shows how sensational material can, in the right hands, be fashioned into a novel of substance and lasting significance.

The Secret Agent also exemplifies the curious interrelationship of fact and fiction. The fate of Verloc's brother-in-law Stevie recalls that of the French anarchist Martial Bourdin in the Greenwich bombing of 1894, while Conrad's subtle exploration of the nature of terrorism became a long-term obsession of the American Unabomber, Ted Kaczynski.[10]

John Buchan admired *The Riddle of the Sands*: 'the atmosphere of grey Northern skies and miles of yeasty water and wet sands is as masterfully reproduced as in any story of Conrad's.' A Scot, Buchan published a handful of novels before taking a job as an editor with Nelson's. His literary circle included Henry James, Hugh Walpole and E. C. Bentley, whose *Trent's Last Case* appeared on his list.

While convalescing from illness in 1913, he wrote *The Power-House*, describing it to Walpole as 'a real shocker'. When war broke out, a duodenal ulcer prevented him from joining the army. Frustrated, he wrote a second 'shocker', which in pitting a lone individual against a sinister and powerful conspiracy set a template for the 'man on the run' thriller. The protagonist was Richard Hannay, and the book was *The Thirty-Nine Steps*.[11]

Hannay's real-life counterpart was Edmund Ironside, whom Buchan had met in South Africa. Known as 'Tiny' because he was six feet four and seventeen stone, Ironside spoke fourteen languages and worked in Intelligence; in later life, he became a field marshal and was raised to the peerage. Buchan's master-stroke was to raise the stakes by making Hannay a resourceful amateur rather than a professional daredevil. After a mysterious stranger whom he has sheltered in his flat is murdered, Hannay becomes the prime suspect, and in a series of breathless set pieces, he fights against the odds to survive and keep his country safe from harm.

This short book was very different from *The Riddle of the Sands*, not least because the story concerned 'the enemy within'. Buchan kept detail to a minimum, and his characterisation was straightforward; the essential ingredients were pace and incident. Hannay returned in four more novels, starting with *Greenmantle* (1916), a thriller with a plot about a scheme to fuel unrest in the Middle East.

There was much more to Buchan than the Hannay books. He joined British Intelligence during the war, served as an MP, and as Lord Tweedsmuir became Governor-General of Canada. A versatile author, he had no lofty ambitions for his 'shockers'. Yet the quality of his writing[12] lifted them out of the ordinary, and their influence proved pervasive.[13]

Buchan encouraged the war correspondent Valentine Williams to write a 'shocker' too. Williams had time on his hands after being blown up by a German shell in France, so he came up with a thriller about being a British agent without papers in wartime Germany; he termed it his 'shell-shocker'. Debarred by army regulations from writing under his own name, he published *The Man with the Clubfoot* in 1918 under the pseudonym Douglas Valentine. The book's success paved the way for a long line of thrillers that appeared under his own name, but as a writer he was no match for Buchan.

Nor were other thriller writers of the time. H. C. McNeile, who wrote as 'Sapper', created the heroic Hugh 'Bulldog' Drummond, but the jingoistic tone of the stories has aged badly. The same is true of the vast output of Sydney Horler, whose 'Tiger' Standish was a Drummond clone. His publishers' slogan, 'Horler for Excitement!', captured the nature of his appeal, but it did not survive his death.

To modern readers, the racism and homophobia that disfigure many of the books of 'Sapper' and Horler are self-evidently unacceptable, but even in their day, the crudeness of blood-and-thunder fiction was evident. Dorothy L. Sayers, whose reviews often flayed badly written thrillers (her verdict on T. C. H. Jacobs' *Sinister Quest* in 1934 was: 'plenty of thrills and assaults, you see; plenty of clichés, a fair amount of bosh'), couldn't even bring herself to comment on Horler's *Harlequin of Death* (1933).

The superficial sophistication of E. Phillips Oppenheim's thrillers, meanwhile, earned him the tag 'The Prince of Storytellers'. Oppenheim combined a career as a leather merchant with author-ship until he was forty; in later years, the wealth brought by colossal sales enabled him to live in luxury on the French Riviera. He wrote fast and sometimes carelessly, but *The Great Impersonation* stands out for its clever use of doppelgängers and confusion of identities between the Englishman Everard Dominey and German Leopold von Ragastein. In the year of publication, 1920, the novel sold over one million copies.

When war broke out, William Somerset Maugham was too short and too old to enlist. Instead, he joined an ambulance unit and, while at the Front, he fell in love with a young man called Gerald Haxton. In 1915, his life became exceptionally complicated. His finest novel, *Of Human Bondage*, was published; his married female lover, Syrie Wellcome, gave birth to his daughter; her husband threatened to divorce her; she took an overdose; and Haxton was charged with gross indecency. Maugham must have been relieved to be offered the escape route of becoming a secret agent, a role for which he was fitted by his linguistic proficiency and his crea-tive imagination

He drew on his experience of working in Intelligence for a series of cynical, credible short stories, collected in *Ashenden: Or the British Agent* (1927)[14]. The best espionage stories are usually novels, but this book is an exception.[15] Legend has it that Winston Churchill persuaded Maugham to withhold some of his stories from publication, lest too many secrets be given away to Britain's enemies. Maugham never returned to spy fiction, and endured an unhappy marriage to Syrie before separating from her in order to live with Haxton.

Ashenden, an early example of those protagonists whose first names are not revealed, was neither brilliant nor courageous. He is merely a small cog in a large wheel, a spy hired by 'R', a fictional incarnation of 'C', the code name of Captain Sir Mansfield Cumming, head of MI6 at the time Maugham was recruited. He is acutely aware of the callousness and double standards of his superiors, who 'shut their eyes to dirty work so that they could put their clean hands on their hearts and congratulate themselves that they had never done anything that was unbecoming to men of honour'.

The outbreak of war in 1939 marked the beginning of the end for the Golden Age of detective fiction, if not for books written in that tradition. Authors such as Sayers and Berkeley stopped writing detective stories. Others experimented briefly with spy fiction. An example was Nicholas Blake,[16] whose *The Smiler with the Knife*, published in 1939, nevertheless still featured his gentleman detective, Nigel Strangeways.

The same watershed year brought a remarkable novel of pursuit[17] in the Buchan tradition. Geoffrey Household's *Rogue Male*[18] traced an unnamed protagonist's attempt to assassinate an unnamed European dictator. Household caught the mood of the times, but he thought it prudent not to name Adolf Hitler as the intended victim.

Eric Ambler's masterpiece also appeared in 1939. *The Mask of Dimitrios*, aka *A Coffin for Dimitrios*, follows Charles Latimer, a detective novelist, in his quest to uncover the truth about the life of a mysterious individual whose corpse he has been shown in a mortuary. Ambler's literary accomplishment is evident in the way he allows much of the story to unfold through flashbacks, a structural device often used ineptly by genre writers.

Ambler had a flair for evoking sinister settings and shady characters. Although he wrote a handful of detective stories,[19] and occasionally adapted their tropes, as in *Epitaph for a Spy* (1938),[20] he was in the vanguard of a new breed of thriller writers, writing from an anti-establishment perspective that Buchan would never have contemplated.

As an unhappy schoolboy at Berkhamsted, Graham Greene[21] imagined himself as a character in Hannay's mould, 'making his hidden way across the Scottish moors with every man's hand against him'. Like Buchan, he was self-deprecating about his work in the genre, describing the books as 'entertainments'. This defensiveness illustrates crime writers' perception of the snobbery of the literary establishment about the quality of their work.

In 1939, Greene was recruited to work in Intelligence, and

published his first novel of espionage, *The Confidential Agent*. Set in an unnamed country, clearly based on Spain during its civil war, the story has a bleak flavour captured in the reflections of D, the protagonist: 'People were united only in their vices . . . It was as if the whole world lay in the shadow of abandonment.'

Sent on a mission to West Africa, Greene whiled away the voyage reading a novel by Michael Innes. The story didn't appeal to him, but he was prompted to write an escapist thriller of his own. *The Ministry of Fear* (1943) borrows ingredients from classic detective fiction, such as a charity fete, a séance and a mystery surrounding the contents of a cake, while the hero, Arthur Rowe, wryly observes that 'the world has been remade by William Le Queux.'

Notes

The main sources are *Literary Agents* by Anthony Masters, *The Riddle*, by yachtsman Maldwin Drummond, the biographies of Le Queux by David Ian Chapman and Chris Patrick and Stephen Baister, LeRoy L. Panek's history of the British spy story and Peter Lewis's biography of Ambler.

1   *He waited patiently for the light to improve*: Accounts of the execution vary; some suggest that the delay was of his choosing, because he wanted to see the sun rise one last time.

2   *his yacht Asgard*: At the time of writing, *Asgard* is on display at the Collins Barracks, now a site of the National Museum of Ireland. *Asgard*, a gift from his American father-in-law, was not the model for the *Dulcibella*, which Childers based on his previous boat, *Vixen*.

3   *some of his Irish colleagues suspected him of being a spy*: Charles Townsend has noted that Childers' wife Molly may have passed inside information from Sinn Fein to Basil Thomson, who headed the Special Branch, 'Stories of the Revolution: The riddle of Erskine Childers', *Irish Times*, 11 December 2015. Given Molly's commitment to the cause, this seems unlikely.

4   *Childers saw his son in his cell*: Erskine Hamilton Childers became President of the Republic of Ireland from 1973 to 1974; he claimed he'd made good on his promise to his father, and that all but one of the men concerned accepted his handshake.

5   *The Riddle of the Sands*: Sam Llewellyn, an author of sailing thrillers and two authorised sequels to Alistair MacLean's *The Guns of Navarone* and *Force 10 from Navarone*, also wrote *The Shadow in the Sands*, a follow-up to Childers' novel. Another Childers fan is Ken Follett, whose thrillers include the Edgar-winning *Eye of the Needle*, aka *Storm Island*; the title of his *The Key to Rebecca*, a novel inspired by the story of the real-life Nazi spy Johannes Eppler, alludes to a cipher based on Daphne du Maurier's *Rebecca*.

6   *The defence establishment strove, with mixed results, to address the threat*: A curious analogy concerns Ewen Southby-Tailyour, a Royal Marine who

was posted to the Falkland Islands in the late 1970s. He charted the coastal waters for the benefit of yachtsmen, and this work proved of considerable value to the British authorities after Argentina invaded the Falklands in 1982. His books, published after rather than before the war, included *Reasons in Writing: A Commando's View of the Falklands War*.

7 *William Le Queux*: Le Queux was an accomplished self-promoter, although David Ian Chapman points out that he twice declined a knighthood for 'personal reasons'. He claimed improbably that he'd met Hawley Harvey Crippen, who discussed committing the perfect murder a couple of years before the death of Cora Crippen. Le Queux and George R. Sims also seized the chance, during the Brides in the Bath murder trial, to try out the infamous zinc bath for themselves during a lunchtime adjournment at the Old Bailey.

8 *'invasion fiction'*: Other examples include *The Spies of the Wight*, published in 1899 by Headon Hill (Francis Edward Grainger) and Maurice Drake's 1913 novel *WO2*, aka *The Mystery of the Mud Flats*.

9 *The Secret Agent*: Conrad himself adapted the book for the stage, and other versions of the story in various forms include Hitchcock's *Sabotage*, and two operas.

10 *the American Unabomber, Ted Kaczynski*: Kaczynski, responsible for a lengthy bombing campaign from 1978 to 1995, identified closely with Conrad's character 'the Professor'.

11 *The Thirty-Nine Steps*: The novel has been filmed and televised. A comic stage version by Patrick Barlow, which owed more to Hitchcock's 1935 movie than to Buchan, ran for nine years in London's West End, and also enjoyed success on Broadway.

12 *the quality of his writing*: In *Snobbery with Violence*, Colin Watson seized on a remark made by the spy Scudder (not Hannay) in *The Thirty-Nine Steps* to accuse Buchan of antisemitism, but more recent commentators have argued that this is unfair and misleading: see e.g. 'On the trail of John Buchan's *Thirty-Nine Steps*', a *Guardian* podcast presented by Eva Krysiak, 14 August 2015.

13 *their influence proved pervasive*: Hitchcock told François Truffaut that his first version of *The Man Who Knew Too Much*, although loosely based on a Bulldog Drummond story, was shaped by reading Buchan: 'What I find appealing . . . is his understatement of highly dramatic ideas.'

14 *Ashenden: Or the British Agent*: Hitchcock's film *The Secret Agent* conflated a couple of the Ashenden stories. He was dissatisfied with the movie, telling Truffaut that the story didn't allow the audience to root for the hero, and that 'there was too much irony, too many twists of fate.' In the 1960s, Maugham's stories were a major influence on John le Carré and Len Deighton.

15 *this book is an exception*: So are Michael Gilbert's two collections featuring the agents Calder and Behrens.

16 *An example was Nicholas Blake*: Margery Allingham, whose *Traitor's Purse* features Albert Campion, is another. Julian Symons said that Allingham was capable of grafting espionage on to her usual style of writing with engaging results; he argued that Michael Innes' spy stories, starting with *The Secret Vanguard*, were more in the Buchan tradition. Agatha Christie wrote an 'enemy within' wartime mystery, *N or M?*, featuring Tommy and Tuppence Beresford as undercover agents who follow up a 'dying message' clue.

17 *a remarkable novel of pursuit*: Its admirers include David Morrell, whose debut *First Blood* spawned the popular Rambo films. He sent the manuscript to Household hoping for an endorsement, but explained in *Thrillers: 100 Must-Reads*, co-edited with Hank Wagner: 'The author of a novel in which a rotting polecat is skinned and its guts are used to build a catapult to drive a stake through someone's forehead told me that he couldn't possibly give me a quote. "Your novel is far too bloody."'

18 *Geoffrey Household's Rogue Male*: The book was filmed by Fritz Lang as *Man Hunt*. Household, an Oxford-educated former banker who also had a spell as a banana salesman, continued to publish novels for almost half a century, including a long-awaited sequel to his debut, *Rogue Justice*, but none matched the first book for impact.

19 *he wrote a handful of detective stories*: The stories in *The Intrusions of Dr Czissar* concern a retired detective who helps Scotland Yard to solve mysteries. He also collaborated with Charles Rodda (who wrote prolifically under the pen-name Gavin Holt) on crime novels published under the name Eliot Reed.

20 *Epitaph for a Spy*: Thomas Jones sees the novel as 'a sly variation on the traditional English country-house murder mystery – a crime has been committed; one of the guests must be guilty; the mystery has to be solved within a limited time frame – but displaced to a hotel on the French Riviera, and with espionage the crime rather than murder', 'Dangerous Games', *Guardian*, 6 June 2009.

21 *Graham Greene*: Greene and Dorothy Glover catalogued their painstakingly assembled collection of nineteenth-century mysteries in *Victorian Detective Fiction*. Greene's early thrillers included *Brighton Rock*, a story of gang violence at the English seaside inspired by a report of a trial at Lewes Assizes, and filmed with Richard Attenborough as the sociopathic Pinkie. Greene categorised these books as 'entertainments', separate from his worthier literary novels, but later abandoned the distinction; it was a mistake to treat them as inherently second-rate.

FOURTEEN

The Mistress of Deception

Agatha Christie

'Are we still going to the dance at the Prospect Hotel tonight?'
Mrs Robson asked one December morning in 1926. She was
breakfasting in a Yorkshire hotel with the woman from room five.

'Yes, of course.'

Fair-haired and in her mid-thirties, the woman from room five
was pleasant but reserved. This hotel, the Hydropathic, was elegant
and discreet and seemed to suit her. She'd told people that until
recently she'd been living in Cape Town. At times she had an air
of quiet melancholy, and Mrs Robson gathered that she'd suffered
a recent bereavement.

Her evenings were usually spent in the Winter Gardens Ballroom,
dancing to the music of the Happy Hydro Boys or filling in a
crossword puzzle. Once or twice she'd played billiards with a wine
merchant called Pettleson, whose singing she'd accompanied on
the piano.

She usually had her nose in a book. She'd registered with the
lending library run by the Harrogate branch of W. H. Smith, and
among six titles she'd borrowed were two recently published crime
books: *The Double Thumb*, a collection of short mysteries by Francis
D. Grierson featuring chemistry expert Professor Wells, and Douglas
Timins' *The Phantom Train*.

After breakfast she went for a walk and in the afternoon she had a game of billiards. When Pettleson asked her to autograph the sheet music of the song he'd sung to her accompaniment, she signed herself Teresa Neele.

She bathed and changed for dinner. Wearing a salmon-pink georgette dress, she came down the stairs. Close to the fire was a man, reading a newspaper. He lowered the paper, and their eyes met.

His name was Archie Christie, and he'd come under suspicion of murdering his wife, who had disappeared in mysterious circumstances eleven days earlier. All the time, Agatha Christie was safe and well in the Harrogate Hydropathic, masquerading as Teresa Neele. Neele was the surname of her husband's mistress.

The Christies' strange reunion brought to an end a disappearing act that had captivated press and public alike.[1] The novelist had vanished on 3 December 1926, driving away from home in Sunningdale after kissing her daughter Rosalind goodnight. Her two-seater Morris Cowley coupé was discovered by a quarry close to the Silent Pool, at the foot of the North Downs. The headlights were blazing. Inside the car were items of clothing and an expired driving licence. The police were called, and they soon established that Christie's personal life was troubled. Her mother had died earlier in the year, and Archie had recently confessed to having fallen in love with a vivacious secretary called Nancy Neele.

Speculation raged. Had Archie killed her, had she committed suicide, or suffered an accident? Or was her vanishing trick a publicity stunt, designed to boost sales of her latest novel, *The Murder of Roger Ackroyd*? Fellow crime writers couldn't resist the temptation to play detective themselves. Sir Max Pemberton[2] told the *Daily Mail* that she was probably dead, whereas Edgar Wallace suggested[3] that her disappearance was 'a typical case of "mental reprisal" on somebody who has hurt her'. After discussing the mystery in the *Daily News*, Dorothy L. Sayers[4] joined in 'the Great Sunday Hunt', a large-scale search of the area where Christie's car had been found. She discovered no clues.

Once he'd found his wife, Archie Christie issued a statement saying that she was 'suffering from a complete loss of memory and identity'. In fact, Christie had written to Archie's brother, letting him know that she intended to spend time recuperating in a Yorkshire spa town, but once the press sensationalised the story, matters quickly got out of hand. The Christies' marriage was broken beyond repair. They divorced in October 1928, and less than three weeks later, Archie married Nancy Neele.

Agatha Christie offered no explanation of her disappearance, other than a single newspaper interview, which was economical with the facts,[5] and her lengthy autobiography was silent about the most remarkable episode in her life. Her later short stories and novels offer only limited hints[6] as to the state of mind that led to her trip to Harrogate, but it seems safe to say that the widespread criticism of her at the time, for perpetrating a hoax that wasted police time and money, was unfair.

Debate continues to swirl around the disappearance, including expert discussion about whether she experienced 'psychogenic amnesia secondary to trauma', also known as dissociative amnesia,[7] as a result of calamities in her personal life. The death of her mother and potential loss of her husband had shaken her world to its foundations, and, as a result, the woman whose principal detective emphasised the importance of 'the little grey cells' became deeply distressed and behaved irrationally. The international scandal caused by her disappearance was mortifying. Public humiliation at a time when she was at her most vulnerable led to lifelong reticence, coupled with an instinctive distrust of the media.

Mental anguish sapped her creative powers. Although she needed to earn money to look after herself and Rosalind, she struggled to come to terms with what had happened. Her published output during the next three years was thin in terms of quantity and quality. But as time passed, her fortunes improved.

The year 1930 marked a turning point. She married an archaeologist called Max Mallowan, whom she'd met while travelling in the Middle East as part of the process of recovery. She became a founder member of the Detection Club, a social network of like-minded writers to which she retained a lifelong devotion.[8] And she published an accomplished whodunit, *The Murder at the Vicarage*. This was the first novel to feature a character originally introduced in a short story three years earlier.[9] In a wretched misjudgement, Ronald Knox had dismissed her as 'the stupidest' character in the story. She was an elderly spinster called Jane Marple.

Agatha Christie is often seen as quintessentially English, and so is her detective fiction. Yet her father was American, and she was widely travelled. Many of her novels are set far from that mythical Home Counties village Mayhem Parva:[10] in continental Europe, in the Middle East, in the Caribbean, even in ancient Egypt.

Born Agatha Mary Clarissa Miller in 1890, her comfortable upbringing in Torquay was disrupted by her father's death. She gained personal experience of life in a country house when visiting her older sister Madge,[11] who had married into money and lived at Abney Hall in Cheshire. Young Agatha accompanied her mother on a three-month trip to Cairo, which she used as the setting for a story. A family friend in Devon, the novelist Eden Phillpotts,[12] encouraged her literary ambitions and introduced her to his agent, who turned the book down.

On Christmas Eve 1914, she married Archie Christie, a dashing army officer. While her new husband was away in France, she contributed to the war effort by joining the Voluntary Aid Detachment as a nurse. Moving to the hospital dispensary, she trained as an apothecary's assistant and acquired a knowledge of poisons that was to prove invaluable in her career as a crime writer. On one occasion, a pharmacist who was giving her tuition took a brown lump from his pocket and asked what she thought it was. The answer was curare, a poison used on arrow tips in parts of South America; he told her that he carried it around with him because it made him feel powerful. The remark stuck in her mind, and more than forty years later, she introduced his fictional counterpart into a novel.[13]

Christie started *The Mysterious Affair at Styles* in 1916, when Madge bet her that she couldn't write a detective story. The novel was accepted (after two years of deliberation) by John Lane, who exploited her inexperience by shackling her to a six-book contract on less than generous terms. But Christie was, at first, simply glad to be published. The book appeared in 1920 and introduced Hercule Poirot, a retired Belgian police officer, in a story narrated by

Captain Arthur Hastings. Christie borrowed from writers she admired. The brilliant, vain, eccentric detective and his loyal, obtuse friend represented an amusing makeover of the Holmes–Watson partnership.

Her original manuscript contained a climactic courtroom scene inspired by Leroux's *The Mystery of the Yellow Room*, but Lane felt this denouement didn't work. Thus Poirot revealed the solution to the puzzle not from the witness box, but rather to the suspects gathered in the drawing room. This device became a Christie trademark, and the book also featured a 'dying message' clue, two floor plans and three reproductions of handwriting. Above all, she took the 'least likely suspect' solution that Bentley had used in *Trent's Last Case* to satirise omniscient detectives, and treated it seriously as a means of mystification.

Christie gave readers the information they needed to unravel the mystery while distracting them from the truth. She exploited the space afforded by a full-length novel to shift suspicion from one character to another, deploying clues and red herrings with cool detachment before supplying a final twist when all is finally revealed. She had created the classic Golden Age whodunit, but years passed before the scale of her achievement was fully appreciated, even by Christie herself.

War and a global influenza pandemic had cost millions of lives. In Britain, if not in the United States, unemployment remained high, yet there was a widespread mood of euphoria. People were desperate to have some fun for a change, to solve puzzles and play games. Detective stories, like crossword puzzles, offered an enjoyable way of escaping from personal problems by solving someone else's.

When psychological crime fiction is discussed, Christie's name seldom springs to mind, because she doesn't explore her characters in depth.[14] Yet Poirot made clear, as early as *The Murder on the Links* in 1923, the importance in the detection of crime of recognising a killer's 'signature', and the psychology of criminals became a recurring theme in her work.

Throughout the 1920s she varied her approach, producing light, lively thrillers more regularly than full-length whodunits, as well as using an assortment of backgrounds. In *The Man in the Brown Suit*

(1924), set in part in South Africa, she hid the culprit's identity with an ingenious storytelling device that she took a stage further when she ditched John Lane in favour of Collins and published perhaps the most famous of all detective novels, *The Murder of Roger Ackroyd* (1926).[15]

The peace of King's Abbott is shattered when the suicide of a wealthy widow is swiftly followed by the murder of the man she'd hoped to marry. This time the story is narrated by a local GP, whose sister, Caroline Sheppard, is an inquisitive gossip who might almost have stepped from the pages of Elizabeth Gaskell's *Cranford*. The unorthodox solution[16] tested the boundaries of 'fair play' plotting, but stayed within them.

Caroline Sheppard never returned, but aspects of her personality resurfaced in Jane Marple of St Mary Mead, a village whose tranquillity was disrupted by ingenious murderers with alarming regularity.[17] Miss Marple was the antithesis of Sherlock Holmes: an elderly woman[18] who has seen little of the world beyond her back garden, yet possesses great wisdom. Experience of village life had given her a deep understanding of human nature, which she deploys in solving puzzles. Like Father Brown, she often relies on intuition rather than on making deductions from physical evidence in the conscientious manner of Dr Thorndyke.

When her nephew, the trendy novelist Raymond West, asks the artist Joyce Lemprière to marry him, Miss Marple irritates him by comparing it with the local milkman's proposal, drawing a horrified protest: 'Joyce and I aren't like the milkman and Annie.' 'That is where you make a mistake, dear,' Miss Marple replies. 'Everybody is very much alike, really. But fortunately, perhaps, they don't realise it.'

This retort captures Christie's view of the world. She disdains smug intellectuals and their patronising attitudes towards apparently less sophisticated folk, in particular women. Millions of readers empathise with this and identify with her views about the common themes of human behaviour. This, rather than scientific or other expert know-how, is at the heart of Miss Marple's success – and Christie's.

*

Christie achieved fresh heights in the 1930s. In a foreword to *Cards on the Table* (1936), she spelled out her challenge to the reader. There were only four suspects: 'widely divergent types, the motive that drives each one of them to crime is peculiar to that person, and each one would employ a different method. The deduction must, therefore, be entirely *psychological* . . . when all is said and done it is the *mind* of the murderer that is of supreme interest.'

This underestimated novel is a showcase for Christie's skills. Mr Shaitana, a wealthy foreigner who has taken up the dangerous hobby of collecting people who have got away with murder, invites Poirot to dinner to meet his 'exhibits' only to be murdered himself during a game of bridge.[19] In a characteristically concise opening chapter, Christie not only sets the scene for a clever puzzle, but also pokes fun at the racism of insular Britons who 'rightly' despise exotic foreigners, and casts a cold eye on the arrogance of those, like Shaitana, who are scornful of the '*bourgeois* sensibilities' of Poirot, and indeed Christie and many of her readers.

Golden Age detective novelists wrote about serial killers[20] long before that term was invented. Christie was not first in the field, but *The ABC Murders* (1936) is a *tour de force*; the much-borrowed central concept is itself a development of an idea of Chesterton's. Equally dazzling, for very different reasons, is *Curtain*, a novel underestimated mainly because it was published at a time when classic detective fiction was hopelessly out of fashion.

Curtain's subtitle is *Poirot's Last Case*. Having written the book early in the Second World War, Christie withheld it from publication until 1975, the year before her death. The central idea is dazzling,[21] and stronger characterisation, especially of the culprit, might have made it as powerful as her finest book.

This was *And Then There Were None* (1939). Collins said that 'probably . . . the world will declare it the greatest detective story ever written' and, astonishingly, the novel lived up to the publishers' hype. Again, the central idea was not wholly original,[22] but the storytelling was exceptionally assured. What was so innovative was Christie's handling of the concept of ten strangers, invited to a small island by an unknown person, who are murdered one by one, their fates mirroring those of characters in a nursery rhyme.

The novel also gained power, as did *Murder on the Orient Express* (1934) and *Curtain*, from the way that Christie integrated into an elaborate plot a theme that preoccupied her and other leading detective novelists of the 1930s: how can one achieve true justice, when the established legal system fails to deliver it?

Decades after her death in 1976, there is no sign of Christie's phenomenal success coming to an end. Her detective stories, and adaptations for television, film and other media, remain popular around the world. Her stage play *The Mousetrap*[23] has been running in the West End since 1952. Christie is unique, and attempts by others to match her, or to belittle her achievements, invariably end in failure.

Her straightforward prose style is an asset rather than a weakness. Unpretentious and unburdened by lengthy descriptive writing, her stories remain readable today, while some ostensibly sophisticated Golden Age novels provoke yawns. The value of her quiet touches of humour is often underestimated, although she numbered P. G. Wodehouse among her admirers. If her characters are sometimes ciphers, at least they are ciphers representing universal human types.

And then there is her plotting. Many of the tricks of Christie's trade were far from original or unique to her, but she reinvented them so effectively that they became unrecognisable. At first sight, Chesterton's 'The Invisible Man' and *Death in the Clouds* (1935), where murder is committed on board an aeroplane in which Poirot is a passenger, have little in common, yet the method of masking the culprit's identity is comparable.

For Emma Lathen,[24] Christie's brilliance lay 'in her rare appreciation of the Laocoön complexities inherent in any standard situation . . . she lets the cliché [misdirect the reader] for her. When a sexually carnivorous young woman appears on the Christie scene, the reader, recognising the stock figure of the home wrecker, needs no further inducement to trip down the garden path of self-deception . . . the solution, the keystone of which is simply the durability of the original marriage or attachment, comes as a startling *bouleversement*.'

In her books, appearances keep deceiving. Even the central

premise is frequently not what it seems. In one book, an apparently inexplicable killing proves simply to have been a rehearsal for a second murder, with death a matter of bad luck for the victim. In another, someone about to kill for an inheritance diverts suspicion by suggesting that a person who died a natural death was murdered. In one of the cleverest novels, an apparent series of murders is conceived to disguise a particular crime.[25]

Christie took hackneyed tropes of the genre, such as 'the butler did it' or 'the body in the library', and gave them a fresh spin.[26] Her 'least likely person' culprits include a Marple-esque spinster, a child, an investigating policeman, a Watson figure and even Poirot himself. As Robert Barnard pointed out,[27] a favourite method was to place the reader in a 'position of sympathy' with the murderer.[28] In one novel, the killer is the supposed target of a failed series of attempted murders, and in another the investigating police superintendent. *All* the suspects in one book conspire to commit the crime; Raymond Chandler said of this solution that 'only a half-wit could guess it'. In other words, he'd played the game and lost.

Notes

The main sources are the biographies by Janet Morgan and Laura Thompson, Jared Cade's *Agatha Christie and the Eleven Missing Days*, John Curran's books about Christie's notebooks, and Robert Barnard's *A Talent to Deceive*.

1   *a disappearing act that had captivated press and public alike*: It has also captured the imagination of writers such as Andrew Wilson, who fictionalised it in *A Talent for Murder*. In 1979, Vanessa Redgrave starred as Christie in the film *Agatha*, the screenplay of which paid scant attention to the facts.
2   *Sir Max Pemberton*: Pemberton's adventure stories sometimes ventured into the field of crime. Along with Bertram Fletcher Robinson and Arthur Conan Doyle, he was a member of 'Our Society', a select band of students of criminology. After Fletcher Robinson's death, he completed his story *The Wheels of Anarchy*. In 1914, he published the first part of a mystery called 'The Donnington Affair', and invited other writers to complete it. G. K. Chesterton's second part turned it into a Father Brown story.
3   *Edgar Wallace suggested*: 'My Theory of Mrs Christie: Either in London or Dead', *Daily Mail*, 11 December 1926. The following year, he published a story, 'The Sunningdale Mystery', about the disappearance of a woman from Berkshire.
4   *Dorothy L. Sayers*: Aspects of Christie's disappearance found their way into Sayers' *Unnatural Death*.

5   *other than a single newspaper interview, which was economical with the
    facts*: She talked to the *Daily Mail* on 15 February 1928, and claimed to
    have developed amnesia after a failed suicide attempt.

6   *Her later short stories and novels offer only limited hints*: Examples are
    'The Edge' and 'The Harlequin Tea Set', together with some of her romantic
    novels written under the name Mary Westmacott, notably *The Burden*.

7   *dissociative amnesia*: In *Scientific American* on 2 August 2017, Stefania de
    Vito and Sergio Della Sala pointed out that it is now recognised that partial
    amnesia can occur, and concluded that the case 'remains a mystery'.

8   *the Detection Club . . . to which she retained a lifelong devotion*: Christie
    wasn't a natural 'joiner', but despite her retiring nature, she served on the
    Club's committee in the late 1930s and, after Sayers died, became its
    President until her death.

9   *a character originally introduced in a short story three years earlier*: Jane
    Marple made her debut in 'The Tuesday Night Club'; originally published
    in *The Royal Magazine*, it became the first chapter of *The Thirteen Problems*.
    The story centred around a group of amateur mystery-solvers, a concept
    which recurs in Ellery Queen's Puzzle Club stories, Isaac Asimov's Black
    Widowers series, and novels such as Berkeley's *The Poisoned Chocolates
    Case* and Richard Osman's *The Thursday Murder Club*.

10 *'Mayhem Parva'*: A term coined in *Snobbery with Violence* by the crime
    novelist Colin Watson.

11 *her older sister Madge*: Madge wrote a play, *The Claimant*, which was
    produced in 1924. It was based on the Tichborne inheritance case of the
    1860s–70s, which inspired later novels such as Josephine Tey's *Brat Farrar*
    and Julian Symons' *The Belting Inheritance*.

12 *the novelist Eden Phillpotts*: Phillpotts was a popular regional novelist and
    also achieved success as a crime writer, sometimes under his own name,
    sometimes as Harrington Hext. *The Red Redmaynes* has a pleasing twist,
    while *The Grey Room* is a locked-room mystery.

13 *she introduced his fictional counterpart into a novel*: This was *The Pale
    Horse*; her description of the symptoms of thallium poisoning is more
    authoritative than Ngaio Marsh's in *Final Curtain*. Christie's novel has been
    claimed as an inspiration for real-life murders and also the saving of lives.
    The first murderer known to have used thallium, the serial poisoner Graham
    Young, denied having read the book, although Christie was unfairly criticised
    in some quarters for having publicised a previously little-known murder
    method. Conversely, a woman from Latin America wrote to Christie saying
    that she had saved someone from slow poisoning by recognising the symp-
    toms from the novel. Similarly, a nurse in London identified the cause of a
    child's sickness after reading *The Pale Horse*. Police investigating George
    Trepal, the so-called 'Mensa Murderer' of Florida, who poisoned a family
    of neighbours with thallium, found a copy of *The Pale Horse* at his property.

14 *she doesn't explore her characters in depth*: It is often argued that the need
    to withhold information about character from readers of detective fiction
    renders the genre inherently second-rate. This is an oversimplification. As
    Reginald Hill has pointed out, even novels of the highest quality do not
    reveal everything about the characters at once.

15 *The Murder of Roger Ackroyd*: First serialised in the London *Evening News*
    as *Who Killed Ackroyd?* Laura Thompson's biography perpetuates the myth

that 'the Detection Club committee proposed a motion that Agatha should be expelled as she had broken the "rules"; only a vote by Dorothy L. Sayers saved her.' The Club didn't exist in 1926, and its members would have regarded such a motion as ridiculous. In fact, Sayers rebutted the suggestion that Christie did not play fair in *The Murder of Roger Ackroyd*, pointing out that it was the reader's job to suspect *everybody*. Conversely, she rebuked Canon Victor L. Whitechurch for unfairly concealing a crucial piece of evidence from the reader in *The Crime at Diana's Pool*.

16 *The unorthodox solution*: Christie credited Madge's husband with the original idea, although Lord Mountbatten also claimed to have suggested it to her. The solution was anticipated by Anton Chekhov in *The Shooting Party* and by the Norwegian Stein Riverton. Other detective novelists who have used a similar ploy include Isabel Ostrander, Virgil Markham, Anthony Berkeley and more recently Kate Ellis, while Christie herself reworked it cunningly in *Endless Night*. The French professor of literature and psychoanalyst Pierre Bayard argued in *Who Killed Roger Ackroyd?* that the murderer was a character unsuspected by Poirot. Separately, Bayard has contended that Sherlock Holmes' solution to *The Hound of the Baskervilles* was wrong.

17 *a village whose tranquillity was disrupted . . . with alarming regularity*: Although not as often as Midsomer, created by Caroline Graham in a series featuring DCI Barnaby and starting with *The Killings at Badger's Drift*. The body count in the long-running television series *Midsomer Murders*, broadcast since 1997, has run to several hundred.

18 *the antithesis of Sherlock Holmes: an elderly woman*: Her principal literary predecessor was Miss Amelia Butterworth from Anna Katharine Green's *That Affair Next Door*. Patricia Wentworth's Maud Silver, created at much the same time as Marple, was a former private governess who becomes a private inquiry agent.

19 *a game of bridge*: Bridge also features prominently in a shipboard whodunit published three years earlier, *S.S. Murder* by Q. Patrick (Richard Wilson Webb and Mary Louise White Aswell). The story is told in a series of letters from a female journalist to her fiancé.

20 *Golden Age detective novelists wrote about serial killers*: Examples include John Rhode's *The Murders in Praed Street*, Anthony Berkeley's *The Silk Stocking Murders*, *The Silent Murders* by Neil Gordon (A. G. Macdonell), *The Edge of Terror* by Brian Flynn, and Philip MacDonald's *X v Rex* (as Martin Porlock) and *Murder Gone Mad*.

21 *The central idea is superb*: It is drawn from *Othello* and the now obscure *John Ferguson* by St John Ervine; Christie deploys both plays as clues in her story. Ellery Queen's final, never completed novel *The Tragedy of Errors* employs the same concept, seeking to present 'the insanity of today's world' within the confines of a 'fair play' detective novel, as Frederic Dannay expressed it. Dannay wrote the book's outline, which was finally published in 1999.

22 *Again, the central idea was not wholly original*: *Six Dead Men* by S.-A. Steeman anticipated some aspects of the story. Other elements were prefigured in *The Invisible Host* by the American couple Gwen Bristow and Bruce Manning, a novel said to have been inspired by the constant disturbance caused by a neighbour's raucous radio. Owen Davis turned the book into a play, *The Ninth Guest*, which was filmed.

23 *Her stage play The Mousetrap*: Based on a radio play, *Three Blind Mice*, written to celebrate Queen Mary's eightieth birthday. The plot was influenced by the case of Dennis O'Neill, a twelve-year-old boy killed in 1945. Julius Green argues in *Curtain Up* that she 'challenged the male hegemony in West End theatre more successfully than any other female playwright before or since.' The run was interrupted by a pandemic in 2020, but not even Covid-19 was lethal enough to end it permanently.

24 *For Emma Lathen*: In 'Cornwallis's Revenge' in *Agatha Christie, First Lady of Crime*, edited by H. R. F. Keating. The Lathen name was used by economist Mary Jane Latsis and lawyer Martha Henissart for a series featuring one of the genre's few likeable bankers, John Putnam Thatcher. The books benefit from an authentic presentation of the business world. Lathen was sometimes called 'the Agatha Christie of Wall Street'. The pair also collaborated as R. B. Dominic, whose books featured a congressman as amateur detective.

25 *an apparent series of murders is conceived to disguise a particular crime*: As Father Brown pointed out in 'The Sign of the Broken Sword', the best place to hide a leaf is in a forest. This idea has been adapted by writers as diverse as Ed McBain and Lee Child. Philip MacDonald used it in an Anthony Gethryn story, 'The Wood-for-the-Trees'. On TV, Glenn Chandler's 'The Killing Philosophy' in the *Taggart* series made inventive use of the trope, which also crops up in films such as Roland Joffé's black comedy *Goodbye Lover*.

26 *took hackneyed tropes of the genre, such as 'the butler did it' or 'the body in the library', and gave them a fresh spin*: In *Three Act Tragedy* and *The Body in the Library* respectively. In the former novel, remarkably, the murderer's motive is different in the UK edition from that in the US edition.

27 *As Robert Barnard pointed out*: In *A Talent to Deceive*. An academic who wrote concise, witty whodunits, Barnard analysed Christie's techniques with intelligence and insight. The fact that even he could not come close to matching her global success illustrates the extraordinary nature of her achievements.

28 *to place the reader in a 'position of sympathy' with the murderer*: As Barnard says, this technique was also regularly deployed by Ross Macdonald, whose private eye Lew Archer is so frequently hired by the person who turns out to be the villain 'that one has the gravest doubts about the financial viability of the Archer detective agency'.

FIFTEEN

American Tragedy

Van Dine and the American Golden Age

In August 1924, Willard Huntington Wright was nursing a shameful secret. He confessed the truth to his estranged wife Katharine and their daughter Beverley, but was desperate to keep his friends in the art and literary world in the dark. Above all, he begged her not to allow his younger brother, Stanton,[1] an avant-garde artist, to find out how low he'd sunk.

'I hope you have impressed upon Beverley,' he wrote to Katharine, 'not to mention, or let on a word to Stanton . . . If the facts got out it might hurt me a great deal . . . In any event, he is not to be told anything. I can't explain, but it's important.'

Wright was in dire straits. He was only thirty-five, but his days as a prominent art and literary critic, and as editor of the influential magazine *The Smart Set*, were now a distant memory. A fellow critic sneered[2] that Wright was 'someone who had once given the impression of being someone important'. Deep in debt and short of work, unhappily married, and with his mental and physical health ravaged by years of drug-taking, he was at his wits' end.

The turning point came when, to keep depression at bay, his doctor recommended reading detective stories,[3] and a friend gave him the run of the two thousand mysteries in his library. Back in

1912, he'd written that 'any serious detective story is of necessity bad. It appeals to the most primitive cravings within us.' Now the time had come for desperate measures.[4] He would write a best-selling detective novel himself.

Wright produced outlines for three books with a distinctive sleuth, an emphasis on 'fair play' plotting, and a veneer of intellectual sophistication. Despite telling his wife he was penniless, he invested in new clothes and a set of business cards. This, he explained to her, was 'to impress the publishers and editors with my opulence . . . If they think you're prosperous, they imagine you're a better writer!'

He fixed up lunch with an old classmate, Maxwell Perkins, now a high-profile editor with Scribner's. Emphasising the need for strict secrecy, he handed over the story outlines. Perkins made him an offer of three thousand dollars, more than he'd earned in the past five years.

A burst of feverish activity resulted in the completion of *The Benson Murder Case* (1926), based on an unsolved cause célèbre, the shooting of a wealthy bridge player called Joseph Bowne Elwell.[5] The detective, Philo Vance, took smugness, eccentricity and brilliance to extremes.

To avoid soiling his good name by association with detective stories, Wright adopted the pseudonym S. S. Van Dine. The narrator had the same name. Scribner's conjured up a mystery about their new star author's identity. They spent lavishly on newspaper adver-tising and the distribution of facsimile cards of an NYPD crime report about the murder of Alvin Benson. Philo Vance, they boasted, would 'inevitably find a literary niche alongside of that triumvirate of immortal sleuths, Monsieur Lecoq, Auguste Dupin, and Sherlock Holmes'.

The publicity blitz worked like a dream, although one sceptic complained in *The Saturday Review of Literature* that the solution to the puzzle was obvious and that Vance had the 'conversational manner . . . of a high-school girl who has been studying the foreign words and phrases in the back of her dictionary'. The voice crying in the wilderness belonged to a young writer called Dashiell Hammett.

Van Dine's next novel, *The 'Canary' Murder Case* (1927), was based on another famous unsolved crime, the killing of Dot King, the 'Broadway Butterfly'. Philo Vance allows the killer to commit suicide, saying to the District Attorney: 'Pray don't give way to conventional moral indignation.'

The publishers repeated their stunt with facsimile crime report cards, announcing the murder by strangulation of Margaret Odell, only to find that, by embarrassing coincidence, a woman of the same name had gone missing from Toledo, Ohio. At least this underlined the topicality of Philo Vance's cases. Their aura of glamour and excess tapped into the zeitgeist of the Roaring Twenties. President Calvin Coolidge, and his Secretary of Commerce Herbert Hoover, were numbered among Van Dine's admirers. The book became a runaway bestseller, and so did the fourth in the series, *The Bishop Murder Case* (1929).[6]

Scribner's described Van Dine coyly as 'a man in his thirties who has had some legal experience, and was educated at Harvard'. Speculation about his identity raged. When the secret leaked out, he rewrote history so as to present the emergence of Van Dine as a miraculous consequence of Willard Huntington Wright's tragic collapse from overwork and nervous strain. Claiming to have been 'saved by illness', he said he'd been forbidden by his doctor to write anything before New Year's Day 1926. All this was 'hokum', as he admitted to his long-suffering wife, but it made a terrific story. The article's rueful title said it all: 'I Used to Be a Highbrow, but Look at Me Now'.

His self-absorption was encapsulated by the title of a semi-autobiographical novel, *The Man of Promise*, published in 1916. He admired Theodore Dreiser[7] and wrote, rather in the Dreiser style, about a young man whose ambitions are throttled, essentially because 'one by one . . . the women who had crossed his life had taken something vital out of it'. Misogyny was, as his unsparing biographer John Loughery has demonstrated, only one of his vices; others included racism, homophobia, meanness, vanity and cruelty to those close to him. At least he was kind to dogs and treated his second wife much better than the luckless Katharine and Beverley.

He poured scorn on commercial fiction, just as he scoffed at patriotism, monogamy and religion. As a young critic, one of his editors proclaimed him a 'Literary Vivisectionist'. What he lacked in self-awareness he made up for in self-esteem. Ezra Pound remarked drily in a letter to James Joyce: 'Wright thinks me a bit cracked and regards himself as the sane and normal and practical male.'

Throughout his life, he was his own worst enemy. A brief period of study at Harvard culminated in exclusion from his course, while an expenses fiddle ended his tenure as editor of *The Smart Set*. When the United States declared war on Germany, he dodged the call-up on health grounds, and his friend H. L. Mencken helped him to find a job on the *New York Evening Mail*. He lost it when a stupid prank led people to suspect him, mistakenly, of being a German spy. As Mencken said, his provocative behaviour was 'a masterpiece of imbecility'. In the years following the war, he lost his way, becoming increasingly jealous of his brother Stanton's charisma and success, until his luck turned.

Van Dine set himself up as an expert on crime, factual and fictional. Shortly after his first novel came out, the sensational Hall–Mills murder trial[8] took place. A woman and her two brothers were accused of the savage killings of her husband, an Episcopalian priest, and his married lover. The trio were ultimately acquitted, and nobody was ever convicted of the crimes. During the media circus surrounding the trial, Scribner's promoted Van Dine's opinions on the mystery, although he could do no more than pontificate about the significance of psychological clues.

He published 'Twenty Rules for Writing Detective Stories', but unlike Ronald Knox, he took his strictures seriously. As regards 'fair play' plotting, he leapt on to the moral high ground, always treacherous territory. He complained that the trick in *The Murder of Roger Ackroyd* was 'hardly a legitimate device' and argued that the novel's effect was 'nullified by the denouement'. This was ludicrous, especially given that he didn't always play entirely fair with his own readers.

The Rules said something about the times, as when Van Dine decreed: 'There must be no love interest in the story.' This reflected a distrust of sentimentality prevalent in the Jazz Age. The Rules also revealed something about their author, who warned: 'A servant . . . must not be chosen by the author as the culprit . . . The culprit must be a decidedly worth-while person . . .'

Van Dine sold film rights in the Vance stories to Paramount. When the original screenplay for *The 'Canary' Murder Case* enraged him (by no means a unique experience for authors whose 'masterpiece' is rewritten by others), the studio had to placate him by bringing in a talented screenwriter, Florence Ryerson,[9] to improve the script. Hollywood feted him, and he was given a cameo role long before it became commonplace for authors to appear in screen adaptations of their books, but that scene finished up on the cutting-room floor. The film became the first detective 'talkie', and a series of Philo Vance movies[10] was launched.

Van Dine's sales helped Scribner's to survive the aftershocks of the Wall Street Crash. Maxwell Perkins told F. Scott Fitzgerald that it was almost as if the Vance books had benefited from the Depression. Van Dine felt invulnerable. Never mind that the comedians Abbott and Costello spoofed Vance in a film; no matter that humorous poet Ogden Nash said that 'Philo Vance / Needs a kick in the pance.' Corey Ford, writing as John Riddell, satirised Vance in *The John Riddell Murder Case* (1930), a book brightened by droll illustrations and an amusing floor plan. Van Dine even joined Ford at bookshop signings, presumably on the premise that no publicity is bad publicity.

At a party on board an ocean liner, he met a socialite who had changed her name from Eleanor Rulapaugh to Claire de Lisle. He divorced Katharine and married Claire, and the newly-weds became fascinated by dogs. Van Dine bought ten acres of kennels in New Jersey and this new obsession supplied background for his sixth and supposedly final detective novel, a locked-room mystery, *The Kennel Murder Case* (1933).

His personal trademarks were a Van Dyke beard and a pearl-handled cane, and his striking looks and self-indulgent lifestyle made him seem like a character from one of his books. He and his new wife entertained guests in their penthouse overlooking Central Park, a stone's throw from a 'Hooverville' shanty town for the homeless. The apartment housed a team of servants, sixty-eight aquaria for two thousand exotic fish,[11] collections of Chinese ceramics and modern art, and a blackjack table and roulette wheel. The American Dream, a term recently popularised by James Truslow Adams,[12] seemed to have become Van Dine's reality.

Van Dine's phenomenal sales prompted other writers to follow his lead. Among them was Ellery Queen, the pen-name of two Jewish cousins, Manfred Lee and Frederic Dannay.[13] It was also the name of their gifted amateur detective, the son of a New York cop. The Queen stories weren't written in the first person, and this allowed for greater narrative flexibility. Despite the debt to Van Dine, the cousins began to hone their craft in a distinctive fashion. Crucially, they paid increasing attention to characterisation, plausibility and style.

Dannay and Lee were advertising men who had been enticed by the prospect of a $7,500-prize contest to collaborate on a detective novel. *The Roman Hat Mystery* (1929) was duly submitted, and they were overjoyed by an unofficial tip-off that they had won the prize. The magazine co-sponsoring the contest then went out of business, and its successor awarded the prize to someone else.[14] This galling experience gave them an early insight into the vicissitudes of authorship but they had a $200 publishing deal for consolation.

Ellery's second case, *The French Powder Mystery* (1930), reached a climax that Anthony Boucher described as 'probably the most admirably constructed denouement in the history of the detective story'. The explanation of the mystery is lengthy and complex, yet the culprit's identity is only revealed by the book's last two words. The cousins were showing a zest and inventiveness which Van Dine couldn't match.

The influence of Anthony Berkeley is evident in the multiple solutions to *The Greek Coffin Mystery* (1932). The novel boasts a cast of thirty-nine characters, a map, two floor plans, a challenge to the reader, and an acrostic hidden in the chapter titles. The first edition included 'How to Read the Queen Stories', a pamphlet that emphasised the interactive nature of the crime-solving game. Readers were urged to use the pamphlet 'as a bookmark while reading a Queen story'.

Success led Dannay and Lee to create a second alter ego. The series of four Barnaby Ross books,[15] featuring veteran Shakespearean actor and sleuth Drury Lane, opened in 1932 with *The Tragedy of X*. A 'dying message' clue subtly points to the solution of the mystery, and this became a familiar ingredient of the cousins' puzzles. Lane offered a neat rationalisation of the prevalence of victims in Golden Age whodunits uttering cryptic clues to their fate with their expiring breath: 'There are no limits to which the human mind cannot soar in that unique, god-like instant before the end of life.'

Dannay and Lee made a palaver of guarding the real identities of both Ellery Queen and Barnaby Ross. A rumour spread, perhaps started by the cousins themselves, that Ellery Queen was really Van Dine, and that Barnaby Ross was Alexander Woollcott. They attended autograph parties and literary teas wearing black masks, and even debated each other in masks, with Lee as 'Queen' and Dannay as 'Ross'. Typically, Ross would outline a complicated mystery before challenging Queen to solve it. Given that their performance was carefully rehearsed, this proved less testing than the occasion when they were invited to lunch at the Authors' Epicure Club. They discovered that 'speaking through a mask is one thing. But eating through one, or under one, is something else again.'

Fulton Oursler,[16] the editor of *Liberty* magazine, adapted the Van Dine formula[17] under the pen-name Anthony Abbot. Abbot narrated the cases of Thatcher Colt,[18] a wealthy dilettante who makes a hobby of criminology and improbably becomes New York's Police Commissioner. The idiosyncrasies of Van Dine were tempered by down-to-earth police work, and occasionally a startling candour about police brutality, which both Colt and his creator seemed to regard as a necessary evil.

Oursler's most interesting project in the genre sprang from an unlikely source, a conversation with Franklin Delano Roosevelt.[19] The President floated an idea for a mystery that intrigued him: how can a man disappear with five million dollars in any negotiable form and not be traced? Oursler encouraged him to turn it into a detective story. FDR felt unable to do so, but half a dozen crime writers contributed to a 'round-robin' story based on the premise. Van Dine was among those who wrote a section of *The President's Mystery Story*,[20] which was duly serialised in *Liberty*, published in book form in 1935, and even filmed.

Irritatingly omniscient detectives such as Vance make a natural target for satire. At around the same time that Anthony Berkeley created Roger Sheringham, T. S. Stribling[21] launched the psychologist Henry Poggioli on a detecting career of 'illustrious obtuseness'. Poggioli's first five cases were collected in *Clues of the Caribbees* (1929). In the final story, 'A Passage to Benares', set in Trinidad, his career apparently came to a unique and shocking conclusion.

Stribling was one of those authors of distinction who felt embarrassed about slumming it in the detective genre. He told a friend, 'Right at this moment I am lost to morality and the hope of eternal life, even in hell, by doing a mystery story for *Adventure*. I wouldn't have done it, but I needed the money.' At least he admitted that he enjoyed 'doing tripe just as well as . . . tender loin.' Poggioli not only returned unscathed in 'A Pearl at Pampatar' but proved remarkably resilient. Although Stribling's last non-criminous fiction appeared in 1940, he published Poggioli stories for a further seventeen years.

Van Dine wasn't alone in shrouding his stories in a fog of erudition. The American detective novelist on whom Dorothy L. Sayers bestowed the accolade 'the highbrow of highbrows' was C. Daly King, whose books took quirkiness to a new level. He coined the term 'obelist',[22] which he defined as 'one who harbours suspicion', and which featured in the title of three novels. An author of books such as *Beyond Behaviourism*, King gave his police detective Michael Lord a Watson called Dr Love Rees Pons; he had a weakness for weirdly punning character names. Like his creator, Pons was an 'integrative psychologist'.

King's books occasionally descend into psychobabble and his characters make cardboard seem multifaceted. Yet the fantastic convolutions of his plotting offer guilty pleasures to connoisseurs of the bizarre. Trevis Tarrant, a wealthy man-about-town whose butler-valet Katoh happens to be a Japanese spy, is a colourless version of Philo Vance who appeared in the short story collection

The Curious Mr Tarrant. Published in Britain in 1935, it failed to find an American publisher,[23] a sign of evaporating enthusiasm for stories in the Van Dine mould.

That same year, Ellery Queen tackled the question that so preoccupied leading British crime writers at the time: in what circumstances can murder be justified? At the end of *The Spanish Cape Mystery* (1935), Ellery becomes introspective: 'I've often boasted that the human equation means nothing to me. But it does, damn it all, it does!' Van Dine's influence was fading. Barnaby Ross's brief career had concluded with *Drury Lane's Last Case* (1933), and the cousins revealed their real names. It was time to take Ellery Queen in a fresh direction.

Van Dine's extravagance left him with no choice but to keep writing about Philo Vance, but Dorothy L. Sayers was moved to say:[24] 'If any criminal ever does succeed in slaying Mr Vance, I shall heartily sympathise . . . something lingering with boiling oil in it should be reserved for tormentors of the King's English.'

Description, dialogue and characterisation had never been strong points of the series. Now even the quality of the plots declined. Vance was at last allowed the luxury of unrequited love, but his doomed infatuation with Zalia Graem in *The Garden Murder Case* (1935) lacked the humanity of Lord Peter Wimsey's yearning for Harriet Vane.

Hardboiled crime fiction was growing in popularity, although the cerebral whodunit was still alive and kicking in America. As well as Ellery Queen, Rex Stout[25] was making a name for himself as a writer after seeing the fortune he'd made in business wiped out by the Great Depression. *Fer-de-Lance* introduced his brilliant, orchid-loving, armchair detective Nero Wolfe[26] in 1934. The series ran for more than forty years, while a club of enthusiasts called the Wolfe Pack formed in 1969 and is still going strong. Wolfe's cases are narrated by his intrepid sidekick Archie Goodwin,[27] whose witty and distinctive voice enabled Stout to straddle two horses. He gave traditional detection a hardboiled gloss.

Van Dine failed to adapt to changing times. To fund his lifestyle, he began endorsing products as diverse as a radio console, alcohol, board games and Goodrich tyres. His disdain for emerging rivals was summed up in a letter to Florence Ryerson that described Dashiell Hammett's stories as 'all booze and erections'.

Drinking heavily and depressed by slumping royalties, he started writing *The Powwow Murder Case*,[28] only to run out of steam and (perhaps mercifully) abandon it. When asked to produce an outline for a film parodying Vance and starring the comic actor Gracie Allen, he was glad to take the money and write. The outline became a short, lamentable book and reviews were predictably brutal.

His health was deteriorating, and his publicity photographs suggested a man of seventy, rather than fifty. Stanton, aware of his brother's capacity for self-harm, feared he would commit suicide, but it didn't quite come to that. Van Dine struck a deal to write a new story showcasing the ice skater Sonja Henie, only to suffer a heart attack and die before completing it. To the end, he was unrepentant about his self-destruction. 'I'm so glad for all the brandy I've had,' he said to his editor at one of their last meetings. 'I only regret that I didn't drink more of it.'

Notes

The main sources are John Loughery's biography of Van Dine, Francis M. Nevins' *Ellery Queen: The Art of Detection*, the Ellery Queen website, Howard Haycraft's *Murder for Pleasure* and correspondence with Art Scott.

1   *his younger brother, Stanton*: Stanton Macdonald-Wright was a pioneer of the abstract form of painting known as Synchronism. His portrait of Willard was bought by the Smithsonian and hangs in the National Portrait Gallery.
2   *A fellow critic sneered*: This was the equally egotistical Edmund Wilson, in 'The All-Star Literary Vaudeville'.
3   *his doctor recommended reading detective stories*: Jacob Munter Lobsenz, MD was rewarded with a cameo role in *The Kennel Murder Case*, and became Vance's personal physician.
4   *desperate measures*: Brooks Hefner describes long-forgotten pseudonymous stories featuring an intellectual criminal, written by Wright a decade before his success as Van Dine, in *Clues*, vol. 30, issue 1.
5   *Joseph Bowne Elwell*: Elwell was found murdered in his locked Upper Manhattan brownstone in 1920.
6   *The Bishop Murder Case*: The crimes are based on the Mother Goose nursery tales. Agatha Christie integrated nursery rhymes into several of her storylines, such as the excellent 'cold case' mystery *Five Little Pigs*; sometimes the device adds little, as in the sub-par *Hickory, Dickory, Dock*, aka *Hickory, Dickory, Death*, but the rhyme in *And Then There Were None* works brilliantly.

7 *Theodore Dreiser*: Dreiser's *An American Tragedy*, published a year before the first Van Dine novel, was also based on a real-life murder but otherwise very different.

8 *the sensational Hall–Mills murder trial*: Damon Runyon attended the trial, as did Mary Roberts Rinehart, and the case inspired Frances Noyes Hart's *The Bellamy Trial*. Did F. Scott Fitzgerald adapt elements of the story for the later parts of *The Great Gatsby*? According to Sarah Churchwell in *Careless People: Murder, Mayhem and the Invention of The Great Gatsby*, the answer is yes.

9 *Florence Ryerson*: Ryerson was a co-author of the screenplay for *The Wizard of Oz*. She collaborated with her husband Colin Clements, also a screenwriter, on mystery novels featuring Hollywood detective Jimmy Lane. *Sleep No More* was praised by Sayers as 'scrupulously fair'.

10 *a series of Philo Vance movies*: Vance was played by various actors, notably William Powell, later a popular Nick Charles in the *Thin Man* films inspired by Dashiell Hammett's book, and Basil Rathbone, who subsequently earned fame as Sherlock Holmes.

11 *exotic fish*: Vance lectures about tropical fish in *The Dragon Murder Case*. In this story, a man dives into a swimming pool, only to vanish; the same situation occurs, but is more satisfactorily explained, in Carter Dickson's *A Graveyard to Let*. The film of Van Dine's book was credited with creating a craze for tropical fish.

12 *James Truslow Adams*: Author of *The Epic of America*.

13 *Manfred Lee and Frederic Dannay*: Their real names were Emanuel Benjamin Lepofsky and Daniel Nathan.

14 *its successor awarded the prize to someone else*: Ironically, that successor was *The Smart Set*. The new winner was *Murder Yet to Come*, a locked-room puzzle by Isabel Briggs Myers. With her mother, she devised the Myers–Briggs Type Indicator, which remains a widely used form of personality test. Her brief foray into detective fiction ended with *Give Me Death*, a mystery tarnished by a racist element in the storyline, which concerns a sequence of deaths in the Darnell family.

15 *four Barnaby Ross books*: The second, *The Tragedy of Y*, is notable for a daring choice of 'least likely suspect'. Agatha Christie did something similar in one of her post-war whodunits.

16 *Fulton Oursler*: After converting to Catholicism, Oursler wrote *The Greatest Story Ever Told*, which became an epic film. His son, Will Oursler, also wrote mysteries, including the casebook novels *The Trial of Vincent Doon* and *Folio on Florence White*.

17 *adapted the Van Dine formula*: The police work reflects Freeman Wills Crofts' sober influence, as did Milton Propper's series about Philadelphia cop Tommy Rankin. Propper was among those writers who struggled to come to terms with the fading of the Golden Age. His last book appeared in 1943 and after suffering mental illness he took his life in 1962.

18 *Thatcher Colt*: The Hall–Mills case inspired *About the Murder of the Clergyman's Mistress*, while *About the Murder of a Man Afraid of Women* was based on William Desmond Taylor's unsolved murder. The final Colt novels, *The Creeps* and *The Shudder*, were (according to Francis M. Nevins in *Cornucopia of Crime*), ghostwritten by Oscar Schisgall.

19 *Franklin Delano Roosevelt*: FDR was reading Carter Dickson's *The Punch*

and Judy Murders at the time of his death. His wife Eleanor was presented as an amateur detective in a series of novels written by their son Elliott. A second Presidential offspring, Margaret Truman, wrote mysteries set around Washington DC, while Gerald Ford's daughter Susan has co-written crime fiction. Jon L. Breen indicates in 'The Ghost and Miss Truman', reprinted in *A Shot Rang Out*, that both Elliot Roosevelt and Margaret Truman utilised ghostwriters.

20 *The President's Mystery Story*: The puzzle was ultimately resolved when Erle Stanley Gardner wrote a final chapter thirty years later, and the book was reissued as *The President's Mystery Plot*.

21 *T. S. Stribling*: Thomas Sigismund Stribling won a Pulitzer Prize in 1933. His biographer Kenneth W. Vickers and Arthur Vidro, editor of *Dr. Poggioli: Criminologist*, credit Fred Dannay for encouraging him to keep writing about Poggioli, whose detective work becomes increasingly astute. Stribling's language and ideas in the context of race relations may now seem dated and inappropriate, but by the standards of his time he was progressive.

22 *'obelist'*: The UK first edition of *Obelists at Sea* said the term meant 'a person of little or no value', prompting King's tetchy comment when inscribing a copy: 'It's not my fault that the English don't know their own language'.

23 *it failed to find an American publisher*: This omission was not rectified until 1977, and an expanded version, *The Complete Curious Mr Tarrant*, was published in 2003. Edward D. Hoch noted in his introduction that King wrote a novel about Tarrant called *The Episode of the Demoiselle D'ys*, which nobody wanted to publish. Attempts to trace the manuscript have so far come to nothing.

24 *Dorothy L. Sayers was moved to say*: When eviscerating *The Casino Murder Case* in a review for *The Sunday Times*.

25 *Rex Stout*: Stout was a prominent campaigner for authors' rights, and *Plot It Yourself*, aka *Murder in Style*, is arguably the best detective novel about plagiarism. In the course of a long life, Stout dined with Chesterton at the Savoy and corresponded with Ian Fleming after James Bond and M discussed Wolfe in *On Her Majesty's Secret Service*. Fleming's jokey suggestion that Bond and Wolfe should collaborate came to nothing, but another fan, René Magritte, named several artworks after Stout's novels.

26 *Nero Wolfe*: Introducing a reprint of *The Silent Speaker*, Walter Mosley argued that: 'Wolfe was lazy, agoraphobic, prejudiced against many different kinds of people (most notably women), and a glutton. He was arrogant, vengeful, spiteful, and sometimes cruel . . . But I always knew that he had high moral values and that people sitting before him could trust him if they themselves could be trusted . . . I learned from him . . . I learned that real heroes rarely exist, if indeed they ever do. I learned that life is not so much the struggle of good against evil as the struggle to survive.' As Art Scott has said to me in correspondence: 'Apart from the steady stream of novels & novellas . . . there were three Hollywood movies, a comic strip, two radio shows . . . two American TV series, and, as recently as 2012, a handsomely mounted eight-episode TV series made in Italy. I would argue that, of the Great Detectives, the Nero Wolfe "media franchise" has lasted as long as any, apart from Holmes, Poirot, Marple, and maybe Maigret.'

27 *Archie Goodwin*: Archie is, Walter Mosley says, 'the distilled optimism of

America as it was . . . His voice is the voice of all the hope and humor of a new world.'

28 *The Powwow Murder Case*: Van Dine apparently wrote a mere four pages of this story about witchcraft, but this did not deter his publishers from producing a mock-up with an excited blurb: 'The series of crimes which Philo Vance is called upon to solve is the most sinister and unusual in the whole repertory of the famous Philo Vance stories, but the solution, though startling, is wholly rational and logical.' The only known copy of this little curiosity sold at auction in 2020.

SIXTEEN

Superfluous Women

Queens of Crime

In 1929, Gordon Daviot achieved a writer's dream. The young Scottish novelist had dashed off a detective novel, *The Man in the Queue*, featuring a likeable Scotland Yard man called Alan Grant. Methuen were running a competition, offering £250 for the best detective novel submitted, and Daviot scooped the prize, as well as a publishing deal. In the United States, the book earned the Dutton Mystery Prize. What more could a newly published novelist wish for?

Complications arose when the American publishers wanted an author photo and biographical note. Daviot decided that there was nothing for it but to travel down from home in Inverness to London, and meet the publishers in person to confess the truth.

'The trip was worth it,' Daviot told a friend, 'if only to see the look on their faces.'

Nobody had guessed that Gordon Daviot was a woman, whose real name was Elizabeth MacKintosh.

MacKintosh had called herself Gordon Daviot because she shared the view of another female crime writer, Lucy Malleson, that 'there were still plenty of people who didn't believe in women as writers of crime stories'. One option was to choose a gender-neutral name. Malleson's first books were published as by J. Kilmeny Keith, and when Edith Caroline Rivett introduced Scotland Yard's Inspector Macdonald in her first detective novel, *The Murder on the Burrows*, she called herself E. C. R. Lorac.[1] Similarly, Margery Allingham published thrillers as Maxwell March, although her more serious crime writing appeared under her own name.

Lucy Malleson metamorphosed into Anthony Gilbert with *The Tragedy at Freyne* (1927), which introduced Scott Egerton, a young politician with a taste for amateur detection. Collins agreed to publish the novel, and asked for some promotional material, an interview, and a photograph. Unlike Elizabeth MacKintosh, Malleson decided to hide the truth. Gilbert, she wrote back, was 'a retiring sort of chap, whose hobbies were breeding Scotch terriers on the Sussex Downs and photographing ancient churches'. Because he was seldom in town, there was no interview, but the photograph presented a challenge which she met with the help of that stand-by of classic detective fiction, a disguise.

She made for the hairdressing department of the Army and Navy Stores, and ordered a wig ('not marcelled, of course, but luxuriant') and 'a good square beard'. Duly made over, she borrowed a Homburg hat, and took a taxi to a photographer: 'a peculiar figure, clad as to its upper portions in gentlemen's attire, but, in place of the anticipated trousers, a rather elongated kilt'. One of the pictures achieved the right effect: the 'apple-cheeked, smooth-skinned' young woman had transformed into a 'benevolent Germanic professor in tortoiseshell horners'.

Unfortunately, the publishers abandoned the idea of promoting an elderly man with a beard. On the principle of waste not, want not, Lucy Malleson kept the photograph on her mantelpiece. Collins made a mystery out of Anthony Gilbert's identity, prompting wild speculation, such as the claim that he was a well-known amateur aviator. For years, nobody knew that Anthony Gilbert was a woman. Even after the secret leaked out, novels continued to appear under that name for the rest of her life.[2]

Elizabeth MacKintosh, Lucy Malleson and Edith Rivett all belonged to that generation of women who saw so many of their male contemporaries killed during the First World War. They'd survived the slaughter only to be confronted by repeated challenges, not least being offensively labelled 'superfluous'. In writing detective stories they found fulfilment.

MacKintosh had abandoned her career as a PE teacher after the death of her mother, and stayed at home in Inverness to look after her father. Although the name of Gordon Daviot became famous as a result of her work as a playwright,[3] she remained in the north of Scotland for the rest of life, making occasional forays to London and the bright lights. It took her seven years to produce a second novel about Alan Grant. *A Shilling for Candles*[4] (1936) was published under the name Josephine Tey, to create a brand for her detective fiction separate from her work for the theatre.

Gladys Mitchell, another teacher who never married,[5] published her first detective novel in the same year as MacKintosh, but proved much more prolific. Excessive productivity results in books of variable quality, and even Mitchell's admirers admit that her work is uneven. At her best, she wrote such energetic and entertaining mysteries that Philip Larkin lauded her as 'the great Gladys'.

Few detectives make such a memorable entrance as Mrs Bradley in Mitchell's *Speedy Death* (1929). She is invited to a country-house party, and the corpse of a renowned explorer is promptly discovered in a bath. The deceased proves to have been a woman masquerading as a man. Melodrama is piled on melodrama as Mrs Bradley commits murder and is improbably defended at her trial by her son, an eminent barrister. The storyline offers an early example of a theme that came to obsess leading Golden Age writers: how can one ensure that right prevails in a society where applying the law strictly threatens to result in injustice?

Not content with one successful homicide, Mrs Bradley took the law into her own hands again in her fourth case, *The Saltmarsh Murders* (1932). The story, narrated by a naive curate, reads like a zany pastiche of *The Murder at the Vicarage*, published two years earlier. Saltmarsh proves to be a hotbed, not merely of adultery, intrigue and murder, but also of pornography, incest, 'sadism plus inverted nymphomania' and suspected infanticide. An appendix containing extracts from Mrs Bradley's notebook ends on a note of satisfaction: 'And I have committed my second murder.'

*

For many people, the post-war years were no 'Golden Age'. Detective fiction afforded writers as well as readers the chance of flight from reality. The pressures faced by young working women were illustrated by the experiences of Dorothy Leigh Sayers. She finished her first novel, nicknamed 'Lord Peter', only to be dismayed by the expense of having her manuscript typed: 'I expect he'll cost about £7, curse him!' Shortly after this, she asked her parents to help to keep her going until the following summer, 'then, if Lord Peter is still unsold I will chuck the whole thing, confess myself beaten, and take a permanent teaching job.'

She wasn't beaten. After joining an advertising agency, Benson's, where she coined the phrase 'it pays to advertise', she managed to publish her book, now called *Whose Body?* (1923). Emotional calamities wrecked her happiness. An affair with a fellow writer, John Cournos, came to an unhappy end, and a relationship on the rebound with a man who worked in the motor trade resulted in her becoming pregnant. Her lover abandoned her when she broke the news.

Under a pretext of ill health, she took herself off to a nursing home to give birth in secret, terrified lest her parents and her employers discover the truth. She arranged for her aunt and cousin, experienced foster parents, to look after her son, John Anthony. For the rest of her life she went to extraordinary lengths to conceal the truth about her illegitimate child.

Just as Agatha Christie[6] felt humiliated by her husband's infidelity, and the publicity surrounding her irrational flight to Harrogate in response to the collapse of her marriage, so Sayers felt an acute sense of shame about becoming an unmarried mother. She believed that she'd sinned, and never told her parents that they had a grandson.

Her hero, Lord Peter Wimsey, possessed wealth, charm and – most important of all to Sayers – a formidable brain. Sayers was an intellectual elitist and has often been accused of snobbery, although in addition to Lord Peter she also created a detective who was a bourgeois wine salesman and another who was a cleaning lady,[7] neither of whom made much impact. The truth is that readers on both sides of the Atlantic relished escapist fantasies featuring well-bred detectives.

At first, Wimsey was simply a Bright Young Sleuth with a top hat and a monocle in lieu of a deerstalker and pipe, but as Sayers' confidence as a novelist grew, she sought to transform him into a rounded character, and to write stories that integrated mystery with meaningful themes and literary polish.

She married a motoring correspondent from the *News of the World*, 'Mac' Fleming. The pair of them collaborated in a fruitless investigation of the mysterious death of Nurse May Daniels, whose decomposed body was found in a field near Boulogne; a hypodermic syringe and empty morphine box were found near the corpse. The mystery was never solved, but it supplied a plot detail for the third Wimsey novel. *Unnatural Death* (1927) is famous for an innovative (if controversial) method of murder: Sayers often seemed more interested in 'howdunit' than 'whodunit'.[8] Her attempts in the novel to portray both racism in English society and a manipulative lesbian relationship were flawed but ahead of their time; the book illustrates her growing ambition as a writer.

Her career in advertising provided background for *Murder Must Advertise* (1933), an early example of a detective novel set in a workplace other than a newspaper office. Having learned the importance of branding, she insisted on being known as 'Dorothy L. Sayers', with the all-important middle initial: 'The name as it stands on the title page . . . is part of the author's "publicity".'

Sayers realised that if the detective novel was to be humanised, to be something more than a mere puzzle, she had to abandon her doubts about the relevance of 'love interest' to the genre. In *Strong Poison* (1930), she introduced Harriet Vane, a strong and independent-minded detective novelist and something of a self-portrait. Wimsey falls for Harriet after she is accused of murdering her former lover, a fictionalised version of John Cournos. He saves her from the gallows with the help of undercover work by Miss Climpson and members of her detective agency, the Cattery, through whom Sayers mocks the absurd prejudice that such talented women were somehow 'superfluous' because they were unmarried. Today, the word 'spinster' is often seen as freighted with misogyny, but Sayers was among those pioneering women writers whose concern was not with niceties of terminology but the reality of female experience.

Wimsey continued his pursuit of Harriet,[9] although several years (and books) passed before she agreed to marry him; Sayers being Sayers, the proposal is accepted in Latin. The couple's protracted courtship was something new in detective fiction. Sherlock Holmes, Hercule Poirot, Jane Marple and John Rhode's irascible Dr Priestley never grew as characters, and their emotions seldom played a part in the story.[10]

Wimsey's development did not impress everyone (Agatha Christie described him as 'a good man spoiled'), but Sayers' focus on characters whose relationships evolve over time changed the shape of detective fiction. Today's crime series have something in common with television soap operas, with the ups and downs of the protagonists' personal lives, and the development of their characters and careers as integral to their appeal to readers as the mysteries they confront.

Sayers was a pioneering cartographer of detective fiction[11] and also a perceptive student of real-life crimes. She reviewed for *The Sunday Times*[12] with her characteristic blend of wit, erudition and blunt speaking. A leading light in the Detection Club, she became its President when E. C. Bentley's health failed, but her zest for writing fiction faded. Through Harriet Vane, she expressed her self-doubt: 'The books were all right, as far as they went; as intellectual exercises, they were even brilliant. But there was something lacking about them; they read now to her as though they had been written with a mental reservation, a determination to keep her own opinions and personality out of view.'

This passage comes from *Gaudy Night* (1935),[13] a book which lacks a murder,[14] although poison pen letters[15] disturb the scholarly calm of an all-female college in Oxford. Sayers told her publisher, Victor Gollancz, that it was her only novel embodying any kind of 'moral', in its emphasis on intellectual integrity, which she always regarded as a fundamental and permanent value in an emotionally unstable world. Yet she acknowledged that to make a detective story a vehicle for such a theme was 'reckless to the point of insanity'.

The gamble paid off. *Gaudy Night* has often been described as the first major feminist detective novel, not least by younger women who set out to follow in her footsteps.[16] Sayers didn't regard herself as a feminist, but her speech to a women's society titled 'Are Women Human?' is a characteristically powerful plea for equal treatment of women.

She cultivated a distinctive personal image: strong-minded, highly opinionated, increasingly eccentric.[17] The feminist academic and crime writer Carolyn G. Heilbrun argued[18] that Sayers' disdain of efforts of dress, cosmetics and hairdressing required both great courage and great talent. It also reflected a technique of misdirection as effective as Agatha Christie's. Nobody guessed at the sexual passions that had driven her in her younger days, or at the misery caused by the unhappiness of her relationships with men.

Like Josephine Tey, the New Zealander Ngaio Marsh created a sympathetic detective inspector from Scotland Yard, loved the theatre with a passion, never married and was fiercely protective of her personal privacy. Marsh and Tey were both Anglophiles, but they contemplated England from the perspective of outsiders. Their most compelling evocations of place[19] came when they captured the landscape of their home countries.

Marsh was a theatre director whose love of the stage is evident in much of her detective fiction. Pirandello's influence can be detected in *Death and the Dancing Footman* (1942), in which Jonathan Royal invites a group of people who hate each other to a country-house party; with the manor cut off from the outside world by snow, the suspense builds towards an inevitable tragedy.

Marsh's detective Roderick Alleyn was one of the suave, well-educated police inspectors to emerge during the 1930s.[20] Yet although Marsh remains one of the most popular writers of Golden Age fiction, natural reserve inhibited the full flowering of her literary talents. For her, 'tekkery' always came second to theatre work, and the strength of many of her novels lies in the characterisation, comedy and setting rather than in the murder investigation, with its relentless and sometimes wearisome interviewing of suspects.

Margery Allingham's family had a talent for storytelling; her father, Herbert, described it as 'our little fiction factory'. Albert Campion, who became her Great Detective, made his first appearance in 1929, taking a subordinate role in *The Crime at Black Dudley*, a country-house mystery. The principal amateur sleuth was a pathologist called George Abbershaw. If Allingham had persisted with Abbershaw, she might have become an exponent of forensic detective work, but he was too colourless a character, and she was no Austin Freeman.

Her husband was a young artist called Philip Youngman Carter, and to an extent *The Crime at Black Dudley* was a collaborative effort, begun just two months after their wedding. He encouraged her, and contributed ideas. They continued to work together, and inscribed some of the early books to family and friends from 'the clever authors', but in their essentials, the novels were Allingham's.

Campion, originally conceived as a minor criminal from the upper classes,[21] seemed like a 'silly ass' in the mould of Bertie Wooster. Like Lord Peter Wimsey, he transformed as his creator gained in confidence and strove to develop him into a rounded individual.

The Fashion in Shrouds (1938) prompted the *Observer*'s influential detective fiction critic 'Torquemada' to rhapsodise: 'To Albert Campion has fallen the honour of being the first detective to figure in a story which is also a distinguished novel.' Today, this seems like over-praise, and it is significant that when the book was republished in 1965, its length was cut. But Allingham's determination to avoid the constraints of literary formula won her distinguished admirers.

A. S. Byatt, for instance, has said[22] that: 'Allingham can do both good and evil convincingly. But her nature is generous – her readers must understand as well as shudder at these truly nasty persons. Her own inventive energy, her own curiosity, her pace, are incomparable. I have often thought that Iris Murdoch learned from her to make up odd worlds with their own laws that relate to the real world half in a fairytale way. She turned puzzles into true drama, but with a conscious artificer's grace.'

Allingham, like Sayers, was bedevilled by personal difficulties. The carefree mood of the early days of marriage didn't last. 'Pip' proved an erratic husband, although their marriage continued, and after her death he completed her final novel and wrote another about Campion. She experienced severe mood swings, and it seems that for much of her life she suffered from a thyroid deficiency and from a failure to diagnose bipolar disorder that was compounded by the adverse effects of electro-convulsive therapy.

Josephine Tey also suffered from depression and deteriorating physical health. She told a newspaper interviewer that, in comparison to historical plays, writing a thriller was 'like a piece of knitting; it's my way of relaxing'. But she took her crime writing seriously, and also compared it to crafting a sonnet. Her output was modest, but of high calibre.

Her series police officer Alan Grant plays a subsidiary role in *The Franchise Affair* (1948). The lead is taken by a solicitor, Robert Blair, engaged to defend Marion Sharpe and her mother on a charge of abducting a girl called Betty Kane. The germ of the story came from an eighteenth-century case concerning the supposed kidnapping of Elizabeth Canning,[23] which Tey refashioned into an intriguing novel of psychological suspense.[24]

Grant's most famous case, *The Daughter of Time* (1951), typifies Tey's unorthodoxy as a detective novelist. The Scotland Yard man, laid up in hospital with a broken leg, believes that he can recognise a criminal when he sees one. When he considers a picture of Richard III, he refuses to accept the conventional view that the hunchback monarch was a child killer. Grant's conclusions may not be wholly original, but that is beside the point. The story is a classic of armchair (or hospital bed) detection.[25]

Brat Farrar (1949)[26] was a stand-alone mystery about an apparent imposter, influenced by the story of the Tichborne Claimant. As Val McDermid has pointed out,[27] questions of identity permeate Tey's novels: 'it is that fascination with who we really are and what actually shapes our relationships that is the key to Tey's role as the bridge between the golden age and contemporary crime fiction . . . Tey was never vulgar nor titillating; she left space for the reader to forge their own understanding of what was underpinning her characters' behaviour.'

When Tey's father died at the age of eighty-seven, she was at last free to pursue her own interests, but it was too late. She was thrilled when Sayers invited her to join the Detection Club, replying:[28] 'I have an odd feeling that your charming and unexpected letter has altered the foundations of my life.' Before it could, cancer took hold of her, and she died prior to becoming a member. Her eighth and final detective novel, *The Singing Sands*, was published posthumously in 1952.

Men dominated British crime fiction for the first three decades of the twentieth century. From then on, Christie, Sayers, Allingham and Marsh took centre stage. Even the most gifted male contemporaries – the likes of Nicholas Blake (a pen-name of the poet Cecil Day-Lewis) and Michael Innes – never quite matched their sales or reputations.

Many leading members of the Detection Club were female, including Clemence Dane, who was primarily a playwright, and the Australian Helen Simpson. They collaborated on three novels, the first of which was filmed by Hitchcock,[29] before going their separate ways. Other women to make a mark ranged from the prolific Patricia Wentworth to Mary Agnes Hamilton and Ellen Wilkinson[30] ('Red Ellen'), two Labour MPs who each published a mystery set in the House of Commons.

Georgette Heyer, although mainly a purveyor of historical romance, produced a dozen crime novels. She subcontracted the plotting to her husband, although Sayers was probably unaware of that when she damned *The Unfinished Clue*[31] (1934) with faint praise, saying that 'good writing would often carry a poor plot.'

Rebecca West was puzzled by 'this curious flight that so many intelligent women make into detective writing'.[32] A feminist such as West might have realised that gifted women relished the chance to establish themselves in a vibrant field of popular culture. In an era when female civil servants or teachers who married were required to give up their jobs, crime writing was an eminently suitable occupation for so-called 'superfluous women'. The preeminent figures in British detective fiction were no longer male; they were the 'Queens of Crime'.[33]

Notes

The main sources are the biographies of Tey by Jennifer Morag Henderson, Sayers by Barbara Reynolds, James Brabazon and Ralph E. Hone, Marsh by Margaret Lewis and Joanne Drayton, and Allingham by Julia Jones; Lucy

Malleson's autobiography *Three-a-Penny*; and Gladys Mitchell's website, run by Jason Half. The essays by Heilbrun, Hart, and Gilbert mentioned below appear in *Dorothy L. Sayers: The Centenary Celebration*, ed. Alzina Stone Dale.

1 *Lorac*: More than forty years later, H. R. F. Keating wrote in *Murder Must Appetize* of his shock on eventually learning that Lorac was a woman. She wrote another long series under the name Carol Carnac. 'Carol' is 'Lorac' spelled backwards.

2 *novels continued to appear under that name for the rest of her life*: Anthony Gilbert's final book, *A Nice Little Killing*, appeared in 1973, the year she died. Like almost all the other Gilbert books, it formed part of a long series featuring solicitor Arthur Crook. *The Woman in Red*, a 'woman in jeopardy' mystery, became a gripping film noir, *My Name is Julia Ross*, with Crook cut out. The film was loosely remade as *Dead of Winter*.

3 *her work as a playwright*: *Richard of Bordeaux*, a success for John Gielgud as director and actor in 1933. In *The Daughter of Time*, Alan Grant says that he saw the play four times. Nicola Upson's first novel featuring Tey, *An Expert in Murder*, takes its title from a phrase in the script. Upson's series reinvents Tey as an amateur detective.

4 *A Shilling for Candles*: Filmed by Hitchcock as *Young and Innocent*, with an unrecognisable storyline. Nicola Upson's *Fear in the Sunlight* imagines an encounter between Hitchcock and Josephine Tey at Portmeirion in Wales, but the pair never met in real life.

5 *Gladys Mitchell, another teacher who never married*: Mitchell's life companion, Winifred Blazey, occasionally dabbled in detective fiction.

6 *Agatha Christie*: At the start of her career, Christie contemplated calling herself 'Martin West' or 'Mostyn Grey'. After her divorce, she wanted to revert to her maiden name, but Collins persuaded her that this would cause a damaging loss of name recognition.

7 *a bourgeois wine salesman and . . . a cleaning lady*: Montague Egg and Jane Eurydice Judkin, both of whom were confined to short stories; the latter only appears in 'The Case of the Travelling Rug', which was published posthumously.

8 *Sayers often seemed more interested in 'howdunit' than 'whodunit'*: Sometimes the m.o. was over-elaborate. As Raymond Chandler said in 'The Simple Art of Murder' of the method in Sayers' final novel, *Busman's Honeymoon*: 'a murderer who needs that much help from Providence must be in the wrong business.'

9 *Wimsey continued his pursuit of Harriet*: It is striking that, in an age when sex discrimination was rife in the real world, fictional male detectives often met and married strong women with successful careers. Marsh's Roderick Alleyn was married to Agatha Troy, a painter; Campion's wife, Amanda Fitton, was an engineer; Nicholas Blake's Nigel Strangeways married an explorer, and after her death has a relationship with a sculptor.

10 *their emotions seldom played a part in the story*: However, Jane Marple shows genuine anger at the cruel murder of a housemaid in the closing lines of *A Pocket Full of Rye*.

11 *a pioneering cartographer of detective fiction*: Her long introduction to the first anthology she edited for Gollancz was, at the time, the most important study of the genre.

12 *She reviewed for The Sunday Times*: The reviews are collected in *Taking Detective Stories Seriously*.

13 *Gaudy Night*: Few detective novels divide critical opinion so sharply. P. D. James rated the book as 'one of the most successful marriages of the puzzle with the novel of social realism and serious purpose'. However, Q. D. Leavis was patronising: Sayers 'performed the function of giving the impression of intellectual exercise to readers who would very much dislike that kind of exercise if it was actually presented to them'. The novelist and critic Jessica Mann offered a trenchant rebuttal of Leavisite snobbery in *Deadlier than the Male*: 'generations of schoolgirls have been inspired to try for a place at one of the Oxford or Cambridge women's colleges because of reading *Gaudy Night* . . . one such, myself, is unchanged in her admiration for the book.' As an archaeology student at Cambridge, Mann was taught by Glyn Daniel, himself the author of two detective novels.

14 *lacks a murder*: As do James M. Cain's *Mildred Pierce* and Tey's *The Franchise Affair*, not to mention those (mostly) anticlimactic books where a presumed murder proves to be suicide.

15 *poison pen letters*: Postmen in Golden Age fiction were constantly delivering anonymous and abusive correspondence to luckless English villagers. Writers may have been inspired by a real-life case involving a miscarriage of justice, explored by Christopher Hilliard in *The Littlehampton Libels*. An early poison-pen story is Herbert Jenkins' 'The Gylston Slander'; others include Ethel Lina White's *Fear Stalks the Village*, Edmund Crispin's *The Long Divorce*, John Dickson Carr's *Night at the Mocking Widow*, and *The Voice of the Corpse* by Max Murray, a neglected writer who was actually born in the Australian bush. The trope is used inventively in *The Crimson Madness of Little Doom* by the underrated Mark McShane and in Charles Palliser's *Rustication*. Stereotypically the letter writer is a sexually frustrated spinster, but readers' expectations are often subverted, as in Agatha Christie's *The Moving Finger*.

16 *younger women who set out to follow in her footsteps*: The Americans Carolyn G. Heilbrun and Carolyn G. Hart were among them. In her essay 'Gaudy Night', Hart, author of a long series set at a mystery bookstore, credited Sayers with inspiring not only Heilbrun but others such as Nancy Pickard and Sharyn McCrumb.

17 *a distinctive personal image . . . increasingly eccentric*: Michael Gilbert's essay 'A Personal Memoir' recounts examples, recalling Sayers' enthusiasm for wearing men's clothing, including a man's hat and a rugby shirt, as well as her taste for using coarse language. He also quotes James Brabazon's insightful comment: 'she never made a fool of herself except in her own, particular, calculating way.'

18 *Carolyn G. Heilbrun argued*: In her essay 'Biography between the Lines'.

19 *Their most compelling evocations of place*: For instance, in Tey's *The Singing Sands*, and Marsh's *Died in the Wool*. No fewer than four of Roderick Alleyn's cases take place in New Zealand: unusual for a Scotland Yard man.

20 *one of the suave, well-educated police inspectors to emerge during the 1930s*: Others included E. R. Punshon's Oxford graduate Bobby Owen, who starts as a police constable, but climbs the ladder rapidly, and Michael Innes' John Appleby, whose career is so distinguished that he earns a knighthood.

21 *Campion, originally conceived as a minor criminal from the upper classes*:

Allingham liked to tease friends and readers about his true identity. His real name was supposed to be Rudolph, and she hinted that he had royal blood.

22 *A. S. Byatt, for instance, has said*: A. S. Byatt, 'Why I Love Margery Allingham', *Daily Telegraph,* 8 December 2007. Introducing a Folio Society edition of *Traitor's Purse*, which she described as 'a wartime masterpiece', she noted that after John le Carré took part in a joint interview with Allingham, he sent a cable to the reporter saying: ALLINGHAM MARVELLOUS BUT GREATLY REPEAT GREATLY UNDERPLAYS HERSELF. J. K. Rowling has named Allingham as her favourite of the Queens of Crime and *The Tiger in the Smoke* as her favourite detective novel.

23 *the supposed kidnapping of Elizabeth Canning*: Tey had read *Elizabeth is Missing*, an account of the case by Lillian de la Torre.

24 *Tey refashioned into an intriguing novel of psychological suspense*: In 'The Lost Girl', *The Guardian,* 29 May 2009, Sarah Waters argues that Tey 'adapted the Canning story to meet the conservative middle-class concerns of the time' and that *The Franchise Affair* was closely informed 'by the specific moral panics . . . of post-war life'; Tey's novel was an influence on Waters' very different novel, *The Little Stranger*, just as the Canning case influenced Tey.

25 *The story is a classic of armchair (or hospital bed) detection*: A Most Contagious Game by Catherine Aird is in part a homage to Tey's book.

26 *Brat Farrar*: Improbably, the book formed the basis for Jimmy Sangster's lurid screenplay, with a gaslighting storyline, for the Hammer horror movie *Paranoiac*. Tey didn't have a screen credit, and probably wouldn't have wanted one.

27 *As Val McDermid has pointed out*: In the *Daily Telegraph* on 15 November 2014.

28 *She was thrilled . . . replying*: On 19 March 1949.

29 *the first of which was filmed by Hitchcock*: *Enter Sir John* became *Murder!* Actor-manager Sir John Saumarez takes up the cause of Martella Baring when she is tried for murder. This scenario probably inspired Lord Peter Wimsey's attempt to clear the similarly accused Harriet Vane. Helen de Guerry Simpson, a close friend of Sayers, enjoyed literary acclaim until cancer cut her life short.

30 *Mary Agnes Hamilton and Ellen Wilkinson*: Both women lost their seats in 1931, victims of a Conservative landslide, although Wilkinson gained re-election and became a minister. Hamilton became a civil servant and broadcaster.

31 *Sayers was probably unaware of that when she damned The Unfinished Clue*: In *The Sunday Times* on 1 April 1934.

32 *Rebecca West was puzzled by 'this curious flight that so many intelligent women make into detective writing'*: She made this comment during a BBC radio interview with Jessica Mann, who recorded it in *Deadlier Than the Male*.

33 *the 'Queens of Crime'*: This term, still widely used, encompassed Christie, Sayers, Marsh, Allingham, and sometimes Tey, occasionally Mitchell. It may have been coined by the critic for the *Observer*, Maurice Richardson. In May 1937 he used the phrase to describe Christie, Sayers and (with tongue in cheek) Ellery Queen.

SEVENTEEN

Challenging the Reader

Detection and game-playing

'I'm planning a big advertising stunt,' the young journalist remarked casually to a colleague at the *Daily Mail*. 'I need some money to start things moving.'

Wareham, the colleague, kept a tight grip on the purse strings, but was in a benevolent mood. 'How much do you want?'

'About a thousand pounds.' In other words, ten times the annual wage for an ordinary working man.

'All right,' Wareham said breezily. 'We'll fix that up.'

Securing the cash had proved easier than even the journalist, a born optimist, had dared to hope. Thirty years old, he was married with a young child, and perennially short of cash. The bailiff's shadow loomed over his little house in Notting Hill, but now Edgar Wallace had come up with a scheme to make his fortune.

He loved writing and his imagination fizzed constantly. Already he'd turned out a handful of stories, as well as a play called *An African Millionaire* (1904), which ran for only six nights. The way forward was to write a bestselling novel, a thriller with a difference. He'd whip up public excitement by offering big prizes for solving his mystery.

He came up with an 'impossible crime' puzzle about the assassination of the Foreign Secretary by a quartet of exotic foreigners, but the editors he approached showed little interest. Undaunted, he came up with the same solution as so many present-day writers frustrated by the publishing industry's lack of enthusiasm for their gems. He would self-publish.

Never a man to do anything by halves, he rented a room in Temple Chambers, which became the official address of the Tallis Press, sole proprietor Edgar Wallace. He was willing to face up to the unpalatable truth that it isn't enough to write a good book; it needs to be effectively marketed, and this requires the investment of time and money. He told his wife Ivy that he was 'most anxious to get on with the advertising part of it . . . really the most important part.'

His ambitious promotional campaign showed what was possible before the era of Facebook, Twitter and the blogosphere. *The Four Just Men* (1905) was advertised on hoardings and in shop windows all over London, in newspapers and in theatres. He posted a copy to the prominent politician Joseph Chamberlain, urging him – in vain – to mention the story in a speech. The book was bound with a detachable competition form in the back page, and included an appendix describing Wallace's literary style as placing him 'in the forefront of living impressionistic writers'. He dreamed of establishing book agencies in all the principal towns, and tried in vain to secure investment from Alfred Harmsworth, owner of the *Daily Mail*. Early reviews were good, but solutions to the puzzle started pouring in, and Wallace realised he hadn't stipulated a limit on the number of potential winners.

He couldn't afford to pay up. When he delayed announcing the competition winners, disgruntled readers flooded the *Daily Mail*, the novel's principal cheerleader, with letters of complaint. Fearing bankruptcy, Wallace begged Harmsworth for help. Desperate to avoid the *Mail*, never mind his star reporter, being ruined by the scandal, the newspaper baron wired him a thousand pounds, to be deducted in monthly instalments from his salary. Edgar Wallace lived to write another day.

From its unhappy beginnings to its premature end at the height of his fame,[1] the life of Edgar Wallace unfolded with as many

unexpected twists as his most outlandish thrillers. He was illegitimate, the product of a brief fling between a merchant navy
captain's wife and an actor who was about to marry someone else.
The naval captain died while his wife was pregnant; following the
birth, she arranged for her baby to be cared for by the family of
a fishmonger called Freeman. Growing up, he was known as
Richard Horatio Edgar Freeman. He felt his mother had abandoned
him, and never forgave her.

After leaving school at twelve, he was sacked from working on
a milk round for stealing from his employer and became a plas-
terer's assistant. He enlisted in the army under the name Wallace,
taken in tribute to the author of *Ben-Hur*, but military life didn't
suit him, so he bought himself out. Writing, he thought, offered a
route to fame and fortune. At a banquet in Cape Town, he met
Rudyard Kipling, who said: 'For God's sake, don't take to literature
as a profession. Literature is a splendid mistress, but a bad wife.'
Wallace was undaunted.

The debacle of *The Four Just Men* did nothing to dent his
self-confidence. The Just Men returned in five later books, suffering
the traditional fate of series villains; they grew ever closer to the
forces of law and order. Their intelligence work during the war
earned them a pardon from a grateful government, and eventually
one of their number, George Manfred, ran the Triangle Detective
Agency in Curzon Street.

Wallace took to dictating his stories on to wax cylinders for his
secretary to type up, a method that boosted his productivity[2] and
gave his writing a characteristic immediacy. He wrote a play called
The Terror (1927) in the space of 'five nervous and preoccupied days'; it enjoyed a lucrative seven-month run at the
Lyceum, and was adapted into Warner Brothers' second 'all-talking
picture' before Wallace turned it into a novel. His plays usually
enjoyed huge popular if not critical success; in 1928, three of them
were running in the West End at the same time.

The public appetite for Wallace's stories was insatiable, and his
publishers claimed that he wrote one in four of all novels read in
Britain. Perhaps his most attractive series character was the
mild-mannered John G. Reeder, who worked in the office of the
Public Prosecutor, and claimed to have 'a criminal mind'. Wallace's

other detectives included a policeman called Elk, solved mysteries such as *The Fellowship of the Frog*[3] (1925).

G. K. Chesterton expressed his bewilderment[4] that a reissue of *Trent's Last Case*, which carried on its back cover encomia from Christie, Sayers, Austin Freeman and Crofts, carried on the *front* cover a quote from Edgar Wallace: 'Evidently, it is his compliment alone that really counts.' Chesterton damned Wallace's fiction with faint praise: 'To despise such stories is of all things the most despicable. It is like despising pantomimes or public-houses or comic songs.' Giving pride of place to Wallace was 'vulgar . . . connected with mere size or noise or notoriety or mass-production.' Then, as now, it wasn't easy to disentangle legitimate reservations about the literary merit of a bestselling author – whether Edgar Wallace or Dan Brown – from snobbery and jealousy.

Occasionally there was more to Wallace's writing than met the eye. *The Four Just Men* remains interesting as an example of a murder mystery with a plot driven by social and political imperatives. Sir Philip Ramon, courageous but seen as representing a 'corrupt and vengeful government', is targeted for assassination because he is determined to clamp down on immigration, including those who find in England 'an asylum from the persecution of despots and tyrants'. But the main significance of *The Four Just Men* lay in Wallace's demonstration that detective fans wanted to solve the puzzle themselves.

Wallace was an ideas man, frequently ahead of his time. During the Golden Age, the detective story became a battle of wits between reader and author. 'The detective fan . . . who knows all the tricks and all the devices is like a hound on the scent, and a writer has to be a veritable fox to escape his guesswork,' claimed the American writer Gelett Burgess, who compared[5] the construction of a mystery to 'the Art of Warfare, with the Reader as the Enemy'.

Competitions were popular[6] and took increasingly ingenious forms. In 1930, Agatha Christie was hired to devise a detective puzzle in the form of a treasure hunt to help promote tourism to the Isle of Man. 'Manx Gold' was published in five instalments in the Manchester *Daily Dispatch* and as a pamphlet, 'June in

Douglas', which was distributed around the island. The 'treasure' took the form of four snuff boxes hidden in various Manx locations.

Perhaps the most fiendish competition was devised by Edward Powys Mathers, who compiled crosswords for the *Observer* under the appropriate name 'Torquemada'. He was also a leading detective fiction critic and, in *The Torquemada Puzzle Book* (1934), his interests coalesced. The first part of the book, dedicated to E. C. Bentley, was 'a miscellany of original crosswords, acrostics, anagrams, verbal pastimes and problems'. The second part, dedicated to Dorothy L. Sayers, was *Cain's Jawbone*, a detective story one hundred pages long. The pages were printed in a random order and a prize was offered for anyone who could deduce the correct sequence. The eccentric style of storytelling meant that working out the mystery was a Herculean task. Only two people solved it.

The challenge that detective writers posed to readers became explicit when Ronald Knox, co-editor of *The Best Detective Stories of the Year 1928* (1929), offered people a chance to exercise their ingenuity: 'I shall give in each case a "cue", the last few words of a sentence; on reaching those words let the reader switch his eyes off the page at once, for fear of finding out too much before he attempts the solution for himself.'

Ellery Queen became the leading exponent of the formal challenge to the reader.[7] The third Queen book, *The Dutch Shoe Mystery* (1931), includes a fourteen-page chapter, 'Interlude', printed with wider margins 'for the use of the reader in jotting down his personal notes about the solution'. In an anthology called *Challenge to the Reader* (1938), Queen changed the names of the authors and detectives of the twenty-five chosen stories. The drawback was that readers unfamiliar with the authors in question had no chance of deducing who wrote what.

The corollary of the challenge to the reader was the cluefinder,[8] setting out at the end of the book the clues to the solution in the text; this disciplined writers into playing fair. The first book to include a cluefinder seems to be J. J. Connington's *The Eye in the Museum* (1929). The idea was quickly borrowed by others, including Freeman Wills Crofts, John Dickson Carr, Elspeth Huxley[9] and Rupert Penny.[10]

C. Daly King adopted a high moral tone in *Obelists at Sea* (1932), instructing readers not to consult the cluefinder before finishing the whole story: 'Personable readers, even though they cheat at solitaire, never cheat at this.' King presented the ultimate cluefinder in *Obelists Fly High* (1935). No fewer than thirty-eight clues were identified, and categorised as to the murderer's relations with the victim, his motive, his ingenuity, his anxieties, the time of death and the detective's mistake. As if this were not enough, King supplied three diagrams as well as a list of characters; he also began the story with an epilogue[11] and ended it with a prologue.

Visual clues[12] adorned *Murder in Black and White* (1931) by Evelyn Elder, a pen-name of Milward Kennedy. The artist Austin Blomfield drew half a dozen pictures, presented as pages from the sketch-book of Sam Horder, which illuminated the mystery of a shooting at a French chateau. Across the Atlantic, this concept was refined by the husband-and-wife duo Willetta Ann Barber and R. F. Schabelitz in *Murder Draws a Line* (1940); no fewer than forty sketches indicate artist-detective Christopher Storm's view of the evidence. Five more books featuring 'Kit' Storm and artistic clueing were published. Schabelitz, a professional book illustrator, provided the images, while Barber, formerly his model, wrote the stories.

Two linked novels published by America's most eccentric crime writer, Harry Stephen Keeler,[13] typified his surreal methods of Dalí-ing with detection. *The Marceau Case* and *X. Jones – of Scotland Yard*, both published in 1936, dealt with investigations of a single impossible murder. The books reproduced letters, cable-grams, cartoons, diagrams and photographs, one of which featured Keeler himself.

Van Wyck Mason's *The Castle Island Case* (1937), investigated by Major Roger Allenby, purported to be 'a sensational NEW kind of detective story which departs radically from the time-worn molds . . . for the first time the candid camera has collaborated with the author to produce, through pictures which are an integral part of the text,[14] the story of a dramatic murder in Bermuda.' One photo-graph depicted a naked female corpse spread out on the sand, a form of candour expurgated from the second edition. The book was meant to kick-start a series of 'Candid Clue Mysteries', but

Mason wrote no more of them. *LOOK* magazine subsequently hailed *Photocrime* as yet another supposedly 'new type of detective fiction'. The reader competed against 'the masterful Hannibal Cobb' in the race to solve puzzles posed in pictures and text.[15]

Ingenious detective plots were complemented by imaginative forms of publishing. In Walter Eberhardt's *The Jig-Saw Puzzle Murder* (1933), the victim plays a game with jigsaw pieces in his New York apartment, in the presence of five people who wish him dead before the inevitable happens. The book was supplied with two hundred jigsaw pieces; put together, they unmasked the culprit.

Harrap adapted mysteries by authors as different as J. S. Fletcher and Erle Stanley Gardner into jigsaw puzzles. The hardback novel was sold together with jigsaw pieces in a box attached to the inside back cover; the completed puzzle gave the solution in visual form. Although the series was soon discontinued, jigsaw puzzle murder mysteries[16] (usually written to order) remain popular to this day.

The Baffle Book (1928), according to its authors Lassiter Wren and Randle McKay, 'grew out of a game . . . to amuse studio gatherings in New York'. The book contained twenty-eight mystery puzzles,[17] illustrated by diagrams and charts, and including solutions, a score sheet and guidelines on 'How to give a Baffle Party'. The British edition was edited by F. Tennyson Jesse. She admitted that a puzzle book had to dispense with 'the finer points of detection – those based on knowledge of character', but praised the authors for playing fair, and recommended the pleasures of the Baffle Party.

Wren and McKay produced two more Baffle Books, as well as *The Mystery Puzzle Book* (1933), boasting '45 illustrations of documents, diagrams, and clues'. S. S. Van Dine contributed a foreword that captured the puzzles' timely appeal, saying the book helped him to forget for a time 'the present great epochal world change which we euphemistically call a "depression"'.

Evelyn Johnson and Gretta Palmer produced *Murder: Thirty-Two Thrilling Crimes* (1928; the UK edition (1929) included one puzzle fewer and added *'and Mystery'* to the title). The publishers boasted that 'the insipid and irritating love-interest that is an integral part of the conventional detective story, has in all cases been omitted', but dropped a broad hint about the literary limitations of this type of book, saying: 'Short of having the stories read like excerpts from a dry-goods catalog, we have presented our cases as tersely as possible.' The unique selling point of J. C. Cannell's *100 Mysteries for Arm-Chair Detectives* (1932) was that most of them were supposed to be 'based on actual crimes and mysteries investigated at Scotland Yard'.

In 1937, under the name Tally Mason, the versatile writer August Derleth[18] published *Consider Your Verdict*. Witness testimony in ten coroner's cases was presented, giving readers a chance to solve the mystery before opening a sealed section in which the coroner pinpointed the culprit through rigorous examination of the evidence. 'Can you tell a lie as quickly as Dr Webster?' the jacket copy demanded. 'Might be developed into a game,' suggested *Kirkus Reviews*.

Detective games flourished[19] throughout the 1930s. Collins Crime Club produced a spin-off card game devised by the thriller writer Peter Cheyney.[20] The cards featured characters ranging from Hercule Poirot to the now-forgotten Janet Murch, from Philip MacDonald's *The Nursemaid Who Disappeared*.[21] Cheyney, like Wallace, was a skilled self-publicist, and his likeness appeared on a card gummed to the inside of the box.

Murder mystery and interactive games combined in the first Crime Dossier written by Dennis Wheatley and planned by J. G. Links. *Murder off Miami* (1936), known in the US as *File on Bolitho Blane*, was presented by the authors as the start of a 'new era in crime fiction': 'Cablegrams, original handwritten documents, photographs, police records, criminal records, and even actual clues in the form of human hair, a piece of blood-stained curtain etc., are all contained in this folder . . . forming the complete Dossier of a crime.' A sealed section at the back of the folder contained the solution, and a note on the back cover proclaimed:

Keep this carefully

It is a First Edition of the first Crime Story ever presented
in this way. Should others follow, it is possible that an
undamaged copy of 'Murder off Miami' may be
of considerable interest one day.

Wheatley was another smart salesman. *Murder off Miami* sold over 100,000 copies[22], and had three successors before rising production costs and the advent of war put paid to the series. In the US, dossiers in the same format were called Crimefiles; as well as the first Wheatley–Links collaboration, the series included stories by detective novelists such as Helen Reilly[23] and Q. Patrick.

The craze for Crime Dossiers[24] was short-lived. Far from launching a new era, they seemed to represent a cul-de-sac, as Julian Symons indicated in an austere obituary for Golden Age game-playing: 'To insulate your writing totally from life is also to make it trivial . . . The Golden Age . . . was a minor road full of interesting twists and views which petered out in a dead end.' Like most critics,[25] he underestimated the flexibility and potential of Golden Age tropes and traditions. Reports of the death of the game-playing puzzle mystery proved to be greatly exaggerated.

Notes

The main sources are the biographies of Wallace by Margaret Lane and Neil Clark.

1 *its premature end at the height of his fame*: He was hired to work on the script of RKO's 'gorilla picture', better known as *King Kong*, in December 1931, but died shortly afterwards, aged fifty-six. The flags of Fleet Street flew at half-mast, and the bells of St Bride's tolled in mourning. Characteristically, he left an estate mired in debt; equally typical, the debts were paid thanks to a continuing inflow of royalties.
2 *a method that boosted his productivity*: Neil Clark says that Wallace wrote 170 books, twenty-three plays, sixty-five sketches and almost a thousand short stories, but the precise numbers are, despite the assiduous work of his bibliographers W. O. G. Lofts and Derek Adley, anyone's guess.
3 *The Fellowship of the Frog*: This lively piece of nonsense about a master criminal in a frog mask was adapted for the stage by Ian Hay. Film versions were made in the US, Britain and (like many Wallace stories) Germany.
4 *G. K. Chesterton expressed his bewilderment*: In the *Illustrated London News* on 25 October 1930.
5 *Gelett Burgess, who compared*: In 'Strategy of the Mystery Story', possibly unpublished; the manuscript of the article was sold at auction in 2020. Burgess developed the warfare analogy in suitably ingenious fashion.
6 *Competitions were popular*: Especially with newspapers that serialised mysteries. In 1907, the *Daily Mirror* offered £10 to the reader 'who most satisfactorily solves the mystery of the death of Lord Queste' in *The Love That Kills* by the husband-and-wife duo Coralie Stanton and Heath Hosken.

In 1926, the same newspaper offered prizes totalling £500 to those who solved the puzzle in *The Wintringham Mystery*, later published as *Cicely Disappears*, under the name A. Monmouth Platts, another pen-name of Anthony Berkeley Cox. Mystery competitions have continued to appear ever since. In 1956, The *Australian Women's Weekly* published two instalments of *Murder of Olympia* and invited readers to write, in up to 400 words, how they would finish the story; the winner received two tickets to the Melbourne Olympics. The author was Margot Neville (a name used by two sisters, Margot Goyder and Anne Neville Goyder Joske).

7   *the leading exponent of the formal challenge to the reader*: British writers who used the device included Anthony Berkeley and Rupert Penny.

8   *the cluefinder*: Twenty-first-century cluefinders appear in Martin Edwards' *Mortmain Hall* and *Blackstone Fell*. In 1973, a note on the dust-jacket blurb of Kingsley Amis's homage to the Golden Age, *The Riverside Villas Murder*, said: 'Those who may wish to pit their wits against the author's and solve the mystery for themselves are advised to study pages 61, 82 and 160.' Amis's *The Crime of the Century* was a 'summer holiday' competition mystery serialised in *The Sunday Times* over six weeks. When published as a book, it included the winning entry as well as Amis's solution.

9   *Elspeth Huxley*: Her detective novels were set in colonial Africa, as is her memoir *The Flame Trees of Thika*. Her cousin Aldous wrote one famous short crime story, 'The Gioconda Smile'.

10 *Rupert Penny*: Penny's real name was Ernest Basil Charles Thornett. *The Talkative Policeman* introduced a Scotland Yard man whose Watson was a stockbroker. As Penny admitted in his preface, the cerebral detective story was falling out of fashion by 1936, but he produced seven more ingenious whodunits crammed with maps, floor plans, sealed rooms and ciphers, plus one thriller, before devoting his talents to cryptography at Bletchley Park and later at GCHQ.

11 *King . . . began the story with an epilogue*: Philip MacDonald employed a similar device in *Rynox*, aka *The Rynox Mystery*; the novel opens with an unexpected delivery of a fortune in banknotes before describing the events leading up to it.

12 *Visual clues*: The music critic Eric Blom included plot information in the form of musical notation in his epistolary mystery *Death on the Down Beat*, published as by Sebastian Farr.

13 *Harry Stephen Keeler*: See *A to Izzard: A Harry Stephen Keeler Companion*, edited by Fender Tucker. In Keeler's younger days, his mother confined him to an asylum. He enjoyed a brief vogue with his labyrinthine 'webwork' stories, which sometimes wove in short stories written by his wife Hazel Goodwin. Inscribing *The Box from Japan* in 1932, he claimed that, at 360,000 words, it was the longest mystery novel ever published, adding wryly 'and probably no living person has ever read it through'. The storylines became increasingly outlandish; among the questions posed by *The Case of the Transposed Legs*, co-authored by Hazel, were: 'Why did the killer of banker Nils Pederson chop off his legs and sew them back on with silver wire in transposed position?' and 'How was a book on cats the key to escape from a great prison?'

14 *pictures which are an integral part of the text*: Among those posing as a character in a photograph was C. Daly King. Francis Van Wyck Mason was

a historian and popular novelist; his book was revised in 1960 as *The Multi-Million-Dollar Murders*.

15 *puzzles posed in pictures and text*: The main writer was Austin 'Rip' Ripley, whose solve-it-yourself 'minute mysteries' or 'Detectograms' were widely syndicated in the US, and also collected in book form as *How Good a Detective Are You?*

16 *jigsaw puzzle murder mysteries*: In 1949, Clayton Rawson's 'Pictures Don't Lie' combined a mystery in a pamphlet with a photographic clue in jigsaw form. Twenty-first-century versions of this concept are often tied in to television series, such as *Death in Paradise*, created by Robert Thorogood, and often feature Golden Age tropes.

17 *The book contained twenty-eight mystery puzzles*: 'The Sandy Peninsula Footprint Mystery' contains a plot device similar to that in John Dickson Carr's *The White Priory Murders*.

18 *August Derleth*: Derleth was H. P. Lovecraft's first publisher and himself a prolific author whose Solar Pons pastiches of Sherlock Holmes were widely admired.

19 *Detective games flourished*: Detective card games include 'Sexton Blake', 'Krimo' and 'I Commit'. In 1953, Wheatley produced *Alibi*, a detective board game. The most enduring mystery board game is *Cluedo*, aka *Clue*, which first appeared in 1949 and has given rise to innumerable spin-offs, including a novel (Ronald Barker's *Clue for Murder*), a television series, a film with three different endings, a play and an off-Broadway musical. The thirst for interactive detective puzzles on TV has led to shows such as *Whodunnit?*, in which celebrities competed to solve the puzzle over six series from 1972 to 1978, and *Armchair Detectives*, with members of the public playing detective, in 2017. *Murder in Small Town X*, combining reality TV and interactive mystery, was screened in the US in 2001; a British version, *The Murder Game*, came two years later. This concept resurfaced in 2021's *Murder Island*, with a storyline by Ian Rankin.

20 *Peter Cheyney*: Cheyney's books mostly represent an Englishman's attempt to mimic the style of tough American writers. Unexpected admirers of his protagonist Lemmy Caution included Jean-Luc Godard, who borrowed the name for a character in his dystopian film *Alphaville*.

21 *The Nursemaid Who Disappeared*: Also known as *Warrant for X*, the novel was filmed in 1939 and remade in 1956 as *23 Paces to Baker Street*. MacDonald's Great Detective Anthony Gethryn races against time to save a man from *The Noose* in the first novel to appear under the Collins Crime Club imprint. *The Maze* is a 'challenge the reader' puzzle, told mainly through documents. MacDonald was inventive if sometimes slipshod, and a first-rate Hollywood screenwriter.

22 *Murder off Miami sold over 100,000 copies*: In his autobiography, Wheatley claimed that Queen Mary bought all six of the copies available in Hatchards on the day of publication.

23 *Helen Reilly*: Reilly's novels feature New York cop Christopher McKee. Her brother, James Kieran, and her daughters Ursula Curtiss and Mary McMullen, were also crime writers. Curtiss's psychological suspense novels include *The Forbidden Garden*, filmed as *Whatever Happened to Aunt Alice?* *Out of the Dark* was filmed as *I Saw What You Did*.

24 *Crime Dossiers*: Billy Butlin, an entrepreneur as keen on self-promotion as

Wheatley, tried in vain to persuade him to set a dossier in a Butlin's holiday camp. However, in 1954, John Creasey had his series character Hon. Richard Rollison investigate the disappearance of three 'Redcoats' from a camp Phwelli in *The Toff at Butlin's* and even gave Billy Butlin a cameo role in the story.

25 *Like most critics*: Reg Gadney (later a spy novelist who also adapted Minette Walters' *The Sculptress* for television) was a far-sighted exception. In 'The Murder Dossiers of Dennis Wheatley and J. G. Links', in the *London Magazine* in March 1969, he quoted Howard Spring's dismissal of the first Dossier: 'It is not for me to criticize *Murder Off Miami* any more than it would be for an art critic to criticize the artist's haystack.' As Gadney said, 'Spring was no doubt unaware that Duchamp had already exhibited a urinal and that the barriers between artefacts and reality were starting to collapse.' Gadney saw the Crime Dossiers as a form of 'literary collage . . . distinctly related to Dada and certain forms of Concrete poetry', and argued that: 'If any future alterations are to be made to the physical aspects of the book, then the dossiers suggest some of them. Reading habits, rather than the habit of reading, might change for a start . . . .' During the past half century, technological advance has brought about some of the changes Gadney envisaged, with certain Dossiers adapted into computer games. Continuing developments will take the interactive mystery in fresh directions. 'Crime Fiction and Digital Media' by Tanja Valisato, Maurit Piipponen, Helca Mantymahi and Aino-Kaisa Koistinen in *The Routledge Companion to Crime Fiction* explores a wide range of recent developments, including a Twitter story by Ian Rankin, an iPhone app developed from Stieg Larsson's *Millennium* trilogy, the true-crime podcast *Serial*, and the digital game *Miss Fisher and the Deathly Maze*, inspired by Kerry Greenwood's historical mysteries.

EIGHTEEN

Locked Rooms

'Impossible crime' mysteries

Carnegie Hall in New York on 10 April 1927 was the scene of a musical catastrophe, a public humiliation that provoked a novel of revenge. The occasion was the American premiere of the *Ballet Mécanique*, composed by George Antheil. Antheil was the self-styled 'Bad Boy of Music'. His avant-garde compositions were so controversial that performances sometimes led to brawling in the audience.

For Antheil, this was a proud moment. In Europe, he was mentioned in the same breath as Stravinsky and Gershwin. Now came his chance to conquer his home country. Originally he'd conceived the piece as a suitably strange soundtrack for a Dadaist film. His orchestration called for sixteen player pianos, two grand pianos, three xylophones, seven electric bells, four bass drums, three aeroplane propellers of different sizes, a tam-tam and a brass drum.

'Artistic differences' (in other words, Antheil was difficult to work with) led to a change of direction, and the film became a silent movie. Discovering that the technology to make his original concept of synchronised pianolas work did not exist, Antheil reworked the music into a concert piece, which premiered in Paris. Jean Cocteau, Erik Satie and James Joyce were among its admirers, and Aaron Copland said it 'outsacked the Sacre'. Antheil agreed to allow two performances of *Ballet Mécanique* at the Carnegie Hall, produced by his friend Donald Friede. Copland was to play one of the pianos.

Excitement mounted as Friede warned of a concert so sensational that it might provoke riots. Unfortunately, everything that could go wrong on the night did go wrong. There weren't even any riots. The fans simulating the sound of propellers blew straight at the audience, causing mayhem as programmes, handkerchiefs and (it was reported) even wigs and hats went flying. The climactic siren wail was delayed, so that it did not sound until the audience was heading for the exit. There were no fist fights, only mocking laughter. The reviews were savage, the second performance was cancelled and Antheil's reputation lay in shreds.

Antheil lived for another thirty-two years, but his brief heyday was over. *Ballet Mécanique* wasn't performed again until after his death. For him, solace took the form of a detective novel in which thinly disguised versions of people he blamed for his undoing were murdered. In bringing this about, he was helped by three people who won a Nobel Prize, albeit not for detective fiction.

George Antheil was born in Trenton, New Jersey, and studied music before moving to Berlin, and then to Paris, where he lived above the Shakespeare and Company bookshop. He married Boski Markus, a niece of Arthur Schnitzler, and his social circle included Ernest Hemingway, Gertrude Stein and Dr Louis Berman, an expert on endocrinology. Ezra Pound was a friend, even though he nicknamed him 'infAntheil'. In honour of his lover Olga Rudge,[1] Pound commissioned three violin sonatas from Antheil, whose life seemed charmed until the debacle at Carnegie Hall.

Antheil and Boski returned to Europe, but he ran short of money after Friede failed to honour promises to finance his work. Pound invited him to Italy and introduced him to W. B. Yeats and Gerhart Hauptmann[2]. Boski had learned English from reading mysteries, while Yeats, Hauptmann and Pound were all fans of detective fiction. Antheil decided to write a locked-room puzzle, with input from his friends and flavouring from Berman's book on endocrinology. Pound sent the manuscript of 'The Denny Murder Case', with the author named as Theilan Brent, to a literary agent, who submitted it to Faber.

T. S. Eliot,[3] a director at Faber, praised the book, while noting that it was 'too closely patterned on Van Dine.[4] This would not matter quite so much if the author did not here and there sneer at the methods of his model . . .' Antheil revised his story, but it was never published in the United States. In Britain it appeared in 1930 as *Death in the Dark*[5] by Stacey Bishop, and enjoyed minimal success.

Antheil's next failure was a satirical opera called *Transatlantic*; the Nazis, those enthusiastic pioneers of no-platforming and cancel culture, subsequently blacklisted it as 'Degenerate Music'. He returned to the United States and became a composer of film scores.[6] The mind that had delighted in devising a locked-room mystery amused itself with practical science. In an unlikely collaboration with the actor Hedy Lamarr, he invented a 'frequency hopping spread spectrum', a forerunner of modern wireless technology.

The breathless preface to *Death in the Dark* describes four apparently impossible shootings, three murders (one of them in a locked and guarded prison cell, with nobody in sight) and one attempt: 'The murders themselves, and the motives underlying them, were . . . the most cruel and morbid murders that criminal history has known for a long time. Devilish and diabolical in their intent, they harboured an almost incredible hatred and greed, and were executed with a cold-blooded grace and perfection.' Thankfully, the Vance-like amateur sleuth Stephan Bayard is on hand to solve the puzzle, drawing on generous helpings of pseudo-scientific mumbo-jumbo to explain the culprit's 'thymocentric' personality.

Cunningly concocted yet clumsily written, and stuffed with in-jokes that meant nothing to outsiders, *Death in the Dark* is a bizarre book. For Antheil, it offered catharsis. He was taking revenge on Donald Friede, whom he blamed for the calamity of Carnegie Hall. The first victim, David Denny, is a concert manager who has ruined the career of the young violinist and composer John Alvinson. Antheil had studied the violin, and amused himself by having Bayard say of Alvinson, 'I grow jealous before the fiery talent of that young man!'

Friede learned the truth but put a brave face on it in his autobiography, saying that Antheil 'came to hate me so very much that
. . . he wrote a detective story about me, in the opening pages of
which he had the reader discover me dead . . . In the balance of
the book he managed to kill my mother, my wife,[7] and my brother,
as well as a psychiatrist whom he had met through me. It was a
very thorough job . . .'

Antheil may have chosen his book's title as a hat-tip to a novel that
appeared two years before his. *Death in the Dusk* (1928) was the
first detective novel by Virgil Markham,[8] son of the once-renowned
poet Edwin Markham. Set 'among the sorcerous hills of Wales', the
novel is an extravaganza, complete with maps, a floor plan and a
striking twist – not to mention a host of Gothic trappings, such as
a mystic bone, and a legend about an imperishable arm. The tone
is set in Markham's own 'Prefatory Words': 'The nine days' terror
became a nine days' wonder, and without hyperbole it may be said
that the fate of one nation hung upon the Radnorshire riddles.'

Markham's second locked-room mystery, *The Black Door* (1930),
was renamed *Shock!* when it appeared in the Collins Crime Club,
a rare example of a British Golden Age title outdoing its American
equivalent for melodrama. The subtitle was less concise: *The
Mystery of the Fate of Sir Anthony Veryan's Heirs in Kestrel's
Eyrie Castle Near the Coast of Wales, Now Set Down from the
Information Supplied by the Principle* [sic] *Surviving Actors and
Witnesses*.

During his brief crime-writing career, Markham specialised in
'impossible crime' stories. But before his last novel appeared in
1936, a young fellow American had emerged with a passion for
detective stories and a flair for literary conjuring tricks. John
Dickson Carr shared Markham's taste for grotesquerie, but
displayed much greater staying power. He became the master of
the locked-room mystery.

Carr owed his love of 'impossible crime' stories not just to Poe
but also to Leroux's *The Mystery of the Yellow Room*, and to the
Father Brown stories that he read while growing up in Pennsylvania.

Real-life murder cases fascinated him and references to them ripple through his writings.

After college, he travelled to Paris, the backdrop for his first novel, *It Walks by Night* (1930)[9], in which a *juge d'instruction*, Henri Bencolin, investigates a beheading in a guarded room. The book was published in Harper's series of 'Sealed Mysteries',[10] a clever marketing riff on the challenge to the reader. The final section was protected by a paper seal; a purchaser who could resist the temptation to read to the end and returned the novel with the seal unbroken was entitled to a refund. Carr's story brims with youthful zest. Leroux is name-checked, and so are historical murderers who demonstrated 'the artistry of crime', such as Crippen. Naturally, Bencolin has an admiring friend to narrate his cases, the American newspaperman Jeff Marle.

Carr married an Englishwoman, and the couple settled in England. His romanticism and Anglophilia are captured in the lyrical opening of Dr Gideon Fell's debut, *Hag's Nook* (1933), with the American Tad Rampole haunted by 'a feeling that the earth is old and enchanted'. Fell, whose appearance was modelled on Chesterton's, is described as a lexicographer, although he never seems to have compiled any dictionaries, and was quickly established as a beer-loving historian and student of the supernatural. His wife soon vanished from accounts of his cases; family members tended to get in the way of Great Detectives.[11]

The Mad Hatter Mystery (1933) earned a rapturous review from Dorothy L. Sayers,[12] who praised Carr's ability to 'create atmosphere with an adjective, and make a picture from a wet iron railing, a dusty table, a gas-lamp blurred by the fog. He can alarm with an illusion or delight with a rollicking absurdity. He can invent a passage from a lost work of Edgar Allan Poe which sounds like the real thing. In short, he can write.' Sayers' influence was such that Carr later told an interviewer that the review meant he 'was established overnight'.

He tried to revive Bencolin in 'Vampire Tower', begun early in 1935, with a plot inspired by an illusion from a popular magic show that gave flavour to several of his storylines, the Maskelyne Mysteries. The trouble was that he now felt Bencolin was lifeless. Abandoning the unfinished typescript, he reworked the raw material into a Fell novel. *The Three Coffins*, aka *The Hollow Man*, was lauded as one of the finest locked-room mysteries, a triumph of atmospheric writing and seductive sleight of hand.

The novel is equally famous for a chapter called 'The Locked Room Lecture', in which Fell breaks the fourth wall: 'We're in a detective story, and we don't fool the reader by pretending we're not . . . Let's candidly glory in the noblest pursuit available to characters in a book.' He analyses different types of locked-room story[13] with gusto, citing authors as diverse as Anna Katharine Green, Israel Zangwill[14] and Ellery Queen, as well as Thomas W. Hanshew's 'magnificent' but now-forgotten detective Hamilton Cleek.[15]

For Carr, clueing a mystery was an art: 'Write a lie as though it were true[16] . . . The most important clue should sound like the wildest nonsense; in placing a cryptic clue, be sure that your reader never sees it at eye-level. This can be done by using love scenes or comic scenes.' And so, although detection remains the priority, romance and comedy recur in Carr's fiction.

At first under the name Carr Dickson, and then as Carter Dickson, he wrote about a third Great Detective, Sir Henry Merrivale,[17] alias 'H. M.'. Merrivale is essentially a comic character. In the short story 'The House in Goblin Wood',[18] the last line of which is as chilling as any in Golden Age fiction, Merrivale slips on a banana peel while walking along a pavement. The slapstick typifies Carr's technique of misdirection, since the comedy distracts attention from a revealing snippet of dialogue.

And then there was Colonel March,[19] head of Scotland Yard's unforgettably named Department of Queer Complaints, who investigated reports 'which do not seem to bear the light of day or reason'. Carr based March on John Rhode, with whom he co-wrote *Drop to His Death*, aka *Fatal Descent* (1939), in which they amused themselves by killing off a publisher. The victim meets his end not in a locked room, but in a sealed lift.

For Carr, detective fiction was 'the grandest game in the world'.[20] He was the first American elected to membership of the Detection Club, remarkably achieving this feat before reaching the age of thirty. He was excited by the prospect of his 'literary idol' presiding

over his initiation into Club membership, but Chesterton died
before the dream could come true.

Locked-room mysteries are supremely artificial. To devise a
baffling 'impossible crime' scenario is one thing, to explain matters
in a credible and convincing way quite another. Readers need to
suspend their disbelief, and this is often easier with a short story
than a novel. It helps if the premise is irresistibly tantalising[21] –
as when a man is wounded by a bullet fired two hundred years
earlier, or a victim is shot when alone in a guarded room and
the smoking gun is found in a sealed envelope. The best locked-
room mysteries have the same mesmerising appeal as miracles
and magic.[22]

Clayton Rawson,[23] an advertising artist with a passion for magic
tricks, conjured up his own Great Detective. The Great Merlini is
an illusionist and amateur detective who maintains that nothing
is impossible. Rawson and Carr were friends and exchanged plot
ideas. Rawson's concept of a victim killed in a room whose doors
and windows are sealed on the inside with gummed tape inspired
Carr to write *He Wouldn't Kill Patience* (1944).[24] Rawson's very
different solution to the same puzzle appeared in a short story,
'Out of this World'.

In 1939, William A. P. White, who was establishing a reputation
as a novelist and reviewer under the name Anthony Boucher, urged
Carr to produce another book in the vein of *The Burning Court*
(1937),[25] a non-series novel with a tantalising and controversial
finale. Classic detective fiction gave rational explanations to the
mysteries of life, but for once Carr had hinted that supernatural
forces were at work. Carr replied that if he repeated the performance, 'the faithful customers would murder me'.

Boucher reckoned that Carr violated the principles of fair play
in *Seeing is Believing* (1941), but was a fervent admirer. *Nine
Times Nine* (1940), published under the pen-name H. H. Holmes,
is dedicated to Carr, and chapter fourteen pays tribute to Dr Fell's
famous lecture. The unique solution is revealed by a sleuthing
nun.[26] Sister Ursula of the Sisters of Martha of Bethany's familiarity
with the Rheims translation of the Bible, the Catholic version,
contributes to her deductions. She remarks of a police detective's

disbelief of a woman's evidence, 'the reasoning that leads him to this suspicion is perfectly sound – for a Protestant.'

From Poe's 'The Murders in the Rue Morgue' onwards, American writers led the way in popularising the locked-room mystery. But they were not alone. Crime writers from around the world,[27] including many leading figures,[28] have been tempted by the challenge of inventing a seemingly impossible crime.

Scotland's Anthony Wynne[29] was a specialist who delighted, as Dorothy L. Sayers said,[30] in 'the hermetically sealed chamber, the sand without a footprint, the open field without cover, and a dead man in the midst of it all'. There are crafty tricks in books such as *Murder of a Lady*, aka *The Silver Scale Mystery* (1931), but his Great Detective Dr Eustace Hailey[31] was too thinly characterised to make a lasting impression.

English-born Norman Berrow[32] spent most of his adult life in Australia and New Zealand. *Don't Jump, Mr Boland!* (1954) is an 'impossible crime' story set in Sydney: a man is witnessed jumping from the edge of a high cliff, but his remains are not found at the foot of the cliff. The scenario of *The Footprints of Satan* (1950) originated in a real-life incident. In the 'Great Devon Mystery' of 1855, a trail of hoof marks appears in the snow, seemingly made by a cloven-footed creature walking on its hind legs.

There is a long tradition of French locked-room mysteries,[33] although during the Golden Age few were translated into English.[34] Noël Vindry prioritised plot over people in his 'impossible crime' mysteries investigated by an examining magistrate, Monsieur Allou. Vindry's compatriot, Gaston Bocahut, another of those Golden Age authors who trained as an engineer, published four novels as Gaston Boca, including *The Seventh Guest* (1935), a puzzle investigated by dilettante detective Stéphane Triel.

Marcel Lanteaume wrote locked-room mysteries to overcome boredom while a prisoner of the Nazis. He escaped and joined the resistance, but had to wait until France's liberation for *The Thirteenth Bullet* (1948), an ingenious serial-killer puzzle, and two more novels, to be published. By then, they seemed old-fashioned.

After being dropped by his publisher, he destroyed the other manuscripts he'd written in captivity.

Not until the twenty-first century were English-speaking readers treated to translations of Vindry, Boca and Lanteaume. At the time of writing, even *Six Crimes Sans Assassin* remains unavailable in translation, even though it is a notable 'impossible crime' novel by one of France's finest crime writers, Pierre Boileau.

Many locked-room mysteries written in other languages were long unknown in the Anglosphere. Franco Vailati's[35] *The Flying Boat Mystery* (1935) poses the question of how a man can disappear from a locked bathroom on a plane during an internal Italian flight: was it suicide, accident, murder or deliberate escape? Vailati only published one mystery, whereas Japan's Seishi Yokomizo's enthusiasm for Poe, Conan Doyle, Christie and above all Carr, drove him to build a long career in the field.

Yokomizo's award-winning debut, *The Honjin Murders*, introduced his brilliant detective Kosuke Kindaichi. First published in 1946, it was set nine years earlier. The book is a homage to the cerebral locked-room mystery. Leroux, Van Dine and Carr are name-checked, and there is mention of *Murder among the Angells* (1932), a mystery set in a strange L-shaped Boston mansion by the long-forgotten Roger Scarlett. Locked-room and 'impossible crime' mysteries are mostly written by men,[36] possibly because they are drawn to the Heath Robinson-like contraptions sometimes employed to commit murder in a sealed space. But Roger Scarlett was really two women, Evelyn Page and Dorothy Blair.[37]

Locked-room mysteries are commonly associated with Golden Age detection, and in 1942, Howard Haycraft advised[38] would-be crime writers to 'avoid the Locked Room puzzle. Only a genius can invest it with novelty or interest today'. Three-quarters of a century later, Brian Skupin argued that, if John Dickson Carr were alive today, 'he would be witnessing the second Golden Age of the locked room mystery'. With crime fiction, nothing is impossible.

Notes

The main source about Antheil is Mauro Piccinini's afterword to Locked Room International's 2017 reprint of *Death in the Dark*. Douglas Greene's biography and Carr's correspondence held in the Detection Club archives are the main sources in relation to Carr. Robert C. S. Adey's *Locked Room Murders*, posthumously updated by Brian Skupin, remains an indispensable guide to this sub-genre.

1   *his lover Olga Rudge*: Pound and Rudge collaborated on a detective novel, *The Blue Spill,* but failed to finish it; an edition with a commentary was published in 2018.
2   *W. B. Yeats and Gerhart Hauptmann*: Both men, like Eliot, won the Nobel Prize in Literature. Yeats thought Antheil 'adorable, quite crazy, and probably a genius, so one forgives him being exceedingly tiresome and hysterical'.
3   *T. S. Eliot*: Eliot briefly reviewed detective novels. His love of the genre was shared by his older brother, Henry Ware Eliot Jr, who published *The Rumble Murders* under the name Mason Deal.
4   *patterned on Van Dine*: Clyde B. Clason's Theocritus Lucius Westborough, who had an erudite preoccupation with art, culture and impossible crimes, was another detective in the Philo Vance mould.
5   *Death in the Dark*: Along with *To Be Hanged* by Bruce Hamilton, *Death in the Dark* was issued by Faber with pictorial boards rather than a dust jacket. The experiment was discontinued, and copies became legendary for their scarcity. Julian Symons thought there was a second Stacey Bishop novel; he was probably confused by the fact that Antheil later published *Every Man His Own Detective: A Study of Glandular Criminology*. This was a work of non-fiction, although 'glandular criminology' is a concept which owes more to the imagination than to science.
6   *composer of film scores*: Antheil scored *In a Lonely Place*, and the expressionistic, experimental *Dementia*, aka *Daughter of Horror*. He also wrote the music for a comic opera version of *Volpone*. Ben Jonson's play also inspired Thomas Sterling's novel *The Evil of the Day*, which was in turn adapted for the stage by Frederick Knott as *Mr Fox of Venice*, and filmed as *The Honey Pot*.
7   *he managed to kill . . . my wife*: Friede was married to Evelyn Johnson, whose fictional alter ego possesses 'a cold, calculating mind'; she co-authored *Murder: Thirty-Two Thrilling Crimes*.
8   *Virgil Markham*: In 1929, Markham is said to have launched at the University of California the first academic course on mystery literature, 'The Development and Technique of the Mystery Story'. *The Devil Drives*, another locked-room mystery, exemplifies his offbeat crime-writing style.
9   *It Walks by Night*: The story began life as a novella called 'Grand Guignol', patterned on the Parisian theatre of the macabre, with Bencolin parting the curtains to reveal the horrors lurking behind. Mike Wilson, an expert in the Grand-Guignol, argues that its relationship with writers of detective and crime fiction (such as Christie and Frédéric Dard) has been underappreciated.
10 *'Sealed Mysteries'*: Carr's UK publisher, Hamish Hamilton, borrowed the gimmick and also used it for British mysteries, such as Mary Agnes Hamilton's *Murder in the House of Commons*.
11 *family members tended to get in the way of Great Detectives* : Dr Priestley's daughter April, who plays a major role in John Rhode's *The Paddington Mystery*, disappears from view once safely married to Harold Merefield, the

great man's secretary and general dogsbody. Ellery Queen's wife and child also vanish during the course of his detective career. Edmund Crispin gave Gervase Fen a wife, but she and their offspring are rarely mentioned.

12 *a rapturous review from Dorothy L. Sayers*: In *The Sunday Times* on 24 September 1933.

13 *He analyses different types of locked-room story*: Even more comprehensive is Adey's analysis in *Locked Room Murders* of twenty different solutions to locked-room puzzles, i.e.:

1. Accident.
2. Suicide.
3. Remote control – poison gas, or impelled to do so with his own hands.
4. Mechanical and other devices.
5. Animal.
6. Outside agency made to look like inside agency – e.g. a dagger fired through window.
7. The victim was killed earlier but made to appear alive later.
8. Presumed dead but not killed until later – e.g. by the first person to enter the room.
9. The victim was wounded outside but died inside.
10. Turning key, bolt, catch, etc., from outside with pliers, string, etc.
11. Unhinging and rehinging door or window.
12. Taking out and replacing windowpane.
13. Acrobatic manoeuvre.
14. Door locked or wedged on outside. Key replaced or bolt thrown before re-entrance.
15. Door locked on the outside. Key returned before re-entrance.
16. Other methods of gimmicking doors, windows, etc.
17. Secret passages, sliding panels, etc.
18. The murderer was still in the room when entrance was forced.
19. Alibi provided while the murder was committed in an apparently guarded area.
20. Other impersonation stunts.

The more extravagant 'solutions' to over two thousand stories include 'Giant octopus in attendance' and 'Midget descending from a helicopter'.

14 *Israel Zangwill*: Zangwill was a leading figure in cultural Zionism. A champion of the oppressed, he earned the sobriquet 'the Dickens of the Ghetto'. His short novel *The Perfect Crime*, aka *The Big Bow Mystery*, broke new ground in the 'impossible crime' field, and featured a Scotland Yard detective called Wimp. His story 'Cheating the Gallows' is also notable.

15 *Hamilton Cleek*: Cleek's mastery of disguise earned him the sobriquet 'The Man of the Forty Faces'. He is a former criminal who becomes a private detective often consulted by Scotland Yard.

16 *'Write a lie as though it were true . . .'*: Greene quotes these remarks from Dorothy Gardiner's account of an MWA (Mystery Writers of American) meeting in which Carr shared a panel with Hugh Pentecost, Manfred Lee, and Fred Dannay.

17 *Sir Henry Merrivale*: He first appears halfway through an atmospheric locked-room puzzle, *The Plague Court Murders*, which Carr originally

conceived as a 'Chief Inspector Masters Mystery'. Like Allingham's Albert Campion, he soon took centre stage. The wartime Merrivale novel *She Died a Lady* offers an unusual twist on the notion of the unreliable narrative.

18 'The House in Goblin Wood': Fred Dannay's afterword to the story in the November 1947 issue of *Ellery Queen's Mystery Magazine* provides a thoughtful analysis of Carr's gift for subtle only 'fair play' clueing.

19 *Colonel March*: March appeared in only nine short stories, but the series formed the basis for a TV series, with Boris Karloff cast as the Colonel and mysteriously given an eyepatch to wear.

20 *'the grandest game in the world'*: Carr's essay with that title, reprinted in Douglas Greene's revised edition of *The Door to Doom and Other Detections*, is a hymn of praise to the classic mystery.

21 *the premise is irresistibly tantalising*: The 'bullet' story is 'The Duel of Shadows' by Yorkshireman Vincent Cornier, creator of secret service agent Barnabas Hildreth, aka 'The Black Monk'. The 'smoking gun' story is 'The X Street Murders', one of Joseph Commings' stories about Senator Brooks U. Banner.

22 *miracles and magic*: The outstanding modern exponent of 'impossible crime' stories with a magical dimension is David Renwick, creator of TV's *Jonathan Creek*; in this witty series, Creek starts out as an assistant to magician Adam Klaus. 'Misdirection' in Steve Pemberton and Reece Shearsmith's anthology series *Inside No. 9* is equally accomplished.

23 *Clayton Rawson*: Writing as Stuart Towne, he created a second magician-detective, Don Diavolo. Rawson, a founder member of the MWA, coined its heartfelt slogan, 'Crime Doesn't Pay – Enough'. In 1948, he told a correspondent: 'Maybe some day if mystery writers can figure out some way of making rental libraries give the author a cut of their profits, I'll write another Merlini, but not until then.'

24 *He Wouldn't Kill Patience:* Like Crofts' *Antidote to Venom*, the story is set in a zoo; otherwise the books are very different.

25 *The Burning Court:* Greene's biography discusses the book in depth, and even offers an alternative solution.

26 *a sleuthing nun*: Sister Ursula is far from alone. Peter Tremayne's Sister Fidelma, for example, solves mysteries in the seventh century, while Alison Joseph's Sister Agnes fled from a violent marriage to become a member of an open order based in London, and an amateur detective.

27 *around the world*: For instance, Bertil Falk's anthology *Locked Rooms and Open Spaces* comprises Swedish stories. Martin Edwards' *Foreign Bodies* includes examples from Bengal, France and Japan.

28 *many leading figures*: Examples of their work include Agatha Christie's *Hercule Poirot's Christmas*, Margery Allingham's *Flowers for the Judge*, Georges Simenon's 'The Little House at Croix-Rousse', Christianna Brand's *Death of Jezebel* (which she described as 'an attempt to write like the early Ellery Queens'), Edmund Crispin's *The Moving Toyshop*, Ed McBain's *Killer's Wedge*, Peter Dickinson's *The Poison Oracle* and Michael Dibdin's *Vendetta*.

29 *Anthony Wynne*: In real life, Dr Robert McNair Wilson. Like Antheil, he was a friend of Ezra Pound.

30 *as Dorothy L. Sayers said*: In a *Sunday Times* review on 6 January 1935 of Anthony Wynne's *The Toll House Murder*.

31 *Dr Eustace Hailey*: Hailey was known as 'the Giant of Harley Street' because

of his physical bulk, and his other gimmick was a snuff habit. Wynne strove to humanise him, saying that 'he never blames the criminal so wholeheartedly as to be unable to see and feel his tragedy'. But Wynne's love of pontificating got in the way. In *Death of a Banker*, a marvellous 'impossible crime' scenario is squandered as Wynne preaches tediously about the evils of high finance. E. C. Bentley made similar points with much greater panache in the opening pages of *Trent's Last Case*.

32 *Norman Berrow: The Terror in the Fog* is set in Gibraltar, where Berrow lived prior to settling in the southern hemisphere. The leading Australian-born exponent of locked-room mystery novels during the Golden Age was Max Afford, who published four.

33 *French locked-room mysteries*: Since 1987, Paul Halter has become a notable specialist in impossible crimes. He has a lower profile in the Anglosphere, but lately his works have become available in English translation.

34 *few were translated into English*: Exceptions included Francis Didelot's *Murder in the Bath* and Jean Toussaint-Samat's *Shoes that Had Walked Twice*. Didelot, whose mother was a descendant of Edgar Allan Poe, had a career lasting for half a century; two of his books were televised in the 1960s BBC anthology series *Detective*. Toussaint-Samat's principal detective was Maurice Levert.

35 *Franco Vailati*: His real name was Leo Wollenborg Jr. He fled to the US to escape antisemitism and became an American citizen. Igor Longo's afterword to his English translation of the novel discusses Italian Golden Age fiction.

36 *mostly written by men*: Kay Cleaver Strahan wrote two, including *Footprints*, a cold-case mystery that won the Scotland Yard Prize. Strahan's career was brief and her indulgence in Had-I-But-Known writing has obscured the merit of her books about 'crime analyst' Lynn Macdonald.

37 *Evelyn Page and Dorothy Blair*: The pair published five Scarlett novels and later taught creative writing. A nineteen-year old pupil described Blair as 'a compelling, ugly, dynamic character' who had been 'in the army, worked in factories, lived in sin'. The student, who seems not to have been tempted to write a locked-room mystery, was Sylvia Plath. Evelyn Page taught at Smith College, and the writer Lucy Lippard recalls being allowed 'one violent death per semester' (Garth Greenan Gallery website, 13 December 2017). The eccentric architecture and Gothic mood of the Angells' mansion influenced Japanese novels such as Soji Shimada's *Murder in the Crooked House*.

38 *Howard Haycraft advised*: In *Murder for Pleasure*. Brian Skupin's upbeat comments appear in his introduction to the 2019 *Supplement* to Adey's *Locked Room Murders*.

NINETEEN

The Long Arm of the Law

Early police stories

'Don't come back without him,' Sir Robert Anderson told his detective inspector. The Assistant Commissioner of the Metropolitan Police had just briefed Frank Froest, an officer experienced in crimes with an international dimension, about a case of the utmost sensitivity.

Froest's mission was to travel to Argentina, arrest a notorious swindler and bring him back to England to stand trial. As if that were not challenge enough, in February 1895 no extradition treaty was in force between the two countries. An earlier attempt to capture Jabez Balfour had failed. Two Scotland Yard detectives had set off for South America with a warrant, only to find themselves thwarted by their quarry, who bribed people to obstruct his pursuers, and then fled to Salta, in the foothills of the Andes.

Balfour was the most notorious fraudster in British history. He'd served as a magistrate and mayor of Croydon before becoming a high-profile Liberal MP. Pious, teetotal and philanthropic, Balfour cultivated a holier-than-thou image while building a business empire whose assets were wildly overvalued.

The bubble burst in 1892 and several of his fellow directors were arrested, but by then Balfour was in Buenos Aires. His mistress and her sister completed an unusual *ménage à trois*; his wife was conveniently incarcerated in a mental institution in Roehampton. The combined debts of his empire were estimated at seven million pounds, roughly £1 billion today.

Once in Argentina, Froest persuaded a judge to order Balfour's handover. Suspecting that his prisoner would try to escape before the next train to Buenos Aires was due, Froest hired a train of his own. An armed British Consul guarded Balfour while Froest rode on the engine footplate. The detective kept his revolver handy, knowing they had to travel a thousand miles through wild country, and that local officials would argue that he'd kidnapped Balfour. A sheriff's officer pursued them on horseback, demanding that the train stop; he fell from his horse in a vain attempt to board, and was killed.

The train broke down during the journey, and local police came to detain Froest and his party, but he'd taken the precaution of ordering a replacement train. Once he received a signal that his captive was on board and steam was up, he said that he wanted to relieve himself, and instead jumped on the train, which promptly set off for Buenos Aires. When they arrived, they were greeted by an Argentinian cutter carrying envoys of the judiciary, demanding Balfour's release.

Froest wasn't to be denied He managed to get Balfour on board a ship sailing for Southampton and their progress across the ocean was gleefully recorded by the British press. Back in England, Balfour was tried and sentenced to fourteen years in jail, while Frank Froest became a celebrity, the most famous policeman in the world.

Froest's career included many high points, as well as occasional lows. He played a minor role in the fruitless hunt for Jack the Ripper, and took part in the investigation that led to the arrest of Adolf Beck for fraud, following a mistaken identification that gave rise to a notorious miscarriage of justice. In 1910, two friends in the theatrical world, John Nash and Lil Hawthorne, came to him to express concern about the mysterious disappearance of a music-hall artiste. Froest called in Detective Inspector Walter Dew, who interviewed one Dr H. H. Crippen about his missing wife, and eventually uncovered an extraordinary story of lethal passions lurking behind a seemingly respectable domestic façade.

Two years after Crippen's execution, Froest retired from Scotland Yard. His fame was such that King George V, who had presented him with the King's Police Medal, gave the speech marking his retirement. But Froest wasn't ready to put his feet up. Like many police officers before and since, he'd made a habit of cultivating sympathetic journalists, among them a young reporter called George Dilnot, who had aspirations to write fiction.

The Grell Mystery (1913), Froest's first novel, features Superintendent Heldon Foyle, executive chief of the Criminal Investigation Department, who 'rarely wore a dressing gown and never played the violin'. Plainly, this is a story about not a brilliant and implausible amateur, but rather a professional. The story is a marriage of entertainment and propaganda on behalf of the police.

For Foyle, 'there are times when it is necessary for a police officer to put a blind eye to the telescope and to do technically illegal things in order that justice may not be defeated.' This philosophy, not so very different from Sherlock Holmes', reflects the spirit of Balfour's capture. The enduring question is whether, in police work, the end justifies the means.

Dilnot probably acted as ghostwriter. The book was filmed, and so was *The Rogues' Syndicate*, which appeared three years later under the joint names of Froest and Dilnot. They also collaborated on short stories about a secret group of international crime-fighters[1] operating from a small hotel off the Strand. The casebook of this 'most exclusive club in the world' was published in 1915 as *The Crime Club*.

Froest's know-how assisted Dilnot in writing a book about Scotland Yard, and although Froest's literary career soon came to an end, Dilnot became a prolific author.[2] Collins republished *The Crime Club* in its Detective Story Club series, and Dilnot was hired to compile a spin-off magazine called *Hush*, nominally (but not actually) edited by Edgar Wallace. The magazine lasted a year, by which time Collins were ready to launch a new imprint; perhaps as a nod to Froest and Dilnot. So began the legendary Collins Crime Club.[3]

*

Froest was a trailblazer, a cop turned crime novelist. But none of his innumerable successors had a career quite as colourful as Sir Basil Thomson. Following spells as a farmer in Iowa, a stipendiary magistrate in Fiji and a senior colonial administrator in Tonga, Thomson became a prison governor before moving to Scotland Yard to take charge of the CID in June 1913. He 'found that the London detectives were naturally divided into two classes, the detective and the "thief-catcher". The latter belonged to the class of honest, painstaking policemen without sufficient education to pass examinations for promotion, but who made up for this deficiency by his intimate knowledge of the rougher class of criminals.'

While at the Yard, Thomson interrogated both Roger Casement and Mata Hari, when each was suspected of being an enemy of the state. He was contemptuous of Communism, and fear about shock waves following the Russian Revolution made him determined to root out suspected left-wing plots to overthrow the establishment: the final chapter of his memoirs is titled 'Curbing the Reds'. He was knighted, and appointed Director of Intelligence at the Home Office, but he left office after falling foul of the Prime Minister, David Lloyd George.

Disaster struck four years later. Thomson was fined for an act of indecency with Thelma de Lava, a woman he'd just met in Hyde Park. He claimed he'd met her with a view to researching a book he was writing, but it emerged that she was a prostitute. Was he framed by enemies, or simply caught out in a moment of weakness? It was at least true that he was already an established author, having published his first book more than twenty years earlier.

Thomson was in his sixties, and the public humiliation would have destroyed many men, but whatever his faults, they didn't include a lack of resilience. Shrugging off the scandal, he pursued his literary ambitions. In the year of his conviction, he published a book of short stories about a private detective called Mr Pepper, one of which – 'The Vanishing of Mrs Fraser' – was inspired by a famous urban legend.[4] After passing his seventieth birthday, he made use of his professional experience by creating a Scotland Yard detective called Richardson. In the course of eight novels published in just five years, Richardson enjoys a meteoric rise through the ranks, starting as a police constable, and reaching the dizzy heights of chief constable.

The short, snappy series was ahead of its time in emphasising the importance of teamwork in police investigations, and although characterisation is thin, occasional touches lend authenticity, as with Thomson's frankness about police officers' dread of criticism in the newspapers. *Milliner's Hat Mystery* (1937) is remarkable for inspiring Ian Fleming[5] while he was working in Intelligence during the Second World War. Fleming borrowed Thomson's idea of using a corpse dressed as an airman for a plan to conceal the invasion of Italy from North Africa, known as 'Operation Mincemeat'.

Thomson was not the first British crime writer to record a police officer's scramble up the greasy pole. Almost a quarter of a century before Richardson made his debut, the husband-and-wife duo Alice and Claude Askew[6] published *The Adventures of Police Constable Vane M.A., on Duty and Off* (1908), recounting 'the startling incidents in the career of a gentleman of birth and education, who joined the London police'.

The Askews were storytellers pure and simple, and Vane's exploits pay little attention to police procedure. But even before Froest turned to fiction, George R. Sims recognised that it made sense to give stories about police detectives an air of realism. His Detective Inspector Chance solved mysteries taken from real life; 'The Mystery of a Midsummer Night', for instance, reworks the Constance Kent murder case (see note 12 on p. 47). But Chance made no impression, and his exploits were not even collected in book form until more than sixty years later.

The breakthrough for stories about police investigation came after the First World War, with the appearance of Freeman Wills Crofts' *The Cask* (1920). The story opens in London, with the discovery of a human hand and gold sovereigns in a cask that is unloaded at St Katherine's Docks. Displaying a doggedness which became the hallmark of Crofts' cops, Inspector Burnley leaves no stone unturned in his hunt for the truth about the victim, the motive for the murder and the identity of the culprit.

Apparently impregnable alibis,[7] as in the highly elaborate *The Hog's Back Mystery*, aka *The Strange Case of Dr Earle* (1933), became a Crofts trademark. Regular readers deduced that if it seemed impossible that suspects had committed the crime, they must have come up with a highly ingenious scheme to get away with murder, although Crofts managed to introduce some variety into his storylines, for instance by writing inverted mysteries.

At first, he avoided series characters. The title of his fifth book, *Inspector French's Greatest Case* (1924), indicated another stand-alone, but Joseph French, nicknamed 'Soapy Joe' because of his technique of soft-soaping witnesses, became a fixture, establishing himself as the leading Scotland Yard detective of the Golden Age. In the early books, French was allowed traces of individuality, including the loss of a son during the war, and a wife who contributes ideas about cases when he is struggling for answers, but these soon faded. He retained a love of foreign travel, shared with his creator, and several cases took him overseas. The murder of Mant Carrington in *Found Floating* (1937) even enables him to join a cruise to the Eastern Mediterranean.

French's willingness to break the law in his early cases is striking. In *The Box Office Murders*, aka *The Purple Sickle Murders* (1929), he searches premises without a warrant and persuades a subordinate to help him burgle a garage. But given the attitude of real-life officers such as Froost, this was hardly unrealistic. Pedantic writing and unsophisticated characterisation typified the 'Humdrum' school of detective novelists,[8] but Julian Symons, who coined the term, acknowledged that Crofts was the head of that school.[9] Crofts' avoidance of literary fireworks did at least give an impression of verisimilitude. As Raymond Chandler said,[10] Crofts was 'the soundest builder of them all when he doesn't get too fancy'.

Henry Wade's early detective fiction shows Crofts' influence, but he had a closer understanding of the realities of police work. Like Crofts, he was instinctively a supporter of the status quo, but his cynicism and pessimism fed through into increasingly ambitious novels. Crofts was prepared to tolerate policemen behaving badly; Wade did not flinch from exploring the consequences of their human frailty.

Wade excelled at describing rivalries between police officers, their ambitions and their petty jealousies, and the temptations to bend the rules in the hope of securing a desired result. The steady rise up the ladder of Scotland Yard detective and Oxford graduate John Poole is slower than that of Vane or Richardson, and much more believable. Yet his progress provokes resentment, and in *The Duke of York's Steps* (1929), Wade acknowledged the reservations felt about young, intelligent detectives by career cops.

Fallibility in a supposedly heroic investigator, such as Bentley's Philip Trent and Berkeley's Roger Sheringham, is even more arresting in a detective presented as credibly as Poole. His mistakes typically result from trusting people too much. In *Bury Him Darkly* (1936), his lack of discretion leads to the murder of a colleague. The time-served Superintendent Fraser is sardonic: Poole 'was a good officer . . . but . . . obviously too fond of making friends with people in the cases which he investigated . . . It all came . . . from the modern practice of admitting public school men to the police force; they might have their good qualities but they were inclined not to "know their place".'

Tensions between police officers surfaced when Lord Trenchard, who became Metropolitan Police Commissioner in 1931, proposed a military-style officer corps of senior policemen, trained at a special college. This development was fiercely opposed by the Police Federation and politicians such as Aneurin Bevan, but Hendon Police College opened its doors in 1934.

John Rhode's novel *Hendon's First Case*, a mystery about ptomaine poisoning published in 1935, was thus highly topical. Jimmy Waghorn, a graduate of Cambridge and Hendon, matched wits with the case-hardened Superintendent Hanslet and cerebral Dr Lancelot Priestley. But Rhode never overdid the realism. The puzzle was solved not by the professionals, ancient or modern, but by the brilliant professor.

Leading lights in the Detection Club became increasingly interested in the minutiae of police work. Crofts was one of five Detection Club members who, together with Russell Thorndike, collaborated in a unique project pitting crime writers against the professionals. The authors each wrote a story about a 'perfect murder', a crime they regarded as insoluble, and then challenged the recently retired ex-Superintendent Cornish to explain in each case precisely how the police would set about bringing the perpetrator to justice. Dorothy L. Sayers was among the contributors to the resulting book, *Six against the Yard*[11] (1936), and she inscribed a copy to Norman Kendal, an Assistant Commissioner of the Metropolitan Police with an interest in fictional crime, who became the only non-writer ever to be elected to membership of the Club.

Knighted in 1937, Kendal was consulted during that year by Dorothy L. Sayers. Out of the blue, a Dr John Dancy had telephoned her, explaining that his wife had been murdered, and wondering if Sayers would like to examine the scene of the crime. He thought it might provide her with useful first-hand research. Baffled, Sayers asked Kendal what she should do, and with characteristic diligence sent him a six-page memo summarising her strange conversation with the bereaved doctor.

Naomi Dancy, also a doctor, had died in the early hours on 23 November, at her home in Richmond. She'd been shot at close range through each eye as she slept. According to her husband, her brother Maurice Tribe was the killer, and had also tried to shoot him before locking himself in the lavatory and cutting his own throat. Tribe, an alcoholic who had suffered severe wounds during the war, had apparently murdered his sister in a frenzy of rage. Kendal told Sayers that the police were satisfied, and she resisted the temptation to pursue the matter, or use the strange invitation as material for a novel.

Well-born, Oxbridge-educated police detectives became commonplace. E. R. Punshon abandoned a series about a pair of traditional cops called Carter and Bell to introduce Bobby Owen in *Information Received* (1933). Bobby, the affable and good-looking grandson of Lady Hirpool, joins the police after finding jobs hard to come by at a time of economic slump. Sayers heaped praise on Punshon's 'entrancing portraits of Scotland Yard officials . . . His Scotland Yard is a creation peculiarly his own. It is not realism in the dull and pedestrian sense . . . His policemen are just a little brighter and more beautiful than earthly policemen.'

Duly encouraged, Punshon charted Bobby's progress through the ranks over the course of thirty-five novels and more than twenty years. Yet Bobby never attained the popularity enjoyed by

Ngaio Marsh's[12] Roderick Alleyn or Michael Innes' John (later Sir John) Appleby. Appleby made his debut in Innes' *Death at the President's Lodging*, aka *Seven Suspects* (1936), set in a college in a fictitious Oxbridge-style university. Gollancz described the book as the best first detective story that had ever come their way.

Crofts, Punshon, Marsh and Innes lacked a detailed knowledge of police work, and had little or no interest in acknowledging police corruption or brutality. Their focus was on entertainment. So was Wade's, but he faced up to the darker side of criminal investigation.[13] His masterpiece, *Lonely Magdalen* (1940), shows John Poole making uneasy compromises with his conscience.

Poole hunts the murderer of a prostitute, a daring choice of subject for a Golden Age novelist. The highly original construction of the narrative enables Wade to marry a gripping account of police investigative procedure to a poignant human drama. The book is divided into three parts. In the first, 'Working Back', the discovery of a female corpse on Hampstead Heath leads to a revelation about the dead woman's identity. The second, 'Twenty Five Years Ago', is an extended flashback, as Wade returns to his eternal theme: the havoc that war wreaks on people's lives. The third, 'Working Forward', sees Poole and his colleagues close in on the culprit. But once a suspect is identified, Poole is troubled by Chief Inspector Beldam's conduct of the interrogation.

When the case reaches court, Poole is cross-examined, and cannot 'bring himself to let Beldam and the Force down; he declared there had been no bullying . . . when he left the box he was sweating and miserably conscious of having been as near perjury as ever he had been in his life.' After the verdict is delivered, Poole consoles himself that justice has been done. But – shockingly, by the standards of the time – the book's final paragraph suggests that he may have been deceiving himself.

Like Wade, John Bingham was heir to a baronetcy and a pillar of the establishment, but equally prepared to confront the ugly side of policing. His first novel, *My Name is Michael Sibley*, which appeared seven years after the end of the Second World War, is narrated by Sibley, a writer who is interrogated by the police following the death of an old school friend, John Prosset, for whom he had nursed a secret hatred.

Sibley doesn't help himself by lying and trying to dispose of a knuckleduster that he'd carried around in his pocket for years.[14] At first, the unnamed inspector treats him pleasantly, but as circumstantial evidence of Sibley's guilt mounts, the questions become menacing: 'I was a threat to his reputation or another rung in the ladder to promotion . . . he was only indirectly an inspector trying to fight crime for the protection of the community. He was much more dangerous. He was fighting for himself and his family. Primeval. Out to win the meat.'

Bingham's focus is on characterisation and suspense rather than twisty plotting, but for Julian Symons, the book was a logical progression from the pioneering work of Francis Iles, 'a classic example of the crime story's new direction' after the Golden Age. The same could be said of Symons' *The Thirty-First of February* (1950), in which the question is whether Anderson, an advertising copywriter, has pushed his wife down the cellar stairs, or whether she simply suffered a fatal accident. 'I had been rereading Dostoevsky', Symons said, 'and my police inspector carries echoes of the Grand Inquisitor.'

The police story had become more sophisticated in the course of half a century, and so had policing, but crime writers continued to wrestle with the eternal question: when do ends justify means?

Notes

The main sources are Sir Basil Thomson's *My Experiences at Scotland Yard*, Joan Lock's *Scotland Yard Casebook* and David Brawn's introduction to the 2016 reprint of *The Crime Club*. Henry Wade is discussed in Curtis Evans' *The Spectrum of English Murder*, and John Poole in Leah A. Strong's chapter in Earl F. Barguinnerier and George N. Dove's *Cops and Constables*.

1   *a secret group of international crime-fighters*: The American author Carolyn Wells had previously created the International Society of Infallible Detectives, five pastiches of famous sleuths; the detectives in the Crime Club were created by Froest and Dilnot, and included Heldon Foyle.
2   *Dilnot became a prolific author*: He was general editor of a series of *Famous Trials*, and wrote Sexton Blake stories as well as detective novels. His last book, *Counter-Spy*, was a wartime thriller.
3   *the legendary Collins Crime Club*: John Curran's *The Hooded Gunman* surveys the imprint's history.

4   *a famous urban legend*: The legend appears to date back to the Paris Exposition Universelle of 1889. The most effective version of the story is Anthony Thorne's *So Long at the Fair*, filmed in 1950. Evelyn Piper's *Bunny Lake is Missing*, which makes reference to the legend, was an even more successful film.

5   *Milliner's Hat Mystery is remarkable for inspiring Ian Fleming*: A further connection is that Thomson presented copies of his books to Kathleen Pettigrew, who was personal assistant to Stewart Menzies, the director of MI6, and seems to have been the model for Miss Moneypenny in the James Bond books.

6   *the husband-and-wife duo Alice and Claude Askew*: They also created Aylmer Vance, a 'ghost seer' or investigator of psychic phenomena. Their partnership came to a tragic end in 1917 when they were travelling on an Italian steamer torpedoed by a German submarine. Both drowned, and Claude's body was never recovered.

7   *Apparently impregnable alibis*: 'Miracle in Crooked Lane', an episode in David Renwick's series *Jonathan Creek*, is a brilliant reinvention of this trope for the television age. Renwick scripted four episodes of the TV series *Agatha Christie's Poirot*, and even his popular sitcom *One Foot in the Grave* was peppered with detective fiction references.

8   *the 'Humdrum' school of detective novelists*: Symons cited R. A. J. Walling, J. S. Fletcher, and G. D. H. and Margaret Cole as other Humdrums. Walling, a newspaperman, created the private investigator Philip Tolefree. Symons also characterised Henry Wade as a 'Humdrum', a strange misjudgement.

9   *Crofts was the head of that school*: The Superintendent Wilson novels of G. D. H. and Margaret Cole were originally inspired by Crofts' success, but suffer by comparison because the authors became bored with detective fiction. Wilson is dull, although the Coles allowed him to take a dig at Sir Basil Thomson, to whom they were politically opposed, in *The Death of a Millionaire*: 'Wilson's little differences with Sir Basil had been notorious . . . they used to discover at least a couple of great revolutionary plots a week before, Sir Basil went.' Wilson resigned to become a private detective, only to resume his career at Scotland Yard as if nothing had happened.

10 *As Raymond Chandler said*: In 'The Simple Art of Murder'.

11 *the resulting book, Six against the Yard*: Known as *Six against Scotland Yard* in the US. The other contributors were Margery Allingham, Anthony Berkeley and Ronald Knox.

12 *Ngaio Marsh*: *Money in the Morgue*, a continuation novel set in New Zealand and based on an unpublished fragment written by Marsh, was published in 2018 by Stella Duffy.

13 *he faced up to the darker side of criminal investigation*: For example, in *The High Sheriff* and *Bury Him Darkly*, as well as in *Lonely Magdalen*. A police superintendent is suspected of a child kidnapping in his final novel, *The Litmore Snatch*, published in 1957 and an early example of a British detective novel in which a female police sergeant, Mary Wittam, plays a significant part in the investigation.

14 *a knuckleduster that he'd carried around in his pocket for years*: This was a strange habit of Bingham's, which he bestowed on his protagonist. A knuckleduster also features in *Deadly Picnic*, a feeble police novel written late in his career.

TWENTY

Blood-Simple

Dashiell Hammett

In the early hours of 1 August 1917, a black Cadillac stopped outside a boarding house in Butte, Montana. Five masked men jumped out of the car and strode into the building while a sixth kept watch. The men told the landlady that they were police officers, and wanted Frank Little. Terrified, she said that Little was in room 32.

The masked men smashed down the door, and found their quarry asleep in his underwear and a leg cast. The intruders gagged him with a towel, and manhandled him out to their car. After tying him to the bumper, they dragged him along the road for a block, scraping off most of his knee caps, before pulling up and hanging him from the Milwaukee railroad trestle on the outskirts of town. They left a note in red letters pinned to his underwear: Little's death was a FIRST AND LAST WARNING.

Frank Little had come to Butte to support local mineworkers in their bitter dispute with the Anaconda Copper Mining Company. Copper mining earned Butte the nickname of 'the richest hill on earth', but 168 miners had died during the Speculator Mine disaster, a horrific fire which had provoked a strike.

Nobody was charged with Frank Little's murder, but long afterwards a former Pinkerton's detective confided in his lover that an official from Anaconda Copper had offered him five thousand dollars to carry out the killing. The lover was the dramatist Lillian Hellman, and the ex-gumshoe was a man whose experience of dirty detective work gave his private-eye novels a sharp edge of authenticity. His name was Dashiell Hammett.

Samuel Dashiell Hammett helped out his father as a salesman of seafood before becoming, as he put it, 'the unsatisfactory and unsatisfied employee of various railroads, stock brokers, machine manufacturers, canners and the like'. At the age of twenty-one, he joined the Baltimore office of the Pinkerton National Detective Agency.[1]

Hammett went on to become a bit-part player in one of the sensations of the Roaring Twenties. He shadowed prosecution witnesses on behalf of the lawyers defending Roscoe 'Fatty' Arbuckle,[2] a silent film comedian who was tried no fewer than three times for the rape and manslaughter of an aspiring actress. Hammett reckoned that Arbuckle had been framed by an ambitious DA, and victimised by the press; the fallen star's 'eyes were the eyes of a man who expected to be regarded as a monster but was not yet inured to it'.

But was it really true that someone offered Hammett money to kill Frank Little? It seems unlikely. He was a storyteller, and often embellished anecdotes about his colourful early life to suit his audience. He joined the army, but succumbed first to influenza and then tuberculosis. In hospital, he met a nurse called Josephine 'Jose' Dolan, and married her shortly before she gave birth to their daughter. He returned briefly to Pinkerton's, but detection was dangerous work, and he bore the scars to prove it. During the course of his career as a private eye, he was hit with a brick after bungling a tailing job, and had his leg badly cut by a member of a gang he was trying to arrest for the theft of dynamite. Poor health forced him to find a safer way to earn a living.

He started selling pieces to *The Smart Set*. The magazine was running at a loss, and its co-editors, H. L. Mencken and George Jean Nathan, set up more commercially focused publications to keep it afloat. One of them, with a mission to publish 'the best stories available of adventure, the best mystery and detective stories, the best romances, the best love stories, and the best stories of the occult', was a pulp magazine called *The Black Mask*.[3]

'Pulps' sold up to a million copies per issue. Printed on porous grey wood-pulp paper, they were cheaper to produce than the higher quality 'glossies' or 'slicks', and their content was often lurid and sensational, aimed at the same market as the nineteenth-century's 'penny dreadfuls'. Most contributors churned out hack work for a 'penny a word', but some of their stories brimmed with an energy found in crude British thrillers written by the likes of 'Sapper' and Sydney Horler but often absent from more sophisti-cated detective novels. *The Black Mask* soon achieved a circulation of 250,000, but Mencken was disdainful of his 'new louse', and he and Nathan sold the magazine for a quick profit.

Carroll John Daly's 'The False Burton Combs', published in December 1922, is widely regarded as the first of the hardboiled crime stories for which *The Black Mask* became legendary. Daly introduced the private eye Race Williams in 'Knights of the Open Palm' the following June, six months after Hammett's first story for the magazine appeared. 'The Road Home' was published under the by-line Peter Collinson, perhaps because 'Peter Collins' was slang for a nobody.

Under his own name, Hammett produced a series of stories narrated by a private eye known only as the Continental Op. The Op is short, fat and unglamorous, but a ruthlessly effective gumshoe. Hammett refined a sparse, visceral prose style, influenced by the economical style of reporting practised by Pinkerton's men. Conveying the violence, corruption and sexual promiscuity of the Prohibition years demanded something very different from the genteel, cerebral approach of plotsmiths working in the Golden Age tradition. As Julian Symons put it, Hammett, like Ernest Hemingway, 'eliminated the author's voice as much as possible in an attempt to make the final product genuine and not synthetic – life rather than literature'.

The birth of a second child meant that Hammett and his family couldn't survive on his earnings from short fiction. After a brief spell as advertising manager for a local jeweller, he had a lucky break when Joseph T. Shaw became editor of *The Black Mask*. Hammett was encouraged that Shaw didn't want crossword-puzzle type mysteries, saying: 'As I see it, the approach I have in mind has never been attempted. The field is unscratched and wide open.'

Shaw gave him the freedom to develop as a writer, a freedom mirrored in his personal life as his family moved to San Anselmo while he stayed behind in San Francisco.[4] Frequent use of slang gave his crisp, witty writing about a sleazy world a believability that other crime writers struggled to match. The Continental Op's increasing callousness seemed equally credible.

Hammett's next step forward came with a novel serialised over four issues of the magazine, another first-person narrative from the Op. The story was set in Butte, Montana, fictionalised as Personville and nicknamed Poisonville. Dedicated to Shaw and originally titled *Poisonville*, the novel was renamed *Red Harvest* (1929) and became the first of five novels in which Hammett redefined American crime fiction.

Hammett's ability to capture the corruption and abuse of power that made Poisonville toxic is evident from the start: 'For forty years old Elihu Willsson . . . . had owned Personville, heart, soul, skin and guts', but when he hired gunmen to crush a labour dispute, 'he lost his hold on the city and the state. To beat the miners he had to let his hired thugs run wild . . . they took the city for their spoils.'

The dissection of a rotten civic society makes *Red Harvest* a kind of bleak morality tale. The Op cleanses the city by pitting gangsters against each other, and letting their brutality do the rest. As the body count rises (one chapter is called 'The Seventeenth Murder'), and he orchestrates one death after another, he acknowledges that he's become 'blood-simple like the natives'.[5]

Such a turn of phrase is as memorable as it is pithy, and Symons rightly disputed Raymond Chandler's view[6] that, in Hammett's hands, the American language 'had no overtones, left no echo', pointing out that Hammett's dialogue was as raw as his characters' lives. As James Ellroy says[7], 'It's the language of suspicion, alienation and the big grasp for survival. It's a constant jolt of physical movement and conversation.'

*

The Op returned in *The Dain Curse*, again spread over four issues of *Black Mask*. Shaw asked Hammett to ensure that each instalment was effectively a stand-alone story, and although the book links them together, the joins are visible. The novel is often regarded as Hammett's weakest, partly because of its structural flaws, partly because he'd trespassed into Golden Age territory, weaving a family curse and multiple solutions into the complex plot. Hammett later called it 'a silly story . . . all style', but it's gleefully melodramatic and offers glimpses of a compassion absent from *Red Harvest*.

Hammett reviewed crime fiction with wit and insight[8] and his scathing condemnations of Philo Vance (that jokey comparison to 'a high-school girl who has been studying the foreign words and phrases in the back of her dictionary') are frequently quoted. Less familiar, perhaps because it does not fit the narrative spun by those who regard a love of hardboiled crime fiction as incompatible with a taste for intricate whodunits, is his praise for traditional mysteries. J. J. Connington's *The Two Tickets Puzzle* (1930) was 'an excellent straight detective story', for instance, while he described H. C. Bailey's *The Garston Murder Case*, aka *Garstons* (1930), as 'first-rate entertainment'.

Hammett began a short-lived relationship with a music teacher called Nell Martin, and moved with her to New York. His third novel, *The Maltese Falcon* (1930), represented a leap forward in terms of quality: Alexander Woollcott said it was 'the best detective story America has yet produced'. Hammett abandoned first-person narration. The characters' thoughts and feelings are never revealed; he simply recounts what they say and do, and shifts the serious violence off-stage.

This time the protagonist was Sam Spade, who achieved the remarkable feat of becoming fiction's quintessential private eye despite never appearing in another novel.[9] Spade reflects Hammett's belief that a private detective doesn't 'want to be an erudite solver of riddles in the Sherlock Holmes manner; he wants to be a hard and shifty fellow, able to take care of himself in any situation'. A memorable film version starring Humphrey Bogart ensured Spade's iconic status.

Shortly after Spade and his partner Miles Archer are hired by an attractive woman who gives her name as Miss Wonderly, Archer is shot dead. In trying to find out whodunit, Spade discovers that Miss Wonderly is an alias of Brigid O'Shaughnessy, who – like a gang led by the obsessive Casper Gutman – is desperate to find the eponymous falcon, a statuette of extraordinary value and rarity.

The plot is not original; some of the material was adapted from two of the Op's cases, 'The Whosis Kid' and 'The Gutting of Couffignal'. Hammett's intense writing lifts the novel out of the ordinary and so does his treatment of sex. Spade sleeps with a suspect, and the homosexuality of two of Gutman's sidekicks is obvious. And Hammett's inclusion of the so-called 'Flitcraft parable', a story that has nothing to do with the main plot, is so intriguing that students of the genre have long argued over its interpretation.[10]

Spade tells Brigid O'Shaughnessy about being hired to find a real-estate agent called Flitcraft who vanished from home one day 'like a fist when you open your hand'. Using a false name, Flitcraft had begun a new life with a new wife and child after a narrow escape when a beam fell from a tall building and nearly killed him: 'He knew then that men died at haphazard like that, and lived only when blind chance spared them.'

Hammett dedicated *The Maltese Falcon* to Jose, but like Flitcraft, he'd given up on family life and soon he gave up on Nell Martin too. When he wasn't writing, he spent most of his time drinking in the company of fellow *Black Mask* contributors Frederick Nebel[11] and Raoul Whitfield.[12]

Hammett and Whitfield enjoyed arguing about how many murders a crime novel could sustain; the number increased the more they drank. Whitfield, a former pilot and steel-mill worker, was a dapper, charismatic, ambitious figure, and for a while his star shone as brightly as Hammett's. Hammett gave a favourable review to his friend's first novel, *Green Ice* (1930): 'naked action pounded into tough compactness by staccato, hammerlike writing'. The two men had much in common: war service, alcoholism, tuberculosis and unhappy marriages. And Whitfield's first wife, Prudence, had a relationship with Hammett.

In Whitfield's second novel, *Death in a Bowl* (1931), private eye Ben Jardinn investigates the murder of a conductor during a concert at the Hollywood Bowl. Whitfield signed a contract with the film company Paramount on terms so lucrative that, according to *Black Mask*, they took 'all the press out of Depression'. He divorced Prudence, married a wealthy socialite, Emily Vanderbilt, and relocated to the Dead Horse ranch in New Mexico. But the marriage broke down and Emily died one night with a gunshot wound to her chest, a presumed but mysterious suicide.[13]

Whitfield was in California at the time of Emily's death; he inherited her estate and married again, but his writing career was destroyed by TB. Eventually the money ran out and his third wife threw herself out of a hotel window. At one point Hammett sent a cheque to the sanatorium where Whitfield was slowly dying.

Hollywood beckoned Hammett too, although he was not flattered when the Paramount executive and future movie mogul David O. Selznick described him as 'another Van Dine' in terms of commercial potential. The film world offered vast riches, and Hammett set about spending them on women and lavish parties. After a 'five-day drunk', he met a young woman with literary aspirations at a Hollywood party and they discovered a shared enthusiasm for T. S. Eliot. Her name was Lillian Hellman; she was married but Hammett became the love of her life.

The Glass Key (1931),[14] Hammett's fourth novel, combines a cleverly clued mystery[15] with a study of loyalty and the abuse of power. Paul Madvig, a crooked political boss in a nameless city is suspected of killing a senator's son. His trusted friend and fixer Ned Beaumont[16] tries to solve the crime in order to clear Madvig's name, and falls for the senator's daughter, Janet Henry.

The book's title comes from Janet's account of a strange dream about finding a house in a forest that has a table piled high with food but hundreds of snakes slithering over the floor; at the end of the book she says that the key to the door 'was glass and shattered in our hands just as we got the door open . . . We couldn't lock the snakes in and they came out all over us and I woke up screaming.'

The symbolic significance of Janet's dream has excited

speculation. Does it mean that Beaumont is impotent? Does Janet harbour incestuous fantasies about her father? A less high-flown interpretation is that human relationships, including the love of Beaumont and Janet for each other, are fragile. Despite weaknesses stemming from over-hasty writing, Symons argued that they 'do not seriously affect the book's originality nor its quality as a view of one kind of American life at the time. Its technique of revealing character by indirection was pushed much further by Hammett than by Hemingway and was not attempted by any other American novelist between the wars'.

William Faulkner was another of Hammett's drinking buddies. Although their political opinions were at opposite ends of the spectrum, they admired each other's work, and when Faulkner described *Sanctuary*,[17] his dark novel about rape, abduction and murder, as a potboiler, Hammett would have none of it.

Drink sloshes through the pages of Hammett's fifth and final novel, *The Thin Man* (1934). He was spending even faster than he earned, keeping his wife and children short of money, and producing only a trickle of short stories. Hellman lived with him on and off, but she too was broke until her play *The Children's Hour* enjoyed a long run on Broadway.

The narrator of *The Thin Man* is Nick Charles (really Charalambides), an alcoholic former Pinkerton man whose wife Nora is an heiress. Hammett and Hellman never married, but their teasing relationship and their love of partying is reflected in the lifestyle of Nick and Nora. A woman is found dead and the prime suspect, an inventor called Claude Wynant, has gone missing. The storyline carries pinches of sadomasochism, and after Nick grapples with one of the female characters, Nora asks, 'Tell me the truth, when you were wrestling with Mimi, didn't you have an erection?' When he says, 'Oh, a little', she laughingly says, 'If you aren't a disgusting old lecher.'

This passage was cut from the magazine serialisation, and the UK edition of the novel,[18] but retained in the American edition. When the book was filmed with William Powell and Myrna Loy as Nick and Nora, the sexual references were removed. Even the booze was consumed in moderation, but the chemistry between the stars and the fashionable screwball comic elements resulted in a hit that spawned a sequence of 'Thin Man' movies.

Hammett also invented a comic-strip hero, Secret Agent X-9, and wrote the captions for over a year. A film producer signed him up, but he devoted most of his time to solving crossword puzzles or hiring prostitutes. Three times he was taken off the payroll, and each time he charmed his way back on to it. The scriptwriter Nunnally Johnson[19] reckoned that Hammett's self-destructive behaviour derived from 'an assumption that he had no expectation of being alive much beyond Thursday'.

Three magazine stories in 1934 proved to be his last published fiction. The years before his death in 1961 saw a slow, relentless decline. Hammett became ensnared in radical politics, and during the post-war purge on 'un-American activities', he was sent to prison for six months for contempt of court. Asked why he never wrote in jail, he said he was never bored enough to want to do so. The McCarthyite era saw his work blacklisted, and in later life he was ravaged by emphysema and cancer. His final attempt to produce a novel, unpromisingly titled *Tulip*, yielded just an auto-biographical fragment.

Hammett often behaved shamefully, especially towards women. Once he hit Hellman on the jaw and knocked her down during a quarrel at a party. A starlet called Elise De Viane sued him for battery and attempted rape; the truth about what happened is unclear, but Hammett's writing about violence is disturbingly convincing. Hellman said when delivering his eulogy, 'Never, in all the years, did he play anybody's game but his own.'

'Everyone who reads Hammett seems to read their own needs into his work,' according to private eye writer Sara Paretsky,[20] who sees 'a dangerous female sexuality which Hammett found so terrifying that he needed to destroy it'. Her own detective was intended as 'a rebuttal of Brigid O'Shaughnessy . . . a physical, sexual person without being evil . . . if Sam Spade had never existed, neither would V. I. Warshawski.'

Notes

The main sources on Hammett's life and work are the biographies by Julian Symons, William F. Nolan and Nathan Ward.

1   *Pinkerton National Detective Agency*: The Agency was founded in the 1850s by Allan Pinkerton and was, at its peak, the largest private law-enforcement agency in the world. Birdy Edwards, who appears in the Sherlock Holmes novel *The Valley of Fear*, was a Pinkerton agent, and so for a time was Felix Leiter, a recurrent character in Ian Fleming's James Bond books. Pinkerton agents feature in numerous films, notably *American Outlaws*.

2   *Roscoe 'Fatty' Arbuckle*: Arbuckle starred in Mack Sennett's movies about the Keystone Cops, and is a character in Peter Lovesey's mystery *Keystone*.

3   *The Black Mask*: Later, it became simply *Black Mask* and appeared until 1951. Contributors included Paul Cain (pen-name of George Caryl Sims), whose solitary novel *Fast One* was described by Raymond Chandler as the 'high point in the ultra-hardboiled manner'. George Harmon Coxe created 'Casey, Crime Photographer' for the magazine, and Jack 'Flashgun' Casey ultimately became a media franchise, extending to radio, film, theatre, novels and comic books.

4   *he stayed behind in San Francisco*: This period of his life was covered in Wim Wenders' film *Hammett*; the screenplay was co-written by Ross Thomas, who wrote crime novels under his own name and also as Oliver Bleeck. The film was based on a novel by Joe Gores, who worked as a private eye prior to becoming a full-time author. Gores' novel *32 Cadillacs* shared material with *Drowned Hopes* by his friend Donald Westlake, with the events told from different viewpoints. An earlier crossover occurred in their novels *Dead Skip* and *Plunder Squad* respectively.

5   *'blood-simple like the natives'*: The Coen brothers' film *Blood Simple* took its title from this phrase. In 2007, the New York City alternative metal band Bloodsimple recorded an album called *Red Harvest*.

6   *Raymond Chandler's view*: Expressed in 'The Simple Art of Murder', in which Chandler also says Hammett 'wrote scenes that seemed never to have been written before'. Edmund Wilson dismissed *The Maltese Falcon* as 'not much above those newspaper picture-strips in which you follow . . . the ups and downs of a strong-jawed hero and a hardboiled but beautiful adventuress', a judgement illustrating Wilson's knack for the snobbish misreading of popular fiction.

7   *As James Ellroy says*: In 'The Poet of Collision', *Guardian*, 29 September 2007.

8   *Hammett reviewed crime fiction with wit and insight*: He complimented books ranging from J. S. Fletcher's *Sea Fog* to A. E. W. Mason's *The Prisoner in the Opal*. Philip MacDonald's *The Noose* offered 'the neatest plot I have seen in months. It is logical, it is simple, and it is baffling.' Among amateur sleuths, he found Anthony Berkeley's Roger Sheringham 'the most amusing – well, anyhow, the least annoying'.

9   *despite never appearing in another novel*: Hammett featured him in three short stories.

10   *students of the genre have long argued over its interpretation*: George J. Thompson said in *The Armchair Detective*, May 1974, that the parable

suggests 'the absurdity of assuming that the external world is necessarily stable'. Julian Symons was sceptical about such fine-spun theories.

11 *Frederick Nebel*: Nebel, a former dockhand and farmworker, was best known for stories about Steve MacBride and Kennedy, a tough police captain and a hard-drinking crime reporter.

12 *Raoul Whitfield*: Whitfield wrote stories for *Black Mask* under the name Ramon Decolta about a Filipino private eye, 'the Island detective', whose cases have been collected in *Jo Gar's Casebook*.

13 *a presumed but mysterious suicide*: When Walter Satterthwait moved to Santa Fe in the early twenty-first century, he became fascinated by the case, and wrote *Dead Horse*, in which cop Tom Delgado (a fictitious character) becomes obsessed with the idea that Whitfield was responsible for Emily's death.

14 *The Glass Key*: René Magritte, a crime fiction fan who also referenced Poe and Fantômas in his art, borrowed the title for his painting *La Clef de Verre*. The Coen brothers wove threads from the novel into their film *Miller's Crossing*.

15 *a cleverly clued mystery*: In Symons' opinion, 'The stick and the hat are as good as any such clues in Agatha Christie'.

16 *Ned Beaumont*: In 'The Decline and Fall of the Detective Story', Somerset Maugham described Beaumont as 'a curious, intriguing character whom any novelist would have been proud to conceive'.

17 *Sanctuary*: Faulkner's interest in crime and detection is also evident in books such as *Light in August* and *Absalom! Absalom! Intruder in the Dust* features the attorney Gavin Stevens, who also appears in the stories collected in *Knight's Gambit*.

18 *This passage was cut from . . . the UK edition of the novel*: As Symons says: 'Erections did not exist in English fiction at that time.'

19 *Nunnally Johnson*: His screenplays included *The Three Faces of Eve* (based on a non-fiction book by two psychiatrists) and *The Woman in the Window*, arguably the first movie to be labelled 'film noir'. The script employs a storytelling cliché in order, as David Bordwell says, to explore 'seamy psychological terrain' while offering an upbeat ending untypical of film noir. The source novel, *Once Off Guard*, was a stand-alone written by J. H. Wallis, who tried in a series featuring Inspector Jacks, a college-educated New York cop, to do something a little different with the detective novel. *Murder by Formula* includes a claim *in verse* by Wallis that he has 'played fair' by the reader. *The Servant of Death* is an inverted mystery, and the formal 'challenge to the reader' is to deduce how he will be caught.

20 *according to . . . Sara Paretsky*: In an introduction to the Folio Society's 2000 edition of *The Maltese Falcon*.

TWENTY-ONE

Murder and its Motives

True crime

On a hot August morning in 1933, a murder trial began in
Pasadena's small courthouse. A British woman with a passion for
criminology took a seat in the front row; it was reserved for the
Alabama Star, but an influential friend had pulled strings on her
behalf. She was staying in Santa Monica with her husband, a
playwright who had succumbed to the lure of Hollywood. She'd
gone bathing in the ocean with Laurence Olivier, and her husband
had swum with a topless Greta Garbo before the startling news
came that Pasadena's 'cloistered calm' had been shattered by a
sensational murder case.

The press called the case 'the Pent-roof killing', because Harold
Wolcott was accused of shooting his lover, Helen Bendowski, in a
garishly decorated penthouse flat above a florist's shop. Wolcott
had inherited the property from his unusually forgiving ex-wife
– who had divorced him because of his affair with Helen – after
she died of cancer.

The British criminologist was within touching distance of
members of the jury. Each juror sat in a rocking chair, and because
of the heat, everyone rocked to and fro, fanning themselves. The
scene seemed like 'something fantastic, as though out of an impres-
sionist play'.

The defence lawyers made sure that all but two of the jurors were female, because they reckoned the accused – whom they always referred to as 'the boy Harold' – had a way with women. The criminologist, however, 'saw no charm in the puffy, pasty man, already over-heavy for his thirty-three years, who sat sulkily between his counsel'. The evidence against Wolcott appeared damning, but the jury returned what she described scathingly as 'the only verdict which the circumstances did not warrant'. He was found guilty of manslaughter and jailed for ten years.

When she wrote the case up, the criminologist made little secret of her opinion that 'the boy Harold' had got away with murder.

Wynifried Margaret Jesse preferred to be called Fryniwyd or Fryn and published as F. Tennyson Jesse. Writing ran in the blood; she was the great-niece of Alfred, Lord Tennyson.[1] Perhaps she also owed her interest in crime to the great poet, a devotee of the *Newgate Calendar*. She became a reporter for the *Daily Mail* and also wrote fiction and poetry. Attractive and charismatic, she numbered the playwright H. M. 'Tottie' Harwood among her admirers.

Tottie invited her to Windermere, and promised her a flight over the lake in an aeroplane offering joyrides. As the plane took off, unaware of the danger of being caught in the propeller, she put out her right hand to wave. As she said, 'it got stuck. It didn't really hurt. I pushed my hand back into my lap and watched fascinated as a pool of blood reached to my knees.' Her hand was severely mutilated, and she lost more of it with each of the six operations she endured in the next twelve months, but the wounds would not heal. Eventually she had to wear artificial fingers, and teach herself to type with her left hand. Morphia injections helped her to cope with the pain but she became addicted to the drug.

This horrific misfortune set the pattern of a life that glittered without being golden. She and Tottie married when he was forty-four and she was thirty. The couple kept their marriage a secret for three years because of the complication that Tottie was still embroiled in a relationship with a married woman who was the mother of his son.

In the same year as the wedding, 1918, Jesse created Solange

Fontaine,[2] daughter of an English mother and French father, and 'a naturalised citizen of the world'. Solange was the author of a book about criminology, and her unique feature as an amateur detective was that she'd been gifted with an extra spiritual sense that warned her of evil.

Six of her cases were collected in *The Solange Stories* (1931); in the foreword Jesse discussed detective novelists ranging from Marie Belloc Lowndes and Agatha Christie to Philip MacDonald and the mysterious A. Fielding.[3] She revealed that her ambition was 'to write a good detective novel, keeping strictly to the rules – and I very much doubt if I shall ever be able to fulfil it. It is a pity, because I should play the game so honourably.'

Jesse never did master the classic detective novel, but her contribution to crime writing was distinctive. Introducing the first Solange stories in *The Premier Magazine*, she said: 'I've always been very interested in criminology, and when in the USA used to visit prisons, night courts, etc., a great deal. I have sat in the death-chair of Sing-Sing Prison. Murder, to my mind, is the most fascinating of all phenomena, because it is the one in which the game can never be worth the candle, also because it has behind it a more endless combination of motives than any other act.'

She explored this theme in *Murder and its Motives* (1924),[4] classifying murder motives under six headings: murder for gain; for revenge; for elimination; for jealousy; for lust of killing; and from conviction. The motives were illustrated by case studies, with William Palmer and Constance Kent among her chosen murderers. Equally fascinated by the complexity of victimhood, she used the word 'murderee'[5] to describe that 'race of human beings who lay themselves out to be murdered'. Her way with words ('Women in crime are like those artists who always paint a picture "with a story"') and provocative opinions (of capital punishment, she said: 'We should kill a great many more people') ensured the book's success.

She and Tottie travelled extensively. While staying on the Riviera, they handed their motor yacht over to E. Phillips Oppenheim, while in America, they socialised with Dorothy Parker and Alexander Woollcott. Yet as Jesse's literary career prospered, her private life became increasingly troubled. After a number of miscarriages, her inability to have a child became a source of distress. Her health was fragile, and her extreme mood swings may be a clue to un-diagnosed bipolar disorder, but she refused to seek psychiatric help. In 1931 she took an overdose of sleeping pills and was found the next day in a coma. Her stomach was pumped, and she made a recovery, but this proved to be the first of a long sequence of failed suicide attempts, often accompanied by farewell letters to Tottie; some were loving, some recriminatory.

Following an approach by Harry Hodge, whose family firm published *Notable British Trials,*[6] she began to contribute to the series, starting with the Madeleine Smith case. Her incisive intro-duction to the *Trial of Samuel Herbert Dougal* (1928), which concerned the Moat Farm case,[7] highlighted the abuse of vulner-able women by predatory men. Her prose was enlivened by an eye for telling detail. Of Reginald Ivor Hinks, hanged for killing his father-in-law, she said: 'He was the only prisoner whom I have ever seen who wore a black tie and a black mourning-band round his arm as signs of sorrow for the person whom he was accused of killing.'

Jesse was deeply troubled by a famous miscarriage of justice. An affair between a married woman, Edith Thompson, and a sailor, Frederick Bywaters, ended in tragedy when Bywaters stabbed Edith's husband to death in October 1922. Edith witnessed the attack, but took no part in it; she had, however, written a series of letters to Bywaters contemplating her husband's death. She had, for instance, referred him to *Bella Donna* (1909), a novel by Robert Hichens[8] in which a woman plans to poison her husband. This was interpreted as an incitement to murder.

Edith's adultery sparked moral outrage. The couple were tried for murder and found guilty, and she and her lover were hanged. Although Edith was unquestionably a liar, she was essentially a dreamer, a fantasist. Francis Iles argued that she was 'executed for adultery'.[9]

Novelists quickly identified the fictional potential of the Thompson–Bywaters case, with its tangled emotions, deceit and sudden, irrational violence. The press dubbed Edith 'the Messalina of Ilford', and this lurid reference to the promiscuous and homicidal wife of the Roman emperor Claudius gave E. M. Delafield[10] a title for a novel based upon the case, *Messalina of the Suburbs* (1924). The couple's correspondence inspired an element of A. E. W. Mason's third novel about Inspector Hanaud, *The Prisoner in the Opal* (1928), while their doomed relationship was reimagined by Dorothy L. Sayers and Robert Eustace in *The Documents in the Case*. But Sayers' lack of sympathy for Edith is evident in her characterisation of Margaret Harrison.

Jesse was so moved by Edith's fate that she felt inspired to write the novel for which she is still remembered, *A Pin to See the Peepshow* (1934). Despite a disingenuous disclaimer, Edith was the model for Julia Almond, the unhappy protagonist. Jesse consulted the woman who had been Deputy Governor of Holloway at the time Edith went to the gallows, and authentic detail complements the narrative's emotional gravity. According to Jesse's occasionally overwrought biography, she immersed herself so deeply in her characters' lives that 'she almost suffocated'.

The year after the novel's publication saw an Old Bailey murder trial bearing uncanny similarities to the Thompson–Bywaters case. The Rattenbury–Stoner case[11] concerned a *ménage-à-trois* at the Villa Madeira in Bournemouth, which culminated in Alma Rattenbury's youthful lover clubbing her elderly husband to death with a mallet. At first, in a hysterical state, Alma confessed to the crime, but, in court, Stoner took full responsibility. Both were charged with murder; Alma was acquitted, but Stoner was sentenced to death. She committed suicide, and his sentence was commuted to life imprisonment. Jesse wrote up the case for *Notable British Trials*.

Francis Iles shared Jesse's fascination with real-life crime and the failings of British justice. Public faith in the legal system was generally high, but Iles thought his scepticism was justified by the treatment of women like Edith Thompson and Alma Rattenbury. *As for the Woman* (1939), his final novel, concerns a *ménage-à-trois*; its title came from a dismissive line in the judge's hostile summing-up, which contributed to Edith Thompson's conviction.

In 1936, seven Detection Club members produced a book examining real-life cases, *The Anatomy of Murder*, and Iles tackled the

Rattenbury trial in a pungent essay. The book included fresh revelations from John Rhode about the Constance Kent case, as well as Dorothy L. Sayers' closely reasoned study of the Wallace mystery.[12]

The close connections between crime in fiction and in fact were illustrated when John Dickson Carr used the techniques of the detective novelist in a book about the unsolved murder of Sir Edmund Godfrey in 1678. People are even keener to solve the puzzles of real life than those in books, and Carr, John Rhode and other authors contributed theories to a series run by *The Star* about unsolved crimes, with readers competing for a prize of five guineas for the best solution they could offer.

Shortly before the Second World War, Fryn Tennyson Jesse hosted the initial meeting of the Black Maria Club. The Club provided a forum in which criminal cases could be discussed by novelists and others with a professional interest: it was agreed that members of the judiciary would be allowed to join 'if they behaved'. Marie Belloc Lowndes read a paper about Lizzie Borden, and other members included A. E. W. Mason, John Dickson Carr and Harry Hodge, but following the outbreak of hostilities, the Club never met again.[13]

Fryn Tennyson Jesse's literary gifts and range of interests set her apart from most 'true crime' writers. She was the most influential female criminologist of the twentieth century, although sometimes her judgements prompted disagreement or courted controversy.

Jesse showed sympathy towards Madeleine Smith, acquitted of murder but an inspiration for several of crime fiction's most dangerous women. She argued that Madeleine was 'born before her time' and lacked the outlets for her passions available to women during the interwar years. This view was challenged by William Roughead, who reckoned that 'even in the wider freedom offered by this golden age of lipstick, cocktails, and night clubs, she would infallibly have gone wrong.'

Roughead was a Writer to the Signet, a Scottish lawyer who for sixty years attended every significant murder trial in Edinburgh. An early contributor to *Notable British Trials* whose criticisms of Oscar Slater's prosecution assisted Arthur Conan Doyle's fight for justice in the case, Roughead had a diverse band of admirers including Hugh Walpole, Dashiell Hammett[14] and President Franklin Delano Roosevelt, while Dorothy L. Sayers, reviewing Roughead's *Mainly Murder*,[15] described him as 'far and away the best showman that ever stood before the door of a Chamber of Horrors'. Sayers argued that his ability to combine factual accuracy with an entertaining narrative style made him the leader in his field.

Books about criminology date, as novels date,[16] but despite shifts in public attitudes to crime and punishment, Roughead's reputation has survived relatively unscathed. As Joyce Carol Oates puts it,[17] he 'wrote in a style that combined intelligence, witty skepticism, and a flair for old-fashioned storytelling and moralizing; his accounts of murder cases and trials have the advantage of being concise and pointed, like folk tales'. She even detects a Borgesian flavour in his writing. Introducing a contemporary collection of his essays, the Belgian-born American critic Luc Sante said that, in Roughead's hands, 'Madeleine Smith might be the template of the lethal film noir heroine'.

Roughead's American counterpart was the librarian and bibliophile Edmund Pearson,[18] who established himself as the leading authority on the case of Lizzie Borden, acquitted in 1893 of murdering her parents with an axe. Nobody else was ever charged with the crime, and Pearson was not alone in suspecting that she was guilty. Pearson and Roughead corresponded with each other from the early 1920s, and when Pearson visited Edinburgh, Roughead helped him to experience at first hand the city's 'criminous sites and sanguinary memories'.

In 1948, fourteen years after the first publication of *A Pin to See the Peepshow*, Fryn and Tottie collaborated on a stage version, which enjoyed less good fortune. Public performance of Frank Vosper's play[19] based on the Thompson–Bywaters case, *People Like Us*, written not long after the trial but banned by the Lord Chamberlain, was finally permitted at much the same time. Nevertheless, the brother of Edith's murdered husband protested against the staging of *A Pin to See the Peepshow*, without having read or seen it. The Lord Chamberlain withheld a licence, a costly calamity given that thirty-two actors had been rehearsing for a fortnight. When the play eventually reached the West End, it flopped, and on Broadway it lasted just one night.

Despite deteriorating health, Jesse continued to research and write about crime. *Comments on Cain* (1948) examined three trials that she had witnessed in Britain, the US and France, including that of 'the Boy Harold'. In each case, the culprit was a predatory, youngish man. The book's reception was mixed, with Roy Fuller[20] especially negative.

Her final contribution to *Notable British Trials* covered the highly controversial Christie and Evans case, better known by the address of the murder scene, 10 Rillington Place.[21] She agonised over the factual complexities, telling the crime novelist Nigel Morland[22] that Timothy Evans was 'not a completely innocent man' and a congenital liar. But Evans was hanged for a murder that was the work of John Reginald Christie, and Jesse said to Morland that she thought he was, at most, an accessory to manslaughter.

Edgar Lustgarten, the first prominent criminologist of the television age, made use of his experience as a barrister when writing both fiction and fact. His first novel, *A Case to Answer*, aka *One More Unfortunate* (1947), combined courtroom drama, an ironic twist worthy of Francis Iles, and a powerful argument against capital punishment. Graham Greene said it was the best crime story he'd read since *Malice Aforethought*. Lustgarten wrote only a handful of novels but became a household name[23] as a result of presenting TV programmes such as *Scotland Yard* and *The Scales of Justice*.

Ever since Thomas De Quincey's satiric consideration of murder as one of the fine arts, literary interest in real-life crime has been accompanied by an awareness that the human suffering that is inseparable from crime can be, and often is, exploited and exacerbated by inferior writers. There is a never-ending tide of books that are prurient or shoddily sensational, including some of the more mind-boggling efforts of 'Ripperologists' claiming to have unearthed proof that yet another 'hitherto unsuspected' individual committed the Whitechapel murders.

Even the more sophisticated studies are often flawed and driven by a desperation to say something new. As Raymond Chandler said:[24] 'Nobody ever writes a book about a famous case to prove that the jury brought in the right verdict.'

Occasionally, however, Fryn Tennyson Jesse's successors have produced books of high distinction, such as Truman Capote's 'non-fiction novel'[25] *In Cold Blood*[26] (1966). Capote was apt, like many less talented writers, to play fast and loose with the truth. But he shared something in common with Jesse as well as with Norman Mailer, whose Pulitzer Prize-winning *The Executioner's Song* (1979) concerns the murderer Gary Gilmore, and the Nobel Laureate Bob Dylan, whose 'Murder Most Foul' tackles the assassination of John Fitzgerald Kennedy. They were all storytellers.[27]

Notes

The main sources are Joanne Colenbrander's biography of Jesse, Steve Haste's *Criminal Sentences*, Albert Borowitz's *Blood and Ink* and Victoria Stewart's *Crime Writing in Interwar Britain*.

1   *the great-niece of Alfred, Lord Tennyson*: Her sister Stella married Eric Simson, whose fiction written under the name Laurence Kirk included a village poisoning mystery, *Whispering Tongues*, and a novel of suspense, *The Farm at Santa Fe*, aka *The Farm at Paranao*.
2   *Solange Fontaine*: All the stories were finally collected in 2014 as *The Compleat Adventures of Solange Fontaine*. In his introduction, Douglas Greene points out that some of the early stories have racist elements, and that another recurrent feature is repugnance about sex.
3   *the mysterious A. Fielding*: Fielding was a prolific author for the Collins Crime Club whose identity remains unclear.
4   *Murder and its Motives*: A revised and expanded edition was published in 1952.
5   *'murderee'*: Jesse thought she'd coined this word but it cropped up earlier, for example, in *Women in Love* by D. H. Lawrence.
6   *Harry Hodge, whose family firm published Notable British Trials*: The series ran from 1905 to 1959, and was revived in 2017.
7   *the Moat Farm case*: Camille Holland was killed for her money by her lover Samuel Herbert Dougal, who was hanged in 1903. Edmund Pearson examined the case in 'Miss Holland's Elopement', while the culprit's extraordinary confession is included in Sandoe's *Murder: Plain and Fanciful*. The case inspired Douglas G. Browne's *Rustling End*, featuring his series detective Harvey Tuke, and R. J. White's *The Smartest Grave*, which won a Collins Crime Club competition for the best detective novel written by a university don. The case also provides an ingredient of the multilayered historical mystery *Bleeding Heart Square* by Andrew Taylor, whose grandmother's family sold the Moat Farm to Dougal.
8   *Robert Hichens*: Hichens is best remembered for a novel filmed by Hitchcock.

The Paradine Case concerns a barrister who falls in love with a woman on trial for murder.

9 *'executed for adultery'*: René Weis, who wrote a book about the case, arranged for Edith Thompson's remains to be reburied in the same grave as her parents in 2018.

10 *E. M. Delafield*: Delafield later became famous as author of the amusing *Diary of a Provincial Lady*. Her story 'They Don't Wear Labels' shows the influence of Francis Iles. Her association with him is discussed in *The Golden Age of Murder*.

11 *The Rattenbury–Stoner case*: John Van Druten's play *Leave Her to Heaven* was inspired by the case, as were Terence Rattigan's play *Cause Célèbre*, and Simon Gray's television drama *Death of a Teddy Bear*, and his play based on it, *Molly*. Shelley Smith's *The Woman in the Sea* tells the story in the form of a novel. Sarah Waters used details from the case, as well as from that of Thompson and Bywaters, in *The Paying Guests*, although the relationship which becomes the catalyst for murder is lesbian rather than heterosexual.

12 *Dorothy L. Sayers' closely reasoned study of the Wallace case*: William Herbert Wallace was found guilty of murdering his wife in 1931, but the conviction was quashed on appeal. Sayers' assessment of his personality – an amateur's attempt at retrospective offender profiling – led her to believe that he was innocent. John Dickson Carr agreed, while Raymond Chandler called the story 'the nonpareil of all murder mysteries'. Elements drawn from the case appear in many crime novels, including *The Last Sentence* by Jonathan Goodman, who also wrote an influential study of the mystery. Lady Ralston's murder in P. D. James' *The Skull beneath the Skin* parallels the killing of Julia Wallace, while James also references the case in *The Murder Room*. James later argued that Wallace was guilty (*Sunday Times Magazine*, 27 October 2013). Most of those who have examined the case argue that the killer was Wallace's junior business associate, Richard Gordon Parry.

13 *the Club never met again*: Carr, however, referenced it – under the name the Murder Club – in *He Who Whispers* and *In Spite of Thunder*. The better-known Crimes Club was founded in 1903, and is still going strong. Arthur Conan Doyle was among its members.

14 *Roughead's diverse band of admirers included . . . Dashiell Hammett*: At Hammett's suggestion, Lillian Hellman adapted a story from Roughead's *Bad Companions* into a Pulitzer-Prize nominated play, *The Children's Hour*.

15 *Dorothy L. Sayers, reviewing Roughead's Mainly Murder*: In *The Sunday Times* of 30 May 1937.

16 *Books about criminology date, as novels date*: In October 2017, however, *The Signet* magazine argued that Roughead's 'inheritors are not only those regularly cited by scholars – the Christies, Sayers and others of crime writing's "Golden Age" – but also the true crime documentaries of the twenty-first century, Netflix's "Making a Murderer", the BBC's "Storyville" and the podcasts of "Serial".'

17 *Joyce Carol Oates puts it*: See 'The Mystery of JonBenét Ramsey', *New York Review of Books*, 24 June 1999. Oates' interest in crime, real and fictional, has often surfaced in her work, under her own name, and under the names Rosamund Smith and Lauren Kelly. Her story 'Landfill', published in the *New Yorker* in 2006, drew on the death of a student at a New Jersey college.

18 *the librarian and bibliophile Edmund Pearson*: Improbably, in 1934 he went
    to Hollywood, and worked as an uncredited writer on *Bride of Frankenstein*
    and *Werewolf of London*.
19 *Frank Vosper's play*: Vosper, an actor and author of *Murder on the Second
    Floor*, a novelisation of one of his plays, adapted Agatha Christie's 'Philomel
    Cottage' as *Love from a Stranger*, which became a popular success. He
    drowned in mysterious circumstances in 1937 while travelling back to Britain
    from performing in the play on Broadway.
20 *Roy Fuller*: Best known as a poet, Fuller wrote three crime novels, including
    a sardonic, Freudian story about an amnesiac, *Fantasy and Fugue*.
21 *10 Rillington Place*: This became the title of Ludovic Kennedy's book (filmed
    in 1971 with Richard Attenborough as Christie and John Hurt as Timothy
    Evans), which argued that Evans suffered a grotesque miscarriage of justice.
22 *. . . telling, Nigel Morland*: In an unpublished letter of 13 March 1956, while
    still working on the book.
23 *became a household name*: Lustgarten acquired a curious form of immor-
    tality, inspiring the narrator's character in *The Rocky Horror Picture Show*,
    and being sampled in Severed Heads' 1984 pop hit 'Dead Eyes Opened'.
24 *As Raymond Chandler said*: In a letter to Dale Warren of Houghton Mifflin,
    2 September 1948. Chandler left Knopf because of their feeble handling of
    apparent plagiarism by James Hadley Chase. In 1933, Hammett's English
    publishers had successfully sued a young Englishman, Cecil Henderson, for
    a wholesale plagiarism of *The Maltese Falcon* called *Death in the Dark* (the
    title was also lifted, from George Antheil).
25 *'non-fiction novel'*: Meyer Levin's *Compulsion*, based on the Leopold and
    Loeb case, is ostensibly a novel but in some ways anticipates Capote's and
    Mailer's books. It was adapted for stage and film.
26 *In Cold Blood*: This exploration of the murder of four members of the Clutter
    family in rural Kansas was acclaimed as a pioneering example of narrative
    non-fiction. 'Handcarved Coffins', published towards the end of Capote's
    tumultuous life, and purportedly another account of a real-life crime, seems
    to have been pure invention: see Peter Gillman, 'Cracking the Case of Capote,
    the Cold Blooded Literary Thief', *The Sunday Times*, 17 February 2013.
27 *They were all storytellers*: The Northern Irish crime writer Paul Charles
    makes the connection between Capote, Mailer and Dylan in 'Rough and
    Rowdy Ways by Bob Dylan: The Event Album is Back!', *Hot Press*, 1 July
    2020.

TWENTY-TWO

Twists of Fate

Frances Iles and ironic crime fiction

Sybil da Costa was a former singer who took up a new career as a landlady. Likeable, hard-working and attractive, she quickly found tenants for her boarding house at Pembridge Villas in Notting Hill. She made a striking contrast to the man she called her husband. At fifty-seven, James Starr was twenty-two years older, morose and depressive. Born James Achew in Ohio, of American and Japanese parentage, he was a former juggler and cabaret performer. Now he lived on Sybil's earnings and passed the time by hiding in wardrobes to spy on their paying guests.

Among the tenants was a young South African writer. William Plomer had landed in Britain after three years in Japan, and was undergoing a process he termed 're-Westernisation'. Plomer's publishers were Leonard and Virginia Woolf of the Hogarth Press,[1] and Virginia described their author as a 'compressed, inarticulate young man, thickly coated with a universal manner . . . tells a nice dry prim story; but has the wild eyes which I once noted in Tom [T. S. Eliot] & take that to be the true index of what goes on within.'

James Starr misinterpreted the look in those wild eyes, and persuaded himself that Plomer was having an affair with Sybil. On the morning of 24 November 1929, he tried to force his wife to confess her infidelity. When she protested her innocence, he slashed her throat repeatedly with a razor. She died in front of their six-year-old daughter.

Her body was found at the top of the stairs, while Starr was discovered in the kitchen, with his head in the gas oven. For good measure, he'd cut his own throat, but neither of his attempts at suicide proved fatal. Tried for murder, he was found guilty and sentenced to death. An appeal failed, but ultimately he was reprieved because of his insanity, and detained in Broadmoor for the rest of his life.

Plomer was away from Pembridge Villas at the time of the killing. The scale of Starr's jealousy and capacity for violence horrified him. He'd had no designs whatsoever on Sybil's virtue. Although he was reluctant to admit it, even to himself, Plomer was gay.

Some authors write accounts of real-life murders, some authors fictionalise them. William Plomer wrote about a real-life murder case in which he might have been a victim. He had liked Sybil, 'a lively, pretty, fresh-looking Jewess', and was convinced that he'd had a narrow escape. Writing a thinly veiled account of the crime offered him a form of catharsis.

In *The Case is Altered* (1932), he becomes young Eric Alston, while the Starrs are Mr and Mrs Fernandez. Plomer's evocation of boarding-house life, and of the tensions between members of different social classes, is compelling. So is his account of Paul Fernandez' descent into madness and murder. Eric's excursions into politics and his devotion to his girlfriend's brother are more crudely handled, but *The Case is Altered* became one of Hogarth's most commercially successful titles.[2]

Plomer became a prominent editor and a well-regarded poet. During the Second World War, he met Ian Fleming, who helped him to avoid prosecution after being arrested for propositioning a sailor. A few years later Plomer returned the favour, reading the manuscript of *Casino Royale*, which introduced James Bond. Fleming dedicated *Goldfinger* to the man who had, a generation earlier, narrowly escaped death at Pembridge Villas.

*

Plomer was one of a number of talented young authors whose novels explored the wellsprings of murder during the Golden Age. Their books were not whodunits of the kind then in vogue, but precursors of the modern crime novel, even though the authors didn't think of themselves as 'crime writers'.[3] James Hilton's *The Dawn of Reckoning* (1925) begins as a character study, which develops into a story about a killing, with a murder trial and a race against time to prevent injustice. The book was freely adapted into *Rage in Heaven*, a film noir co-written by Christopher Isherwood. Hilton wrote a single detective novel in the classic vein[4] under a pen-name before becoming the bestselling author of novels such as *Goodbye, Mr Chips* and *Lost Horizon*.

A. P. Herbert[5] was another versatile writer who dipped a toe into criminous waters. In *The House by the River*[6] (1920), the key question is what will happen to Stephen Byrne, who kills a pretty housemaid by mistake when she rebuffs his advances. He disposes of the corpse in the Thames, helped by a friend, who becomes the prime suspect. The irony of the story's ending was echoed in many later novels as Herbert left it to others to explore the fallibility of conventional justice through crime fiction.

Joanna Cannan's[7] *No Walls for Jasper* (1930) anatomises the quiet desperation of middle-class life and the craving for financial security and respectability at a time of economic hardship. Julian Prebble, who works in publishing, becomes besotted with a female historical novelist, and unwisely concludes that murdering his rich and unpleasant father offers a route to happiness. Cannan modelled the object of Julian's attentions in part on her friend and fellow writer Georgette Heyer, to whom she dedicated the book. Her accomplished treatment of criminal psychology made little impression, however, and she soon turned to more conventional stories.

The Irishman Lynn Brock[8] followed a different path, digressing from elaborate puzzles solved by his Great Detective Colonel Gore to produce what his publishers described as 'a character study of a normal man turned murderer'. *Nightmare* (1932) was, they claimed, one of the most remarkable books they had ever published. Unfortunately, nobody took much notice.

Nightmare is strange and surreal. Brock pours much emotional energy into his account of the misfortunes of Simon Whalley, an

Irish playwright. Whalley and his wife Elsa are tormented by their neighbours, and after Elsa dies, he determines on vengeance. The nihilistic mood – for instance in a disturbing passage about an attempted rape that follows discussions about 'Freud and birth control and homosexuality and totemism and infinity and things of that sort' – reflects Brock's adherence to Arthur Schopenhauer's pessimistic philosophy. This, coupled with an unusual and downbeat finale, doomed the book to failure. No doubt demoralised, Brock refrained from publishing another crime novel for six years. This was *The Silver Sickle Case* (1938), but by then Brock had lost his place in the vanguard of detective novelists.

The most powerful British novel of the 1920s to focus on homicidal psychology was C. S. Forester's *Payment Deferred* (1926). Personal experience of financial hardship sharpened his portrayal of a bank clerk, William Marble, who is in debt and at his wits' end when a nephew newly arrived from Australia and with a wallet full of cash pays an unexpected visit. Having poisoned the young man and buried his corpse in the garden, Marble indulges in profitable financial speculation with the proceeds before his luck turns sour.

In *Payment Deferred*, the legal system fails to guarantee true justice, and the deficiency is supplied by a savage twist of fate. The book, adapted for the stage with Charles Laughton playing Marble, and subsequently filmed, proved highly influential. Forester's second crime novel followed a similar pattern. *Plain Murder*[9] (1930) features a murderous conspiracy between three men who face dismissal from an advertising agency after being caught out in a minor fiddle. Their apparent success in carrying out the perfect murder feeds the ringleader's ego, with disastrous consequences.

Forester's third crime novel, *The Pursued*, was a dark tale of domestic abuse, murder and revenge in the suburbs. Written in 1935, the book was frank in its treatment of sex and ahead of its time in the way it portrayed discrimination against women. This time, the ironic twist in the narrative was matched by the book's own fate.

Forester wrote the story in California, having been lured to

Hollywood by a film deal. He submitted the manuscript, but publication, as well as payment, was deferred. Forester began writing about the Napoleonic era naval officer Horatio Hornblower; meanwhile the publishers managed to mislay the manuscript of *The Pursued*.

The Hornblower books enjoyed such success that Forester didn't return to crime writing. He regretted the book's loss, saying mournfully: 'It is just possible that a typescript still exists, forgotten and gathering dust in a rarely used storeroom in Boston or Bloomsbury.' Decades after his death in 1966 it surfaced.

In 2011, *The Pursued* finally appeared in print. Its prolonged disappearance was an extreme example of the neglect suffered by several British novels of psychological suspense during the interwar years. The outstanding exceptions were two books published by the mysterious Francis Iles.

In a preface to *The Second Shot*, Anthony Berkeley identified the potential of 'a puzzle of character', and this led him to write a different type of crime novel. He chose a new persona, borrowing the name of Francis Iles, a smuggler who was a distant ancestor. In keeping with his obsessive desire for privacy, he insisted that his new publisher, Victor Gollancz, must not disclose that Iles was Anthony Berkeley.

The first Iles book, subtitled *The Story of a Commonplace Crime*, reflected his interest in real-life crime, borrowing from the case of Major Herbert Armstrong, the only British solicitor hanged for murder. But *Malice Aforethought* (1931) broke away from his previous work by exploring the culprit's mindset rather than the intricacies of detection.

The misadventures of a meek, philandering doctor who sets out to murder his domineering wife are recounted with cool wit. Dr Bickleigh's criminal career follows a similar course to William Marble's in *Payment Deferred*, but Forester's dreary suburban landscape gave way to a charming Devon village, and an upper-class milieu where people play tennis and go to tea parties, and never have to scratch around to make ends meet.

Malice Aforethought caught the moment. Gollancz's cunning leak of the news that the Iles name masked the identity of a well-known writer prompted feverish, and often hilariously inaccurate, guess-work. These stabs in the dark amused Berkeley, until Alexander Woollcott infuriated him by suggesting that the Iles name disguised a collaboration in which E. M. Delafield – with whom Berkeley was infatuated – had improved the original work.

Naomi Royde-Smith shrewdly argued that the way women were presented in the book did not suggest a female author, although the names of Marie Belloc Lowndes and F. Tennyson Jesse were among those put forward. Gollancz gleefully stoked the speculation, demanding 'Who is Francis Iles?' on the dust jacket of his second novel, *Before the Fact* (1932), and listing twenty candidates mooted in the Press.

Before the Fact, sardonically subtitled *A Murder Story for Ladies*, is a story about a victim. In orthodox whodunits, the victim was usually a cipher whose main purpose in life (and in death) was to provide suspects with potential motives for murder. Heartless black-mailers and rich, unpleasant old folk who gleefully threaten to disinherit impoverished dependants were done to death with monotonous regularity.

Iles' focus was very different. The doomed marriage of Johnnie and Lina Aysgarth teems with subtle horrors. Johnnie Aysgarth is an updated version of William Palmer, the nineteenth-century Rugeley Poisoner, but the main focus is on Lina. Her masochistic willingness to hope for the best in the face of mounting evidence of her husband's cruelty and criminality is tragic and horrifying.

Iles argued that women such as Palmer's doomed wife Annie sometimes demonstrated an 'instinctive submissiveness' when threatened by male cruelty. He later admitted that he hadn't adequately captured Lina's psychological make-up, but the story remains an extraordinary study of coercive control. Light relief is afforded by Isobel Sedbusk, a detective novelist modelled on Dorothy L. Sayers, and an 'ardent feminist'. Alfred Hitchcock filmed the story as *Suspicion*, but not even he dared to adopt Iles' night-marish ending, and the movie ends in anticlimax.

After years of writing non-stop, Iles was burned out. *As for the Woman*, produced after a gap of seven years, was rejected by Gollancz, who regarded the story as sadistic. Iles' new publishers did him no favours by subtitling the novel *A Love Story* and insisting in the jacket description that the book 'is not a thriller, and is not intended to thrill'.

There is more to the story than the unpromising blurb intimated. Young Alan, the femme fatale Evelyn and her threatening husband Pawle had real-life counterparts in the author, Delafield and her husband Paul. Having poured his obsessions into the story, Iles was distraught at its failure. His emotional life plunged into turmoil when Delafield succumbed to cancer, and his creative spark died.[10] *As for the Woman* was proclaimed as the first of a trilogy, but he never published another novel.

Iles' blend of chilling irony and unorthodox plotting inspired fellow authors for decades. Milward Kennedy[11] said that Iles had discerned a new road for the crime novel – 'the "inner history" of the murder itself'. Iles' followers developed the inverted mystery, experimenting with story structure[12] while charting the malign workings of Fate. Their books were sometimes witty and frequently cynical.

Dedicating *Sic Transit Gloria* (1936) to Victor Gollancz, Kennedy described the book as an 'experiment' reflecting his belief that 'if the detective-novel becomes too stereotyped . . . the genre may be destroyed'. James Southern discovers the corpse of glamorous Gloria Day in his London flat, yet Kennedy's priority was not to create a whodunit puzzle but to tackle a burning issue of the times.

The 1930s were a decade of anxiety: economic, social and political. People worried about the outlook for a world in which dictators like Hitler, Mussolini and Stalin seemed all-powerful. Critics who patronise Golden Age detective fiction routinely neglect the way authors such as Kennedy used the framework of a crime story to explore questions of the kind put by James Southern: 'A jury could only have secured injustice. What did the law matter – if the law could not have secured justice? People talked of judicial murder: was not judicial failure to secure the just punishment of a murderer just as bad?'

Kennedy was a thoughtful writer, but lacked Agatha Christie's verve. She wrapped up similar questions in entertainments such as *Murder on the Orient Express* and *And Then There Were None*, novels so popular and so dazzlingly original that their preoccupation with combating injustice is routinely overlooked.

The wittiest account of an 'altruistic crime' came in *Trial and Error* (1937). The novel was published as by Anthony Berkeley rather than Francis Iles, because one of Berkeley's recurrent characters, Ambrose Chitterwick, is called on to achieve justice against the odds. On discovering that he is terminally ill, Lawrence Todhunter decides to kill someone in order to benefit mankind. He toys with the idea of becoming a political assassin before settling for a domestic murder, intended to rid the world of a malign presence. He seems to commit the perfect crime, but, when an innocent person is accused, he confesses his guilt. The irony is that the police refuse to believe him.

Iles' youngest disciple was Leonard O. Mosley,[13] who wrote *So I Killed Her* (1936) in his early twenties. The narrator is a detective novelist whose determination to commit the perfect murder is compromised by the collapse of his sanity. Set mainly in the United States, and unusually frank about sex, this ice-cold novel has been strangely overlooked by critics.

Iles' influence also pervades the work of C. E. Vulliamy,[14] Bruce Hamilton and Richard Hull, one of crime writing's few chartered accountants.[15] The dust jacket of Hull's first novel, *The Murder of My Aunt*[16] (1934) trumpeted the freshness of his approach: 'There is no C.I.D. Inspector, no medico-legal pundit, no erudite dilettante with lightning intuition; yet there is murder and there is detection. The author plays the game with fair rules, but new rules of his own making.'

In charting the odious Edward Powell's attempts to dispose of his almost equally repellent Aunt Mildred, Hull achieved, in Dorothy L. Sayers' words, 'originality and unlikeness to anything else'. The book was 'a study of unbalanced reactions to delight the heart of the psychologist . . . The insensitive might even find it as funny as it appears to be on the surface; the sensitive will find it painful, but continuously interesting and exciting.'

Hull's novels brimmed with trickery, and Jorge Luis Borges was among his admirers. *Murder Isn't Easy* (1936; the title encapsulates the haplessness of Hull's homicidally inclined puppets), set in an advertising agency, tells the story from multiple viewpoints, manipulated to ingenious effect. His darkest book, *My Own Murderer*

(1940), has a solicitor-narrator with a boundless capacity for self-deception. Hull gave the character his own real name, Richard Henry Sampson.

For all Hull's flair, his work suffered from two recurrent faults. One clever idea alone will not sustain a full-length novel, and over-reliance on unpleasantness – however amusingly conveyed – as a defining personality trait is not enough to create characters whom readers care about. *Last First* (1947) pokes fun at those who peek at the ending of detective stories by presenting the final chapter at the start, but the story is turgid. The clever set-up in *A Matter of Nerves* (1950), with events narrated by a murderer[17] whose identity is concealed, is also squandered. By the time of his final book, *The Martineau Murders* (1953), Hull was reduced to reworking the plot of his memorable debut.

A particular irony deprived two interesting novels of the attention they deserved: both were published just as the Second World War broke out. Roland Wild's debut *The Trial of Mary Court* ends tantalisingly, with the jury about to deliver its verdict on whether a woman is guilty of murdering her husband; it is left for the reader to decide. Wild was an Englishman who emigrated to Canada, as was John de Navarre Kennedy, whose *Crime in Reverse* is even more striking: Nicholas Chetwynd K.C. accepts the brief to defend Eric Ricardo, who is accused of murdering a private detective called Makin. But we know from the start that Chetwynd himself is the killer.

Iles and most of his fellow Ironists wrote about the world they knew: middle-class English society. An exception was Peter Drax,[18] whose insight into the everyday existence of ordinary people strengthens taut books such as *High Seas Murder* (1939), set in a working-class fishing port. *Death by Two Hands* (1937) describes how the theft of valuable fox-skins leads to murder. There isn't a country house in sight, far less a secret passage or locked room, but Drax offers a neat twist – of character – in the book's last line.

If Drax understood how poverty blights lives, Donald Henderson experienced it at first-hand. Henderson was an actor and writer whose inability to find work during the Slump led to his sleeping rough for months on end. He shared Iles' fascination with criminal cases from real life.[19] Just as William Palmer's homicidal career supplied material for *Before the Fact*, so it helped to shape the storyline of Henderson's undeservedly neglected novel about a loathsome serial killer, *Murderer at Large* (1936).

Procession – to Prison (1937), a crime novel about a 'trunk murderer', was well received, but after that Henderson 'could sell nothing . . . for fully two years . . . The irony of the literary life . . . seems to lie in the fact that, when you are all but down and out, you can write well, but your luck is never any good from the *selling* point of view. Poverty breeds more poverty.'

Henderson tramped the streets of London and Edinburgh looking for work 'with my press cutting book under my arm'. He lost his nerve as an actor, and following a spell in hospital, and when war broke out, his attempt to enlist was rebuffed. Instead, he became an ambulance driver but suffered severe injuries during the Blitz.

He began a new novel with the unlikely ingredients of serial killings and a religious theme. The result was *Mr Bowling Buys a Newspaper* (1943), which was successfully adapted for the stage. The film rights were bought and Henderson's praises were sung by Raymond Chandler. His luck seemed to have changed, but *Goodbye to Murder* (1946), a black comedy concerning domestic abuse, sexual repression and a female serial killer, proved to be Henderson's last novel. That brief upturn in fortune was brought to a cruel end by lung cancer.

He was soon forgotten. The most telling epitaph came from Chandler, who said that *Mr Bowling Buys a Newspaper* was 'one of the most fascinating books written in the last ten years . . . Yet I doubt whether it has sold 5,000 copies over here. There is something wrong with the book business.'

Lauded in his prime as a mainstream novelist, and ultimately knighted, Hugh Walpole relished the company of fellow writers. His circle included such diverse figures as Marie Belloc Lowndes, Edgar Wallace and William Plomer, and he collaborated with Clemence Dane on an appreciation of Claude Houghton, author of books such as the unorthodox psychological mystery *I Am Jonathan Scrivener* (1930).

Literary fashion is fickle. Walpole's reputation declined during his lifetime and has calcified since his death. Yet to write him off as a thin-skinned hack with a gift for self-promotion is an unfair caricature. A closeted homosexual, he wrestled with his own demons, and his occasional ventures into crime are psychologically intriguing. His memorably sadistic villains include Leroy Pengelly in *Above the Dark Circus* (1931), a novel admired by Borges.

The Killer and the Slain offers a chilling variation on the Jekyll and Hyde theme. John Ozias Talbot is bullied by a degenerate school friend, James Oliphant Tunstall, whose subsequent reappearance drives Talbot, a sensitive novelist, to murder. The crime leads to fresh torment, as Talbot (whose most successful book is rather like *Before the Fact*) begins to resemble his loathsome enemy. Walpole died before publication in 1942, and his novel failed to earn the attention it deserved.

Iles' principal post-war heirs[20] were John Bingham and Julian Symons, but the most unorthodox mystery in this vein was written by a woman,[21] Constance Lindsay Taylor,[22] under the pen-name Guy Cullingford.

In *Post Mortem* (1953), the murder of detestable author Gilbert Worth is investigated by Worth's own ghost.[23] This conceit allows for wry humour, as the deceased discovers that his nearest were by no means his dearest. Even his mistress, Rosina, is quick to transfer her affections. Rosina emphasises post-war changes in class relations, arguing: 'This is the day when belted earls show people round their grounds for half a crown a time, and all the slum kids boast about their television sets.'

In an epilogue, a publisher makes the eternal complaint that: 'Publishing is a tricky business at the best of times, and these were not the best of times.' A member of Worth's family wryly notes that 'nothing can keep a writer from scribbling, probably not even death.'

Notes

The main sources are Donald Henderson's unpublished memoir and the research into his life by Paul Harding.

1   *Plomer's publishers were Leonard and Virginia Woolf of the Hogarth Press*:
    The Woolfs also published *Death by Request*, the sole detective novel by
    Augustus John's son Romilly and his wife Katherine, a mystery with a
    striking if unoriginal twist.

2   *The Case is Altered became one of Hogarth's most commercially successful
    titles*: In a review for the *Spectator*, L. A. G. Strong quoted Hugh Walpole's
    view that Plomer possessed 'unqualified genius'. Strong's detective Inspector
    Ellis McKay was a composer in his spare time. In *All Fall Down*, a tyrannical
    bibliophile appears to have been crushed to death by an avalanche of books.

3   *the authors didn't think of themselves as 'crime writers'*: Theodore Dreiser's
    An American Tragedy was included in the Howard Haycraft–Ellery Queen
    'definitive library' of 'detective story cornerstones', as indeed was Victor
    Hugo's *Les Misérables*. Dreiser's book, based on the murder of Grace Brown,
    brims with irony but is hardly a genre novel; the crime is a metaphor for
    fault lines in American society. Similar crimes in the early 1930s were
    dubbed 'the American Tragedy murders'. Dreiser argued that they weren't
    copycat killings but illustrations of the societal ills he described.

4   *a single detective novel in the classic vein*: This was *Murder at School*, aka
    Was it Murder?, published as by Glen Trevor. The amateur sleuth, Colin
    Revell, proves as fallible as Philip Trent or Roger Sheringham. Benn, the
    publishers, offered a ten pound prize for the first person to guess Trevor's
    real identity.

5   *A. P. Herbert*: Herbert's achievements included a campaign for divorce law
    reform, a long stint as an independent MP and authorship of a series of
    'misleading cases' illustrating the absurdities of English law.

6   *The House by the River*: Fritz Lang's film of the book is an example of
    'Gothic noir', with music by George Antheil.

7   *Joanna Cannan*: Her *Ithuriel's Hour*, aka *The Hour of the Angel*, recounts
    a Himalayan expedition that culminates in a killing. She later wrote two
    short series featuring police detectives.

8   *Lynn Brock*: Brock's real name was Alister McAllister. He was (like Simon
    Whalley) an Irish playwright and his play *The Riddle* (as by Anthony Wharton,
    with Morley Roberts co-credited) drew on the Maybrick case.

9   *Plain Murder*: The setting anticipates that of Sayers' *Murder Must Advertise*,
    published three years later.

10 *his creative spark died*: Iles continued to review, proving as opinionated
    and perceptive as Sayers and Symons. He championed Patricia Highsmith,
    among others, describing *The Glass Cell*, with its 'savage indictment of the
    American penal system', as 'a major event in the progress of crime-fiction'.

11 *Milward Kennedy*: His real name was Milward Rodon Kennedy Burge. The
    way in which justice is thwarted at the end of *Death to the Rescue*, and the
    cynicism of the finale to *I'll be Judge, I'll be Jury*, reflect Iles' influence.
    Kennedy tipped a hat to his mentor in the equally innovative *Poison in the
    Parish* (which opens with a 'Prologue or Epilogue') by naming his narrator
    Francis Anthony; the novel explores the concept of the altruistic crime.
    Kennedy too gave up writing detective fiction to concentrate on reviewing.

12 *experimenting with story structure*: Writing in *CADS* 77, Kate Jackson
    highlights the crossovers between Golden Age fiction and modernist
    literature in terms of themes and techniques, a fruitful field for further
    study.

13 *Leonard O. Mosley*: He became a prolific writer but was best known as a biographer.

14 *C. E. Vulliamy*: His early crime novels, published as by Anthony Rolls, display his gift for satire, although sometimes the jokes wore thin, as in *The Vicar's Experiments*, aka *Clerical Error*, about a homicidal clergyman; Peter Lovesey's *The Reaper* handled comparable material more effectively almost seventy years later. *Family Matters* deals with attempts to commit murder, which, in Dorothy L. Sayers' words, led to 'a most original and grimly farcical situation, and an ironic surprise-ending, pregnant with poetical injustice.' After a break of almost twenty years, he relaunched his career with *Don among the Dead Men*, filmed as *A Jolly Bad Fellow*.

15 *one of crime writing's few chartered accountants*: Brian Flynn, a local government accountant, created the gentlemanly private detective Anthony Bathurst and wrote three thrillers as Charles Wogan. Frank Arthur Ebert, who worked as an accountant in Fiji and New Zealand before returning to his native Britain, published a brief series with a Fijian background as well as the stand-alone *Confession to Murder*, all under the name Frank Arthur. Today, Abir Mukherjee, formerly an accountant, has Sam Wyndham and Surendranath Banerjee investigating crime in Raj-era India.

16 *The Murder of My Aunt*: The book is also 'the best, and by far the most entertaining, of the early English mystery novels with a gay angle', at least according to Anthony Slide in *Lost Gay Novels: A Reference Guide to Fifty Works from the First Half of the Twentieth Century*.

17 *events narrated by a murderer*: A similar gimmick is used in *They'll Never Find Out* by Francis Duncan, a pen-name of William Underhill.

18 *Peter Drax*: This was the pseudonym of Eric Elrington Addis. A practising barrister, he published half a dozen crime novels in a four-year burst. Work on his next book was interrupted when war broke out. He became a warship commander, but was killed during a German air raid on Alexandria. *Sing a Song of Murder*, completed by his wife Hazel, appeared posthumously.

19 *He shared Iles' fascination with criminal cases from real life:* With John Dickson Carr's encouragement, he wrote a radio play about the Borden case.

20 *Iles' principal post-war heirs*: Although F. Addington Symonds remains obscure in Britain, the French scholar François Rivière praised the originality of his ironic mysteries, including *Smile and Murder*.

21 *written by a woman*: Yolanda Foldes' *Mind Your Own Murder*, in which a millionaire invites one of his four nephews to murder him, also bears some of the Ironists' hallmarks. Foldes' real name was Jolán Földes; born in Hungary, she emigrated to England in 1941.

22 *Constance Lindsay Taylor*: Her first book, *Murder with Relish*, published as by C. Lindsay Taylor, is a witty examination of the class divide; a domestic cook turns detective in order to achieve justice for her late employer. As Cullingford, Taylor continued to write interestingly but infrequently.

23 *the murder . . . is investigated by Worth's own ghost*: This plot device seems to have originated in Robert Barr's novella *From Whose Bourne*, in which a ghost helps to clear his wife of poisoning him. In *Dead to the World*, by the American pulp merchant David X. Manners, a mystery writer solves his own death, while in a 1951 comedy film, *You Never Can Tell*, a dog poisoned for money is reincarnated as a private eye who solves the crime. In the same year, another post-mortem investigation was recounted by Olivier

Séchan and Igor Maslowski in *You Have Never Been Murdered* (*Vous qui n'avez été tués*), which won the *Prix du Roman d'Aventures*, but has yet to be translated into English. F. Addington Symonds' *Murder of Me* follows a similar pattern, while Robertson Davies' *Murther and Walking Spirits*, on the fringe of the genre like a number of his books, begins with the murder of the narrator and then charts his afterlife. A televisual variation on the theme came in the Flemish-language serial *Hotel Beau Séjour*, first aired in Belgium in 2017.

TWENTY-THREE

The Sound of Mystery

Radio mysteries

Spring 1930, and the BBC is barely three years old. Modest in size but not in ambition, the Corporation has already commissioned the building of a new Broadcasting House at Portland Place. Sir John Reith, the Director General, aims to focus on 'all that is best in every department of human knowledge, endeavour, and achievement . . . The preservation of a high moral tone is obviously of paramount importance.'

What better way to achieve these high-minded objectives than by broadcasting a detective story written by half a dozen authors in collaboration?

Anthony Berkeley and Dorothy L. Sayers were determined to raise the profile of the newly established Detection Club, and they seized the moment. They went to lunch at the Savoy with the BBC's Howard Marshall and were joined by Agatha Christie, Hugh Walpole, E. C. Bentley and Father Ronald Knox. Walpole agreed to circulate a synopsis of a story, and it was agreed that those writing later instalments could ask their predecessors to foreshadow the plot twists they had in mind.

So far, so good. The BBC's magazine *The Listener* introduced the story, *Behind the Screen*, as the work of 'the well-known Detection Club', and promised that it would build to a 'nerve-shattering and brain-racking conclusion'. The authors would not only write the episodes, but broadcast them as well. There was even an interactive element, with Milward Kennedy supervising a competition for armchair detectives.

Bold, innovative and exciting as the project was, it bristled with complexity. The story would be told over six weeks. On the first Saturday evening, Walpole, one of the most popular writers in the country, and also an accomplished broadcaster, would read the first instalment. An eighteen-hundred word transcript would appear in *The Listener* the following Wednesday. This timescale proved nightmarishly tight.

Walpole refused to write out his instalment. Insisting that he must be spontaneous, he spoke from notes. Hilda Matheson, in charge of the Talks Department, arranged for two parliamentary reporters to take down his words, and type them up on the Sunday morning, so that she or Marshall could check the transcript that afternoon, and post the corrected version to the printers so that they had it at half past seven on Monday morning. Even then, publication of *The Listener* was delayed.

As instalment succeeded instalment, the challenges increased, for the BBC as well as for listeners trying to fathom the puzzle. Milward Kennedy even disagreed with *The Listener*'s edict that sufficient clues should be supplied by the middle of the story to enable the solution to be guessed. 'My view is less mathematical,' he said.

Eventually the story reached a conclusion that more or less made sense, even if Ronald Knox's solution was scarcely a model of fair play. Sixty people who entered the competition were lured into suggesting that the victim died by accident, and nobody answered all the questions correctly.

As a postscript, the BBC arranged a broadcast in which Berkeley and Sayers plotted a detective story together.[1] Having planned their mystery off-air, they edited it to fit a fifty-minute time slot, and concluded by inviting their audience to suggest a title. By modern broadcasting standards, their audience of twelve million people was big enough to kill for.

The BBC was delighted and persuaded Sayers to mastermind a follow-up mystery. Despite continuing squabbles with J. R. Ackerley of the Talks Department, the Detection Club's second round-robin mystery, *The Scoop*, set in a newspaper office and suggested by a real-life crime,[2] proved a triumph. A survey of listeners resulted in almost fifteen hundred appreciations; a few super-sensitive souls criticised Sayers' 'vulgarity and profanity', but she was also the most popular speaker.

Ackerley hoped to commission a new mystery, either written entirely in dialogue or taking the form of a complete murder trial, but the Detection Club members had other ideas. They contemplated expanding *The Scoop* into a full-length book, but decided instead to write a new collaborative novel, and the success of *The Floating Admiral*[3] (1931) led to three more published joint ventures, before they returned to the BBC in 1940 with a series of six radio mysteries.[4]

Val Gielgud was not involved with the Detection Club's two cross-media initiatives,[5] but played a central role in the Corporation's ventures into criminal entertainment. At the age of sixteen, he'd made his debut as a producer with 'a shameless plagiarism of *Raffles* – with my brother John as the adventuress swathed in ropes of remarkable sham pearls – before no less an audience than G. K. Chesterton in his studio at Beaconsfield'.

Gielgud understood that a skilled writer who took account of 'the blindness of the audience . . . and the ineffectiveness of purely physical action', could exploit 'the peculiar advantages of radio,[6] where time and space can be travelled without impediment'. He became embroiled in controversy when the left-wing *Daily Herald*, improbably supported by the right-wing British Empire Union, attacked the broadcasting of Patrick Hamilton's *Rope*, but his colleague Eric Maschwitz consoled him that any publicity was better than none. Gielgud's exotic lifestyle – he married five times, and often wore a cloak and carried a sword-cane – was certainly a gift for the gossip columnists.

Maschwitz reckoned that the BBC would make a perfect setting for a murder mystery, so he and Gielgud duly set off to the south of France with a Corporation secretary, dictating seventy thousand words to her in the space of sixteen days. The result was *Death at Broadcasting House*, aka *London Calling!* (1934), with Maschwitz adopting the pen-name of Holt Marvell. The book was turned into a film starring Jack Hawkins, with Gielgud – a competent actor, if no match for his illustrious brother John – playing Julian Caird, the Director of Drama.

Dorothy L. Sayers reviewed the book favourably, but questioned a detail of the plot; Gielgud proudly referred to blueprints of the Broadcasting House studio plans in order to prove her wrong. But he and Maschwitz got their comeuppance when they exploited their experience of moviemaking. Sayers disapproved of *Death as an Extra* (1935) and its reliance on 'a bunch of the most tedious American gangsters who ever bumped their victims off in season and out of season'. She had a point: the appearance of American gangsters (let alone quasi-Ruritanian politicians and aristocrats) in Golden Age detective fiction is an unmistakable clue to second-rate stories.

Maschwitz's success in writing lyrics for songs such as 'These Foolish Things' eventually took him away from the BBC and from crime writing. Gielgud never fulfilled his hopes of achieving success as a literary novelist, but continued to write detective fiction. His main contribution to the genre came in encouraging fellow crime novelists to write for radio.

He had a nightmarish relationship with the thriller writer Peter Cheyney, though, whose interest in broadcasting 'lay in the medium's advertising rather than its literary or dramatic attractions'. Cheyney enjoyed some success with his early radio work, notably *The Adventures of Alonzo MacTavish*, featuring a clone of Leslie Charteris' Simon Templar, but his intolerance of criticism meant Gielgud found him impossible to work with.

In contrast, Gielgud respected Sayers, and produced her controversial and groundbreaking religious play *The Man Born to Be King*. He, like many others, was startled on meeting her for the first time: 'I had expected to meet a feminine version of Lord Peter Wimsey . . . I confess to having felt a mingling of shock and disappointment when I came face to face with a square-shouldered, tweed-clad, evidently practical woman in pince-nez with something of the air of an amiable bull-terrier.' They found they had much in common, however, including a love of Oxford, a hatred of time-wasting and bad cooking, and a warm friendship with John Dickson Carr.

*

Encouraged by Gielgud, Carr became a leading exponent of radio crime drama,[7] demonstrating a flair for macabre atmospherics, snappy dialogue and ingenious plots. His radio plays, which included an eight-part mystery set in Regency England, *Speak of the Devil*, often dispensed with a series detective, but Dr Gideon Fell was on hand to answer the question posed in Carr's BBC debut, *Who Killed Matthew Corbin?*

Once the USA entered the war, Carr was ordered home. CBS aired an adaptation of his non-series novel *The Burning Court* in its anthology series *Suspense*, and he began to contribute fresh material, performed by actors including Peter Lorre, whose sinister tones were heard in three of Carr's plays, and Sydney Greenstreet,[8] perfectly cast as Gideon Fell in *The Hangman Won't Wait*. Add to the mix music by Bernard Herrmann, and the entertainment for listeners was as compelling as it was melodramatic.

Returning to Britain in 1943, primarily to write wartime propaganda, Carr was given an office at Broadcasting House. Among his colleagues was the actor-turned-writer Ernest Dudley, creator of the sinister psychoanalyst Dr Morelle,[9] and host of a book programme called *Armchair Detective*.

Carr persuaded Gielgud to broadcast 'a series of thrillers in the American manner, with all the trimmings of atmospheric bass-voiced narrator, knife-chords and other specially composed musical effects'. The result was a British counterpart to *Suspense*, the popular series *Appointment with Fear*, introduced by Valentine Dyall, alias 'The Man in Black'.

Carr and Gielgud also wrote stage plays. *Inspector Silence Takes the Air* featured an impossible crime in a cellar used as a BBC studio; among the characters was Julian Caird, from *Death at Broadcasting House*. Carr was also responsible for a radio play about Jack Silence, but the Scotland Yard man wasn't one of his own creations. He'd first appeared in a serial called *Death Comes to the Hibiscus* by Gielgud and a British co-author using the pen-name Nicholas Vane. The Vane pseudonym concealed the identity of a man already renowned for his radio work, Francis Durbridge.

*

Francis Durbridge's life changed when, at the age of twenty-five, he wrote a serial featuring a new character for broadcast by the BBC Midland Region. By 1938, Durbridge was one of the few writers earning a living solely from work for the BBC. His break-through came with the invention of a suave and successful novelist with a penchant for solving mysteries that defeat Scotland Yard. The paragon's name was Paul Temple.

Send for Paul Temple comprised eight episodes, each lasting twenty-five minutes. Temple meets a chic and charming journalist, Louise Harvey, who has changed her name to Steve Trent in her quest to unmask the Knave of Diamonds, leader of a ruthless gang of jewel thieves. After Steve's brother, a police officer, is murdered by the gang, she and Temple collaborate to work out the meaning of a dying message clue – 'the Green Finger!' – uttered by one of the gang's victims.

The Green Finger proves to be a pub on the outskirts of Evesham, a counter-intuitive choice of headquarters for 'the most sensational criminal organisation in Europe'. The combination of cliffhanger endings to each episode, pacy, action-packed writing, Temple's sophisticated lifestyle and the corkscrew plot proved enormously popular. Seven thousand listeners demanded that the BBC send Paul Temple back to the airwaves, and Durbridge quickly obliged with another mystery in the same vein, *Paul Temple and the Front Page Men*. A star was born.

Paul and Steve celebrated their first joint investigation by marrying, and their light-hearted banter became a recurrent feature of the stories. The BBC had previously broadcast Dashiell Hammett's *The Thin Man*, and the popularity of Nick and Nora Charles demonstrated the potential of a husband-and-wife team of investigators, but Paul and Steve were much more genteel. Whereas their American counterparts battled alcoholism and (by the standards of the time) talked dirty, the Temples' endless cocktail-quaffing never seemed to have any adverse effects, and Paul's strongest oath was 'By Timothy!'[10]

Durbridge didn't aspire to Hammett's literary excellence. He stuck to a formula, with regular attempts to run the Temples' car off the road, bomb them out of existence or lure them to lonely spots where murder victims survived just long enough to gasp out cryptic messages. Their friend, Scotland Yard Commissioner Sir Graham Forbes, proved so dependent on their help as to seem clueless. Yet Durbridge's storytelling flair kept listeners glued to the wireless.

Under assorted names, Durbridge was immensely prolific, although, like many American pulp writers, he had a habit of recycling material; different titles often conceal the same plot. He created a host of investigators. During the Second World War, with Val Gielgud, he wrote *The Girl at the Hibiscus*, six short radio plays about Amanda Smith, a nightclub dance hostess. Amanda returned in *Death Comes to the Hibiscus*, the twelve-part serial that introduced the enigmatic Inspector Silence, but her career proved short-lived. Durbridge's next idea was to create a female counterpart to A. J. Raffles, but the BBC shared Arthur Conan Doyle's disapproval of any attempt to glamorise the criminal, and the character became another female journalist, Gail Carlton.

Neither Gail nor any of Durbridge's other detectives came close to matching Temple's longevity or global appeal. Far from fading from the post-war scene, the character became ubiquitous. The radio serials were now introduced by the famous 'Coronation Scot' theme tune, with Peter Coke[11] portraying Temple. The stories were novelised, and adapted for film and (much later, with scripts written by others) for television. There was even a Paul Temple comic strip, which ran in daily newspapers for over twenty years.

Durbridge's stand-alone television serials enjoyed huge success. Among the finest were two six-part serials in the 1960s: *Melissa* concerned the murder of a writer's wife, while the untypical *Bat Out of Hell* was a first-rate inverted mystery. More than thirty years after its original screening, *Melissa* was re-written by Alan Bleasdale, a leading television dramatist and long-standing Durbridge fan.

Bleasdale, renowned for gritty social realism rather than cunning plot twists, undoubtedly possesses superior literary gifts, but the homage misfired. His attempt to graft character-driven writing on to a clever plot lacked grip. Writing taut, compelling mysteries is not as easy as Durbridge made it look.

*

The United States had no equivalent to the BBC, and rival broad-casters were soon fighting each other for audience share and advertising revenue. The popularity of mysteries meant that detectives became as ubiquitous on the airwaves[12] as on the printed page. Many of fiction's private eyes had their own shows, while many detectives were created especially for radio.

Chester Gould introduced Dick Tracy in a comic strip for the *Detroit Mirror* in 1931. Three years later Tracy was given his own radio series. Chisel-jawed Tracy battled against an array of dastardly villains,[13] thrilling youthful listeners but allowing little scope for audience participation.

George Zachary, a radio producer with CBS, felt that radio audiences would relish pitting their wits against those of a detective. After discovering the Ellery Queen novels, Zachary proposed to the co-authors Fred Dannay and Manny Lee that Ellery should star in his own weekly series of hour-long shows.

At first the cousins were dubious. As Dannay said, writing for radio requires 'different muscles' from collaborating on novels. But the prospect of writing for an audience of millions proved irresistible, and the pair undertook an apprenticeship in the unfamiliar medium, writing scripts for existing series. They also created a game show called *Author! Author!* Each week's episode began with a dramatised version of a mysterious incident, after which a panel of four, including Dannay and Lee, would be asked to devise a scenario which made sense of it. Listeners were also invited to contribute.

The Adventures of Ellery Queen, which introduced Ellery's secretary Nikki Porter,[14] began its run in 1939, with Bernard Herrmann[15] as music director. The last scene of the script was even withheld from the actors until the last minute, and the radio equivalent of the novels' Challenge to the Reader involved guest celebrities such as Dorothy Parker putting forward solutions. With the exception of Lillian Hellman, quick to solve the puzzle of 'Napoleon's Razor', the famous guests often failed to distinguish themselves, and Zachary's attempt to involve the public met with limited success. But audiences loved the show.

To turn out weekly scripts was punishing, and eventually the cousins took a fifteen-month break. During that time Dannay launched *Ellery Queen's Mystery Magazine*,[16] which flourishes to this day. The pair also honed their skills as novelists. *Calamity Town*,[17] the first of a more sophisticated run of books, has long been regarded as one of their finest achievements. Yet at first it failed to find a publisher, and so they resumed their radio work.

Writing to schedule became too much for Dannay. Anthony Boucher took over from him, but without earning a credit, and developed the series to reflect his socially liberal views. *Murder for Americans*,[18] for instance, is a story about hate pamphlets attacking Jews, Catholics and black people; the culprit is a white man, motivated by personal gain.

The radio series finally ended in 1948, but novels continued to flow. Ellery also turned up on television, notably in a series created by Richard Levinson and William Link and screened in the mid-1970s. Jim Hutton starred as Ellery and the pilot episode featured a dying-message clue. In deference to tradition, each story challenged the viewer to solve the puzzle before Ellery revealed all.

Notes

The main sources include Alexis Weedon's article '"Behind the Screen" and "The Scoop": A Cross-Media Experiment in Publishing and Broadcasting Crime Fiction in the Early 1930s', *Media History*, vol. 13, no. 1, 2017; Val Gielgud's memoirs *Years of the Locust* and *Years in a Mirror*; Douglas Greene's biography of John Dickson Carr; the biographies of Patrick Hamilton by Nigel Jones, Sean French and Bruce Hamilton; Melvyn Barnes' *Francis Durbridge: A Centenary Appreciation*; and Francis M. Nevins and Martin Grams Jr's *The Sound of Detection: Ellery Queen's Adventures in Radio*

1 *Berkeley and Sayers plotted a detective story together*: The transcript was published by Tony Medawar as 'Plotting a Detective Story' in *CADS* 51, April 2007.
2 *The Scoop . . . suggested by a real-life crime*: Patrick Mahon's murder of Emily Kaye in 1924, known variously as 'the Bungalow murder' and 'the Crumbles murder', was the source. The contributors were Sayers, Christie, Berkeley and Bentley again, plus Freeman Wills Crofts and Clemence Dane. *The Scoop* was finally published in book form, together with *Behind the Screen*, in 1983.
3 *The Floating Admiral*: In 2016 Simon Brett masterminded *The Sinking Admiral*, a modern homage to the book, and a collaboration between contemporary Detection Club members. The Club's most recent collaborations have been *Motives for Murder*, a book of short stories, and *Howdunit*, about the art and graft of crime writing.

4 *a series of six radio mysteries*: The authors were Anthony Gilbert, Anthony Berkeley, John Rhode, Nicholas Blake, Gladys Mitchell, and G. D. H. and Margaret Cole. A further series of radio plays by Club members in 1948 included Christie's *Butter in a Lordly Dish* and Cyril Hare's *The Murder at Warbeck Hall*, later expanded into *An English Murder*, his only novel featuring Dr Wenceslaus Bottwink.

5 *Val Gielgud was not involved with the Detection Club's two cross-media initiatives*: He did, however, become a member of the Club in 1947, having attended as John Dickson Carr's guest prior to war breaking out.

6 *the peculiar advantages of radio*: Gielgud made these points in an introduction to the printed version of Patrick Hamilton's *Money with Menaces* and *To the Public Danger*. He regarded the latter, which focuses on dangerous driving, as 'one of the very best of radio plays'.

7 *Carr became a leading exponent of radio crime drama*: Douglas Greene, who argues that Carr's plays 'were probably the best mystery dramas ever created for the radio', has been responsible for editing or publishing several volumes of them.

8 *Peter Lorre . . . and Sydney Greenstreet*: Lorre and Greenstreet teamed up with Humphrey Bogart, playing Sam Spade, in a memorable film version of Hammett's *The Maltese Falcon*.

9 *Ernest Dudley, creator of the sinister psychoanalyst Dr Morelle*: Dudley, the pen-name of Vivian Ernest Coltman-Allen, was a prolific and versatile writer for print, radio and television whose long, colourful life is summarised in Jack Adrian's obituary (*Independent*, 4 February 2006). Morelle, supposedly modelled on the film director Erich von Stroheim, was a sarcastic misogynist – 'The Man You Love to Hate!' After beginning life on radio, he appeared in novels, short stories, a film and a play. In the second series of radio plays, Morelle was portrayed by Heron Carvic, creator of the amateur detective Miss Seeton. The Seeton books, quintessentially English yet most popular with American readers who have a particular vision of England, were continued after Carvic's death by Roy Peter Martin – who also wrote as James Melville (as 'Hampton Charles') – and Sarah J. Mason ('Hamilton Crane').

10 *Paul's strongest oath was 'By Timothy!'*: In *Paul Temple and the Spencer Affair*, a villain's cunning impersonation of Temple is undone by his lamentably careless use of the phrase 'By George!' instead.

11 *Peter Coke*: That year, Coke also played the lead role in *Gravelhanger*, a six-part television series based on Gielgud's thriller of that name, but the show was poorly received.

12 *detectives became . . . ubiquitous on the airwaves*: Leading stars often played the gumshoe; examples include Frank Sinatra (Rocky Fortune), Dick Powell (Richard Diamond) and Edmond O'Brien (Johnny Dollar). *On the Air: The Encyclopedia of Old-Time Radio* is a definitive study by John Dunning, also a detective novelist and creator of the bookseller and former cop Cliff Janeway.

13 *Chisel-jawed Tracy battled against an array of dastardly villains*: Dick Tracy has become an American pop culture icon. A 1990 film starring Warren Beatty as Tracy earned three Oscars, including one for Stephen Sondheim, who contributed five songs.

14 *Ellery's secretary Nikki Porter*: Nikki was not herself a detective, but

American radio didn't lack female detectives who were smart, self-reliant and usually single. Among the many crime-solvers discussed in Jack French's *Private Eyelashes: Radio's Lady Detectives* is the singer and international crime-fighter Diane LaVolta, played by Marlene Dietrich in *Time for Love*. Diane was a reincarnation of Mademoiselle Madou, played by Dietrich in *Cafe Istanbul*; that show in turn drew heavily on *Everybody Comes to Rick's*, a then unproduced play by Murray Burnett and Joan Alison and the basis for the classic Bogart movie *Casablanca*.

15 *Bernard Herrmann*: Herrmann composed soundtracks for Hitchcock's *Vertigo* and *Psycho*, and Roman Polanski's *Chinatown*. His first wife was Lucille Fletcher, and he wrote the music for her radio play *The Hitch-Hiker*. Orson Welles called her *Sorry, Wrong Number* the greatest radio script ever written; it was filmed, novelised by Fletcher and Allan Ullman and formed the basis of three different operas.

16 *Ellery Queen's Mystery Magazine*: In its first eighty-one years of existence, the magazine has had only three editors: Dannay, Eleanor Sullivan and Janet Hutchings. This continuity has been a source of enduring strength, as has the magazine's emphasis on showcasing both leading writers and newcomers.

17 *Calamity Town*: The story gives a fresh spin to plot devices previously employed by Christie, Sayers and Francis Iles. It begins with Ellery relocating to a small New England town that became the background for a septet of mysteries, the Wrightsville novels.

18 *Murder for Americans*: Aired on 17 July 1947. The culprit did have a black accomplice, prompting Ellery to intone: 'Virtue and vice co-exist in all races. No race has a monopoly on either.'

TWENTY-FOUR

In Lonely Rooms

Raymond Chandler

At the height of his fame in the summer of 1950, Raymond Chandler took a call. Warner Brothers wanted him to work on a new Alfred Hitchcock movie. Two of his four screenplays had been nominated for an Academy Award,[1] but Chandler's love-hate relationship with Hollywood erred on the side of hatred; 'what happens on the set is beyond the writer's control', he moaned to his literary agent. Even so, the approach was flattering.

He didn't know that he wasn't Hitchcock's first choice. John Steinbeck and Thornton Wilder weren't interested in the project, and Dashiell Hammett wasn't capable. Hitchcock wanted to film a debut novel by an unknown woman writer, a book that Chandler called 'a silly story'.

Chandler didn't need the money,[2] but allowed himself to be persuaded, on condition that he could work from home, since his wife Cissy was in poor health. Hitchcock agreed that script meetings could be held at Chandler's home in the swish coastal resort of La Jolla. Cissy made herself scarce while the two men sat on a davenport, drinking tea and discussing how to make something of Patricia Highsmith's *Strangers on a Train*.

Both men had formidable egos. Chandler's success with the screenplay for *Double Indemnity* had earned him far more clout in Tinseltown than most writers could dream of, but Hitchcock simply wanted the script to capture his vision for the film. For Chandler, character and motivation were at the heart of Highsmith's story, whereas what mattered to Hitchcock was building suspense. Conflict was inevitable.

Chandler sent the first part of his treatment to Hitchcock, and the second a fortnight later. In between, he heard nothing, which felt like 'the Chinese water torture'. Hitchcock took Chandler to lunch at his club in Los Angeles, but Chandler found the director's thinking hard to digest, and the meal gave him food poisoning. He invited Hitchcock over to tea at La Jolla before he'd fully recovered, and his mood was foul.

The meeting ended with Chandler calling the director a 'fat bastard'. That insult destroyed whatever was left of their relationship. For Hitchcock, writers were as disposable as tissues, and the moment the script came in, Chandler was pulled off the payroll. It was a very swift goodbye.

Hiring a little-known writer, Czenzi Ormonde,[3] to rework the screenplay, Hitchcock held his nose as he dropped Chandler's version into the bin. Ormonde shared an agent with Chandler, and so Chandler was sent a copy of her final screenplay. She'd kept some of his lines, but he thought she'd 'castrated' them. He wrote to Hitchcock, pouring scorn on 'a flabby mass of clichés, a group of faceless characters, and the kind of dialogue every screen writer is taught not to write', but his name stayed on the credits, which was all Hitchcock needed.

One name absent from those credits was Edmund Crispin. Hitchcock bought the rights to use the fairground scene from the finale of a whodunit utterly different from Highsmith's novel, the Gervase Fen detective story *The Moving Toyshop* (1946). The film revived Hitchcock's career, but Chandler never worked in Hollywood again.

Raymond Chandler met Dashiell Hammett only once, at a dinner for *Black Mask* writers held in Los Angeles on 11 January 1936. A photograph of the assembled group suggests a convention of affable salesmen. Almost everyone is smiling and looking at the camera. The exceptions are Chandler, sucking his pipe in contemplative mood, and Hammett, tall and preoccupied, looking as if he wished he were somewhere else.

The two men couldn't have imagined that, in years to come, they would be bracketed together as the men who transformed American crime fiction. Chandler was the elder by six years, although his career as a crime writer was just beginning, while Hammett's was already over. At first glance, they seemed to have plenty in common. Each had a wretched relationship with his father, each wrote his first crime fiction for *Black Mask*, each created legendary private eyes, each cared passionately about the quality of his work, each made a fortune in Hollywood, each succumbed to alcoholism.

Obvious similarities masked sharp differences, in upbringing and education, in their working lives, in their politics, in their married lives, in their attitudes towards women and in their understanding of the world outside the United States. Apart from a brief spell in Canada, Hammett never left his native country, while Chandler was well travelled. Their contrasting experiences fed through into their writing. Each man developed a distinctive literary voice, compelling enough to stand the test of time, so that their books continued to sell long after their *Black Mask* colleagues were forgotten.

Raymond Thornton Chandler's parents divorced when the boy was seven, and his mother took her son back to her native Ireland before moving to London. Chandler's uncle paid for him to attend Dulwich College,[4] and he arrived there the year that P. G. Wodehouse left. He struggled to find a vocation, and in 1912 he headed for California. During the war, he joined the Canadian army, and fought in France. He later claimed his service was brought to an end when German shelling knocked him unconscious, although he may have made that story up. At thirty-one he returned to Los Angeles, where he fell in love with a friend's stepmother.

The woman was Pearl Eugenie ('Cissy') Pascal, and her husband Julian was a pianist, with whom – bizarrely, as it now seems – Chandler wrote a comic opera, 'The Princess and the Pedlar'.[5] Eighteen years older than Chandler, Cissy was still beautiful, lovely enough to be able to lie convincingly about her age. Her past was veiled in sexy, glamorous mystery: she'd been married twice, had socialised with opium-taking high-livers in New York City, and supposedly modelled in the nude. She divorced Julian and married Chandler in 1924, when she was fifty-three. Chandler meanwhile earned rapid promotion in an oil company along with a great deal of money.

As the years passed, reality intruded. Chandler was bored by his job and took to drink. It is unclear when he found out Cissy's true age, or how he reacted to it, but several times he separated from her and moved into hotel rooms. Occasionally he threatened suicide, more often he suffered alcohol-induced blackouts. In 1932 he was fired. His self-destructive streak differed from Hammett's, because he fought to master it. He sobered up, returned to Cissy, and started writing pulp fiction.

For a man of forty-four with no job and no money, he showed astonishing discipline in honing his new craft. At a time when some pulp writers churned out a million words a year, Chandler served a patient apprenticeship, believing he had 'to learn American like a foreign language', studying and analysing the pulps. As an exercise in technique, he rewrote a novelette by Erle Stanley Gardner about an ex-con called Rex Kane before devoting five months to writing a story of 18,000 words. Joseph Shaw accepted 'Blackmailers Don't Shoot' for *Black Mask*, paying $180.

Working in solitude, he continued to write slowly, with painstaking observation of detail, evolving a literary style so rich and distinctive that in time it became widely imitated, and eventually much-parodied. His use of slang, even his judgements as to whether to provocatively split an infinitive, were conceived as meticulously as any locked-room mystery. His unrelenting focus remained not on puzzle, but on people and place.

His luck turned when he was fifty. The publisher Alfred Knopf encouraged him to write a novel, and his response was to create a distinctive private eye. Philip Marlowe told the story of *The Big Sleep* (1939) in a sardonic tone as fresh as it was arresting: 'It was about eleven o'clock in the morning, mid October, with the sun not shining and a look of hard wet rain in the clearness of the foothills . . . I was neat, clean, shaved and sober, and I didn't care who knew it. I was everything the well-dressed private detective ought to be. I was calling on four million dollars.'

Chandler crammed his lurid storyline with pornography, adultery, alcohol, a psychotic nymphomaniac and a homosexual assassin. If the plot was confused, this was because he cannibalised parts of his earlier stories, 'The Curtain' and 'Killer in the Rain', and cared little about whodunit. What mattered was Marlowe's view of the world. Everything is seen through his eyes, but with Chandler's double vision, half cynical, half romantic.

Unlike the typical pulp fiction detective, Marlowe has his own code of ethics, but is far from infallible. As his case draws to a close, he faces up to his own shortcomings: 'You were dead, you were sleeping the big sleep, you were not bothered by things like that, oil and water were the same as wind and air to you. You just slept the big sleep, not caring about the nastiness of how you died or where you fell. Me, I was part of the nastiness now.'

Knopf loved the book, and advertised it on the front page of *Publishers Weekly* with three telling lines:

In 1929 Dashiell Hammett
In 1934 James M. Cain[6]
In 1939 Raymond Chandler

Initial reaction to the novel was muted. In *The Postman Always Rings Twice*, Cain set out to shock, but the wry tone of Chandler's tale of debauchery and murder seemed even more unsettling. Marlowe returned in *Farewell, My Lovely* (1940), but sales were modest. The same fate befell his next two novels. Selling film rights earned him only a pittance by Hollywood standards, and although versions of *Farewell, My Lovely* and *The High Window* (1942) reached the screen, they were mangled out of recognition.

Chandler was gnawed by frustration. Cissy was debilitated by fibrosis of the lungs and the couple led an eremitic existence. He continued to refine his style, above all in his evocation of California, 'the department store state: the most of everything and the best of nothing'.

Romanticism permeates the stories. One of Marlowe's forerunners in *Black Mask* was called Mallory, a clue that Chandler saw his detective, trying his best for his clients in a California drenched in booze and corruption, as a man of honour, like a knight on a chivalric quest.

The unromantic truth about attempting to succeed as a writer is that talent is seldom enough. It may not even prove necessary. What everyone needs is a slice of luck. Chandler's came when Knopf, who had feared that marketing the books as pulp fiction would undermine his reputation, finally decided there was nothing to lose by selling pulp rights in *The Big Sleep*. Hundreds of thousands of copies were bought in no time, and when a twenty-five cent edition of *Farewell, My Lovely* appeared on the shelves, sales topped a million. As sometimes happens after a long period of neglect, one breakthrough was swiftly followed by another. Chandler was hired by Paramount Studios to write a film adaptation of Cain's *Double Indemnity*.

'They threw me off the hay truck about noon,' is the opening line of Cain's *The Postman Always Rings Twice* (1934). In this short book, every word earns its keep. The same is true of *Double Indemnity*, written a couple of years later: a man's infatuation with a beautiful woman leads to conspiracy and catastrophe, as in the chilling real-life case that caught Cain's imagination. Ruth Snyder persuaded a besotted corset salesman called Henry Judd Gray to help her to chloroform and then garrotte her heavily insured husband. Their scheme was uncovered, and they were sentenced to death. An illicitly taken photograph of Snyder in the electric chair at Sing Sing captured the reality of capital punishment.

Billy Wilder, the director, wanted to co-write the screenplay of *Double Indemnity* with Cain, but the author was contracted to another film company. Although Chandler lacked experience in screenwriting, that didn't worry Paramount, who were unaware that a year earlier he'd written to Alfred Knopf's wife Blanche: 'James Cain – faugh! Everything he touches smells like a billygoat. He is every kind of writer I detest, a *faux naïf*, a Proust in dirty overalls.'

Chandler started drinking heavily again, and at one point stopped coming in to work. But the final screenplay was taut and Fred MacMurray and Barbara Stanwyck[7] were perfectly cast as the doomed lovers. The result was a memorable film noir. Cain said later that: 'It's the only picture I ever saw made from my books that had things in it I wish I had thought of.'

John Houseman invited Chandler to write a vehicle for the actor Alan Ladd, but although he was the sole author of *The Blue Dahlia*, he struggled with the co-operation and compromises inherent in moviemaking. The story, a whodunit about the murder of an ex-serviceman's wife, lacks the tension of *Double Indemnity*.

Shortly after the film's release, the mutilated corpse of Elizabeth Short was discovered in Los Angeles. The murder was never solved, although forty years later James Ellroy wrote a novel about the crime. Because Elizabeth always wore black and dyed her hair the same colour, the press nicknamed her 'The Black Dahlia'.

When the critic James Sandoe asked him about the ghettoising of detective stories, which were often reviewed separately from literary fiction, Chandler responded: 'the detective or mystery story as an art form has been so thoroughly explored that the real problem for a writer now is to avoid writing a mystery story while appearing to do so.'

The Atlantic Monthly magazine offered him the chance to spell out his opinions, which he did with gusto in 'The Simple Art of Murder'. No essay about the genre has exerted as much influence or been quoted as often. Through sheer verve of advocacy, Chandler disguised the holes in his case. For all his talk about realism, Marlowe is himself a fantasy figure.

Hammett, he said, 'gave murder back to the kind of people that commit it for reasons, not just to provide a corpse; and with the means at hand, not with hand-wrought duelling pistols, curare, and tropical fish'. He also singled out for praise an eclectic mix of books[8] by the Americans Percival Wilde, Kenneth Fearing and Richard Sale, and Britain's Raymond Postgate and Donald Henderson. In a rousing finale, he laid out a personal manifesto for the urban private-eye novel: 'In everything that can be called art there is a quality of redemption . . . But down these mean streets a man must go who is not himself mean, who is neither tarnished nor afraid. The detective in this kind of story must be such a man. He is the hero; he is everything.'

Chandler is often misrepresented as despising the traditional detective story, but he admired a range of Golden Age writers, including Austin Freeman and Crofts, and regarded Philip MacDonald as the writer with 'best natural charm'. He also had an eye for neglected books, including two powerful studies of Depression-era America. Edward Anderson's *Thieves Like Us*[9] (1937) was 'one of the the the best crook stories ever written', and James Ross's *They Don't Dance Much*[10] (1940) 'a sleazy, corrupt but completely believable story of a North Carolina town'.

In 'Casual Notes on the Mystery Novel', Chandler argued again for realism in the genre and credibility of motivation. The perfect mystery novel, he concluded, couldn't be written, because something always had to be sacrificed. It was 'a form which has never really been licked, and those who have prophesied its decline and fall have been wrong for that exact reason . . . It is still fluid, still too various for easy classification, still putting out shoots in all directions.'

Chandler enjoyed speculating about real-life crimes such as the Wallace and Maybrick mysteries, the Penge murder,[11] and the 'completely goofy' Adelaide Bartlett case. As for Crippen: 'I cannot see why a man who would go to the enormous labor of de-boning and de-sexing and de-heading an entire corpse would not take the rather slight extra labor of disposing of the flesh in the same way, rather than bury it at all . . . For a man with a cool head . . . he also did many things which simply didn't make sense.' Chandler found Crippen intriguing: 'You can't help liking this guy somehow.'

With a novelist's eye for the telling detail, he told Sandoe that 'one needs a little touch of something out of the ordinary . . . Mrs Rattenbury's rat race around the whisky bottles on the night of the murder, Fox's hair smelling of smoke and the exact timing of his murder to get the insurance, the Crippen friend's account of the Crippen ménage . . . These are the things that make murder cases fascinating.'

Chandler's new-found affluence meant that he and Cissy were able to move to upmarket La Jolla. Somerset Maugham, whose *Ashenden* he admired, visited them there, and Chandler confided that Cissy was terminally ill: 'her suffering is killing me.' Chandler's gruff,

often adversarial manner formed a protective shell, masking loneliness, and Marlowe's scepticism reflected his creator's sense of
isolation. Even when Cissy was well enough to entertain, the tea
parties to which they invited friends like the hardboiled writer
Jonathan Latimer[12] were stilted and uncomfortable.

Chandler shared with Sayers a need for a curmudgeon's carapace, along with the insistence on taking infinite pains over each
story, the love of analysing real-life murders and a flair for correspondence. Both authors felt adrift from the outside world.
Compensating for their private pain shortened their lives. Sayers
ate voraciously, and put on too much weight, while Chandler took
refuge in the bottle.

The Long Goodbye (1953) is his most ambitious novel, dealing
with friendship and betrayal, police brutality and the danger of
concentrating too much power in the hands of a few media tycoons.
A year later, Cissy died, and having lost her, he too was lost. He
drank himself into oblivion and on one occasion phoned the
police, saying he was going to kill himself. He was found trying
to put a revolver in his mouth, and spent the night in a psychiatric
ward.

Still grieving, he returned to Britain, making friends with Ian
Fleming, who was struck by his kindness and melancholy. Michael
Gilbert, the crime writer who acted as his London solicitor, never
forgot the lunch in Soho when Chandler used salt cellars and wine
glasses to illustrate precisely how Marlowe would fight off two
assailants. All the waiters gathered round to watch.

He became besotted with women such as Natasha Spender, wife
of the gay poet Stephen, and the literary agent Helga Greene.[13] He
completed the seventh Marlowe novel, *Playback* (1958), but his
tax affairs were in a mess, despite Gilbert's efforts. When Fleming
interviewed him for the BBC, he was so drunk that the recording
had to be heavily edited before it could be broadcast.

Helga's cousin, Maurice Guinness, who co-wrote a quintet of
Golden Age detective novels under the pen-name Newton Gayle,[14]
argued that it was time for Marlowe to find a wife. Chandler started
'The Poodle Springs Story',[15] in which the private eye has married
the heiress Linda Loring, but, a month before his death, he told
Guinness that he thought Marlowe unsuited to matrimony: 'I see

him always in a lonely street, in lonely rooms, puzzled but never quite defeated . . .'

A squabble about which of the women in Chandler's life should inherit his estate was resolved in favour of Helga, to whom he was engaged at the time of his death. A letter to her captured his credo: 'To accept a mediocre form and make something like literature out of it is in itself rather an accomplishment . . . [writers] are not always nice people, but essentially we have an ideal that transcends ourselves.'

Notes

The main sources are the biographies of Chandler by Tom Hiney and Tom Williams, and *Raymond Chandler Speaking,* edited by Dorothy Gardiner and Kathrine Sorley Walker.

1 *Two of his four screenplays had been nominated for an Academy Award*: *Double Indemnity* and *The Blue Dahlia*. His screenplay of Elisabeth Sanxay Holding's *The Innocent Mrs Duff* was never made; nor was his screenplay of *Playback*, which later became the seventh Marlowe novel. He also contributed to rewrites of *The Unseen*, based on *Midnight House*, aka *Her Heart in Her Throat*, by Ethel Lina White.

2 *Chandler didn't need the money*: He turned down a lucrative offer to turn Philip Marlowe into a comic-strip character, and to give his name to a mystery magazine. Hitchcock seized the latter opportunity, and *Alfred Hitchcock's Mystery Magazine* was launched in 1956.

3 *Czenzi Ormonde*: Ormonde's other screenwriting credits included *Step Down to Terror*, aka *The Silent Stranger*, a remake of Hitchcock's *Shadow of a Doubt*, and *Once You Meet a Stranger*, a TV movie remake of *Strangers on a Train* with the protagonists' genders reversed.

4 *Dulwich College*: Dulwich alumni and crime novelists include A. E. W. Mason, C. S. Forester and Simon Brett.

5 *'The Princess and the Pedlar'*: Chandler wrote the libretto, Pascal the music, but it was neither produced nor published, which may be as well for Chandler's reputation, given that it was a fantasy about fairy folk in the royal palace of Arcadia. Kim Cooper discovered it in the Library of Congress in 2014.

6 *James M. Cain*: James Mallahan Cain continued to write into his eighties, but his reputation rests mainly on his early work, which receives an explicit salute in Laura Lippman's stand-alone *Sunburn*.

7 *Fred MacMurray and Barbara Stanwyck*: MacMurray made Walter Neff credible as a nice guy who gets in over his head. Stanwyck, sultry and dangerous, made a speciality of playing the femme fatale.

8 *an eclectic mix of books*: Namely *Inquest, Dagger of the Mind, Lazarus No. 7, Verdict of Twelve* and *Mr Bowling Buys a Newspaper*. Although Chandler claimed that without Hammett these books might never have been written, the prime influence on Postgate and Henderson was Francis Iles.

9 *Edward Anderson's Thieves Like Us*: Anderson based his protagonists on Bonnie and Clyde. Nicholas Ray directed the movie version, *They Live by Night*, and Robert Altman directed a remake.

10 *They Don't Dance Much*: Flannery O'Connor said 'it didn't sell much.' Ross's original title was 'Dine and Dance', but as he said when inscribing a copy, his editors 'seemed to think there wouldn't be much dancing in Smut's joint'. Ross failed to find a publisher for his second book, 'In the Red', and resorted to becoming a literary agent. His laconic style has been compared to Cain's, while the unvarnished presentation of racism is today as shocking as the protagonists' casual approach to torture and murder. When *They Don't Dance Much* was reprinted in 1975, Ross mused that Chaucer's 'The Pardoner's Tale' might have been an unconscious influence on his story. Today it reads as a compelling early example of 'rural noir'. So, in a very different way, is *The Hex Murder*, published in 1936, by Alexander Williams under the name Forrester Hazard, and apparently based on a real-life crime. The story deals extensively with Amish culture, also explored in Peter Weir's crime film *Witness* half a century later.

11 *the Penge murder*: The horrific starving to death of Harriet Staunton in 1877 was fictionalised in *Harriet*, by Elizabeth Jenkins, an underestimated novelist who lived to 104. Her favourite among her own books was *Dr Gully*, about the Bravo poisoning case.

12 *Jonathan Latimer*: Latimer wrote five novels about private eye William Crane. His stand-alone *Solomon's Vineyard*, one of many crime stories featuring a weird cult, was so lurid that although it was published in Britain in 1941, it was banned in his home country; a sanitised version, *The Fifth Grave*, subsequently appeared in the US. As private eye Karl Craven says, the story has got 'everything but an abortion and a tornado'. Latimer's screenplays include *The Glass Key* and *The Big Clock*. For television he wrote scripts for *Checkmate* (created by Eric Ambler) and *Perry Mason*, and an episode of *Columbo*.

13 *the literary agent Helga Greene*: The former wife of Hugh Greene and sister-in-law of Graham Greene.

14 *Newton Gayle*: Guinness's co-writer was poet and activist Muna Lee. 'Newton Gayle' was elected to the Detection Club, but when the writing partnership ended, Guinness didn't produce a novel until the 1960s, when he published three thrillers under the name Mike Brewer.

15 *'The Poodle Springs Story'*: The novel, renamed *Poodle Springs*, was completed by Robert B. Parker, who also wrote a sequel to *The Big Sleep* called *Perchance to Dream*. Parker's own private eye Spenser was carved in Marlowe's image. After Parker's death, Ace Atkins continued the Spenser series.

TWENTY-FIVE

Brothers in Crime

Patrick and Bruce Hamilton

Bruce and Patrick Hamilton were brothers who shared a fascination with crime. One Sunday in January 1932, they lunched together in Earl's Court, where their sister Lalla had a flat, and afterwards went for a few drinks. Patrick's latest play, inspired by an extraordinary real-life murder, had become a hit in the West End, and that very day the *Sunday Referee* had published his article arguing the merits of the 'true thriller', and claiming that it was 'the grown-up sequel to the fairy-tale'. Before parting, the brothers agreed to meet the following morning and visit the law courts. For them, watching trials was 'fascinating if a little horrifying'.

Patrick, his wife Lois, and Lalla set off for the pub, which was due to open again at seven o'clock. As they turned into a narrow street lacking pavements, a car hurtled towards them and hit Patrick at high speed. It carried him along the road before throwing him off the bonnet and on to the ground. He sustained compound fractures and multiple lacerations. For several days his life hung in the balance.

When Bruce visited the hospital and saw his younger brother's injuries, he almost fainted. He, Lois and Lalla maintained a vigil at Patrick's bedside, and he rented a room nearby. For years he'd suffered from nightmares, and on his first night there he woke up

at three in the morning in a state of incoherent terror. He jumped
out of bed, smashed the window of his room and finished up on
a flimsy veranda roof, forty feet above the road, crying for help.
His landlord came to the rescue and, Bruce reckoned, saved his
life. He finished up in the hospital bed next to Patrick.

Bruce was lucky that this bizarre episode left him only with
gashes, which healed in weeks. Patrick's injuries changed his life.
He was left with a severely damaged arm and stiff leg, and despite
the efforts of a plastic surgeon, his face was badly disfigured. The
psychological effects of the accident proved devastating. His confidence was destroyed and he thought he'd become a grotesque.
He referred to the accident as the time 'when I was killed'.

Although Bruce spent much of his life working in Barbados,
and they went for long periods without seeing each other, his
devotion to Patrick never faltered. Two years after the accident,
he married a woman he'd met in Barbados, but Patrick discouraged him from having children, and refused to allow Aileen
Hamilton into his life. Bruce didn't protest at this interference:
'Perhaps I should have stood on my dignity . . . But I was not
prepared to forsake all others, virtually to give up Patrick to save
Aileen some mortification.'

The brothers' lives remained strangely intertwined, and they
continued to feed off each other's obsessions, everything from
cricket to Marxism. Bruce recalled their being reunited following
a lengthy separation during the Second World War. They'd spent
a few enjoyable days together at the Albany when Patrick 'said a
strange thing. "What a pity one of us isn't a woman. Then we
could have got married and been together always." I answered
jokingly that it would have required a change of family provenance
as well as of sex. The next evening he came home rather tight,
and . . . tried to get me to abuse Aileen . . . Presently he realised
he was hurting me, and became full of compunction and tender-
ness.'

After Patrick's alcohol-fuelled decline and death, Bruce kept the
flame alive by publishing a memoir about him. The last photograph
of Bruce, taken shortly before his own death, shows him surrounded
by Patrick's books, not his own. Shortly before Patrick died,
however, Bruce wrote a novel that presented a thinly disguised

study of their relationship, and was called 'A Case for Cain.'[1] His fictional alter ego spends his life 'practically dedicated to something hardly short of the worship of his brother'. And yet, as the story reaches a climax, he leaves his wife, and beats his brother to death with a golf club.

Bruce never published the book.

The Hamilton brothers represent a missing link in the story of crime fiction as it evolved from the cerebral puzzles that dominated the Golden Age into a post-war preoccupation with psychological darkness. They came from a family of writers, although only Patrick achieved significant success. And even he has become, in the words of his biographer Sean French,[2] 'an eerie non-presence in modern British literary history', who attracted admirers as diverse as John Betjeman, Doris Lessing and Graham Greene, while remaining a shadowy figure. He divided his life into compartments, with a handful of friends who seldom if ever met each other.[3]

The other Hamiltons were, in French's opinion, notable mainly for careers of 'dogged literary failure'. The father, Bernard Hamilton, dedicated one of his novels to an illustrious neighbour in Sussex, Arthur Conan Doyle. For a while, Bernard shared Conan Doyle's interest in the occult, but although Conan Doyle became Bruce's godfather, the friendship didn't last, and Bernard later wrote a book attacking Conan Doyle's spiritualist beliefs.

Bernard's life was a saga of dismal relationships, soiled by his self-indulgence. On his twenty-first birthday, he inherited £100,000, and celebrated by meeting a prostitute at the Empire Theatre. He squandered his money; as for the prostitute, he married her. His quixotic ambition to 'reclaim' her owed more to vanity than gallantry, and his mission proved calamitous. They separated, and his wife threw herself in front of a train at Wimbledon Station, although not before writing a letter helpfully exonerating Bernard from blame.

Bernard's second wife, also a writer, was the mother of Bruce, Patrick and Lalla. As Bernard's fortunes declined, his temper darkened, and he became an alcoholic. So did Patrick and Lalla. Like Bernard, Patrick became obsessed with a prostitute, but rather than marrying Lily Connolly, he fictionalised her in *The Midnight*

Bell (1929). This novel was not a mystery, but its evocation of London's sleazy side set a pattern for his later work.

His breakthrough came when he anglicised the story of a *folie à deux* thrill-killing in Chicago, and turned it into a stage play. Nathan Leopold and Richard Loeb were teenagers from wealthy families who fell under Nietzsche's spell, and persuaded themselves that they were supermen exempt from the legal and moral constraints binding less favoured mortals. A series of petty crimes escalated into a scheme to commit the perfect murder as an experiment. After months of planning, they kidnapped fourteen-year old Bobby Franks, killing him with a chisel before pouring hydrochloric acid on his body with a view to concealing its identity, and hiding the remains in a culvert. Their incompetence and vanity soon led to the scheme unravelling, and to their arrest and conviction. They escaped the death penalty, but were sentenced to life imprisonment in 1924.

Hamilton called his play *Rope*, and it was first performed in 1929. He was oddly defensive about it, claiming that he hadn't been influenced by the Leopold–Loeb case, and wasn't interested in crime. In a preface to the published version, he said that '*Rope* is not intended to be a highbrow play . . . when *Rope* is accused of delving into morbid psychologies . . . of being anything but a sheer thriller . . . I am at a wretched loss.' Perhaps he protested too much because he feared his own fascination with Nietzsche, cruelty and crime was unhealthy. The strength of his play derived not only from the values of compassion and humanity expounded by his character Rupert Cadell when denouncing the crime, but also from Patrick's insight into the sadistic mentality of the two killers.[4]

With help from Patrick, Bruce found an agent for his first crime novel, *To Be Hanged* (1930), and it was published by Faber in Britain and Doubleday in the US. When Bruce asked Arthur Conan Doyle for a supportive quote, the great man expressed reservations about the credibility of the book's ending, and even claimed to have forgotten he was Bruce's godfather. But generosity prevailed, and the American dust jacket carried his encomium: 'It is one of the cleverest detective stories I have read.'

Whatever its flaws, this unorthodox story is notable for its recognition of the fallibility of the English justice system, and for the portrayal of the ruthless killer, a 'pure and logical egoist . . . ready to destroy without compunction anything, or anybody, that might obstruct his least designs'.

Patrick married, but the relationship was doomed from the start. According to Bruce, 'Patrick discovered that he was quite unable to manage a satisfactory sexual relationship with Lois.' Bruce put this down to 'psychological incompatibilities', and after the honeymoon Patrick turned to drink. During a quarrel between the brothers, Patrick was dismissive of Bruce's writing, although he sent a grovelling letter of apology later that day: 'How could I not be interested in your work – seeing that I love you as no one else?' But Bruce was stung, and didn't show his next manuscript to Patrick.

This was *Hue and Cry*; Faber rejected the book, but the Collins Crime Club published it in 1931. Again, the storyline is unusual, and Bruce makes no secret of his left-wing political sympathies. The protagonist is a professional soccer player who is victimised by the club chairman, an odious capitalist. The young goalkeeper murders him and flees to London, where he has a series of encounters with a prostitute, a novelist based on Patrick, an 'extreme socialist', and a disgraced former policeman who has become a rancorous radical. The outcome is at odds with conventional notions of justice, as it is (contrary to critical mythology) in so many crime novels of the 1930s.

Bruce's fourth novel, *Middle-Class Murder* (1936), blended an ironic storyline patterned on Francis Iles' *Malice Aforethought*[5] with a Marxist perspective that Iles would have derided. The superb opening finds Tim Kennedy, one of the genre's few sociopathic dentists, writing a fake suicide note from his wife. Whether the power of the scene derives from Bruce's recollection of the exculpatory suicide note written by Bernard Hamilton's first wife is open to question, but the story did refract the private traumas of both brothers; Kennedy's unfortunate wife, like Patrick, had been disfigured in a road accident.

No Golden Age author so explicitly equates the bourgeois way of life with psychological degeneration as Bruce, when he dissects 'the true middle-class murderer, a figure of awful menace and awful fascination', but his didacticism was a weakness. Too often he succumbed to the temptation to make a polemical point, to shout rather than show. The avowedly political *Rex v. Rhodes: The Brighton Murder Trial* (1937) sought to lambast a failing society and a flawed legal system. The structure, borrowing the format of the *Notable British Trials* series, was highly original, but wasted on a dull story with a crude pro-Soviet agenda. *Traitor's Way* (1938) is a lively Buchanesque manhunt story, marred by a risible misreading of contemporary geopolitics.

Let Him Have Judgment (1948) focused on a specific miscarriage of justice; Erle Stanley Gardner called the novel 'a mystery master-piece', and it was adapted for the stage by Raymond Massey under its American title, *The Hanging Judge*. Yet Bruce's career as a crime novelist faltered, and he published only one more mystery. *Too Much Water* appeared in 1958 but belonged in spirit to the mid-30s. It was a traditional whodunit set on board a cruise ship, and its plot was lifted (with explicit acknowledgement) from Christie's *The ABC Murders*. The naive young Marxist had given way to a weary conservative bereft of ideas.

Val Gielgud's determination to raise the standards of radio drama led him to urge successful playwrights to write for the BBC. In 1936, he asked Patrick to try his hand at a radio play: 'a psycho-logical thriller along the lines of *Rope* would be good.' The result was *Money with Menaces*, a story of vengeance that captures the idea that committing a crime can be empowering. The villain tells his victim: 'I have not only revenged myself personally on you . . . I have also . . . symbolically taken revenge for all those who were like me against all those who were like you.' This fascination with the power of the criminal began to preoccupy Patrick, as it would other writers of psychological thrillers such as Patricia Highsmith.

Almost a decade after writing *Rope*, Patrick enjoyed fresh success with a Victorian thriller in which a woman who seems to be losing her mind is in fact suffering mental torture at the hands of her husband. This time, key elements of plot and psychology came not from a real-life crime, but from fiction, and in particular from Bruce's work.

In Bruce's *To be Hanged*, a landlady says of the doomed Emily Clifford: 'I always knew when she'd gone, because the gas in the kitchen went up brighter when she turned it out in the sitting-room.' Patrick borrowed this idea, with Bruce's approval, for a highly effective stage device which supplied him with an evocative title, *Gas Light*, which is usually rendered as *Gaslight*. The play's ironic twist is in the Francis Iles tradition, while the veteran detective, Rough, is modelled on Sergeant Cuff from *The Moonstone*.[6] Patrick told his brother that he'd written 'a sort of dramatic "*pastiche*" of Wilkie Collins or Gaboriau'.

Bruce's portrayal of superficially likeable villains in *To be Hanged* and *Middle-Class Murder* influenced Patrick's own version of the middle-class murderer, the sociopathic charmer Jack Manningham. In the house where he once cut a woman's throat, Manningham sets out to drive his wife insane. Melodramatic as the material is, what lifted it out of the ordinary was, in Bruce's phrase, its 'breadth of humanity'. *Gas Light*'s presentation of cruelty disguised as concern is chillingly credible. Here a woman is placed in jeopardy by a subtle yet extreme form of domestic emotional abuse.

Gas Light premiered in 1938, doing well in London and even better in New York; under the title *Angel Street*, it enjoyed the longest run by a foreign drama on Broadway. Film versions (titled *Gaslight*) were directed by Thorold Dickinson in Britain, and George Cukor in the US, and Patrick became rich on the proceeds. The play's enduring legacy is unique. 'Gaslighting' has become a term to describe psychological manipulation, typically suffered by a woman at the hands of a man.[7]

Patrick Hamilton is remembered mainly for two stage plays, although the obscure *The Man Upstairs* employs a trick of disguise that Anthony Shaffer reinvented brilliantly in *Sleuth*. Patrick regarded himself primarily as a novelist, reminding Bruce that 'your godfather took as poor an opinion of his Sherlock H. stories as your brother does of his plays.'

Like Conan Doyle, Patrick was not always the best judge of his own work. He was a chronicler of the rootless, the people who frequent dingy saloon bars and grubby boarding houses for want of anything better to do. He toyed with the idea of writing a three-volume Victorian thriller in the Wilkie Collins tradition, before producing his finest novel, *Hangover Square* (1941),[8] an early example of the crime novel focusing on mental disturbance that became increasingly common after the war. Two murders occur, but there is no mystery about them. The story's power comes from the atmospheric account of the decline of a melancholy alcoholic George Harvey Bone, which parallels Britain's stumbling descent towards war.

Patrick's final novels composed a trilogy about Ernest Ralph Gorse, an amoral confidence trickster. J. B. Priestley thought it significant that the stories were set in the 1920s and 30s: 'he could no longer cope with the post-war world.' In the first book, *The West Pier* (1952), set in Brighton,[9] Gorse is bracketed with real-life murderers such as the poisoner Thomas Neill Cream and the Brides in the Bath killer George Joseph Smith. In the second, *Mr Stimpson and Mr Gorse* (1953),[10] he's likened to a host of villains, from Dr Pritchard and Dr Palmer, and 'the strangely acquitted Miss Madeleine Smith', to twentieth-century killers such as 'Ronald True . . . Mahon, Neville Heath and George Haigh'. So much for the author who claimed to have no interest in crime.

After such a build-up, it comes almost as a let-down to reach the end of the third and weakest book, *Unknown Assailant* (1955),[11] and realise that Gorse never actually murders anyone. Patrick's focus was on the mindset of a man who enjoys hurting others. A revealing passage talks about 'the sadistic or masochistic element underlying every physical relationship between man and woman, or, if it comes to that, man and man, or woman and woman'.

The Gorse trilogy is the work of a writer sinking into a quagmire of despair. Bruce also suffered from intense depression, although he didn't seek solace in the bottle. The brothers' political allegiances crumbled. Patrick, long an admirer of Stalin and the Soviet Union, had developed a portfolio of blimpish Tory opinions by the time of the Suez crisis, while Bruce became such a pillar of the establishment as to earn a chivalric honour, the CMG – Companion of the Order of St Michael and St George.

Divorce and remarriage failed to bring Patrick happiness. His mother had taken her own life, and he too contemplated suicide.

He underwent electro-convulsive therapy, which saved his life for a time, perhaps at the cost of destroying his literary verve. Drink finally killed him at the age of fifty-eight. The literary dynasty died out when Bruce succumbed to brain cancer – by macabre coincidence, the same fate suffered by his fictional alter ego in 'A Case for Cain'.

The suppressed resentment and jealousy revealed by the storyline of 'A Case for Cain' reflects the psychological complexity of the brothers' relationship. That obsessive fascination with criminal mentality and behaviour sets their work, and above all Patrick's plays and novels, apart. Ernest Ralph Gorse is much less well remembered than his transatlantic counterpart Tom Ripley, but Patrick Hamilton and his overlooked brother explored the psyches of charming, cruel criminals long before the flowering of the talents of the equally troubled Patricia Highsmith.

Notes

The main sources are the biographies by Bruce Hamilton, Nigel Jones, and Sean French, J. B. Priestley's introduction to *Hangover Square* and Jonathan Frost's collection of Hamilton books, correspondence and related materials.

1   'A Case for Cain': Jones refers to the book under an alternative (but equally revealing) title, 'Fall of an Idol'.
2   *Sean French*: French, with his wife Nicci Gerrard, is co-author of novels of psychological suspense, under the joint pseudonym Nicci French. A dozen stand-alones were followed by a series about a psychoanalyst, Frieda Klein.
3   *a handful of friends who seldom if ever met each other*: They included Michael Sadleir, whose firm Constable published Henry Wade, among other detective novelists, and John Davenport. Davenport and his friend Dylan Thomas co-authored a spoof detective story bristling with libels and in-jokes, *The Death of the King's Canary*; it was not published until 1977, after the authors' deaths. By then most of the jokes were incomprehensible.
4   *Patrick's insight into the sadistic mentality of the two killers*: Among the actors who have appeared in *Rope* was Donald Henderson, whose own crime fiction bore some resemblance to Patrick's. *Rope* was filmed by Alfred Hitchcock, who shared Patrick's fascination with sadism.
5   *an ironic storyline patterned on Francis Iles' Malice Aforethought*: Bruce's choice of character names, such as 'Berkeley', 'Cox', 'Milward' and 'Kennedy', pays tribute to his literary influences.
6   *the veteran detective, Rough, is modelled on Sergeant Cuff from The Moonstone*: Rough reappeared in a much less successful play, *The Governess*.
7   *'Gaslighting' has become a term to describe psychological manipulation, typically suffered by a woman at the hands of a man*: In 'From Westworld

to Homeland: Pop Culture's Obsession with Gaslighting', *Guardian*, 21 January 2017, Zoe Williams argued that: 'Gaslighting as metaphor has the resonance of a human truth, but takes its relevance from this particular time: when the cod intimacy of scattergun sharing traps us behind masks, and a new brutality in popular discourse goes straight to "You're mad" without even pausing at "You're wrong."' At the murder trial in 2019 of Ben Field and a co-accused (a part-time magician, who was ultimately acquitted), the prosecution alleged that the pair 'gaslighted' two elderly victims, a man and a woman, seeking to convince them that they were losing their minds as a prelude to killing them for money (Bill Gardner, *Daily Telegraph*, 1 May 2019). Hamilton's play has enjoyed a resurgence, although one production in 2019 'pruned the text to remove some of the lazy sexism and the patronising attitudes'. Another was inspired by the director's view that 'its depiction of abusive relationships has not dated and remains alarmingly relevant', although she deprecated the way in which 'gaslighting' has become a buzzword that has 'in some ways lost any attachment to the actual gravity of this kind of abuse' (Natasha Tripney, 'Gaslight: The Return of the Play that Defined Toxic Masculinity', *Guardian*, 8 October 2019).

8   *Hangover Square*: The novel, which is prefaced with a definition of schizophrenia, was made into a film noir with a soundtrack by Bernard Herrmann that Stephen Sondheim credited as an influence on his own musical *Sweeney Todd*.

9   *set in Brighton*: Graham Greene suggested to the theatrical producer Gilbert Miller in an unpublished letter that Hamilton would be well qualified to dramatise his own *Brighton Rock*. Hamilton, he said, 'can put real horror into a play, knows how to get realistic atmosphere, and could manage the good-and-evil theme very well'.

10 *Mr Stimpson and Mr Gorse*: Patrick's original title, 'Signature to Crime', seems so superior that the change is baffling. In 1987, the novel was adapted into the television series *The Charmer*, starring Nigel Havers.

11 *Unknown Assailant*: In correspondence, Patrick talked about writing a fourth Gorse novel, but it never materialised.

TWENTY-SIX

Cracks in the Wall

Georges Simenon and European crime fiction

After the First World War, a bunch of young Belgian writers and painters living in Liège formed a group known as 'La Caque'. The fear and hardship of the years of German occupation of their home town were fresh in the memory. Moral standards were a luxury, and the young men grew up contemptuous of authority and social norms. They amused themselves with endless philosophising, as well as drink, drugs and sex. They gloried in the dissolute and relished the macabre. The artists among them specialised in painting hanged men.

One member of the group was a teenage journalist who used the pen-name Georges Sim. As Georges Simenon, he earned enduring fame by writing about murder. Years later, he said: 'I was born in the dark and in the rain, and I got away. The crimes I write about are the crimes I would have committed if I had not got away . . .'

Joseph Jean Kleine, one of La Caque's founders, developed a taste for cocaine, morphine and ether; poverty forced him to devote his artistic talents to working as a painter and decorator in order to fund his addiction. Early one winter morning in 1922, after a night spent drinking with his colleagues in La Caque, Kleine was found dead. A sacristan came across his corpse, dangling by a scarf from the door knocker of the church of St Pholien.

The police could not rule out the possibility that Kleine had been murdered, perhaps by a disgruntled drug dealer, and that the killer had attempted to disguise his handiwork as a suicide. The *Gazette de Liège* promptly ran a story with a headline that seemed authoritative: 'Man in despair hangs himself from church door – A victim of drugs'. This became the accepted interpretation of the tragedy of St Pholien.

More than sixty years later, it emerged that the report was written by young Georges Sim; he'd also spent the night drinking with Kleine, and seems to have been the last person to see him alive. He didn't murder Kleine, but if the police had suspected accidental death resulting from a prank gone wrong, he would have become a prime suspect. Not that he escaped scot-free. A sense of guilt tormented him. In his memoir *Three Crimes*, he reflected: 'In the last resort wasn't it us who killed him?'

Georges Simenon abandoned formal education at the earliest opportunity, and took a job at the *Gazette de Liège*, a conservative, Catholic newspaper, shortly before his sixteenth birthday. He'd devoured the stories of Gaston Leroux, and fancied himself as a Belgian Joseph Rouletabille, even dressing in the same way, with snap-brimmed hat, pipe and mackintosh. Reporting for the *Gazette* gave Simenon the chance to learn about human nature, and how to write at speed.

Still in his teens, he tried his hand at fiction; an early, unfinished novel written in collaboration with a friend was a parody of Sherlock Holmes, featuring an English detective called Gom Gutt. He spotted the growing popularity of detective stories and foresaw the day when writing them would become a suitable job for a serious novelist.

Crime fascinated him even more than detection. Stints as a court reporter taught him about the criminal law and the people caught in its web. His ambivalent attitude towards conventional notions of right and wrong can be traced to his formative years. His father died young, and he had a problematic relationship with his mother. At a time when previously respectable citizens were ready and willing to break the laws imposed by an occupying force, he developed a sympathy for ordinary people, 'les petites gens'.

He moved to France, returning briefly to Liège to marry his girlfriend Tigy, and soon became as industrious an author as he was a womaniser. His biographer calculates that he churned out one hundred and forty-seven 'pulp fictions' in the space of seven years, while Simenon once bragged to Federico Fellini that he'd had sex with ten thousand women, most of them prostitutes. The true figures don't matter; his egotism undeniably matched his energy. A more complicated question is whether accusations of misogyny[1] are unfair.

Simenon's flair for dramatic self-advertisement made Dorothy L. Sayers look self-effacing, and the stories he told about himself were so contradictory that sorting out the truth would test the patience of Inspector Maigret himself. In 1927, he signed a contract requiring him to be locked in a glass cage for a week while he wrote a novel for serialisation in a new daily, *Paris-Matinal,* with the theme, title and characters to be chosen by a readers' vote and communicated to him by a court official as he entered the cage. The paper folded before the stunt could take place, but he kept the advance and made the most of the publicity. To his amusement, people came up to him for years afterwards, claiming to have watched him writing his story in his see-through prison.

When the publisher of a French author trumpeted his 'first novel for three years', the irrepressible Belgian released flyers welcoming 'the first Simenon for eight days'. Never a reticent man, he published twenty-odd works of autobiography. One of his lovers was the legendary dancer Josephine Baker, 'the Black Pearl', and Simenon said he would have married her but for his fear that he would simply have become known as 'Monsieur Josephine Baker'.

The early Georges Sim detective stories, such as 'The Two Engineers', a locked-room mystery, rank low in comparison to his more serious work, but illustrate a knack for plotting. In Liège, he'd encountered Commissaire Arnold Maigret,[2] head of the city's transport police, who supplied him with the name for a detective who appeared in a handful of stories prior to the publication of *Pietr the Latvian,* aka *The Strange Case of Peter the Lett*, a novel which appeared in 1931 under his real name.

Jules Maigret is a Parisian cop who seems strikingly ordinary. His unglamorous genius derives from patience and focus: 'what he waited and watched out for was the *crack in the wall*. In other words, the instant where the human being came out from behind the opponent.'

The Maigret series was launched at a sensational ball for four hundred guests (and many more gatecrashers, even though everyone was fingerprinted at the door) at La Boule Blanche, a Montparnasse nightclub. Newspapers described the ball as 'a night of madness', and *Le Canard enchaîné* complained that 'Georges Simenon wants to be famous at any price.' The cost exceeded the publishers' budget, and Simenon had to put his hand in his pocket, but the ball was a shrewd investment. The publicity ensured the book's success. He became a celebrity who loved the good life.

When he and Tigy rented a mansion on the outskirts of La Rochelle, he delighted in riding into the old walled city on an Arab stallion. The mayor obligingly arranged for a ring to be put in the pavement, so that Simenon didn't need to pay a boy to hold the horse's head while he played bridge at the Café de la Paix. The Simenons travelled widely, and in Istanbul he secured a coup, interviewing the exiled Leon Trotsky[3] for *Paris-Soir*.

The ingredients that set the Maigret stories apart from other detective fiction were evident from the start. Simenon's literary style is sparse, his books short, his vocabulary limited. To reach out to a mass readership, he restricted himself to a vocabulary of about two thousand words. Literary, cultural, religious and political references are rare. As Julian Barnes has pointed out,[4] 'There is . . . no authorial presence, no authorial judgement, and no obvious moral signposts. Which helps make Simenon's fiction remarkably like life.'

In *The Hanged Man of Saint-Pholien*,[5] aka *The Crime of Inspector Maigret* and *Maigret and the Hundred Gibbets* (1931), Maigret is working in Belgium when he becomes intrigued by a shabby and nervous traveller with a cardboard suitcase. On 'the off chance', he switches the suitcase for an identical one that he has bought. This is hardly the behaviour of a conventional cop, and Maigret's eccentric intervention leads to tragedy when the other man kills himself.

Suffering from 'a choking sense of anguish', Maigret discovers that the suitcase contains an old suit. He determines to unravel the puzzle of character that led the traveller to place a revolver in his mouth and pull the trigger after losing something so seemingly valueless. The explanation has its roots in a shocking incident from the past; once Maigret ferrets out the truth, he is content to let sleeping misdemeanours lie.

The story fictionalises Kleine's death; as Simenon's biographer Patrick Marnham noted: 'Life, having inspired art, had started to repeat it.' Three months after the novel's publication, another former member of La Caque, Frédéric Deblauwe, murdered a rival pimp in a hotel. The investigation was led by Inspector Guillaume, who had attended the ball in Montparnasse; he gave Simenon advice about police procedure, and to an extent Jules Maigret's methods were modelled on his.

Deblauwe pleaded *crime passionnel*, and escaped the guillotine. Simenon decided not to attend the trial of an old friend: 'It occurred to me that Deblauwe risked losing his head and I had no right to go to court and risk . . . him losing the slightest drop of his *sang-froid*.' Like Maigret, his priority was to understand criminals, not to judge them.

Another of his former compatriots, Hyacinthe Danse, murdered his mistress and his mother in France before fleeing to Belgium. There he killed one of his former teachers, a Jesuit priest. He confessed, was tried for all three murders and received a sentence of life imprisonment. His defence was conducted by a lawyer called Maurice Garçon, who had acted for Simenon a few months earlier, when he'd been accused of libelling a woman who claimed to be the inspiration for the amoral Adele in his novel *Tropic Moon* (1933).[6]

Simenon wrote about Kleine, Deblauwe and Danse in *Three Crimes*, an uncharacteristic book conceived and often described as a novel, but in truth a personal memoir, with names not changed to protect either the innocent or the guilty. *Three Crimes* was written in 1937, by which time Simenon had deserted Maigret. His destiny, he felt convinced, was to win the Nobel Prize in Literature. And it is a truth universally acknowledged that writing detective stories is no passport to becoming a Nobel Laureate.

*

After he stopped writing about Maigret, Simenon concentrated on *romans durs*, 'hard' novels of psychological suspense. Two of the finest are *The Man Who Watched the Trains Go By* (1938)[7] and *Monsieur Monde Vanishes* (1945).[8] Both title characters are men trapped by respectability who abandon comfortable existences for an uncertain future. Kees Popinga becomes a murderer, while Norbert Monde's epiphany transports him to a new life on the French Riviera.

Simenon's brother Christian was killed in an ambush while serving with the Foreign Legion in Vietnam. Simenon had encouraged Christian, whose involvement with Belgian fascists during the early part of the war had put his life in jeopardy, to sign up with the Legion under a false name. Christian's death wasn't Simenon's fault, yet a sense of responsibility haunted him. This bleak mood was reflected in a book sometimes claimed as a masterpiece of existentialism,[9] *The Snow Was Dirty*, aka *The Stain of the Snow, Dirty Snow* and *The Snow Was Black* (1948).

In an unnamed country occupied by a foreign army, a small town is fouled by fear, corruption and betrayal. Even the snow is tainted. Nineteen-year-old Frank Friedmaier admits he is 'not a fanatic, or an agitator, or a patriot. I'm a lowlife.' His mother Lotte runs a brothel, and he plays the peeping Tom, watching the prostitutes at work when he's not having sex with them himself. He graduates to murder, and facilitates the rape of Sissy, a girl who is devoted to him. The question Simenon poses, perhaps thinking of Christian and the thugs he'd consorted with prior to joining the Foreign Legion, is whether such a man is capable of redemption.

Simenon so overshadowed other crime novelists from continental Europe as to eclipse their reputations, especially in English-speaking countries, but this neglect was often undeserved. One of his most successful contemporaries was also a native of Liège who became a journalist in his teens. Yet although Simenon and Stanislas-André Steeman corresponded briefly, they never met, and Steeman's work is closer in spirit to that of the Golden Age puzzle-makers. *The Mystery of Antwerp Zoo* (1928), his first novel, co-written with Herman Sartini, alias Sintair, was conceived as a skit on the traditional mystery. Like *Trent's Last Case*, it was taken seriously by publisher and public alike.

After three further collaborations, Steeman flew solo, and at the age of twenty-three he published *Six Dead Men* (1931), introducing the detective Wenceslas Vorobeïtchik, known as Wens. The story concerns a sequence of deaths connected to a tontine, and Wens' explanation of the murderous scheme in the final chapter is prefaced by one of those teasingly enigmatic remarks beloved by Great Detectives: 'what first roused my suspicion was the disappearance of the bedspread.'

The novel won the Prix du Roman d'Aventures, and Steeman brought Wens back in a series of 'fair play' mysteries as well as experimenting with other types of crime fiction. Wens featured in a serial-killing mystery, *The Murderer Lives at Number Twenty-One* (1939), which became the first film directed by Henri-Georges Clouzot. *Legitimate Defence* (1942), a psychological thriller, became *Quai des Orfèvres*, one of Clouzot's most admired films, albeit with a script so far removed from the source material that the culprit's identity was changed.

Unlike so many writers of puzzle-oriented mysteries, Steeman adapted to the changing demands of the post-war reading public. His novels became increasingly dark in tone, and his literary career culminated with a courtroom-based story set in the US, *Autopsy of a Rape* (1964).

Frédéric Dard, a French friend of Simenon, published hundreds of books under a host of pen-names, including a long series of thrillers featuring a protagonist called Antoine San-Antonio. The best of Dard's stand-alone 'novels of the night' bear comparison with Simenon's *romans durs*, and also have bizarre touches worthy of John Dickson Carr. *Bird in a Cage* (1961), set in Paris at Christmas, is a story of paranoia and a vanishing body, which ends with the narrator reflecting: 'I could try telling them the truth, but . . . How could I get them to believe . . . ? Nightmares are personal things that become absurd when you try to tell them to other people.'

Dard won the Grand Prix de Littérature Policière for *The Executioner Weeps* (1956), a doom-laden story about a man who falls in love with a woman suffering from amnesia, but fame and fortune came at a price. The break-up of his first marriage caused him to attempt suicide, and in 1983 the family endured a severe trauma while living in Switzerland. Dard's young daughter Josephine was kidnapped; he paid a ransom of two million Swiss francs, and she survived her fifty-hour ordeal.

The abductor proved to be a freelance cameraman accompanying a television crew that had been reporting on her father. Dard fictionalised the crime, and for him and ultimately for Josephine, the novel seems to have proved therapeutic. In English translation, its title is *Should We Kill Children Who Have Their Hands on Their Hips?*

In Europe, as elsewhere, leading mainstream authors dabbled in detection. Among them were two Frenchmen. In 1932, the poet and publisher Claude Aveline[10] wrote *The Double Death of Frédéric Belot*, a mystery combining narrative game-playing with insight into character. Despite killing off the eponymous master detective, Aveline subsequently revived him.

George Bernanos' *A Crime* (1935) was a detective story mainly written for financial reasons, before writing *The Diary of a Country Priest*, which helped to secure his reputation as a leading Catholic novelist and polemicist. He argued that Simenon's stories were parables of spiritual life.

The sense that detective fiction was an Anglo-American preserve took time to dissipate, and even crime writers who made a mark in their home countries struggled to break through into English-speaking markets. Among authors who were translated, Simenon remained pre-eminent.

Italian *gialli*[11] (gaudy yellow crime paperbacks published by Mondadori from 1929 onwards) were at first predominantly translations of Christie, Ellery Queen and their compatriots, but local writers strove to compete. Augusto De Angelis, who made his debut with *The Murdered Banker* (1935), produced mysteries that, in Chesterton's phrase, aimed to express 'the poetry of modern life'. De Angelis published fifteen books featuring the Milanese cop Carlo De Vincenzi, but the Fascist Ministry of Popular Culture eventually banned detective stories, and in 1943 De Angelis' provocative journalism led to his arrest. Following his release from custody, he was beaten up by a Fascist thug, and died in Bellagio of his wounds.

The pattern in Spain was much the same. Enthusiasm for spoofing Sherlock gave way to a growing interest in writing contemporary crime fiction that was snuffed out by the civil war, and the hostile environment for detective novelists fostered by the Franco regime.

In Germany, Bertholt Brecht and Walter Benjamin were detective fans who wrote essays about the genre, but their plans for collaborating on a mystery were disrupted by Hitler. Benjamin, who was Jewish, killed himself with an overdose of morphine tablets rather than face repatriation from Catalonia to France and thence into Nazi hands'. Curiously, neither of the two most interesting crime novelists working in the German language to emerge on either side of the Second World War happened to be born in Germany.

Friedrich Glauser, sometimes referred to as 'the Swiss Simenon', despite having been born in Vienna, had one of the unhappiest life stories of any writer. Thrown out of college in Geneva prior to graduating, he was diagnosed with schizophrenia, developed an addiction to morphine and opium, and made sporadic attempts at suicide. Much of his life was spent in psychiatric wards, asylums and (after being arrested for forging a prescription) prison, while service with the Foreign Legion in North Africa was followed by a long series of poorly paid jobs. He worked as a coal miner in Belgium, a dishwasher, a farm-hand and a hospital orderly. A fall caused by the effects of insulin shock therapy left him with a fractured skull and brain damage, and extreme poverty caused him to postpone his marriage to a former psychiatric nurse. He died in 1938 at the age of forty-one, just before the wedding was finally due to take place.

As a result, he never knew that the film made of *Thumbprint*, his first crime novel about Sergeant Studer, released the year after his death, would earn critical and commercial acclaim. Far less could he have anticipated that his name would endure through the Friedrich Glauser Prize for crime fiction, Germany's answer to the Edgars and the Daggers. The humanity and empathy with ordinary people that are second nature to Maigret are also evident in Sergeant Studer. *In Matto's Realm* starts with an escape from a psychiatric clinic in Berne; the title is a reference to the spirit of insanity.

Friedrich Dürrenmatt, a Swiss-born playwright, turned his hand to crime writing with two novels examining the nature of justice[12] and featuring the terminally ill Inspector Bärlach, a lineal descendant of Maigret. *The Judge and His Hangman* (1950) gives an existential flavour to the old question of whether it is legitimate to prevent or avenge murder by killing someone, while *The Quarry*, aka *Suspicion* (1951), explores the consequences of Nazi war crimes and how to punish them.

In *The Pledge* (1958), a cop's obsessive hunt for a serial killer is thwarted by chance. Rational detective work would reap a just reward, in a traditional mystery, but Inspector Matthäi's fate is to suffer, despite having discovered the truth. In Dürrenmatt's universe, tidy outcomes only happen as a matter of luck; life is ruled by random happenstance. The subtitle is *Requiem for the Detective Novel*, and Dürrenmatt, who introduces himself into the story,[13] finds himself on the receiving end of a sobering lecture: 'You fellows in the writing game . . . don't try to grapple with a reality that keeps eluding us, you just set up a manageable world. That world may be perfect, but it's a lie.'

Simenon never made the mistake of hurling Maigret into the Reichenbach Falls, and, during the Second World War, he revived his detective. Returning to the familiar offered comfort for his readers, as well as himself, during the miserable years of German occupation.

Controversy about his work for a German film company[14] led him into self-imposed exile from France after the war ended. During a decade spent on the other side of the Atlantic, he divorced the long-suffering Tigy and married his former secretary. Following a return to Europe, this second marriage disintegrated into bitterness and divorce. His devoted but troubled daughter Marie-Jo took her own life in 1978, after six previous attempts; she left, he said, 'a void that nothing can fill'. In his later years, he became reclusive, sharing his life with a woman who had worked as his second wife's maid.

'Some people collect stamps. I collect human beings,' Simenon once said. The novelist Thomas Narcejac argued that Simenon realised that he, like his detective, was 'a connoisseur of souls'.

Everything turned upon atmosphere and character. As Narcejac says, Simenon 'never loads his narrative with hairs, specks of mud or dust or bloodstains . . . A clue, to him, is something much vaguer and more rewarding: a gesture, a word, a glance . . . he reveals the criminal little by little, gently bringing us to admit the psychological necessity of his act.'

His admirers included André Gide, who was awarded the Nobel Prize in Literature in 1947, the year Simenon had predicted he would receive it. Maigret novels continued to appear until 1972,[15] and the British authors Simenon influenced include Alan Hunter, Gil North and W. J. Burley,[16] while Ireland's John Banville took inspiration from Simenon for his crime fiction written under the name Benjamin Black.[17]

Julian Symons described Simenon as 'in some ways the most extraordinary literary phenomenon of the century', but that Nobel Prize remained out of reach. Admiring yet merciless, Symons suggested this was because there was 'something lacking at the highest level . . . it appears that he dissects his people rather than entering their personalities . . . The best books are fine small works of art, but they are *small* works of art . . . his talents have been those of a literary surgeon rather than a great creator.'

Yet Simenon, as David Hare has pointed out,[18] believed that 'a book, like a Greek tragedy, should be experienced in a single session . . . Typically, in one of Simenon's stories, a single crime is enough to ensure that a hitherto normal life falls apart . . . as though any of us might at any time suddenly encounter a crisis that we will turn out to be powerless to overcome . . . The thrill of reading a novel, said Simenon, is to "look through the keyhole to see if other people have the same feelings and instincts you do".'

Notes

The main sources are the books about Simenon by Patrick Marnham, Thomas Narcejac and John Raymond, as well as Boileau and Narcejac's *Le Roman Policier* and Marnham's review of *Three Crimes* in the *Spectator*, 14 July 2007. Xavier Lechard's blog *At the Villa Rose* is the main source in relation to Steeman's books. Pushkin Press's website and Josephine Dard's article in *L'Express* of 4 June 2010 are the main sources about Dard.

1   *accusations of misogyny*: In 'The Genius of Georges Simenon', *Guardian*, 25 September 2016, David Hare defends him: 'A small man's fear of women is often his subject, and he describes that fear with his usual pitiless accuracy . . . loss of control is seen to be a particularly masculine terror.'

2   *Commissaire Arnold Maigret*: He was deported during the Second World War and died in a concentration camp.

3   *the exiled Leon Trotsky*: Trotsky and his secretary, Rudolph Klement, subsequently secured visas to enter France, where they became targets for assassins. Klement was sheltered by Léo Malet – an anarchist, poet and former cabaret singer whose later crime fiction included stories about private eye Nestor Burma – but his luck ran out, and his headless corpse was fished out of the Seine. One of Trotsky's previous secretaries, Evgenia Petrovna Shelepina, fared better, marrying the British writer Arthur Ransome. Although best known for children's fiction, Ransome also wrote a biography of Poe and (as William Blunt) reviewed detective stories for the *Observer*.

4   *As Julian Barnes has pointed out*: In 'Georges Simeon Returns', *TLS*, 7 May 2014.

5   *The Hanged Man of Saint-Pholien*: The story resurrects a moral dilemma about crime and consequences raised by Balzac in *Old Goriot*: 'if all you had to do was push a button to kill a wealthy mandarin way off in China to inherit his riches, would you do it?' The same question arises in an otherwise very different detective novel by Ruth Rendell, *The Speaker of Mandarin*.

6   *Tropic Moon*: Set in Gabon, the novel examines the consequences of French imperialism. It was filmed half a century later as *Équateur*; the writer and director was Serge Gainsbourg.

7   *The Man Who Watched the Trains Go By*: John Banville described the book as 'insouciantly gruesome'. The post-war film version, starring Claude Rains, ranks among the best movies made from a Simenon novel.

8   *Monsieur Monde Vanishes*: The premise is suggestive of the 'Flitcraft parable' in Hammett's *The Maltese Falcon*, although Monde is not struck by a falling beam.

9   *sometimes claimed as a masterpiece of existentialism*: The novel has been likened to Camus' *The Outsider*, while Thomas Narcejac compares it to Greene's *Brighton Rock*: 'It strikes as deeply into the evil, and deeper still into the good.'

10 *Claude Aveline*: His real name was Evgen Avtsine. Detective fiction was a sideline for him, but Pierre Boileau and Thomas Narcejac admired his writing and were perhaps influenced by it.

11 *Gialli*: The first *giallo* movie was *Ossessione*, adapted in 1943 from James M. Cain's *The Postman Always Rings Twice*, which has been filmed seven times in all, as well as adapted for radio, the stage (twice) and as an opera. The leading director of *giallo* films, Dario Argento, made his debut with *The Bird with a Crystal Plumage*, influenced (although the author was not credited) by Fredric Brown's *The Screaming Mimi*.

12 *novels examining the nature of justice*: Justice is also a key theme of *Die Panne*, a novella adapted from a radio play, and also known as *The Breakdown* and *Traps*. The television film version, *A Dangerous Game*, was adapted from a play based on Dürrenmatt's story by James Yaffe, an American detective writer.

13 *Dürrenmatt . . . introduces himself into the story*: He also makes a cameo appearance in *End of the Game*, a film version of *The Judge and His Hangman* for which he co-wrote the screenplay. *The Pledge* became a critically lauded movie, transplanted to the US, and starring Jack Nicholson.

14 *Controversy about his work for a German film company*: Mark Lawson, whose *The Man Who Had 10,000 Women* is a radio play celebrating Simenon's centenary, concluded that accusations of collaboration are too harsh: 'he was more pro-Simenon than pro-Nazi. With the egotism and political naivety of many artists, he simply could not accept that something as trivial as a world war could interrupt his career' ('Would You Believe It?', *Guardian*, 23 November 2002).

15 *Maigret novels continued to appear until 1972*: In Britain alone, there have been three major TV series featuring Maigret over the course of more than half a century. The most renowned was the 1960–63 series; the principal scriptwriters included the crime novelists Roger East and Margot Bennett and the playwright Giles Cooper. Cooper also wrote scripts for the Sherlock Holmes TV series starring Douglas Wilmer, while his radio play *Unman, Wittering and Zigo*, adapted for stage, television and film, is surely the most chilling mystery set in a school.

16 *Alan Hunter, Gil North and W. J. Burley*: Creators of George Gently, Caleb Cluff ('the Maigret of the Dales') and Charles Wycliffe, based in East Anglia, Yorkshire and Cornwall respectively. North's real name was Geoffrey Horne. The influence of Maigret and Cluff can also be seen in Peter Robinson's long series about DCI Alan Banks.

17 *crime fiction written under the name Benjamin Black*: In 'The Escape Artist', *LA Weekly*, 28 May 2008, Banville described this as 'a completely different process than writing as John Banville. It's completely action-driven, and it's dialogue-driven, and it's character-driven.'

18 *as David Hare has pointed out*: In 'The Genius of Georges Simenon'. Hare's play *The Red Barn* is an adaptation of Simenon's *La Main*.

TWENTY-SEVEN

Sensation in Court

Legal mysteries

William Marvin Lindley was known as 'the red-haired killer'. A convicted sex murderer on the condemned row in San Quentin prison, he was awaiting execution. The case against him seemed so strong that nobody took much interest in his fate until Al Matthews, a freelance lawyer from Los Angeles, studied the case and came to the conclusion that Lindley wasn't guilty.

The crime dated back three years, to 1943. In the aftermath of the Depression, poor people were living in ramshackle temporary camps on the banks of the River Yuba in California. Three young sisters went for a swim, and shortly afterwards thirteen-year-old Jackie Marie Hamilton was found dying. She'd been battered and raped. Her last words to her father were that it was 'that old red-headed liar in the boathouse'.

Armed with a 'dying message' clue worthy of Ellery Queen, and testimony from a witness who had seen the girl struggling with Lindley, a mentally unstable drifter who had red hair and treated the boathouse as home, the police soon got their man. A guilty verdict was a foregone conclusion. Al Matthews discovered that the witness was actually colour blind, but, on appeal, the Supreme Court upheld the conviction. Lindley was destined for the gas chamber.

Matthews read an article in the *Saturday Evening Post* in which the writer Erle Stanley Gardner described his early experiences as an attorney, defending all manner of criminals. Gardner had an affinity for underdogs, and Matthews wrote to him, seeking help with Lindley's defence.

Gardner studied the evidence and reconstructed the crime. He concluded that the prosecution case was far from watertight, and that Lindley's alibi hadn't been properly analysed. What is more, *another* red-headed man, a hop picker present in the vicinity on the day of the murder, was seen with scratch marks on his face, and had promptly left the area. In a race against the clock worthy of his fiction, Gardner persuaded the authorities to grant a stay of execution. Lindley's sentence was commuted to life imprisonment, and eventually he was exonerated.

The case prompted Gardner to form a group of experts in criminal investigation who were willing to donate their services in the cause of justice. They set about examining apparent wrongful convictions and their first case involved an Oregon lumberjack, Clarence Boggie, who was serving a life sentence for murder. As a result of their work, publicised in *Argosy* magazine, Boggie was pardoned. The group became known as the Court of Last Resort.[1]

After graduating from high school, Erle Stanley Gardner decided that rather than waste time in college pursuing his ambition to become an attorney, he'd learn in a law office. In his mid-twenties, he joined a legal practice, and after a brief digression as a salesman, he returned to the law. The lessons he'd learned about marketing proved invaluable as he supplemented his income through writing.

He began by producing pulp fiction, with an emphasis on quantity rather than quality; his first series character was Speed Dash, a 'human fly detective' with a photographic memory. Concluding that a story plot was 'composed of component parts, just as an automobile is', Gardner devised a 'plot machine', a cardboard wheel with spokes radiating from the centre. The spokes indicated characters, situations and unexpected complications. As the wheel revolved, the points of contact where the spokes came together supplied the nucleus of the plot: 'If I couldn't get a plot within thirty seconds, I thought I was slipping.'

Churning out stories in industrial quantities, he created investigators under a host of pen-names, and didn't brook rejection. The editor of *Black Mask* once printed alongside a 'Phantom Crook' story the covering letter: '"Three O'Clock in the Morning" is a damned good story. If you have any comments on it, write them on the back of a check.'

He dashed off two novels utilising his legal know-how, *Reasonable Doubt* and *Silent Verdict*. The books prioritised pace and conflict rather than detection, and were published in 1933 as *The Case of the Velvet Claws*[2] and *The Case of the Sulky Girl*. They introduced Perry Mason, a lawyer conceived as 'a fighter who is possessed of infinite patience', together with his secretary Della Street and the young investigator Paul Drake. The second book contained a trial, and courtroom drama became a key ingredient of the series.

Perry Mason triumphed in every case, a feat at which mortal lawyers can only marvel. Mason was Gardner's glamorised self-portrait, a combative attorney's wish fulfilment. His luckless opponent, District Attorney Hamilton Burger, prosecuted so many innocent people that it's a wonder he kept his job. Long after Mason's first appearance, the jacket copy of *The Case of the Terrified Typist* (1956) made clear that, this time, the tables would be turned, and the jury would find his client guilty. The hook for the reader was: how could Mason possibly prevail?

Gardner's skills as a literary detective were modest. When he was sent a copy of Francis Iles' *Before the Fact*, he deduced that the author was 'rather a plain woman who bared the real facts of her sex life', adding, 'If I'm wrong on this, the sex angle of the book is a masterpiece of imaginative writing.' He also startled Raymond Chandler by saying that he considered Edgar Wallace the greatest man that ever lived.

Gardner and Chandler were friends. In blurbing *The Big Sleep*, Gardner described the debut novelist as 'a star of the first magnitude'. Chandler was underwhelmed by the stories Gardner wrote as A. A. Fair featuring private detectives Bertha Cool and Donald Lam.[3] For him, they suffered from the same defect as Rex Stout's Nero Wolfe mysteries: 'an eccentric character wears out its welcome'. Perry Mason, on the other hand, was 'the perfect detective because he has the intellectual approach of the juridical mind and at the same time the restless quality of the adventurer.'

Gardner practised law by day and wrote furiously at night. Perry Mason's name became a byword for brilliant advocacy, and a decade after his first appearance, the Pocket Book paperback imprint was selling millions of copies of Mason's cases. In the mid-1950s, the total passed fifty million, and that figure had doubled by 1962.

The success of the Court of Last Resort burnished Gardner's reputation. Naturally, he wrote a book about the Court's work, and a television series followed. The Mason stories were adapted for radio and film, and most successfully of all for television, with Raymond Burr playing Mason. Gardner's capacity for hard work remained breathtaking, and he rattled out twenty Mason novels during the 1960s, as well as ten under the A. A. Fair name and a string of travel books.

Such relentless productivity led to rumours that the books were the work of a syndicate, like the books about the Hardy Brothers and Nancy Drew.[4] Gardner described himself as 'a fiction factory' and treated writing as a business. For many years he dictated his stories at great speed to a secretarial team of three sisters, one of whom became his second wife. His enthusiasm for the Dictaphone led him to urge Chandler to use it too. His publisher offered one hundred thousand dollars to anyone who could prove that Gardner didn't write his own stories, but nobody claimed the prize. A writer who writes so many words (twenty million is one guess) so fast will never achieve consistent quality. The Mason stories are formulaic, but found admirers as diverse as Chesterton, Sinclair Lewis, Somerset Maugham and Evelyn Waugh.

The ambiguous nature of justice has long troubled lawyers who write crime fiction. Melville Davisson Post's Randolph Mason sailed on the windy side of the law in his early days, but Ephraim Tutt's moral compass never fluctuated. Arthur Train, a Harvard-educated New York attorney, was daring enough to create a lawyer both wise and kindly, bent on using his legal wiles to help the vulnerable. Tutt, who arrived on the scene shortly after the First World

War, was 'the Quixote who tries to make things what they ought to be in this world of things as they are . . . following the dictates of his heart when his head says there is no way.' For more than a quarter of a century, this paragon waged battle with prosecutor Hezekiah Mason, and was called 'the best-known lawyer in America' until yet another Mason supplanted him. As with Perry, Tutt's record of winning cases was enviable.

Yankee Lawyer: The Autobiography of Ephraim Tutt, published in 1943, described how the great man came to be a champion of the underdog. Train's name didn't appear on the cover, and photographs of members of his family purported to depict Tutt's relatives. The *New York Times* treated the book as a genuine autobiography, and Train amused himself by reviewing the story of his friend for the *Yale Law Journal*. The hoax convinced an astonishing number of readers, and letters flooded in, thanking Tutt for his years of unstinting public service.

Train was driven to publish an article in the *Saturday Evening Post*,[5] confessing the truth and headed 'Should I Apologise?' In a Borgesian aside, he noted the editor Maxwell Perkins' suggestion that 'fifty years hence, as between Tutt and myself, Tutt will be remembered as the real person and I as the fictional character.'

Not everyone saw the joke. For Train, the outcome was a surreal version of every lawyer's nightmare – becoming personally embroiled in litigation. Lewis Linet sued him and his publisher for a refund, and sought an injunction to prevent the book being published as Tutt's autobiography. The injunction was denied, but Train died before a court could adjudicate on Linet's claim for reimbursement of the $3.50 he'd paid. Linet, predictably, was also an attorney.

Preparing a client's case for trial requires the lawyer to build a narrative convincing enough to persuade a judge or jury. It is a form of storytelling, and the need to make sense of conflicting strands of evidence requires the skills of a detective. No wonder so many lawyers have turned to writing crime fiction.

In Britain, the division of the legal profession into barristers (in simple terms, the lawyers who conduct trials) and solicitors (typically, those who prepare cases and brief barristers to advise or appear in court) may explain the absence of a British equivalent to Erle Stanley Gardner.[6] Dorothy L. Sayers was also struck by the different methods and manners of American attorneys, saying of Perry Mason's second case:[7] 'The trial is excellent fun when once the English reader has reconciled himself to what seems to him the undignified and incomprehensible behavior of American lawyers and judges . . . Perry Mason's methods of cross-examination would hardly go down well at the Old Bailey.'

Among British lawyers,[8] the most talented detective novelist was Cyril Hare,[9] a barrister who became a county court judge. His fourth novel, *Tragedy at Law* (1942), set in the early months of the Second World War, drew on his experience of life as a marshal on a judicial circuit, and follows the misadventures of an able but unsympathetic judge as he travels around dispensing justice. The story reintroduces Hare's series policeman, Inspector Mallett, but the central character is a barrister. Francis Pettigrew is a reluctant detective, because of his sensitivity to the pain that crime leaves in its wake.

Pettigrew opposes capital punishment, scarcely a fashionable view in the British legal profession at the time, and finds it impossible to treat 'murder in the raw' as a game. He resorts to 'eking out a precarious practice by the drudgery of legal authorship', and has a self-awareness as rare in Golden Age detectives as his lack of professional success. He believes he lacks 'some quality that was neither character nor intellect nor luck, but without which none of these gifts would avail to carry their possessor to the front'.

The novel's plot is equally unorthodox. Tension builds, but Hare's prime focus is on the people. Murder does not occur until late in a story, which is scarcely a model of fair play, given that the culprit's motive springs from an arcane piece of legislation. The unique tang is reflected in Pettigrew's bitterness at the story's end, even though he has solved the mystery. Nothing could be further from Perry Mason's ebullience.

Over a span of twenty-one years, Hare produced nine novels.[10] His short stories were equally accomplished, and following his death, his Detection Club colleague Michael Gilbert[11] edited a compilation of them. Gilbert, a solicitor rather than a barrister, enjoyed a much longer and more prolific career[12] as a crime writer. Police stories, whodunits, espionage fiction, adventure stories, thrillers, over the years he mastered them all.

Gilbert created a long line of carefully differentiated crime-solvers, mostly policemen and lawyers. Some featured in several stories, but Gilbert's unwillingness to repeat himself meant that none became a high-profile series character. His failure to create a 'Great Detective' and his determination not to write the same book twice counted against him. Despite the excellence of his work, he was never a household name.

Smallbone Deceased (1950) was a workplace detective story set in a firm of solicitors based (like his own practice) in Lincoln's Inn. The novel captures the austerity of post-war Britain, with electricity cuts relevant to the establishing of alibis, while Gilbert's wit adds savour. A young lawyer, Henry Bohun, collaborates with Chief Inspector Hazlerigg to discover the person responsible for the death of a small trustee whose corpse is found in a capacious deed box.

Death Has Deep Roots (1951) opens with a murder trial at the Old Bailey. The young defence solicitor Nap Rumbold races against time, travelling to France to establish his client's innocence, only to find his own life in jeopardy. Gilbert's awareness of the law's foibles adds to the reader's pleasure. One onlooker is bemused by the initial exchanges between learned counsel and the judge: 'How excruciatingly polite they all are. What does it all mean?'

Gilbert blends courtroom drama with an action thriller with its roots in the activities of the French Resistance. Mixing two very different types of story is bold and unusual, but Gilbert was ideally equipped for the task, given his legal knowledge and wartime experience as a soldier. In the US, Anthony Boucher led reviewers in a chorus of praise: 'It's hard to recall any technical tour de force of fusion quite so admirably integrated as this.'

Scott Turow's *Presumed Innocent,*[13] published in 1987, gave the legal mystery fresh impetus. Rusty Sabich, a married prosecution lawyer, is assigned to handle the murder of a fellow prosecutor, Carolyn Polhemus, with whom he had a brief affair. When he himself is indicted for the crime, he hires a savvy defence lawyer, Sandy Stern. The novel benefits from Turow's own experience as a prosecutor.[14] The combination of legal know-how, astute characterisation and a cunning whodunit twist was strengthened by sharp prose.

Four years later, John Grisham's second novel, *The Firm*, became another bestseller, prompting a tsunami of slick legal thrillers, many of them written by American lawyers. Mitchell McDeere, a bright Harvard graduate, secures a lucrative job in a tax law firm in Memphis, only to discover that a number of lawyers who worked in the business have died in mysterious circumstances. The story is a workplace mystery set in a legal office, but as different from *Smallbone Deceased* as could be imagined.

Grisham, like Turow, has maintained his connection with the law, and has also served on the board of the Innocence Project. Founded in 1992, the Innocence Project aims to exonerate people who have been wrongly convicted, with the aid of DNA testing, and to reform the criminal justice system. It is as if the Court of Last Resort has been reinvented, a sobering reminder that injustice is timeless.

Notes

The main sources are Dorothy B. Hughes' biography of Gardner, Jon L. Breen's *Novel Verdicts* and Molly Guptill Manning's book about the Tutt autobiography.

1   *the Court of Last Resort*: Melville Davisson Post's second collection of Randolph Mason cases, published in 1897, was originally titled *The Man of Last Resort.*

2   *The Case of the Velvet Claws*: Slick marketing was a hallmark of Gardner's career. The jacket of the first book boasted that Mason was 'going to be famous', and the UK edition included a sealed jigsaw puzzle giving 'a valuable clue to the solution'. The second Mason book featured a different gimmick, a scene previewing the next Mason novel. 'Teasers' of this kind are now commonplace.

3   *Bertha Cool and Donald Lam*: The duo first appeared in *The Bigger They Come*, which exploited a defect in the extradition laws of the state of Arizona. In a nutshell, it was possible to get away with murder provided one was willing to spend the rest of one's life in Arizona. The novel's publication provoked a public outcry, forcing the legislature to plug the loophole. The Cool and Lam series ran to twenty-nine novels in Gardner's lifetime; in 2016, *The Knife Slipped* became the thirtieth, after being rediscovered by the writer and publisher Jeffrey Marks.

4 *the Hardy Brothers and Nancy Drew*: Both series were aimed at children and young adults. The Hardy Boys were created in 1927 by Edward Stratemeyer, and the stories have been written by a long list of authors under the collective pseudonym Franklin W. Dixon. Stratemeyer conceived their female counterpart, Nancy Drew, in 1930; the stories appear under the by-line Carolyn Keene.

5 *an article in the Saturday Evening Post*: On 26 February 1944.

6 *the absence of a British equivalent to Erle Stanley Gardner*: Raymond Postgate's *Verdict of Twelve* and two books published by Edward Grierson in the 1950s stand out for sophistication rather than adherence to a Gardner-like formula. *Reputation for a Song* charts the unjust destruction of a man's good name with irony worthy of Francis Iles; a 1970 film version, *My Lover, My Son*, was underwhelming. *The Second Man* features a female barrister, Marion Kerrison.

7 *saying of Perry Mason's second case*: In *The Sunday Times*, 22 April 1934.

8 *Among British lawyers*: The barrister Sarah Caudwell and the solicitor Frances Fyfield were talented, if very different, novelists who emerged in the 1980s. Caudwell's books narrated by Hilary Tamar (whose gender remains a mystery) were witty light entertainments featuring a group of Chancery barristers. Fyfield's novels include a series about the prosecutor Helen West, who has been portrayed on television by Juliet Stevenson and Amanda Burton.

9 *Cyril Hare*: His real name was Alfred Alexander Gordon Clark. The pen-name came from Cyril Mansions, where he lived, and Hare Court, the barristers' chambers where he worked. His first novel, *Tenant for Death*, began life as a play, *Murder at Daylesford Gardens*, which was later revised as *The Noose is Cut*, but still failed to earn a professional production.

10 *Hare produced nine novels*: Pettigrew appears in five, finding love in the wartime mystery *With a Bare Bodkin*. He served as a judge in *That Yew Tree's Shade*, aka *Death Walks the Woods*, which has a plot derived from litigation concerning the destiny of Dr Crippen's estate following his execution.

11 *Michael Gilbert*: While serving during the Second World War, Gilbert was captured by enemy forces, although he later escaped. Good writers waste nothing, and his time as a prisoner provided material for *Death in Captivity*, aka *The Danger Within* (under which title it was filmed). An excellent whodunit concerning an apparently impossible crime is set against the backdrop of an Italian POW camp. *The Night of the Twelfth* is an uncharacteristically chilling mystery set in a school, about a sadistic sex killer and with echoes of the Moors Murders.

12 *a much longer . . . career*: He published thirty novels and 185 short stories, as well as four stage plays (one of which, *A Clean Kill*, borrowed a trick for unmasking the culprit from Philip MacDonald's *The White Crow*) and scripts for radio and television. His non-fiction included *The Tichborne Claimant*, and for the CWA he edited a book of essays, *Crime in Good Company*.

13 *Presumed Innocent*: The novel was filmed by Sydney Pollack. In the sequel, *Innocent*, Sabich's wife is the murder victim, and Turow deploys multiple points of view rather than relying on Sabich alone as narrator. *The Burden of Proof* traces Sandy Stern's life following his wife's suicide.

14 *The novel benefits from Turow's own experience as a prosecutor*: However, Julian Symons thought Turow overdid the legal detail and the improbabilities, feeling 'admiration without a flicker of emotional involvement. To compare Turow with the just as legally knowledgeable George V. Higgins is to put a skilled artisan beside an artist.'

TWENTY-EIGHT

California Dreaming

Crime writers and Hollywood

Howard Hawks bought the film rights to *The Big Sleep* for Warner Brothers shortly after scoring a hit with *To Have and Have Not*, released in 1944 and starring Humphrey Bogart and Lauren Bacall. He saw the story as a perfect vehicle for the two actors, but Chandler was not available to write the screenplay. Hawks therefore turned to William Faulkner, who had collaborated with Jules Furthman on *To Have and Have Not*. But Faulkner was contemptuous of Hollywood, and Hawks wanted input from another writer.

Hawks had directed crime films as diverse as *Trent's Last Case* and *Scarface*. A Los Angeles bookstore owner supplied him with a first novel written by a friend called Leigh Brackett. *No Good from a Corpse* (1944) featured a tough private eye and a glamorous but amoral adversary. The gumshoe, Edmond Clive, isn't merely determined to solve the murder of a woman he'd loved; he is prepared to kill the culprit.

The mood of Brackett's novel is macho, and the debt to Chandler unmistakable. Hawks knew nothing about the author, but was impressed by Brackett's ear for dialogue and had a knack of spotting potential.

'Call in this guy Brackett,' he told his secretary. 'He'd be good to write the screenplay.'

The message was sent, and Leigh Brackett duly appeared in his office.

Hawks found himself greeting a twenty-eight-year-old woman. As Brackett later recalled, he 'rallied bravely and signed me anyway'. Later he bestowed upon her his version of a compliment, saying she wrote 'like a man'.

The testosterone-fuelled world of hardboiled crime writing was almost, but not quite, an exclusively masculine preserve. Several women contributed to *Black Mask*, although Leigh Brackett was not among them. Her first love was science fiction, but refusing an offer to work on *The Big Sleep* was unthinkable, even though she was in the middle of writing *Lorelei of the Red Mist* for *Planet Stories*. She solved the dilemma by persuading an even younger writer, Ray Bradbury, to complete it for her.

She hit it off with Hawks, but William Faulkner was a different matter. On her first day in the studio, he announced that they would work on alternate scenes, and she never saw him again. When he left the project, Hawks brought in Furthman for the rewrites. According to Brackett, 'Faulkner went down in history as the screenwriter whose every single line was rewritten in Hollywood.'

Making the film taught Brackett story construction. When Chandler was asked to clarify who killed the chauffeur in the novel, he wired back to say that he didn't know. Bogart was infatuated with Bacall, and so overwhelmed by drink and despair that at one point he required sedation and couldn't work. But the stars' on-screen chemistry and the smartness of the screenplay created a Hollywood classic to rank alongside *The Maltese Falcon*.

The need to collaborate when working on a film (unless one is William Faulkner) makes the experience very different from writing a novel. As Brackett said, 'If I sit down to write a novel, I am God at my own typewriter,[1] and there's nobody in between. But if I'm doing a screenplay, it has to be a compromise.' She 'went off into corners and wept a few times at things that made me very unhappy', but her career flourished.[2]

Brackett's career in Hollywood was, by and large, a 'happy ever after' story, unlike that of many of her peers. Thirty years after *The Big Sleep*, she adapted *The Long Goodbye* for Robert Altman, advancing the storyline to the 1970s, taking plenty of liberties with the original story and adding a dash of satire. She continued to dabble in crime fiction, ghostwriting *Stranger at Home* (1947) for the actor George Sanders,[3] and collaborated again with Hawks and Furthman on the western *Rio Bravo*.[4] At the time of her death, she was working on the screenplay for a *Star Wars* movie, *The Empire Strikes Back*.

A struggling young writer, William Riley Burnett, worked as a night clerk in a disreputable hotel, gaining an insight into Chicago's dark side. The city was the headquarters of the gang empire run by Al Capone, who served as the model for the hoodlum Cesare 'Rico' Bandello in Burnett's first novel, *Little Caesar* (1929). The nod to Shakespeare reflects Burnett's emphasis on the politics and power plays of gang life, while his mix of terse dialogue and action has proved highly influential.[5]

The film of the book made a star of Edward G. Robinson and set a standard for gangster movies such as *Scarface* (1932), another fictional version of Capone's criminal career. Burnett, now working in Hollywood, co-wrote the screenplay,[6] which was based on a novel by pulp writer Armitage Trail. Trail (whose real name was Maurice Coons) set a calamitous benchmark for crime novelists lured by the siren call of Tinseltown, squandering his new-found wealth on drink before succumbing to disaster. His downfall came with astonishing speed; he died of a heart attack before *Scarface* even hit the screens. He was twenty-eight.

Burnett's early work in the cinema included *The Beast of the City*, a film reflecting Herbert Hoover's wish to portray the police in a positive light. A dedicated police captain finds the fight against crime is compromised by legal loopholes and crooked counsellors. He resorts to vigilantism,[7] and the film's climax is violent.

When Burnett's heist story *High Sierra* (1940) was filmed, the challenge he and John Huston, who co-wrote the screenplay, faced was not to fall foul of the Hays Code,[8] which prescribed moral guidelines for American films, and sought to ensure that criminals were not glamorised. The pair succeeded and managed to slip past the censors a story about a woman who lived with two different men.

Huston also directed the film version of Burnett's *The Asphalt Jungle* (1949). A criminal recently released from jail masterminds a jewel heist in a Midwestern town; the gripping eleven-minute sequence during which the raid is carried out[9] helped to popularise the caper movie.

Burnet also contributed to the scripts of films as diverse as *This Gun for Hire*, based on a novel by Graham Greene, and *Ice Station Zebra*, a messy version of Alistair MacLean's Cold War thriller. Like Brackett, he remained level-headed and pragmatic, saying: 'I pretty much know the limitations of humanity and the possibilities in life, which aren't very great for anybody. You're born, you're gonna have trouble, and you're gonna die.'

Horace McCoy wrote about one hundred screenplays, but none were as memorable as his first novel. A journalist who also contributed to *Black Mask* and other pulps, he lost his job during the Depression, and found work as a boxer and fruit picker before making his way to Hollywood to earn a crust as a film extra.

Hollywood was a ravenous and indiscriminate beast, chewing up actors and writers and spitting most of them out. McCoy ended up sleeping in alleyways and on park benches, and working as a bodyguard, a soda jerk, and a bouncer at a dance marathon contest in Santa Monica. His luck turned when a studio gave him a writing contract and he married an heiress (Dashiell Hammett inscribed McCoy's copy of *The Thin Man*: 'To Horace McCoy, who married my dream woman'). Even so, he contrived to go bankrupt.

The nightmarish dance marathons had given him the idea for a screenplay that was rejected. Undeterred, he used the same background for a short but stunning novel: *They Shoot Horses, Don't They?* (1935). Dance marathons were a Depression-era forerunner of reality television shows and *The Hunger Games*. Contestants desperate for food, shelter and the chance of a cash prize danced until they dropped to provide cheap entertainment for voyeurs with a taste for sadism. Sleep deprivation became a spectator sport. One woman in Seattle attempted suicide after dancing for nineteen days and only making fifth place in the contest. A young man in New York State who danced for eighty-seven hours without a break died of heart failure.

McCoy wasn't writing a whodunit or a private-eye novel, but a first-person account of a man driven to commit a shocking crime. His protagonists are two Hollywood wannabes, Gloria and Robert, who join a marathon in the hope of winning a thousand dollar prize, or at least catching the eye of one of the film moguls who might drop in to watch their suffering.

They Shoot Horses, Don't They? captures the bitter taste of Depression-era America, with the dance marathon a metaphor for life's bleakness. An ambitious literary stylist, McCoy hated being labelled as a 'hardboiled' novelist. His admirers included Gide and Sartre, while Simone de Beauvoir called the book 'the first existentialist novel to have been written in America'. In France he was compared to Steinbeck and Hemingway, but in the US his reputation never reached the same heights.

After the Second World War, he devoted more time to writing fiction, notably *Kiss Tomorrow Goodbye* (1948),[10] a brutal stream of consciousness novel about a ruthless gangster[11] who happens to be a Phi Beta Kappa scholar. McCoy's love-hate relationship with Hollywood endured, and he inscribed a first edition to a woman friend: 'For Sally / From a bit player / who still adores her / with love and a / small sigh for the / good old days'.

When a heart attack cut short his career at the age of fifty-eight, his widow found that to pay back the advances he'd received, she needed to sell his library and record collection, raising a paltry $750. The books sold included a first edition of *The Great Gatsby* inscribed: 'From Scott Fitzgerald / of doom a herald / To Horace McCoy / no harbinger of joy'.

It was typical of McCoy's life as a nearly man that Sydney Pollack's *They Shoot Horses, Don't They?*, the best screen version of any of his stories, did not appear until 1969, fourteen years after his death. It won one Academy Award, and was nominated in eight other categories.

Richard Hallas was the unlikeliest of tough-guy writers. Born Eric Knight, he was a Yorkshireman whose best-known book was the tear-jerker *Lassie Come-Home*. He moved to the United States, and experience as a Hollywood screenwriter informed his solitary crime novel.

The title of *You Play the Black and the Red Comes Up* (1938) suggests that life is a game of chance, while the style verges on a burlesque of the *Black Mask* school. Dempsey, the narrator, a naive and easy-going army deserter whose wife leaves him at the start of the story, is the antithesis of the tormented protagonist of *They Shoot Horses, Don't They?*

Like so many writers and would-be film stars in the 1930s, Dempsey heads for California and becomes involved in a crooked scheme. Not only does he evade justice, he enjoys his ill-gotten gains in the company of a woman called Mamie. Cynical and witty, the story takes unexpected turns, and his attempt to confess to the cops is treated as a hoax: 'Go on, you've had your headlines, brother . . . . Beat it.' Dempsey is forced to conclude that his pal Genter was right: 'the minute you crossed into California you went crazy.'

Knight's death was marked by the same randomness of fate as Dempsey's life. Having attained the rank of major in the US Army during the Second World War, he was killed in a plane crash in Dutch Guiana while heading for a war zone.

David Goodis[12] came from a family of prosperous Jewish émigrés, and after finding work in Hollywood married Elaine Astor, who soon left him, supposedly because of his lack of culture. He worked out his bitterness by writing stories in which a femme fatale taunts and torments a luckless man.[13]

He reinvented Elaine as Gert Parry, the murdered wife in *Dark Passage* (1946), a coincidence-heavy yet compelling story about an innocent man on the run. The book was filmed with Bogart and Bacall, but Goodis's lifestyle became increasingly eccentric. Whereas most Hollywood writers found plenty of ways to squander their wealth, Goodis hated spending his money, and was renowned for wearing threadbare suits and driving a battered Chrysler. Moving out of his hotel, he rented a sofa from his lawyer, Allan Norkin, so as to get closer to Norkin's wife, with whom he was infatuated.

When Ruth Norkin proved unattainable, Goodis resorted to what he termed 'going to the Congo', paying for the company of African-American women who frequented sleazy clubs. A dispute about his sofa rental charge caused him to desert the Norkins in favour of the Hollywood Tower on Franklin, the street where Philip Marlowe was supposed to live.

During the 1950s, Goodis wrote paperback originals[14] for Gold Medal;[15] these were not reprints of hardbacks, but new stories with garish cover artwork[16] promising thrills aplenty. As pulp magazines faded away, paperback originals cornered the market. Goodis's protagonists were troubled outsiders: the novelist Ed Gorman[17] said that Goodis 'didn't write novels, he wrote suicide notes'. Caring for his parents and a brother who suffered from schizophrenia took a heavy toll, and so did a long-running claim for copyright infringement against ABC TV. Goodis insisted that the television series *The Fugitive*,[18] in which Dr Richard Kimble is wrongly convicted of killing his wife, plagiarised *Dark Passage*.

He checked himself into a psychiatric hospital, and died with the lawsuit unresolved. Five years later, the appeal court ruled in favour of his estate. In death, he achieved a critical acclaim that eluded him while he was alive; even so, his biography, written in French,[19] was not translated into English for thirty years.

'There are thirty-two ways to write a story, and I've used every one,' Jim Thompson claimed, adding, 'but there is only one plot – things are not as they seem.'

Thompson liked to joke that he'd been born in jail, and it wasn't far from the truth. He came into the world in an apartment over the cell block in Anadarko, Oklahoma Territory. His father, the sheriff of Caddo County, overreached himself in the murky world of politics before fleeing to Mexico when accused of embezzlement.

At seventeen, Thompson took a job as a hotel bellboy in Fort Worth. He moonlighted as a bootlegger, drug peddler, con man, pimp and male escort. Cigarettes and whiskey kept him going, but he finished up in hospital after suffering a breakdown coupled with a bout of TB. During the Depression years, he married a telephone operator but adopted a hobo's lifestyle, harvesting for farmers and digging ditches for sewers.

A piece for *True Detective*[20] about the murder of a young drifter called Eugene Kling launched him on a fresh career. His true-crime stories were illustrated with photographs, sometimes showing his wife, his sister or himself sprawled on the ground and posing as murder victims. 'Ditch of Doom – The Crimson Horror of the Keechi Hills', published in *Master Detective*, was a typically vivid account of a serial killer whose habit of burying his victims on a farm in Oklahoma turned the landscape into 'a shovel-scarred battlefield'.

Thompson conjured stories out of newspaper reports and the need to recount a complicated case in a short span taught him not to waste words. 'You don't have to describe the furniture' became his catchphrase, and he honed his ability to capture atmosphere and build suspense through changes of pace and using a first-person viewpoint.

He was briefly a member of the Communist Party prior to trying his luck in Hollywood. Driving to California, he was robbed by a hitch-hiker, and when the studios showed no interest, he headed back home again. Although he became disillusioned with Marxism, empathy with society's underdogs pervaded his fiction. His first crime novel was a subversive reworking of James M. Cain's *Double Indemnity* called *Nothing More than Murder* (1949).

When Robert Wade,[21] a younger crime writer, asked him for advice, Thompson snapped: 'Take up plumbing.' Yet paperback original publishing – like digital publishing sixty years later – offered the potential for a good income. Lion Books were developing an American equivalent to the *série noire* fiction pioneered by Gallimard in France, and an idea suggested by Arnold Hano, the editor at Lion, was developed into Thompson's first book for them. *The Killer Inside Me* (1952), narrated by an affable deputy sheriff who proves to be a sadistic sociopath, was pitch-black fiction.

In a frenetic burst of activity, Thompson wrote thirteen books in next to no time. A few misfired, but others give startling insight into the working of warped minds. The narrator of *After Dark, My Sweet* (1955) is a handsome but troubled former boxer on the run from an institution, and Thompson makes telling points about the treatment of people suffering from mental illness. *Savage Night* (1953), a story about a hitman with TB, is tense yet surreal.

After the Lion imprint closed, Thompson struggled to find a new American publisher, although, like McCoy and Goodis, he was admired in France. Stanley Kubrick gave his career fresh impetus, hiring him to work on a screenplay of Lionel White's *Clean Break* (1955), a 'one last job' novel about a racetrack heist. The result, *The Killing,*[22] gave Thompson a taste of the film world's own brand of savagery: Kubrick was credited with the screenplay, and Thompson learned, to his fury, that he'd merely contributed 'additional dialogue'.

Thompson wrote short books and wrote them fast. When he took twice as long as usual to craft *The Getaway* (1958), he fretted that 'this page a day stuff . . . is undoubtedly best in the long run; but . . . it's sure hard on the pocket book.' A ruthless bank robber, Doc McCoy, takes flight with his wife Carol and his ill-gotten gains, with the police and a crazed accomplice hot on his trail. Thompson's insight gives an air of authenticity to the bizarre elements of their story – such as a terrifying underwater hideout where Doc and Carol take refuge until the coast is clear – before the book reaches a climax that is horrific and unique.

His bleak, powerful novels included *The Grifters* (1963) and *Pop. 1280*[23] (1964), while to pay the bills he wrote for the TV soap opera *Dr Kildare* and a novel tied in to the crime show *Ironside*. He was hired to script Sam Peckinpah's screen version of *The Getaway*, but Steve McQueen disliked the ending, and another writer was hired to produce a finale more to the star's taste. In a suitably eccentric coda to his relationship with Hollywood, Thompson played Judge Grayle in the film version of Chandler's *Farewell, My Lovely*.

'Just you wait,' Thompson said to his wife in 1977, not long before a never-ending sequence of health problems caused him effectively to starve himself to death, 'I'll become famous after I've been dead about ten years.' At that time all his books were out of print, and only twenty-five people turned up to his memorial service. In 1990, however, Stephen Frears' film of *The Grifters* earned four Academy Award nominations. Screen versions of *After Dark, My Sweet* and *The Kill-Off* (1957), plus a star-studded re-make of *The Getaway*, soon followed. Thompson's prophecy had come true.

Notes

The main sources are Woody Haut's *Heartbreak and Vine*; Max Décharné's *Hardboiled Hollywood*; Lee Server's *Encyclopedia of Pulp Fiction Writers*; Tony Hilfer's *The Crime Novel*; Robert Polito's biography of Jim Thompson; Brian Ritt's *Paperback Confidential*, edited by Rick Ollerman; and Jay A. Gertzman's *Pulp according to David Goodis*.

1   *'If I sit down to write a novel, I am God at my own typewriter'*: Much depends on a writer's priorities. Daniel Mainwaring wrote whodunits under the name Geoffrey Homes before publishing *Build My Gallows High*, which became *Out of the Past*, a classic film noir later remade as *Against All Odds*. He then abandoned fiction for a lucrative career as a Hollywood screenwriter.

2   *her career flourished*: As a novelist, her finest achievements were in science fiction and she was nicknamed 'Queen of the Space Opera'. After she died, work on the script for *The Empire Strikes Back* was continued by Lawrence Kasdan, who wrote and directed the masterly film noir *Body Heat*.

3   *George Sanders*: Sanders appeared in many crime films, including Hitchcock's *Rebecca* and *Foreign Correspondent*. In 1957 he hosted a thirteen-episode TV series, *The George Sanders Mystery Theater*, which included dramas based on stories by Frederick Nebel, Charlotte Armstrong and Cornell Woolrich. The appearance of two crime novels under his name cashed in on his success; the first, *Crime on My Hands*, was ghostwritten by Craig Rice.

4   *collaborated again with Hawks and Furthman on the western Rio Bravo*: Brackett enjoyed an excellent working relationship with both men, but it is salutary to note that Furthman was paid four times as much as her for working on the picture.

5   *his mix of terse dialogue and action has proved highly influential*: Barry Graham argues in 'W. R. Burnett: The Iron Man Who Chose to Rust' that the hoodlums' conversation in the first chapter of *Little Caesar* inspired crime novelists such as George V. Higgins and Elmore Leonard, as well as Quentin Tarantino. In Graham's view, 'Burnett . . . invented the crime novel as it's now written by George Pelecanos and Dennis Lehane, and invented the narrative style of such TV shows as *The Wire*.'

6   *Scarface . . . co-wrote the screenplay*: The principal writer was the accomplished Ben Hecht, whose collaborations with Hitchcock included *Spellbound*, distantly based on Francis Beeding's *The House of Dr Edwardes*, and famous for its dream sequence; David Bordwell calls it 'the best-known psychoanalytic film of the era'. Hecht also worked on *Notorious*, and (without credit) on *The Paradine Case*, adapted from Robert Hichens' novel.

7   *A dedicated police captain finds the fight against crime is compromised by legal loopholes . . . He resorts to vigilantism*: This concept recurs in films such as *Dirty Harry* and its four sequels.

8   *the Hays Code*: The Motion Picture Production Code, introduced in 1930, was strictly enforced from 1934.

9   *the gripping eleven-minute sequence during which the raid is carried out*: *The Asphalt Jungle*'s influence can be traced in films as diverse as *Rififi*,

Ocean's Eleven (and its remake), *The Italian Job*, *Deadfall* (based on a novel by Desmond Cory), *Dog Day Afternoon* and *The Usual Suspects*.

10 *Kiss Tomorrow Goodbye*: Tony Hilfer described the book as a 'gross, bizarre, heavy-handed, pretentious, naive, weird, sick psychological extravaganza.' A film version starring James Cagney was banned in Ohio.

11 *a ruthless gangster*: Perhaps the most memorable of Britain's fictional gangsters was Ted Lewis's Jack Carter: *Jack's Return Home* was filmed as *Get Carter*. Lewis, like many of his American counterparts, had a self-destructive streak and died at forty-two. Other notable British gangster films include *The Long Good Friday*, which has a stunning final scene, and *Layer Cake*, based on J. J. Connolly's novel.

12 *David Goodis*: His novel *Nightfall* was filmed by Jacques Tourneur, while François Truffaut filmed *Down There* as *Shoot the Piano Player*. Jay A. Gertzman draws parallels between Goodis's life and work and Franz Kafka's. For him, Goodis was 'the pulp Kafka of Philadelphia'.

13 *a luckless man*: Gertzman argues that Goodis even 'makes his lonely gangsters into another variety of his noble loser' and does this even more effectively than underestimated writers of genuine talent. Those writers include Peter Rabe (who had a doctorate in psychology and wrote a textbook on psychotherapy as well as gangster stories) and Gerald Kersh, an author with a wide literary range who is best known for *Night and the City*, filmed by Jules Dassin.

14 *paperback originals*: Rick Ollerman, crime writer and author of *Hardboiled, Noir and Gold Medals*, argues that paperback originals 'had a huge influence on the genre and on culture and they sold millions'. Citing the success of authors such as John D. MacDonald, Donald E. Westlake and Lawrence Block, he suggests that 'this post-war, post-pulp phenomenon was as influential as anything else in the annals of crime fiction.'

15 *Gold Medal*: Gold Medal, an imprint of Fawcett, built on the impact made by the paperback edition of *I, the Jury*, a sex-and-violence thriller by Mickey Spillane that launched the career of tough private eye Mike Hammer. Gold Medal fans included Truffaut and Jean-Luc Godard, whose *Pierrot le Fou* was based on Lionel White's *Obsession*. Godard named a character after Goodis in *Made in USA*, based on a novel by Donald E. Westlake. The French directors' work in turn influenced film-makers such as David Lynch and Quentin Tarantino.

16 *garish cover artwork*: Typically featuring scantily clad women. Some of these books are now pricey collectors' items: see for instance *The Paperback Covers of Robert McGinnis* by Art Scott and Wallace Maynard. The more traditional Dell paperback mysteries, often reprinted hardbacks, became famous for their 'mapbacks', back-cover diagrams showing – often in attractive and inventive ways – where key events in the story occurred. These too are now highly collectible.

17 *Ed Gorman*: Gorman, a stylish writer and commentator, co-founded the magazine *Mystery Scene*.

18 *the television series The Fugitive*: The series ran for 120 episodes from 1963 to 1967, and the second instalment of the two-part finale was, at the time, the most-watched television episode ever, with an estimated audience of seventy-eight million. The show's creator, Roy Huggins, denied suggestions that the storyline was loosely based on a 1954 case in which a physician,

Sam Sheppard, was acquitted of the murder of his wife, and said Kimble was inspired by Victor Hugo's Valjean. He also created the private-eye series *77 Sunset Strip* and co-created *The Rockford Files*.

19 *his biography, written in French*: Philippe Garnier's *Goodis: A Life in Black and White*.

20 *True Detective*: Launched in 1924 as *True Detective Mysteries*, it phased out fiction and became a factual counterpart to *Black Mask*, surviving until 1995. Later contributors included Ann Rule, who became a bestselling true-crime author after publishing a book about the serial killer Ted Bundy, *The Stranger Beside Me*. The title *True Detective* was adopted for a highly successful TV series created and written by Nic Pizzolatto which first aired in 2014.

21 *Robert Wade*: Bob Wade and Bill Miller began writing together as schoolboys. Their debut, *Deadly Weapon*, appeared under the name Wade Miller, and boasts a notable final twist. As Whit Masterson they wrote *Badge of Evil*, which became *Touch of Evil*, a film noir directed by Orson Welles. As Dale Wilmer they wrote *Memo for Murder*, featuring an episode of dental torture predating a similar but more famous scene in William Goldman's *Marathon Man* by twenty years. Wade deplored the literary establishment's snobbery about paperback-original publishers, joking: 'Don't tell my mother that I write for Gold Medal. She thinks I'm a pimp.'

22 *The Killing*: Among the memorable films which it influenced were John Boorman's *Point Blank*, based on *The Hunter* by Richard Stark (a pen-name of Donald E. Westlake), and Tarantino's *Reservoir Dogs*.

23 *Pop. 1280*: Robert Polito describes Charles Brockden Brown's *Wieland*, in which the protagonist feels compelled by the voice of God to murder his family, as 'a sort of early American *Pop. 1280*'. Thompson's novel, narrated by a sheriff with his own methods of cleaning up town, was filmed by Bertrand Tavernier. It supplied the name for a New York City cyberpunk band.

TWENTY-NINE

Carnival of Crime

Mystery and the macabre

In the summer of 1946, William Lindsay Gresham hoped the good times were coming. At thirty-six, he'd survived TB and mental health problems, and he and his wife Joy had two young boys. His first novel, *Nightmare Alley*,[1] dedicated to Joy, had just been published, and he breezily inscribed a copy to a good friend and fellow member of the International Brotherhood of Magicians, Clayton Rawson:

> For / the Great Merlini – / who can stretch a / rope without stretching / his neck, same time / Bill Gresham / Dep. Sheriff / Maricopa Co. / Arizona.

Magic fascinated Gresham, and so – ever since a childhood trip to Coney Island – did carnivals. Biographical notes on dust jackets of first books routinely exaggerate the colourful nature of authors' lives, but Gresham was a publicist's dream. Rinehart & Company claimed he had 'held just about every job any one man can do in a relatively short life. He was a clerk for a fire insurance company, editor of the Western Electric Kearny newspaper, typewriter salesman, demonstrator of magic tricks, a laundry worker, a secretary in a private detective agency (until they discovered he couldn't take shorthand and had been doing the correspondence by memory) and wanted to become a Unitarian minister.'

He worked as a freelance writer until, the publishers said, 'a close friend of his was killed in the Spanish Civil War. Gresham joined a group of volunteers and crossed the Pyrenees in the dead of night to fight for the Spanish Republic. Cut off in the South by Franco's breakthrough he managed to escape by tramp steamer and sealed train across the border into France . . . Due to malnutrition, an aftermath of the blockading of Spain, he spent several months recuperating and during this time began to study psychiatry . . . Friends claim they used to catch him strolling down Broadway of a summer evening magnificently clad in shirt, slacks and bedroom slippers.'

These experiences coalesced to produce a delirious American nightmare for the post-war world. Rinehart proclaimed it was 'not a nice book . . . It is charged to the point of explosion with the necessary quality of its own violence.' For the cultural commentator Michael Dirda, it is 'more than just a steamy noir classic. As a portrayal of the human condition, *Nightmare Alley* is a creepy, all-too-harrowing masterpiece.'

At the Ten-in-One carny, young Stanton (Stan) Carlisle watches a geek,[2] a wild man who bites off the heads of chickens and snakes and drinks their blood. Clem Hoately, boss of the Ten-in-One, explains how to groom alcoholics into performing as geeks by bribing them with the promise of drink: 'All the while you're talking he's thinking about sobering up and getting the crawling shakes. You give him time to think it over . . . Then throw in the chicken. He'll geek.' A geek is the lowest of the low.

The freakish outcasts in the carny include tattooed Sailor Martin ('the living picture gallery'), tiny, tap-dancing Major Mosquito and the Half-man acrobat Joe Plasky, who teaches Stan how to kill. The pretty brunette Molly performs an electric chair act as scantily clad Mamzelle Electra: 'only by wearing the briefest of covering can she avoid bursting into flame.' Madame Zeena, 'miracle woman of the ages . . . she tells you the innermost secrets of your past, your present, and your future', educates Stan sexually, in the Tarot and in the mind-reading racket.

Stan is adept at sleight of hand and loves an audience: 'While they're watching and listening you can tell 'em anything. They believe you. You're a magician.' He tries to knock out Zeena's drunkard husband by supplying him with wood alcohol rather than rye whiskey, and manages to kill him. Not only does he escape justice, he seduces Molly and runs away with her to put into practice everything he's learned about how to manipulate people. The credo is simple: 'Human nature is the same everywhere. All have the same troubles. They are worried.'

But Molly isn't as smart as Zeena, and Stan becomes restless in his pursuit of 'a wad of dough', reinventing himself as a spiritualist, the Rev. Stanton Carlisle, skilled at conning the gullible into parting with their money. Flashbacks reveal the childhood traumas that shaped his character, and the meaning of the book's title.

Stan's life takes a fresh turn when he consults a gorgeous, cynical psychologist, Dr Lilith Ritter. She becomes his lover and a ruthless partner in crime as they plot to swindle wealthy Ezra Grindle out of a fortune. But Stan is destined for his own nightmare alley.

The carnival stood outside the bounds of conventional society,[3] its madness[4] in keeping with a post-war world numbed by warfare and darkened by a nuclear cloud. Gresham's authentic portrayal of life in the carney combines with the bitter irony of Stan's fate to give the story a visceral power.

Some readers found the language so unwholesome that reprints were expurgated, while the presentation of sadomasochism, as when Molly begs Stan to hurt her, horrified some critics. 'If you like your meat raw, this is your dish,' said a reviewer in the *Atlanta Constitution* under the headline 'Beware Geeks Bearing Gifts'.

Nightmare Alley was filmed a year after publication, with matinee idol Tyrone Power cast against type as Stanton Carlisle. Twentieth Century Fox hired a carnival to supply an authentic background covering ten acres of the studio's back lot,[5] but toned down the bleakness of the storyline. This wasn't enough to prevent a box office failure, with the *New York Times* lamenting a 'shocking lack of good taste'. The film eventually achieved cult status,[6] but too late for Gresham. His personal descent into nightmare bore a tragic resemblance to the trajectory of Stanton Carlisle's life in the story.

Gresham was born in Baltimore. His family moved briefly to Fall River, Massachusetts, scene of the Borden axe murders, before settling in New York. After leaving high school, he drifted from job to job and sang folk songs in Greenwich Village. Communism seduced him, and while serving as a medic with the loyalists in Spain, he met Joseph Daniel Halliday, a former sideshow worker, whose tales about carnival life gave him much of the background for his writings.

After returning to the United States, Gresham failed in a suicide attempt before gradually recovering his health. He met and married Joy Davidman, an ethnically Jewish atheist. She was an award-winning poet who shared Gresham's radical political instincts, although both became disillusioned: 'We taught paranoia,' Gresham said, 'and called it Political Education.'

Shortly before *Nightmare Alley* was published, he suffered a breakdown. He was drinking heavily and was occasionally violent. Seeking solace in religion, he and Davidman became interested in the writings of C. S. Lewis. The sixty thousand dollar sale of the film rights enabled the couple to move to a mansion in New York, but Gresham remained restless and unhappy. He dabbled in folk-singing, and tried to ease his misery by exploring Dianetics, the precursor of Scientology, and taking an assortment of lovers. On one occasion he'd tried to hang himself on a hook, but it broke.

Davidman travelled to England, where she met C. S. Lewis and became infatuated. At first her devotion was not reciprocated, and when Gresham broke the news that he was living with his cousin, Renée Rodriguez, and wanted a divorce, Davidman returned home in the hope of saving their marriage. Gresham's drunkenness, violence and infidelity persuaded her that the relationship break-down was irretrievable. She left for England with her two sons, and eventually married Lewis, although her early death from cancer severely tested her new husband's faith.[7]

Gresham married Renée, but his next novel made little impression and, as his prosperity slipped away, so did his health. He wrote a book about Harry Houdini[8] as well as magazine articles, such as a piece describing 'Magic's Most Dangerous Trick', in which a shot is fired at a magician, who catches the bullet between his teeth. The 'bullet catch' was not for the faint-hearted, given that a dozen magicians were said to have died while performing it.

When Clayton Rawson formed the Witchdoctors' Club, an informal but exclusive magicians' social club, he invited Gresham to join; members performed an evening of conjuring tricks each summer at a picnic at Rawson's home in Mamaroneck, New York. Gresham also became a close friend of John Dickson Carr, who returned from England in 1958.

The following year, Gresham invited Carr over for lunch to meet his editor and his wife. A lengthy discussion ensued about classic detective fiction and the mystery of Julia Wallace's murder. Gresham was so short of money that his editor's wife recalled 'it really strained Gresham's purse to entertain, even with ground beef, but he had the air of a Spanish don. Carr behaved like he was dining in the grandest of London Clubs.' Three years later, Carr dedicated his historical mystery *The Demoniacs* to Gresham, but shortly before the book was published, Gresham died.

He was still in his early fifties, but his eyesight was failing and he was diagnosed with cancer of the tongue. The carnival was over. On 14 September 1962, he checked into the Dixie Hotel in Manhattan, where he'd hung out with carnival workers while researching *Nightmare Alley*. There he took a fatal overdose of sleeping pills.[9] Legend has it that his pockets were stuffed with business cards bearing the inscription: *No Address. No Phone. No Business. No Money. Retired.*

Luis Montana, aka Lew Mountain, the protagonist of Bill S. Ballinger's[10] *The Tooth and the Nail*[11] (1955), is a magician who learned his trade in the carny. When his wife is killed, he utilises his skill as an illusionist in order to take revenge. 'Death,' he says, 'is the greatest necromancer of all.'

Lew's first-person narrative alternates with chapters recounting a murder trial in which the accused's identity is withheld from the reader. At first, the two storylines lack any apparent connection, but Ballinger keeps the reader engaged while weaving them together and creating an illusion of his own.

Anthony Boucher declared Ballinger 'a major virtuoso of mystery technique'. He'd introduced the parallel-plot technique in *Portrait in Smoke*, published in 1950, handling it so inventively that Harper published the novel (and *The Tooth and the Nail*) as a 'Sealed Mystery',[12] reviving the sales gimmick employed for Golden Age whodunits.

Fredric Brown held a series of dead-end office jobs until he was thirty. He struggled to make ends meet during the Depression years, when he and his wife Helen (to whom he'd proposed by letter, without their ever having met) were raising two small children. Years later, he worked out his frustrations in a literary novel called *The Office* (1958), but his reputation as a crime writer rests mainly on his daring and often dazzling experiments with storytelling technique.

Brown began with stories for the pulps, but they were in decline by this point, prompting him to try a novel. He spent two weeks with a mentalist in a carnival, studying the people, learning about their work, and listening to the slang terms they used, as research for 'The Freak Show Murders', a novella expanded five years later into *The Dead Ringer* (1948). After writing two shorter stories also set at a carnival, he was ready to write a novel with a carnival background.

The result was *The Fabulous Clipjoint*,[13] written in 1944 but only published three years later, after being rejected by a dozen publishers. The title refers to Chicago, a brutal yet dazzling city where 'the craziest things can happen . . . and not all of them are bad'. After the murder of his father, young Ed Hunter runs off to join his uncle Am(brose), a former private eye. Am now works in the carnival, which to Ed offers the prospect of freedom. And it seems saner than the world he has escaped.

Anthony Boucher described *The Fabulous Clipjoint* as 'sordidly compelling', and the book won the Edgar Award for best first novel. Brown's post-war breakthrough coincided with Gresham's, and once he could afford to write full time, his life changed. He divorced Helen and remarried, having met his second wife

Elizabeth at a writers' group in Milwaukee, where he worked as a proofreader by day and author by night. They began a relationship despite his temerity in criticising Elizabeth's work-in-progress.

Ed and Am Hunter appeared in six further books, but they moved on from the carnival and Brown's interest in them faded. His restless imagination was liberated when he took literary risks. As the mood took him, his writing was playful, witty, macabre or gruesome.

He returned to the carnival in a stand-alone novel, *Madball* (1953), but this time he focused on the seamy realities beneath the slick surface: prostitutes working as 'show girls' and an exhibit called 'Mystery of Sex' featuring a two-headed calf foetus and pornographic books for sale. During the war, the world of the carnival had excited him and offered light relief from the horrors. Now, like Gresham, he saw the carnival's rotten side as well as its craziness. It became a metaphor for American society during the Cold War.

While working on *The Fabulous Clipjoint*, Brown wrote one of the most stunning short stories in the genre. From the opening words of 'Don't Look Behind You', the reader becomes a terrified prospective victim of a deranged killer: 'Just sit back, and relax now. Try to enjoy this; it's going to be the last story you ever read . . .'

Brown's short stories dazzle in range and originality. 'Mistake' is a mere fifty words long, while 'I'll Cut Your Throat Again, Kathleen' is a dark study in mental disintegration and cruelty. 'Obit for Obie' became one of his most effective novels, *The Deep End* (1952), in which newspaperman Sam Evans becomes convinced that a sequence of apparently accidental fatalities are the work of a sociopathic killer.

'The Laughing Butcher' is one of the darkest 'impossible crime' stories, with a 'footprints in the snow' puzzle embellishing a tale of revenge. Brown enjoyed chess – the game plays a part in 'The Laughing Butcher' – and his gift for plotting enabled him to conjure up bizarre, dreamlike scenarios[14] before rationalising them with the rigorous logic of a chess grand master.

He followed his own dream, living the bohemian life of a writer in a small town famed for its artistic colony. This was Taos, New

Mexico, where he set *The Far Cry* (1951), a doom-laden novel flavoured with autobiographical seasoning. George Weaver, recovering from a breakdown, rents an adobe house where eight years earlier Jenny Ames was murdered by a man called Nelson, who was never caught. George is acutely conscious of the painful contrast between the dead innocent and his hard-drinking wife Vi, and his obsession with Jenny has catastrophic consequences.

Jenny and Nelson are supposed to have met through a Lonely Hearts Club, like Brown and his first wife. 'What', Weaver muses, 'is a Lonely Heart murder? Isn't every heart lonely, always?' Jack Seabrook suggests the novel 'may be read as Brown's attempt to exorcise the memory of his first wife[15] by splitting her into two characters and having George Weaver's soul torn apart by the difference between them.'

Off-kilter mysteries such as *His Name Was Death* (1954; expanded from the short story 'Who Was that Blonde I Saw You Kill Last Night?') and *The Lenient Beast* (1956) are admirable for their technical accomplishment as well as their chilling tone and unusual plots.[16] Both tales are told through multiple points of view, in the third and first person respectively. The murder motive in *The Lenient Beast* may be unique; Brown, who described himself as an 'ardent atheist', creates a serial killer driven by a warped sense of mercy. The tantalising question is: what tipped him over the edge into madness?

Brown was a heavy drinker who suffered from asthma and allergies; eventually he was diagnosed with emphysema. His fiction became ever more preoccupied with homicidal insanity,[17] and his cynical wit was not enough to lighten the darkness. Like Gresham, by the early 1960s he was physically and creatively burned out. An attempt to write for television came to nothing, and his late novel *The Murderers* (1961) was uncharacteristically derivative of Highsmith's *Strangers on a Train*. His mysteries disappeared from the bookshelves, and at the time of his death he was more celebrated for his science fiction. The title of his final book was typical Fredric Brown: *Paradox Lost*.

Notes

The main sources are Douglas Greene's biography of John Dickson Carr, Pat H. Broeske's 'The Hypnotic Allure of *Nightmare Alley*', *Mystery Scene* 159, 2019, Leslie Fiedler's *Freaks*, Nicholas Litchfield's introduction to *The Tooth and the Nail*, Jack Seabrook's biography of Brown, and Newton Baird's *A Key to Fredric Brown's Wonderland*.

1   *Nightmare Alley*: The title pays homage to Thomas Love Peacock's satiric novella *Nightmare Abbey*. Michael Dirda acclaimed the book's 'raw, Dostoevskian power' ('A "Nightmare" to Remember', *Washington Post*, 13 May 2010). Dirda brackets the novel with Albert Camus' *The Outsider*, translated into English in the year *Nightmare Alley* was published. Camus acknowledged Cain's *The Postman Always Rings Twice* as an influence on his book.

2   *a geek*: *Nightmare Alley* is often credited with bringing the word into common currency, long before it acquired a fresh meaning.

3   *The carnival stood outside the bounds of conventional society*: *The Fair Murder*, aka *The Carnival Murder*, by Nicholas Brady (who also wrote under his real name, J. V. Turner, and as David Hume) illustrates this in bizarre fashion. On the surface this is a conventional British Golden Age mystery, with a Great Detective in the form of eccentric parson Ebenezer Buckle assisting sceptical Inspector Doby after the fatal stabbing of 'Sandra, The Fattest Woman the World Has Ever Seen'. The story behind the crime is as gruesome as anything in detective fiction. Cosy it isn't.

4   *its madness*: Captured so horrifically in Robert Bloch's carnival-based TV version of his own 'weird tale', 'The Sorcerer's Apprentice', for *Alfred Hitchcock Presents*, that the show's sponsor refused to allow it to be screened.

5   *an authentic background covering ten acres of the studio's back lot*: Hollywood stars such as Joan Crawford and Lana Turner came along to have fun. Gregory Peck tried the 'Test Your Strength' machine and Rex Harrison took lessons in fire-eating.

6   *The film eventually achieved cult status*: Jules Furthman wrote the screenplay a year after *The Big Sleep*. Jonathan Brielle adapted the story into a musical in 2010. A graphic novel version was published by Spain Rodriguez. Guillermo del Toro started work on a remake in 2020, only for filming to be interrupted by the appropriately nightmarish intrusion of the Covid-19 pandemic.

7   *her early death from cancer severely tested her new husband's faith*: Richard Attenborough's film *Shadowlands* portrays Lewis's relationship with Davidman. Lewis adapted an epitaph he'd originally written for Charles Williams to place on Davidman's grave.

8   *Harry Houdini*: Houdini's own publications include a short thriller, *The Zanetti Mystery*. There has been speculation on the internet about who ghostwrote it; the candidates include Fulton Oursler. In recent years, Daniel Stashower has written a series featuring Houdini as a detective.

9   *he took a fatal overdose of sleeping pills*: Gresham was by then a forgotten man. The only New York journalist to record his passing was a bridge columnist who said that 'the card-playing world lost one of its best students'.

10 *Bill S. Ballinger*: William Sanborn Ballinger also wrote extensively for radio,

TV and film. David Bordwell argues that Laura Lippman's novels, such as *I'd Know You Anywhere*, develop Ballinger's method of parallel chronology, paving the way for Gillian Flynn's *Gone Girl*.

11 *The Tooth and the Nail*: Stripped to essentials, this is a story about a manhunt. Francis Iles said it showed the author as 'one of the most competent, and perhaps the most ruthless, of American murder-writers'. Lawrence Block cites the book (which became a South Korean thriller film in 2017) as an influence on his early novel *Lucky at Cards*, featuring a magician's son.

12 *a 'Sealed Mystery'*: After *The Tooth and the Nail*, the gimmick was used just twice, for Nicholas Blake's *A Penknife in My Heart* and Nicolas Freeling's *Question of Loyalty*, aka *Gun before Butter*.

13 *The Fabulous Clipjoint*: Introducing a paperback omnibus of Brown novels, H. R. F. Keating described Ed Hunter as 'an earlier – by four years – Holden Caulfield of J. D. Salinger's *Catcher in the Rye* . . . a later Jim Hawkins, of R. L. Stevenson's *Treasure Island*'.

14 *bizarre, dreamlike scenarios*: *The Fabulous Clipjoint* opens with the words 'In my dream . . .' , as does *Night of the Jabberwock*, in which recurring connections between the storyline and *Alice in Wonderland* are eventually rationalised. Brown's knack of coming up with quirky and memorable titles is typified by one of his finest novels, *The Screaming Mimi*. Occasionally, love of an arresting phrase carried him away, as with *The Case of the Dancing Sandwiches* and *Mrs Murphy's Underpants*.

15 *Brown's attempt to exorcise the memory of his first wife*: In 1955, he presented her with an inscribed copy of his latest novel, but she may have winced at its title, *The Wench is Dead*.

16 *unusual plots*: He contributed a chapter to the MWA's *Mystery Writer's Handbook* called 'Where Do You Get Your Plot?', arguing that: 'a writer plots by accretion . . . plots aren't "got"; they are constructed one step at a time.'

17 *His fiction became ever more preoccupied with homicidal insanity*: *Knock Three-One-Two* opens: 'He had a name, but it doesn't matter; call him *the psycho*.' A 1975 film version, *L'Ibis Rouge*, was directed by France's Jean-Pierre Mocky. The novel is told in the third person, from eight points of view.

THIRTY

Waking Nightmares

Noir fiction

Steve Fisher[1] and Frank Gruber[2] were friends with plenty in common. They'd served in the military, they were based in New York City and they wrote pulp fiction. They also discovered they shared an admiration for the dark, emotional thrillers of a New Yorker called Cornell Woolrich.

After failing to become a second F. Scott Fitzgerald, failing to make the grade as a Hollywood screenwriter and failing to consummate a brief marriage, Woolrich had moved into a hotel apartment with his controlling mother. He'd written for the pulps before publishing his first crime novel, a story of obsessive revenge called *The Bride Wore Black* (1940).

Fisher and Gruber liked to go out drinking, and one night while in Yorkville, they phoned Woolrich's hotel to ask him to join them. The call was answered by Claire Attalie Woolrich, who made it clear that there was no question of her son accepting the invitation. She even refused to put him on the phone.

On occasion, Woolrich did manage to escape the apron strings into the company of his fellow authors, only to dismay Fisher with his 'deep, brooding bitterness about life' and his habit of speaking in a dismal whine. One night, he plucked up the courage to call H. N. Swanson, a top Hollywood agent, in Fisher's presence: "'Hello,

Swanie," I heard Woolrich's sad, nasal voice say into the telephone, "This is that tired, washed-up hack, Cornell Woolrich."'

This strange, troubled man inspired Fisher's breakout novel, *I Wake Up Screaming* (1941). A Hollywood screenwriter is hounded by a vengeful police officer, and there is a compelling portrayal of the detective, a sexually impotent sadist: 'He had red hair and thin white skin and red eyebrows and blue eyes. He looked sick. He looked like a corpse. His clothes didn't fit him. He wore a derby . . . He was a misfit. He was frail, grey-faced and bitter. He was possessed with a macabre humour. His voice was nasal. You'd think he was crying. He might have had T.B. He looked like he couldn't stand up in a wind.'

As if borrowing his fellow author's physical description wasn't bruising enough, Fisher called his psychotic cop Cornell.

Thin-skinned as he was, Woolrich didn't bear a grudge, if Fisher is to be believed. When Fisher set about writing a film script of Woolrich's novella *I Wouldn't be in Your Shoes*, the absence of a rational resolution to the story defeated him. He rang to arrange a meeting with Woolrich in the hope of clarification. Woolrich's mother didn't permit him to leave his hotel room, so the two men spoke on the phone. Woolrich said simply, 'Use the ending you had on *I Wake Up Screaming*.'

In his unpublished memoir 'Blues of a Lifetime', Woolrich pinpointed a moment in his childhood[3] that shrouded him with a lifelong sense of doom: 'I was eleven and . . . looked up at the low-hanging stars of the Valley of Anahuac, and knew I would surely die finally, or something worse . . . I had that trapped feeling, like some sort of a poor insect that you've put inside a downturned glass, and it tries to climb up the sides, and it can't, and it can't, and it can't.'

Cornell George Hopley-Woolrich was the only child of an unhappy marriage. His parents separated and, after graduating, he launched himself as a Jazz Age novelist. He wrote articles for *The Smart Set*, provoking controversy with an attack on trendy young women which demanded, 'Why do they have to show their thighs all the time?'

At twenty-five he moved to Hollywood, working on a film version of his second book, *Children of the Ritz*. While in California, he married a film mogul's daughter after a brief and improbable romance. He and Gloria split up three months later, following her discovery of a diary recording his homosexual encounters; apparently he liked to cruise the waterfront at night, wearing a sailor's uniform. She sought to annul the marriage on the ground of non-consummation.

In the depths of the Depression, Woolrich ran out of money and moved with his mother into an apartment in the Hotel Marseille, New York City, which became his home for the next quarter of a century. Having published half a dozen mainstream novels, he succumbed to commercial reality, and his first pulp story appeared in *Detective Fiction Weekly* in 1934. 'Death Sits in the Dentist's Chair' featured elements that recurred in his later work:[4] black humour, a vivid account of imagined horror-to-come, and the frantic suspense of a race against time.

Woolrich's unfulfilled yearning for love is reflected in the emotion of his prose as agony upon agony piles on luckless protagonists. He never created a series character, so readers couldn't be confident that a Woolrich story would have a happy ending. Many did not.

His writing wasn't laconic like Hammett's or wisecracking like Chandler's, but feverish. In Woolrich's hands, ironic plot twists expose not the fallibility of conventional justice, as in the books of Francis Iles and his followers, but life's chaos. His doom-drenched world view enabled him to create what Francis M. Nevins calls 'waking nightmares'.[5]

Who can I trust? is a familiar refrain in crime fiction. In *The Black Curtain* (1941), Frank Townsend confronts an even more terrifying question: *can I even trust myself?* Suffering from amnesia and suspected of murder, he becomes the quarry in a deadly manhunt. The story was filmed as *Street of Chance*, and movie versions of Woolrich's work became emblematic of a new form of film-making influenced by social upheaval and the terrors of war, a genre of foreboding and malevolence that became known as film noir.[6]

In *Phantom Lady* (1942),[7] Scott Henderson walks into a bar and on a whim invites a woman to dinner and a show. They agree not to talk about themselves, or even exchange names. Later, his wife is found murdered, and he is charged with the crime. Only one person can clear him, but nobody can find her, and the witnesses all swear they saw him alone. Henderson is sentenced to death, the chapter headings recording the number of days left before his execution.

A simple-minded recluse with supposedly uncanny powers predicts in *Night Has a Thousand Eyes* (1945)[8] that a millionaire called Harlan Reid will die at midnight in three weeks' time, in the jaws of a lion. Tension mounts as a lion escapes from a local circus, and Reid's helpless horror is to know his fate.

Woolrich's strengths as a writer of emotional thrillers – fear-jerkers – were inseparable from his literary shortcomings.[9] His prose often turned purple, and the mood of despair sometimes descended into hysterical shrillness. The scenarios of his finest stories seize the imagination, and Chandler described him as the 'best ideas man', but he was often unable to resolve the terrifying situations he'd created with matching flair. Flukes and coincidences abound in real life, but novelists who overindulge in them risk testing the suspension of disbelief to breaking point.

I Married a Dead Man[10] (1948) opens with a pregnant woman's switch of identities following a train crash, but fails to explain the events of the story before twisting towards a maudlin conclusion: 'I don't know what the game was. I'm not sure how it should be played . . . I only know we must have played it wrong somewhere along the way . . . We've lost. That's all I know. We've lost. And now the game is through.'

For moviemakers more concerned with creating suspense than solving puzzles, Woolrich's scenarios were perfect. One of Alfred Hitchcock's masterpieces was based on a Woolrich novella which began life under the drab title 'Murder from a Fixed Viewpoint' before being published as 'It Had to be Murder'. The narrator, Hal Jeffries, is confined to his New York apartment by a broken leg. He whiles away the time by spying on his neighbours, and becomes convinced that one of them, Lars Thorwald, has committed a murder. But when he calls in the police, there is no evidence to back up his claim.

The characters are ciphers, but Woolrich conjures up unbearable suspense through Jeffries' obsession, his helplessness and the threat posed by Thorwald: 'Suddenly, death was somewhere inside the house here with me. And I couldn't move, I couldn't get up out of this chair.' Renamed *Rear Window*, the story made a compelling and influential movie.[11]

Hitchcock's film emphasises the story's voyeuristic aspects,[12] but a key driver of *Rear Window* is the wretchedness of isolation. Loneliness tormented Woolrich, and the toxic mix of his mother's suffocating devotion, sexual misery, acute lack of self-esteem and out-of-control drinking slowly destroyed him. By the end of the 1940s, he'd produced all his best work and become old before his time. Once his mother died in 1957, he all but gave up on life, despite lingering on for another eleven years. His neglect of a foot infection led to gangrene, and the amputation of a leg.

Woolrich died a millionaire, consumed by self-loathing. He left behind a manuscript aptly titled 'The Loser'; appropriately, he never managed to finish it.[13] His estate founded scholarships in his mother's memory, but his greatest legacy was a body of work that dazzled like a garish neon sign in pitch darkness.

Not even Woolrich's delirious urban nightmares are as disquieting as Joel Townsley Rogers' novel of rural paranoia, *The Red Right Hand* (1945).[14] Heading in their car from New York to Vermont, the recently betrothed Inis St Erme and Elinor Darrie pick up a strange-looking tramp. Murder swiftly follows. The narrator is a potential witness – but might he also be a suspect? From the opening paragraph, the surreal events 'of the dark mystery of tonight' present questions as intriguing as they are macabre. Where is the killer of Inis St Erme? What did he do with St Erme's right hand? And what is his purpose?

Bizarre locales such as the Swamp Road and Dead Bridegroom's Pond enhance the phantasmagoric mood, as do the character names: Riddle, St Erme, Dexter, Quelch, Flail. The narrator is haunted by recollections of 'the distant baying of the hounds', and 'the voices of the locusts . . . the gray bird fluttering frantically in my face' as he tries to make sense of the inexplicable. What should we believe? Whom should we trust? Nothing is as it seems.

The dizzying stream-of-consciousness narrative is not split into chapters, and seems far removed from a Golden Age puzzle. Yet

Rogers is as adept at misdirection as he is generous with his clues – one of which takes the form of a word game – and although coincidences abound, the novel is an 'impossible crime' story and a febrile version of the 'fair play' mystery.

The heady brew of *The Red Right Hand* disconcerted some critics,[15] but the book found favour in France, winning the Grand Prix de Littérature Policière. But such originality is rare. Rogers lived for almost another forty years without coming close to matching his masterpiece.[16]

In 1948, the fledgling Mystery Writers of America voted to present Woolrich with an Edgar Award, recognising the 'lifetime achievement' he'd crammed into little more than a decade. On the other side of the Atlantic, the much longer-established Prix du Roman d'Aventures for best French crime novel of the year was given to Thomas Narcejac,[17] a graduate of the Sorbonne and former teacher whose real name was Pierre Ayraud, for his debut mystery *Death on Tour*.

At the ceremony, Narcejac met Pierre Boileau, who had won the same prize ten years earlier for *The Sleeping Bacchus*.[18] The two men decided to write together. Despite their shared love of the classic stories of Conan Doyle, Chesterton and Leblanc, they understood that the Second World War had changed the market for crime fiction. They admired the American hardboiled writers, and Woolrich's dark, hallucinatory storylines inspired them to take a new direction with books that became known as *suspense à la française*. Their first joint effort, *The Shadow and the Prey*, appeared under an anagrammatic pen-name, Alain Bouccarèje.

Their second collaboration was published in 1952 under their own names. *Les Diaboliques, She Who Was No More* and *The Fiends* (filmed as *Diabolique*), concerns a travelling salesman and his mistress who conspire to murder his wife in order to collect on her life insurance. The frightening plot twists are worthy of Woolrich, but Boileau and Narcejac, with their shared love of classic detection, plotted with greater finesse. Their brand of ingenuity coupled with vivid atmospherics proved irresistible to moviemakers.

Henri-Georges Clouzot snapped up the film rights – according to legend, he was just ahead of Hitchcock in the race – and created a masterpiece of French cinema. When Boileau and Narcejac learned of Hitchcock's enthusiasm for their work, they set about writing a novel they hoped would appeal to him. The result was *The Living and the Dead* (1954), a puzzle about the slipperiness of identity.[19] Hitchcock loved the premise: 'the hero's attempt to re-create the image of a dead woman through another one who's alive . . . To put it plainly, the man wants to go to bed with a woman who's dead; he is indulging in a form of necrophilia.' His version, *Vertigo,*[20] although not an instant success, is today one of the most revered movies of the twentieth century.

In *Spells of Evil* (1961), a much less celebrated novel, Boileau and Narcejac employ the familiar set-up of a charming yet weak-willed man who falls in lust with a sexy but duplicitous woman with fatal consequences. The story is told by a vet who is called out to help a mysterious widow, Myriam Heller, who lives with a tame cheetah and an African maid. He embarks on a dangerous liaison with Myriam but soon has cause to fear that she possesses the ability to use dark arts to murderous effect.

With Boileau and Narcejac, as with Woolrich, one can never be confident that the disorientated protagonist – such as Richard Hermantier, the blind, tormented inventor from *Faces in the Dark* (1952) – will survive. Similar uncertainty surrounds what will happen to lead characters created by the duo's disciples, notably Hubert Monteilhet,[21] Catherine Arley,[22] Frédéric Valmain[23] and Robert Thomas.[24]

The lasting appeal of Thomas' play *Trap for a Lonely Man*[25] is reflected in the regularity with which it has been performed on the stage since its premiere in 1960 and also adapted for film. Daniel Corban, whose wife has vanished, finds himself confronted in his Alpine chalet by a woman claiming to be the missing Madame Corban. Daniel has never seen her before, but witnesses come forward to insist that she is indeed his wife. Is he going mad, or is he the victim of an extraordinary conspiracy? And if the latter, what is the plotters' motive?

The most gifted French writer to follow in the footsteps of Boileau and Narcejac was Jean-Baptiste Rossi. While working in an advertising agency, he turned to crime writing with a vengeance. He adopted the anagrammatic pseudonym Sébastien Japrisot[26] and, so it is said, wrote two novels in the space of a month. In the first, *The 10.30 from Marseille*, aka *The Sleeping-Car Murders* (1962), a woman's body is discovered when a train reaches the end of its journey, and her death is followed by the murders of other occupants of her sleeping car. The solution to the mystery is as unlikely as those favoured by Woolrich and Boileau and Narcejac, but Japrisot skates over thin ice with panache.

He repeated the feat in *Trap for Cinderella* (1962). Two women are trapped in a house fire, and only one of them survives. Shockingly burned, and in need of reconstructive surgery, she also suffers from amnesia. What is her true identity, and how unreliable is she as a narrator? Once again, plot twists and narrative drive distract the reader's attention from multiple improbabilities.

One Deadly Summer (1977) is ingenious but subtler, a showcase for Japrisot's technical skill in allowing an elaborate story to unfold through multiple viewpoints. A beautiful but mysterious nineteen-year-old seduces a naive volunteer fireman; evidently, she has an ulterior motive, and the atmosphere of menace implies that the outcome will be catastrophic. Like Woolrich, Japrisot makes the reader desperate to discover the fate of his characters, but fearful that there won't be a happy ending.

Notes

The main sources are Francis M. Nevins' writings on Woolrich, in particular *First You Dream, Then You Die*, and Truffaut's *Hitchcock*.

1   *Steve Fisher*: After running away to sea at sixteen, Fisher wrote his first story aboard a submarine. During the Depression, he dined on crackers and ketchup and was evicted from cheap hotels for non-payment, but with Gruber's help he began to earn a living from the pulps. Fisher scripted *Lady in the Lake*, based on Chandler's novel, and *Dead Reckoning*. Later he wrote TV scripts for *77 Sunset Strip*, *Starsky and Hutch*, *McMillan & Wife* and *Barnaby Jones*. Fisher is said to have inspired Humphrey Bogart's portrayal of Dix Steele in *In a Lonely Place*.

2   *Frank Gruber*: Gruber also made the transition from pulp fiction to writing for television and film; he adapted Eric Ambler's *The Mask of Dimitrios* for the big screen.

3   *a moment in his childhood*: Nevins compares Woolrich's real-life experience to the Flitcraft parable in Hammett's *The Maltese Falcon*, arguing that they represent 'each man's revolt against religion'.

4   *elements that recurred in his later work*: Nevins categorises Woolrich's
    main types of story thus: Noir Cop (featuring a sadistic police officer); Clock
    Race; Waking Nightmare (the protagonist comes to after a blackout and
    becomes convinced he did something appalling while out of himself);
    Oscillation (the viewpoint figure's trust in someone close to him or her is
    eaten away by suspicion); Headlong through the Night (the last hours of a
    hunted man as he flails desperately across the dark city to his doom);
    Annihilation (a male protagonist finds the perfect woman only for her to
    vanish without a trace); and stories where 'we are compelled to share the
    final hours and minutes of someone torn apart by the ultimate torture:
    knowing that he or she will die in a particularly awful way and at a
    particular moment'.
5   *'waking nightmares'*: One of Woolrich's finest novellas is simply called
    'Nightmare' and was filmed twice.
6   *film noir*: The title of Sherwood King's *If I Die Before I Wake* captures the
    sense of nightmarish dread permeating film noir. Orson Welles filmed the
    story as *The Lady from Shanghai*, compensating for an incoherent screen-
    play with a sumptuous visual feast, notably a memorable and much-imitated
    climax in a hall of mirrors.
7   *Phantom Lady*: First published under the name William Irish, the screen
    version was directed by Robert Siodmak, whose other films include *The
    Spiral Staircase*, based on Ethel Lina White's *Some Must Watch*, and *The
    Suspect*, based on James Ronald's ironic *This Way Out*.
8   *Night Has a Thousand Eyes*: The story developed an earlier novella called
    'Speak to Me of Death', but appeared under a new pseudonym, George
    Hopley. Woolrich was attempting to 'break out', but sales didn't live up to
    his hopes. A film version was co-written by Jonathan Latimer.
9   *his literary shortcomings*: Julian Symons said harshly that those shortcom-
    ings 'preclude him from serious consideration'.
10 *I Married a Dead Man*: The book, another 'William Irish', has been filmed
    several times, initially as *No Man of Her Own*.
11 *a compelling and influential movie*: Similarly, one may detect touches of
    The Bride Wore Black in Tarantino's *Kill Bill*.
12 *Hitchcock's film emphasises the story's voyeuristic aspects*: In *Hitchcock*,
    by François Truffaut (who directed *The Bride Wore Black*), the British director
    responded to the film reviewer C. A. Lejeune's criticism of Jeffries as a
    Peeping Tom: 'Sure he's a snooper, but aren't we all?' Hitchcock said his
    presentation of Thorwald's murder was influenced by the real-life cases of
    Crippen and Mahon.
13 *he never managed to finish it*: Woolrich also abandoned *Into the Night*, a
    book posthumously completed by Lawrence Block. Block created private eye
    Matt Scudder and burglar Bernie Rhodenbarr, who (like Peter Lovesey's cop
    Peter Diamond) has a cat named after E. W. Hornung's A. J. Raffles.
14 *The Red Right Hand*: The novel, published in 1945, expanded a novella
    published in *Detective Fiction Weekly*. Two of Rogers' other three novels
    were also elaborations of shorter stories.
15 *The heady brew . . . disconcerted some critics*: The acerbic Jacques Barzun
    and Wendell Hertig Taylor dismissed the book as 'bore-dumb'.
16 *without coming close to matching his masterpiece*: Perhaps Rogers was
    insufficiently haunted by demons. A Harvard graduate, he was happily

married for more than sixty years, and had five children, one of whom established a website with a detailed bibliography of his father's work.

17 *Thomas Narcejac*: Narcejac wrote a book about Simenon, and a genre study, *The Crime Novel*.

18 *The Sleeping Bacchus*: Boileau's novel is yet to be translated into English, but it inspired a novel with the same title by Hilary St George Saunders, one half of the duo who wrote as Francis Beeding.

19 *a puzzle about the slipperiness of identity*: This favourite genre theme is at the heart of the duo's clever and strangely overlooked *Who Was Claire Jallu?*

20 *Vertigo*: The screenplay was co-written by Alec Coppel, whose other work included *A Man about a Dog*, a play about a doctor who sets out to kill his wife. Coppel turned the story into a novel, and it too became a film, *Obsession*, aka *The Hidden Room*. He also wrote the screen version of his novel *Mr Denning Drives North*, about the consequences of an accidental killing.

21 *Hubert Monteilhet*: Monteilhet's debut *The Praying Mantises* won the Grand Prix de Littérature Policière and presents a murder story worthy of Woolrich in epistolary form. His most famous book, *Return from the Ashes*, aka *Phoenix from the Ashes*, plays with notions of identity in the context of plastic surgery, and has been filmed twice.

22 *Catherine Arley*: Arley, whose real name is Pierrette Pernot, is an actor, playwright and novelist. Oddly, her most famous novel, *Woman of Straw*, was not published in her native France for many years after its original appearance in Switzerland. The book, filmed with Sean Connery and Gina Lollobrigida, is a suspenseful account of a conspiracy to murder a rich old man.

23 *Frédéric Valmain*: Valmain was a shadowy figure, an Algerian-born actor and writer; most sources say that Valmain was a pen name for Paul Baulat, who also wrote as James Carter. Occasionally, it has been claimed that Valmain was a pseudonym of Frédéric Dard. Valmain has been credited with a stage adaptation of Simenon's play *Liberty Bar*, but his most notable crime novel is *The Jackals*, which transplants a murderous conspiracy in the tradition of Cain's *Double Indemnity* to a small town on the Algerian coast.

24 *Robert Thomas*: The success of *Trap for a Lonely Man* encouraged Thomas to rewrite his first play, and *Eight Women*, set in a snowbound country house, was filmed by François Ozon, with musical numbers and a starry cast. Thomas also translated Agatha Christie's play *The Unexpected Guest*. Like Thomas, Yves Jacquemard and Jean-Michel Sénécal were actors and playwrights. They collaborated as Jacquemard-Sénécal and *The Body Vanishes* was filmed. After Jacquemard died young, Sénécal pursued a solo career under their joint brand name.

25 *Trap for a Lonely Man*: The play, whose title has had numerous variants, supplied the storyline for no fewer than three American TV movies: *Honeymoon with a Stranger*, *One of My Wives is Missing* and *Vanishing Act*. Hitchcock contemplated filming the play, but may have been deterred by the similarity to the plot of *Chase a Crooked Shadow*, a film whose premise itself resembled that of an earlier radio play, *Stranger in the House*.

26 *Sébastien Japrisot*: Japrisot published his first novel aged seventeen, and then turned to translating westerns featuring Hopalong Cassidy. Most of his novels of suspense have been filmed, *Trap for Cinderella* twice. His movie scripts included *And Hope to Die*, the film version of David Goodis's *Black Friday*, and *Mad Enough to Kill*, based on a book by the novelist, screenwriter and translator Jean-Patrick Manchette.

THIRTY-ONE

Dagger of the Mind

Casebook novels

Vera Caspary turned to writing crime fiction as a form of escapism: she was desperate to cleanse her system of political poison. A Hollywood-based novelist, screenwriter and (under the alias of Lucy Sheridan) a member of the Communist Party, she was among the legion of radicals left distraught by Stalin's decision to sign a non-aggression pact with Hitler.

'Losing faith is a slow process,' she wrote in her memoirs, 'and painful. A last desperate effort to cling to belief attacks the nerve roots . . . "I can never quit being a Communist," I had once declared. The recollection sickened me because I knew that even while I said it I had practised self-deceit . . . my devotion had never been complete.'

She held a gathering at her home that led to a bitter debate between Van Wyck Brooks, a critic who shared her sense of betrayal, and the Soviet apologist Anna Louise Strong. When Brooks challenged her about Hitler's invasion of Poland, Strong could only respond with a rant about statistics: her 'blows fell heavily, but never upon the target'. Ashamed and embarrassed to have hosted a debacle, and sickened by political bigotry, Caspary sought solace in writing a mystery play.

Her first effort was feeble, but she rewrote it with a different culprit, and a friend encouraged her to turn it into a novel. When she complained that 'you can't write a mystery without cheating', he urged her to try. 'Mysteries have never been my favourite reading,' she admitted. 'The murderer, the most interesting character, has always to be on the periphery of the action lest he give away the secret that can be revealed only in the final pages . . . The novel demands a full development of each character. This was my problem.'

Another friend, the screenwriter Ellis St Joseph,[1] recommended solving the difficulty through storytelling technique. Why not take a leaf out of Wilkie Collins' books, by 'having each character tell his or her own version, revealing or concealing information according to his or her own interests'?

This structural ploy liberated Caspary's imagination:[2] 'After all those barren mechanical years, I worked with the zest of a young writer with a first novel.' She came up with a book that changed her life and defined her reputation, a novel that became a famous film and gave a name to a haunting song: *Laura*.

Vera Caspary was born into a Jewish family. A broad-minded education meant that she was 'robbed of simple faith but relieved of superstition', and 'could honestly echo my mother's "I'm Jewish and proud of it"'. While serving her apprenticeship as a writer, she worked as a stenographer in her native Chicago, before taking a job in advertising. She amused herself by promoting a mail-order scheme known as the Sergei Marinoff School of Classic Dancing, although Marinoff didn't exist. When customer inquiries flooded in, panic ensued until a ballet teacher could be found to provide advice that Caspary refined into a correspondence course.

Her local community was left reeling by the news that Bobby Franks had been killed by Leopold and Loeb. The crime that inspired Patrick Hamilton's *Rope* shocked Caspary, partly because it came close to home, but also because it was so hard to comprehend: 'If gangsters had kidnapped and done murder at the bidding of a racketeer boss . . . the crime would have been dismissed as another evidence of Chicago lawlessness. But the Loebs! The Leopolds! Not only respectable but respected; not only millionaires, but an institution . . . Both boys were brilliant students at the university. Why? Why? Why?'

Caspary was struck by the compassion people felt for the families of the killers as well as the family of the wretched victim. And even at times of tragedy, life goes on. Richard Loeb's aunt was trying to sell a beach cottage, but was desperate to avoid being pestered by prurient time-wasters. She asked Caspary to act as an intermediary, and lent her the key. This was a chance too good to miss. The cottage became an illicit shelter where Caspary and her boyfriend had sex.

This wasn't the only way she benefited from the tragedy: 'Until then I'd never had the slightest interest in violence . . . the shock of murder by and among members of our conservative world, the intensity of horror in the neighbourhood . . . scarred my mind. Had anyone told me in the summer of 1924 that I was to become a writer of murder stories I'd have been no less startled than I was when [two friends] confided the names of the two "nice Jewish boys" who had kidnapped and killed one of their own kind.'

Moving to New York, she worked for a magazine called *Dance Lovers*, where her outspokenness led to her being sacked by the chief editor, Fulton Oursler. She was establishing herself as a playwright and novelist when the Depression intervened, 'the chemistry of dread that touched us all'. The suffering of those ruined by the Wall Street Crash dismayed her and brought out her rebellious streak. During the hot summer of 1931, she sat naked at her window, 'my authoring costume . . . a pair of spectacles and a pair of sandals', heedless of her mother's warning that two men in the apartment opposite were watching, and typing out a novel that excoriated prejudice and the love of material possessions.

A lucky break came with an invitation to write for Paramount Pictures. During her time in advertising, she'd worked on a correspondence course about plotting that now came in handy. She managed to sell essentially the same story eight times before the truth dawned on Paramount. Her attitudes were sharpened by the plight of those ruined by economic catastrophe. A long struggle to write a book reflecting her radical political sympathies ended in dismay: 'How could I write a proletarian novel when I had never known a proletarian?'

In 1939, Caspary travelled to Europe. She'd agreed to make a marriage of convenience to enable the brother of a friend to escape from the Nazis, but when she met the man in Switzerland, their mutual detestation made her think better of it. She fled to Russia, but the sense of a society under constant surveillance caused her doubts about Stalin to grow. Abandoning Communism proved an emotional wrench, but she found solace with her future husband, the film producer Isidore 'Igee' Goldsmith, and in the success of *Laura*.

While preparing to write *Laura*, Caspary studied *The Woman in White*, making detailed notes about Collins' method of structuring his mystery. As any prosecuting or defence counsel knows, and as any jury quickly learns, each witness called to give evidence in a trial views events through a lens clouded by their personal concerns. The casebook form of novel, offering a sequence of testimonies, is inherently flexible.[3] Contrasts between the different points of view allow a writer to explore character, build suspense and craft subtle plot twists.[4]

The early scenes of the story are narrated by Waldo Lydecker, an aesthete perhaps based on Alexander Woollcott. He denounces 'the conventional mystery story as an excess of sound and fury, signifying, far worse than nothing, a barbaric need for violence and revenge in that timid horde known as the reading public'. Waldo offers his account 'not so much as a detective yarn as a love story', apparently because Mark McPherson, the detective called in to investigate the murder of Laura Hunt, becomes obsessed with her.

Waldo's manipulative behaviour owes something to Collins' portrayal of Count Fosco, while Laura is a twentieth-century version of Marian Halcombe, an emancipated woman who has (like her creator) earned respect as well as a good living in the cut-throat advertising business. McPherson represents Caspary's ideal of a New York detective and is almost as much a fantasy figure as Lord Peter Wimsey. For all his smart-alec dialogue, he's far removed from the stereotypical hardboiled cop; not only has he read Gibbon and a history of the Jews, he nurses 'proletarian prejudices'.

Wry, witty prose combined with a mid-story plot twist and slick characterisation to produce a compelling novel, published in 1943. Caspary sold the film rights (signing 'one of the worst contracts ever written . . . as carelessly as a five-dollar check'), but was infuriated by Otto Preminger's 'Hollywood version of a cute career girl'. *Laura* was a hit, but the most memorable character is Waldo Lydecker.

The colossal popularity of a breakthrough novel is a mixed blessing. Even authors who avoid being labelled as one-hit wonders may find their later careers have a lingering whiff of anticlimax. For the rest of her life, Caspary battled in vain to come up with a better story. Film-makers begged her to 'write me another *Laura*', but she was handicapped by her lack of interest in plot construction. She cared little for conventional mysteries, although her novella *Murder in the Stork Club* boasts a Christie-style gathering of the suspects in the eponymous Manhattan nightclub, and a 'least likely person' solution.

Caspary admired the work of Cornell Woolrich, while her favourite crime novel was *Before the Fact*. The hapless protagonist of Francis Iles' novel is gnawed by the suspicion that her husband is a murderer, and Caspary borrowed this idea for *Bedelia* (1945), reversing the genders of suspect and potential victim, and setting her story in Connecticut in the winter of 1913–14. The film version shifted the location to Europe, and was produced by Goldsmith.

Caspary regretted being typecast as a suspense writer, but concluded her memoirs by saying, 'This has been the century of the Woman and I know myself fortunate to have been part of that revolution.' Despite her embrace of the high life after marrying Goldsmith, her fiction continued to reflect her preoccupation with politics, gender issues and social class.

Her enthusiasm for Wilkie Collins and the casebook method of storytelling never waned. In her final mystery, *Elizabeth X*, aka *The Secret of Elizabeth* (1978), a young woman is found wandering, apparently suffering from amnesia. Who is she? Through a sequence of first-person testimonies, a shocking story unfolds about the abuse of power. Elizabeth, like Laura Fairlie in Collins' novel, proves to have been confined in a 'place of safety' at the behest of a rich and ruthless male oppressor.

Kenneth Fearing, also born in Illinois, had much in common with Caspary. His political sympathies resembled hers, and he too took up crime fiction as a sideline only to find it more lucrative than the work he cared for most. Although his mother was Jewish, his father was not, and his parents split up when he was young. When Fearing married a Jewish woman, she regarded him as a gentile.

During the 1920s, Fearing published poetry and wrote pulp fiction, some of it pseudonymous soft-core pornography. Alcohol held a fatal attraction for him, and on one occasion he was jailed for drunkenness. He helped to found the left-wing magazine *Partisan Review*, and his Depression-era verse reflected his Marxist leanings.

In 1938, he stayed at Yaddo, a writer's colony in Saratoga Springs, which he fictionalised three years later in *Dagger of the Mind*, aka *Cry Killer!* There is no shortage of literary backbiting in a novel lauded by Raymond Chandler as 'a savage piece of intellectual double-talk'. The story is told through multiple viewpoints and ends with a murderer condemned to die in the electric chair: 'My lips, beneath the mask they had placed over my face, opened and started to speak. I said, "The truth is simple. The truth is . . ."'

For his masterpiece, *The Big Clock*,[5] Fearing borrowed from both real life and fiction. The year 1944 saw the sensational trial of Wayne Lonergan, a bisexual playboy convicted of murdering his wife, an heiress. In the same year, Sam Fuller's[6] *The Dark Page* was published while its author was serving as an infantryman; the setting is a tabloid newspaper, whose star reporter investigates a murder he has committed himself. In Fearing's story, a magazine boss called Earl Janoth murders his mistress, and then instructs his right-hand man George Stroud to track down a witness to the killing. For Stroud, there is a snag. He is the witness, and Janoth wants the witness dead.

Again Fearing juggled multiple viewpoints. His aim was not to hide the killer's identity or motivation, but to create suspense. Rapid shifts of perspective build tension as Stroud hunts himself,[7] pretending to seek out the truth while at the same time frantically trying to hide it. Although he is far from heroic, the reader identifies with his terror, and wants him to survive. Fearing satirises the business empire of the right-wing publisher Henry Luce, and employs the metaphor of a ticking clock not only to capture the race against time and to convey a business conglomerate eating away at the lives of those trapped within it, but also as a symbol of mortality.

The Big Clock (1946) earned Fearing a fortune. He divorced his first wife and married a woman he'd met at Yaddo, but, as drink took its toll, he spent all his money and lost his literary verve. Institutions fascinated him, and provided the backdrop for his best novels, but he saw them with an outsider's eye. He remained an individualist in whom incoherent idealistic thinking warred with instinctive scepticism. When the House Un-American Activities Committee asked him if he was a member of the Communist Party, he mumbled, 'Not yet.'

Notes

The main sources are Caspary's *The Secrets of Grown-Ups*; A. B. Emrys's, *Wilkie Collins, Vera Caspary and the Evolution of the Casebook Novel* and introduction to *The Murder in the Stork Club*; and Robert M. Ryley's articles about Fearing on the Modern American Poetry website.

1 *Ellis St Joseph*: St Joseph wrote a film script, *A Scandal in Paris*, loosely based on the memoirs of Vidocq.
2 *This structural ploy liberated Caspary's imagination*: As it has for many other writers. Examples include Sayers and Eustace's *The Documents in the Case*, C. H. B. Kitchin's *The Birthday Party*, Michael Innes's *Lament for a Maker* and Robert Player's *The Ingenious Mr Stone* in the twentieth century, and Michael Cox's history-mysteries *The Meaning of Night* and *The Glass of Time*, Joseph Knox's *True Crime Story* and Janice Hallett's *The Appeal* in the twenty-first.
3 *The casebook form of novel . . . is inherently flexible*: In *Here Comes a Candle*, Fredric Brown included a radio play, a screenplay, a sportscast, a teleplay, a stage play and newspaper articles. Marketed as a serious novel, the book failed to achieve the breakthrough Brown yearned for, perhaps because for once he failed to match the originality of the book's format with an equally zestful storyline. More than half a century later, Riku Onda's *The Aosawa Murders*, a multilayered casebook novel about mass poisonings at a family party, illustrated the potential of the form for ambitious novelists.
4 *Contrasts between the different points of view allow a writer to explore character, build suspense and craft subtle plot twists*: Nevertheless, the form challenges literary technique. E. R. Punshon, a prolific detective novelist admired by Sayers, was wise to publish his attempt to use the casebook method for an inferior thriller, *Documentary Evidence*, under a pen-name, Robertson Halkett. Paula Hawkins' *Into the Water* juggles no fewer than eleven viewpoints. As Val McDermid pointed out: 'To differentiate 11 separate voices within a single story is a fiendishly difficult thing. And these characters are so similar in tone and register – even when some are in the

first person and others in third – that they are almost impossible to tell
apart, which becomes monotonous and confusing' (*Guardian*, 26 April 2017).

5   *his masterpiece, The Big Clock*: The novel began life in an abridged magazine version as 'The Judas Picture', and was filmed, with a screenplay by
Jonathan Latimer. *No Way Out*, a 1987 remake which updated the storyline
to the Cold War, offered an additional plot twist. The book was also the
uncredited source of the French film *Police Python 357*. There are strong
echoes of Fearing's story in *The Killing of Francie Lake*, which is one of
Julian Symons' less successful novels, as well as in his psychological mystery
The Narrowing Circle.

6   *Sam Fuller*: Fuller was a crime reporter and war hero who became a novelist,
screenwriter and film-maker; he wrote and directed an admired film noir
Pickup on South Street. He acted in several movies, including Godard's
Pierrot le Fou and Wenders' *The American Friend*, based on Patricia
Highsmith's *Ripley's Game*. *The Dark Page* was filmed as *Scandal Sheet*.

7   *Stroud hunts himself*: Early examples of this type of story include Maurice
Leblanc's *813* and Bruce Graeme's *Not Proven*, in which a police sergeant
murders his wife's lover, and is then tasked with investigating the crime.
Later versions include Derek Marlowe's spy thriller *A Dandy in Aspic*.
Marlowe's erratic career is discussed in Joseph Goodrich's *Unusual Suspects*.

THIRTY-TWO

Whose Body?

Whowasdunins: mysteries about the victim's identity

On a visit to the Fitzroy Tavern in London in 1953, a writer and a young Indian friend met two twenty-year-old naval cooks. The writer was an urbane fellow of fifty with a good war record. He was called Rupert Croft-Cooke and most of his books appeared under his own name, but for slumming it with detective novels, he used a pseudonym, Leo Bruce. Joseph, his Indian companion, lived with him in Sussex and worked as his secretary.

Croft-Cooke invited the sailors to stay over the weekend. After the guests departed from the house, they became involved in an altercation with two other men. Unfortunately, one was a policeman, and the sailors found themselves charged with assault. While they were being interviewed, they told the police that the writer and his companion had plied them with drink and committed acts of 'gross indecency' upon them.

At the time, Britain was in the grip of one of its periodic moral panics about crime. The Home Secretary, Sir David Maxwell Fyfe, spearheaded a crackdown against vice; pornographers, prostitutes and gay men easy targets. Homosexuals, Sir David said, were 'exhibitionists and proselytisers, and a danger to others, especially the young'. The number of prosecutions for homosexual offences soared.

The author Sir Compton Mackenzie and the historian Lord Kinross (himself homosexual, although this was naturally not mentioned) told the East Quarter Sessions at Lewes about Croft-Cooke's reputation for decency and clean living. To no avail. It did not help that the Fitzroy Tavern was a well-known haunt of gay men in search of rough trade. The author was found guilty on three counts of gross indecency, and sentenced to nine months in jail, of which he served six. Joseph was also imprisoned.

Croft-Cooke never admitted guilt. Rejecting 'any suggestion that I was a homosexual of the inverted, effeminate type', he argued that he had been victimised by 'filthy-minded officialdom'. Did his accusers frame him, hoping to be treated more leniently by the police in return? Whatever the truth, the author's life would never be the same again.

Upon his release, he fled with Joseph to Tangier, and they remained there for fifteen years. In Morocco, he wrote an impassioned denunciation of his treatment and the penal system in *The Verdict of You All*. He and Joseph continued to travel before returning to England in the early 1970s, settling in a flat in Bournemouth.

Books continued to pour from his pen after his time in prison. They included a new series of pseudonymous whodunits. Perhaps a streak of contrariness prompted him to buck the trend. Whereas authors such as Nicholas Blake and Helen McCloy moved away from traditional detection, Croft-Cooke's whodunits remained relatively conventional, even if his final mystery had the trendy 1970s title *Death of a Bovver Boy*.

In *Dead Man's Shoes* (1958), partly set in Tangier, he satirised establishment complacency and prejudice. A senior police officer says: 'You must have a nice few convictions for sex offences. The Home Office expects it . . . Get someone well known in the dock and you're well away . . . Work for weeks on some murder and what happens? Chummy gets off . . . and you're criticised for having charged him. Morality before murder, that's my motto.'

In *Who's Who*, Croft-Cooke stated that his recreations were 'All', but made no mention of his crime fiction. His obituary in *The*

Times said that the remarkable variety of his books reflected an 'exuberant thirst for experience'. His magnum opus was an auto-biographical sequence, *The Sensual World*, which ran to no fewer than twenty-four volumes (twenty-seven, including supplementary titles).

He hoped this marathon project would be his principal legacy, but his memoirs were curiously reticent. A man who produces so many books about himself[1] is no shrinking violet, yet Croft-Cooke hated talking about his sexual orientation. Just as embarrassing, apparently, were his thirty-one detective novels published under the name Leo Bruce. They earned only a couple of passing mentions in the whole of *The Sensual World*.

Literary life, like crime fiction, teems with ironies. Croft-Cooke's obituarist thought he was 'likely to be assured of a lasting place in English literature both as a recorder and as a commentator on the events and attitudes of his generation'. Yet since his death, Croft-Cooke's most popular writings have been the traditional mysteries which he preferred to keep in the closet.

Rupert Croft-Cooke worked as a teacher, freelance journalist and antiquarian bookseller before establishing himself as a writer whose versatility (he wrote books about darts, cooking, sherry and the circus as well as fiction) and productivity facilitated an agreeable lifestyle. He developed a wanderlust early, working in Argentina and travelling around continental Europe in a motor caravan.

Despite rebelling against his privileged upbringing, he was at heart a compassionate conservative. During the war he received the British Empire Medal for his service in the army intelligence corps. He also developed a friendship with Lord Alfred Douglas, Oscar Wilde's 'Bosie', and wrote his biography. While in India, and attached to the Gurkhas, he met Joseph Susei Mari, a 'sixteen-year-old Indian boy who formed a habit of confiding in me while I was drinking gassy orangeade'. They became close and Joseph remained his secretary and companion until Croft-Cooke's death.

The first Leo Bruce detective novel, published in 1936, was a tour de force reflecting the 'gay debonair charm and mordant wit' for which, according to his obituary, he was noted. *Case for Three*

Detectives is a locked-room mystery satirising Golden Age detection in general and Lord Peter Wimsey, Hercule Poirot and Father Brown in particular. The darts-playing and apparently obtuse Sergeant Beef solves the puzzle while the Great Detectives tangle themselves in elaborate knots.

Two of Beef's subsequent cases[2] take the classic detective story a stage beyond the usual question of whodunit. *Case without a Corpse* (1937) begins splendidly, with Beef's darts match interrupted by a man who says he has committed a murder and promptly takes a fatal dose of poison. But who has he murdered and where is the body? As Beef says, 'I always supposed a murder case started with a corpse, and then you had to find out 'oo done it. This time we know 'oo's done it, but we can't find the corpse.'

In *Case with Four Clowns* (1939), Bruce reworked this theme. Beef has recently left the police, and gets word from a relative who is involved with a circus travelling around Yorkshire that a gypsy fortune teller has predicted that a murder will take place in connection with the circus. But who will be the killer and who the victim?

Bruce was not the first detective novelist to play games with the concept of 'whowasdunin'. Here, as so often, Anthony Berkeley led the way. In *Murder in the Basement* (1932), a couple move into their new home after their honeymoon, only to discover a body buried in the cellar. The corpse belongs to a woman who has been shot. Through a combination of diligent forensic work and good luck, the police discover who she is, and that she previously worked at a prep school. Enter Roger Sheringham, who taught at the school and began to write a novel featuring his former colleagues ('nobody could imagine a character and make it live', he claims). But which of them became a murder victim?

Sheringham's manuscript is reproduced, enabling the reader to compete with him in trying to identify the potential victim. She is identified long before the end of the book, but Berkeley had freshened up the puzzle story, blending a new type of riddle with sober detective work. At the end of the story, Sheringham helps to thwart justice – or, perhaps, to do justice in a very unconventional way.

Detective novels often make a mystery of the murder victim's identity. Milward Kennedy, for instance, had published the lamentably titled *Corpse Guards Parade* (1929), in which Inspector Cornford starts to entertain doubts about whether the corpse in question really is that of missing 'black sheep' Henry Dill. But Berkeley was giving the reader an additional challenge. The question wasn't only whodunit, but also – which of the characters was murdered?

Leo Bruce wasn't alone in following his lead. In 1939, Anita Boutell published *Death Has a Past.* Odious Claudia Hetherton summons five female family members to her country house. We know from the start that one person is shot, and the other person commits suicide after writing a short confession. Again the questions are: who killed whom, and why?

This country-house mystery is set in Britain, so convincingly evoked that, in 1941, in his study of the genre *Murder for Pleasure*, Howard Haycraft listed Boutell alongside Dorothy Bowers in a group of young British women authors of promise. Yet Boutell was an American who had spent less than a decade living in the UK. Like Bowers, she seemed destined for success, but her career, like Bowers', came to a premature end.[3]

A similar fate subsequently befell Bernice Carey,[4] whose first novel, *The Reluctant Murderer* (1949), offers a post-war slant on the 'whowasdunin'. The story is narrated by Vivian Haines, a Californian career woman who plans to commit murder during the course of a weekend with her sister. The identity of her proposed victim is craftily withheld, and tension mounts as it dawns on Vivian that her own life is also in danger.

Patricia McGerr[5] showed greater staying power. Another American, she made an immediate impression with her debut. In *Pick Your Victim* (1947), a group of bored Marines stationed on the Aleutians come across a torn newspaper cutting. Tantalisingly, it reveals that Paul Stetson has admitted to murdering an officer of the Society to Uplift Domestic Service, but does not identify the victim. To while away the time, a Marine who once worked for the Society recounts what he knows, so that his colleagues can wrestle with questions of motive and opportunity as they try to deduce who was killed.

McGerr continued to experiment with the whowasdunin and was rewarded with the Grand Prix de Littérature Policière,[6] awarded for *Follow, as the Night,*[7] aka *Your Loving Victim* (1951). Someone plunges from a balcony to their death. The reader learns that Larry Rock, a deeply unpleasant man even by the standards of newspaper columnists, invited the four women in his life to a party, intending to kill one of them. But for all the antipathy between members of the group, what reason could he have for committing murder – if, indeed, he was responsible for the crime?

J. C. Masterman's long-awaited follow-up to his Golden Age mystery *An Oxford Tragedy* appeared in 1956. *The Case of the Four Friends* brought the Viennese lawyer Ernest Brendel back to the city of dreaming spires to recount a story of 'pre-detection' in which he foresaw a murder, but had to discover the identities of both victim and killer. The concept is similar to that of *Case with Four Clowns*, but the execution very different.

Brendel relies on psychological clues to solve the puzzle, and the cerebral approach is reflected in Masterman's low-key story-telling. The book includes an introduction, which evolves into a postscript, rather as if 'a diagnosis became a post-mortem'. Masterman muses on the approach he took in writing the novel, and on the nature of the genre; he suggests that the novella might be the ideal length for the classic detective story, an indirect admission that he'd padded out his puzzle.

The challenges of writing a whowasdunin are daunting.[8] The story structure may seem contrived, and cramp the author's style, leading to compromises on characterisation and credibility. Tricky as it is to master, in skilled hands the whowasdunin can prove as flexible and as gripping as the casebook mystery novel.

Two of the finest crime writers to emerge in Britain during the post-war period published whowasdunins that won awards for best novel of their year. Julian Symons' *The Colour of Murder* (1957) begins with a long statement given by John Wilkins to his psychiatrist. We presume that murder has been done, but the identity of the victim only becomes clear at the end of the first section of the book. Then a body is discovered; there is a long trial scene and an ironic coda worthy of Francis Iles.

The structure of Mary Kelly's *The Spoilt Kill* (1961) is different. After an unidentified corpse is found in a Stoke-on-Trent pottery, there is a long flashback before the investigation proceeds to a bleak conclusion. The fusion of plot, characterisation and unusual workplace setting results in one of the most accomplished British novels narrated by a private investigator.

At the start of Stanley Ellin's[9] *Mirror, Mirror on the Wall*, a divorced businessman called Peter Hibben finds 'a large, fleshy, terrifyingly lifeless woman on the floor, apparently shot to death'. The victim lies on the bathroom floor in his Greenwich Village apartment and the murder weapon seems to be his own gun. Peter hopes that the bizarre events of the next sixty minutes are nothing more than a nightmare, but his quest for answers becomes a horrific journey into his past. What has happened, to whom, and why, only becomes clear at the end of a novel that explores with graphic candour questions of identity, sexual obsession and mental disturbance.

The book was published in 1972, and Ellin took full advantage of the new era of sexual outspokenness. A writer of distinction, he set out not to titillate but to tantalise. *Mirror, Mirror on the Wall* blended classic elements, including a cunningly disguised cipher (the meaning and profound significance of which only emerges in the final lines of the novel), with a storyline dependent on sexual psychology.

For once the publishers' claim that the novel 'is unlike anything else you have ever read' was scarcely an exaggeration. The book won the Grand Prix de Littérature Policière, while H. R. F. Keating included it in his list of the hundred best crime and mystery books: 'Dialogue and narration are in sinewy, fresh-minted, no-holds-barred prose in the very best traditions of American crime writing.'

Time can rub the shine off pioneering fiction. As Keating admitted, 'writing about sex . . . is a tricky business', and what was once admired as audacious and unorthodox ceases to shock, and no longer seems progressive. Ellin's book now shows its age, but remains a landmark in the development of the modern crime novel.

*

The whowasdunin has continued to evolve.[10] When David Fletcher[11] combined a whowasdunin puzzle and psychological suspense in *The Accident of Robert Luman*, he sought to present his brain-damaged protagonist with a realism and understanding that (in 1988) seemed ahead of its time. An introductory section reveals that a murder of extraordinary savagery has been committed, but the victim's identity is not revealed. Fletcher's main focus, however, is on building the tension as the luckless Robert Luman finds himself the prime suspect in the murder inquiry, trapped in a web of suspicion.

Julian Symons' *Something Like a Love Affair* (1992) begins with the discovery of an unidentified body in a ditch. He explores the nature of sexual obsession as wealthy but neglected Judith Lassiter embarks on a passionate affair with her young driving instructor. The mystery is married to a study of mental disintegration, accompanied by acute touches of social observation.

With *The Hunting Party*[12] (2018), Lucy Foley blended the classic 'closed circle' whodunit, the casebook technique and the 'whowasdunin' with a contemporary take on toxic relationships. A group of Londoners gather at a hunting lodge in the remote Scottish Highlands to see in the New Year. A body is found in the snow, but its identity is not revealed until late in the story. The set-up is a homage to Christie, the result an international bestseller.

'The deaths are discovered because of the country's sudden obsession with perfect coffee.' So begins Mark Lawson's[13] *The Deaths* (2013). But who is dead, and who is responsible? The juxtaposition of social satire and dark reality is maintained throughout. Set in the aftermath of the global financial crisis of 2008, the story traces the misadventures of four wealthy couples who live cheek by jowl, and whose apparently charmed lives are destined to be transformed by murder. The result is a condition-of-Britain crime novel which demonstrates the rich possibilities opened up by imaginative storytelling.

Notes

The main sources are information supplied by Croft-Cooke's godson Richard Hardwick, Croft-Cooke's obituary in *The Times*, B. A. Pike's introduction to *Murder in Miniature*, and Curtis Evans' 'The Man Who Was Leo Bruce' in *American Culture*, 13 November 2010.

1 *A man who produces so many books about himself*: David Holloway described him as 'an obsessive autobiographer . . . His method was generally to present the more outstanding events of his life first in fictional form and then . . . more prosaically as a part of his autobiography' (*The Times*, 12 June 1979).

2 *Beef's subsequent cases*: Beef is said to have been modelled on a village darts player of Croft-Cooke's acquaintance. The series benefits from the relationship between Beef and his snobbish Watson, detective novelist Lionel Townsend. Townsend keeps patronising Beef, but always gets his come-uppance. Curiously, Croft-Cooke admitted to his godson in the 1970s, and confirmed in an inscription in the book, that Beef's seventh case, *Neck and Neck*, was written up not by himself but by his brother, L. A. B. (Laurie) Cooke, also an author. Following his release from prison, a new Leo Bruce series featured a schoolteacher sleuth, Carolus Deene; one of his most interesting cases offers a version of the plot idea in Christie's *The ABC Murders*.

3 *a premature end*: Bowers succumbed to TB, but why Boutell abandoned crime fiction is unclear. Her first husband was Patrick Kearney, a playwright who adapted Dreiser's *An American Tragedy* for the stage. Following their divorce, Kearney was granted custody of their daughter, only for Boutell to seize her, prompting an extensive search for her and scandalous headlines, six months before Agatha Christie's even more famous disappearance. After her second marriage foundered, she took a third husband, Henry Boutell, but he died in 1931; in the same year, Kearney committed suicide after being ruined by the Wall Street Crash. The Boutells had settled in England, where Anita wrote her first three novels; she returned to the US after war broke out.

4 *Bernice Carey*: Carey's eight novels appeared from 1949 to 1955; she lived for another thirty-five years, but did not publish another novel.

5 *Patricia McGerr*: McGerr believed that the success of *Pick Your Victim* discouraged Ellery Queen from a plan to write a novel with a similar premise. *The Seven Deadly Sisters* is also a 'whowasdunin'. She later created Selena Mead, a spy's widow who takes to espionage herself; a television series was mooted, but the project never got beyond an eight minute 'demonstration film'.

6 *Grand Prix de Littérature Policière*: The highest award for a detective novel in France, the prize was founded in 1948 by author and literary critic Maurice-Bernard Endrèbe. Two awards are made each year, one for the best French novel and the other for the best foreign novel.

7 *Follow, as the Night*: The book became a Franco-Italian film, *One Step to Eternity*.

8 *The challenges of writing a whowasdunin are daunting*: Clifford Witting, a talented writer of traditional mysteries, rose to the challenge in *Measure for Murder*, where the victim is identified halfway through the story. Richard Hull's *Until She Was Dead* begins with a murder trial, without the deceased's name being revealed. A long flashback follows, but the book lacks suspects and narrative energy, although Hull offers amusing compensation in the shape of a policeman who sees the best in everyone.

9 *Stanley Ellin*: Ellin's reputation rests primarily on his short stories, above all 'The Specialty of the House' (the twist in which has been borrowed by

many other writers) and the stunning 'The Question', but he was also a gifted novelist. His eclectic output included several novels that were the sources for films. *Dreadful Summit*, about a troubled young man's sixteenth birthday, is a precursor of *The Catcher in the Rye*, but much bleaker; it was filmed as *The Big Night*. *Leda, aka Web of Passion*, starring Jean-Paul Belmondo, was based on *The Key to Nicholas Street*. *The Eighth Circle* is an Edgar-winning novel about private eye Murray Kirk, but Ellin had no interest in writing a long series. Another PI, John Milano, appears in two later books, including *The Dark Fantastic*, which was turned down by Ellin's long-term publisher because sections of the book are narrated by a crazed racist. Ellin, a Quaker, abhorred racism, but wrote the story as a means of trying to understand what drives a person to commit shocking crimes.

10 *The whowasdunin has continued to evolve*: Julian Symons' *The Criminal Comedy of the Contented Couple*, aka *A Criminal Comedy*, and *The Hand of Strange Children* by Robert Richardson, a journalist whose relatively brief career as a novelist encompassed classic detection, Sherlockian pastiche and psychological suspense, are neglected examples.

11 *David Fletcher*: Fletcher was a pen-name for a talented novelist, Dulan Barber, whose death at the age of forty-eight prevented him from quite fulfilling his considerable potential. In this novel and its predecessor, *On Suspicion*, he updated the earlier work of John Bingham and Julian Symons, showing how an innocent person can appear guilty when put under pressure by the police.

12 *The Hunting Party*: Foley's *The Guest List* follows the same pattern. Janice Hallett's *The Appeal* is a whowasdunin in the form of a casebook, with documents in the case in the form of a bundle of emails. Two law students presented with a bundle of emails and other documents are tasked with solving three puzzles: who was murdered; who was convicted; and who was really guilty.

13 *Mark Lawson*: Lawson is a cultural commentator who has done much to promote interest in crime literature in translation.

THIRTY-THREE

Private Wounds

Transitioning from the Golden Age

In October 1938, a man and a woman met in the bar of the Red Lion pub in Musbury. Both were recent arrivals in the Devon village, both were good-looking and both were married. He was a poet and member of the Communist Party who supplemented his income by writing detective fiction under a pen-name. She was a farmer's wife but a free spirit. The mutual attraction was instant.

After an interval of more than twenty years, he recalled the 'wild, preposterous and devouring love-affair which I had embarked on, or rather been shanghaied aboard – a product partly, perhaps, of the hallucinatory and irresponsible Munich period'. Perhaps realising that blaming the Munich Agreement was a bit much, he also referred to it as 'a shameless, half-savage, inordinate affair which taught me a great deal about women, and about myself, that I had never known.'

His lover's name was Edna Elizabeth Currall, but she liked to be known as Billie. After discovering that he wrote poetry, she nicknamed him Po. Their passion blazed through the summer months before war broke out, but early in 1940 Billie announced that she was pregnant. Their son William was born in September, but the two families agreed to carry on as before. Billie's husband John agreed to treat the child as his own, and they resolved not to reveal the truth about his parentage. Po's contribution was to buy a pram, and according to his son Sean, who was a small boy at the time, 'on one notorious afternoon, as an act of confession and defiance', his father wheeled his half-brother in the pram through the middle of the village.

Po had nothing more to do with William, and although he wrote a number of poems about Billie, their relationship petered out. He soon involved himself with another woman, although once he and his wife divorced, he married someone else.

Billie dropped hints that their relationship revived from time to time; what is certain is that his memories of her didn't fade. The last novel he published, almost thirty years after their first meeting, was a fictional account of their affair, although in the story their infidelity results not in the birth of a child but in two murders.

John Currall read the book and said to Mary, who still lived in the neighbourhood, 'He may think I don't know what his story is about, but I do, damn his eyes.' And after John died, and Po himself had been diagnosed with terminal cancer, Billie wrote to him. She proposed marriage, even though he was still married to his second wife. He sent Billie a copy of his novel, the last he ever published. Sexual repression, as in his first detective story, was at the heart of the mystery. The book was published a few months after he was appointed Poet Laureate.

Cecil Day-Lewis was born in Ballintubbert in Ireland but brought up in England. He became part of W. H. Auden's circle and his first volume of poetry appeared in 1925. Ten years later, while working as a schoolteacher, and heavily involved with left-wing politics, he wrote a whodunit. From the start, he had a habit of quarrying his own experiences for his fiction, and the setting was based on Summer Fields, where he taught.

Like Auden, he was addicted to detective stories. *A Question of Proof* (1935) was well received, but quickly surpassed by *Thou Shell of Death* (1936), which reworks *The Revenger's Tragedy* into a dazzling 'impossible crime' mystery. Day-Lewis's pen-name, Nicholas Blake, came from the first name of his newly born second son, and a family name. His gentlemanly detective, Nigel

Strangeways, was modelled on Auden, although as Auden's influence on his poetry waned, Nigel came to resemble a self-portrait.

He published three mainstream novels under his own name, but these made much less of an impression than *The Beast Must Die*[1] (1938), his most ambitious detective novel. When his son Sean had a narrow escape from being hit by a dangerously driven car, he came up with the idea of a story about Felix Lane, a crime writer whose son is killed by a hit-and-run driver.

The book begins: 'I am going to kill a man. I don't know his name, I don't know where he lives, I have no idea what he looks like. But I am going to find him and kill him . . .' This is an opening worthy of Francis Iles, but by quoting Lane's diary, Blake intensifies its emotional force. Psychological suspense is supplemented by traditional detection; the story becomes more orthodox once Nigel Strangeways turns up,

Blake's star was in the ascendant. Orson Welles planned to film Strangeways' next case, *The Smiler with the Knife* (1939), only to abandon the project and make *Citizen Kane* instead. Along with Margery Allingham and Michael Innes, Blake was one of the 'young masters' applauded by the Marxist John Strachey, who argued in 'The Golden Age of English Detection' that 'some of these detective novels are far better jobs . . . than are nine-tenths of the more pretentious and ambitious highbrow novels'. This was the origin of the phrase 'Golden Age detective fiction'. Yet even as Strachey coined the term[2] in 1939, war was looming, and bringing with it the end of the Golden Age.

During the 1940s, Cecil Day-Lewis gave up on the Communist Party, but continued to juggle writing poetry and a complicated personal life with producing whodunits as Nicholas Blake. Under his own name, he published *The Otterbury Incident* (1948),[3] one of the finest mystery stories for young adults.[4] He recognised that the traditional detective story, with 'its knack of disarming the hideous facts of violence and turning all "to favour and to prettiness"' now seemed old-fashioned.

He rose to the challenge posed by the new order of things.[5] Writing *The Beast Must Die* required 'the fullest stretch of imagination and an unusual degree of emotional involvement', and, by the mid-1950s, he was ready to furlough Strangeways and try a serious crime novel.

The idea for *A Tangled Web* (1956) came from an account in the memoirs of Sir Patrick Hastings, KC, of 'The Case of the Hooded Man', the murder of a policeman in Eastbourne in 1912. The culprit, John Williams, was a burglar who, Day-Lewis thought, 'bore the most remarkable resemblance, in temperament and actions, to Hornung's "Raffles"'. The case took its nickname from the hood worn by Williams on his way to and from the trial that resulted in his conviction and subsequent execution. In updating the events to post-war Britain for his novel, Day-Lewis also borrowed from John Bingham in his presentation of a ruthless police investigation.

The novel's alternative title, *Death and Daisy Bland*, reflects Day-Lewis's sympathy for the character he based on Williams' pregnant lover, Florence Seymour. Edgar Power, supposedly a friend of Williams, who gave damning evidence against him, was even more fascinating. The author based his character Jacko on Power, whom he described 'as the nearest thing to Iago I have ever heard about in real life'. Once again, Day-Lewis's emotions were thoroughly engaged with the book, and even though the outcome is predictable, the focus on character rather than plot suited the mood of the times.

Day-Lewis admired writers such as Simenon, Bingham and Highsmith for seeking to add 'another dimension to the crime novel'. The idea for his next stand-alone mystery came from a friend who suggested a story 'in which two men, previously unknown to each other, and both needing to get rid of certain human encumbrances, meet by chance and decide to swap victims'. The result was *A Penknife in My Heart*, published in 1958.

Day-Lewis found he 'had to work myself into the minds of two very different men . . . plunge as deep as I could into their weird relationship, and *be* each of them as he made his murder-attempt . . . and live with them through the aftermath. It needed a pretty strenuous stretching of the invention.'

Simenon is name-checked in the novel, but Highsmith is not. Day-Lewis said that neither he nor his friend had read *Strangers on a Train* or seen Hitchcock's film of the novel. After his book went to press, he discovered the similarity of premise: 'Later, I found that Miss Highsmith's treatment was entirely different from mine; but its starting-point was identical – and, horror of horrors, I had given two of my characters the same Christian names as she had used for two of hers.'

Day-Lewis said he didn't remember hearing about the idea behind Highsmith's book or the film, and blamed the long arm of coincidence, but perhaps some memory had lodged in his subconscious.[6] Ironically, P. D. James' *Original Sin* (1994), set in a London publishing house, bears a resemblance to a Nigel Strangeways novel, *End of Chapter* (1957), and this prompted mischievous chatter from some journalists at the time of publication. But James, like Day-Lewis, had no need to copy anyone else. The depressing truth is that it is exceptionally difficult to be entirely original.

Like Highsmith, Day-Lewis was developing the modern crime novel, but with uneven results. 'It is discouraging', he confessed, 'to find a character, whom you believe you have furnished with flesh and blood, leaking nothing but sawdust when he is stabbed.'

The Private Wound[7] (1968), his final stand-alone, gains power from his vivid evocation of the affair with Billie Currall. The story is narrated by a novelist called Dominic Eyre, who stands in for Day-Lewis, while Billie becomes Harriet 'Harry' Leeson. She calls Eyre Boo, rather than Po, and the setting is the west of Ireland rather than Devon, but there are many parallels with the old affair. Day-Lewis's first wife, Mary, becomes Harriet's sister-in-law Maire in the novel, while Flurry Leeson is the counterpart of the luckless John Currall.

The former Communist was now a pillar of the establishment. He started another Nigel Strangeways novel with a Swinging Sixties title, 'Bang, Bang, You're Dead', but never completed it. At one point, a character in the manuscript says of reviews: 'I never read them now. What's the point? Why suffer from heartburn when you can keep away from the food that causes it?'

Day-Lewis felt 'fated to be a good starter but a poor finisher'. His reputation as a poet declined, even as public honours were being heaped upon him. Half a century after his death, to the consternation of distinguished writers[8] ranging from Andrew

Motion and Melvyn Bragg to A. S. Byatt and Ben Okri, he has yet
to be commemorated by a plaque in Poets' Corner at Westminster
Abbey.

Writers working in the Golden Age style and tradition continued
to emerge.[9] Christianna Brand[10] and Edmund Crispin began to
produce clever, high-spirited whodunits in the war years and
became doyens of the Detection Club, but by the mid-50s they
were running out of steam. Game-playing mysteries had fallen out
of critical favour, even if plenty of readers agreed with a remark
in the final Nigel Strangeways novel, *The Morning after Death*
(1966): 'crime novelists today are trying to write variations on
Crime and Punishment without possessing a grain of Dostoevsky's
talent. They've lost the courage of their own agreeable fantasies,
and want to be accepted as serious writers.'

Talented novelists, even if they are not Dostoevsky, like to stretch
themselves. Margery Allingham, never content to focus on the
tricky whodunit puzzle, adapted more readily than most of her
Detection Club colleagues to the nuclear age. Her detective Albert
Campion evolved, and so did his relationship with a new friend
from Scotland Yard, Charlie Luke.

The historian Jane Stevenson underscores the value of detective
stories[11] as social documents when she says that Allingham's
'crisply observant evocation of the specific textures and concerns
of the present moment' are valuable 'precisely because she wasn't
intentionally writing a commentary on the times . . . Though her
work is fantastical, it is rooted in observation of the differences
between the formative experiences of one generation and the next.'

Stevenson argues that a recurrent theme in Allingham's work
is how individuals react to a changing world: 'The question that
always interests her most is "why". Her plotting is a device to
express character . . . She must have been one of the first writers
to observe the alienating potential of tower blocks, even while the
concrete was still setting in the first wave of postwar town planning. "It's not quite like a street," says a policeman in *The China
Governess*, contemplating a tower-block corridor. "A lot can happen
without the neighbours knowing." Equally, she was the first mass-
market British writer to involve computers in a plot, as early as

1952 – a Hollerith, in fact, the punch-card precursor to true computers.' This was in *The Tiger in the Smoke*, where Albert Campion is confronted by Jack Havoc, an escaped convict who is the embodiment of evil.

Helen McCloy[12] was in the vanguard of American crime novelists whose fiction bridged the gap between the genre's pre-war and post-war preoccupations. She wanted to examine the criminal mind as well as to concoct crafty puzzles. The opening pages of her first novel, *Dance of Death*, aka *Design for Dying* (1938), demonstrate her twin concerns.

On the first page, a debutante's corpse is dug out of the snow – however, the body is not frozen but hot, and the dead woman's beauty has been disfigured by a yellow stain. On the second page, the Police Commissioner confidently informs Basil Willing, a forensic psychiatric assistant to the New York County District Attorney, that 'there's no place for psychology in police work'; he is to be proved hopelessly wrong.

Basil is an updated version of the Great Detective, 'living proof of the theory that a successful doctor to the mad must be slightly mad himself in order to understand his patients'. His knowledge of Freud and Jung means that his interpretation of the psychology of crime seems more authoritative than that of his fictional predecessors.

As an investigator, he searches for 'psychic fingerprints', arguing that: 'The blunders a suspect makes, the things he drops and breaks and forgets . . . might tell the psychologist as much about his mind as the marks on a bullet tell the ballistics expert about the gun from which it is fired.' When it comes to motive, he does not ask 'whom does this crime benefit [but] what psychological type would be gratified emotionally by this type of crime?' To solve the puzzle of Katherine Jocelyn's death in the absence of material clues, he displays an understanding of female emotions rather than merely 'the fundamental male emotions, greed and lust'.

McCloy's gift for buttonholing her readers is illustrated by the opening to *Cue for Murder* (1942): 'The murder mystery at the Royalty Theatre was solved through the agency of a house fly and a canary. The fly discovered the chemical evidence that so

impressed the jury at the trial, but the canary provided a psychological clue to the murderer's identity before the murder was
committed.'

McCloy kept moving with the times. Only two Willing novels
appeared after 1956, including a story in the Jekyll and Hyde
tradition,[13] *Mr Splitfoot*[14] (1968). Increasingly she favoured stand-
alone novels. An early example was *Panic*, a wartime confection
of whodunit, suspense story and a puzzle about a field cipher so
intricate that American book clubs declined to publish it, although
the government snapped up copies for editions catering for the
armed services.

The book was first published in 1944 but did not appear in the
UK until 1972, at which time the wartime references were excised,
since 'as we are now living in the state of perpetual warfare fore-
seen by George Orwell, any war story can be brought up to date
simply by changing the name of the enemy.' McCloy later realised
this was a mistake. A key aspect of the enduring appeal of crime
stories published long ago lies in the light they cast on the age in
which they were written.

McCloy married Davis Dresser,[15] who was a prolific writer of
'drugstore fiction' prior to creating the tough private eye Mike
Shayne under the pen-name Brett Halliday. His sales far exceeded
his wife's, although she was the superior literary stylist. The couple
helped to found the Mystery Writers of America, and McCloy
became its first female President. She and her husband reviewed
crime fiction and were partners in a literary agency and publishing
business.

McCloy said that she began with the classic detective story, 'a
form as rigid as the sonnet or the haiku', but moved 'further and
further away from the classic . . . pattern. Apparently I was
responding to a trend which came after the war demanding more
suspense and less detection.' But she concluded that this was
another mistake. Forecasting a revival of the traditional mystery,
she said: 'The only thing about fashion that is certain is that it
will change.'

As they adjusted to the new normal of the Atomic Age, McCloy's
fellow authors experimented with different approaches. Rex
Stout confronted his Great Detective Nero Wolfe with a new and

formidable adversary, the master criminal Arnold Zeck, a reworking of the battle between Holmes and Moriarty. But after three books, Wolfe triumphed and normal service was resumed. The cousins who wrote together as Ellery Queen were bolder in their experiments as they fought to keep their ingenious mysteries fresh and relevant in rapidly changing times.

Notes

The main sources are the biographies of Day-Lewis by his son Sean and Peter Stanford, his introduction to the *Nicholas Blake Omnibus*, the Poetry Foundation website and McCloy's remarks in *Twentieth-Century Crime and Mystery Writers*.

1   *The Beast Must Die*: A key plot twist anticipates a similar development in Gillian Flynn's *Gone Girl*. The novel was filmed twice, notably by Claude Chabrol in 1969, and televised by the BBC in 1968. A new TV series inspired by the novel was screened in 2021, with the story changed almost out of recognition.

2   *even as Strachey coined the term*: In *The Saturday Review of Literature*.

3   *The Otterbury Incident*: The story was adapted from a French screenplay, *Nous les Gosses*.

4   *one of the finest mystery stories for young adults*: Young adult mystery fiction is a crowded field; among the leading contemporary practitioners is Anthony Horowitz, creator of the Diamond Brothers and Alex Rider.

5   *the challenge posed by the new order of things*: In contrast, the actor V. C. (Victor Vaughan Reynolds Geraint Clinton) Clinton-Baddeley, a lifelong friend of Day-Lewis, published the first of five highly traditional detective novels featuring Dr Davie, a sleuthing don, as late as 1967. Day-Lewis fagged for Clinton-Baddeley at school, and addressed to him a romantic poem, 'Once in Arcady'.

6   *perhaps some memory had lodged in his subconscious*: Jamie Sturgeon suggested in *CADS* 80 that Blake might have recalled 'The Police are Baffled' by his friend Alec Waugh, which features a similar concept.

7   *The Private Wound*: The title comes from *The Two Gentlemen of Verona*. The book was originally called *Take Her Up Tenderly*, also the title of an as yet unpublished novel by Mary Kelly. The story was described by Day-Lewis's biographer as a powerful mea culpa, 'yet there is no hint of the son – or even sons – that resulted from the affair'.

8   *to the consternation of distinguished writers*: Catherine Milner, 'Dean Denies Poet Laureate His Plaque in the Abbey', *Daily Telegraph*, 2 February 2003.

9   *Writers working in the Golden Age style and tradition continued to emerge*: John Dickson Carr, John Rhode and Ngaio Marsh kept going for years, but their later books seldom matched their best. Among the newcomers in the 1950s, the most gifted were Peter and Anthony Shaffer, whose detective stories represented a brief outpouring of youthful *joie de vivre*. Beverley Nichols, a popular author and public speaker, created Horatio Green, a Great Detective blessed with an exceptionally keen sense of smell. When Lynton

Lamb, an illustrator and postage stamp designer, and V. C. Clinton-Baddeley started writing detective fiction during the Swinging Sixties, both were themselves in their sixties. These authors wrote pleasant conventional mysteries, but none of them made a significant impact.

10 *Christianna Brand*: Brand digressed to write children's books about Nurse Matilda, which led to the popular film *Nanny McPhee* (and a sequel). Her late crime novel *The Rose in Darkness* was more intriguing than Edmund Crispin's underwhelming swansong *The Glimpses of the Moon*, but received little attention. In the 1970s, their style of mystery was firmly out of fashion.

11 *Jane Stevenson underscores the value of detective stories*: In 'Queen of Crime', *Guardian*, 19 August 2006. A similar point was made by C. H. B. Kitchin in 1939. His *Death of My Uncle* ends with an unorthodox catechism and musings on the traditional mystery: 'A historian of the future will probably turn, not to blue books or statistics, but to detective stories if he wishes to study the manners of our age . . .'

12 *Helen McCloy*: Helen Worrall Clarkson McCloy studied at the Sorbonne and spent several years as an art critic based in Europe before returning to the US. As Helen Clarkson, she published a science fiction novel about the menace of nuclear warfare, *The Last Day*.

13 *the Jekyll and Hyde tradition*: McCloy's interest in split and multiple personalities is reflected in *Through a Glass, Darkly*. This expansion of a short story explores the idea of doppelgängers in a school setting.

14 *Mr Splitfoot*: H. R. F. Keating included this novel, and *The Private Wound*, both from 1968, in his list of the hundred best crime and mystery books.

15 *Davis Dresser*: Dresser, who lost an eye in a childhood accident with barbed wire and subsequently wore an eyepatch, enlisted in the US Cavalry at the age of fourteen, and it is said that he rode with Pershing, chasing the Mexican revolutionary Pancho Villa. His first wife, Kathleen Rollins, was also a writer with whom he occasionally collaborated. He wrote under a host of pen-names, but the Shayne stories were his most successful, and were adapted for radio, television and film, eventually becoming a franchise, with Dresser hiring other authors to write under the Halliday name. The *Mike Shayne Mystery Magazine* was founded in 1956 and survived for almost thirty years. The 2005 film *Kiss Kiss Bang Bang* was loosely based on a Halliday novel, *Bodies Are Where You Find Them*. After his marriage to McCloy ended, Dresser married yet another writer, Mary Savage; they had a son they called Halliday.

THIRTY-FOUR

Out of this World

Traditional detective fiction evolves in the United States

'We are two howling maniacs in a single cell, trying to tear each other to pieces. Each suspects the other of the most horrible crimes . . . We ought never to speak . . . until someday, mercifully, we both drop dead and end the agony.'

A wild rant, yes, but there was a grain of truth in Manny Lee's words to Fred Dannay. Writing together as Ellery Queen, they formed crime fiction's ultimate Jekyll and Hyde. Queen was not only a split personality, but a tormented one.

The two cousins depended on each other for their financial survival. They'd even signed a contract binding them to write together without limit of time. Although their collaborative methods were a jealously guarded secret, the division of labour was straightforward: Dannay planned the stories, and Lee wrote them. This approach played to their strengths, and neither of them ever published a solo crime novel. On the surface, they had plenty in common; both were short, bald, bespectacled Jewish men who shared a love of books. Yet they were ferociously competitive, and each felt the other didn't appreciate his talents.

Ellery Queen's fame, as a fictional detective as well as an author, peaked just after the Second World War, when the cousins' bitterness towards each other was at its most acute. They collaborated long distance, by telephone and letter, but their correspondence oozed with bile. Conflict was fuelled by the frustration of being yoked together by economic necessity. Both felt under severe domestic pressure; Lee had eight children, while Dannay's son Stephen was born with brain damage and died at six. Illness plagued both men.

Lee's high-flown aspirations as a writer meant he felt embarrassed about his inability to publish anything more sophisticated than detective stories. An unhappy, emotional man with no other literary escape valve, he resented the time Dannay devoted to *Ellery Queen's Mystery Magazine* (*EQMM*), and crime fiction criticism. Dannay was unrepentant. He became an evangelist for the genre, aiming to raise its reputation in the US, much as Dorothy L. Sayers and Anthony Berkeley had done in Britain through the Detection Club.

'You get sick after you open my letters,' Lee said. 'I get sick before I open yours. The mere sight of your handwriting on the envelope upsets me.' On another occasion, he said: 'Your letters are poisonous. You keep dropping little atom bombs under me.' Dannay was no less brutal, saying that one of Lee's letters ruined his dinner because his 'stomach turned over'.

The end of the Ellery Queen radio show's run provoked Lee into mocking Dannay's earlier episodes for their outdated dependence on cerebral deduction: '*Things* didn't happen; *ideas* happened.' In contrast: 'I went out after . . . stories of people.' Theirs was the eternal argument between traditionalists who emphasise the importance of plot in a mystery novel and those who focus on its characters.

'I honestly think that there is more realism in a good fantasy than in bad realism,' Dannay said. He was proud of their achievements: 'there is no one in the field . . . who can do the sort of thing Queen is known for.' But he felt wounded that Lee regarded him simply as 'a clever contriver' with limited interest in characterisation, and raged when Lee told him, 'flatly and arbitrarily, that I am not as well informed on psychiatry as you'.

Lee was equally thin-skinned: 'You have never once in twenty years been able to resist rubbing my nose in the dirt when events have proved me wrong . . . You take a joy in my failures, a bitter satisfaction . . . We're both bad losers, but you're also a bad winner . . . What does all this vomit accomplish? . . . The hell with it.'

Their venom wasn't entirely reserved for each other. They had harsh words for Mickey Spillane, and also for Raymond Chandler's *The Little Sister*, while the *Saturday Evening Post* provoked Dannay's fury by turning down one of their stories: 'They want shit, they are shit, and it takes a shit expert to satisfy them.'

Arguments about their books often descended into sneering sarcasm. During a row over *Cat of Many Tails* (1949), Dannay said, 'I did not think seven brutal murders, all obviously by the same Jack the Strangler, insufficient to panic a city.'

Time and again over the years, the two men bared their souls to each other. Lee confessed: 'I am so full of tensions, guilts, fears, stresses, strains, cross-purposes, confusions . . . and lack of under-standings.' He described their relationship as a 'marriage made in hell'. But when he thought he might be dying from the heart-related problems that eventually killed him, he made a reluctant concession: 'In our respective weaknesses, psychologically, we needed each other.'

After the Second World War, literary critics buried the Golden Age detective novel; it seemed like a body in a building bombed in the Blitz. Agatha Christie, an exception to most rules, survived and prospered. She even exploited the uncertainties of post-war life with characteristic cunning. In *A Murder is Announced* (1950), a puzzle of identity,[1] Jane Marple points out that: 'Fifteen years ago one knew who everybody was . . . But it's not like that any more[2] . . . people just come – and all you know about them is what they say of themselves.'

One of Christie's enduring strengths was her clear-eyed insight into the human capacity for wickedness. But the war had changed perceptions. As Hilary Mantel has said,[3] 'books are born in a certain cultural moment. They surf on the tide of the times.' After the death camps and the torture, after so many ordinary people had carried out so many monstrous crimes, elegant and rational explanations for evil acts no longer seemed enough.

Readers craved fiction in keeping with the zeitgeist and so did

a new generation of writers. Julian Symons became their spokesman,[4] arguing that 'the moral attitudes involved in crimes of
violence have a special significance' following the decision to drop
atomic bombs on Hiroshima and Nagasaki in pursuit of 'peace
and order'. He wondered: 'What shifts of individual morality
relating to violent action are implied in such fateful decisions, and
in the very general acceptance of a greater wrath to come?'

Those shrewd traditionalists Dannay and Lee recognised the
need to adapt to reflect the changed climate. Their post-war novels
bore little resemblance to the convoluted whodunits that had established Ellery Queen's reputation during the Golden Age.[5] *Ten Days'
Wonder* (1948) was the third Ellery Queen novel set in Wrightsville,
but Dannay's concept was audacious. More conventionally religious
than his cousin, he wanted to explore the nature of good and evil.
A war veteran's amnesia becomes not merely a plot device, but a
springboard for character development. He rebuked Lee for failing
to grasp the ambition of his detailed outline: 'The basic theme . . .
is the Ten Commandment crimes. If that is pedestrian, then I give
up.'

Cat of Many Tails[6] was equally bold. The presentation of a
city terrorised by multiple murders mirrored the chaos of
post-war society. Race plays a part in the storyline, and Dannay
said: 'After all, even though we would be subtle about it, the
authors of the books are Jews, and in all the deepest senses, so
is Ellery Queen the character.'[7] The novel ends with a quotation
from the Bible.

Perfectionists with fragile egos, the cousins suffered an infinite
capacity for self-doubt. Yet Lee was excited by the potential of
Dannay's outline for *The Origin of Evil* (1951): 'The Darwinian
concept in this story is an excellent example of where our eternal
race has taken you. It is a great concept, bold, original, "big".'

The novel fashioned from that concept illustrates how the
series had evolved, with a metaphorical portrayal of Hollywood
murdered by television, and a vivid forecast of the likely impact
of nuclear war. The action takes place just as the brief post-war
peace came to an end, and hostilities commenced in Korea. What
had gone wrong with the world? One character voices Lee's
melancholy conclusion: 'It's about envy and suspicion and malice

and lust . . . and a thirst for hot, running blood. It's about man, Mr Queen.'

Dannay needed his cousin to bring his characters and situations to life. When Lee succumbed to writer's block, the series ground to a halt. Dannay eventually found a ghostwriter, Theodore Sturgeon[8], to help him produce an Ellery Queen novel. *The Player on the Other Side* (1963) opens with Ellery himself suffering from writer's block. The enjoyable story, which involves a tontine, benefited from the input of both Lee and Dannay and its success led to a long list of ghostwritten novels of more variable quality. They made money but, in the long run, passing them off as the work of the original writing team harmed the reputation of the Queen novels.

The brand was sustained by Dannay's tireless efforts as an anthologist,[9] as an author of books about the genre[10] and above all as editor of *EQMM*. As early as 1949, he was complaining to Lee that it was 'getting harder and harder to find good *new* material'. Finding good *old* material, and clearing the rights, was no easier, but he remained editor-in-chief until his death.

His vision for *EQMM* was threefold. First, he aimed to encourage good crime writing by offering a reliable market. Second, he wanted 'to develop new writers seeking expression in the genre', a goal that has resulted in an astonishing achievement: more than eight hundred new writers have broken into print thanks to the magazine. Finally, he was determined to 'raise the sights of mystery writers generally to a genuine literary form'.

Dannay loathed the view that crime fiction was inherently second-rate, and few have done more to wipe away that slur. *EQMM* has featured over forty Nobel and Pulitzer Prize-winning authors, ranging from Kipling and Hemingway to Norman Mailer and Alice Walker. Given the cold economic realities of publishing, such a venture might have withered quickly on the vine, but *EQMM* celebrated its eightieth anniversary in 2021.

The other leading champion of American detective fiction at the time was Anthony Boucher. This was the pen-name that William Parker White adopted in his youth, prior to publishing his first short story at the age of sixteen. Boucher's life was dogged by asthma, but defined by his devout Catholic faith and a lifelong passion for both crime and science fiction.[11]

His first novel, *The Case of the Seven of Calvary* (1937), was plucked by the editor Lee Wright from Simon & Schuster's slush pile. The story is a homage to the traditional whodunit, complete with a 'challenge to the reader' and a cluefinder. Dr John Ashwin,[12] a professor and armchair detective, name-checks Erle Stanley Gardner, Stuart Palmer[13] and John Dickson Carr, while the structure is borrowed from the early Ellery Queen mysteries. Boucher even introduced himself as a character; the tale of Ashwin's investigation is told to 'Tony Boucher'.

Boucher's brash private detective Fergus O'Breen appeared in three novels and also short stories blending mystery with science fiction; they included the pleasingly titled 'Elsewhen', which features a time machine. O'Breen's sister Maureen featured in *The Case of the Baker Street Irregulars* (1940), a piece of Sherlockian fun with a cipher on the dust jacket 'written in the Code of the Dancing Men', but Boucher's most memorable female detective was Sister Ursula, who featured in two novels published under the jokey pen-name H. H. Holmes.[14]

Rocket to the Morgue (1942) is a *roman-à-clef* in which Boucher's love of mysteries and science fiction coalesced. He appeared under his real name, along with his wife; other characters were thinly disguised sci-fi writers, such as Robert A. Heinlein and L. Ron Hubbard. Hilary St John Foulkes, a disagreeable heir to a great literary estate, was an unflattering version of Arthur Conan Doyle's son Adrian.

The book was Boucher's seventh novel in the Golden Age tradition, and his last. The sorrowful tone of an inscription to the Mexican crime writer Antonio Helú[15] suggests that his creative career stalled because of a collapse in confidence. *The Case of the Seven of Calvary*, he said, was 'my first novel, which people still keep calling my best and what does that make me?'

Fluent in French and Spanish, Boucher started to translate stories by Georges Simenon for *EQMM*, and before long Fred Dannay sent him five mysteries by Helú for translation. At a time when crime fiction written in languages other than English was seldom available in Britain or the US, Boucher's work broke fresh ground, above all when he translated Jorge Luis Borges' 'The Garden of Forking Paths' for the magazine.

In a rare lapse of editorial judgement, Dannay rejected Boucher's version of Borges' 'Death and the Compass', but accepted for publication in *EQMM* translated stories by Pierre Boileau and Thomas Narcejac, written separately before they began to collaborate. Dannay did, however, worry about Narcejac's stories, giving the instruction: 'Go easy on sex! Avoid such words as damn, bastard, and bitch. Avoid all political references, especially contemporary ones – they go out of date fast.'

Boucher busied himself writing a long series of radio plays featuring Sherlock Holmes and Ellery Queen, producing crime anthologies and editing a sci-fi equivalent to *EQMM*, *The Magazine of Fantasy and Science Fiction*. His crime fiction reviews for *EQMM* and the *New York Times* secured his reputation.

He had a knack of spotting talent early, whether in the first novels of Ira Levin, Ed McBain or H. R. F. Keating. Boucher's choices of the best books of the year identified outstanding debuts by authors as diverse as Edward Grierson and Patricia Moyes,[16] alongside novels that have become acknowledged classics, from *Psycho*[17] to *The Spy Who Came in from the Cold*.

An influential advocate for crime in translation, Boucher lauded not only Simenon and Borges but also Hubert Monteilhet's *The Road to Hell* (1964) and Julian Semyonov's[18] *Petrovka 38* (1963), the title of which alludes to the telephone number of Moscow's police headquarters; the book was promoted as 'the first thriller to come out of the Soviet Union'.

He contributed an introduction and (to avoid spoilers) an afterword to Leo Perutz's[19] remarkable *The Master of the Day of Judgement* (1921). He described Perutz as 'a Jew from Prague who became Viennese by adoption . . . an individual, unpredictable and fascinating writer who blends realism and fantasy in a disconcerting way'. The book plays a new trick on readers, and as Boucher said, it is the counterpart among psychological crime novels to one of the classic detective stories.

*

Boucher's faith in the future of the detective story, although ultimately vindicated, was not shared by everyone. In 1954, John
Wyndham forecast that science fiction would replace detective
stories[20] in the public's affections. Wyndham had published one
light thriller[21] before the war, but two others had been rejected.
A switch of genre transformed his career, and in 1951 he achieved
international success with *The Day of the Triffids*, a highly readable
story in which blinded humans are terrorised by malevolent plants.
Wyndham argued that 'there has been too much murder going on
for too long . . . The present outbreak of rockets may be seen as
the assault weapons softening up the detectives.'

Elizabeth Ferrars joined battle with him,[22] insisting that detective fiction deals with 'human emotions, with violence, fear, guilt,
suspicion, courage, intelligence, and moral values . . . suspense
must be created, curiosity stimulated'. Science fiction 'cannot be
redeemed by answering that fascinating question, whodunit? or
give the reader the satisfaction of winning or losing in a game of
wits with the writer'.

The squabble was needless. The two genres continue to coexist,[23]
and there are almost as many connections between them as there
are fictional detectives and monsters from outer space.

A founder member of the Mystery Writers of America in 1945,
Boucher masterminded a collaborative novel by twelve members
of the MWA's Northern California chapter, *The Marble Forest*[24]
(1951), which appeared under the name Theo Durrant[25] and
concerned a doctor's race against time to save his kidnapped
daughter. He served as MWA President, and in 1962 he edited an
MWA collection of true-crime essays,[26] *The Quality of Murder*.
Contributors included Patrick Quentin, who wrote about the
Maybrick case and claimed to have met Florence Maybrick, and
Robert Bloch, author of an essay about Ed Gein, 'the Butcher of
Plainfield', who was an inspiration for *Psycho* (1959).

Boucher campaigned for better remuneration for writers; the
MWA's early slogan was 'Crime Doesn't Pay – Enough'. He strove
to bring authors closer to their readers, encouraging Allen Hubin[27]
to launch the first crime fiction fanzine, *The Armchair Detective*,
in 1967; it ran for thirty years. Boucher also supported efforts to

establish an annual conference about mystery fiction. But his health deteriorated, and he died in 1968. Two years later, the convention was duly held in Los Angeles, attracting eighty-two fans. In his honour, it was named Bouchercon.

Bouchercon takes place each year, but these days the attendance ranges between one and two thousand. Festivals and other events celebrating the genre attract enthusiastic audiences around the world, and more are established each year. Fanzines and magazines have proliferated,[28] although, in the twenty-first century, blogs and podcasts have become key sources of information, reviews and discussion about the genre. The battle that Dannay and Boucher fought for so long is being won.

Notes

The main sources are Joseph Goodrich's *Blood Relations*, Francis M. Nevins' books about Ellery Queen, Jeffrey Marks' biography of Boucher, and Marvin Lachman's *The Heirs of Anthony Boucher.*

1   *a puzzle of identity*: In discussing Christie's appeal, John Lanchester highlights this novel as an example of 'a cocktail of orderly settings and deep malignity, of comfiness and coldness, and at its heart it asks one of the most basic questions of all, modernity's recurring preoccupation: who are you?' ('The Case of Agatha Christie', *London Review of Books*, 20 December 2018).
2   *it's not like that any more*: Other writers working in the Golden Age tradition made comparable use of post-war confusion about identity, including Christianna Brand in *Death of Jezebel*, C. H. B. Kitchin in *The Cornish Fox* and Carol Carnac (aka E. C. R. Lorac) in *Crossed Skis*.
3   *As Hilary Mantel has said*: See Alison Flood, 'Hilary Mantel: I am "Disappointed but Freed" by Booker Decision', *Guardian*, 25 September 2020. She was discussing fashions in literary award-giving.
4   *Julian Symons became their spokesman*: See 'The Face in the Mirror' in *Crime in Good Company*, edited by Michael Gilbert.
5   *the convoluted whodunits that had established Ellery Queen's reputation during the Golden Age*: Symons concluded that retaining 'a Golden Age figure out of place in the kind of stories that the cousins were trying to write' was a mistake. Nor was he convinced by *The Glass Village*, from which Ellery is absent: 'this attempt to comment critically on McCarthyism, then at its height, loses much of its intended impact through the melodramatic way in which the material is treated.'
6   *Cat of Many Tails*: A 1971 TV film version starring a miscast Peter Lawford, *Ellery Queen: Don't Look Behind You*, was written by William Link and Richard Levinson, credited under a joint pen-name, Ted Leighton. Four years later, *Ellery Queen: Too Many Suspects*, the pair's TV film version of *The Fourth Side of the Triangle*, spawned a TV series starring Jim Hutton.

7 *the authors . . . are Jews, and in all the deepest senses, so is Ellery Queen the character*: Joseph Goodrich observes in *Blood Relations*: 'Ellery's sense of ethics, his love of justice, of books and learning is quintessentially Jewish.'

8 *Theodore Sturgeon*: Sturgeon, born Edward Hamilton Waldo, was a science fiction author who wrote two screenplays for *Star Trek*. Several Queen ghostwriters, such as Jack Vance and Avram Davidson, were better known for sci-fi. Others included Edward D. Hoch, a prolific writer of short stories, and Gil Brewer, a writer of paperback originals who produced in *The Red Scarf* a gripping thriller about the fatal attractions of a glamorous woman with a suitcase full of banknotes.

9 *an anthologist: 101 Years' Entertainment: The Great Detective Stories 1841–1941* was designed to 'paint a whole picture' of the genre's history. *The Misadventures of Sherlock Holmes* gathered Sherlockian parodies and pastiches, but the Conan Doyle estate objected, and the book was withdrawn from circulation.

10 *books about the genre*: *Queen's Quorum*, which catalogues 'cornerstone volumes' of short detective fiction, was described by Boucher as 'indispensable'.

11 *a lifelong passion for both detective and science fiction*: Major crime novelists who also wrote highly regarded science fiction included Margot Bennett, Fredric Brown and Howard Browne. Among the dabblers in sci-fi was W. J. Burley, creator of the Cornish cop Charles Wycliffe, and also author of *On the Sixth Day*, set in the far-distant future. Reginald Hill's Dalziel and Pascoe novella *One Small Step* sees Yorkshire's finest investigating the first murder on the moon. Distinguished science fiction writers who have turned to crime include Jack Finney and Isaac Asimov, creator of the Black Widowers, a dining club whose members try to solve mysteries; the best 'armchair detective' turns out to be the waiter, Henry Jackson. John Sladek, a specialist in sci-fi and the surreal, created Thackeray Phin in the Great Detective tradition, while Randall Garrett's Lord Darcy books are alternative history whodunits featuring another Great Detective. Kate Wilhelm, a leading science fiction author, also wrote mysteries, notably *Smart House*, a locked-room puzzle for the computer age, from a series about private investigators Charlie Meiklejohn and Constance Leidl. *Great North Road*, by Peter F. Hamilton, in which a cop investigates serial killings in 2143, is a contemporary sci-fi novel with detective interest.

12 *Dr John Ashwin*: Ashwin returned to investigate 'The Case of the Toad-in-the-Hole', concerning a sequence of murders patterned on real-life crimes, such as the Maybrick case. The book plays with the genre's conventions but failed to find a publisher.

13 *Stuart Palmer*: Palmer's first detective novel, *The Penguin Pool Murder*, launched a series featuring the sleuthing spinster Hildegarde Withers. The final entry, *Hildegarde Withers Makes the Scene*, was completed after his death by Fletcher Flora, who also ghostwrote three Ellery Queen novels.

14 *H. H. Holmes*: This was the alias of a legendary mass murderer, con man and bigamist from Chicago, Herman Webster Mudgett. Mudgett confessed to murdering twenty-seven people, although less than half of his supposed killings were proved, and some victims turned out to be alive. Erik Larson's *The Devil in the White City* is a narrative non-fiction account of his misdeeds.

15 *Antonio Helú*: Better known as a film-maker, Helú is said to have been the

first Mexican writer to create a series detective. Máximo Roldán is a petty criminal, but more a victim of circumstance than a Latin American Raffles. Helú's fiction reflects his radical politics and disdain for a corrupt society and unreliable system of justice.

16 *Patricia Moyes*: Boucher's pick was *Dead Men Don't Ski*, the first of nineteen novels featuring Scotland Yard's Henry Tibbett. *Who is Simon Warwick?* is a cunning 'long lost heir' story.

17 *Psycho*: Robert Bloch's novel became a legendary Hitchcock film; although he is usually regarded as a horror writer, crime features in much of Bloch's fiction.

18 *Julian Semyonov*: Julian (or Yulian) Semyonov was an investigative journalist, screenwriter and author of detective and spy fiction; his main series characters were a spy, Stierlitz, and militia colonel, Vladislav Kostenko, who appeared in *Petrovka 38*, a Soviet version of the police procedural. Previously, the anti-Stalinist Polish writer Leopold Tyrmand, who later emigrated to the US, had published *The Man with White Eyes* (1955), a thriller in which the mysterious protagonist fights organised crime in Warsaw.

19 *Leo Perutz*: Exiled from Vienna in 1938, Perutz settled in Tel Aviv. His eclectic band of admirers included Graham Greene, Italo Calvino and Ian Fleming, who called *Little Apple*, a thriller set during the Russian Revolution, 'a work of genius'. *St Peter's Snow*, aka *The Virgin's Brand*, opens with a protagonist coming round in hospital after an accident to find himself the apparent victim of a conspiracy. Perutz's portrayal of fanaticism and an experiment to induce mass hysteria caused the novel to be banned by the Nazis, and his description of a powerful hallucinogenic drug anticipated the discovery of LSD.

20 *John Wyndham forecast that science fiction would replace detective stories*: The spat is recorded in Elizabeth Foxwell's blog *The Bunburyist*, 1 October 2010. 'Roar of Rockets!' appeared in *John O'London's Weekly* on 2 April 1954. In the same year, Isaac Asimov laid the argument to rest by publishing *The Caves of Steel*. His mentor John W. Campbell had warned him that sci-fi and detective fiction were incompatible, but Asimov's novel successfully combined the two forms and many books occupy the literary borderlands. Examples include V. A. Van Sickle's *The Wrong Body*, in which a medical experiment switches the characters of a Chicago racketeer and a senator; the pseudonymous author was Arthur Hawthorne Carhart, a prominent conservationist.

21 *Wyndham had published one light thriller*: This was *Foul Play Suspected*, published under the name John Beynon.

22 *Elizabeth Ferrars joined battle with him*: 'No Danger to Detectives!' appeared a week after Wyndham's article. Ferrars was born Morna Doris MacTaggart; in the US, her pen-name was given an added tweak of mystery, and became E. X. Ferrars. Her crime-writing career lasted more than half a century; a founder member of the CWA, she was elected Chair in 1977.

23 *The two genres continue to coexist*: The 1985 TV movie *Murder in Space* was first broadcast without the ending. Viewers could enter a competition to solve the mystery; a tie-in novelisation that also included an entry form rather than the answer was written by the Canadian crime novelist Howard Engel and his second wife, Janet Hamilton, under the pen-name F. X. Woolf.

24 *The Marble Forest*: Boucher's co-authors included such capable writers as

Lenore Glen Offord, also a reviewer and the first female member of the Baker Street Irregulars, and Darwin Teilhet, who wrote an early anti-Nazi mystery, *The Talking Sparrow Murders* (1934). William Castle's 1958 film *Macabre* was loosely based on the novel. Castle promoted the movie by taking out an insurance policy in respect of any member of the audience who died of fright while the film was running. His other marketing gimmicks included hiring people to pretend to be nurses, waiting in the cinema foyer, and parking a hearse outside the cinema.

25 *Theo Durrant*: William Henry Theodore Durrant was another notorious American murderer; known as 'the Demon of the Belfry' because the mutilated body of one of his two female victims was found in a church belfry, he protested his innocence until his execution.

26 *an MWA collection of true-crime essays*: His earlier anthology, *The Pocket Book of True Crime Stories*, included an essay by Q. Patrick that argued for Lizzie Borden's innocence.

27 *Allen Hubin*: Hubin subsequently produced a monumental bibliography of the genre.

28 *Fanzines and magazines have proliferated*: For instance, *CADS*, edited by Britain's Geoff Bradley, has run for over thirty years, and, in the US, so has *Mystery Scene*, founded by the crime novelist and anthologist Ed Gorman.

THIRTY-FIVE

Perfect Murders

Crime and the end of empire

In 1929, Arthur Upfield was working in the Australian bush as a boundary rider maintaining the Rabbit-Proof Fence.[1] A desperate measure intended to protect crops and pastures from hordes of hungry rabbits, the Fence crossed vast stretches of inhospitable terrain. The men employed to look after it travelled on bicycles, or drove a buckboard drawn by two camels.

Upfield was a regular visitor to the Government Camel Station[2] just south of the twin summits of Dromedary Hill, a remote homestead occupied by George Ritchie. So were several other men, including a young stockman known as Snowy Rowles.[3]

Upfield had already published a couple of detective novels whose sales were modest. The secret of success, he decided, was to come up with a fresh idea: 'Fiction plots are like nuggets of gold dug out of a unique mine . . . much digging is necessary to unearth them.' The challenge for any murderer was: what to do with the victim's body? Was it possible to come up with a perfect method of disposing of a corpse, using only simple materials available at a homestead?

Around the campfire, he shared his dilemma with his colleagues and Ritchie said: 'Supposing I wanted to do you in . . . I'd shoot you dead and burn your body. When the ashes were cold, I'd go through the lot with a sieve, getting out every burnt bone and all metal things . . . The metal I'd put into a pot of sulphuric acid . . . and your burnt bones I'd put through a prospector's dolly-pot, and toss out the dust for the wind to scatter. There'd be none of you left.'

Sulphuric acid was kept at every homestead for tin-smithing. Ritchie also suggested burning a couple of kangaroo carcases as a means of explaining the fire; carcases were frequently burnt to keep flies away, so this wouldn't seem suspicious. Upfield used Ritchie's scheme in *The Sands of Windee* (1931),[4] the second book to feature his detective Inspector Napoleon Bonaparte,[5] also known as 'Bony', the son of an Aborigine mother and an Englishman.

Sales of the book were good enough to allow Upfield to quit his job, but then he received a startling reminder of his discussions about the perfect crime. The police arrested Snowy Rowles on three counts of murder. The bodies of three male victims were missing, but telltale clues – teeth and a gold wedding ring – left in a large pile of ash had been found. It seemed that Rowles had put Ritchie's plot into practice.

The Murchison Murders, so called after the place where the crimes were committed, became a cause célèbre. Rowles was tried for a single murder, the alleged killing of a New Zealander called Louis Carron. Called as a prosecution witness, Upfield became belligerent when the defence argued that Rowles might not have listened to the discussion about the perfect crime, retorting: 'Look! . . . you don't think he sat there dumb all night. Certainly he joined in.'

Upfield's evidence amounted to marvellous publicity for his book, but disaster for the man in the dock.[6] Rowles went to the gallows, implausibly protesting his innocence. After the trial, a detective who worked on the case said that Upfield's imagination was 'a danger to the human race'. Upfield retorted that if he came up with any original murder method in future, he'd patent it in order to collect royalties.

Arthur William Upfield is closely associated with Australia, and an ability to evoke its atmospheric landscape strengthens his fiction. Yet he was born in England[7] and lived there until he was twenty-two. At that point, his father sent him to the other side of the world to make something of himself.

A truculent individualist,[8] Upfield drove cattle, herded sheep, picked grapes and gouged opals. He also fell in love with the Outback. While serving in the Australian Imperial Force during the First World War, he married and had a son. He subsequently tried to settle again in England, but the call of the bush proved irresistible, and he left his wife and child to sail back on his own.

The post-war vogue for detective fiction tempted Upfield to experiment with a whodunit, writing by hurricane lamp in the evening after a day's work. Dissatisfied with the result, he produced a second book, a thriller that found a publisher. So the story goes, while working as a cook in New South Wales, he met 'Tracker' Leon Wood of the Queensland Police,[9] whom he'd known during the war. Wood's father was white, his mother Aboriginal. Wood gave him a copy of a biography of Napoleon Bonaparte, and inspiration struck.[10]

Upfield rewrote his first book, abandoning its white detective for a character modelled on Wood; he called him Inspector Napoleon Bonaparte, or Bony for short. *The Barrakee Mystery* (1929) was accepted, launching Bony on a career that extended to twenty-nine cases recorded over more than three decades. The books sold well in Britain and the United States, but reaction in Australia has long been mixed,[11] partly because of the perception that, despite his admiration for Aboriginal people, Upfield's presentation of them was flawed.

Upfield was for many years the most famous crime writer to set his stories in Australia, but he was not the first. In the mid-nineteenth century, a Belfast-born woman moved to Australia to write about the gold rush for the *Ladies' Companion*. She wrote poetry as well as journalism, and married a police trooper – perhaps bigamously. In 1866, she wrote a crime story. This was 'The Dead Witness', at first published anonymously and later as by 'Waif Wander'.

So began the career of Mary Fortune, seven of whose police stories featuring Mark Sinclair were collected in *The Detective's*

Album in 1871. In the course of a remarkable life she had both a racehorse and a greyhound named after her, but was arrested several times for drunkenness and vagrancy. She became impoverished and her later years were marred by loss of sight. In 1911 she was buried in an unmarked grave that was forgotten until its rediscovery more than a century later.[12]

Helen Simpson, meanwhile, whose adult life was spent in Britain, where she collaborated with Clemence Dane as well as writing novels on her own, was a prominent Australian-born author of the Golden Age. So was Paul McGuire,[13] who was in the mould of those British dons and clergymen who took up the genre as a sideline.[14] McGuire's awareness of life's fragility was shaped by the First World War, in which four of his older brothers were killed. A journalist, he spent several years in London, where he belonged to a circle of Catholic writers including G. K. Chesterton.

He published mysteries throughout the 1930s. Rather than create a significant series detective, he preferred to explore a wide variety of settings, including a remote Pacific island in *Burial Service*, aka *A Funeral in Eden*[15] (1938). Contemporary Europe was the background for *The Spanish Steps*, aka *Enter Three Witches*, but, by the time it was published in 1940, war had broken out again. A wistful prefatory note said that the story 'belongs to the months before September 1939, an epoch now as remote as the First Byzantium'. The publishers optimistically compared McGuire to Sayers and Allingham, but this proved to be his final detective novel. He devoted the rest of his life to promoting the Catholic faith and international diplomacy, serving as Australian Ambassador to Italy and as an envoy to the Holy See.

In 1954 Charlotte Jay,[16] Adelaide-born and widely travelled, won the first Edgar for best novel, with *Beat Not the Bones*, tracing a woman's quest to find the truth about her husband's death in New Guinea. After setting her first novel, *The Knife is Feminine* (1951), in her home country, Jay explored a range of exotic locations.

In contrast, British-born Pat Flower[17] preferred to use Australia as a background, initially with Inspector Swinton as an Antipodean Maigret. The jokiness of titles such as *Fiends of the Family* (1966) matured into a flair for ironic plotting. Swinton appears in the inverted mystery *Hell for Heather* (1962), but the key character is Paul Baxter, who sets out to kill his rich wife; Flower portrays his psychological disintegration with panache. Writing in 1997, Stephen Knight said she 'stands out as the most unfairly overlooked of Australia's crime authors, a parallel to Mary Fortune in that respect'.

Jon Cleary[18] enjoyed a higher profile. His Sydney cop, Scobie Malone, first appeared in *The High Commissioner*[19] (1966), conceived as a stand-alone. After writing two more Malone novels, Cleary turned his attention elsewhere, but, following a long break, he revived Malone, whose career ultimately extended to twenty books.

In the twenty-first century, authors from Australia, Peter Temple,[20] Michael Robotham[21] (twice) and Jane Harper,[22] have won the CWA Gold Dagger for best novel of the year four times. Harper's *The Dry* (2016) evokes the Outback: after two years without rain in Kiewarra, tensions in the community become unbearable when three members of the same family are found dead. Seemingly it is a case of murder followed by suicide, but people become fearful when federal agent Aaron Falk, returning to the place where he grew up, starts to ask questions.

For the first half of the twentieth century, detective novels set in Africa and the Middle East[23] were usually written by authors born in Britain.[24] During the Golden Age, the most accomplished African mysteries came from Elspeth Huxley, who spent her formative years living in Kenya. On the night the atom bomb fell on Hiroshima, a young South African journalist, Peter Godfrey,[25] wrote the first of hundreds of short stories. His detective Rolf Le Roux assisted the Johannesburg police, often in cases featuring impossible crimes or other trickery in the Golden Age tradition.

Godfrey's opposition to apartheid caused him to leave for England in 1962. Three years later the same path was followed by a fellow journalist, James McClure,[26] who would later be described as the father of South African crime writing.[27] His determination to report what he saw, such as a black prisoner, handcuffed to the back of a police van, being dragged through the streets, had made him unpopular with the authorities. After six years in Britain, he made an impact with his first crime novel.

In *The Steam Pig* (1971), the Afrikaner Lieutenant Tromp Kramer and his black Bantu detective sergeant Mickey Zondi investigate the fatal stabbing of a white woman by a suspected Bantu intruder. The story cast light on the realities of life in South Africa, and won the CWA Gold Dagger.

Kramer and Zondi appeared in seven further books that portrayed the interactions between people of different races, and the tensions between the English- and Afrikaans-speaking whites, with wit as well as realism. The final book in the series, *Song Dog* (1991), was a prequel to the first, describing how the pair first met in Zululand.

Apartheid is dead, and today McClure's books have value not only as entertainment but also as records of an unmourned period of his country's history. Social divisions continue to trouble post-apartheid South Africa,[28] and the crimes to which they give rise lie at the heart of Deon Meyer's novels. Meyer, formerly a journalist and advertising executive, writes in Afrikaans rather than English. He broke through with *Dead before Dying* (1996), in which Cape Town cop Mat Joubert investigates a seemingly random series of murders committed with a Mauser pistol from the Boer War.

Long before the sun set on the British Empire, writers outside Europe whose first language was not English were turning their attention to crime fiction. A striking example is Sharadindu Bandyopadhyay.[29] Educated in Calcutta, he wrote poetry and studied law before creating Byomkesh Bakshi[30] in 1932. The Bakshi stories, originally written in Bengali, have evocative titles such as 'The Gramophone Pin Mystery', and are narrated by a writer called Ajit. Bakshi is a Satyanweshi, or truth-seeker, and he and Ajit form a duo broadly in the Holmes–Watson tradition but distinctively portrayed. Among the best of the stories is 'The Venom of the Tarantula', an 'impossible crime' mystery featuring an ingenious poisoning.

The Sherlock Holmes stories also exerted a profound influence on the series about the cerebral Bengali private detective Prodosh

Chandra Mitra, generally known as Feluda, which the film-maker Satyajit Ray started writing in the mid-1960s. The series continued until Ray's death in 1992, and Feluda has been kept alive in film and other adaptations. Feluda enjoyed immense popularity in India but remained little known further afield. The same was true, for instance, of the Urdu mystery and spy writer Asrar Ahmed, who wrote as Ibn-e-Safi.[31]

The Indian detective most celebrated in Europe and the US was created by an Englishman who had never set foot in the sub-continent. The ironically titled *The Perfect Murder* (1964), H. R. F. Keating's[32] first novel about Inspector Ganesh Ghote of the Bombay CID, earned a CWA Gold Dagger, and Keating wrote about Ghote for ten years before finally visiting his detective's homeland.

Keating's books, widely read in India,[33] owed their success primarily to the characterisation of Ghote, a humane and humble man, and an underdog who persevered against the odds; the very fact that he was the antithesis of Great Detectives such as Holmes made him much more sympathetic. After the series, Keating resurrected Ghote in two prequels; by setting the books in the 1960s, he acknowledged that his detective was a man of the past, ill-suited to life in twenty-first-century Mumbai.

Vaseem Khan[34] introduced a contemporary Mumbai detective (albeit retired from the police force) in *The Unexpected Inheritance of Inspector Chopra*, which launched the Baby Ganesh Detective Agency series in 2015. The presence of a baby elephant, which does not age, suggests the gentle whimsy of Alexander McCall Smith's[35] books set in Africa, but the stories have a darker edge, while Chopra's modesty and determination to fight crime and corruption make him an heir to Ghote's mantle.

Notes

The main sources are Ray B. Browne's book about Upfield, Upfield's *The Murchison Murders, Follow My Dust!*, a biography by his partner Jessica Hawke, apparently based on a memoir he wrote, Kelly Handson's article 'Outback Murder: a How-to Guide' in *University of Melbourne Collections*, issue 12 (June 2013), Stephen Knight's *Continent of Mystery* and *Dead Witness*, and Eugene Schleh's *Mysteries of Africa*.

1   *the Rabbit-Proof Fence*: Now less vividly known as the State Barrier Fence
     of Western Australia, in fact it consists of three fences, completed in 1907,
     and totalling over 2,000 miles in length. Unfortunately, the Fence's effec-
     tiveness was compromised by the rabbit population's skill at jumping and
     burrowing.
2   *the Government Camel Station*: In 2018, it was included on the State Register
     of Heritage Places, perhaps illustrating the appeal of dark tourism.
3   *Snowy Rowles*: His real name was less memorable: John Thomas William
     Smith. He'd adopted his alias after escaping from police custody, but his
     attempts to commit the perfect murder were compromised by repeated
     blunders. He cashed Carron's pay cheque, and kept his victim's possessions
     in his cabin, wrapped in an oilskin. His failure to destroy Carron's wedding
     ring led to its identification by a jeweller who had marked it uniquely, albeit
     by mistake.
4   *The Sands of Windee*: Julian Symons noted that Bony's tracking skills were
     reminiscent of those in James Fenimore Cooper's stories, but concluded:
     'the characters apart from Bony are uniformly wooden, and none of the
     books really moves outside well-worn Humdrum tracks.'
5   *Inspector Napoleon Bonaparte*: Two television series have been made
     featuring Bony, while a TV movie, *3 Acts of Murder*, told the story behind
     the Murchison Murders.
6   *Upfield's evidence amounted to . . . disaster for the man in the dock*: Upfield's
     book about the case, *The Murchison Murders*, emphasised his personal
     liking for Rowles, whom he regarded as a Jekyll and Hyde character.
7   *Yet he was born in England*: So too was Ilford-born Alan Geoffrey Yates,
     who settled in Australia after the Second World War and found fame and
     fortune writing as Carter Brown. A mass-producer in the pulp tradition, he
     sold paperback original thrillers, often set in California, by the million.
8   *A truculent individualist*: In later life, he used stationery printed with the
     heading 'All Fame and No Bloody Money'.
9   *he met 'Tracker' Leon Wood of the Queensland Police*: This story about Bony's
     creation has often been repeated, although questions have been raised as to
     whether Wood existed, or was simply the product of Upfield's imagination.
10   *inspiration struck*: Tony Hillerman, whose series featuring Joe Leaphorn
     and Jim Chee of the Navajo Tribal Police began with *The Blessing Way* in
     1970, cited Upfield as an inspiration. Introducing a new edition of Upfield's
     A Royal Abduction, he said: 'When my own Jim Chee . . . unravels a mystery
     because he understands the ways of his people, when he reads the signs
     in the sandy bottom of a reservation arroyo, he is walking in the tracks
     Bony made 50 years ago.' Since Hillerman's death, his daughter Anne has
     continued the series.
11   *reaction in Australia has long been mixed*: Some of the language in the
     books is racist, and Stephen Knight portrayed the creation of Bony as 'at
     once respectful and contemptuous of Aboriginals'. But Knight has acknowl-
     edged that: 'Upfield meant his texts to honour the blacks as well as the
     bush, and few in the twenties took even that radical a view.'
12   *an unmarked grave that was forgotten until its rediscovery more than a
     century later*: The discovery was made by Lucy Sussex (Jason Steger, 'Solved!
     The Case of Mary Fortune, the Pioneering Crime Writer Who Vanished',
     Sydney Morning Herald, 7 July 2016).

13 *Paul McGuire*: Dominic Mary Paul McGuire worked in Intelligence during
the war, serving as deputy director for psychological warfare. His post-war
writing on social policy led to his becoming personal adviser to the Australian
Prime Minister.

14 *took up the genre as a sideline*: Similarly, the British-born dentist Arthur
Gask took up crime writing while waiting for his patients to arrive. He
emigrated to Australia and became a prolific novelist with a Great Detective
called Gilbert Larose. A celebrity dabbler in fictional crime was Miles
Franklin, renowned as author of *My Brilliant Career*. *Bring the Monkey*, a
whimsical story set in an English country house, was her solitary venture
into the genre.

15 *A Funeral in Eden*: Barzun and Taylor chose this book as one of their fifty
classics of the genre.

16 *Charlotte Jay*: Jay's real name was Geraldine Halls. Dorothy B. Hughes
called her 'one of the most important writers of far-off places and their
mysterious qualities'.

17 *Pat Flower*: Patricia Flower's family emigrated to Australia during her teens.
The *Australian Dictionary of Biography* notes that 'The two sides of her
writing – comedy and horror – reflected aspects of her personality.' There
is a tragic irony in her portrayal of Martin Briggs, the murderer in *Cobweb*;
as his self-confidence collapses, he is unable to sleep and starts taking pills.
Flower suffered from insomnia, and at sixty-three took a fatal overdose of
pentobarbitone.

18 *Jon Cleary*: Born in Sydney, Cleary left school at fourteen. *Peter's Pence* was
an Edgar-winning thriller about an IRA plot to rob the Vatican that misfires
and leads to the Pope being kidnapped.

19 *The High Commissioner*: The book was filmed as *Nobody Runs Forever*, with
Rod Taylor playing Malone.

20 *Peter Temple*: Born in South Africa, Temple moved to Australia in 1980.
His series investigator was Jack Irish, but he won the Gold Dagger for a
stand-alone, *The Broken Shore*.

21 *Michael Robotham*: A former journalist and ghostwriter for Lulu, Rolf Harris
and others, Robotham turned to crime fiction with *The Suspect*. The Gold
Dagger-winning *Life or Death* is set in the US.

22 *Jane Harper:* Harper was born in England but lived in Australia as a child
and returned there as an adult.

23 *detective novels set in . . . the Middle East*: The most popular by far, such
as *Appointment with Death* and *Murder in Mesopotamia*, were written by
Agatha Christie. Claude Vernon Frost, who worked with Military Intelligence
in Iraq during the Second World War, subsequently wrote, under the name
Charles B. Child, a long series of short stories featuring Inspector Chafik J.
Chafik of the Baghdad police; these were posthumously collected in *The
Sleuth of Baghdad*.

24 *authors born in Britain*: Godfrey Warden James, a former colonial civil
servant who wrote as Adam Broome, is an example. An exception was John
Canaday, an American art historian who wrote crime fiction as Matthew
Head. He drew on his experience of life in the Belgian Congo to write three
novels set there featuring Dr Mary Finney ('I'm a perfectly honest missionary
and I'm a damn good tropical doctor'). Ngũgĩ wa Thiong'o's *Petals of Blood*,
published in 1977, could hardly be more different. A political novel with a

satirical edge, it was summed up by Steven R. Carter in *Mysteries of Africa* as 'an anti-detective novel with a radical social vision'.

25 *Peter Godfrey*: Godfrey tackled racism head-on in 'The Face of the Sphinx'. 'Wanton Murder' was filmed as *The Girl in Black Stockings*, with the action shifted from Muizenberg to Utah.

26 *James McClure*: McClure produced two non-fiction books that gave insight into life in the police. While researching *Spike Island: Portrait of a Police Division*, he was given access to 'A' Division of Merseyside Police, and presented a compelling picture of attempts to maintain law and order in a deprived city. Four years later, he adopted the same method in San Diego, California; the result was *Cop World*.

27 *the father of South African crime writing*: The description comes from 'Michael Stanley's Top 10 African Crime Novels', *Guardian*, 30 June 2010; the Stanley name conceals the identities of African-born Michael Sears and Stanley Trollip, creators of David 'Kubu' Bengu of Botswana CID. Their choices included *The Screaming of the Innocent* by Unity Dow, a human rights activist and Botswana's first High Court judge; based on a real case, it is 'a powerful and disturbing book. A young girl vanishes; the police guess that she has been eaten by a lion, but the reader knows that she has been ritually murdered for body parts reputed to bestow great power.'

28 *Social divisions continue to trouble post-apartheid South Africa*: Wessel Ebersohn's recent novels also explore the complex legacy of South Africa's past. Ebersohn's early books were written during the apartheid years, and introduced the Jewish prison psychologist Yudel Gordon, whom he revived in the twenty-first century in an attempt to explore the wellsprings of violence in a country where much has changed, but crime remains endemic.

29 *Sharadindu Bandyopadhyay*: Bandyopadhyay, a versatile writer, moved to what is now Mumbai to work in the film industry.

30 *Byomkesh Bakshi*: Pinaki Roy argues in *The Manichean Investigators: A Postcolonial and Cultural Rereading of the Sherlock Holmes and Byomkesh Bakshi Stories* that the Bakshi stories are 'generally aimed at solving principally social problems of the ordinary Indians in and around the subaltern metropolis of colonial Kolkata . . . Bandyopadhyay thus first of all negates the Eurocentric convention of granting primacy to the bourgeoisie.'

31 *Ibn-e-Safi*: His work includes *The House of Fear*. Claims that Agatha Christie admired his work might just be wishful thinking, but he did influence the prominent screenwriter Javed Akhtar.

32 *H. R. F. Keating*: Keating's diverse output included *Jack, the Lady-Killer*, set in India during the 1930s, which is a crime story in verse.

33 *widely read in India*: Arjun Raj Gaind, author of a trilogy of mysteries set during the height of the British Raj, has recorded his admiration of *The Perfect Murder*: 'the corruption and the endless bureaucracy, the vibrancy of the packed streets and the distinct patois of Bombay-wallah English, even that sense of relentlessly sweaty optimism that was so prevalent before the dawn of liberalisation – it was all spot-on, capturing the city of my childhood with a panache that was blindingly intoxicating' ('A Very Pukka Murder', *Firstpost*, 13 November 2016).

34 *Vaseem Khan*: The author's latest series, set in India after the Partition, shows how classic tropes, including a detective duo in the Holmes–Watson mould (a female cop, Persis Wadia, and her sidekick Archie Blackfinch), can

be deployed against a backdrop of a society in transition and racial and other injustices in the context of an entertaining murder mystery.

35 *Alexander McCall Smith*: Alexander McCall Smith, the author of a bestselling series set in Botswana that began with *The No. 1 Ladies' Detective Agency*, said when introducing a reprint of *The Perfect Murder* that the Ghote novels are timeless because they 'are about how the good man . . . preserves his integrity in a world of false values, greed and rampant injustice'.

THIRTY-SIX

Mind Games

Post-war psychological suspense

On a wet February evening in 1956, after drinking two bottles of cheap wine, sixteen-year-old Linda Millar got behind the wheel of her Ford Tudor sedan. Her father had bought it for her as a present for good grades, although two of her friends had recently been killed in car accidents, and she'd already earned a reprimand for speeding.

Linda drove into a group of three thirteen-year-old boys, two of whom were thrown seventy feet, before ramming a concrete wall and driving away. The third boy ran for help. Minutes later, she crashed into the rear of a stationary Buick. The sedan rolled on to its roof, and came to rest. A passer-by found Linda sitting on a kerb, weeping and screaming. When he tried to reassure her, she said, 'God damn, what will I tell my parents?'

The police picked her up, and took her to hospital; her two victims arrived there shortly afterwards. A check revealed that she'd only suffered minor injuries. But one of the boys was dead on arrival, and his friend was seriously hurt. At first, Linda denied that she'd caused the collision with the boys, but the police quickly found evidence to prove she was lying, and arrested her.

Linda was medically examined and diagnosed as 'schizoid personality type'. She slashed her wrists with a razor, and was

admitted to a rest home. A week later, her mother won the Edgar
Allan Poe award for best novel of the year. *Beast in View* was a
story of suicide, sudden death, and schizophrenia.

Margaret Ellis Sturm was born in 1915, in Berlin, Ontario; the
following year, the town changed its name to Kitchener. As a child,
she walked to school past a slaughterhouse. The smell and the
screaming of the animals haunted her for years. She enjoyed
escaping into the stories in *Black Mask*, saying that she was
'practically weaned on South American poisons and Lunge's
reagent'.

She read Classics at the University of Toronto, but her mother's
death was a shock from which she struggled to recover. An unhappy
affair was followed by a mild episode of schizophrenia, which
culminated in an attempt at suicide. Hoping to come to terms with
her inner demons, she studied psychiatry.

At this point, she met Ken Millar. They'd attended the same
school and both wanted to be writers. They married, but on
becoming pregnant she considered abortion. She decided to keep
the baby, Linda, but became a semi-invalid with a heart ailment
that she later described as imaginary.

The experience of typing Ken's stories and submitting them to
magazines in the hope of paying the maternity-ward bill spurred
her to start writing again. Ken encouraged her to try a mystery,
supplying her with a plot and editing her manuscript. The result
was *The Invisible Worm*, its title taken from William Blake. The
name of Margaret Millar alone appeared on the book cover, but
the contract with Doubleday treated the couple as co-authors
entitled to an equal split of royalties. The book was published in
the same week in 1941 as *I'll Eat You Last*, the debut of a Michigan
native, Henry Clay Branson.[1] The Millars and the Bransons became
friends, although Anna Branson said that she was 'always a little
bit afraid' of Maggie.

Maggie's detective was, almost inevitably, a psychiatrist.[2] Paul
Prye featured in two further novels and in 'Mind over Murder', a
novella in the Christie vein. Ken continued to make editorial suggestions, but his contribution diminished as her confidence grew, and
he branched out on his own under the name Ross Macdonald.

Wall of Eyes (1943) opens with Alice Heath pretending to be blind, like her embittered sister. Kelsey Heath lost her sight when a car she was driving crashed, killing a young woman passenger. After murder is committed within the dysfunctional Heath family household, Toronto cop Inspector Sands[3] is confronted by a puzzle about identity, conscience and the yearning for security. Sands treats suspects like his puppets, and plays 'the disillusioning role of God'.

Sands plays God again at the end of *The Iron Gates*, aka *Taste of Fears* (1945). A married woman's disappearance from home after receiving a mysterious parcel precipitates a sequence of murders. The crimes arise from long-buried family secrets, and are motivated by a yearning for justice twisted into lust for revenge. Sands' case against the murderer is circumstantial, so he leaves the culprit to commit suicide,[4] saying: 'You have nothing left to live for.'

Authors too play God. Sands never appeared in another novel. Freed from the shackles of writing a series, Maggie produced the stand-alones that were her finest novels. She wove teasing mysteries into subtle explorations of sexual relationships and the female psyche.

A stint as a Hollywood scriptwriter enabled Maggie to buy a family house in Santa Barbara and hire a nanny to help look after Linda. Her daughter had already exhibited worrying patterns of behaviour, some of it attention-seeking, some of it macabre. She stole money from her parents, and Anna Branson was startled to see that, in her dolls' house, Linda had gagged and bound to a chair several dolls.

Morbid psychology forms the core of *Beast in View* (1955).[5] Lonely Helen Clarvoe is stalked by someone giving the name Evelyn Merrick. Maggie learned that her plot, based on the real-life case of Christine Beauchamps,[6] was replicated in Gore Vidal's first television screenplay[7] *Dark Possession*. Ken suggested a clever final twist, although its shock value has diminished over the years, because so many other writers have borrowed it. The book has dated (the presentation of Helen's gay brother Dougie now seems like a caricature), but the story remains a tense read.

The Millars' respect for each other's writing wasn't tarnished by rivalry. But Maggie seems to have felt jealous of Ken's devotion to their troubled daughter, and Linda's errant behaviour culminated in the tragedy of the fatal car crash.

Linda faced the prospect of up to ten years in jail, and the legal proceedings were conducted in the glare of hostile press publicity. The judge sentenced her to eight years' probation, subject to conditions: she wasn't to drink alcohol, and had to undergo psychiatric treatment. The Millars fled to northern California for a year and licked their wounds. They'd racked up heavy legal and medical expenses, but at least their daughter had survived the crash, unlike the victim.

Maggie kept writing and served as President of the MWA, but neither she nor her husband realised that Linda was drinking again. Their daughter's doctors didn't tell them, believing she needed to establish a 'psychological distance' from her parents.

Linda drove off with two men to a casino in Nevada, and didn't come back, a flagrant breach of her probation. Her disappearance prompted the issue of a warrant for her arrest, and once more the Millars found themselves caught in the public spotlight at a terrifying point in their lives. Linda was eventually found unharmed, and given a suspended sentence rather than a spell in jail, but needed to be sedated under a doctor's care. So did her mother.

Fiction supplied Maggie with a refuge from nightmarish reality. She wrapped her psychological puzzles in stories that traced the fault lines in seemingly well-ordered lives. Confounding readers' expectations was a speciality. *An Air That Kills*, aka *The Soft Talkers* (1957), begins with Ron Galloway's disappearance and confirmation of his wife's suspicion that he'd been having an affair. Troubled marriages are at the heart of the story, but the final revelation is classic Millar. As Julian Symons put it, she 'shakes the kaleidoscope and shows us an entirely different pattern from the one we have been so busily interpreting'.

Her next three books comprised, in the words of Edward D. Hoch,[8] a 'special trio':[9] each is set in California and features a private eye, and each, with virtuosity worthy of Ellery Queen, 'withholds the key element of its solution to the very end'. Maggie noted in a reprint of her 1960 novel *A Stranger in My Grave* that

she'd summed up the premise in her notebook: 'A woman dreams
of visiting a cemetery and seeing engraved on a granite tombstone
her name, the date of her birth and the date of her death four
years previously. Write your way out of that one, kiddo.'

She rose to the challenge, contriving a brilliant structural device
that enabled her to reveal a crucial secret in the book's final two
words. Daisy Harker, 'a good daddy-loving girl', is plagued by a
dream about seeing her own tombstone. At first, Daisy is not
worried by the realisation that 'any good marriage involves a
certain amount of play-acting', but family deceptions lie at the
book's heart. Stevens Pinata, a bail bondsman and investigator,
helps her to discover the way in which, on her supposed date of
death, she was 'psychically murdered'.

Linda married and gave birth to a son, and for a time Maggie
felt able to relax. While Ken's career reached fresh peaks, she
wrote no fiction between 1964 and 1970. She'd just published
another crime novel when Linda died in her sleep at the age of
thirty-one, as a result of what Ken described as 'a cerebral incident'. Grief-stricken, Maggie insisted that she'd given up writing
for good. Six years later she resumed her literary career, but the
magic had gone. Her later crime novels, accomplished as they
were, failed to reach the heights of her best work.

Ken succumbed to Alzheimer's disease, and Maggie suffered
from macular degeneration. Long before the end came, she lost
her sight. Of all the connections between fact and her fiction, the
strangest and saddest is that the fatal car crash and the blindness
integral to the storyline of *Wall of Eyes* anticipated catastrophes
in her own life.

The trick in *Beast in View* was anticipated in Helen Eustis' *The
Horizontal Man*. Seasoned fans of contemporary crime fiction will
foresee the solution to Eustis's mystery, and not only because of
a shortage of credible suspects. Today the attitudes to unconventional sexual behaviour no longer seem advanced,[10] but at the time
of publication in 1946, the book was daring and different. Eustis
was in the vanguard of those post-war writers who recognised the
potential of the crime story for exploring the dark recesses of the
human mind[11] as well as for entertaining readers.

Kevin Boyle, a charismatic womaniser and professor at a women's college, is battered to death – by someone apparently devoted to him. Eustis based the setting on her experience as a student at Smith College, where, as she said in a biographical note, she 'won a medal for creative writing . . . and her first husband', who happened to be a professor, and may have been the inspiration for Boyle.

Psychological clues abound – and a psychiatrist unmasks the culprit. Eustis had undergone psychoanalysis, and the story reflects her insistence 'that psychoanalysis is an important force in world thought and behaviour today'. The darkness is leavened by touches of satire: 'Personally, I think there are not enough murders. They feed us in some way.'

The Horizontal Man never became a film noir: a missed opportunity. Eustis merrily admitted that there were many people at Smith she wanted to kill, and writing the book afforded long-term catharsis. She lived for a further sixty-nine years, but never published another murder mystery.[12]

Dorothy B. Hughes[13] climbed into the mind of a serial strangler in *In a Lonely Place*[14] (1947). Dickson 'Dix' Steele's story, albeit told from a third-person viewpoint, is a precursor to Lou Ford's nihilistic narrative in Jim Thompson's *The Killer Inside Me*. Dix is also a forerunner of the young men who charm and kill their way through the books of Patricia Highsmith and Ruth Rendell. The strange, disturbing nature of sociopathy is captured by one of Highsmith's titles, *This Sweet Sickness*.

Dix has come back from the war to Los Angeles – superbly evoked, from foggy waterfront to dark urban bowels. Living a life of apparent ease at the home of a rich, absent friend, he's pretending to write a crime novel, borrowing from Hammett, Chandler and Gardner, 'with a touch of Queen and Carr'. In truth, he is a deeply disturbed fantasist who 'had found nothing yet to take the place of flying wild . . . that feeling of power and exhilaration and loneness in the sky'.

Murdering women whom he encounters by chance offers him only fleeting release. Through his wartime buddy Brub Nicolai, now working as an LAPD cop, he tries to keep track of the investigation into his killings, all while beginning an affair with a mercurial actress called Laurel. Angered by the stupidity of public reaction to his crimes ('It took imagination to think of a man, sane as you and I, who killed'), troubled by the suspicious attitude of Brub's wife and frustrated by Laurel's elusiveness, his mood swings become ever more sudden and violent, and the risks he takes become more extreme.

The cultural context was significant. Hughes was writing, as Megan Abbott has emphasised,[15] in 'an era of gender realignment and perceived masculinity under siege. What we see in Dix's tale is a cunning, prescient analysis of post-war sexual panic still underway as Hughes was writing. This was the time, and place, of the Black Dahlia Murder, which tore the roof off a Los Angeles thick with sexual violence, missing women, unsolved crimes, and general mayhem.'

Abbott links the darkness of post-war crime fiction 'to the return of soldiers to a changed America. Gone are the economic opportunity, the glory, the innocence of their own youth.[16] And, perhaps most of all, their women. Out of the kitchen and into the workforce. Potentially into their jobs. And who knew what else they had been up to while he was gone?'

Abnormal psychology obsessed John Franklin Bardin, whose most distinctive crime fiction appeared just after the war. Bardin's mother suffered from paranoid schizophrenia, and family misfortunes forced him to leave university. For a time he worked as a bouncer in a roller-skating rink. In a furious burst of energy, he produced three novels in eighteen months. Powerful studies of disturbed states of mind[17] were knotted together with extravagant storylines.

The outlandish mood of *The Deadly Percheron* (1946), narrated by the psychiatrist George Matthews, is set in the opening paragraph: 'Jacob Blunt was my last patient. He came into my office wearing a scarlet hibiscus in his curly blond hair. He sat down in the easy chair across from my desk, and said, "Doctor, I think I'm losing my mind."'

When Blunt explains that he keeps seeing little men in green and purple suits who pay him to wear flowers, Matthews is flummoxed. After seeing one of the tiny men for himself, he is drawn into an eccentric charade. Amnesia and confusions about identity complicate his battle to untangle a web of murder and mystery.

In *The Last of Philip Banter* (1947), an advertising executive with a drink problem and an unhappy marriage finds a typed manuscript on his desk.[18] The manuscript, seemingly written by himself, is headed 'Confession', and mingles the past with the present. As the events described begin to come true, he starts to lose his grip on reality.

Equally unsettling, *Devil Take the Blue-Tail Fly* begins with Ellen Purcell, a harpsichordist, who is about to leave a mental hospital, but finds the staff members reluctant to turn their backs on her. Unlike fellow crime novelists who wrote about psychiatrists solving problems, Bardin was a sceptic as a result of his visits to his mother while she was undergoing treatment. He does not disguise his hostility towards electro-convulsive therapy and 'psychiatric mumbo-jumbo'.

Good or bad luck with timing helps to determine whether a novelist achieves commercial success or remains in the shadows. Bardin was a trailblazer who for many years failed to receive his due. Discouraged, he turned to writing less remarkable, pseudonymous crime fiction[19] while working in advertising and then editing magazines.

Julian Symons championed Bardin's first three books, which he described as 'powerful, not perfect, novels. They suggest more than they ever say about the incestuous feelings[20] of parents and children, and the solutions . . . seem to be rooted in psychology rather than reason.' He admired Bardin's ability to shock and terrify, arguing that the novels were unlike anything else in modern crime fiction.

Bardin enjoyed a brief revival in the 1970s, as Symons' advocacy[21] resulted in his first three books being reissued in a paperback omnibus. Encouraged, Bardin wrote a final novel. By this time, the world had changed again. The *Lady Chatterley's Lover* obscenity trial and controversy about Philip Roth's *Portnoy's Complaint* were old news. Sexual candour was in vogue, and male writers in particular were quick to exploit their new freedom.

Unfortunately, *Purloining Tiny* (1978) reads like an erratic pastiche of Bardin's early work. The eponymous Tiny, an attractive young woman who happens to be a famous contortionist, is kidnapped and held captive in an apartment by her long-lost father. The focus on incestuous desires is more explicit[22] than in Bardin's early books, with bizarre results. Symons' understated verdict was 'a sad disappointment', while Stanley Ellin gave a bemused endorsement, calling the book 'one of the strangest mystery novels I have ever read'.

Devil Take the Blue-Tail Fly appeared in Britain in 1948, but failed to find an American publisher. In the same year, Robert M. Coates'[23] *Wisteria Cottage* did make a splash. The blurb trumpeted it as 'a terrifying book . . . that takes you into the mind of a psychotic and lets you follow, step by engrossing step, down the path to explosive violence'.

Richard Baurie, the protagonist, 'would seem a pleasant young man . . . You would not have reason to suspect that he was a schizophrenic and a potential murderer.' The account of his mental disintegration begins with a snippet from a psychiatrist's report, and further extracts are included as events move to a grimly foreseeable conclusion.

The relentless one-note tone suggested a flawed storytelling technique and Coates failed to progress as a crime novelist. A younger writer fascinated by disturbance and depravity believed that her fiction would be better than *Wisteria Cottage* because, as she said in her private journal, it would be written 'primarily . . . as entertainment'. Her name was Patricia Highsmith.

Notes

The main sources are Tom Nolan's introduction to Margaret Millar's collected stories, *The Couple Next Door*, and his biography of Ross Macdonald.

1   *Henry Clay Branson*: Branson's series character was a doctor-turned-private eye called John Bent.
2   *Maggie's detective was . . . a psychiatrist*: Psychiatric sleuths were in vogue. In addition to Helen McCloy's Basil Willing, Rosemary Kutak introduced Marc Castleman in the intriguing multiple-viewpoint mystery *Darkness of Slumber*; he returned in *I am the Cat* before disappearing.
3   *Inspector Sands*: Sands first appeared in the third and final Prye novel, and also in 'The Couple Next Door'.

4   *he leaves the culprit to commit suicide*: As does, among other detectives, Lord Peter Wimsey in *Murder Must Advertise*.

5   *Beast in View*: The novel edged past Highsmith's *The Talented Mr Ripley* to win the Edgar. For Laura Lippman, a leading writer of series fiction and stand-alone novels of psychological suspense, it is 'a timeless story, one that reminds the twenty-first-century reader that we may have new technological tools with which to taunt and stalk our enemies. But . . . human nature doesn't really change' (*Women Crime Writers of the 1940s and 50s* website).

6   *Christine Beauchamps*: The case of Christine 'Sally' Beauchamps, an alias for Clara Norton Fowler, was reported on by American neurologist Morton Prince in 1906.

7   *Gore Vidal's first television screenplay*: Vidal's three detective novels, written under the name Edgar Box, featured Peter Cutler Sargeant II, a heterosexual version of himself. In *Death in the Fifth Position*, Sargeant reflects on a visit to a gay bar: 'it was like those last chapters in Proust when everybody around starts turning into boy-lovers until there isn't a womanizer left on deck.'

8   *Edward D. Hoch*: Hoch specialised in short stories. Among his novels, *The Shattered Raven* features murder committed at a Mystery Writers of America banquet.

9   *'a special trio'*: The other two books are *The Listening Walls* and *How Like an Angel*. Symons praised the former's 'apparent double bluff and brilliant trick ending'. The latter sees a former casino cop tasked to find a dead man and is one of many crime novels featuring an eccentric cult, in this case the reclusive True Believers. Symons contrasted Maggie's thoughtful portrayal of the Brothers and Sisters of the Tower of Heaven with the approach of Margery Allingham and Ngaio Marsh: 'For them, the cult is merely a background, ridiculous and distasteful.'

10 *the attitudes to unconventional sexual behaviour no longer seem advanced*: Golden Age novelists usually flinched from addressing sexual deviation. Even in Lynn Brock's promisingly titled *The Kink*, the kinkiest part of the story is the plot. Philip MacDonald's post-war story 'Love Lies Bleeding' was a little more ambitious, but MacDonald never wrote a novel in the Millar vein. His final book, *The List of Adrian Messenger*, Colonel Gethryn's last hurrah, was a throwback to the Golden Age.

11 *the potential of the crime story for exploring the dark recesses of the human mind*: The film-maker François Ozon has taken stories by distinguished writers such as Ruth Rendell as starting points for psychological thrillers about sexuality and identity. *Double Lover* was adapted from Joyce Carol Oates' *Lives of the Twins*, aka *Kindred Passions*.

12 *never published another murder mystery*: She became a prolific translator, of Simenon among others.

13 *Dorothy B. Hughes*: Hughes took inspiration from the sharp prose of Eric Ambler, to whom she dedicated *The Fallen Sparrow*. Sarah Weinman described Hughes as 'the world's finest female noir writer' in the *Los Angeles Review of Books*, 12 August 2012. At the height of her career, family commitments led to an eleven-year break from writing novels. She returned briefly with *The Expendable Man*. The story turns on a mid-story revelation about the protagonist Hugh Densmore, which, Weinman argues, helps one to understand 'how things stood in America at the time'; it elaborates an idea

from Hughes' earlier book, *Dread Journey*. After another gap, of fifteen years, she published her last book, a biography of Erle Stanley Gardner.

14 *In a Lonely Place*: In Nicholas Ray's film version, Andrew P. Solt's screenplay transformed Hughes' story, with Dix becoming a screenwriter with a violent streak who is suspected of killing a woman.

15 *as Megan Abbott has emphasised*: In 'The Origins of American Noir', *The Paris Review*, 1 August 2017, in which she emphasises Hughes' 'abiding interest in the psychology of difference, in taking on the perspectives of those unlike herself: from street punks to political prisoners, from an African American doctor to a war refugee among the Tesuque Indians'. Abbott, whose own work includes *You Will Know Me*, a striking novel of domestic suspense about a teenage gymnast and her family, also points out the historic significance of *In a Lonely Place*: 'From Patricia Highsmith and Jim Thompson to Bret Easton Ellis and Thomas Harris, nearly every "serial killer" tale of the last seventy years bears its imprint – both in terms of its sleek, relentless style and its claustrophobic "mind of the criminal" perspective. But its larger influence derives from Hughes's uncanny grasp of the connection between violence and misogyny and an embattled masculinity.'

16 *Gone are the economic opportunity, the glory, the innocence of their own youth*: The first two novels of Britain's Michael Gilbert showed how much the war changed detective fiction as well as society. His debut, *Close Quarters*, was a classic whodunit set in a pre-war cathedral close. But in *They Never Looked Inside*, aka *He Didn't Mind Danger*, a gang leader who is a 'perverted psychologist' exploits the natural lawlessness and dissatisfaction of recently demobilised young men to engage in large-scale organised robbery.

17 *Powerful studies of disturbed states of mind*: Dissociative identity disorder, formerly known as multiple personality disorder and frequently mis-described as schizophrenia, continues to feature in crime fiction and films. An example is *Identity*, a 2003 film that utilises reverse chronology and has a scenario reminiscent of Christie's *And Then There Were None*.

18 *a typed manuscript on his desk*: The tantalising possibilities of a supposedly fictional manuscript that seems to come true have been explored by crime writers ranging from Roger East in his Golden Age puzzle *Murder Rehearsal* to Renee Knight, whose *Disclaimer* begins with Catherine Ravenscroft receiving a book about her life. Knight employs this device to explore the 'Who can be trusted?' dilemma at the heart of so many twenty-first-century novels of psychological suspense. Fredric Brown's *Murder Can Be Fun* varies the theme, with an unknown killer mimicking the crimes described in radio scripts that have yet to be broadcast.

19 *less remarkable, pseudonymous crime fiction*: Bardin adopted the pen-names Gregory Tree and Douglas Ashe; *A Shroud for Grandmama* appeared under both names.

20 *They suggest more than they ever say about . . . incestuous feelings*: As late as 1958, the very thought of incest horrified the clean-living young lawyer Kirk Halstead in Evelyn Berckman's *No Known Grave*. It was 'a hearsay thing, something known only among the degraded, the degenerate and the bestial'.

21 *Symons' advocacy*: He introduced a Bardin omnibus volume that features in *Mona Lisa*, a crime film directed and co-written by Neil Jordan, which

makes several references to Bardin's work. Jordan's other thrillers include *The Crying Game* and *Greta*.

22 *The focus on incestuous desires is more explicit*: As in *First Person Plural*, a novel by Richard Wiseman (whose real name was Nick Bartlett) about obsessive love in a family of three orphaned children, told from their points of view. Published in 1975, it anticipated by three years a comparable scenario in Ian McEwan's *The Cement Garden*. Wiseman's other crime novel, *Duncan Is In His Grave*, also has a psychosexual focus.

23 *Robert M. Coates*: Coates' 1926 novel *The Eater of Darkness*, said to be 'the first surrealist novel in English', has spoof detective elements, including a mad scientist, and has been compared to Flann O'Brien's much better-known *The Third Policeman*. *Wisteria Cottage*, aka *The Night before Dying*, was filmed as *Edge of Fury*, but Coates' principal reputation was as an art critic.

THIRTY-SEVEN

Deep Water

Patricia Highsmith

Patricia Highsmith adored snails. Her fascination with gastropods was no childish fancy, beginning when she was twenty-five years old. Walking past a fish market, she spotted two snails locked in an embrace. Intrigued, she rescued them from the cooking pot, and kept them at home in a fish bowl. Close study of their mating rituals prompted her to write 'The Snail-Watcher', the first of her published tales[1] about macabre encounters between snails and people destined for a very sticky end.

This devotion to snails proved not to be a brief infatuation, but rather a long-term love affair. In *Deep Water* (1957), Vic Van Allen keeps two snails, named Edgar and Hortense after Highsmith's own favourites. Studying his pets in peace and quiet gives Vic temporary respite from the unhappiness of his marriage: 'How they did adore each other and how perfect they were for each other.' Vic seems meek and decent at first, but it becomes clear that he is a sociopath who does not flinch at murder.

In the 60s, while living in Suffolk, Highsmith kept three hundred snails in her back garden. She told the magazine *Reveille* she admired 'their self-sufficiency' and even became reluctant to travel without them. On one occasion, when invited to a cocktail party, she packed dozens of snails into a vast handbag, together with a head of lettuce. Opening the handbag, she showed off to a fellow partygoer her 'companions for the evening'.

After leaving England, Highsmith moved to continental Europe, but crossing international borders with her pets presented a serious challenge. She rose to it, as she explained to her American editor, by smuggling her snails in her bra,[2] six to ten per breast, he reported: 'That just wasn't on the one trip – no, she kept going back and forth . . . And she wasn't joking – she was very serious.'

Keeping snails, she told a radio interviewer, gave her 'a sort of tranquillity'. Highsmith's relationships with fellow human beings were rarely as tranquil. Her fictional characters are often weak individuals who find themselves attracted to predatory types with disastrous results. Graham Greene, expressing his admiration for 'The Snail-Watcher', pointed out that she regarded her most famous creation, Tom Ripley, with the same 'emotionless curiosity' with which Knoppert the snail-watcher observes the snails' sexual antics.

Highsmith's troubles began before she was born. Her parents' relationship faltered, and her pregnant mother drank turpentine in the hope of disposing of her unborn child, to no avail. The couple divorced on 10 January 1921; Mary Patricia Plangman was born nine days later, in Fort Worth, Texas. Her mother subsequently married Stanley Highsmith, but their family life seemed to the young girl to be a form of 'living hell'.

Edgar Allan Poe was an early literary influence on Highsmith, and her life proved as dysfunctional as his. The two of them shared a birthday, and, rather like Poe, Highsmith developed a taste for alcohol and young women that failed to bring her lasting contentment. Her apprenticeship as a crime writer comprised seven years spent writing for magazines such as *Black Terror*.

In 1948, Truman Capote recommended her to spend time at the artists' colony Yaddo.[3] There she finally made progress with her first novel. Years later, she told her lover Marijane Meaker[4] (who wrote pulp crime fiction under the name Vin Packer) that she owed Yaddo 'everything'. Chester Himes, soon to carve a reputation as an influential black writer, had a room across the corridor from her at Yaddo, but Highsmith bonded more closely with another writer, an Englishman called Marc Brandel.[5]

Brandel's real name was Marcus Beresford, and he was the son of the author J. D. Beresford.[6] Most of Highsmith's lovers, before and after Brandel, were women, but in May 1949, she and he celebrated the news that her first novel was to be published by agreeing to marry on Christmas Day. It was an improbable match. Before long, Highsmith fell for another woman, and the wedding never took place.

Highsmith had an idea for a novel about two men who agree to exchange murders, so that neither of them will be suspected. This wasn't a new idea[7] – Alec Waugh's[8] 'The Police are Baffled', for instance, used the same device in 1931 – but there can be little doubt that Highsmith thought it up independently.

Like so many other young writers in the post-war years, she was fascinated by the psychology of murder and 'the opposing planes, drives of good and evil . . . How by a slight deflection one can be made the *other*'. *Strangers on a Train* (1950) duly shifted the moral centre of the novel of psychological suspense, emphasising the ambiguity of guilt and innocence.

A chance encounter on a railway journey introduces Guy Haines, a wealthy architect, to a playboy called Charles Anthony Bruno. Guy longs to be rid of his unfaithful wife Miriam, while Bruno wants his father dead. Bruno proposes that each of them murders the person standing in the way of the other's happiness. Guy does not take the proposal seriously until Bruno murders Miriam. Fearing that he will become implicated if he reports Bruno to the police, Guy finds himself drawn into the homicidal conspiracy.

Real-life crimes echo in the story. Bruno's surname came from Bruno Hauptmann, executed in 1936 for kidnapping and murdering Charles A. Lindbergh Jr,[9] the infant son of the legendary airman. His forename came from the victim. The fatal attraction between Guy and Bruno is reminiscent of the Leopold and Loeb 'thrill-killers' murder case fictionalised by Patrick Hamilton in *Rope*. But Highsmith fashions melodramatic plot material into something haunting and unforgettable.

The Blunderer (1954) traces another destructive relationship between two men.[10] Walter Stackhouse, an unhappily married lawyer, becomes obsessed with Melchior Kimmel, surely the most brutish bookseller to be found in the entire genre. Kimmel has killed his wife, but evaded arrest. Walter's wife falls off a cliff, and although he has not murdered her, his behaviour arouses the suspicion of a relentless police officer – and he also makes an enemy of the menacing Kimmel.

Self-harming behaviour is in the DNA of Highsmith's protagonists, such as the crime writer Sydney Bartleby in *A Suspension of Mercy*, aka *The Story-Teller* (1965). This book, relatively light in tone, is set in East Anglia, where Highsmith was living at the time.[11] Sydney fantasises about killing his wife Alicia, rolling up her body in a carpet, and burying it in woodland. When Alicia vanishes, people wonder if he has actually murdered her. One of Highsmith's techniques for getting into Sydney's head entailed burying dead snails in the woods behind her Suffolk cottage.

Tom Ripley,[12] charming, amoral and Highsmith's most famous character, lives even more dangerously, but is adept at the art of self-preservation. In *The Talented Mr Ripley* (1955), Tom kills an acquaintance and assumes his identity. He has a gift for reinventing himself, constantly skating on thin ice, yet somehow sliding out of reach of the police. No one in crime fiction's pantheon of anti-heroes has made such a deep and lasting impression as Ripley.

Francis Iles praised the brilliance of the novel's 'cynical, credible, yet quite unexpected ending' and found Highsmith's 'ruthless inhumanity' refreshing. Julian Symons was another admirer, although he admitted that she 'is an acquired taste, which means a taste that some never acquire'.[13] For him, Highsmith was the crime writer 'who fuses character and plot most successfully'. She even dashed off – in a month – a book about plotting suspense fiction. Yet plotting was not her main strength. Her supreme gift was an ability to come up with off-beat situations that are pregnant with menace and then explore how they impact on her characters.

Graham Greene, another writer who spent a lifetime wrestling with demons,[14] described Highsmith as 'a poet of apprehension'. As he said, she 'created a world of her own . . . a world claustrophobic and irrational . . . a world without moral endings'. In *The Tremor of Forgery* (1969), Howard Ingham, an American staying in Tunisia, thinks he has killed an intruder, but the truth is never made clear. This novel barely qualifies as crime fiction, but Greene thought it her finest.

Edith's Diary (1977) is a poignant study of mental disintegration in which, over the years, a woman's contented family life gradually falls apart. She keeps a secret diary that, as things go from bad to worse in the real world, records a fantasy of an alternative existence. Highsmith doesn't exploit the full potential of this brilliant device, and her usual publishers rejected the book. Nevertheless, it is among her most powerful.

Symons conceded that some of her later novels became self-indulgent and preposterous, and Tom Ripley's charm was wearing thin by the time of his fifth and final appearance. In the last quarter-century of her career, much of her best work came in the short story form; its disciplines suited her literary gifts.

Highsmith had no time for convention. She found 'the public passion for justice quite boring and artificial',[15] and claimed that criminals are 'dramatically interesting because, for a time at least, they are active, free in spirit, and they do not knuckle down to anyone'. Few of her books have happy endings.[16]

She confessed that *A Game for the Living* (1958), set in Mexico, and the closest of her novels in spirit to a whodunit, was a misfire. This was because she 'tried to do something different from what I had been doing . . . [which] caused me to leave out certain elements that are vital for me: surprise, speed of action, the stretching of the reader's credulity, and above all that intimacy with the murderer himself. I am not an inventor of puzzles.'

Nevertheless, in one of her private journals (or *cahiers*, as she called them), she wrote that the 'old-fashioned morality' of E. C. Bentley's *Trent's Last Case* would be remembered when Mickey Spillane was forgotten. She argued that Ernest Bramah's stories about the blind amateur detective Max Carrados deserved to be remembered:[17] 'the artistry and literary elegance of his stories entertain as much as the ingenuity of his plots.' Unpredictable as ever, she accepted an invitation to join the Detection Club[18] and contributed a short story to *Verdict of 13* (1978), an anthology of the work of Club members, including such stalwarts of traditional detective fiction as Michael Innes, Christianna Brand and Ngaio Marsh.

The game-playing ethos of the Club appealed to her. She believed that: 'Writing fiction is a game, and one must be amused all the time to do it.' This may account for her willingness to take part in an eccentric and unique project[19] in 1975. She and seven other leading writers, including Brand, Marsh, Dick Francis, Len Deighton and the American Helen McCloy, agreed to collaborate with the record company EMI by writing instalments of a mystery story lasting ten minutes each. They were to feature on a double LP and cassette tape, but with the ninth and final episode missing.

Each author was to be recorded reading his or her contribution, and crime fans would be invited to try to solve the puzzle. Highsmith's episode featured Tom Ripley – the only short story in which he appears – but the recording was never produced, and the story never published in book form. This is a shame, since the concept of a joint venture by such an eclectic group and featuring fiction's favourite psychopath seems irresistible. The reasons for its non-appearance remain shrouded in mystery.

The playfulness of Highsmith's writing tends to be overlooked. No other crime writer of her generation would gleefully have produced a collection of stories called *Little Tales of Misogyny* (1975). For all the game-playing, contentment eluded her, just as it eluded Poe. As the years passed, she suffered from ill health, and her personal life was disfigured by deeply troubled relationships with her mother and an endless stream of lovers.

She could be as charming as Ripley, and as antagonistic as Melchior Kimmel. People close to her complained of stinginess, racism and antisemitism. She died alone in Switzerland, her last visitor an accountant. Alcoholism exacerbated her unpleasant behaviour, and the theory that she was a high-functioning individual on the autism spectrum[20] seems plausible. She left her millions to Yaddo.

As Graham Greene pointed out, Highsmith's territory is far distant from 'the heroic world of her peers, Hammett and Chandler', but her work has spoken to her successors for more than half a century. Gillian Flynn, whose *Gone Girl* (2012), like *Deep Water*, charts the lethal consequences of a loveless marriage, believes[21] that the secret of Highsmith's enduring appeal and influence is that she 'does a great job of trusting her characters . . . Her stuff isn't overly plotted. It has this sense of wonderful inevitability about it . . . She kind of takes you by the hand and walks you toward the cliff.'

Notes

The main sources are the biographies of Highsmith by Andrew Wilson (himself a crime novelist) and Joan Schenkar, and Marijane Meaker's account of her 'Romance of the 1950s' with Highsmith.

1   *the first of her published tales*: 'The Quest for Blank Claveringi' describes the ill-fated visit of a zoology professor to a remote island inhabited by gigantic snails. A third story, contemplated in 1969 but apparently not completed, told of a post-nuclear world in which the only survivors are a small group of people and snails, some of which develop a taste for human flesh.

2   *She rose to it, as she explained to her American editor, by smuggling her snails in her bra*: The editor, Larry Ashmead, is quoted by Wilson. Joan Schenkar suggests that Highsmith's claim was 'theatrical', and that usually she smuggled the snails in cottage-cheese cartons. Her reasoning, based on the modest size of Highsmith's breasts, reminds one of Lestrade rather than Sherlock Holmes.

3   *Yaddo*: Elizabeth Fenwick was at Yaddo at much the same time. Her early detective stories, as by E. P. Fenwick, gave way to novels of psychological suspense.

4   *Marijane Meaker*: Meaker's Vin Packer novel *The Evil Friendship* fictionalised New Zealand's Parker–Hulme murder case long before Juliet Hulme reinvented herself as the crime novelist Anne Perry.

5   *Marc Brandel*: Brandel married three times. After publishing several crime novels, he focused on writing for TV series such as *The Four Just Men*, *Danger Man* and *Paul Temple*. In 1956, he adapted *The Talented Mr Ripley* for television, and in 1985 Highsmith paid him to write a film version of *The Blunderer*, but the project never got off the ground. His sister Elisabeth created the Wombles of Wimbledon Common.

6   *J. D. Beresford*: John Davys Beresford dabbled in various genres. In Dorothy L. Sayers' *The Unpleasantness at the Bellona Club*, he is mentioned alongside Wells and Galsworthy, but his main contribution to the crime genre was recommending Collins to publish Freeman Wills Crofts' debut *The Cask*.

7   *This wasn't a new idea*: Julian Symons suggested that Baroness Orczy thought of it first. The notion of exchanging murders has become a familiar ingredient of crime fiction, and is to be found at the heart of novels as different as Sheila Radley's *This Way Out* in her Inspector Quantrill series, Evelyn Berckman's suspense novel *Stalemate*, Amanda Craig's *The Golden Rule* (which also draws on the fairy tale 'The Beauty and the Beast') and Peter Swanson's twisty thriller *The Kind Worth Killing*; Swanson's *Eight Perfect Murders* also reflects his fascination with Highsmith. Peter Lovesey's *On the Edge*, aka *Dead Gorgeous*, has a comparable starting point, and Lovesey has also written a short story called 'Strangers on a Bus'. Variations on the theme may be found in novels by Leo Bruce and Kate Ellis, as well as the play *Dead on Nine* by Jack Popplewell, a playwright, songwriter and rhubarb farmer. In *The Third Lady* by Shizuko Natsuki, a close encounter

in a hotel is the catalyst for a story about love and obsession, in which the apparent 'murder by proxy' of a professor specialising in chemical research leads to an exploration of culture and morality in Japan.

8   *Alec Waugh*: Brother of the more famous Evelyn, he wrote prolifically. 'The Police are Baffled' appeared in *The Bystander* on 25 February 1931.

9   *Bruno Hauptmann, executed in 1936 for kidnapping Charles A. Lindbergh Jr*: The child was abducted and murdered in 1932; the horror induced by the crime informs the plot of Christie's *Murder on the Orient Express*.

10 *another destructive relationship between two men*: *Two Faces of January* and *Those Who Walk Away*, both of which benefit from vividly evoked European settings, offer further examples of this favourite Highsmith scenario.

11 *East Anglia, where Highsmith was living at the time*: Jill Dawson's *The Crime Writer*, published in 2016 but set in 1964, presents a fictional version of this period of Highsmith's life. Dawson also fictionalised the Thompson–Bywaters case in *Fred & Edie*.

12 *Tom Ripley*: In a remarkable article about the suspense novelist A. J. Finn (a pen-name for Dan Mallory), Ian Parker points out that, at Oxford, Mallory studied the Ripley novels and quotes his view that Highsmith 'persuades us to root for sociopaths' ('A Suspense Novelist's Trail of Deceptions', *New Yorker*, 11 February 2019).

13 *a taste that some never acquire*: Dorothy B. Hughes, for instance, declined to give an endorsement to *A Game for the Living*, saying, 'I don't like her writings' and that she disliked her presentation of Mexican people.

14 *Graham Greene, another writer who spent a lifetime wrestling with demons*: *Brighton Rock* combines an exploration of sin with a thriller plot, while *Our Man in Havana* is a comedy about espionage.

15 *She found 'the public passion for justice quite boring and artificial'*: This view is expressed in *Plotting and Writing Suspense Fiction*, as are her reservations about *A Game for the Living* and her contention that writing fiction is a game.

16 *Few of her books have happy endings*: Highsmith's second novel, *The Price of Salt*, aka *Carol*, about a lesbian relationship between a shop assistant and a customer, is an exception. During her lifetime, the book appeared under a pen-name, Claire Morgan.

17 *She argued that Ernest Bramah's stories . . . deserved to be remembered*: In *The Times Literary Supplement*, 5 June 1981.

18 *she accepted an invitation to join the Detection Club*: She drew a wide-eyed self-portrait of herself on the occasion of her initiation into the Club on 21 November 1975 and captioned the picture 'Happy Evening'.

19 *her willingness to take part in an eccentric and unique project*: The project is discussed in 'Serendip's Detections XV' by Tony Medawar in *CADS* 71. Len Deighton, the one surviving contributor, told me in an email in October 2015 that he had no recollection of the project. Is it possible that the whole business was some form of literary hoax?

20 *the theory that she was a high-functioning individual on the autism spectrum*: See, for instance, *Asperger Syndrome: A Gift or a Curse?* (2005) by Viktoria Lyons and Michael Fitzgerald.

21 *Gillian Flynn . . . believes*: See 'Gillian Flynn on Patricia Highsmith', *Wall Street Journal*, 24 April 2014.

THIRTY-EIGHT

Forking Paths

Borges and postmodernism

On Christmas Eve, 1938, a bookish middle-aged man suffered an accident in his home city, Buenos Aires. Running up a flight of stairs, he cut his head on a casement window that had been freshly painted and left open to dry. The wound became infected, and for seventeen days his life hung in the balance. His poisoned blood made him delirious, and he suffered terrifying hallucinations.

The wound left a permanent mark, physical and psychological. His father had recently died, and in his mind the two disasters were linked. Like his father, he loved writing; he'd published poems and critical essays, and translated Kafka into Spanish. He hated his poorly paid job as a clerk, even though he worked in a library; to him, literature was everything. Had the fever damaged his brain? Would he now find himself unable to write?

He dipped a toe back in the water with short stories, crammed with images that obsessed him – maps, mirrors and labyrinths. His love of the classical English detective puzzle shone through. One of his earliest ventures supplied the title for a volume published in 1941; 'The Garden of Forking Paths' was translated into English by Anthony Boucher. The following year, he produced the remarkable 'Death and the Compass', and co-authored a book of short mysteries paying tribute to past masters such as Conan Doyle.

Jorges Luis Borges became one of South America's most influential men of letters, arguably the most distinguished writer to have been denied the Nobel Prize in Literature. But he never lost his love for detective fiction. In 1969, during a lecture tour in the United States, he lunched with his friend and translator Donald Yates and crime aficionado Francis M. Nevins. A fellow diner came to their table brandishing a camera, and asked permission to take a photograph.

'Say cheese!' he commanded.

'Might I say Chesterton instead?' asked Borges.

Fanny Haslam, whose family came from Staffordshire, was widowed three years after marrying a colonel in the Argentinian army. He was shot dead in a feud, leaving her with two small boys. One son trained as a lawyer and married a woman from a military family; they had two children, one of whom, born in 1899, was nicknamed Georgie. His full name was Jorge Francisco Isidoro Luis Borges Acevedo.

Fanny taught her grandson English and he was enthralled by what she told him about her home country. His mother taught him Spanish, and constantly recounted the glorious exploits of his ancestors, believing that he would be proud of his military heritage, but it made him feel inadequate. Near-sighted and frail, he knew he could never be a man of action. His father had literary ambitions and a library extending to over a thousand English-language volumes. Borges wrote later: 'If I were asked to name the chief event in my life, I should say my father's library.'

He became a frequent contributor to a magazine called *Sur*, owned by the writer and intellectual Victoria Ocampo.[1] She introduced him to Adolfo Bioy-Casares, who shared his love of detective fiction and literary jokes. In 1942, the two men published *Six Problems for Don Isidro Parodi*, often cited as Argentina's first home-grown book of detective stories.

A foreword by Gervasio Montenegro, 'Member, Argentine Academy of Letters', pays tribute to 'the blood-curdling cruelties of the *roman policier*', and talks about Sherlock Holmes, Lecoq and Max Carrados, as well as Poe, M. P. Shiel and Baroness Orczy. Among those referenced are John Dickson Carr, Edgar Wallace and the long-neglected Lynn Brock. Montenegro ranks the book 'on the same level as those recommended to keen London enthusiasts by the incorruptible Crime Club!' But Montenegro was a figment of the authors' imagination, and he became a character in their stories.

The book was published under the pseudonym H. Bustos Domecq, with a hoax biographical note about Domecq supplied by a schoolteacher, Miss Adelina Badoglio. In-jokes abound, while Montenegro's antisemitism reflects the authors' scorn for racism and fascism; Nazi-supporting extremists had suggested that Borges was Jewish, and not a 'true' Argentinian.

Parodi is introduced in 'The Twelve Figures of the World' as a victim of a miscarriage of justice, which, for the authors, typifies corruption in Argentina. Fourteen years ago, he was sent to prison for a murder he did not commit, and never leaves his cell. He proves to be a master of armchair detection, solving the weird problems brought to him. 'Tai An's Long Search', dedicated to the memory of Ernest Bramah, is a riff on Poe's 'The Purloined Letter', while 'Tadeo Limardo's Victim', dedicated to Franz Kafka, features characters named after Father Brown and Count Fosco.

'Death and the Compass' concerns a series of killings; despite echoes of Chesterton and *The ABC Murders*, the story is wholly distinctive. Borges called it 'a nightmare in which elements of Buenos Aires appear, deformed by the horror of the nightmare'. He traces the destiny of a brilliant detective, Erik Lönnrot, who 'believed himself a pure reasoner, an Auguste Dupin, but there was something of the adventurer in him, even a little of the gambler'. Lönnrot plays for the highest stakes in a battle of wits with a criminal known as Scharlach the Dandy.

Borges and Bioy-Casares produced an anthology of crime stories featuring their fellow countrymen alongside Christie, Berkeley, Milward Kennedy and Ellery Queen. They argued that critics underestimated detective fiction, 'simply because it does not enjoy the prestige of being tedious'. Their mission to raise awareness of the pleasures of the genre in their home country took a fresh direction in 1945, when they founded a detective fiction imprint that introduce traditional mysteries to readers in Argentina. With a nod to Dante's vision of hell, they called it the Seventh Circle.

Nicholas Blake's *The Beast Must Die* was the first Seventh Circle title, and novels by Michael Innes and Anthony Gilbert soon followed. The series proved successful and influential;[2] as Borges said: 'those books did a lot of good, because they reminded writers that plots were important. If you take up detective novels, and if you take up other novels afterwards, the first thing that strikes you – it's unjust, of course, but it happens – is to think of the other books as being shapeless.'

Although the Seventh Circle emphasised British Golden Age detection, the imprint also represented Americans such as Cornell Woolrich and Vera Caspary, together with home-grown mysteries that used Golden Age tropes to make sly comments about the state of Argentina[3] at a time of populism and Peronistas, when the country was a magnet for displaced Nazis searching for a safe haven.

By the time Borges was fifty-five, his blindness rendered him unable to read novels by Alain Robbe-Grillet,[4] one of the postmodernists he inspired. In the English-speaking world, despite Boucher's advocacy, his own work remained relatively unknown until he and Samuel Beckett jointly received the prestigious Prix International in 1961. Although he preferred to work on a small canvas, concentrating on essays, poems and short stories, his metafiction became increasingly influential.[5]

María Angélica Bosco's[6] first novel, *Death Going Down* (1955), became a Seventh Circle title. Frida Erlinger's corpse is discovered in the lift of an apartment block, and at one point the detective Ericourt describes the crime as 'the Argentinian version of *The Mystery of the Yellow Room* with a fifty-year-old Rouletabille weighing eighty-five kilos. That's me.'

Because she was a woman,[7] Bosco was dubbed 'Argentina's Agatha Christie',[8] a hopelessly misleading label. Her fiction addressed contemporary issues such as the role of women in society, and there's a Borgesian flavour to a remark made by

Ericourt's assistant, Blasi: 'I don't like clues. Their interpretation often leads us the wrong way.'

Bosco championed the work of Guillermo Martínez,[9] Argentina's most successful crime writer of the early twenty-first century. Martínez's international breakthrough came with a recent-history mystery, *The Oxford Murders* (2003), in which events that took place ten years earlier are recounted by a twenty-two-year-old mathematician from Argentina.

A graduate in algebraic topology, the unnamed narrator is studying at Oxford when he meets the legendary mathematician Arthur Seldom outside his lodgings. They promptly find the body of a widowed landlady, who has been smothered by a pillow. Seldom has been summoned to the house by a mysterious message, stating the address and time, together with a neatly drawn circle and the words *the first of the series*. The plot fuses murder and mathematics,[10] and the focus is on the cerebral rather than the characters.

Borges' political views were less radical than those of many Latin American crime writers. The region has seen so much violent disorder, torture and corruption that distrust of the police is ubiquitous.[11] Just as Hammett and Jim Thompson despised the crookedness of people with power in the United States, so crime novelists like Paco Ignacio Taibo II have railed against social injustice in Latin America.

Taibo wrote a biography of Che Guevara and co-authored *The Uncomfortable Dead* (2004) with the masked revolutionary Zapatista leader Subcomandante Marcos. This literary odd couple wrote alternating chapters of the book. Taibo's sections feature his series private eye Héctor Belascoarán Shayne. The jokey dimension to the story is evident as early as page two, when Marcos namechecks Pepe Carvalho and his creator, the Spanish crime writer Manuel Vázquez Montalbán.[12]

Barcelona-born, Montalbán was imprisoned in 1962 for demonstrating in support of striking miners, and suffered torture during his incarceration. A lifelong Communist, he wrote novels reflecting his ideology and tendency to sermonise.[13] Carvalho finds himself caught up in Argentina's tormented past in *The Buenos Aires*

Quintet (1997). He undertakes a missing person search on behalf of his uncle, and at one point he encounters a man arrested for pretending to be Borges' son (and grandson of a dancer from Samarkand and an English lord). Borgesian references abound.

European writers whose criminal ventures owe a debt to Borges[14] include Friedrich Dürrenmatt[15] and Umberto Eco.[16] The Spanish writers Arturo Pérez-Reverte[17] and Carlos Ruiz Zafón also reflect an eclectic mix of literary interests in their crime novels. Game-playing, libraries and labyrinths fascinate both men as they did Borges.

Pérez-Reverte's *The Flanders Panel* opens with an extract from Borges' poem 'Chess', the game at the heart of a story about murders in the past and present. Dupin, Holmes and Lupin are all name-checked in a detective story that begins with the discovery of a puzzling inscription hidden in a fifteenth-century Flemish painting. Zafón's fantastical 'Cemetery of Forgotten Books' gives its name to a quartet of bestselling historical bibliomysteries in the Gothic vein, starting with *The Shadow of the Wind*.[18]

Among British crime novels in the Borgesian vein is Desmond Cory's[19] *Bennett*[20] (1977). It begins with an illusion,[21] a list of other books by the eponymous detective novelist, William Bennett. Part of the novel takes the form of a journal, ostensibly written by Bennett, who has gone missing in Spain. A policeman called Hunter tries to find him, in connection with the death of an au pair girl back in Britain. There are echoes of the Lord Lucan case, but Cory's concern is not to offer a solution to that mystery, but to play an intellectual game with the reader.

Are there two journals? Are there two men claiming to be Bennett? And does Hunter have a close personal connection with the man he is . . . hunting? Original and unrepeatable, the book includes nods to Chesterton, Carter Dickson and Philip MacDonald's little-known whodunit *The Wraith* (1931), but its anticlimactic nature is summed up in the final lines, with a risky, taunting irony: 'Yes, he's wasted a lot of time on Bennett, all right. But then, he won't be the only one.'

Borges enthusiasts rebuked Julian Symons for omitting the Argentinian man of letters from the first edition of *Bloody Murder*, only to be slapped down when he revised the book: 'Major Borges tales . . . are similar to minor ones in convincing or amusing only on the level of jokes . . . games played by a writer amusing himself with the *idea* of the puzzle rather than making an effort to construct one.'

Symons feared that Borges and his disciples were attempting 'to destroy the crime story from within'. Perhaps he disapproved of Borges' fascination with the Golden Age puzzles, for which *Bloody Murder* sought to provide an obituary. One reason why Eco's *The Name of the Rose* (1980) enjoyed widespread popularity as well as critical acclaim was precisely because enthusiasm for the game-playing tradition of the Golden Age lives on.

There is a limit to the number of new games that any novelist, however imaginative, is able to play with the genre. Moonlighting from his day job as a movie critic, David Thomson wrote *Suspects* (1985), an ingenious 'life of crime' for film noir fans. Eighty-five biographical sketches of characters such as Waldo Lydecker from *Laura* and Dix Steele from *In a Lonely Place* disclose a host of unlikely connections and coincidences. An overarching storyline gradually emerges from the shadows. A map and family tree help to cast light on the contrivances.

It is hardly surprising that postmodernists such as Thomson and Paul Auster, author of *The New York Trilogy* (1987), have only dabbled in crime fiction. Even those supreme innovators of the Golden Age, Christie and Berkeley, wrote more orthodox mysteries than mould-breaking novels such as *And Then There Were None* and *The Poisoned Chocolates Case*. Yet in the twenty-first century, writers from across the world continue, consciously or otherwise, to take forward Borges' ideas and methods.

José Carlos Somoza, whose parents emigrated from Cuba to Spain when he was young, emphasised playfulness in *The Athenian Murders* (2000). In ancient Greece, the body of a young student, apparently mauled by a pack of wolves, is found on a mountain slope. The dead man's tutor consults Heracles Pontor, the 'Decipherer of Enigmas', but as their investigation proceeds, another mystery emerges – in the footnotes to the text. The unnamed translator becomes convinced that a message is concealed in the original narrative, and soon his own life is in jeopardy. The device would have delighted Borges.

Traces of Borges' influence can be detected in the recent fiction of Scottish author Graeme Macrae Burnet[22] and also in books *about* crime novels, such as *The Truth about the Harry Quebert Affair*[23] (2012), by Switzerland's Joël Dicker, and *Twisted* (2019), by Ireland's Steve Cavanagh.[24] Borges himself pops up in Gordon McAlpine's *Holmes Entangled*[25] (2018), discovering a manuscript handwritten by Sherlock Holmes in a novel that examines quantum theory.

In *Pulped* (2017), Timothy Hallinan[26] gives the Californian private-eye novel a Borgesian makeover. In the 1990s, Hallinan produced half a dozen novels about the erudite gumshoe Simeon Grist before his publisher dropped the series. Grist was consigned to limbo, only for it to dawn on him that someone else invented his life and the cases he recalls so vividly. Soon he finds himself investigating crime in 'the real world' . . .

Far from being destroyed by Borgesian anti-detective fiction, the crime novel takes in its stride subversion and experiment, just as it shrugs off critical derision, hostility and censorship. Thanks to the centrality of the genre's concerns to contemporary culture,[27] it flourishes across the globe as today's writers[28] explore its infinite possibilities.

Notes

The main sources are Donald A. Yates' anthology *Latin Blood*, Darrell B. Lockhart's *Latin American Mystery Writers: An A-to-Z Guide*, Borges' *Conversations*, Francis M. Nevins' obituary of Yates for *Mystery File*, 2 February 2018, David Lehman's *The Perfect Murder*, Stefano Tani's *The Doomed Detective*, and *The Poetics of Murder*, edited by Glenn W. Most and William W. Stowe.

1 *Victoria Ocampo*: Her sister Silvina later married Bioy-Casares. Graham Greene dedicated *The Honorary Consul*, which is set in Corrientes, to her; Ocampo introduced him to Borges, who rhapsodised about Chesterton and Robert Louis Stevenson from the moment they met.
2 *The series proved successful and influential*: From 1947, Portugal's paperback imprint Coleção Vampiro made a similar splash. Leading writers often translated mysteries written in English, while members of the Second Surrealist Movement supplied the cover artwork. The books were skilfully marketed on a large scale.

3   *home-grown mysteries which used Golden Age tropes to make sly comments
     about the state of Argentina*: Prime examples were a novel co-written by
     Bioy-Casares and his wife Silvina Ocampo, *Where There's Love, There's
     Hate*, set in a seaside hotel at Bosque del Mar, and Manuel Peyrou's *Thunder
     of the Roses*, set in an imaginary country in the grip of an authoritarian
     regime. Borges had met Peyrou in the early 1930s, and encouraged his
     interest in the genre.

4   *Alain Robbe-Grillet*: In Julian Symons' view, 'Robbe-Grillet is interested in
     the technique and minutiae of detection, not its ultimate end.' Frank Kermode
     makes an intriguing comparison between Wallas, the detective in Robbe-
     Grillet's *The Erasers*, and Philip Trent in *Trent's Last Case*: Wallas 'goes
     much more seriously wrong than Trent . . . Trent masters most of the clues;
     the clues master Wallas'. Michael Holquist has argued that: 'If Robbe-Grillet
     knew more about the history of detective fiction, he would not have chosen
     the type of tale he does . . . He would rather have chosen the four [crime
     dossiers] . . . published by Dennis Wheatley and J. G. Links . . . these
     long-forgotten toys provide an easily grasped metaphor for certain essential
     characteristics of recent experimental fiction.' The Kermode and Holquist
     essays appear in *The Poetics of Murder*.

5   *his metafiction became increasingly influential*: His admirers include Michel
     Foucault and John Barth. In Jean-Luc Godard's *Alphaville*, Lemmy Caution
     seeks to outwit a malevolent computer by writing poetry inspired by Borges.

6   *María Angélica Bosco*: Bosco was born in 1909, but when *Death Going
     Down* won the Emecé Prize, she celebrated by 'rejuvenating' herself. She
     reimagined her birth year as 1917, and lived to ninety-seven.

7   *Because she was a woman*: Women crime writers were slower to come to
     the fore in Latin America than in Britain or the US. Among the most prolific
     was Mexico's María Elvira Bermúdez, whose major series characters were
     Armando H. Zozaya, and the detective writer Maria Elena Moran.

8   *'Argentina's Agatha Christie'*: Comparisons between writers, detectives and
     their more famous colleagues are commonplace if often wildly optimistic.
     In the early twentieth century, Chile's Alberto Edwards wrote mysteries
     about Roman Calvo, supposedly 'the Chilean Sherlock Holmes'.

9   *Guillermo Martínez*: *The Oxford Murders* was filmed in 2008. Martinez,
     who published a book about Borges and mathematics, acknowledged in a
     reader's guide to his *The Book of Murder* that Borges casts 'an intimidating
     shadow for many writers in my country . . . in general, Argentinean writers
     are not satisfied if they don't try some kind of rupture of the genre along
     the way.'

10   *murder and mathematics*: Catherine Shaw's *The Three-Body Problem*, set
     in Cambridge in 1888, finds Vanessa Duncan, a schoolmistress, investigating
     the murder of a mathematician who was studying Newton's 'n-body problem'.
     The Shaw name masks the identity of Leila Schneps, an American math-
     ematician specialising in number theory. Desmond Cory's *The Strange
     Attractor*, aka *The Catalyst*, introduced John Dobie, a professor who solves
     murders by applying laws of mathematics and probability. Mathematical
     connections to the detective story are discussed in John T. Irwin's *The
     Mystery to a Solution: Poe, Borges, and the Analytical Detective Story*, an
     erudite tome, although scarcely light reading.

11   *distrust of the police is ubiquitous*: In a blog post for Influx Press discussing

Bosco in 2016, Ben Bollig quotes Carlos Gamerro's claim that 'the "whodunit" is doomed to struggle in his country. There is a simple reason for this. In Argentina, if there is an unsolved murder, everyone assumes, or maybe knows, that the police or the military did it.' This melancholy view led Gamerro to offer ten rules, in the manner of Ronald Knox, for the crime story in Argentina, the first being: 'The police commit the crime.'

12 *Manuel Vázquez Montalbán*: A gourmet, like Carvalho, he wrote a history of Catalan cuisine. His admirers included the Italian writers Leonardo Sciascia and Andrea Camilleri. Camilleri's Sicilian detective bears distinct similarities to Carvalho, and is named Montalbano in tribute to the Spanish writer. The TV series *Montalbano* was so successful that Camilleri's home town, Porto Empedocle, on which the fictional Vigata was based, changed its name to Porto Empedocle Vigata.

13 *reflecting his ideology and tendency to sermonise*: The Marxist critic Ernest Mandel was not impressed, concluding in *Delightful Murder* that: 'In general all Montalban's books are soaked in an atmosphere of spleen, scepticism and fin-de-siècle ennui . . . It is a break with Stalinist dogmatism and hypocrisy, but hardly a step towards greater lucidity of what this society and this world are all about.'

14 *European writers whose criminal ventures owe a debt to Borges*: Stefano Tani argues in *The Doomed Detective* that Borges and Robbe-Grillet, along with Russia's Vladimir Nabokov (in *The Real Life of Sebastian Knight*) and Italy's Carlo Emilio Gadda (in *That Awful Mess on Via Merulana*), 'wreck the pattern of mannerly order and reassurance characteristic of the British detective novel', and describes these authors, none of them crime specialists, as producing 'anti-detective novels'. However, Tani does not examine books by Christie, Berkeley and other British Golden Age novelists, which also defy genre conventions. Tani cites Leonardo Sciascia's *Todo Modo* (which references *And Then There Were None*), William Hjortsberg's *Falling Angel* (filmed as *Angel Heart*) and Thomas Pynchon's *The Crying of Lot 49* as 'deconstructive anti-detective fiction . . . characterised by a more ambiguous perception of reality from the point of view of the detective'.

15 *Friedrich Dürrenmatt*: In *The Perfect Murder*, David Lehman claims that Borges 'is the most radical of detective story writers . . . because he was the first to proclaim the death of the detective – an event comparable in local significance to Nietzsche's pronouncement that God was dead.' Lehman sees Dürrenmatt's *The Pledge* as a variation on the theme of 'Death and the Compass'.

16 *Umberto Eco*: A key character in *The Name of the Rose*, Jorge of Burgos, is blind, like Borges, and works as a librarian; Borges served as director of Argentina's national library. Themes and images drawn from Borges pervade the story. Jorge is a sinister figure, but Eco told Lehman: 'I love Borges, Borges is not Jorge, and the ambiguities that are generated by the text seemed to me as a sort of contribution to the Borgesian poetics of ambiguity.'

17 *Arturo Pérez-Reverte*: *The Flanders Panel* was made into a British film, *Uncovered*, while *The Club Dumas*, a book packed with literary references (to Dumas, Conan Doyle, Paul Féval and Patricia Highsmith among others), was filmed by Roman Polanski as *The Ninth Gate*.

18 *The Shadow of the Wind*: Michael Dirda said of the novel: 'Try to imagine

a blend of Grand Guignol thriller, historical fiction, occasional farce, existential mystery and passionate love story; then double it' (*Washington Post*, 25 April 2004).

19 *Desmond Cory*: Cory's real name was Shaun McCarthy, whose series about the secret agent Johnny Fedora pre-dates James Bond. Cory's *The Circe Complex* became a six-part TV series. His heist thriller *Deadfall* was filmed with a changed ending and a cameo role for John Barry, who ranks alongside Bernard Herrmann as the finest composer of music for crime films.

20 *Bennett*: Edmund Crispin described the book in *The Sunday Times* of 14 August 1977 as: 'Strange, often perplexing . . . an attempt to do something genuinely new with the crime story'.

21 *It begins with an illusion*: This trick was not repeated in the US edition. Miles Tripp's *A Man Without Friends*, televised in 1972, bears a message from the supposed author to his readers on the *back* cover of the dust jacket. Its significance only becomes clear at the end of the story. The idea is clever, but stretched beyond its natural length.

22 *Graeme Macrae Burnet*: *His Bloody Project* was shortlisted for the Man Booker Prize. Macrae Burnet's admiration for Simenon is evident from books such as *The Accident on the A35*. In a positive review, Mark Lawson suggested Macrae Burnet experiments with 'false true crime' but wondered if postmodernism means 'never having to say you're sloppy' (*Guardian*, 10 November 2017).

23 *The Truth about the Harry Quebert Affair*: This prize-winning doorstop of a book left Sam Leith underwhelmed: 'many critics . . . see a masterpiece; I see a completely ordinary, amiably cartoonish and well aerated page-turner that does nothing interesting in literary terms at all' (*Guardian*, 24 April 2014).

24 *Steve Cavanagh*: Cavanagh's books about American attorney Eddie Flynn include *Thirteen*, which features a serial killer as a member of a jury. Flynn is name-checked in *Twisted* but does not appear.

25 *Gordon McAlpine's Holmes Entangled*: McAlpine's other postmodernist ventures included *Woman with a Blue Pencil*, described by Joyce Carol Oates as a book that 'Kafka, Borges, and Nabokov, as well as Dashiell Hammett, would have appreciated' and, as Owen Fitzstephen, *Hammett Unwritten*.

26 *Timothy Hallinan*: Hallinan has also written a series of thrillers set in Bangkok and another featuring the burglar (and private eye) Junior Bender.

27 *the centrality of the genre's concerns to contemporary culture*: As Michael Dibdin says in *The Picador Book of Crime Writing*, the genre provided 'a perfect vehicle for Robbe-Grillet's subversive experiments, as it did for Sjöwall and Wahlöö's political critique'.

28 *today's writers*: Such as Malcolm Pryce, whose Chandleresque novels are set in an alternative universe version of Aberystwyth, Stuart Turton, author of *The Seven Deaths of Evelyn Hardcastle*, and Alex Pavesi, author of *Eight Detectives*, aka *The Eighth Detective*.

THIRTY-NINE

Bloody Murder

Julian Symons and crime fiction criticism

On Guy Fawkes' Night in 1953, two authors met for the first time over tea and corned beef sandwiches at the National Liberal Club in London. One of them, John Creasey, had convened a meeting of fellow crime writers with a view to forming a professional association. Among the dozen people who turned up was Julian Symons.

Creasey was an ebullient man whose limp was the legacy of a childhood attack of polio; he'd conquered the disease with the same single-mindedness that characterised everything he did. The son of an impoverished coach-maker, and the seventh of nine children, he took a series of low-paid jobs while he tried to fulfil his ambition of becoming a published writer. He claimed that he received 743 rejection slips before the first acceptance. After that, there was no stopping him.[1] Soon he was earning enough as a writer to give up working as a grocer's clerk.

Symons came from a modest background, and had also overcome a disability, in his case a severe stammer, but although he shared Creasey's capacity for hard work, they had little in common. Creasey brimmed with bonhomie, while Symons admitted that his manner could be 'truculent, awkward, and intellectually snobbish'.[2]

Their political outlooks also differed: Creasey was a Liberal, while Symons had flirted with Trotskyism before disillusionment set in.

Creasey wrote straightforward light entertainment, but Symons had serious literary pretensions. In the 1930s, he'd founded the magazine *Twentieth Century Verse*, and his circle included George Orwell;[3] the two of them were 'premature anti-Stalinists, deprecating the myths of the virtuous Soviet Union long before it was fashionable to do so'. After the war, he'd published a handful of light detective stories before turning to psychological suspense. Thanks to a recommendation by Orwell, he'd also become a reviewer.

That evening in the National Liberal Club, Creasey persuaded Symons and the others of the benefits they'd gain from promoting their work in collaboration. The upshot was the formation of the Crime Writers' Association; Symons became a founder member and Creasey the Chairman.

Symons regarded Creasey as 'a constantly whirling dynamo', to whom ideas came as naturally as breathing. Creasey understood the value of publicity, for himself and for the CWA. To boost membership numbers of the fledgling organisation, he enrolled under each of his many pen-names. The CWA followed the MWA's lead by giving awards. Independently judged, they became known as the Daggers and remain Britain's most prestigious crime-writing accolades.[4]

Creasey even arranged a crime exhibition at a London department store, displaying weapons used in famous cases. Borrowing an idea from Georges Simenon, he proposed that he be shut up in a glass-sided box in the store, so that people could watch him starting a new book, to be completed before the exhibition closed a few days later. This stunt was abandoned, for fear that showing a book written so fast might provoke doubts about its quality.

'I try to keep myself down to writing twelve books a year,' Creasey told Symons on one occasion. 'It's no good, I can't do it. I write fourteen.'

The unlikely friendship ripened, and Creasey was thrilled when Symons gave a positive notice to one of his novels about Scotland Yard's George Gideon. When Creasey stepped down as Chair of the CWA, his successors were appointed for terms of one year;

Bruce Graeme replaced him, and then Symons took over in 1958. In the same year, following in the footsteps of Sayers and Milward Kennedy, Symons became crime reviewer for *The Sunday Times*.

Creasey still cringed at the memory of Sayers' devastating (but funny) evisceration[5] in that newspaper of his novel *First Came a Murder* (1934): 'the thriller with all its gorgeous absurdities full-blown . . . the English . . . [is] of that curious hit-or-miss variety in which, if you cannot think of the right word, anything vaguely approximated in sound will serve'. Symons' new role gave him, in Creasey's eyes, the opportunity to be more helpful to his friends.

Symons took a different view. He aimed 'to make distinctions in my column, to abandon the alkaline flatness of most writing about crime stories in favour of something sharper, sometimes even picric. The good should be praised, the eccentric tolerated, the bad excoriated, especially if a well-regarded name was on the title page.'

Creasey was shocked, but Symons remained adamant: 'That different levels of writing existed was something John did not understand, and that his books should stay unreviewed, or be reviewed caustically, really upset him.' Punctilious in separating his literary judgements from his personal relationships, Symons was naive enough to think that others could do so with similar ease. In the end, it became too much for Creasey. He tabled a resolution to expel Symons from the CWA until such time as he reviewed in a more collegial spirit.

Val Gielgud was now in the chair. Hands shaking, he implored Creasey to withdraw the motion. Creasey responded by reading out a long account of Symons' alleged misdemeanours. His motion was rejected, and, less than a year later, he resigned from the board of the association, which without him would never have existed. Like the Detection Club and the MWA, however, it continues to flourish, providing crime writers with invaluable support.

Creasey wasn't the only author whose books were scarred by splashes of Symons' critical acid. In 1962, Bruce Graeme published *The Undetective*,[6] narrated by mid-list crime writer Iain Carter. The book features scenes set at CWA meetings and name-checks Edward Grierson, Margot Bennett, Christianna Brand and Michael

Gilbert. At the end of the story, Carter reads Symons' review column:

> I grimaced. Symons hadn't been kind to me:
> 'That Iain Carter's *One Hundred Days Since* appears among the *Best of the Week* is fortuitous, due to the recent printers' strike. Only five crime novels were published last week.'

*

The youngest of seven children, Julian Gustave Symons was the son of a Jewish immigrant who had changed his name to Morris Albert Symons and kept a second-hand shop. Julian never discovered his father's real name, or even which country he'd come from. This mystery about his origins may help to explain the obsessional fascination with masks that runs through many of his stories, either in the form of a disguise or an impersonation – as with Arthur Brownjohn's double life in *The Man Who Killed Himself*[7] (1967) – or to signify the social veneers concealing an impulse to commit crime.

At fourteen Symons left school, and took an office job in an engineering business; this experience helped him to create credible workplace settings in his fiction, but he began with poetry. He socialised with fellow poets, including Roy Fuller and Ruthven Todd,[8] both of whom also dabbled in crime writing. Todd's involvement with the London International Surrealist Exhibition of 1936 gave him an idea for a zany murder mystery, which Symons wrote up. The final version included a character caricaturing Todd. Symons did nothing with it, but six years later his wife found the typescript, on green paper yellowing at the edges, and persuaded him to submit it to a publisher.

Victor Gollancz published *The Immaterial Murder Case* (1945), about an art movement called Immaterialism (you painted only what wasn't there), with a critic's corpse found nestling inside a hinged egg-like sculpture. Todd was infuriated by Symons' caricature of him. Partly because of this, partly because he decided it was a bad book, Symons eventually refused to allow it to be republished.

A job in advertising gave him the background for *The Thirty-*

First of February (1950), the first of his books to explore the nature of guilt and innocence, and to chart progressive mental disintegration. The paradoxes and uncertainties of post-war life are reflected in the notion of a date that doesn't exist – the 31st of February. This decisive change of direction was summed up in Symons' credo: 'a crime story can have the depth and subtlety of characterisation, the moral and social point, of . . . a "straight" novel.'

In Symons' novels, violence often springs from the pressures of urban living. Typically, his murderers go in search of a new life, only to find they are chasing an illusion. He fretted about his 'inability to produce a satisfactory climactic scene, which I know to be a failing transcended only in a few stories', and his refusal to write a conventional series came at a cost. For all his superiority to John Creasey as a literary stylist, his books sold in the thousands, Creasey's in the millions. Compensation came in the form of critical garlands; he was 'perhaps the most honoured crime writer of the second half of the twentieth century'.[9]

Real-life crimes and the ambiguities of justice[10] fascinated Symons. *The Progress of a Crime* (1960) was based on a teenager's murder in Clapham that highlighted the unreliability of eyewitness evidence. *The Players and the Game* (1972) integrated a clever puzzle with a dark account of a *folie à deux* killing partnership suggestive of the Fernandez and Beck case in America and Britain's Brady and Hindley.

He channelled Francis Iles in *The Man Who Killed Himself*, which begins: 'In the end Arthur Brownjohn killed himself, but in the beginning he made up his mind to murder his wife.' *The Man Whose Dreams Came True* (1968) displays the same Ilesian blend of cynicism, wit and ingenuity. For *The Man Who Lost His Wife* (1970), Symons took his lead from Patricia Highsmith, but the brew of psychological study and satire was too thin. For all his emphasis on character as the key to writing a good novel, his stories needed a crafty plot to liberate his imagination.

Irked by Sherlockian fandom, which he thought denigrated Conan Doyle so as to exalt Holmes, he made his feelings plain in a lecture to the Sherlock Holmes Society of London. Realising too late the offence he'd caused, he atoned with a novel that paid

tribute to the sage of Baker Street, featuring an actor who tries
to solve puzzles by Holmesian methods. When Symons confided
to Ngaio Marsh ('the most beautiful and most charming woman
crime writer I have ever met') that he couldn't think of a title, she
came up with *A Three-Pipe Problem*.

His breadth of reading gave him a grasp of the tricks of the
crime-writing trade,[11] and his novels remained inventive. In 1976,
he and his wife suffered a cruel blow when their daughter died
at the age of twenty. Her death coincided with the arrival in England
of Ken Millar, who told Eudora Welty that he found himself 'walking
the London streets, and trying to come to terms with Julian's loss
and the memory of Linda's death seven years ago. Perhaps one
never does come to terms with these matters.'

Symons escaped from misery into Victoriana. The Croydon
Poisonings were reworked for *The Blackheath Poisonings* (1978),
while *Sweet Adelaide* (1980) fictionalised the Pimlico Mystery. After
Adelaide Bartlett was acquitted of killing her husband by admin-
istering chloroform, it was famously said that 'in the interests of
science, she should now say how she did it'; Symons' explanation
of what happened is ingenious, if impossible to prove.

Symons wrote poetry, social and military history, biography, literary
criticism and true crime,[12] and even published a crime and detection quiz. But he is undervalued as a novelist[13] because his fiction
has been overshadowed by the success of *Bloody Murder*. The
first edition of his history of the genre appeared in 1972.

He wasn't crime fiction's first historian. Régis Messac published
a study in France as early as 1929, while, in the English language,
the most important was *Murder for Pleasure* by the American
Howard Haycraft, for whom 'The crime in a detective story is only
the means to an end which is – detection.'

Symons claimed that 'the psychological reason for the weakening
of the detective story in recent years is a weakening in the sense
of sin'. His subtitle *From the Detective Story to the Crime Novel:
A History*, reflected his overarching thesis: 'The detective story
has changed into the crime novel . . . the detective story is an
inferior thing to the crime novel, but it has wholly individual merits
for all except the most priggish.'

He argued that detective writers prioritised puzzling the reader, whereas 'the crime novelist is most often a fictionally split personality.[14] Half of him wants to write a novel about people affected by crime, but the other half yearns to produce a baffling mystery. This split down the middle is very evident in Chandler's own work.' For Chandler, compromise was inherent in the genre, but Symons disagreed: 'When the fusion of characterisation and puzzle is perfect, as in *The Glass Key*, you have books produced in the form of crime novels that have a claim to be considered as works of art.'

Chandler dodged the question when asked to identify the best mystery writer, saying there were 'too many types . . . You have to agree on definitions and standards'. Symons reckoned that reaching agreement was impossible, but insisted that treating writers as gifted as Poe and Faulkner alongside 'hacks with clever ideas' debased 'all criminal coinage'. In other words, he wanted to justify excoriating 'the bad' in his reviews. The snag is that judging a book to be bad suggests universally accepted objective standards. Distinguishing between Shakespeare and Spillane is easy enough, but away from the extremes, opinions will diverge, often sharply. Symons was forced to concede that there is no escaping that most unpredictable of factors, personal taste.

Bloody Murder led to Symons being branded by traditionalists as a scourge of the Golden Age.[15] They were outraged by his habit of stigmatising their favourite writers as Humdrums. The ghosts of all the dead Marxists, socialists and liberals[16] who wrote whodunits must also tremble at being airbrushed from history by his careless claim that 'almost all the British writers of the twenties and thirties . . . were unquestionably right-wing'.

At least he enjoyed Agatha Christie, noting the underappreciated darker side to her imagination. He liked to tell a story of arriving late for a Detection Club dinner at the Moulin d'Or restaurant in Soho. Christie studied him quietly, and he became aware that he'd forgotten to clean his hands. He wondered if he'd given her an idea for a story: *A man comes to table – his hands are grubby . . . faintly marked with some kind of stain – yet half a dozen people are prepared to say he spent the whole day in his office.*

He admired Anthony Berkeley's detective fiction, especially *The Poisoned Chocolates Case* and *Trial and Error*, although he bestowed his highest accolades on the first two Francis Iles novels, for their characterisation, realism and 'the masterly way in which they broke away from the conventions'.

When it came to Sayers, he admitted finding it difficult to assess her work fairly. They were never soulmates. Academically, Symons was Sayers' equal, but he was acutely conscious of his lack of a university education, and her boundless devotion to Oxford probably grated. Of her writing about the genre, he said, 'Everything she says calls for respect, even though some of it may prompt disagreement.' The same can be said of his own opinions. Like Sayers, he prided himself on the integrity of his literary criticism, and like Sayers, he sometimes lacked sensitivity for fellow writers' feelings. For all their differences, he and she shared an uncompromising determination to tell the truth as they saw it, regardless of the risk of causing hurt. This provoked people who disagreed with them to accuse Sayers of snobbery and Symons of arrogance.

Having praised Sayers' craftsmanship, and her incisive mind, Symons flayed her novels: 'there can be no doubt that . . . she was pompous and boring.[17] Every book contains an enormous amount of padding . . .' Bruised by criticism from Sayers fans, Symons adjusted his remarks when revising *Bloody Murder*, and acknowledged that many women readers 'adore' Wimsey, and regarded his analysis as unjust.

The challenge facing anyone rash enough to write a book about the crime genre as a whole is how to integrate a mass of disparate material into something vaguely coherent. In *Bloody Murder*, Symons followed a broadly chronological approach before bolting on a comparison of detective story and crime novel, a short history of the spy story and a set of predictions for the future.

Among women writers, he championed Patricia Highsmith and Margaret Millar. He also praised their leading British counterparts, whose careers proved shorter. Margot Bennett's[18] *The Widow of Bath* (1952) benefits from an evocative setting in a run-down post-war seaside resort as well as Chandleresque wit and ingenious plotting. *The Man Who Didn't Fly* (1955), nominated for the best-novel award on both sides of the Atlantic, offers a puzzle about which man, of a group of four scheduled passengers on a flight which crashed with no survivors, failed to get on board – and why. Her next novel, *Someone from the Past* (1958), won the CWA Gold Dagger, but was also her last.

Shelley Smith's[19] high achievements also gave way to loss of gusto. Her detective Jacob Chaos lasted only two books, and she experimented with various types of story: the woman-in-jeopardy mystery, the impossible crime, ironic psychological crime fiction and the novel of character based on a real-life murder case.[20] *An Afternoon to Kill* (1953) was a tour de force with a remarkable ending, but after publishing *The Lord Have Mercy*, an accomplished story of psychological suspense, in 1956, she managed only three more novels in the next twenty-two years.

Mary Kelly's career followed a similar curve. In a review, Symons described her Gold Dagger-winning novel *The Spoilt Kill*[21] as 'the product of something seen and felt by a writer of individual sensibility', but in later books her writing became too elliptical to retain mass appeal. After 1974, she published no more novels, although she lived until 2017 and began writing a new mystery a few years before her death.

Like contemporaries such as Bennett, Smith, Millar, Highsmith and Symons, Kelly found the constraints of writing about series detectives unduly restrictive. But writing stand-alone mysteries of a consistently high standard, coming up with a fresh set of characters, settings and situations each time, can sap an author's imagination and energy. When P. D. James and Ruth Rendell first emerged in the early 1960s, they went back to basics, introducing police detectives who proceeded to enjoy long and successful careers.

Bloody Murder included a chapter titled 'Big Producers and Big Sellers, Curiosities and Singletons'. This random assortment of snippets about individual authors and books contained much information that, in the pre-internet age, was unfamiliar and intriguing, as with 'the detective story to end all detective stories', *The Face on the Cutting-Room Floor*[22] (1937) by Cameron McCabe. Among twentieth-century novels, Symons highlighted Robert Player's *The*

Ingenious Mr Stone (1945), John Mair's[23] 'intellectual thriller' *Never Come Back* (1941), Miles Tripp's[24] *Kilo Forty* (1963) and Gerald Heard's[25] eccentric Sherlockian pastiche *A Taste for Honey* (1941).

Bloody Murder was widely acclaimed. Thirteen years later, Symons published an updated edition; a third and final version appeared twenty years after the original, and its preface made clear that the book was 'meant for reading, consultation, argument, reasoned contradiction'. The subtle change in emphasis was as close as Symons came to acknowledging an inconsistency between the black-and-white nature of some of his judgements and a frank admission that the book reflected his personal preferences. His revisions hinted at a degree of mellowing, but he remained content to be unfashionably judgemental at a time when he felt outnumbered by 'popularising Philistines'.

In a 'Postscript for the Nineties' to the third edition, he applauded writers whose talent had blossomed, such as Rendell, James, Reginald Hill and Peter Lovesey, but gave some writers then in vogue as fierce a kicking as he had administered to Sayers and the Humdrums. Derek Raymond's[26] books, for instance, were 'repulsive . . . the blood, guts and excrement are detailed in a way that, fortunately, becomes ludicrous.'

Nor were US bestsellers spared the lash. James Ellroy's and Andrew Vachss'[27] 'blood-simple books bear the same relation to the best American crime writing of the period that the Sexton Blake or Nick Carter stories bear to Wilkie Collins and Charles Dickens'. As for the global bestseller *The Silence of the Lambs* (1988), it was 'the literary equivalent of a video-nasty . . . a very unpleasant book pandering to a recent desire for the detailed description of sexual crime'. In writing about his serial killer Hannibal Lecter, Thomas Harris[28] became 'admiring, at times awestruck . . . [and] often descends to the Ellroy–Vachss level of cliché'.

Elmore Leonard's writing suffered a less brutal assault, but Symons delivered a lukewarm verdict on 'a street-smart writer . . . [whose] eminence has been thrust upon him by publishers, journalists, follow-my-leader critics'. He had kinder words for Canada's Howard Engel and Eric Wright,[29] but 'elsewhere little sparkles'. Paul Auster's *New York Trilogy*[30] was 'written in a self-congratulatory way that is deeply disagreeable'.

Readers who took as gospel Symons' opinions about Golden Age novels, which were, at the time, long out of print, may have been shocked by his scathing condemnation of so many modish crime writers. The authors themselves probably felt a spurt of sympathy for John Creasey.

Notes

Symons described his relationship with Creasey in *Criminal Practices*. The other main sources are his autobiographical notes and comments on his work in the bibliography by Walsdorf and Allen, as well as *Julian Symons at 80*, edited by Patricia Craig, his reviews in *The Sunday Times*, his various writings about the genre, and Rosemary Herbert's *The Fatal Art of Entertainment*.

1   *there was no stopping him*: Creasey wrote so much, under more than twenty names, that estimates of his total output remain speculative; he published over six hundred books. His typewriter had three special keys that facilitated writing dialogue by enabling him to type single and double quotation marks and exclamation points without shifting the carriage. He set up the *John Creasey Mystery Magazine*, and ran a literary agency and a publishing business. In spare moments, he married four times, stood regularly for Parliament and even founded his own political party.

2   *his manner could be 'truculent, awkward, and intellectually snobbish'*: Christianna Brand complained about him at length in unpublished correspondence with Robert Barnard, whose *A Hovering of Vultures* included a waspish caricature of Symons, but the warmth of the posthumous tributes in *Julian Symons Remembered* was genuine. Much earlier, Ross Macdonald said in a letter to Eudora Welty that 'apart from a couple of recognised saints, Julian is the best man I know.'

3   *George Orwell*: Charles Garden, in Symons' thriller *The Broken Penny*, was distantly based on Orwell.

4   *Britain's most prestigious crime-writing accolades*: Nevertheless, receipt even of a Gold Dagger for the year's best novel is no guarantee of literary immortality. B. M. Gill, who turned from romantic suspense to crime in her late fifties, won the award for *The Twelfth Juror*, and was twice nominated for an Edgar, but soon faded from view. Joan Fleming won two Gold Daggers, published novels for thirty years, and saw *The Deeds of Mr Deadcert* filmed as *Rx Murder*. Dorothy B. Hughes, among others, heaped superlatives on her writing. Yet she is routinely overlooked by critics. Her determination to vary her approach was admirable, but led to peaks and troughs in quality. Peter Dickinson's first two books won Gold Daggers, but he is mainly remembered as an author of children's fiction.

5   *Creasey still cringed at the memory of Sayers' devastating . . . evisceration*: He talked about it in an interview with Herbert Brean (*LIFE*, 27 April 1962).

6   *The Undetective*: Carter is a modestly successful author who hits the big-time after writing a crime novel under a secret pen-name. The plot thickens once his alter ego becomes a murder suspect.

7   *The Man Who Killed Himself*: The novel was turned into an obscure comedy
    film, *Arthur? Arthur! The Narrowing Circle* was also filmed, again without
    making an impact.

8   *Ruthven Todd*: Under the name R. T. Campbell, Todd dashed off eight novels
    before deserting detective stories and writing *Space Cat* books for children.
    His Professor John Stubbs, who resembles 'a caricature of G. K. Chesterton
    trying to look like Buddha', is a poor man's Sir Henry Merrivale. Todd moved
    to the US in 1947 and joined the MWA. When he could no longer afford
    the subscriptions, Raymond Chandler paid them for him.

9   *perhaps the most honoured crime writer of the second half of the twentieth
    century*: 'It rarely feels like that,' he said in Walsdorf and Allen's bibliog-
    raphy, 'but when the various awards are added up, perhaps it is true . . .
    I have valued particularly the Presidency of the Detection Club . . . and the
    Grand Master Award from the Mystery Writers of America.'

10 *the ambiguities of justice*: The trial scenes in Symons' books benefited from
    the advice of Michael Evelyn, to whom he dedicated *The Colour of Murder*.
    Evelyn, who became Assistant Director of Public Prosecutions, wrote more
    than forty detective novels under the name Michael Underwood, making
    regular use of his legal expertise. Evelyn was gay, and for most of his life
    homosexuality was illegal; the discretion that became a way of life for him
    also prompted a certain restraint in his fiction. *The Crime of Colin Wise*,
    for instance, is an interesting inverted mystery, but Wise is unappealing and
    so the reader doesn't care enough about what will happen to him.

11 *the tricks of the crime-writing trade*: Despite his reservations about tradi-
    tional detection, Symons produced a long series of stories for newspapers
    and magazines featuring a private investigator, Francis Quarles; they were
    written purely for money. The same was true of serials for the *Evening
    Standard* featuring celebrities such as James Mason and Gilbert Harding.
    In a much more sophisticated way, Symons' later novels, in addition to
    examining social mores, frequently employ tricky plot devices with a Christie-
    like cunning that has often been overlooked. *The Criminal Comedy of the
    Contented Couple*, aka *A Criminal Comedy*, for instance, combines a satiric
    picture of the English bourgeoisie with an ingenious plot featuring poison-
    pen letters; disguise and impersonation; an amateur detective who beats
    the official police to the solution; and a modern version of the 'challenge to
    the reader', not to mention a dark final twist that Francis Iles might have
    admired.

12 *true crime*: *A Reasonable Doubt* was a collection of essays about unsolved
    mysteries, of which he said: 'Except in the case of Evelyn Foster, I did no
    first-hand investigating, and the solutions offered are those of an armchair
    detective.'

13 *he is undervalued as a novelist*: Ross Macdonald, writing to Eudora Welty,
    captured the paradox of Symons' achievements when he said, 'I haven't
    found any one book in which his great talent shows itself fully, though I
    enjoy everything he writes.' There is a sense of detachment in Symons'
    fiction; perhaps an innate reserve prevented him from discarding his own
    mask.

14 *the crime novelist is most often a fictionally split personality*: Symons told
    Rosemary Herbert that the need to surprise the reader precluded even the
    best crime novels from achieving the highest literary standards. Sue Grafton,

Barbara Neely and Reginald Hill were among those who disagreed. As Hill said, 'every novel I've read doesn't tell you everything about the characters, not all at once!'

15 *a scourge of the Golden Age*: Because he understood crime fiction, his opinions carry more weight than those of Edmund Wilson, whose essays such as 'Who Cares Who Killed Roger Ackroyd?' rank with his attacks on Tolkien and H. P. Lovecraft for their lack of insight. As an investigator of popular fiction, Wilson was the Captain Hastings of literary critics.

16 *Marxists, socialists and liberals*: Such as Nicholas Blake, the Coles, Patrick and Bruce Hamilton, Raymond Postgate, Mary Agnes Hamilton, Ellen Wilkinson, Ivy Low Litvinov, Leonora Eyles, Christopher St John Sprigg, Lord Gorell, R. C. Woodthorpe, G. K. Chesterton, William Plomer, E. R. Punshon, Anthony Wynne, Nap Lombard (pen-name of Gordon Neil Stewart and Pamela Hansford Johnson) and Helen Simpson.

17 *there can be no doubt that . . . she was pompous and boring*: This confident assertion has often been disputed, not least by Michael Gilbert and P. D. James. Nicolas Freeling contributed an essay extolling the virtues of *Gaudy Night* to a volume celebrating Symons' eightieth birthday. He threw petrol on the flames by condemning Allingham's *The Tiger in the Smoke*, which Symons thought 'a thriller of the highest quality', as 'deplorable trash'.

18 *Margot Bennett*: Bennett, a fervent supporter of CND, also published *The Intelligent Woman's Guide to Atomic Radiation*; her TV scripts included soap operas and seven episodes of *Maigret*.

19 *Shelley Smith*: Francis Iles called her 'the English Patricia Highsmith'. Her real name was Nancy Hermione Bodington, and she too became a scriptwriter.

20 *the woman-in-jeopardy mystery, the impossible crime, ironic psychological crime fiction, and the novel of character based on a real-life murder case*: The main examples were, respectively, *Death Stalks a Lady, He Died of Murder!*, *The Man with a Calico Face* and *Come and Be Killed*, and *The Woman in the Sea*, based on the Rattenbury–Stoner case.

21 *Symons described her Gold Dagger-winning novel The Spoilt Kill*: In *The Sunday Times*, 9 April 1961.

22 *The Face on the Cutting-Room Floor*: Cameron McCabe was a pen-name for Ernst Wilhelm Julius Bornemann, and the novel is an extraordinary essay in postmodernism with an epilogue critiquing detective fiction. Jonathan Coe argues that it is 'a work of wild and desperate youthful romanticism' ('Whodunnit and Whowroteit', *Guardian*, 2 September 2016).

23 *John Mair*: The title of *Never Come Back* proved regrettably prophetic, since Mair was killed while serving in the RAF in 1942. George Orwell admired this thriller, a radical's version of the Buchanesque manhunt story; the closing words are: 'For what, after all, were two small murders in the midst of so much slaughter?'

24 *Miles Tripp*: Symons detected elements of Simenon and Highsmith in *Kilo Forty*, which he regarded as 'outstanding', but Tripp's work fluctuated too often in quality to attract the attention his inventiveness deserved. He created a private eye called John Samson; among his stand-alones, *Woman at Risk* is cleverly structured, while *Five Minutes with a Stranger* calls to mind the macabre sensationalism of Boileau and Narcejac.

25 *Gerald Heard*: Henry FitzGerald Heard, a British historian and writer who

moved to the US before the war, was an advocate for pacifism and psyche-delic drugs. *A Taste for Honey* (admired by Chandler and Nabokov) was filmed in 1966 as *The Deadly Bees*, with a script co-written by Robert Bloch; it prompted a swarm of 'beesploitation' movies, including *Invasion of the Bee Girls*, distantly based on an idea by Nicholas Meyer, but prudently disowned by him. Heard's eclectic body of work included 'The President of the United States, Detective', a prize-winning climate change story with a plot involving Soviet geoengineering; an expanded version, 'The Thaw Plan', is a story about global warming rather than a mystery.

26 *Derek Raymond*: Raymond was the pen-name of Robert William Arthur 'Robin' Cook, adopted to avoid confusion with the American author of *Coma* and other medical thrillers. He dropped out of Eton at seventeen to pursue a lifestyle that encompassed smuggling, writing pornography, a spell in a Spanish jail and five marriages. *He Died with His Eyes Open* was the first in the Factory series, narrated by an unnamed sergeant in the Department of Unexplained Deaths.

27 *Andrew Vachss*: An attorney, Vachss specialised in child protection, the dominant theme in his fiction.

28 *Thomas Harris*: After writing *Black Sunday*, a thriller, Harris produced four books featuring Hannibal Lecter over a period of a quarter of a century. *Cari Mora*, a stand-alone, appeared in 2019.

29 *Howard Engel and Eric Wright*: Engel created the private eye Benny Cooperman, and Wright the cop Charlie Salter. Engel suffered a stroke which left him unable to read but still able to write: in *The Memory Game*, Cooperman is similarly afflicted.

30 *Paul Auster's New York Trilogy*: Auster himself has said that the trilogy is 'rather crude' and that his later work is superior to his 'youthful texts'. See Inge Birgitte Siegumfeldt, 'Paul Auster', *LitHub*, 2 October 2017.

FORTY

People with Ghosts

Post-war private investigators and the legacy of Vietnam

Kenneth Millar was four years old when his father left home. Although the boy had been born in San Francisco, his parents were both Canadian, and they soon returned to Vancouver. Jack Millar was an unsuccessful writer and poet who became a sailor and piloted a harbour boat during the First World War. He and his Christian Scientist wife Annie separated, and, in 1920, Annie took her young son on the transcontinental train across the Rockies and the prairies. Their destination was Kitchener, her home town in Ontario.

Annie had no money, and she and her son were reduced to begging for food. When Ken was six, she took him to an orphanage, only for Jack's cousin and his wife to agree to look after him. At school, he bullied younger classmates, and at his guardians' home he'd discovered sex with the co-operation of a teenage maid, and indulged in petty theft. Reading was another form of escapism, and he discovered Edgar Wallace and Charles Dickens.

Ken was sent to Winnipeg to live with an affluent aunt. She paid for his education at a boarding school, where he gained an insight into how the other half lived. As well as continuing to steal, he started drinking and fighting with other boys; sometimes he had sex with them. His aunt lost her money in the Wall Street Crash, and, before long, he was back in Kitchener, reunited with his emotionally wrecked mother. He yearned to become a writer, but raged inwardly at the unfairness of life. One day he stole an armful of bestsellers from the local library, and dumped them into the sewer.

At the Kitchener-Waterloo Collegiate Institute, he edited the 1931 student annual, *The Grumbler*. He contributed a parody of Sherlock Holmes, his first printed fiction, and included a story by a fellow student, Margaret Sturm. He had a crush on her, and would secretly follow her to her home, although he never spoke to her.

A narrow escape from arrest woke him up to the need to do something positive with his life. He counted the rooms that he'd lived in up to the age of sixteen, and came up with a total of fifty. He gave up stealing, and had an affair with a girl which convinced him that he was heterosexual.

Jack Millar died at the age of fifty-nine. He'd made a mess of his life, but his parting gift was to leave the proceeds of his life assurance to Annie, whom he'd never divorced. She spent some of the money putting Ken through college. His fortunes had changed, but those harrowing early years left scars that never healed.

Ken Millar's mother died in 1936, and in the same year he decided to travel to Europe. Finally, he struck up a conversation with Margaret Sturm and invited her (much to her amazement) to accompany him to Ireland. She declined, but, following his return, they met again. Before long, they married.

Unexpected literary inspiration came from a lecture given by the Governor General of Canada, Lord Tweedsmuir. This was the title taken by John Buchan, 'a small, bright-eyed Scot, who wore the mantle of empire easily'. He told the story of the tortoise and the hare – but, in the Buchan version, the hare won the race. Ken took this moral to heart; he acquired a typewriter and set about writing short stories and sketches.

While teaching at the University of Michigan, Ken met W. H. Auden, and the poet's encouragement and love of detective stories[1] convinced the young academic that writing crime fiction did not amount to frittering away one's talents. During his naval service in 1944, he published his first novel, *The Dark Tunnel*, another example of Buchan's unexpected influence; it was a spy story[2] in the tradition of *The Thirty-Nine Steps*.

Ken and Maggie Millar were befriended by Anthony Boucher, who became an influential advocate for their work. *Blue City* (1947), a thriller reflecting the influence of Hammett and Chandler, didn't achieve sales comparable to those of Mickey Spillane's[3] debut, *I, The Jury*, which introduced the violent private eye Mike Hammer and appeared in the same year, but Ken's writing was plainly superior.

He started to write 'Hit and Run', where an apparent car accident conceals a murder, before settling on a private-eye novel narrated in the first person. He changed his detective's name from Joe Rogers to Lew Archer, and the book's title became *The Moving Target* (1949).

Ken didn't contemplate a long-term career in crime fiction, so he used a pseudonym taken from his father's first names, John Macdonald. The publishers, Knopf, came up with a cunning marketing plan: they would pretend that John Macdonald was a real person, and concoct a fake biography. A moody publicity photograph of Ken in full-length silhouette,[4] wearing a trench coat and soft-brimmed fedora, and smoking a cigarette, completed the illusion.

Boucher said that Ken had 'given the tough tec a new lease on life', but not everyone was impressed. In a private letter to another reviewer, James Sandoe, Chandler was brutally critical[5] of 'the stylistic misuse of language', which was typical of those 'literary eunuchs . . . [who] fall back on oblique terminology to prove their distinction'. When Ken found out about this, much later, he was deeply hurt.

John D. MacDonald, already an established crime novelist, fizzed with anger[6] over Ken's choice of pen-name. An uneasy compromise was brokered with Ken's agent, only for the quarrel to reignite a few years later. By then, John Macdonald had (following a brief incarnation as John Ross Macdonald) already morphed into Ross Macdonald, the name that became inseparable from Lew Archer's.

*

In the years following the birth of the Millars' daughter Linda, tensions grew in their household. Ken idolised Linda, but pressure of work ground him down. He became angry and depressed, ultimately attempting suicide. His idea for 'Hit and Run' had a shocking echo in real life when Linda, driving a car he'd bought for her, killed a young boy.

Ken embarked on a long course of psychiatric treatment. He was tormented not only by Linda's troubles but also by what had gone wrong in his own childhood. These preoccupations came to define his fiction, and he was sometimes accused of writing the same book time and again. His defence was to say: 'Every time you do it, you dig deeper. It's like going to a shrink . . .' Telling stories in the first person suited his purpose. When asked late in life if he planned to write an autobiography, he said: 'I think I have been.'

Like Margaret, he served as President of the MWA, although (unlike her) he never received an Edgar for best novel.[7] In *The Doomsters* (1958), Lew Archer gave voice to his creator's preoccupations: 'I've pretty well got over thinking in terms of good and bad. Those categories often do more harm than – well, good . . . We think we have to punish somebody for the human mess we're in, so we single out the scapegoats and call them evil.'

The driving force of *The Galton Case* (1959), described by one of his literary descendants, Loren D. Estleman,[8] as his 'major contribution to the form', was the myth of Oedipus, and the main source of the characters was the Millar family. As Ken said later, the story 'doesn't tell the naked truth, of course . . . Fiction, when it is working well, lifts out of the writer's life patterns which tend toward the legendary. But the patterns are disrupted . . .'

Narrative unity mattered to him. Alfred Knopf believed that a key distinction between the Archer books and Philip Marlowe's cases was that Chandler 'just can't build a plot'. As Ken said, Chandler thought that good scenes produce a good plot, whereas he saw plot as a vehicle of meaning. He preferred 'plots which extend over a period of two or three generations so that I can show the whole apparatus of family influence or the lack of it.' Even when crafting similes, he strove to capture something essential to the story,[9] in a turn of phrase.

Real-life misfortunes continued to plague him. Soon he was caught up in what Hammett once termed 'a wandering daughter job',[10] when Linda went missing from her campus. Her frantic father hired a private eye,[11] who traced her to a bar in Reno. Again, the Millar family's traumas were played out in the public spotlight: one headline shrieked *Mystery Writer's Toughest Case – Daughter Vanishes*. He mined his life experiences in novels such as *The Chill* (1964), in which Dolly Kincaid, like Linda, disappears on Labor Day weekend. When Dolly is accused of murder, she says she wants to die and is admitted to a rest home.

A major breakthrough came in 1969 with *The Goodbye Look*. William Goldman,[12] who had written the screenplay for a film version of *The Moving Target*,[13] hailed the Archer books as 'the finest detective novels ever written by an American'.[14] They had 'nothing remotely to do with hard-boiled detective novels. He is writing novels of character about people with ghosts.' At a time when the crime novel was still seen as inherently inferior, Ken had become part of the literary mainstream.[15]

Ken Millar lived a snakes-and-ladders life, with triumphs rapidly followed by tragedies. Linda's death delivered a blow sufficient to crush any parent. He considered writing a stand-alone, prompted by Julian Symons' belief that series characters fettered a writer's freedom. But his credo was that, throughout the genre's history, 'the detective hero has represented his creator and carried his values into action in society.'

Remembering the wounds Chandler's criticism had inflicted on him, Ken took pains to support younger writers, giving an endorsement to George V. Higgins'[16] first novel *The Friends of Eddie Coyle* (1970), and heaping praise on an up-and-coming private-eye writer, Roger L. Simon.[17] After a twenty-one-year-old university student sent him a manuscript, he invited the young man to a family dinner, and continued to correspond with him, and encourage his ambitions as a novelist.

The student noticed that Ken kept forgetting things and repeating himself. Before long, memory loss made it impossible for him to keep writing, let alone make the break from Archer. Until his mind failed, he had a sharp eye for talent and potential. It took decades, but, in the twenty-first century, his student protégé, Linwood Barclay,[18] finally established himself as one of the world's most popular thriller writers.

Ken Millar strongly opposed his country's military involvement in Vietnam, but it was younger writers whose books reflected the impact of the conflict on American society.[19] David Morrell's *First Blood* introduced John Rambo, a disaffected Vietnam veteran who became the central figure in a hugely popular film franchise. In the case of James Crumley; reading the Philip Marlowe and Lew Archer stories prompted him to try a private-eye story.

The Wrong Case (1975) introduced affable, hard-drinking Milo Milodragovitch from Montana, and was followed three years later by *The Last Good Kiss*, the first case of C. W. Sughrue, tough and cynical, but equally fond of alcohol. Crumley summed up the differences between the two detectives: 'Milo's first impulse is to help you; Sughrue's is to shoot you in the foot.' They reflected contrasting aspects of Crumley's own character. One or other of them appeared in seven novels over a span of thirty years; *Bordersnakes* (1996) featured both men.

Crumley was not a prolific novelist, but during a long spell in Hollywood he wrote many screenplays for never-to-be-made movies, including James Ellroy's *The Big Nowhere*. He found time to marry five times, although a taste for cocaine and a thirst for whiskey led to long-term health problems. Many of his characters were based on people he'd met, and his writing was at its best when he drew on his own life experiences. His sardonic prose and biting portrayal of a society brutalised by the experience of Vietnam inspired a legion of writers.[20]

Among them was James Lee Burke,[21] who taught at the University of Montana in the mid-1960s along with Crumley. Burke's literary career began in those days, but only took off when he turned to crime fiction in 1987. *The Neon Rain* introduced the New Orleans detective Dave Robicheaux, a recovering alcoholic and Vietnam veteran. Robicheaux is a moral man confronted by moral turmoil, and Burke's insight into the nature of evil has kept the series fresh for over thirty years.

*

Newton Thornburg's witty, macabre and poignant *Cutter and Bone*[22] appeared in 1976, the same year as the final Lew Archer novel, *The Blue Hammer*. Because the story is set mainly in Santa Barbara, Thornburg's name is sometimes bracketed with Ross Macdonald's. But Thornburg wasn't interested in emulating the older man's work.

No crime novel captured the corrosive effect of the Vietnam experience on American society with as much power as *Cutter and Bone*. Richard Bone, having abandoned his marriage and his job as an advertising executive to become a penniless drifter, teams up with scarred and disabled war veteran Alex Cutter in an eccentric conspiracy to blackmail a ranching tycoon called J. J. Wolfe.

Cutter's cynicism bites more sharply than any conventional hardboiled gumshoe's wisecracks, because he has suffered so much. He loathes those who profit from war at the expense of others: 'it's never their ass they lay on the line, man, never theirs, but ours, *mine*.' His comments about the photographs of the My Lai massacre form one of the most memorable passages in the genre, and conclude: 'But you know what you finally say, Rich, after you've studied them all you can? You say – I'm hungry.'

Bone believes (but isn't sure, because he was drunk at the time) that he's witnessed Wolfe dump in a trashcan the body of a teenage girl he'd raped and murdered. He's in it for the money, but also has a hazy justification for what he's doing: 'And if it turned out that the man was not guilty, and therefore not vulnerable, then he simply would not pay. Rather, it would be *they* who paid. Looked at that way, the whole thing seemed almost a moral enterprise, like hunting lion with a spear. One could lose.'

One could lose. Even a man as physically and emotionally strong as Cutter is far from invincible, and he knows it. The book's final sentence delivers an emotional knock-out punch. Thornburg resisted the temptation to write a follow-up, or be trapped into writing a series. The price he paid was unjust neglect of his masterpiece.

Ken Millar liked to say that he was the only American novelist who 'got his early ethical training in a Canadian Mennonite Sunday School'. Kem Nunn's[23] background was, given the graphic sex and violence in his fiction, equally improbable. He was raised as a Jehovah's Witness and trained as a lay preacher before leaving home, drifting to the west coast of America and becoming a passionately enthusiastic surfer.

Nunn's *Tapping the Source* (1984), an example of that unlikely sub-genre surf noir, appeared the year after Ken Millar died from Alzheimer's disease. The Southern Californian background prompted facile comparisons with Chandler, raising expectations in readers that were never likely to be satisfied. As a result it became a cult classic rather than a bestseller. It's a coming-of-age story with not a private eye in sight, about an amateur detective conducting a highly personal investigation.

Ike Tucker, a youthful motorbike mechanic in a small desert town, embarks on a quest to find his sister Ellen, who has been missing for two years. Given the names of three men who may know something about her fate, he heads for Huntington Beach, where he is befriended by Preston Marsh, an alcoholic surfer-turned-biker and Vietnam veteran almost as formidable and unforgettable as Alex Cutter.

Ike learns to surf, but soon finds that the fun, fun, fun associated with the Californian surfing culture has taken a sinister form. For the young people at Huntington Beach, sex and drugs are gateways to a horrifying world of sadism, pornography and murder.

Notes

The main sources regarding Ross Macdonald's life are Tom Nolan's biography, Macdonald's *Self-Portrait*, Ralph B. Sipper's *Inward Journey* and Paul Nelson and Kevin Avery's *It's All One Case*. The main source for Thornburg is Bob Cornwell's article 'Outsider', originally posted on the Tangled Web UK site.

1   *the poet's encouragement and love of detective stories*: Ken didn't share Auden's devotion to Golden Age puzzles. He admired Agatha Christie's invention and refinement of 'light, strong, tragicomic realism', and the 'brilliant and humane' Miss Marple mystery *4.50 from Paddington* (aka *What Mrs McGillicuddy Saw!*), which he regarded as her finest work – a minority view, to say the least. For him, Graham Greene's 'serious interest in the inner life of his characters made the superficial elegance of the Golden Age look like peeling gilt'. He regarded Greene and Hammett as trailblazers whose example liberated successors as diverse as Highsmith, with her 'brilliant tragicomic plots stitching together the fragments of an amoral

society', and the 'exuberantly masculine' Dick Francis, whose *Enquiry*, a story about a jockey robbed of the right to ride, 'takes a hard look at the English class system and its residual cruelties'.

2   *a spy story*: Ken deserted espionage fiction because 'the spy novel by definition is tied to current events . . . At its best the spy novel becomes a kind of historical novel that represents a time.' For him, Greene's *The Confidential Agent* 'stands up as historical fiction long after it has lost its relevance as an immediate commentary on the world'.

3   *Mickey Spillane*: Frank Morrison Spillane turned from writing comic books to producing thrillers awash with sex and violence. The literary establishment shuddered, but Spillane cried all the way to the bank. Ken Millar thought he'd destroyed the hardboiled novel, saying: 'Spillane pulled the plug. I have no intention of plunging after it down the drain.'

4   *A moody publicity photograph of Ken in full-length silhouette*: An even bolder marketing ploy, for the non-Archer novel *Meet Me at the Morgue*, used a frontal X-ray of Ken's skull as a jacket portrait.

5   *Chandler was brutally critical*: Ken couldn't resist the urge to return fire. Accepting that 'Find the Woman' was 'Chandler with onions', he remarked that 'Chandler himself is Hammett with Freud potatoes.' In 'The Writer as Detective Hero', he made a case for the superiority of his work to Chandler's.

6   *John D. MacDonald . . . fizzed with anger*: Entertainingly divergent accounts of this feud can be found in *It's All One Case*, in which Ken Millar describes MacDonald as 'a somewhat angry man anyway', and MacDonald's essay 'Namesake', which indicates that resentment continued to fester. MacDonald's business expertise (he was a Harvard MBA) made him acutely aware of the importance of branding. Millar accepted that MacDonald had 'great imaginative energy', but was dismissive of his series featuring Travis McGee: 'They're not ambitious books.' This is a harsh judgement. The two men had different political views, but did share a passionate concern for the environment. McGee is a 'salvage consultant' who lives on a houseboat, *The Busted Flush*, docked in Fort Lauderdale. *Darker than Amber*, violent, critically acclaimed and now a cult movie, was based on a McGee novel.

7   *he never received an Edgar for best novel*: *The Wycherly Woman* and *The Zebra-Striped Hearse* were nominated for Edgars, but both lost out to British novels: John Creasey's *Gideon's Fire* and Ellis Peters' *Death and the Joyful Woman* respectively. Ken became an MWA Grand Master in 1974 – two years after John D. MacDonald.

8   *Loren D. Estleman*: Estleman created the private eye Amos Walker, and also wrote a series about a hitman, Peter Macklin. The series initiated by *Whiskey River* aims 'to tell the story of America in the twentieth century through the microcosm of Detroit'.

9   *when crafting similes, he strove to capture something essential to the story*: Millar's imagery contrasts with the stripped-down prose of Elmore Leonard, whose style is encapsulated in his principle: 'If it sounds like writing, I rewrite it.'

10 *'a wandering daughter job'*: The phrase comes from 'Fly Paper', a Continental Op story, and was borrowed by the Coen brothers in their screenplay for *The Big Lebowski*.

11 *Her frantic father hired a private eye*: The detective, Armand Girola, became the model for Lew Archer's colleague Arnie Walters.

12 *William Goldman*: Goldman's thrillers and screenplays included *Marathon Man* and *Magic*. His other screenplays included *The Stepford Wives*, based on Ira Levin's novel, and *Masquerade*, based on *Castle Minerva* by Victor Canning. Canning was best known for *The Rainbird Pattern*, filmed by Hitchcock as *Family Plot*.

13 *a film version of The Moving Target*: The film was *Harper*. Paul Newman played Archer, renamed Harper due to a disagreement over rights to the character's name. Newman reprised the role in *The Drowning Pool*.

14 *'the finest detective novels ever written by an American'*: This phrase headlined a laudatory review in the *New York Times Book Review*, which confirmed Millar's status as a leading American novelist. Ben Yagoda, an admirer of the Marlowe and Archer books, argued that Millar's strengths were: 'first, coherent plots; second, an almost journalistic interest in the social and economic strata of contemporary Los Angeles; and, third, a consistent and compelling theme: the power of the past to influence the present.' Yagoda's article, 'The Case of the Overrated Mystery Novel', *Salon*, 6 January 2004, was otherwise a merciless critique of contemporary American crime writers.

15 *Ken had become part of the literary mainstream*: Eudora Welty, the short story writer and novelist, was an admirer of Millar who became a close friend. Their meetings were infrequent, but they conducted an intense correspondence, captured in *Meanwhile, There are Letters*, edited by Suzanne Marrs and Tom Nolan. Marshall McLuhan and the English poet Donald Davie were fans, as was Jerome Charyn, creator of Jewish detective Isaac Sidel, who rises to become US President. Charyn said he couldn't have written crime novels without reading the Archer books. He saw Archer as 'the most reliable unreliable narrator since Nick Carraway in *The Great Gatsby*'.

16 *George V. Higgins*: Higgins, a lawyer, was admired for his dialogue, described by Symons as 'not dreary but at times almost poetic, like that of a Compton-Burnett brought up in Boston's combat zone'. Elmore Leonard claimed that *The Friends of Eddie Coyle*, a gangster story, was the finest crime novel ever written. Symons also admired *Cogan's Trade* (whose eponymous hitman was played by Brad Pitt when the book was eventually filmed as *Killing Them Softly*) and argued that *Outlaws*, an ironic study of a gang of Bostonian Robin Hoods, achieved 'effects beyond the scope of most living novelists'. Conversely, in an obituary, Jack Adrian opined that after his first book, Higgins' novels were 'all just slight variations on the same basic riff' (*Independent*, 10 November 1999).

17 *Roger L. Simon*: Simon's novels about the proudly Jewish, divorced, marijuana-smoking Moses Wine were an attempt to update the private-eye novel, as was the trilogy that another Jewish screenwriter and novelist, Andrew Bergman, wrote about the deceptively polite Jack LeVine. Symons thought both writers suffered from an excess of jokiness; Bergman's flair for humour led him to write the screenplay that became the basis for Mel Brooks' film *Blazing Saddles*.

18 *Linwood Barclay*: After four light-hearted mysteries about columnist Zack Walker, Barclay finally broke through with *No Time for Goodbye*, in which a teenage girl's family suddenly disappears; this was the first in a string of bestselling high-concept thrillers.

19 *younger writers whose books reflected the impact of the conflict on American society*: Nicholas Meyer's *Target Practice* was, he said in his memoir *A View from the Bridge*, 'an attempt to discuss the Vietnam War . . . in the guise of a Lew Archer-type detective story'. The novel was nominated for an Edgar, but lost out to Gregory Mcdonald's droll, dialogue-heavy *Fletch*, introducing the eponymous Vietnam veteran, who declined to accept a Bronze Star.

20 *inspired a legion of writers*: They include George Pelecanos, Daniel Woodrell and Dennis Lehane. Lehane, author of bestsellers such as *Mystic River* and *Shutter Island*, described *The Last Good Kiss* as 'a road novel, a homage to Kerouac and Raymond Chandler, a multilayered mystery, and a heartfelt meditation on the 1970s, the death of idealism, and the inability of men to truly "see" women'. Ray Bradbury paid tribute in a trio of mysteries starting with *Death is a Lonely Business* by calling his detective Elmo Crumley.

21 *James Lee Burke*: Two Robicheaux books, *Heaven's Prisoners* and *In the Electric Mist with Confederate Dead*, have been filmed. While working on *The Neon Rain* he received encouragement from Charles Willeford, who had served an apprenticeship writing pulp paperbacks before breaking through with *Miami Blues*, which introduced Florida cop Hoke Moseley.

22 *Newton Thornburg's Cutter and Bone*: The novel was filmed as *Cutter's Way*. Thornburg was a copywriter turned novelist who bought a cattle ranch in the Ozarks. He described himself as 'a conservative . . . but I'm reasonable', and was acutely aware of capitalism's shortcomings. Introducing a reissue in 2001, George Pelecanos argued that the book, along with *The Last Good Kiss*, *Tapping the Source*, 'and most anything written by Elmore Leonard in the early to mid 1970s . . . seemed to challenge the very foundation of the traditional crime novel'. Pelecanos suggested that the novel refutes 'the Great Lie of the mystery novel', namely the idea that a mystery can be 'solved'.

23 *Kem Nunn*: Nunn has written for TV as well as writing novels such as *Chance*, featuring a forensic neuropsychiatrist, Eldon Chance, and televised in the US with Hugh Laurie playing Chance.

FORTY-ONE

Killing Jokes

Comedy and crime

On 1 May 1948, Craig Rice married for the third time. She was thirty-nine, and two years earlier she'd become the first crime writer to feature on the cover of *Time* magazine. Her sales figures rivalled those of Ellery Queen, Erle Stanley Gardner and Raymond Chandler.

Hank DeMott, her latest husband, was eleven years her junior and – like his two predecessors – a writer. Or at least he liked to think of himself as a writer. The wedding took place in the library of Ned Guymon, a wealthy collector of detective novels and one of Rice's closest friends. Over the past few years, he'd lent her a good deal of money without any hope of seeing it repaid, and he'd footed the bill for the ceremony. The guest list was crammed with celebrities and journalists, and Guymon gave away the bride. She walked down the aisle, carrying not a bible but her novel *The Lucky Stiff*. After the ceremony, she autographed copies for guests. The top tier of the wedding cake was circled by a string of minia-ture skulls.

There was no honeymoon, and marital bliss faded fast. Rice hadn't paid her taxes, and the IRS restricted her budget to forty-five dollars a week. She had to sell her house and car, and to cheer herself up she wrote a story called 'Eyes up in Moonlight', which she sent to *Ellery Queen's Mystery Magazine*. Fred Dannay deemed it unpublishable, because the victim died from over-indulgence in sex. She therefore sent it to Ned Guymon, as collateral for yet another loan. Duly amused, he said it gave a new meaning to the title of Howard Haycraft's study of detective fiction, *Murder for Pleasure*.

Any victim knows that in real life there is nothing funny about crime, but mystery writers use humour in their fiction to entertain, and sometimes to relieve the darkness of murder. Craig Rice's life story has long seemed as mysterious as her books, uncertainty swirling around her family background, the number of her marriages and even her real name. Yet at her peak she was famous for mixing cocktails of crime and comedy, and for earning vast sums almost as quickly as she spent them.

She was born Georgiana Craig in Chicago. Her mother wanted a boy, not a girl, and fled across the Atlantic to rejoin her husband, a painter working in Europe, leaving behind her young daughter. Georgiana was brought up by her father's half-sister and her husband, a couple named Rice, and developed a lifelong terror of rejection. Apart from a three-year period when she was reclaimed by her parents, the Rices looked after her. They adopted her following the Craigs' divorce, and she became Georgiana Craig Rice.

At the age of eighteen, she married and became pregnant with the first of her three children. The marriage, like all her relationships with men, failed to last, but she made a living through journalism. After turning to fiction, she carved a niche in screwball comedy (named after a tricky, unpredictable baseball pitch), a popular source of escapism in Depression-era America.

The flavour of her best stories was distinctive. The neat lattice-work of her plots and a hardboiled milieu were complemented by writing that was satiric, verging on the surreal. *Having Wonderful Crime* (1943) mocks the New York publishing industry, with in-jokes aplenty. The humour had an edge. The storyline of a novel featuring the hard-drinking lawyer John J. Malone, *The Right Murder* (1941), included domestic violence. Rice had suffered at the hands of her second husband, the radical poet Lawrence Lipton. The abuser in the book was called Michael Venning; oddly, she used the same name as a pseudonym for stories about a private eye called Melville Fairr.

Rice overindulged in alcohol, and so did her characters; fictional drunks seemed funny at the time. Her frantic writing sessions alternated with bouts of deep depression. Although undiagnosed in her lifetime, it seems likely that she suffered from bipolar disorder. After she and Lipton moved to Santa Monica, she worked as a screenwriter in Hollywood, partying and boozing as if there were no tomorrow while continuing to pour out detective stories.

When she was hired to ghostwrite *Crime on My Hands* (1944) for the actor George Sanders, she engaged a ghostwriter of her own to cope with the workload. Neither her role nor the sub-ghost's was mentioned when, in her regular review column, she selected the novel as one of the ten best mysteries of the year. Her social circle included the legendary stripper Gypsy Rose Lee, who published a couple of detective novels, although rumours that Rice ghostwrote Lee's *The G-String Murders*[1] (1941) were unfounded.

A messy divorce from Lipton was followed by the marriage to DeMott, which rapidly disintegrated. She attempted suicide and underwent treatment in a psychiatric hospital for chronic alcoholism, but refused to accept she had a problem with drink. Men were a continuing cause of misery. She fell for a fellow mental patient who claimed to be a writer, and they eloped to Chihuahua, where he became her fourth husband. He too proved to be a wife-beater, and the relationship collapsed as rapidly as it had begun. Her habit of becoming besotted with unpleasant and exploitative lovers proved as impossible to kick as the booze. The next man in her life she introduced to friends as her rich husband from Lichtenstein. Henri Maliverni was, however, another unemployed writer only interested in her money. They never made it to the altar.

Rice's health failed, and she was admitted to a sanatorium suffering severe malnutrition and miscellaneous ailments, including anaemia, nerve damage, necrosis of the jawbone, a crippled arm and symptoms similar to multiple sclerosis that confined her to a wheelchair. At forty-six, a once-lovely woman looked decades older. The sight of her, with all her teeth removed and her hair bone-white, horrified her friend and occasional collaborator Stuart Palmer. She sought solace in Roman Catholicism.

On being finally released from hospital, she arranged for Dorothy B. Hughes to meet her at a local church and sponsor her confirmation in the faith. She started writing again, and began a novel called *The April Robin Murders*.[2] But neither medical treatment nor religion had cured her of the instinct to self-harm. She resumed drinking, and got involved with a man she'd met in the sanatorium. Within a few months, she was dead. Her body was found at the bottom of the stairs in her home; close by were cigarette butts, an empty vodka bottle, a cheque of hers that had bounced and several of her books. One of them was *The Lucky Stiff*.

If Rice's story illustrates that the close relationship between comedy and tragedy extends to crime writing, it isn't an isolated example. Poor health exacerbated by alcoholism explains the strange career trajectory of Edmund Crispin,[3] the name under which Bruce Montgomery wrote witty detective novels. An admirer of John Dickson Carr and Michael Innes, Crispin was still an undergraduate when he wrote *The Case of the Gilded Fly*, aka *Obsequies at Oxford* (1944), which introduced the don Gervase Fen.

Crispin quickly established himself as a stylish writer in the Golden Age vein, but he was burnt-out as a novelist by the age of thirty. After more than a quarter of a century, he managed to publish the ninth Gervase Fen novel, the underwhelming *The Glimpses of the Moon* (1977), in the year before his death.

The modesty of Crispin's output is typical of comic crime novelists;[4] Pamela Branch,[5] one of the wittiest British crime writers to emerge in the 1950s, produced just four books. The pipe-smoking barrister Sarah Caudwell published the first of her mannered, erudite, amusingly original legal mysteries in 1980, but only three more appeared over the next twenty years, the last one shortly after her death.

Ever since Lord Peter Wimsey wooed Harriet Vane, authors have kept long-running series fresh by developing the lives and relationships of their cast of characters. Crime novelists who emphasise humour face a challenge. Write stand-alones and you need to come up with strong and funny new ideas at regular intervals. Write a series and you risk becoming formulaic. Tastes in humour change, and even a good joke wears thin if told too often.

The dilemma is illustrated by Joyce Porter, creator of greedy and bone-idle DCI Wilfred Dover,[6] one of the genre's most shameless anti-heroes. In the mid-1960s, the earthy black humour of Dover's cases, like that of Joe Orton's plays, suited the mood of the times. Dover tackled an assortment of grotesque crimes, although if and when he stumbles across the truth, it is thanks to lucky chance or the efforts of his long-suffering sidekick Sergeant MacGregor. *Dover One* (1964) was described by Robert Barnard[7] as 'the funniest crime novel since the war', but Porter found each book harder to write than the last.

One way to keep readers hooked is to create a new series character. Porter's experience in covert operations during the Cold War meant that, like John le Carré, she knew that British Intelligence was often misnamed. She spoofed the spying game[8] by writing about Eddie Brown, a teacher who becomes a reluctant and inept secret agent. The stories made no impact, and she sent Brown on only four missions.

Next came the Honourable Constance Ethel Morrison Burke, a farcical meld of Lady Bracknell and Miss Marple. Porter's decline as a writer had become precipitous, and Julian Symons' verdict was that the books were 'best left unbroached'. Bored with writing fiction, Porter devoted the last decade of her life to researching the life of an aunt of the last Tsar of Russia.

The highs and lows of comic crime writing were encapsulated in Kyril Bonfiglioli's[9] career. *Don't Point that Thing at Me* (1972), the first winner of the CWA award for best debut crime novel,[10] introduced the Hon. Charlie Mortdecai, 'a rich art-dealer who sells stolen masterpieces for kicks, an experienced coward with a flair for dirty fighting, a woman-hater with a weakness for sex'. Mortdecai is an A. J. Raffles for the 'Me' decade, an alcoholic rogue minus a conscience. The blurb gloried in its cluttered plot ('Do not trouble to wonder whodunit'), and the finale reads like a skit on Geoffrey Household's *Rogue Male*.

A disclaimer insisted: 'This is not an autobiographical novel: it is about some *other* portly, dissolute, immoral and middle-aged art-dealer'. Bonfiglioli, the English-born son of an Italo-Slovene book dealer, was a hard-living man-about-town who was repeatedly touched by tragedy. His mother and younger brother were killed in an air-raid shelter, and his first wife died after the birth of their second child. He married again and had three more children, but his enthusiasm for drink and women was destructive.

Mortdecai returned in two books, while a stand-alone novel, *All the Tea in China* (1978), featured one of his ancestors, but Bonfiglioli lacked Charlie's wealth. Beneath the surface insouciance, life became a losing battle against debt and drunkenness. When he was fifty-six, his liver gave up the unequal struggle, although his fiction retained a small but ardent cult following.[11]

A humorous crime series needs to be anchored by more than a single joke or prolonged facetiousness.[12] Colin Watson's[13] Flaxborough Chronicles are grounded in a small port town ('high-spirited . . . like Gomorrah') that bears more than a passing resemblance to Boston in his home patch of Lincolnshire. Flaxborough made a perfect setting for scathing attacks on social pretension. Watson's sly mysteries were investigated by Detective Inspector Purbright, whose tolerance and decency made him a polar opposite to Dover.

The secret behind the longevity of Simon Brett's witty novels starring the actor Charles Paris, which began with *Cast, in Order of Disappearance* as long ago as 1975, is inside knowledge of the worlds of TV, radio and drama. The author of over one hundred books,[14] Brett has published occasional stand-alone novels of psychological suspense, as well as an anthology of parodies and a crime story in verse,[15] but the Paris books remain his signature series.

Each of Ruth Dudley Edwards'[16] detective novels is a satire on a distinct, hallowed institution. Her targets have included the civil service, gentlemen's clubs, Cambridge colleges, the House of Lords, the Church of England, publishing and literary prizes. The books also form a series, unified by a sleuthing odd couple, Baroness Troutbeck and Robert Amiss, and scorn for political correctness.

For most crime writers, humour is a garnish rather than the

main course. Reginald Hill showed that an earthy cop might become something much more than a Porteresque caricature. 'Fat Andy' Dalziel of mid-Yorkshire's finest, made his debut six years after Dover lumbered on to the stage. Over time, Hill's growing confidence and subtlety as a novelist enabled him to transform Dalziel into a multifaceted character. Even in books such as *On Beulah Height* (1998), a complex, disturbing mystery about missing children, Hill's wit gleamed through the darkness.

The Sherlock Holmes canon alone accounts for a vast number of the parodies and pastiches of crime fiction. There are innumerable spoofs of Golden Age detection,[17] including short stories such as E. C. Bentley's 'Greedy Night' and E. V. Knox's 'The Murder at the Towers' and novels including Leo Bruce's *Case for Three Detectives* and *Gory Knight* (1937) by Margaret Rivers Larminie and Jane Langslow. In *Ask a Policeman* (1933), six Detection Club members exchanged detectives and parodied each other's style; thus Anthony Berkeley wrote about Lord Peter Wimsey, while Sayers wrote about Roger Sheringham.

Marion Mainwaring's[18] *Murder in Pastiche, or Nine Detectives All at Sea* (1954) spoofs detectives created by Christie, Sayers, Ngaio Marsh, Michael Innes, Patricia Wentworth, Ellery Queen, Erle Stanley Gardner, Rex Stout and Mickey Spillane. The nine are fellow passengers on RMS *Florabunda*, heading from Liverpool to New York, each adopting their own particular methods of detection when presented with a murder mystery to unravel.

Anthony Horowitz's[19] enthusiasms for comedy and detection coalesced in his first novel for adults, which concerned – a joke. The opening words of *The Killing Joke* (2004) are: 'There's this guy, goes into a bar.' The man in the bar is Guy Fletcher, who embarks on a quest to trace a joke back to its source. This was a fascinating concept, even if the story falters in its later stages. More than a decade later, following the success of his authorised pastiches of James Bond and Sherlock Holmes,[20] Horowitz returned to original detective fiction.

The first half of *The Magpie Murders* (2016) comprises a novel set in 1955. A cleaner has died in mysterious circumstances, and soon her employer is brutally murdered. Shortly before the climax, the story comes to a sudden halt, and we are transported to the present. Alan Conway, author of the story, has apparently committed suicide, and the last two chapters of his novel seem to be missing. Most of the rest of the story is narrated by Conway's editor, Susan, who begins to suspect that Conway was murdered. A 'least likely person' explanation is followed by the solution to the mystery in Conway's novel, which again results in the unmasking of an unexpected culprit.

The book mentions Horowitz's own television writing more than once. In *The Word is Murder* (2017), ex-cop Daniel Hawthorne, a Great Detective for the modern day, recruits his very own Watson to record the brilliance of his deductions. The sidekick is none other than Horowitz himself. Six hours after Diana Cowper walks into a funeral parlour and arranges her own funeral, she is dead, strangled in her own home. The police call in Hawthorne as a consultant, and he persuades Horowitz to write up a story in which red herrings abound. The clueing is worthy of Christie, as is the way in which the truth is disguised.

Gilbert Adair's[21] *The Act of Roger Murgatroyd* (2006), a country-house mystery featuring detective novelist Evadne Mount,[22] was an attempt to celebrate, parody and critique *The Murder of Roger Ackroyd*. The book was well received[23] although Andrew Taylor pointed out[24] that 'this type of parody works best as a sprint and is difficult to sustain over the marathon of full-length novel'. A sequel, *A Mysterious Affair of Style* (2007), deployed the 'least likely culprit' device, which is discussed at length by Evadne during the course of the story.

The title of Adair's final novel, *And Then There Was No One*, represents another hat tip to Christie, to whom the book is dedicated. It was published in 2009, and the events of the story are set in 2011. This time, the story is unreliably narrated by Adair himself. He attends a Sherlock Holmes festival in Switzerland, and a pastiche Sherlock Holmes story is included, together with plentiful references to G. K. Chesterton and Ronald Knox's 'rules'.

Adair fuses elements of reality, a fictional mystery about Gustav Slavorigin's death, and the literary tricks of Christie and Conan

Doyle. In the final scene, Evadne taunts Adair: 'Postmodernism is dead . . . Nobody gives two hoots about self-referentiality any longer, just as nobody gives two hoots, or even a single hoot, about you. Your books are out of sight, out of sound, out of fashion and out of print.' The story ends with a plunge into the Reichenbach Falls.

The critic Jake Kerridge praised the story's[25] 'quiet poignancy. Adair's criticism of his previous Evadne novels is just one example of the honesty with which he writes about the shortcomings of his life and work here, and this lends the novel, for all its meta-fictional tricks . . . an emotional charge rarely found in whodunnits, parodies, postmodern fictions or any combination of the three.'

These remarks about poignancy proved tragically prescient. Adair never published another book. A stroke cost him his sight, a shocking echo of his psychological suspense novel *A Closed Book* (1999), whose protagonist is a blind writer. He died in 2011, the year he'd chosen for his fictional demise.

Notes

The main sources are Jeffrey Marks' biography of Rice, Earl Bargainnier's *Comic Crime*, Bruce Shaw's *Jolly Good Detecting*, John Kennedy Melling's *Murder Done to Death* and the introduction and afterword to Joyce Porter's *Dover: The Collected Short Stories*, by Robert Barnard and J. R. Porter respectively.

1   *The G-String Murders*: Lee Wright of Simon & Schuster, editor of this 'Novel of Murder in Burlesque', promoted it with zest, mailing out a booklet of her correspondence with Lee ('The Belle of the Bistros') to prove the novel was not ghostwritten. This was accompanied by a fold-out bookmark depicting a striptease artiste's lower body.
2   *The April Robin Murders*: Rice never finished the book, and left no notes to indicate how the story might end. Lee Wright hired Ed McBain to complete the novel.
3   *Edmund Crispin*: Crispin became a perceptive crime reviewer and an astute anthologist. His biography by David Whittle explores his fiction and his work as a composer. His music included soundtracks to *Carry On* movies and films of novels by Julian Symons and Michael Gilbert. Among his admirers is Christopher Fowler, creator of Arthur Bryant and John May of the Peculiar Crimes Unit, two 'Golden Age detectives in a modern world'. Their cases include *The Victoria Vanishes*, a homage to Crispin's *The Moving Toyshop*.
4   *The modesty of Crispin's output is typical of comic crime novelists*: Such as his American counterpart, Timothy Fuller, who managed five novels.

Fuller's Jupiter Jones first appeared in *Harvard Has a Homicide* in 1936, and his final case was in 1950.

5 *Pamela Branch*: Branch's *The Wooden Overcoat* opens with Benjamin Cann, found not guilty of strangling his girlfriend, being invited to join the Asterisk Club. To be eligible for membership, one has to be a wrongly acquitted murderer. Before long the Club is thrown into turmoil by the deaths of two members. Branch's final book appeared in 1958, nine years before her own death at the age of forty-seven.

6 *DCI Wilfred Dover*: In a revelation as astonishing as anything Poirot ever managed, Porter's brother explained that the initial inspiration for Dover was Maigret; Porter kept a library of Simenon's novels in the original French. As a beginning writer, she didn't intend to write comedy, but her attempt to create an English Maigret misfired and she 'just turned him inside out'.

7 *Robert Barnard*: Barnard's debut, *Death of an Old Goat*, satirised Australian academe, while targets in other books included politics, religion, romantic novelists and snobbery. The final twist in *A Scandal in Belgravia* illustrates his flair for surprise endings.

8 *She spoofed the spying game*: Sixties spy stories sparked endless parodies, ranging from the farcical to the sophisticated. Among the latter was Anthony Firth's only novel, *Tall, Balding, Thirty-Five*, starring a closeted gay writer-photographer, John Limbo. John Gardner's series about the cowardly secret agent Boysie Oakes led, in an ironic twist of literary fate, to his being hired to write James Bond continuation novels and two books based on Bond films.

9 *Kyril Bonfiglioli*: He was born Cyril Emmanuel George Bonfiglioli, and for a time he edited the magazine *Science Fantasy*. His second wife, Margaret, compiled *The Mortdecai ABC*, which includes personal reminiscences as well as samples of his writing. An overview of his life and work is provided by Leo Carey ('The Genuine Article', *New Yorker*, 20 September 2004).

10 *the CWA award for best debut crime novel*: The award has had various names, including the John Creasey Memorial Dagger. Winners have included Patricia D. Cornwell, Walter Mosley, Denise Mina and Gillian Flynn, and others whose reputations have not lasted as well, such as Sara George, David Serafin and Elizabeth Ironside (in real life Lady Catherine Manning). James Leigh's *The Ludi Victor* had a cliffhanger finale – but this extraordinary thriller had no successor.

11 *a small but ardent cult following*: Julian Barnes' approval of Bonfiglioli's verve is reflected in his four equally breezy books about the private eye Duffy, written as by Dan Kavanagh. Stephen Fry is another admirer, while Craig Brown completed an unfinished novel, *The Great Mortdecai Moustache Mystery*. Thirty years after Bonfiglioli's death, Johnny Depp starred in *Mortdecai*, a film derived from the first novel. Unfortunately the laughter it prompted was derisive.

12 *prolonged facetiousness*: Nancy Spain's nine pun-laden mystery novels have their admirers, but suffer from the author's lack of interest in plotting. Spain was a journalist, broadcaster and celebrity whose flamboyance added colour to the austerity of post-war Britain. Although she had a son, the result of a fling with Margery Allingham's husband Pip, she was a lesbian who died with her partner Joan Werner Laurie in a plane crash, and whose name became the title of a popular song written by Barney Rushe.

13 *Colin Watson*: Four of the Flaxborough Chronicles were televised as *Murder Most English*. Watson also wrote a commentary on between-the-wars crime fiction, *Snobbery with Violence*.

14 *The author of over one hundred books*: *A Shock to the System*, a stand-alone novel in the Ironist vein, was filmed. Mrs Pargeter, a criminal's widow, is another recurring character, while a further series is set in the resort of Fethering (close to Tarring). The Blotto and Twinks books are more broadly comic.

15 *a crime story in verse*: *A Crime in Rhyme* is a skit on the clichés of Golden Age detection.

16 *Ruth Dudley Edwards*: A courageous and sometimes controversial polemicist, she won a Gold Dagger for a non-fiction book, *Aftermath: The Omagh Bombing and the Families' Pursuit of Justice*.

17 *There are innumerable spoofs of Golden Age detection*: In *The Smiling Corpse* (the anonymous authors were later identified as Philip Wylie and B. A. Bergman), G. K. Chesterton, S. S. Van Dine, Dashiell Hammett and Sax Rohmer investigate the murder of a mystery critic at a literary tea celebrating the publication of his book *From Poe to Plethora*. Neil Simon's screenplay for *Murder by Death* parodies Poirot and Marple, plus Nick and Nora Charles, Sam Spade and Charlie Chan; H. R. F. Keating novelized the script.

18 *Marion Mainwaring*: Her tongue-in-cheek humour was admired by Anthony Boucher, who also approved the 'allusive donnish wit' of her other venture into the genre, *Murder at Midyears*. She is best known for completing *The Buccaneers* by Edith Wharton, herself the author of a chilling suspense story, 'The Bottle of Evian', aka 'A Bottle of Perrier'.

19 *Anthony Horowitz*: Formidably productive and possessing a fertile imagination, Horowitz has written TV scripts for *Poirot*, *Midsomer Murders* and his own creation, *Foyle's War*. In his *Crime Traveller*, a detective travels in time to solve crime, but this short-lived 1997 series enjoyed much less success than a very different cop show about time travel, *Life on Mars*, first screened in 2006 and created by Matthew Graham, Tony Jordan and Ashley Pharoah.

20 *authorised pastiches of James Bond and Sherlock Holmes*: *Trigger Mortis* and *The House of Silk*, followed up by *Forever and a Day* and *Moriarty* respectively. *Moriarty* boasts an outrageous Christie-esque twist.

21 *Gilbert Adair*: Adair was also the author of a collection of essays entitled *The Postmodernist Always Rings Twice*. *A Void* was his translation of Georges Perec's lipogrammatic novel, *La Disparition*.

22 *Evadne Mount*: Evadne is the author of mysteries such as *Faber or Faber* (concerning 'identical twin fratricide'), *The Mystery of the Green Penguin* (green being the colour of Penguin paperback detective novels), *Oedipus v. Rex* and *Murder without Ease* – a title that combines a nod to Christie's *Murder is Easy* with a pun about *A Void*, a book without the letter 'e'.

23 *The book was well received*: Scathing dissent came from Michael Dibdin, who dismissed Adair's novel as 'Half-smart and immensely self-reverential', and suggested that Adair had plagiarised Tom Stoppard (*Guardian*, 4 November 2006). His review was churlish, given that his own first novel had been *The Last Sherlock Holmes Story*, a pastiche disdained by many Conan Doyle fans. After his early death, Adair exacted savage retribution in *And Then There Was No One*:

'Got good reviews, too, I noticed. Deserved to.'
'Thanks again.'
'Also a couple of stinkers.'
'Just one, I think. In the *Guardian*. Michael Dibdin.'
'Who died not long afterwards. *Spooooky* . . .'

24 *Andrew Taylor pointed out*: He concluded: 'Adair gives us some excellent jokes but, in the end, his paradoxical achievement is to make us appreciate the solid literary virtues of Agatha Christie' (*Independent*, 17 November 2006).

25 *Jake Kerridge praised the story*: Daily Telegraph, 7 January 2009.

FORTY-TWO

Literary Agents

Post-war spy fiction

In May 1941, the head of British Naval Intelligence, Rear Admiral Bill Godfrey, accompanied by a trusted assistant, flew out to New York. Supposedly, they were to check security in American ports, but they also had a covert mission. The British chiefs of staff had authorised them to promote closer collaboration with the US on security to assist with the war effort.

The two men travelled by a circuitous route, which entailed stopping over in neutral Portugal at Estoril, a notorious haunt for members of the German secret service. The assistant, a lieutenant commander, loved gambling, and he persuaded Godfrey to join him in a trip to a casino. In later life, the lieutenant commander recalled that they came across three German agents at the high table, playing *chemin de fer*. The lieutenant commander had fifty pounds in his pocket, and took on the leader of the German spies, only to lose all his money after three *suivis*. He later said that this humiliation 'added to the sinews of war of the German Secret Service and reduced me sharply in my chief's estimation'.

The encounter later resurfaced in a scene in the lieutenant commander's first novel, published in 1953. In the fictional version, his hero outwits a Communist spy over a game of baccarat. The author was Ian Fleming, the book *Casino Royale*, the spy Le Chiffre and the hero James Bond.

It's typical of Fleming's life, as well as his fiction, that his version of events was a fantasy. Admiral Godfrey's more prosaic recollection[1] was that the successful gamblers were Portuguese businessmen, and that, as he and Fleming left the casino, the younger man tried to give their expensive evening a gloss of glamour: 'What if those men had been German secret service agents, and suppose we had cleaned them out of their money; now that would have been exciting.'

Today, Ian Lancaster Fleming seems almost as unlikely and exotic a character as 007 himself. Fleming's own story is, like that of so many crime writers, hard to disentangle from half-truths and invention. In the case of a hedonistic Englishman who spied for his country long before his hero became a household name, this seems fitting.

Educated at Eton and Sandhurst, Fleming dabbled in stock-broking before discovering that his quick mind suited him to journalism, and in due course to intelligence work. A handsome charmer who pursued women with obsessive zeal and considerable success, he had straightforward tastes in literature, and devoured the thrillers of 'Sapper'.[2]

Fleming spent much of his Naval Intelligence career in Room 39 of the Admiralty, but even while office-bound, he made acquaintances who proved helpful when he began to write fiction. They included Charles Fraser-Smith, ostensibly a functionary in the Ministry of Supply, but in fact the expert who supplied agents with gadgets such as shoelaces that doubled as saws, and golf balls hollowed-out to carry messages. In Fleming's books, he was fictionalised as Boothroyd; in the films, he became 'Q'. Fleming also played a part in developing Operation Golden Eye, a plan to carry out sabotage if the Germans invaded Spain; it was never implemented, but when he bought a house in Jamaica after the war, he called it Goldeneye, and in 1995 that title was given to the seventeenth James Bond movie.

After the war, he oversaw *The Sunday Times'* worldwide network of correspondents. His time in the City had taught him the dark arts of deal-making, and he negotiated three months' leave per annum, most of which he spent in Jamaica. He came up with an idea for a thriller in which a frozen leg of lamb is used as a murder weapon, before being cooked and eaten. Rather than pursuing the idea, he passed it on to his friend Roald Dahl,[3] who transformed it into a famous short story, 'Lamb to the Slaughter'.

He didn't marry until he was forty-three. There was a hurtful edge to his frequent repetition of a joke that he started writing *Casino Royale* days before the wedding in order to take his mind off the horrific prospect of matrimony. The first person to see his manuscript was the poet William Plomer, author of *The Case is Altered*, who supplemented his literary income as a reader for the publishers Jonathan Cape.

Casino Royale, with a scene featuring the hero being tortured with a carpet beater, hardly matched Plomer's work for subtlety, but he recommended it for publication, and Cape bought the book. Reviews were positive: Julian Symons described the novel as 'absorbingly readable' despite a 'staggeringly implausible' plot.

Plomer rhapsodised about the follow-up, *Live and Let Die* (1954): 'sexy, violent, ingenious, & full of well-collected detail of all kinds'. It was banned in Ireland, which made perfect publicity. Bond's third outing, the only book in the series set wholly in Britain, was called *Moonraker* (1955); Noël Coward pointed out to Fleming that Fryn Tennyson Jesse had once used the same title, but her book was long forgotten. Coward was among a *Who's Who* of celebrities drawn into Fleming's circle. Others included Truman Capote, who in later years wrote about a killing involving an American couple, the Woodwards,[4] with whom he and Fleming were acquainted.

Raymond Chandler, another friend, questioned whether Fleming should be content to write fiction that seemed to revel in the sadistic. Critical reaction became increasingly hostile, and the literary scholar Bernard Bergonzi contrasted the constant name-dropping in the books with 'those subdued images of the perfectly self-assured gentlemanly life that we find in Buchan or even Sapper'. Anthony Price[5] said that the Bond stories were thirty years out of date; at least Bulldog Drummond had not been old-fashioned at the time of his creation. To be adversely compared to 'Sapper' must have left Fleming shaken if not stirred.

The title of an attack by Paul Johnson in the *New Statesman* captured the essence of the Bond books: 'Sex, Snobbery and Sadism'. But Johnson's swipe that 'Mr Fleming has no literary skill' was a low blow. Umberto Eco showed more subtlety[6] when analysing Fleming's work, while half a century later Sebastian Faulks said he was 'surprised by how well the books stood up. I put this down to three things: the sense of jeopardy Fleming creates about his solitary hero; a certain playfulness in the narrative details; and a crisp, journalistic style that hasn't dated.'

Discussing Graham Greene's *Our Man in Havana*[7] (1958) on BBC Radio, Fleming argued that any book about secret agents had to be either incredible or farcical. He was 'sufficiently in love with the myth to write basically incredible stories with a straight face', whereas Greene's mocking story about a vacuum salesman who earns extra cash by inventing a spy ring was 'almost too close to those who served in wartime intelligence to be funny'.

Fleming never fulfilled his ambition to write a classic thriller that was 'a mixture of Tolstoy, Simenon, Ambler and Koestler, with a pinch of ground Fleming'. The Bond films brought him vast wealth, but his creative powers faltered, and his mood darkened. Where there is money, there is usually a lawsuit, and he became involved in debilitating litigation over the rights to *Thunderball* (1961). His marriage slowly disintegrated, and so did his health, as years of heavy smoking and drinking, allied to long-term heart disease, took their toll.

At his death, aged fifty-six, he'd been a published novelist for less than a dozen years, but he'd managed to do something that few writers can ever hope to achieve. In James Bond, he'd created a global icon.[8]

John Bingham's interest in clandestine work was sparked by youthful exposure to the books of John Buchan and Edgar Wallace. A journalist from a titled but impecunious family, he joined MI5 in 1940. He was recruited by Maxwell Knight,[9] known as 'M' and the model for Fleming's spy boss, who reminded Bingham of a Buchan hero. Bingham became accomplished at interrogation. He understood that good interrogators do more than ask the right questions; they also listen carefully to the answers.

He returned to journalism after the war, but as the Cold War took Europe in an icy grip he rejoined Knight's team in 1950. In the same year, he published his first novel. The strength of *My Name is Michael Sibley*, like several of his later books, lay in his description of the increasing pressure brought to bear on the suspect by the investigation. Rather than writing spy fiction, he was exploiting know-how gained from intelligence work to create police stories with a difference.[10] In *The Paton Street Case*, one misjudgement by a decent but luckless detective leads to murder; another results in the deaths of two innocent people. Although the plot is ingenious, the case is solved by chance rather than judgement – only for it to emerge that the real villain got away scot free.

As a crime writer, Bingham resembled a gifted amateur rather than a hard-bitten professional. He liked to experiment, and even introduced his publisher as a key character in a curious suspense novel, *Murder Plan Six*, but resisted any mischievous urge to kill him. A crime novelist sends Victor Gollancz a series of tape recordings that explain his intention to commit murder. In dedicating the book to Gollancz, Bingham mentioned that he'd 'occasionally been accused of being "anti-police"', an example of the crass criticisms that are an occupational hazard of the writing life.

Murder Plan Six appeared in 1958, and so did a new face in Maxwell Knight's department, belonging to a young man called David Cornwell. Bingham turned down the chance to take over from Knight, believing he was suited to running secret agents, but not to managing the whole team. He became a mentor to Cornwell, and their wives also became friends.

Cornwell supplemented his income by drawing jokey illustrations for *Talking Birds*[11] by Maxwell Knight, who was a keen ornithologist. Impressed by Bingham's ability to juggle espionage with crime writing, Cornwell decided to follow suit, and Bingham introduced him to his agent Peter Watt, and to Gollancz.

Bingham, by now the 7th Baron Clanmorris, published *Night's Black Agent* in 1961. The title comes from *Macbeth* and puns on the nickname for the spies known as 'Knight's Black Agents'. We know from the outset whom the journalist-narrator intends to kill and (in part) why. His target is a blackmailer and sex killer. The focus is less on the sociopathic villain than on his principal victims.

Cornwell's first novel came out in the same year, after he'd transferred to MI6. He'd given Bingham a teasing nickname, a French translation of 'the square', and decided to use this as a pseudonym for his own fiction,[12] in conjunction with Bingham's first name. The author of *Call for the Dead*[13] was therefore introduced to the world as John le Carré.

The story is a murder mystery set in the world of spies, and the investigation is conducted by a skilled interrogator, the bespectacled George Smiley. Smiley bore a strong resemblance to Bingham,[14] not least in his habit of cleaning his glasses with his tie. Amused, Bingham gave a blurb that Gollancz put on the front cover. Francis Iles said the book was 'outstanding' and Julian Symons thought the author 'undoubtedly a find'.

Smiley returned in *A Murder of Quality* (1962), a whodunit in which he operates as an amateur detective. A year later, le Carré broke fresh ground. *The Spy Who Came in from the Cold* became an instant classic of the espionage genre, but led to fissures appearing in his relationship with Bingham.

Victor Gollancz's marketing remained inventive. He published *The Spy Who Came in from the Cold* in a red (rather than yellow) dust wrapper, to signal that it represented something fresh, a work of literary merit that was also highly topical. This was the era of the Vassall scandal and the Profumo affair; the public was forced to face the truth that spying was more often sleazy than sexy.

Graham Greene and J. B. Priestley endorsed the novel, and advance publicity highlighted comments made in Julian Maclaren-Ross's recent review of Len Deighton's *The IPCRESS File* (1962):[15] 'How peculiar . . . at this time . . . with so many real-life parallels from which to draw, that our spy fiction should be at such a low ebb . . . the really realistic spy novel, as prefigured by Ashenden and Mr Ambler, does not as yet exist.' Colossal sales were matched by critical acclaim from Anthony Price among others; with an irony typical of literary life, the most negative review came from Maclaren-Ross.

The downbeat story about Cold War shenanigans, with both

British and East German intelligence services behaving in an amoral fashion, chimed with the times, and the novel became the first to win both the CWA Gold Dagger and an MWA Edgar. Bingham, a staunch conservative and patriot, was troubled by le Carré's nuanced view of the rival secret services. Bingham knew whose side he was on.

Le Carré's new-found wealth enabled him to abandon intelligence work and concentrate on writing. His next book, *The Looking-Glass War* (1965), went beyond the pale as far as Bingham was concerned. Le Carré conceived the story, about a futile espionage mission in which a man is sent to his death for no good reason, as a satire on the incompetence and cynicism respectively of MI5 and MI6. Bingham regarded the book as a betrayal. For le Carré, his former mentor's attitudes were reflective of a society mired in nostalgia for a glorious past that had vanished for ever.

Bingham riposted in the foreword to his first spy novel,[16] *The Double Agent* (1966), condemning critics of the British intelligence services. The men's friendship faded, but didn't die. When they met in a Wimpy Bar one day, le Carré wistfully compared literary success to a car crash. Like so many other bestselling authors before and since, his life had been transformed by fame and money, and at first he found it hard to adjust.

Le Carré had blurbed Bingham's *A Fragment of Fear*[17] (1965): 'In a nightmare world, he handles his characters with compassion and sincerity, but also with alarm.' In this Woolrichian thriller of paranoia, a writer called Compton remarks: 'We live in dangerous times.' All one can do, he says, 'is keep the spear ready . . . touch the amulet, and hope for the best, and trust that . . . the tribe can after all protect not only the tribe but the individual'. This reflected Bingham's world view; le Carré had little faith in the reliability of the tribe.

The book was filmed and its success seemed to herald a new direction for Bingham. Instead, his career as a novelist lurched into a sad and steep decline.[18] Meanwhile, le Carré revived Smiley in the Karla Trilogy,[19] three novels starting with *Tinker, Tailor, Soldier, Spy* (1974), which cemented his reputation.

*

Female authors tend, in histories of espionage writing, to be invisible women. Yet the female contribution to spy stories goes far beyond fictional Mata Haris and Pussy Galores. Inspiration for James Bond may have come from Phyllis Bottome,[20] an American writer married to a British former spy. She befriended Fleming when he attended their Austrian finishing school in his teens, and encouraged him to write. The hero of Bottome's spy novel *The Lifeline*, published in 1946, is Mark Chalmers, an Eton schoolmaster who is sent by British Intelligence on a special mission to Austria. The parallels between her book and *Casino Royale* are intriguing, and there are similarities between Chalmers and Fleming himself, although the shadows of Carruthers from *The Riddle of the Sands* and Richard Hannay loom over both of them.

Of the relatively few women who have enjoyed lengthy careers as spy writers,[21] Glasgow-born Helen MacInnes achieved the most sustained success. She and her husband Gilbert Highet, who pleasingly combined classical scholarship with working as an MI6 agent, emigrated to the United States. MacInnes' first espionage novel, *Above Suspicion* (1941), was one of her four novels to be filmed. So was *Assignment in Brittany* (1942), which, so the legend goes, became required wartime reading for Allied agents sent to assist resistance workers in Nazi-occupied France.

In the mid to late 1950s, the American writer Holly Roth[22] seemed destined for success. Her early Cold War thrillers, such as *The Mask of Glass* (1954), earned the admiration of Francis Iles among others, but her career came to a premature end that was as tragic as it was mysterious. In October 1964, Roth and her second husband, Josef Franta, set off from Gibraltar in their yacht *Visa*, heading for the Canary Islands. Only Franta made it; Roth was presumed lost at sea.

Palma Harcourt made use of her first-hand experience of intelligence work in thrillers published under her own name before collaborating with her husband, Jack Trotman, on police mysteries under the pseudonym John Penn. But the highest-profile female spy turned novelist is Stella Rimington, formerly the Director General of MI5, who in her late sixties began a commercially successful series featuring the intelligence officer Liz Carlyle.

*

The twin traditions of spy writing, the fantastic and the more realistic, have co-existed since the Second World War. Writers who followed Fleming's lead frequently shared his pro-establishment instincts, but not always. Similarly, the books of Anthony Price and William Haggard[23] have the flavour of the real world, but reflect a conservative world view unlike that of Greene, Ambler, le Carré or Len Deighton.

Deighton stood apart from previous spy novelists. The son of a cook and a chauffeur, he lacked an Oxbridge education, as well as a background equipping him with useful know-how about tradecraft. The catalyst for his literary career was personal and unique. At the age of eleven, he witnessed the arrest by MI5 of a local woman whose dinner parties his mother had cooked for. Her name was Anna Wolkoff, and she was tried *in camera* at the Old Bailey, found guilty of spying and sentenced to ten years in jail. Recollecting the incident, he wrote a spy-orientated screenplay, then a short story, before developing his idea into a novel that appeared the year before le Carré's debut.

The IPCRESS File caught the mood of the Swinging Sixties.[24] The unnamed, working-class narrator[25] works on 'the intelligence fringe' of the War House; he comes from Burnley, the sort of down-to-earth Lancashire town that never featured in a Bond novel. The book opens with a Cabinet memo, includes footnotes and ends with a set of appendices, touches lending an air of verisimilitude to a story told with wit and verve. This was the age of the 'angry young man', but, as Deighton said, although he was a youthful product of the Marylebone Workhouse, he was neither angry nor a class warrior. His protagonist was a literary descendant of Philip Marlowe, a man of integrity.[26]

Deighton's storytelling zest was evident throughout the next three decades, as he experimented with different approaches to his craft.[27] *SS-GB* (1978) is one of the finest 'alternative history' thrillers,[28] set in Britain following its conquest by Adolf Hitler. Deighton's account of a detective's investigation into the murder of an atomic scientist has all the strengths of his ground-breaking spy fiction, together with much the same complexity and cynicism.

He and le Carré made their reputations with books set during the Cold War, but the fall of the Berlin Wall and collapse of the

USSR failed to kill off espionage fiction. Greene and Ambler had already demonstrated their literary range in books as diverse as Greene's *The Honorary Consul* (1973), set in Argentina, and *Doctor Frigo* (the name means 'frozen meat'), published the following year, for which Ambler dreamed up a fictional Caribbean island. Their present-day heirs include Alan Furst,[29] an American specialist in historical espionage.

Charity, Deighton's last novel, and the ninth to feature the spy Bernard Samson, appeared in 1996. Since the 9/11 attacks on the United States and the launching of 'the war on terror', a new generation of writers[30] has found the widespread climate of apprehension about global instability a fertile source of material. Yet books continue to appear that, while facing up to harsh truths, are written with wit as slyly enjoyable as anything to be found in the genre.

Le Carré frequently explored the extremes and excesses of capitalism, which he saw as posing a threat different from that of Communist Russia, but still insidious. In 2017, *A Legacy of Spies* brought his career full circle, with a story narrated by Peter Guillam, Smiley's protégé, who in retirement is summoned by MI6 to explain his part in the events in *The Spy Who Came in from the Cold*; Smiley too reappears, for the first time in more than a quarter of a century.

The trigger for the novel was le Carré's horror about the referendum in which the British people voted to leave the European Union: 'Brexit'. Rather like John Bingham forty years earlier, he expressed the paradox of old age when interviewed by National Public Radio in the US,[31] acknowledging contentment with the illustrious life he'd led,[32] while expressing despair at the state of the contemporary world.

His verdict on post-Cold War society was downbeat: 'We seem to be joined by nothing very much except fear and bewilderment about what the future holds.' But as William Boyd said,[33] his best work shows that 'the tropes of espionage – duplicity, betrayal, disguise, clandestinity, secrets, the bluff, the double bluff, bafflement, shifting identity – are no more than the tropes of the life that every human being lives, except that in the context of spies and spying they are writ large: very much more is at stake.'

Notes

The main sources are Anthony Masters' *Literary Agents*, Andrew Lycett's biography of Fleming, Simon H. King's website, Michael Jago's biography of Bingham and Adam Sisman's biography of le Carré.

1   *Admiral Godfrey's more prosaic recollection*: Even this version has been challenged; some accounts suggest that others were involved in the casino incident, and passed on the story to Fleming.

2   *he . . . devoured the thrillers of 'Sapper'*: Other favourite novels included relatively obscure titles such as Lynn Brock's *Nightmare* and Geoffrey Household's *The Third Hour*.

3   *his friend Roald Dahl*: Dahl was also involved in intelligence work. Introducing the story in the *Tales of the Unexpected* TV series, he claimed that Fleming thought up the idea during a dinner in Vermont when eating a tough piece of lamb. Dahl wrote the screenplays for *You Only Live Twice* and the film of Fleming's children's story, *Chitty Chitty Bang Bang*.

4   *a killing involving an American couple, the Woodwards*: In 1955, Ann Woodward shot her husband, Billy, dead. Tried for murder, she claimed that she'd mistaken him for an intruder and was acquitted, but Capote believed her guilty. After Ann learned that chapters of his book about the case, *Answered Prayers*, were to be published in *Esquire*, she took a cyanide pill. Both her sons also later killed themselves. Dominick Dunne's *The Two Mrs Grenvilles* was also based on the case. Billy Woodward was a posthumous dedicatee of Fleming's *Diamonds are Forever*.

5   *Anthony Price*: Price's first espionage thriller, *The Labyrinth Makers*, introduced historian-turned-spy Dr David Audley. His books blend past and present in sophisticated fashion.

6   *Umberto Eco showed more subtlety*: In his 1966 essay 'Narrative Structures in Fleming'.

7   *Our Man in Havana*: The novel was filmed, and even turned into an opera, with a libretto by Sidney Gilliatt, better known as co-writer of *The Lady Vanishes*.

8   *a global icon*: James Bond continuation novels have been written by authors as notable as Sebastian Faulks, Kingsley Amis, William Boyd and Anthony Horowitz. Over the years the character has been reinvented with considerable commercial success. Robert Ludlum's Jason Bourne and Tom Clancy's Jack Ryan are heroic figures in the Bond mould; like Bond, they have become immensely lucrative franchises which have survived the deaths of the men who originally created the characters.

9   *Maxwell Knight*: He was the inspiration for the character of Jack Brotherhood in le Carré's *A Perfect Spy*. Knight published two crime novels in the 1930s, *Crime Cargo* and *Gunman's Holiday*, the latter dedicated to Dennis Wheatley and his wife. One of his agents – or 'moles' – was Wheatley's stepson William Younger, who wrote a handful of thrillers and crime novels as William Mole, notably *The Hammersmith Maggot* aka *Small Venom*, about the hunt for a blackmailer. Younger's wife also dabbled in the genre under the name Elizabeth Hely; her debut, *Dominant Third*, was a psychological suspense novel dedicated to 'Mole', published and televised in the US as *I'll Be Judge, I'll be Jury*.

10 *police stories with a difference*: The same technique informs *The Third Skin*, aka *Murder is a Witch* (inspired by the Bentley and Craig case), and *The Paton Street Case*, aka *Inspector Morgan's Dilemma*.

11 *jokey illustrations for Talking Birds*: His models were parrots in the cages of the pet department at Harrods. He also illustrated Knight's *Animals and Ourselves*.

12 *a pseudonym for his own fiction*: Cornwell's first suggested pen-name was Jean Sanglas. Victor Gollancz proposed Chunk (or Chuck) Smith or, alternatively, Hank Brown.

13 *Call for the Dead*: The book was filmed by Sidney Lumet as *The Deadly Affair*.

14 *Smiley bore a strong resemblance to Bingham*: He also possessed some attributes of V. H. H. Green, who taught le Carré at that notorious recruiting ground for spies, Lincoln College, Oxford

15 *recent review of Len Deighton's The IPCRESS File*: 'Cloak without Dagger', *TLS*, 8 February 1963. Maclaren-Ross was a Soho oddball who has become a minor cult figure; his *The Doomsday Book* lurks on the outer fringes of spy fiction.

16 *his first spy novel*: Simon King found 'Fugitive from Perfection', an unpublished manuscript by Bingham, locked in Maxwell Knight's filing cabinet. Elements of the story include fascism and a Whitehall cover-up. Was the book too revealing? The story behind the story is yet to be discovered.

17 *A Fragment of Fear*: The film version had a screenplay by Paul Dehn, previously responsible for scripting *Goldfinger*, *The Spy Who Came in from the Cold* and *The Deadly Affair*.

18 *his career as a novelist lurched into a sad and steep decline*: The best book of his later years was a non-fiction study of the real-life criminal Peter Manuel. Edmund Crispin described *The Marriage Bureau Murders* as his 'nadir'; the potential of the tricky and unorthodox central idea of a voyeur of murder is sadly squandered. Bingham tried to emulate the success of Colin Dexter's Morse and Lewis, introducing a pair of cops called King and Owen in a feeble novel called *Deadly Picnic*. A detective called Brock based in a fictionalised Salisbury appeared in two books, but also failed to capture the magic of Morse. Bingham left Brock's third case unfinished.

19 *the Karla Trilogy*: Julian Symons, acknowledging that his was a minority view, complained that the books were 'funereally slow . . . the prose is ponderous, the obliquities often unnecessary', and also dismissed *The Naive and Sentimental Lover* as 'disastrously bad'. Symons much preferred *The Little Drummer Girl*, about an Israeli spy's attempt to kill a Palestinian terrorist.

20 *Phyllis Bottome*: See 'Could This Woman Have Invented James Bond?', *Radio Times*, 10 December 2016.

21 *relatively few women . . . have enjoyed lengthy careers as spy writers*: An exception was Evelyn Anthony (pen-name of Evelyn Ward-Thomas), whose *The Tamarind Seed* was filmed. Among those who sparkled briefly was Sarah Gainham (born Rachel Stainer) and E. H. Clements; both wrote books admired by Francis Iles. Dorothea Bennett's *The Jigsaw Man* was filmed by her husband, Terence Young, who also directed three Bond movies. Today the picture is changing: see Alison Flood, '"Nobody in Tesco Buys Spy Books by Women": How Female Authors Took on the Genre', *Guardian*, 7 January

2020. Charlotte Philby's *The Most Difficult Thing*, aka *Part of the Family*, blends spy fiction with domestic suspense.

22 *Holly Roth*: See Sarah Weinman, 'The Drowning of Holly Roth', *CrimeReads*, 17 May 2018.

23 *William Haggard*: This was the pen-name of Richard Henry Michael Clayton, a former civil servant, who introduced Colonel Charles Russell in *Slow Burner*; the series ran for over thirty years. Francis Iles said Haggard was 'as ingenious an exponent of the international power game as any in the business'. *The Unquiet Sleep* was televised in the BBC's *Detective* anthology series in 1968.

24 *the mood of the Swinging Sixties*: The psychedelic zeitgeist was reflected in the brief, flamboyant career of Adam Diment, whose *The Dolly, Dolly Spy* became an international bestseller in 1967. Three more books about the playboy Philip McAlpine followed before Diment vanished from the scene; see John Michael O'Sullivan, 'The Extraordinary Case of the Missing Spy Novelist', *Esquire*, 24 November 2015. The year 1967 also saw the release of a bizarre spoof film version of *Casino Royale*, boasting five different directors and a soundtrack by Burt Bacharach, while ITV launched *The Prisoner*, starring Patrick McGoohan, who had previously appeared in the more orthodox *Danger Man*. *The Prisoner* was controversial but iconic; in 1968, it was even sent up in 'Wish You Were Here', an episode of an equally stylish cult series, *The Avengers*. George Markstein, the first script editor of *The Prisoner*, later co-wrote the screenplay based on Frederick Forsyth's *The Odessa File* as well as spy novels such as *The Man from Yesterday*.

25 *The unnamed, working-class narrator*: He was called Harry Palmer in films of three of Deighton's books and in a 2022 ITV adaptation.

26 *a literary descendant of Philip Marlowe, a man of integrity*: See Jake Kerridge, 'The Deighton File: A Life of Reluctance and Intrigue', *The Daily Telegraph*, 14 February 2009.

27 *different approaches to his craft*: Among much else, he has written cook books, a book about airship disasters and Bond screenplays, 'which were buried under rewrites'.

28 *one of the finest 'alternative history' thrillers*: Another with a similar premise is *Fatherland*, by Robert Harris, whose later bestsellers include *Enigma*, about code-breaking at Bletchley Park. *Widowland* by C. J. Carey (a pen-name for Jane Thynne) gives the concept of Britain under Nazi rule a feminist slant.

29 *Alan Furst*: The series which takes its name from Furst's novel *The Night Soldiers* shows that espionage fiction of high quality need not be confined to contemporary events. Other American spy writers of note include Charles McCarry, James Grady and Robert Littell, whose first novels, *The Miernik Dossier*, *Six Days of the Condor* (economically filmed as *Three Days of the Condor*) and *The Defection of A. J. Lewinter* respectively, remain arguably their finest achievements.

30 *a new generation of writers*: Notably Mick Herron, whose principal series started with *Slow Horses*. Slough House is a base for a motley crew of secret agents who have suffered career setbacks; the boss, Jackson Lamb, is a memorable character in much the same way as is Reginald Hill's Andy Dalziel. Like Hill, Herron intertwines comedy with clever plotting and incisive social comment.

31 *interviewed by National Public Radio in the US*: The interviewer was Terry Gross, the date 28 December 2017.

32 *the illustrious life he'd led*: Le Carré made cameo appearances in several screen versions of his work, including a televised version of *The Night Manager*. At Oxford, he'd engaged in amateur dramatics, and helped to organise a student production of Patrick Hamilton's *Rope*. In the mid-1980s, he turned down an invitation by Wim Wenders to play the spy Dollman in a proposed film of Erskine Childers' *The Riddle of the Sands*.

33 *as William Boyd said*: *Guardian*, 18 December 2020; for Boyd, le Carré was 'the Dickens of the Cold War' and, like Greene, 'the exemplar of the ultimate literary professional'. In 'Smiley's Success', *The Sunday Times*, 2 May 2021, he argued that 'Smiley endures in the popular imagination not so much because he is an excellent spy but because he is an excellent detective' and that the fact that Smiley is James Bond's polar opposite suited the reinvention of the spy novel. Smiley isn't an agent out in the field, but an intellectual 'and, significantly, a serial cuckold . . . it's his vulnerability, his inadequacies . . . that add to his humanity . . . This is the paradox that makes us remember him.'

FORTY-THREE

Nerve

Adventure novels and thrillers

A quarter of a million people packed Aintree Racecourse in Liverpool for the Grand National steeplechase held on 24 March 1956. Among the crowd was a visiting party of officials from the Soviet Union. The Queen Mother was there to cheer on two of her own horses, including the fourth favourite, Devon Loch. Fifteen days earlier, Devon Loch's jockey had fallen and cracked his collarbone for the ninth time in a career dogged by injuries. He kept quiet about it, determined to fulfil a lifetime's dream by winning the National. His name was Dick Francis.

Twenty-nine horses set off at a ferocious pace, but the Aintree course is full of hazards, and the favourite, Must, fell at the first fence. With three fences to go, Devon Loch took the lead. Only ten horses remained in the field. After taking the final thorn fence with pace and rhythm, Francis' mount was five lengths clear. The crowd roared him on, their cheers deafening. Men were already throwing their hats in the air to salute him. He was only a few yards away from the winning post.

At that moment, Devon Loch buckled in his stride, and collapsed to the ground.

The crowd was stunned into silence. Francis clambered to his feet, and watched in anguish and disbelief as the other horses passed by. The dream had become a nightmare.

Devon Loch's name entered the language, a synonym for defeat snatched from the jaws of victory. What had caused the disaster? Theories flew around: the more imaginative, the better. Had the horse suffered a seizure, or tried to jump a fence that didn't exist? Had it been distracted by the crowd, or a glimpse of a shadow of the Water Jump?

Or might Devon Loch have suffered an electric shock as a result of an underground cable shorting on its racing plates? Lack of oxygen, an excess of glucose, a blood clot, a weak hind leg – did they explain the otherwise inexplicable? Was the calamity the handiwork of a Mafia gambling syndicate, anti-royalist conspirators, or the Russian secret service? Had the wretched creature simply slipped in the mud?

Francis' first thought was that Devon Loch had suffered cramp in its hind legs. Later, he concluded that the horse had been frightened by the gathering swell of noise from the stands. Nobody knows for sure. The mystery remains unsolved.[1]

The Devon Loch disaster changed everything for Francis. A brave and popular jockey, he realised at once that his name would for ever be linked to an astonishing failure in full view of the watching world. Three days after the National, he won a novice chase at Sandown, but what happened at Aintree haunted him for the rest of his life.

Within a few weeks, he was invited to write his autobiography. Francis had left school at fifteen, and never harboured literary ambitions. The obvious solution was to hire a ghostwriter, but Francis' wife Mary had a better idea. She was a former teacher who had a way with words; she'd reviewed in her spare time, and later worked part-time as a reader to sift through thrillers submitted to Michael Joseph.[2] She offered to help with the writing.

Reunited with Devon Loch, he won a hurdle at Nottingham, but a couple of months later he fell off another horse, and was trampled. The Marquess of Abergavenny, a representative of the Queen Mother, invited Francis over to his London flat, and the purpose of the meeting soon became clear. Abergavenny urged Francis to retire at the top, rather than face a slow decline. The conversation was courteous to a fault, but it amounted to a dismissal.

Francis was distraught. He'd lost the Grand National, and now he'd lost the only job he'd ever wanted. He had no hobbies and hated gardening. A few offers came in, and he agreed to contribute a ghostwritten weekly racing column to the *Sunday Express*. With Mary's support, he gained confidence as a journalist, and his autobiography, *The Sport of Queens*, sold well. When the couple watched a thriller play in Oxford, they wondered whether they might be able to do better themselves.

They worked together on *Dead Cert* (1962), a mystery about a murdered jockey. Francis' first-hand knowledge of the racing world added authenticity. The original plan was to name husband and wife as co-authors, but, for marketing purposes, the novel was presented as written by Dick Francis alone. The books grew in popularity, always marketed as Francis' sole work, even though Mary's contribution was indispensable. Francis felt uncomfortable about maintaining this particular fiction, but he was the celebrity, and his wife was content to remain in his shadow.

Even their apprentice works impressed reviewers. The first two books were praised by writers as discriminating as Nicholas Blake and Ross Macdonald, while Anthony Boucher said of *Nerve*: 'One's reaction is not "how can a great jockey write such a good novel?" but rather "how can an excellent novelist know so much about steeplechasing?"'

The Francis books were mostly stand-alone adventure stories that offered appealing variations on the same theme. The narrator was typically a strong but sensitive man who battled against personal setbacks[3] with integrity and determination, qualities that proved invaluable as he strove to foil a criminal plot. The prose was sinewy, the pace fast and the settings cast light on the darker corners of horse racing and its satellite businesses.

Odds Against (1965), with a storyline sparked by the closure of Hurst Park racecourse in order to build housing, introduced Francis' most popular protagonist. Sid Halley,[4] a successful jockey forced to give up racing because of a crippled hand, became a private detective. Halley was more fully characterised than usual, perhaps because he was in part a self-portrait.

Sex and sadism, if not as graphic as in the James Bond series, played a part in the early books, but snobbery was conspicuous by its absence. The novels were much less fantastic than Ian Fleming's. After countless fractures and bruises, Francis knew exactly what severe pain feels like, and so did Mary, whose life was beset by health problems; their protagonists suffered when falling from a horse or beaten by brutal enemies. Realism in detail strengthened the books without slowing their narrative drive.

As the co-authors grew in confidence, their sales and wealth increased immeasurably; they relocated to Florida, and later to Grand Cayman. The background information in the novels was no longer confined to racing, broadening their appeal far beyond readers interested in horses. *Rat Race* (1970) drew on Mary's experience of running an air-taxi business, and she studied equine medicine when researching the plot of *Whip Hand* (1979), in which Halley reappeared; the book won both an Edgar and a CWA Gold Dagger.

The harmonious collaboration between Dick and Mary Francis was the polar opposite of the stormy relationship of the cousins who wrote as Ellery Queen. The couple regarded themselves as running 'a family business'. Their sons Merrick and Felix and their grandson Matthew all supplied inspiration for characters in the books,[5] and, as a physics student, Felix designed a bomb to blow up a plane for *Rat Race*.

Mary's death in 2000 led to five years in which no Dick Francis novel appeared, and again the question arose of whether to bring in a ghostwriter. Instead, Felix wrote *Under Orders* (2006) for publication as by Dick Francis. After that, he was named as co-author for four books, and, following his father's death, he has continued to publish books in the same vein. They appear under his name but are marketed as 'Dick Francis novels'. The brand is too popular and valuable to be allowed to die.

Personal experience was also the catalyst for Alistair MacLean's first novel. A Scottish 'son of the manse', he grew up in Josephine Tey country, the village of Daviot, south of Inverness. As a teenager during the Second World War, he joined the Royal Navy, and served on HMS *Royalist*, taking part in two Arctic convoys.

The war was followed by university, marriage and a job in

teaching. After winning first prize in a short story competition run by the *Glasgow Herald*, he was approached by Collins the publishers, and encouraged to try a novel. On the principle of writing what you knew, he produced a thriller drawing on his experiences during the war.

HMS Ulysses (1955) captured the bleakness and desperation of life on the Arctic convoys. Furious gales and cold, heaving seas were enemies of the men on the ships, as dangerous as German dive-bombers and submarines. The grimly realistic setting, combined with taut prose and narrative momentum, made the book an overnight success.[6] MacLean never surpassed its power and immediacy, but his storytelling gift ensured that his books came to dominate the bestseller lists.

His second novel was another wartime thriller, *The Guns of Navarone* (1957), set on a fictitious Greek island. During the war, he'd spent a few months in Greece, although he admitted he was never at risk of anything worse than sunburn. Next came *South by Java Head* (1958), concerning the fall of Singapore to the Japanese army. MacLean sold the film rights to both books, beginning a long and lucrative association with the movie business. He was soon earning so much money that he fled to Switzerland as a tax exile.

In his early years as a novelist, MacLean entertained some literary ambitions. 1959 saw him venture into Cold War espionage with *The Last Frontier*, set in Hungary, but boredom prompted a change of approach. John Talbot, narrator of *Fear is the Key* (1961), is, if not exactly unreliable, certainly less than straight-forward with his readers. MacLean explained to his nervous publishers that he wanted to 'develop a technique of completely impersonal story-telling in the first person'.[7] Dry wit as well as the single-mindedness of a man on a mission gave the book a distinctive flavour, but sales didn't live up to his expectations.

His next experiment was to write under a pseudonym, to test whether his book would achieve success on merit, rather than on the strength of his reputation. Predictably, his publishers were appalled. Having failed to dissuade him, they were unhappy with the manuscript, only relenting when MacLean threatened to move to a competitor. The outcome was two novels published in quick succession under the name Ian Stuart. *The Satan Bug* (1962), in which germ warfare is used for criminal purposes, was filmed with modest success, but MacLean decided to revert to writing under his own name.

He moved back to live in an English mansion, and, on delivering the manuscript of *Ice Station Zebra* (1963), broke the news to his publishers that he'd never enjoyed writing and proposed to set up in business. He bought Jamaica Inn, made famous by Daphne du Maurier's novel of that name, and reinvented himself as a hotelier. As other thriller writers more committed to the craft[8] emerged, MacLean spent three years demonstrating his ineptitude as a businessman, until rescue came in the form of the film producer Elliott Kastner, who persuaded him to write an original screenplay.

The result was *Where Eagles Dare*, a war story that became the basis for another novel (published in 1967) as well as a film. MacLean began to conceive story ideas in terms of their movie potential rather than as books. He returned to Switzerland, divorced and remarried unhappily; after divorcing his second wife, he tried in vain to persuade her predecessor to take him back. By now, he was drinking as heavily as he was spending. He'd lost enthusiasm for writing, and it showed. As the quality of his fiction declined, readers sensed that he'd lost respect for them. Other writers – known as 'MacLones' in the publishing business – were hired to turn his outlines into novels.[9] Alcoholism hastened his death at the age of sixty-four.

The MacLean method eschewed sex, and he avoided describing violence in stomach-churning detail. He had a habit of calling his female characters Mary, and paid them scant attention. Raymond Chandler and Winston Graham[10] were two of the few popular authors he admired, but he had a particular distaste for Ian Fleming, for years a rival in the bestseller charts.

Pace, plot and place were his strengths. The early books ratchet up the tension, although the descriptions of up-to-the-minute technology quickly dated. He wrote about rugged individualists playing for high stakes, but his unwillingness to create a series character, coupled with the feebleness of the later books and the spin-offs, explain why his work fell out of favour. Today, his attitudes seem old-fashioned, but no more so than Fleming's; the difference is that Fleming created James Bond.

*

Michael Gilbert distinguished the thriller from the adventure story,[11] arguing that the former features 'the continuous and threatening presence of an enemy', while the latter 'is an account of what transpires when someone sets out on a search'. He made a persuasive case, but many books, including several of his own, mix both ingredients. James Patterson, one of the most commercially successful writers who have ever lived, summed up the essence of his craft:[12] 'what gives the variety of thrillers a common ground is the intensity of emotions they create, particularly those of apprehension and exhilaration, of excitement and breathlessness, all designed to generate that all-important thrill.'

Lionel Davidson was a literary chameleon whose career illustrates why there is little to be gained from attempts to categorise and define the different branches of the genre. Spy story, adventure story, serial killer mystery, he switched between them with ease. Although his books offered few cheap thrills, the stylish writing prompted Daphne du Maurier to compare him to Henry Rider Haggard and Graham Greene.

Davidson's origins could hardly have been humbler; born in Hull, as one of the nine children of a Jewish tailor, he taught his illiterate mother to read and speak English after his father died. During the war, he was a submarine telegraphist in the Pacific, and claimed to be one of only two Jews who served in the Submarine Service.

When peace came, he worked as a freelance journalist and edited the magazine *John Bull* prior to publishing his first book, a Cold War thriller. *The Night of Wenceslas*[13] (1960) featured an unlikely hero, an angry young man who finds himself mixed up in international espionage in Soviet-era Prague. A framing device in the next book, *The Rose of Tibet* (1962), enabled Davidson to include himself as a character; there was also an unflattering caricature of the publisher Victor Gollancz.

He spent ten years living in Israel. Many of his relatives had been killed during the Holocaust, and *Making Good Again*[14] (1968) reflected his preoccupation with his Jewish heritage. *The Chelsea Murders*, aka *Murder Games* (1978), was very different, a whodunit with literary clues to a grotesque sequence of sex murders. Another change of direction saw him concentrate on writing screenplays that were never made; although this work paid well, he concluded that he'd rather dig roads. The death of his wife affected him deeply, but he remarried, and published his eighth and final thriller.

Kolymsky Heights (1994), the only novel from the last thirty years of his life, followed a brilliant linguist, Johnny Porter, on a mission to Siberia. Davidson's juggling of classic plot components such as code-breaking and the race against time, allied to his customary three-dimensional characterisation, should have guaranteed the book's success, but it failed to chime with the public mood after the end of the Cold War. Twenty years later, international tensions had risen again, and readers were ready for it. The book was reissued and shot to the top of the bestseller lists.

Francis, MacLean and Davidson lacked interest in writing long-running series. The nature of adventure stories and thrillers means that they tend to be stand-alones.[15] Lee Child[16] has bucked this trend with such success that it is said that one of his books is bought every second of every day. Child was born in Coventry but has lived in the US for many years, and his fame rests on the creation of an American ex-military cop whose popularity illustrates readers' love of memorable series characters.

Killing Floor (1997) introduced Jack Reacher, the quintessential loner, a man who moves from place to place, without possessions or commitments. Sometimes trouble finds him, sometimes he brings it on himself. Fearless and resourceful, he always prevails. Reacher narrates in the first novel, but his later exploits are often written in the third person, where it serves Child's purpose as a means of building suspense.

Reacher's appeal is not that he develops as a character during the series, but rather, as Child has explained,[17] because he represents a tradition both timeless and universal: 'The stories that I love are basically about . . . the mysterious stranger . . . The Westerns were absolutely rock solid with that stuff . . . the mysterious rider comes in off the range, sorts out the problem, and rides off into the sunset. It is . . . a total paradigm . . . not invented in America . . . [but] imported from the medieval tales of Europe. The knight-errant: . . . somehow banished and forced to wander the land doing good deeds. It's part of storytelling in every culture.

Japan has it with the ronin myth; every culture has this Robin Hood idea.'

Notes

The main sources are Graham Lord's biography of Francis, Jack Webster's of MacLean, newspaper reports of the Devon Loch incident, and magazine and newspaper interviews with Lee Child.

1   *The mystery remains unsolved*: Graham Lord points out that the plot of Nat Gould's *The Steeplechaser* (1918) foreshadows the Devon Loch fiasco, although the hero recovers from his horse's collapse and goes on to win the Grand National. Nathaniel Gould was a prolific Manchester-born novelist who spent several years in Australia and specialised in horse-racing stories.

2   *worked part-time as a reader to sift through thrillers submitted to Michael Joseph*: To her husband's amusement, Mary Francis turned down Frederick Forsyth's *The Day of the Jackal*, in which a British assassin is hired to kill President de Gaulle. The apparent defect of the story was that everyone knew that de Gaulle wasn't assassinated. Its strength lay in the painstaking detail of Forsyth's research, which resulted in a compelling story; the question was not whether the killing would succeed, but how a plan so meticulous could fail. Forsyth, an investigative journalist who had also spied for MI6, has enjoyed a long career as a bestselling thriller writer, without ever surpassing the excellence of his debut.

3   *a strong but sensitive man who battled against personal setbacks*: In *Forfeit*, one of Francis' three Edgar-winning novels, racing correspondent James Tyrone delves into a betting scam after the mysterious death of a colleague. Tyrone's wife, a polio sufferer, is confined to a breathing machine. Mary Francis had personal experience of polio, and spent three weeks in an iron lung.

4   *Sid Halley*: Halley appeared in four Dick Francis novels, as well as in Felix Francis' *Refusal*. The character also appeared in a television series, *The Racing Game*.

5   *Their sons Merrick and Felix and their grandson Matthew all supplied inspiration for characters in the books*: Freddie Croft in *Driving Force*, Jonathan Derry in *Twice Shy* and Benedict Juliard in *10 lb. Penalty*.

6   *an overnight success*: When the book was launched in London, those attending included Sir Alan Herbert, who thirty-five years earlier had published *The House by the River*.

7   *a technique of completely impersonal story-telling in the first person*: MacLean's continuing interest in this approach is evident as late as *Bear Island*. In effect a 'closed circle' murder mystery, published in 1971, this was his last thriller of merit. The film version, with Donald Sutherland, bore limited resemblance to the original.

8   *other thriller writers more committed to the craft*: Such as Desmond Bagley. His debut *The Golden Keel* featured a first-person narrator who had, like Bagley, emigrated from Britain to South Africa. *The Tightrope Men* has an opening premise worthy of Cornell Woolrich. Having gone to sleep in London,

Giles Denison wakes in a hotel in Oslo; when he looks in the mirror, he sees another man's face, not his own.

9   *Other writers . . . were hired to turn his outlines into novels*: John Denis wrote two books before MacLean died in 1987. Others who continued the MacLean franchise included the similarly named Alistair MacNeill, who was offered the opportunity on the strength of a manuscript of his own, submitted to MacLean's publishers.

10 *Winston Graham*: The success of Graham's Poldark series of historical novels has obscured the quality of his thrillers. He came into his own in the post-war era, with *The Little Walls* (the first winner of the Crossed Red Herring award, later known as the CWA Gold Dagger), *Marnie* and *The Walking Stick*; the latter two books were filmed.

11 *Michael Gilbert distinguished the thriller from the adventure story*: In 'The Moment of Violence' in *Crime in Good Company*. He argued that 'a thriller is more difficult to write than a detective story.'

12 *James Patterson . . . summed up the essence of his craft*: In his introduction to the anthology *Thrillers*. Patterson introduced Alex Cross, the cop who became his most famous character, in *Along Came a Spider* in 1993. Working with a wide range of collaborators, he has produced a vast number of books. His co-authors include Alafair Burke (daughter of James Lee Burke) and former President Bill Clinton. Typically, a co-author will take Patterson's story outline and do most of the writing. As with so many crime writers, Patterson once worked in advertising, but perhaps none has exploited their expertise in marketing a brand to more lucrative effect.

13 *The Night of Wenceslas*: A film version, *Hot Enough for June*, was scripted by Lukas Heller, whose other screenplays included the psychological thrillers *What Ever Happened to Baby Jane?* and *Hush . . . Hush, Sweet Charlotte*. Heller's daughter Zoe is the author of *Notes on a Scandal*, a mainstream novel cited by Gillian Flynn as one of numerous inspirations for *Gone Girl*.

14 *Making Good Again*: The title is a literal translation of the German word for reparations. Unpredictable as ever, Davidson ended the book not with words, but with three bars of music, representing the song of a woodlark.

15 *they tend to be stand-alones*: This is true almost by definition of conspiracy thrillers, which have often been most effective as films rather than novels; examples include the subtly terrifying *The Parallax View* and *The Conversation*, as well as the more straightforward *All the President's Men*, *Arlington Road* and *State of Play*, and a movie actually titled *Conspiracy Theory*. 'Lip Service', an episode of the TV anthology *Inside No. 9*, draws on movie inspirations in witty and concise fashion.

16 *Lee Child*: Child is a pen-name for James Grant, who has written of his admiration of MacLean's early books, such as *The Golden Rendezvous*. Child took inspiration from John D. MacDonald's books about Travis McGee and was equally impressed by MacDonald's canny marketing, as with the colour-coded titles of the McGee series. Much less expected is his enthusiasm for Dorothy L. Sayers, evident in his introduction to a reprint of *Have His Carcase*, or the fact that a plot twist in one of his novels updates that in Christie's *The ABC Murders*. In 2020, he announced that he planned to collaborate with his brother Andrew (already an established thriller writer) on future Reacher novels prior to handing over the franchise to him.

17 *as Child has explained*: See Alex Berenson, 'What Lee Child Has Learned from Writing the Jack Reacher Books', *Esquire*, 4 December 2014.

FORTY-FOUR

Outsider in Amsterdam

Dutch crime

On a hot morning in the summer of 1958, a twenty-six-year-old Dutchman jumped out of a taxi outside the wooden gate of a Zen monastery. He'd arrived in Kyoto, Japan's 'mystical capital' and home to eight thousand temples. Six-foot-high walls topped with grey clay tiles confronted him. Beyond them, he glimpsed the tops of pine trees, cut by practised hands into exotic and enticing shapes.

His ship had landed at Kobe; from there, he'd come by train. Nobody was expecting him. He'd come in the hope of studying as a monk. When asked why, he said he yearned to understand the purpose of life. The Zen master, an old man in a simple grey gown, said, 'Life has a purpose, but a strange purpose. When you come to the end of the road and find perfect insight you will see that enlightenment is a joke.'

The Zen master accepted the Dutchman as a disciple and permitted him to spend more than a year in the monastery. In the Zendo, the meditation hall, he spent interminable hours preparing his mind to be worthy of being given a *koan*, a riddle of existence to be solved in meditation. But he didn't want to spend the rest of his life as a monk. He loved alcohol too much, and he decided he wasn't even religious. He'd just been looking for some answers.

On an excursion away from the monastery, he was befriended by a wealthy gay man called Leo Marks. On one occasion, Marks took him to a brothel that specialised in catering for transvestites, but the young Dutchman was more interested in the few girls who were present on the premises to keep up appearances in case of a visit from the police.

At Marks' home by the sea, he explored the library, and discovered books written by Robert van Gulik. These were detective stories about the famous magistrate Judge Dee, who 'thinks along strict Confucian lines and believes firmly in morality but when confronted with real Buddhist and Taoist masters, who make fun of him, respects them because Dee himself is a man of genius, with an incorruptible and sincere mind, capable of realising the depth of their teaching'. So began his lifelong fascination with van Gulik, Judge Dee and unusual mystery fiction.

Jan Willem Lincoln van de Wetering enjoyed a silver-spoon childhood. His father was a wealthy Rotterdam commodities trader whose fondness for America prompted his decision to bestow a dead President's name on his youngest child. As he grew up, van de Wetering (who liked to be known as Janwillem) witnessed Dutch military police in bearskin hats shooting people as they rioted over poverty. When war came, he was horrified by the sight of Jewish children being taken away from school for an unknown destination. With peace restored, he rebelled against his comfortable Calvinist upbringing, and embarked on what he termed his philosophical search.

Rotterdam bored him, and he was desperate to escape. A brief spell working for his father in Cape Town ended when he refused to move to Johannesburg, and he joined an 'intellectual motorcycle gang'[1] that took inspiration from Dostoevsky and Rimbaud. A brief marriage to a local artist who taught him 'how ideas can be realized into more substantial forms through pottery and sculpture' did not last. After inheriting money on his father's death, he returned to Europe.

In London, he attended philosophy lectures at University College without attempting to take a degree, and read twenty books recommended by the professor – A. J. 'Freddie' Ayer.[2] Despondent, he told Ayer that none of the recommended books, or his lectures, had brought him any closer to 'the truth'. Ayer filled his pipe, and recommended him to 'go to a monastery, find a master, an adept who has finished his training, and he'll cure you or you'll cure yourself.' With this, he lit his pipe, shook his student's hand, and strolled away. Needing no further encouragement, van de Wetering headed for Japan.

After leaving the monastery, he travelled to Colombia, then Peru. He married for the second time, crossed to Australia, and finally returned to Amsterdam. While running a textile business, he was warned that he faced arrest for having dodged a call-up to military service. A civil servant suggested that, as an alternative to punishment, he work as a part-time unpaid policeman. It was an offer he couldn't refuse, and he spent seven years on the beat, working evenings and weekends.

During that time, he wrote a book describing his experiences in Japan. On leaving the reserve constabulary, he decided to make something out of his knowledge of police work, his taste for Simenon and his continuing quest for answers about the purpose of life. He became a crime novelist.

Outsider in Amsterdam, published in 1975 when van de Wetering was in his mid-forties, introduced a trio of Dutch police officers whose cases, appearing over a span of more than two decades, were as eclectic and outlandish as their creator's life. The story opens with a corpse dangling from a noose in the building that is home to the seventeenth-century Hindist Society. The body belongs to the Society's leader, and his apparent suicide is investigated by Adjutant-Detective Henk Grijpstra and Detective-Sergeant Rinus de Gier.

Grijpstra is heavily built, bourgeois and dreams of being a jazz musician; de Gier is younger, attractive to women, fond of cats and a contemplative flute player with an interest in mysticism. Van de Wetering named them after the Dutch words 'to seize' and 'vulture' respectively, and saw them (rather as Reginald Hill regarded his own cop duo Dalziel and Pascoe) as reflecting different aspects of his own personality. The detectives report to an elderly commissaris, whose surname is never revealed, and whose character reflects aspects of the personalities of van de Wetering's father, the master of the monastery in Kyoto and his boss in the Amsterdam police.

It would be a stretch to describe *Outsider in Amsterdam* as a police procedural. Its offbeat nature is encapsulated in a scene where Grijpstra and de Gier indulge in an impromptu musical jam session. The quirky storyline explores issues ranging from the legacy of colonialism and its impact on contemporary Dutch society to that old favourite, the question of whether murder can ever be justified. The writing has an almost surreal quality, maintained throughout the series. Van de Wetering told an interviewer[3] that he liked to have some sort of dream sequence in every novel.

He decided to join a Buddhist community in Maine, and, although the group soon dissolved, he, his wife and his daughter settled in America. As unconventional in his storytelling as in his life, van de Wetering perplexed critics as often as he enthused them.[4] Even his method of writing was startling: 'I usually write in Dutch, then rewrite in English. The English versions are shorter and I don't get too exuberant with word play. Sometimes the plot lines differ, in some books even the characters differ. I never aim to translate.'

His philosophical musings in *The Japanese Corpse* (1977), which sees de Gier and the commissaris visiting Japan in order to investigate the background to a Dutch killing, baffled the traditionalist critics Barzun and Taylor, who felt that the book 'revels in fantasy and, except in that genre, deserves oblivion'. But even they approved of *The Maine Massacre*[5] (1979), in which de Gier and the commissaris venture to the United States, and solve a series of murders: 'local color is genuine and the plot is respectable'. In France, the novel won the Grand Prix de Littérature Policière.

Van de Wetering's lifestyle, like his books, teetered on the brink of disastrous self-indulgence. As he said, 'hallucinations, mysticism, the spiritual path and messing up on same . . . are subjects dear to my heart.' In the 1980s, he was drinking heavily; as a result, 'my personality fell apart, I needed to build a new mask, set up new habits. That process took eight years. Instead of writing I was mostly puttering about in an old lobster yacht and doing junk sculpture on my acres of coastal land . . . Juanita and I visited Papua New Guinea and Mexico . . . By 1993 I began writing again, using a new formula for my Amsterdam Cops. As private detectives, financed by found drug millions, they can finally be amoral.'

Grijpstra and de Gier finally returned in *Just a Corpse at Twilight* (1994), largely set on van de Wetering's beloved Maine coast. The jokey title had a sad resonance: his career was fading away. In his sixties, he gave up smoking and drinking, but only two more novels appeared before he succumbed to cancer.

Van de Wetering was by no means the first detective writer from the Netherlands. Conan Doyle's shadow loomed over the work of Jakob van Schevichaven, who adopted the pen-name Ivans (i.e. J + van + S) and produced over forty books. His answer to Holmes and Watson was the partnership of Englishman Geoffrey Gill and his Dutch friend Willy Hendriks, while he also created a Great Detective called Mister Monk.[6]

Ivans is often described as one of the two fathers of the Dutch detective story, along with Havank, pseudonym of Hendrikus (Hans) Frederikus van der Kallen. Havank was a translator as well as author of mysteries featuring two French cops, which enjoyed such a high profile that the Dutch national forensic biometric system became known as HAVANK.

Ivans and Havank remained unknown quantities in Britain and America. For years the same was true of A. C. (Albert Cornelius) Baantjer,[7] a police officer whose long experience in law informed a series about Inspector DeKok and Sergeant Vledder. Prior to the arrival of Grijpstra and de Gier, the most celebrated Dutch cop was created by an expatriate Englishman.

Born in London to unhappily married parents who drifted apart, Nicolas Freeling[8] spent his early days on the move, living in Southampton, then Brittany, and later wartime Ireland. His mother was a former Communist whose cousin was Erskine Childers, author of *The Riddle of the Sands*.

After the end of the Second World War, Freeling took a job in the kitchen of a French hotel. Following two years of national service, he wanted to pursue his ambition of becoming a chef. Over the next few years he learned his craft, married a Dutch woman and moved to the Netherlands. The incident that changed his life occurred when he was a senior chef in a hotel in Amsterdam. The local police's investigations into the criminal underworld led them to the hotel. The foreigner in the kitchen was an obvious suspect, and when he pilfered meat for his family – a customary perk of the kitchen – he was arrested.

The policeman who interrogated Freeling was amused, sympathetic and worldly-wise. During the three weeks Freeling spent in prison he was put to work wrapping up bars of soap; he smoothed out some of the papers, and started to scribble down a story about such a man. Deported back to England with his family, he worked the material into a novel that he thought of as a romance and called *Love in Amsterdam*.

When he was introduced to Victor Gollancz, the publisher made clear that the story, featuring a Dutch cop called Piet Van der Valk, should be marketed as a detective novel, and it duly appeared in 1962. This was a haphazard start to a crime-writing career that for the next four decades pursued a similarly erratic course.

In *Criminal Conversation* (1965), Van der Valk refers to himself as 'Philip van der Marlowe'. Freeling also acknowledged the early Maigret novels as a strong formative influence, and even met Simenon once or twice: they shared a 'passion for eccentric hats'. He found Victor Gollancz shrewd but 'tiresome', and infuriated his publisher by 'deviating . . . from his view, formed in the twenties, of what crime fiction should be like . . . But I had been given, technically, the label, stamped upon the famous yellow jackets. It would take me twenty years even beginning to grasp how to get rid of it.'

Before he reached that point, Freeling wrote ten books about Van der Valk. Once established as an author, he returned to the Netherlands, and his experience of Dutch life gave the books an authenticity rare at that time in crime novels written by Englishmen abroad. His fascination with moral conundrums usually took precedence over whodunit or howdunit.

Van der Valk, his creator said, is 'intensely Dutch, characteristically fond of crude personal remarks followed by a guffaw: obstinate, brutal, pragmatic . . . He loved above all his French wife . . . Arlette was his entire secret . . . she was the sharpest and handiest of his tools.' Her confident teasing of the Dutch instinct for conformity gives her husband moral support in his unorthodox approach to police work. The settings are crucial to the stories. In *Double-Barrel* (1964), a spate of poison-pen letters disrupts the calm of smug, self-righteous and repressed Zwinderen.

Guns before Butter (1963) won the Grand Prix de Littérature Policière and was a runner-up for the CWA Gold Dagger. The mingling of love story and smuggling mystery worked well, and Freeling's characterisation of the poor little rich girl Lucienne Engelbert[9] illustrated his gift for humanising his people. In the United States, the MWA awarded *The King of the Rainy Country* (1966) an Edgar.

Van der Valk was a hot property, and Freeling recognised that 'the accepted wisdom is to seize with both hands while the going is good . . . Contracts shower in by every post, movie people invite one to lunch, journalists scratch at the door: the gateway has opened to the sweet life.' His first novel was filmed,[10] and a British television series starring Barry Foster as the Dutch cop was hugely popular; even the theme tune made it to the top of the hit parade.[11]

A long-running series can become a strait-jacket for an ambitious author, and Freeling feared that Van der Valk was starting to parody himself. Having moved to France, he worried that 'the backgrounds would have ceased being exact, slipping into the nonsense chambers of commerce print for handouts.' For him, Maigret's 'Third Republic anachronisms in modern Paris became embarrassing'.

Generations of crime writers have wrestled with this dilemma. Conan Doyle tipped Sherlock Holmes into the Reichenbach Falls, only to bow to pressure and revive his hero. Sayers abandoned Wimsey to matrimony and devoted herself to religion and Dante. Ken Millar didn't move on from Lew Archer. Ian Fleming never freed himself from Bondage.

Freeling's solution was to destroy Van der Valk. While pursuing an inquiry in *A Long Silence* (1972), the detective was shot dead. This quixotic decision Freeling justified by arguing that Van der Valk's demise 'made sure he would stay alive'. In truth, putting a permanent end to such a popular character at the height of his fame rather than opting for a period of benign neglect was an act of literary self-harm.

Freeling then created a provincial French cop, Henri Castang, who plodded through sixteen books. Freeling and his family lived in a large house in Grandfontaine, and the cost of maintaining it and educating his five children led him to admit to 'moments of regret and bitterness' about eliminating Van der Valk. His attempts to explain his reasoning in metaphysical terms, that the death of the detective was somehow 'meant', didn't even seem to convince himself.

His decision to reintroduce Arlette Van der Valk as an investigator in lieu of her husband amounted to an admission of defeat. The experiment proved short-lived and, in 1989, Van der Valk made a comeback in *Sand Castles*, a case pre-dating his demise, but to little fanfare. The parallels between the detective's travels with Arlette and the setting of *The Riddle of the Sands* were more interesting than the story. This proved to be the final Van der Valk novel.

Freeling's other books included *Gadget* (1977), a nuclear thriller that was more of a damp squib, and an entertaining memoir about his time as a chef.[12] Each of his books offers something out of the ordinary, but this isn't always enough to compel a reader to turn the page. After the first heady years, Freeling's books were ignored by award-givers and his readership diminished. He kept writing to the end, but, long before his death in 2003, his time had passed.

Killing Van der Valk was an extreme example of Freeling's fondness for going his own way.[13] His iconoclasm showed itself in his opinions about fellow authors. He loved Dickens, but dismissed *The Mystery of Edwin Drood* as 'trashy'; he admired Chandler, but mocked Hammett as 'a bad writer, lifeless and stilted in the fashionably monosyllabic Hemingway monotone . . . unreadably mannered'. Allingham's *The Tiger in the Smoke* came in for a pummelling – yet he lavished superlatives on *Gaudy Night*, concluding: 'there is grit in a Sayers composition . . . The theme of women's truth to herself is as valid as it was to Ibsen. There is much good social observation of England between the wars. Not for another thirty years would ostensible crime writing reach this level.'

*

For all their idiosyncrasies, Freeling's early novels critiqued society: 'Murder, and any other crime, is not a part of entertainment, but an integral part of life . . . and to choose a crime as the mainspring of a book's action is only to find one of the simplest ways of focussing eyes on our life and our world.'

His cosmopolitanism was significant. During the Golden Age, detective stories set in Europe, even those with recognisable backgrounds rather than variations on Ruritania, offered readers a glimpse into exotic, unfamiliar societies, but little more. Freeling had lived, breathed and loved the Netherlands for long enough to present a three-dimensional picture of the country and its people to British readers. His books aren't travelogues, but novels with a warts-and-all foreign setting integral to each story.

Others followed his lead. Magdalen Nabb's novels featuring Marshal Guarnaccia benefited from her intimate knowledge of Florence, and this impressed an American writer based in Venice, Donna Leon: 'it is evident from her books that she lives in Italy, and that she speaks Italian and she has Italian friends and she has a real sense of the Italian world.'

Leon, yet another advertising copywriter who turned to crime, has mined her love of Venice in a popular series about Commissario Guido Brunetti. For her, that first-hand empathy with the locale is critical. Of Michael Dibdin's Aurelio Zen books,[14] Leon sniffed: 'I think it is quite evident that Dibdin doesn't live in Italy.'

Local knowledge is never the be-all and end-all. It would be crass to claim that one must live in a country in order to write about it, but, as the world has shrunk, widely travelled readers demand authenticity when reading a book with a foreign background. They don't just want to see the sights. They want to experience the sound and the taste and the smell of a place.

Robert Hans van Gulik was born in 1910 in the Netherlands but grew up in the Dutch East Indies, where he learned to read and speak Mandarin. He joined the Dutch foreign service, and during the Second World War served as secretary to the Dutch mission to Chiang Kai-shek's nationalist government in Chongqing. There he married the daughter of a Qing dynasty imperial mandarin.

After returning to Japan in 1949, he produced two books, both privately printed. One was a collection of erotic coloured prints dating back to the Ming dynasty. The other was his translation of an eighteenth-century Chinese *gong'an*[15] detective book, *Celebrated Cases of Judge Dee*, which appeared in a limited edition[16] of twelve hundred copies illustrated by nine drawings, three copied from Chinese art, and six by van Gulik. His aim was to give western readers an insight into Chinese detective fiction.

Judge Dee,[17] a magistrate active during the Tang dynasty, acts as prosecutor, judge and jury, as well as a detective who sometimes conducts his inquiries in disguise. Dee adheres to a strict ethical code, although interestingly this does not exclude torturing someone to extract a confession.

In an afterword, van Gulik mused about the potential of the ancient Chinese detective stories for modern adaptation. He decided to experiment by writing a new case for Judge Dee. *The Chinese Maze Murders* (1951) is set when Dee was alive, but draws on plot material from later times. He wrote the story in English but, doubting that there was a market, had it translated into Japanese. His next step was to translate the book into Chinese; it was published in Singapore and ultimately the English language version appeared in 1956. The book comprises three mysteries, each connected to a garden maze, and the classic nature of the enterprise is captured by the title of the first: 'The Case of the Sealed Room'.

Van Gulik's knowledge of Chinese history and culture gave his stories texture. Publishers couldn't resist the urge to describe Judge Dee as 'the Sherlock Holmes of China' or 'the Maigret of the Tang dynasty', but as van Gulik pointed out, Chinese detective fiction pre-dated its western counterpart. His neat line drawings complemented 'impossible crime' stories and other neatly constructed mysteries, garnished with the casts of characters, diagrams and sketch maps beloved of enthusiasts for the West's Golden Age.

Just as Ken Millar identified with Lew Archer, and Janwillem van de Wetering with Grijpstra and de Gier, so van Gulik saw the Chinese magistrate as a projection of himself, saying: 'Judge Dee, that's me.' He continued to write while rising in the Dutch diplomatic hierarchy, and became ambassador to Japan in 1965, but died from cancer just two years later at the age of fifty-seven.

Throughout his life, van de Wetering remained obsessed with

van Gulik. He wrote van Gulik's biography, and an afterword to a reprint of van Gulik's unsuccessful contemporary novel, *The Given Day* (1964). For van de Wetering, the book symbolised an enduring disconnect, the same conflict that provoked Freeling into murdering Van der Valk. The true artist yearns to grow and move forward. The general public has an insatiable appetite for more of the same.

Notes

The main sources are van de Wetering's *The Empty Mirror*, his biography of van Gulik, a PBS YouTube interview of van de Wetering, Henry Wessels' article 'The Philosophical Exercises of Janwillem van de Wetering' (included on Wessels' Avram Davidson website), Freeling's *Criminal Convictions*, and his obituaries in the *Guardian* and *Daily Telegraph*.

1   *he joined an 'intellectual motorcycle gang'*: His experiences are reflected in his story 'Quicksand' in *Mangrove Mama*.
2   *A. J. 'Freddie' Ayer*: Ayer is among several eminent philosophers – others include Bertrand Russell and Anthony Quinton – to have been a guest speaker at a Detection Club dinner. He is referenced in Alexander McCall Smith's *The Sunday Philosophy Club*, the first novel about Isabel Dalhousie, whose interest in moral philosophy informs her amateur detection.
3   *Van de Wetering told an interviewer*: John C. Carr in *The Craft of Crime*. Carr pointed out that the 'justice in these finely rendered, vivid novels is usually poetic rather than statutory'.
4   *van de Wetering perplexed critics as often as he enthused them*: This was true even of H. R. F. Keating, whose own interest in Buddhism prompted his second novel, *Zen there was Murder*. In *Whodunit?*, Keating described the series as 'curious books, mazy in direction, full of fine insights, gently mad even'.
5   *even they approved of The Maine Massacre*: This goodwill proved short-lived. Their judgement of *The Mind Murders*, published two years later, was crushing: 'Picturesque irrelevance has now turned into a surfeit of surrealist conversations, and credibility would suffer if one could work up an interest in the doings.'
6   *Mister Monk*: Not to be confused with *Monk*, a television series about a San Francisco detective with obsessive compulsive disorder and a gift for solving impossible crimes.
7   *A. C. (Albert Cornelius) Baantjer*: From 1995, his cops featured in a long-running Dutch television series, *Baantjer*, a rare example of a crime show named after the author rather than the detective.
8   *Nicolas Freeling*: Freeling's birth name was Nicolas Davidson, but he took his mother's name. Arlette Van der Valk remarried a man called Davidson.
9   *the poor little rich girl Lucienne Engelbert*: In *Books to Die For*, Jason Goodwin describes her portrayal as 'impeccable and real . . . as autonomous as the Girl with the Dragon Tattoo, but much more believable'.
10 *His first novel was filmed*: As *Amsterdam Affair*.

11 *the theme tune made it to the top of the hit parade*: 'Eye Level', by Simon Park and his Orchestra, spent four weeks at number one in the UK chart in 1973; a lyricised version, 'And You Smiled', was a minor hit for Matt Monro. A lacklustre TV reboot of *Van der Valk* in 2020 received poor reviews, as did its theme music.

12 *an entertaining memoir about his time as a chef*: The Kitchen inspired Anthony Bourdain, a celebrity chef, to write *Kitchen Confidential*. Bourdain also dabbled in crime, publishing *Bone in the Throat: A Novel of Death and Digestion*.

13 *Freeling's fondness for going his own way*: Even the tolerant H. R. F. Keating groaned at the way Freeling 'showers the unprotected reader with opinions . . . He appears to delight in the unusualness of the opinions he holds.'

14 *Michael Dibdin's Aurelio Zen books*: Leon added, in an interview posted at http://italian-mysteries.com: 'Dibdin, particularly with *Dark Spectre* . . . is wonderful . . . . But I don't think the Zen books are fabulous.' Judged as a whole, however, Dibdin's work is broader in range and ambition than Leon's.

15 *gong'an*: Chinese crime-case fiction developed in the Song dynasty and flourished during the Tang and Ming dynasties. Apart from Judge Dee, the best-known magistrate-detective of the era was Judge Bao, or Bao Zheng, whose sense of justice made him enduringly popular. Six of his cases translated by Leon Comber were published as *The Strange Cases of Magistrate Pao*.

16 *a limited edition*: Self-publishing is more widespread today than ever, thanks mainly to technological advances, but it has a long history: J. M. Barrie, for instance, paid for the initial publication of his debut novel, *Better Dead*, a 'shocker' about a society of killers. As van Gulik explained to the bibliophile Vincent Starrett in a letter of 30 January 1951: 'The reason why I published the book myself is that two publishers I sent the MS to informed me that they could consider it only if the text were entirely re-written, so as to adapt it to the taste of the general public. I could not agree . . . As it is, the book in its present form sold well, I have recovered the cost of publication with a nice margin.' Starrett shared van Gulik's interest in historic Chinese literature, but is better known as a Sherlockian, reviewer and occasional detective writer.

17 *Judge Dee*: Barzun and Taylor described themselves as Dee-votees, although Julian Symons was able to curb his enthusiasm for tales 'so far removed from western feeling that in them animals, and even objects, might take voice and give damning evidence.' Among attempts to adapt the Judge Dee stories for the screen, a six-episode series aired on British television in 1969. Five years later Nicholas Meyer scripted the TV movie *Judge Dee and the Monastery Murder*.

FORTY-FIVE

Whodunwhat?

Theatrical murder

One day in 1969, Anthony Shaffer stopped off in New York en route to Puerto Rico, and met up with his twin brother. Peter Shaffer was already a well-established playwright and, within a few years, *Equus* and *Amadeus* would cement his reputation. In his younger days, Anthony had written fiction and reviewed for the *London Mystery Magazine*.[1] Now he worked in the lucrative business of TV advertising, and was on his way to make commercials extolling the wonders of Pepsi Cola.

'Is this the way you really want to live your life?' Peter demanded. 'You're a writer – why don't you stop avoiding it and get on with it?'

Anthony relished the high life – 'expense account, chauffeured car, regular income' – but a tab of LSD given to him by an American girl emboldened him. He resolved to rise to his brother's challenge and become a full-time writer. Although his business partners offered him a year's sabbatical, he turned it down: 'What I needed was terror – the blank page.'

He'd already dabbled in writing for the theatre and he decided to try again. But what sort of play should he write?

The answer came from the literary frolics of his twenties;[2] he set about writing a mystery play that drew on his love of Golden Age detection. He came up with an ingenious piece of 'stage chicanery' for a thriller called 'Anyone for Tennis?' The play was rejected by the legendary West End producer Hugh 'Binkie' Beaumont: 'Everyone will know the trick within a week, dear, no one will keep quiet about that. It won't last a fortnight.'

Shaffer persisted, and gave the play a snappier title. With Anthony Quayle in the lead role of detective novelist Andrew Wyke, *Sleuth* (1970) opened in the provinces before transferring to St Martin's Theatre in London, and became a smash hit. According to his breezy, unreliable memoirs, the only sour note came when Laurence Olivier joined the cast in a Brighton bar during the provincial try-out, and asked Quayle why he was bothering with 'a piece of piss like this'. As Shaffer gleefully pointed out, when the play became a film, Olivier grabbed the role of Wyke, and an Oscar nomination.

During the West End run, Agatha Christie and Max Mallowan came to see the show, and Anthony took them out for dinner. As the alcohol flowed, he heaped praise on *Witness for the Prosecution* (whose central trick is reworked in *Sleuth*) but expressed reservations about *The Mousetrap*; modestly, Christie agreed.

Later that night, in a fit of drunken bravado, Anthony propped up sandwich boards from the St Martin's against the walls of the Ambassadors theatre, home of *The Mousetrap*, and recorded her comments: 'A silly little piece – *A. Christie*', and 'I wish it would go away – *Agatha Christie*'. Retribution came when Peter Saunders, who owned both theatres, banished *Sleuth*, and moved *The Mousetrap* to St Martin's, which could hold a larger audience than the Ambassadors.

Despite this escapade, Anthony maintained a profitable connection with Christie. A film writer whose credits included Hitchcock's *Frenzy*[3] and the horror classic *The Wicker Man,*[4] he adapted *Death on the Nile* and *Evil under the Sun*. Less happily, he co-wrote the screenplay for *Appointment with Death*. He admitted the movie was dreadful, and blamed the director, Michael Winner, 'who made every mistake he could'.

Sleuth was not the first play to satirise the conventions of the country-house murder mystery. Two years earlier, Tom Stoppard's one-act comedy *The Real Inspector Hound* (1968) had poked fun at clichés and clunky writing, whether found in plays like *The Mousetrap* or in the banality of second-rate theatre criticism ('It is hard, it is hard indeed, and therefore I will not attempt, to refrain from invoking the names of Kafka, Sartre, Shakespeare, St Paul, Beckett, Birkett, Pinero, Pirandello, Dante, and Dorothy L. Sayers').

Shaffer's aim was not to bury Christie, but to honour her. The originality of *Sleuth* lay in his subversion of the audience's expectations[5] so as to create plot twists worthy of Dame Agatha. A character who scoffs at the claim of Sayers' friend Philip Guedalla that 'the detective story is the normal recreation of noble minds' pays the ultimate price for his condescension. As the play opens, Wyke is typing a locked-room mystery with a scenario reminiscent of John Dickson Carr's *The Problem of the Wire Cage*. Game-playing is the crux of *Sleuth*. In a world where nothing is as it seems, even the contents of the theatre programme cannot be trusted.[6]

Sleuth set a vogue for comedy thrillers, but Shaffer struggled to match its success. *Murderer* (1975) opens with a memorable *coup de théâtre* inspired by a 'provocative, philosophical idea, that it is most often the victim who seeks out his or her murderer, rather than the other way round . . . it was an attempt to see whether it was possible to outrage and shock an audience whilst still retaining their loyalty.' So the first half hour 'consisted of our hero chopping up his mistress in the bath and then putting the pieces in a stove and burning them.' Critical reaction was predictably mixed, and Shaffer's continued tinkering eventually resulted in three different versions of the play.

References to Golden Age fiction abound in *The Case of the Oily Levantine* (1977), which was quickly retitled *Whodunnit*. A first-act spoof of the country-house mystery, complete with stock characters and villainous blackmailer, turns into a story about a murder game, borrowing a familiar premise.[7] Shaffer's quest for originality yielded diminishing returns, and he admitted that the plot of *Widow's Weeds*, aka *For Years I Couldn't Wear My Black* (1977), was indecipherable. His last play, *The Thing in the Wheelchair* (2001), a dark melodrama freely adapted from a Cornell Woolrich story, 'Eyes that Watch You', has seldom been performed.

*

Striking parallels exist between Shaffer's career and that of his American contemporary Ira Levin. At twenty-three, Levin published *A Kiss before Dying*[8] (1953), the first of seven novels – mostly high-concept thrillers in various genres – to appear over the space of more than four decades. Levin, like Shaffer, moved with conspicuous success into horror writing thanks to *Rosemary's Baby* (1967). Like Shaffer, he was a Christie fan[9] who prized wit and ingenuity.

Levin's macabre *Veronica's Room* (1974), in which a young woman unwisely agrees to impersonate a dead girl, was clever but far from comic. He struck gold when he followed Shaffer's lead. *Deathtrap* (1978) is a witty mystery with a dazzling plot twist that became Broadway's longest-running comedy thriller.

Sidney Bruhl, a playwright with writer's block, contemplates committing murder in order to pass off young Clifford Anderson's play as his own work. The story is often interpreted as presenting a covert gay relationship,[10] and, in a film version, Michael Caine and Christopher Reeve shared a kiss.

Deathtrap is as self-referential as anything written by members of the Detection Club. Levin highlights the challenges posed by the quest for originality in an age when: 'every possible variation seems to have been played. Can I conjure up a few new ones? Can I startle an audience that's *been* on Angel Street, that's dialled "M" for murder,[11] that's witnessed the prosecution, that's played the murder game?'

After *Sleuth*, traditional stage thrillers continued to be written, and Christie novels still kept being adapted for the theatre, while other playwrights strained after originality.[12] Francis Durbridge turned to writing stage thrillers (minus Paul Temple) and, in *Suddenly at Home* (1971), he made crafty use of the fact that the false death had become a trope of the comedy thriller.

Psychological suspense rather than comedy is the focus of Richard Harris's[13] *The Business of Murder* (1981). Again the script features a playwright, and a plot involving a murder that may or may not have been committed. Even the casting of the original West End production – which eventually ran for seven years – played mind games with the audience. The sinister and menacing

Stone was played by Francis Matthews, then familiar as the television incarnation of Durbridge's suave sleuth Paul Temple.

The comedy thriller was becoming tired by the time Stephen Sondheim and George Furth, whose previous collaborations included the hit musical *Company*, wrote a stage play without songs called *The Doctor is Out*, later retitled *Getting Away with Murder* (1996). Sondheim was a lifelong fan of crossword puzzles and Golden Age detection,[14] and this story about the murder of a therapist presents a 'closed circle' of suspects, seven of the dead man's patients. The play closed after seventeen performances on Broadway. The critic Clive Barnes said that it was 'not so much a whodunit as perhaps a whydoit and definitely a whyseeit'.

Andrew Lloyd Webber transformed Gaston Leroux's *The Phantom of the Opera* and Wilkie Collins' *The Woman in White*[15] into big-budget musicals. But combinations of murder and music often hit the wrong note. Monty Norman's *Belle*[16] or *The Ballad of Dr Crippen* ran for a mere forty-four performances in 1961, as it was thought to be in poor taste.

Stephen Sondheim chose in *Sweeney Todd: The Demon Barber of Fleet Street* (1979), his most successful musical with a criminous theme, to keep dialogue to a minimum. The book was written by Hugh Wheeler, better known to detective fiction fans for his Patrick Quentin novels. Sondheim wrote both music and lyrics, as he did for the critically mauled *Assassins* (1990), set at a fairground shooting gallery and featuring seven would-be killers of American presidents.

Ira Levin is said to have laboured for ten years on the book and lyrics for a musical spoof of late-Victorian melodrama, featuring a nineteenth-century female cat burglar. The original title, *Cat and Mouse*, was unwisely abandoned in favour of *Drat! the Cat!* In 1965, the show opened at the Martin Beck Theater (named after a vaudeville theatre manager rather than Sjöwall and Wahlöö's melancholy detective) and closed after eight performances.

Of all the crime novels that might be turned into an opera, Winston Graham's *Marnie* (1961) seems an unlikely choice. The eponymous embezzler is afraid of sex but finds herself blackmailed into marriage by her employer, who rapes her during their honeymoon. Graham's bleak ending was changed in Hitchcock's film version, but preserved in Sean O'Connor's[17] play based on the book.

Nico Muhly decided that the story 'screamed out for operatic treatment', and his version, with a libretto by Nicholas Wright, owed more to Graham than to Hitchcock. The opera's world premiere at the English National Opera in 2017 coincided with extensive publicity about high-profile allegations of sexual exploitation and the abuse of power, but the critical consensus indicated that this ambitious project was off-key.

Singer-songwriter Rupert Holmes[18] enjoyed better fortune with *The Mystery of Edwin Drood* (1985), winning awards for the book, lyrics, music and orchestration. He made a virtue out of Dickens' failure to finish the novel, and after Princess Puffer – in the novel, a strange old woman who runs an opium den – sings 'Don't Quit While You're Ahead', the company joins together, only for voices and music to fall silent. The chairman of the music hall company supposedly staging the show invites the audience to identify the culprit,[19] and while some members of the cast reprise a song from the score, others count the votes. Different versions of the song 'Murderer's Confession' are available, depending on the audience's choice of villain.

Audience participation is taken to a new level in Holmes' *Accomplice* (1990), described by Marvin Carlson as 'the most extreme of the comedy thrillers, in the variety and complexity of its playing with the established codes'. One of the characters speaks to someone watching the play; that person joins the cast on stage, and is revealed as the playwright, Holmes himself.

Holmes also wrote the book for *Curtains*[20] (2006), the outstanding murder mystery musical in an admittedly small field. John Kander and Fred Ebb, the team behind *Cabaret* and *Chicago*, supplied the music and lyrics. A glance at the score gives nothing away. One song is performed both as 'The Woman's Dead' and 'The Man is Dead', while another also has two versions: 'He Did It' and 'She Did It'.

Notes

The main sources are Anthony Shaffer's *So What Did You Expect?* (a memoir published on the day he died), Marvin Carlson's *Deathtraps*, Amnon Kabatchnik's *Blood on the Stage* and Marvin Lachman's *The Villainous Stage*.

1　*London Mystery Magazine*: A story by the Shaffers featuring the brilliant Great Detective in the massive form of Mr Verity, 'Before and After', appeared in one issue, with the next containing an alternative solution that debunked Mr Verity's original explanation. The editor at the time was Austen Kark, whose novelist wife Nina Bawden occasionally wrote detective stories, notably *The Odd Flamingo*. The magazine ran from 1949 to 1982.

2　*the literary frolics of his twenties*: In 1951, Peter published a locked-room mystery, *The Woman in the Wardrobe*, illustrated by E. C. Bentley's son Nicolas (himself an occasional crime writer), and featuring Mr Verity. The book appeared under the name of Peter Antony. Mr Verity returned in *How Doth the Little Crocodile?* and in *Withered Murder*, although, in a suitably mysterious twist, he was ultimately renamed Mr Fathom. For these two novels, Anthony supplied the basic plots, and he and Peter wrote alternate chapters. *Withered Murder* appeared under the brothers' real names, and Anthony – characteristically shameless – contributed a rapturous pseudonymous review to the *London Mystery Magazine*.

3　*Frenzy*: This serial-killer film was based on *Goodbye Piccadilly, Farewell Leicester Square* by Arthur La Bern, who vented his feelings in a letter to *The Times*: 'The result on the screen is appalling. The dialogue is a curious amalgam of an old Aldwych farce, *Dixon of Dock Green* and that almost forgotten *No Hiding Place*. I would like to ask Mr Hitchcock and Mr Shaffer what happened between book and script to the authentic London characters I created.' La Bern, formerly a crime reporter, squandered a fortune, and was later arrested for vagrancy after sleeping rough on Brighton beach.

4　*the horror classic The Wicker Man*: The story has elements of crime fiction and Neil Howie, the protagonist, is a police officer.

5　*subversion of the audience's expectations*: Different media offer different possibilities for subversion. In the 2018 TV miniseries based on Gillian Flynn's *Sharp Objects*, a key revelation in a brief scene during the closing credits of the final episode will be missed if one switches off too soon.

6　*even the contents of the theatre programme cannot be trusted*: A strictly accurate programme would disclose the central plot twist. A similar dilemma confronted Terence Feely (better known as a TV scriptwriter) with *Murder in Mind*, where the heroine insists that three other characters are impostors; the programme preserves the ambiguity of the premise. The same is true of the programme for *Veronica's Room*. The programme for *Double Double* by Eric Elice and Roger Rees reverses the trick played on the reader in the programme for *Sleuth*.

7　*a familiar premise*: Found in novels such as Ngaio Marsh's *A Man Lay Dead* and Christie's *Dead Man's Folly*. The 2018 American comedy film *Game Night* gave the mystery game idea a witty makeover.

8　*A Kiss before Dying*: Levin's use of multiple viewpoints to achieve a stunning mid-story plot twist is complemented by a suspenseful story about a sociopath.

9　*he was a Christie fan*: In his early stage comedy, *Critics' Choice*, a mystery enthusiast says of her books: 'When you've read fifty, you've read them all.' Arguing that other writers of thriller plays had only managed a single masterpiece, Levin once said that Christie was the sole exception, citing *And Then There Were None*, *Witness for the Prosecution* and *The Mousetrap*.

10　*The story is often interpreted as presenting a covert gay relationship*:

Jordan Schildcrout argues in *Murder Most Queer* that the storyline uses the closet as a catalyst for suspense and homicidal violence, although in 2012 the *Los Angeles Times* reported that a revival of the play at the LA Gay and Lesbian Center, featuring a nude scene and an explicit rendering of the gay sub-text, was cancelled after Levin's estate objected.

11 *an audience that's been on Angel Street, that's dialled 'M' for murder*: *Angel Street* is the American title of Patrick Hamilton's *Gaslight*. Frederick Knott's inverted mystery *Dial 'M' for Murder* was a BBC TV play that he adapted for the stage, and turned into a screenplay for a Hitchcock film. Two of Knott's other plays were filmed, *Write Me a Murder* and *Wait until Dark*. He also scripted *The Last Page*, based on a play by James Hadley Chase.

12 *other playwrights strained after originality*: Examples include *Who Killed 'Agatha' Christie?* by the screenwriter and playwright Tudor Gates and Anthony Horowitz's *Mindgame*, set in an asylum.

13 *Richard Harris*: Harris, a leading television writer, co-created *Shoestring*; his other work included the comedy play *Outside Edge* and the screenplay of *I Start Counting*, based on Audrey Erskine Lindop's novel, which won the Grand Prix de Littérature Policière. His work for the stage includes a version of Christianna Brand's debut novel, *Death in High Heels*.

14 *a lifelong fan of crossword puzzles and Golden Age detection*: Sondheim compiled crosswords for the *New York Magazine*, and Anthony Shaffer's *So What Did You Expect?* mentions a murder party game Sondheim invented. Andrew Wyke in *Sleuth* may have been based on Sondheim, but the story that the play was originally called *Who's Afraid of Stephen Sondheim?* is apocryphal. With Anthony Perkins, the star of Hitchcock's *Psycho*, Sondheim wrote the screenplay of *The Last of Sheila*, a whodunit film which offers an explicit 'challenge to the viewer'. They collaborated on another script, *The Chorus Girl Murder Case*. Perkins cited *The IPCRESS File* as an inspiration and Sondheim is said to have written songs including clues to the puzzle. Unfortunately, the film was never made.

15 *The Woman in White*: A performance of the musical supplies an alibi in Woody Allen's *Match Point*, a psychological thriller with touches of Dostoevsky and Dreiser as well as Ruth Rendell.

16 *Belle*: The book was written by Wolf Mankowitz. Although *Belle* flopped, Cubby Broccoli was so impressed that he commissioned Norman to write 'The James Bond Theme'.

17 *Sean O'Connor*: O'Connor has written books about serial killer Neville Heath and the Rattenbury–Stoner case.

18 *Singer-songwriter Rupert Holmes*: Holmes (born David Goldstein) wrote the chart-topping 'Escape (The Piña Colada Song)'; 'Him' was also a top-ten hit. The audience also plays an integral role in his courtroom drama based on John Grisham's novel *A Time to Kill*. Holmes' multimedia mystery *Swing*, set in the big band era, was accompanied by photographs of San Francisco in the 1940s, and a CD of songs containing clues to the mystery. His *Where the Truth Lies* was filmed by Atom Egoyan.

19 *The chairman . . . invites the audience to identify the culprit*: This interactive ploy dates back to 1934 and *The Night of January the 16th*, aka *Penthouse Legend*. The playwright was the right-wing thinker Ayn Rand, who in 'Philosophical Detection' compares studying philosophy to reading detective fiction: by uncovering implicit premises, the philosophical detective

may 'discover who is a murderer and who is a hero'. The idea of treating
the audience as the jury originated in 1915 with George Pleydell's *The Ware
Case*. Pleydell adapted this courtroom drama from his own novel; its storyline
anticipates the approach of the Ironists.

20 *Curtains*: The original book was by Peter Stone, whose screenplays included
the quasi-Hitchcockian *Charade* and *The Taking of Pelham One Two Three*,
based on John Godey's novel.

FORTY-SIX

Black and Blue

British police fiction

'You'll do as you're told, Wainwright,' the detective chief superintendent said.

'Commit perjury?' the constable asked.

'It's not a *request*.'

'No, sir?'

'It's an order.'

'Can I have that order in writing, sir?'

'Don't be such a damn fool.'

'In that case, no, sir.'

'Wainwright, I'm warning you . . . and I keep my promises. Refuse me this, and if you stay in the force a hundred years, you'll *still* be a village bobby.'

'If you say so, sir.'

The police constable left the room. He'd been asked to lie in a court case: a doctor was suing a driver for compensation after being injured in a road accident. Wainwright had recorded the driver's admission of fault in his notebook, but his senior officer was a friend of the driver.

The court case went ahead, and Wainwright told the truth. The DCS did keep his promises, and there was never any chance of promotion. One day Wainwright arrived back at his semi-detached police house one day to find his wife Avis crying. She'd succumbed to distress because 'a simple thing like peaceful living was beyond our grasp'.

He drove to divisional headquarters, and told Superintendent John Craven of his decision to resign. Craven asked why he was still only a beat constable. When Wainwright lied and said he didn't know, Craven said he must have upset somebody, and sent him on compassionate leave. He also arranged a transfer to a village beat. Wainwright never forgot Craven's kindness, and years later he 'tried to give him some small, but belated immortality' in his novel, *Blayde R.I.P.* (1982), as Superintendent John Chapman.

John Wainwright, a gruff, working-class Yorkshireman who left school at fifteen and joined the police in 1947, was determined to do what he thought was right, come hell or high water. His self-discipline was formidable, his moral code stern. On one occasion, he gave a tongue-lashing to a paedophile, whose immediate re-action was to put his neck on a railway line. On hearing the news, Wainwright calmly continued to eat his dinner. In a memoir written years after the event, he said, 'It is possible – even highly probable – that I'd talked a man into committing suicide in a particularly nasty manner, but I felt no guilt . . . I was a much harder man then than I am today.'

He wrote pseudonymous articles for the *Police Review* and persuaded the editor to publish a short story, 'Tergiversation'. He and Avis joined a writers' circle, and after reading Hammett and Chandler, he devoured a batch of inferior crime novels by authors who 'didn't know how coppers talked and hadn't a clue about the sheer chaos of a genuine murder enquiry'.

Wainwright reckoned he could do better, and worked up a story concerning a couple of Mafia executioners[1] on the loose in a northern city. *Death in a Sleeping City* (1965) was snapped up by Collins Crime Club, serialised and translated, and the BBC asked him to adapt it into a radio play.

His burgeoning literary career prompted jealousy from colleagues. 'Quite suddenly,' he recalled, 'I cracked and had to crawl a way through the first nervous breakdown of my life. It left a terrible aftermath. A thing called manic depression, and I wouldn't wish that on *anybody.*' A doctor told him to decide whether he was a policeman or a writer, and he resigned from the force in July 1966. The senior officer who had failed to persuade him to commit perjury signed his certificate of service and added that his conduct was exemplary. On reflection, Wainwright concluded that, for all the man's faults, 'part of me admired him as the greatest policeman I ever met.'

A late starter as a novelist, Wainwright made up for lost time, pouring out scores of books. He was a striking example of that breed of writer who believes a novel should stand or fall on its merits, and need not be supported by marketing efforts on the part of its author. After his death, his reputation faded fast. His industry counted against him; how can someone who produces so much be a writer of distinction?

Wainwright's output was jarringly uneven, but not through any lack of literary ambition; his fiction was eclectic and at its best thought-provoking. *High-Class Kill* (1973) combines a whodunit, a locked-room problem and a study of relationships between the generations. *Brainwash* (1979)[2] gives a highly convincing account of a tough police interrogation.

All on a Summer's Day (1981) is a British counterpart to Ed McBain's 87th Precinct novels, with the imaginary Yorkshire town of Sopworth serving as Wainwright's equivalent to Isola. Choosing it as one of his hundred best crime books, H. R. F. Keating highlighted the 'judgement and compassion that marks Wainwright out from the common ruck of crime writers'.

Georges Simenon was impressed by the originality of *Cul-de-Sac* (1984), calling it 'an unforgettable novel. Every single word counts . . .' The book begins with an extract from the diary of John Duxbury – but is the diary quite what it seems? When Duxbury's wife falls over a cliff, the question of whether her death was suicide, accident or murder is investigated by an obsessive cop. The story deals with yearning for respectability in a very distinctive manner. The finale is startling but inadequately foreshadowed, a flaw that revision could easily have remedied. And that failing illustrates why, for all Simenon's admiration, Wainwright did not achieve the lasting recognition his talent merited.

*

Wainwright wasn't the first post-war British cop to write crime novels. The trail was blazed by Maurice Procter, from Lancashire. Having worked as a weaver in a cotton mill, he crossed the Pennines to become a police constable; at the time, a police officer wasn't allowed to serve in his home town. In 1938, he took part in the investigation into the 'Halifax Slasher', a bizarre case in which reports of a half-crazed, wild-eyed man attacking victims with a mallet or knife prompted an outbreak of mass hysteria. Vigilantes patrolled the streets and Scotland Yard was called in, before several supposed victims confessed to inventing their stories. Four people were jailed for public mischief offences.

In 1946, Procter published *No Proud Chivalry*, covering the period of a policeman's life from recruit to inspector. His purpose, the publisher's blurb proclaimed, was 'to describe – and to some extent to indict – the present police system'. Procter made no secret of his contempt for superior officers who abused their authority, but indicting one's employers is seldom a prudent career move. He departed the force to become a full-time writer.

Procter's realistic portrayal of police work and life in bleak villages, drab towns and dangerous cities broke fresh ground. In *The Chief Inspector's Statement*, aka *The Pennycross Murders* (1951), DCI Philip Hunter investigates crimes that were almost taboo as far as Golden Age writers were concerned,[3] two brutal child murders in a Yorkshire village.

At this point, Freeman Wills Crofts was still writing about Chief Inspector French, but his mysteries couldn't match Procter's for credibility. The ex-cop captured the mundane nature of everyday lives in the era of post-war austerity, while investing his characters with a humanity that appealed to readers weary of omniscient Great Detectives. Procter was scarcely an Angry Young Man, but his gritty writing anticipated the mood of mainstream authors such as John Braine, Stan Barstow and Shelagh Delaney.

Hell is a City, aka *Somewhere in this City* (1954), introduced a tough cop called Harry Martineau. Set in Granchester (a thinly disguised Manchester), the story was filmed[4] with Stanley Baker as the cynical but decent detective. Martineau became a series character, and his continuing duel with the underworld boss Dixie

Costello prefigured the tussles between Ian Rankin's Jack Rebus and 'Big Ger' Cafferty.

John Creasey also spotted the possibilities of the police procedural novel. As J. J. Marric,[5] he created a series about a likeable Scotland Yard man, George Gideon.[6] Anthony Boucher admired the 'technically dazzling handling of a large number of plots in small compass' in *Gideon's Fire*, which represented the high water mark of Creasey's career, pipping Lionel Davidson and Ross Macdonald to the Edgar for best novel in 1962.

Michael Gilbert, who created several memorable police detectives of his own,[7] argued that the way to avoid tedium was to focus on 'the policemen and the policewomen . . . It is their hopes and fears, not the hopes and fears of the murderer that are in the forefront of the story.' For him, Edwin Brock's *The Little White God*[8] (1962) gave 'a real impression of what policemen think about themselves and their work'.

When Bill Knox[9] interviewed fellow Scot Alastair MacLean about *HMS Ulysses*, the thriller writer encouraged him to try writing a novel of his own. Knox duly introduced the Glaswegian detectives Colin Thane and Phil Moss, in *Deadline for a Dream*, aka *In at the Kill* (1957). Experience of crime reporting gave Knox insight into police work, and although his relentless productivity, like Wainwright's, helps to account for his work being undervalued, he has been called 'the forgotten "godfather" of Tartan Noir'.[10]

A new generation of talented authors took the police novel in new directions. P. D. James and Ruth Rendell introduced police officers who became much-loved series characters for half a century but were uninterested in procedural detail. Both women were serious novelists with ambitions to utilise police fiction to investigate character, setting and questions about society.

The minutiae of policing mattered even less to an employee of Oxford University's Delegacy of Local Examinations who decided to see if he could concoct a detective story. He and his family were holidaying in Wales, but as the rain poured down, he sat at the kitchen table and began to write. Given that he'd already published a couple of textbooks and was an obsessive solver of crossword puzzles, he embarked on a cerebral whodunit set in his home city. In the process, he reinvented the traditional mystery.

With a breezy disregard for geographical pedantry, Colin Dexter chose the title 'Ten Miles to Woodstock'. His publishers, equally cavalier about detail, insisted on calling the book *Last Bus to Woodstock*, though the bus in question was not the last of the day. The book was published in 1975 to minimal fanfare.

Dexter's police officers, Inspector Morse and Sergeant Lewis, were an updated Holmes–Watson pairing, their surnames borrowed from fellow crossword champions. They investigate the brutal murder of a young woman whose body is found in a pub car park, but Dexter was uninterested in gritty realism. Critical reaction was muted. Even Edmund Crispin,[11] who loved the elaborate plotting, noted 'a tendency for the prose to lapse into archaic mandarin'.

As the series progressed, Dexter's approach to plotting and narrative structure displayed increasing ambition. He freshened up Golden Age tropes and developed a taste for multiple solutions worthy of Anthony Berkeley. Dexter suffered from deafness, but made clever use of his knowledge of the disability in *The Silent World of Nicholas Quinn* (1977): lip-reading provides a vital clue.

For *Service of All the Dead* (1979), in which a sequence of murders takes place in the vicinity of a fictional church in Oxford's Cornmarket, he adopted a casebook technique, dividing the novel into four sections, each named after a book in the Old Testament. That novel and its successor, the equally convoluted *The Dead of Jericho* (1981), earned Dexter CWA Silver Daggers, but the transformation of his fortunes came thanks to television.

Many enjoyable cop shows are originally written for TV,[12] but *Inspector Morse* became perhaps the most successful adaptation of a series of police novels. The show represented a bold departure from the prevailing wisdom that TV audiences would only be satisfied by something as fashionable and up-to-the-minute as the then-popular American series *Miami Vice*.[13] Each episode was conceived as a one-hundred-minute film, with no expense spared. Along with high-calibre scripts and guest actors, the key ingredients were the chemistry between John Thaw and Kevin Whately as Morse and Lewis (the latter a much younger man than the sergeant in the novels, giving the relationship a fresh dynamic), soundtracks with operatic excerpts as well as melancholy original themes[14] and photography making the most of historic Oxford's beauty.

The gamble paid off. The series became a global phenomenon, with most of the episodes based on original stories and Dexter making Hitchcockesque cameo appearances. The mystery of Morse's first name, the subject of teasing clues prior to its revelation in *Death is Now My Neighbour* (1996), prompted speculation around the world. Two spin-off series, *Lewis* and *Endeavour* (the latter a prequel) ensured that the franchise enjoyed extraordinary longevity.

Some authors ignore, or rage at, the television versions of their work, often with good reason. Dexter embraced his good fortune and even modified his presentation of Morse and Lewis in light of the performances of Thaw and Whately. He had demonstrated that the detective novel was more flexible and enduring than critical groupthink presumed. Reports of the death of the traditional whodunit had been exaggerated.

Ross Macdonald said of William McIlvanney's first crime novel that he'd 'seldom been so excited by a style or so taken by a character as I was by the angry and compassionate Glasgow detective, Laidlaw'.[15] In *Laidlaw* (1977), the cop searches for the murderer of eighteen-year-old Jennifer Lawson, whose corpse is found among bushes in Kelvingrove Park. There is no mystery about the culprit's identity; the question is whether the police will find him before the others who are on his trail. The book's strength lay not in the plot but in the writing. McIlvanney was an accomplished stylist in poetry and prose, regarded in some quarters as the finest Scottish author of his generation.

Only two more books about Laidlaw appeared, but the McIlvanney effect was profound. When a young Ian Rankin told him he hoped to write a crime novel about a cop based in Scotland's capital, the older man inscribed a book: 'Good luck with the Edinburgh Laidlaw'.[16] *Knots and Crosses*, Rankin's second novel, published a decade after *Laidlaw* in 1987, introduced DI John Rebus,[17] who has become one of the genre's most popular cops.

Success did not come to Rankin overnight: his breakthrough book was his fifteenth.[18] *Black and Blue* (1997), Rebus' eighth outing, saw Rankin draw on influences ranging from James Hogg and Robert Louis Stevenson to Irvine Welsh's *Trainspotting*, all while producing a crime novel of distinctive quality. James Ellroy was another model: Rankin 'saw this huge landscape that he was using and his language, and the way he took risks with structure',[19] and wrote a book longer and more ambitious than its predecessors.

The Bible John murders, three unsolved killings in the 1960s, provided a catalyst for the storyline of *Black and Blue*. Rebus's relationship with the crime boss Morris Gerald 'Big Ger' Cafferty, a recurrent and compelling element in the series, is also central: as Rankin says, 'Cafferty is a kind of devil who is always standing behind Rebus with this seductive voice, saying, "It feels good to do bad things, why don't you give it a go?"'

Reginald Hill's rise to prominence took even longer than Rankin's. In 1970, he was lecturing at a college of education in Yorkshire when Collins Crime Club published *A Clubbable Woman*, a story set around a rugby club, in which the murder of Mary Connon is investigated by Superintendent Andrew Dalziel and DS Peter Pascoe.[20]

The contrast between the two detectives is played up from the start: Dalziel was 'a man not difficult to mock. But it was dangerous sport. And perhaps therefore all the more tempting to a Detective-Sergeant who was twenty years younger, had a degree in social sciences and read works on criminology.' Their double act reflected their creator's awareness of his own divided self: the sensitive intellectual and the tough-minded northerner with a fondness for the belly laugh.

Recognising that a series brings dangers of overfamiliarity and stagnation, Hill alternated between series novels and other books. He enjoyed the 'pleochroic puzzles' of the Golden Age, numbering Michael Innes and Francis Iles among his literary heroes, and in *Dialogues of the Dead* (2002), the intricacy of the written codes is worthy of Connington or Rhode. In *Recalled to Life* (1992), Dalziel investigates a cold case, a country-house mystery dating back to 1963, regarded as 'the last of the golden age murders'.

The novel's Dickensian references begin with the first line: 'It was the best of crimes, it was the worst of crimes.'

As his confidence grew, the novels became ever more sophisticated, dealing with issues such as the treatment of shell-shocked soldiers during the First World War and the wars in Iraq.[21] Shocked by the unexpected suicide of a dear friend, Hill mused on psychological secrets in the Gold Dagger-winning *Bones and Silence* (1990). The peaceful cathedral close setting contrasts with the personal turmoil experienced by the characters. By inviting readers to consider which of them was contemplating suicide, he set out to do 'something different within the crime or mystery form'.

Dalziel was at times almost a fantasy figure and the plot convolutions were occasionally over the top, but Hill leavened his literary exuberance with sharp wit. *A Cure for All Diseases*, aka *The Price of Butcher's Meat* (2008), in part narrated by Dalziel, offers an extra level of pleasure for those familiar with Jane Austen's unfinished novel *Sanditon*.

For all his literary daring, Hill prioritised entertainment. His ingenuity was breathtaking – in one novel, the culprit's identity is hidden in plain sight, in the very first line. *The Woodcutter* (2010), his final book, was a stand-alone novel, a revenge tragedy. Almost uniquely among the last-published novels of major crime novelists, the book yielded no hint of diminishing powers.

Notes

The main sources are *Wainwright's Beat*, H. R. F. Keating's *Whodunit?*, Gill Plain's *Ian Rankin's Black and Blue: A Reader's Guide* and Reginald Hill's 'Looking for a Programme' in Robert W. Winks' *Colloquium on Crime*.

1   *a couple of Mafia executioners*: Not having encountered the Mafia on his beat, and at a time before Mario Puzo published *The Godfather*, he researched by reading Norman Lewis's *The Honoured Society* and Estes Kefauver's *Crime in America*.

2   *Brainwash*: The book has been filmed twice, as *Garde à Vue*, aka *The Inquisitor,* and *Under Suspicion*, and adapted for the stage as *Person of Interest*. Stories focusing on police interviews include Ed McBain's *Blood Relatives*, filmed by Chabrol, and John Hopkins' play *This Story of Yours*, filmed by Sidney Lumet as *The Offence*. As a screenwriter, Hopkins adapted Edmund Crispin's *The Moving Toyshop* for the first episode in BBC TV's anthology series *Detective*. He also wrote many episodes of the northern

TV cop series *Z Cars*, co-wrote *Thunderball* and scripted *Murder by Decree*, a Sherlockian film pastiche.

3   *crimes that were almost taboo as far as Golden Age writers were concerned*: Among the exceptions are Dorothy L. Sayers' 'The Leopard Lady', Q. Patrick's *Death Goes to School* and *The Grindle Nightmare*, aka *Darker Grows the Valley*, and Philip MacDonald's *Murder Gone Mad*, which is astonishingly casual about the murder of a small child by a deranged serial killer.

4   *the story was filmed*: Written and directed by Val Guest.

5   *J. J. Marric*: The name was a composite of J (for John), J (his then wife), Mar (for his son Martin) and Ric (for his son Richard).

6   *George Gideon*: A television series, *Gideon's Way*, was screened in the mid-1960s. The first book, *Gideon's Day*, was filmed by John Ford. The screenplay was by T. E. B. Clarke, who also wrote *The Blue Lamp*, which introduced and then killed off PC George Dixon. Dixon returned from the grave to feature in hundreds of episodes of Ted Willis' TV series *Dixon of Dock Green*. Clarke's crime fiction included an 'alternative history' novel, *Murder at Buckingham Palace*.

7   *Gilbert, who created several memorable police detectives of his own*: Hazlerigg and Patrick Petrella were likeable series characters, but Chief Superintendent Knott, who appears in *Death of a Favourite Girl*, aka *The Killing of Katie Steelstock*, is much less scrupulous, as was Mercer from *The Body of a Girl*.

8   *Edwin Brock's The Little White God*: Edgar Wallace and P. D. James wrote about poetical policemen; Brock was a poet who spent eight years as a constable in the Metropolitan Police. He became an advertising copywriter, and joined Dorothy L. Sayers' old firm, S. H. Benson, but wrote no more novels.

9   *Bill Knox*: Knox also wrote a series about Webb Carrick of the Scottish Fishery Protection Service, and books under the names Robert MacLeod, Michael Kirk and Noel Webster. He novelised the television private-eye series created by Edward Boyd, *The View from Daniel Pike*, and his work in the true-crime field included a book about the Peter Manuel case, which was the subject of a non-fiction study by John Bingham and Denise Mina's *The Long Drop*. He hosted a Scottish TV series enlisting the public's help in solving real-life crimes.

10 *'the forgotten "godfather" of 'Tartan Noir'*: The description comes from Stephen McGinty, 'Strange Case of the Scots Crime Novel', *Sunday Times*, 24 December 2017.

11 *Edmund Crispin*: In *The Sunday Times*, 1 June 1975, he observed that: 'Chief Inspector Morse (his addictions are drink, venery, gnomic facetiousness, Wagner and difficult crosswords) emerges . . . as a less appealing character than his creator presumably intended.' Morse's interest in pornography is no more appealing than his miserliness. As for the 'mandarin' prose, Dexter later said, 'I'm still pretending that this fine word was meant to be complimentary.'

12 *Many enjoyable cop shows are originally written for TV*: Notable British examples from the past decade include Jed Mercurio's *Line of Duty*, Chris Chibnall's *Broadchurch* and Sally Wainwright's *Happy Valley*.

13 *Miami Vice*: Anthony Yerkovich's TV series featured two undercover cops, 'Sonny' Crockett and 'Rico' Tubbs, and spawned video games as well as a film directed by Michael Mann.

14 *melancholy original themes*: Composed by Barrington Pheloung. The first *Inspector Morse* soundtrack climbed to number four in the pop charts. Pheloung also wrote music for an episode of *Red Riding*, a television series based on David Pearce's *Red Riding Quartet*, hard-edged novels set in Yorkshire, concerning serial murder and police corruption, and utterly different from Dexter's puzzles.

15 *the angry and compassionate Glasgow detective, Laidlaw*: Television's first major Glaswegian cop was the dour Jim Taggart, played by Mark McManus and created by Glenn Chandler in 1983. The early episodes were distinguished by their blend of action, sardonic wit and dark, dazzling plots. *Taggart*'s popularity helped the series to survive McManus's death in 1994; it ran until 2010.

16 *the older man inscribed a book: 'Good luck with the Edinburgh Laidlaw'*: This anecdote appears in Doug Johnstone's article, 'How William McIlvanney Invented Tartan Noir', *Guardian*, 11 August 2013. Johnstone also discusses whether the term 'tartan noir' was invented by Rankin – or by James Ellroy. The year 2021 saw the appearance of *Dark Remains*, a Laidlaw book started by McIlvanney before his death and completed by Rankin.

17 *DI John Rebus*: On television Rebus has been played by John Hannah and Ken Stott. Rankin has also co-written with Rona Munro *Rebus: Long Shadows*, a play which premiered in 2018.

18 *his breakthrough book was his fifteenth*: This tally includes three thrillers written under the name Jack Harvey.

19 *Rankin 'saw this huge landscape that he was using . . .'*: The quotations come from Gill Plain's book.

20 *Dalziel and Pascoe*: An unhappy television adaptation of *A Pinch of Snuff*, with the comedians Hale and Pace miscast as the detectives, was followed by a superior series on BBC TV, with Warren Clarke and Colin Buchanan in the lead roles. Hill refused to be influenced by the television series: no cameo appearances for him. Once original storylines diverged from his vision of his characters, he did not object, but ceased to watch the shows.

21 *the treatment of shell-shocked soldiers during the First World War and the wars in Iraq*: In *The Wood Beyond* and *Good Morning, Midnight* respectively. The material about Iraq is arguably not handled with Hill's customary finesse, but it is indicative of his range that *Good Morning, Midnight* also includes a Yorkshire family called the Kafkas, death in a locked room, a name-check for John Dickson Carr, and a title and clues from the work of Emily Dickinson.

FORTY-SEVEN

Home Discomforts

Domestic suspense

Celia Fremlin went up to Somerville College twenty-one years after Dorothy L. Sayers. Like Sayers, she was a woman of strong opinions, although their views had little in common. Fremlin joined the Communist Party, but said later that this was largely because 'that was where all the fun was'. She became sceptical about how much her fellow Party members understood about the realities of working-class life. In a spirit of what she called 'armchair socialism', she decided to find out for herself. And so, in 1937, the Oxford classics graduate adopted the pseudonym of Margaret Peters and entered domestic service.

The death of her mother had already given her a taste of domestic work, since she was expected to look after her father. Naively, she thought that: 'by coming down from Oxford and taking a series of jobs as kitchen-hand, charwoman, cook-general and so on, I would get to "know" the domestic servant class . . . would find out where the mistresses were "wrong" and the servants were "right".' Before long, idealism surrendered to reality, and she admitted: 'I did not succeed in doing anything of the kind . . . However much one may will the contrary, one will remain an outsider.'

Fremlin mined these experiences for a non-fiction book. *The Seven Chars of Chelsea* had the misfortune to appear in 1940,[1] a poor moment for a young British writer to make an impression. However, it attracted the attention of Tom Harrisson, who invited her to take part in the Mass Observation project. The immediate fruits of her researches were *War Factory*, co-written with Harrisson, about life in a munitions works, and 'The Crisis', the basis for a never-finished book about the lives of middle-class housewives. The title referred to the crisis of women who had lost a sense of purpose in their domestic lives.

What could women do? Fremlin wondered. Take a job, or volunteer, or 'sell *Daily Workers* in Willesden High Street'? Actually, they could write fiction. And that is what, making use of her apprenticeship in people-watching, Fremlin eventually did.

Fremlin married Elia Goller, a doctor, in 1942, and they had three children. Her second baby, a girl, did not sleep at night: 'I remember one night sitting on the bottom step of the stairs, my baby awake and lively in my arms . . . and it suddenly dawned on me: this is a major human experience, why hasn't someone written about it? . . . it seemed to me that a serious novel should be written with this experience at its centre . . . and then it occurred to me – why don't *I* write one?'

She was too shattered to do so, but years later she found time to write *The Hours before Dawn*, about a harassed mother at the end of her tether. With an unhelpful husband and a sinister female lodger, Louise Henderson is tormented by her baby's crying, and begins to doubt her own sanity. Fremlin's woman-in-jeopardy never ventures into a creepy or remote mansion; she lives in a suburban home and walks drab suburban streets. In such ordinary surroundings, the brooding atmosphere of covert wickedness is all the more terrifying. The husband in the story was not a monster, she said later, and neither were any of the other characters; rather, they were 'ordinary, well-intentioned people caught in a dilemma that is too big for them'.

Published in 1958, the book won an Edgar Award[2] and launched a career of quiet distinction as Fremlin juggled the challenges of parenthood with her urge to develop as a novelist. *Possession* (1969), an often funny yet unsparing account of tensions between mothers and daughters, chronicles the jealousies among competitive women who live vicariously through the achievements of their offspring. Clare Erskine's triumph when her daughter becomes engaged to an accountant proves short-lived when Mervyn Redmayne appears to be tied to the apron strings of a possessive mother. Mervyn's father apparently hanged himself, and it becomes evident that his family nurses dark secrets.

By heart-rending coincidence, shortly after the manuscript was delivered, Fremlin's youngest daughter took her own life at the age of nineteen. A month later her husband did likewise following a severe heart attack. Fremlin fled to Geneva, and three years passed before she published her next novel; it concerned a woman starting all over again.

In *Appointment with Yesterday* (1972), the protagonist runs from a mysterious catastrophe in London – has she killed her second husband? – takes the name Milly Barnes and hides out in a seaside town, taking on a series of part-time cleaning jobs in order to survive. A storyline in which untold horrors bubble beneath the surface of everyday lives is given spice by Fremlin's wit.

Seventeen years after Goller's death, Fremlin remarried. She loved to prowl the streets of London at dead of night, and co-presented a BBC documentary aimed at dispelling the notion that the elderly should be afraid of going out into the city after dark. She was also an outspoken advocate of euthanasia;[3] not long after the Second World War, Goller supplied the barbiturates that enabled a friend of hers suffering from motor neurone disease to take her own life.

Fremlin claimed to have assisted several friends to kill themselves, and insisted on the right to die, but although she found herself caught up in civil proceedings, she was never convicted of a criminal offence. She kept writing, but all three of her children predeceased her, and so did her second husband, while her later years were blighted by blindness and dementia. Despite this appalling sequence of misfortunes, she lived to the age of ninety-four, and died of natural causes.

Long before Fremlin came on the scene, the creepy and remote mansions favoured by early exponents of Had-I-But-Known mysteries had largely given way to the domestic settings favoured by writers interested in the psychology of crime, such as Marie Belloc Lowndes and, later, Elisabeth Sanxay Holding.

In Holding's *Kill Joy*, aka *Murder is a Kill-Joy* (1942), nineteen-year-old Maggie Macgowan is working in domestic service and trying to find her way in the world when out of the blue Dolly Camford, for whose family Maggie works, persuades her to join her in a new career. They leave home in a hurry: Dolly says she is fleeing from a sinister man, but Maggie soon discovers that Dolly's word is not to be relied upon. The plot complications come thick and fast, but Holding also shows Maggie maturing as she battles through a whirl of conflicting emotions.

Family ties and tensions, and the sacrifices women make in order to protect their loved ones, recur as themes throughout Holding's work. Lucia Holley's life takes a nightmarish turn in *The Blank Wall*[4] (1947) when a man who has been involved with her daughter is found dead. In *The Innocent Mrs Duff* (1946), Holding portrays the psychological disintegration of a man who does not appreciate the women close to him.

Holding's prodigious work ethic was fuelled by the need to care for her two daughters after she was left penniless by the Depression. The domestic responsibilities of women writers continued, for all the successes of the 'Queens of Crime', to preoccupy patronising commentators in the post-war era and to prompt debate about whether home-making equipped women with a particular talent for writing detective fiction.

When June Wright[5] made use of three years of working as a telephonist in Melbourne in *Murder in the Telephone Exchange* (1948), newspaper coverage focused on her achievement in publishing a book at the same time as being a domestic goddess: 'At 28, Mrs Wright looks like a French mannequin, keeps a nine-roomed house bright and shining, does all the washing, ironing, cooking and most of the sewing for her quartet of bonny youngsters.'

Wright told one reporter that housewives 'are well-suited to creative writing because they are practical, disciplined and hard-working', and used a domestic image to illustrate her theme: 'writing detective fiction is slow work . . . You must drop your clues, like stitches, on the way out, and pick them up neatly in a pattern when you're coming in.'

The notion that female crime writers may owe some of their success to experience of domestic life has persisted. P. D. James suggested in a memoir 'women have . . . natural advantages, particularly that eye for detail, for the minutiae of everyday living, which is so important in clue-making.' But drive and a determination not to settle for second best matter more. In later life Wright looked back on her short career as a detective novelist and said: 'marriage, motherhood and the suburban lifestyle were not enough – though one would never have dared to voice such sentiments then.'

From the 1940s onwards, female writers freshened the jeopardy story, typically using the home as a claustrophobic setting to ratchet up the tension. As usual, the most interesting books came from novelists willing to take chances.

The woman in peril in Edna Sherry's *Sudden Fear*[6] (1948) turns the tables on her enemies in ruthless fashion. Wealthy playwright Myra Hudson discovers that her husband and his lover intend to kill her and constructs an elaborate scheme of murderous revenge. In *Dread Journey* (1945), Dorothy B. Hughes uses the confined setting of a cross-country train journey to heighten the danger faced by a film star in jeopardy. Suspense is the key, but the novel also concerns race, class and the fact that there is nothing new about Hollywood moguls harassing young starlets.

Jean Potts'[7] remarkable facility for creating menace with a minimum of melodrama[8] is illustrated by *The Evil Wish* (1962). Two unmarried sisters, Lucy and Marcia, live with their domineering father but fare little better than unpaid servants. When their father makes a secret plan to marry a nurse and turf them out of the house, they toy with impractical ideas of murder, only for their father and the nurse to be killed in a car accident. Potts is preoccupied with moral culpability, the consequences of the sisters' 'evil wish', even though they have committed no crime. The sisters display increasingly self-destructive patterns of behaviour and are in jeopardy[9] from themselves as well as from an unscrupulous photographer who enters their lives.

The Little Lie (1968) is even subtler. An inquisitive tenant overhears a quarrel between Dee Morris, his landlady, and the man she loves. When the man walks out on Dee, pride causes her to pretend that nothing has gone wrong. The Panglossian eaves-dropper fantasises that, through his good offices, the break-up will have a happy ending, but Dee's deception gradually unravels with disastrous consequences. Low-key storytelling masks the sophis-tication with which Potts handles a sexual taboo.

Evelyn Berckman[10] attempted to portray tensions and uncer-tainties about sexual orientation in *A Case in Nullity*, aka *A Hidden Malice* (1968). Auriol makes an unsatisfactory marriage to wealthy Ivor Hales, and when she seeks an annulment because her husband refuses to have sex with her, he embarks on a terrifying campaign of persecution. In its day, the storyline was daring, although Berckman's psychological ruminations now seem dated.

Lucille Fletcher's experience of writing for radio gave her a command of dialogue and plot evident in her novels. . . . *And Presumed Dead* (1963) combines woman-in-jeopardy and Gothic flourishes with a post-war international conspiracy thriller – 'an entirely new landmark in the literature of suspense', according to the wild claim on the cover of the Corgi paperback edition. *The Strange Blue Yawl* (1964) is a couple-in-jeopardy mystery combining domestic suspense with unreliable narrative, but perhaps Fletcher's finest novel is *Eighty Dollars to Stamford* (1975), about a part-time taxi driver who becomes intrigued by a mysterious passenger. The plot twists include the deployment of a *male* protagonist in jeopardy.

Charlotte Armstrong's[11] *Mischief* (1950) centres on a nine-year-old girl whose life is at stake. Her parents book into a New York hotel, ready to attend a function, only to be let down by their babysitter. At the last minute, and despite some misgivings, they hire the elevator man's niece Nell to take care of their daughter. But Nell is dangerously disturbed, and not to be trusted. The hotel room setting, with all the action is confined to a single evening, creates a mood of suffocating suspense.

The vulnerability of the young and defenceless makes child-in-jeopardy storylines especially tense. Evelyn Piper's *Bunny Lake is Missing*[12] (1957) captures Blanche Lake's horror when her three-year-old daughter can't be found, while posing the question: does the little girl actually exist, or is she the figment of a troubled imagination? Piper poses a different question in *The Nanny* (1964): is young Joey Fane really a disturbed killer, or is he a prospective victim?

Mary Roberts Rinehart was a favourite author of another wife and mother who turned to crime writing to supplement the family finances. Mary Higgins Clark's[13] first novel, *Where are the Children?*, published in 1975, drew on both the Lindbergh baby kidnapping and the case of Alice Crimmins,[14] a New York cocktail waitress who was convicted of killing her two children. The book's success prompted a publisher to offer $1.5 million for Clark's next novel.

Clark's plots, like Rinehart's, often depend on coincidence, but she compensates with storytelling techniques as slick as her predecessor's. The time span of the action is compressed so as to generate pace, and her protagonists are women with whom her (overwhelmingly female) readership can empathise. What her readers turn the pages to discover is not whodunit – the villain of the piece is often revealed early on – but whether the heroine will survive.

Crime fiction's women in jeopardy are typically twenty- and thirty-somethings, characters with whom readers enjoy identifying. Yet elderly women are often far more vulnerable than the young, a point made by Celia Dale with finesse. In *Sheep's Clothing* (1988), two women tricksters target female pensioners: 'Like as not, the old dears didn't even know they'd been robbed for quite a time . . . and then they probably thought they'd mislaid whatever it was . . . And even when (and if) they did realise what had been done, they were too confused and ashamed to tell anyone.'

Exploitation of the old and helpless, this time by a hypocritical husband and wife, also supplies the storyline for *A Helping Hand*[15] (1966). The fears of Cynthia Fingal, at the mercy of Josh and Maisie Evans, are evoked with insight and pathos: 'Survival was very important. Old, weak, lonely, longing to be finished with it all, tenaciously the young Cynthia still clung, shrunk but unchangeable, inside the husk. Let me give up, but let me not let go.'

Margaret Yorke's[16] understated novels of life in England's villages and small towns were sometimes misdescribed as 'cosy'.[17] There was nothing soft or sentimental about her insights into the minds of criminals, amateur and professional. *The Cost of Silence* (1977) typifies her best work; a touching scenario proves to be anything but. Emma Widnes is an invalid cared for by her devoted shopkeeper husband Norman. Her shocking murder causes skeletons to come tumbling from closets, but the police investigators never uncover the truth disclosed at the story's chilling climax.

Twenty-first century crime novelists have confronted female protagonists with perils of increasing complexity. Their women in jeopardy are often morally ambiguous characters whose nearest and dearest nurse terrifying secrets. Gillian Flynn's *Gone Girl,*[18] published in 2012, breathed fresh life into familiar ingredients. The basic premise draws on a real-life case;[19] the key viewpoints are not so much unreliable as utterly untrustworthy; the tension builds relentlessly; the plot twists startle.

The marriage of Nick and Amy Dunne is as corrosive as that of Vic and Melinda in Patricia Highsmith's *Deep Water*, a book Flynn admires. Nick's account of their lives, told in the present, is interwoven with extracts from Amy's diary. When Amy disappears on their wedding anniversary, Nick is suspected of her murder. The strength of the stunning mid-story twist is that it represents much more than authorial legerdemain. It casts fresh light on the Dunnes' relationship.

Flynn admires Agatha Christie, describing herself as obsessive about 'playing fair': 'One of my biggest peeves is when the writer hasn't given you enough information to figure everything out. You should be able to go back to the beginning of *Gone Girl*, after you've already read it and you know everything, and say: "Check – check – yes, she gave us that information."'

She flayed members of the thought police who attacked the sexual politics of her story and accused her of misogyny: 'To me, that puts a very, very small window on what feminism is[20] . . . Is it really only girl power, and you-go-girl, and empower yourself, and be the best you can be? For me, it's also the ability to have women who are bad characters . . . the one thing that really frustrates me is this idea that women are innately good, innately nurturing.'

Wherever there is a bestseller, a publishing bandwagon rolls close behind. *The Girl on the Train*[21] (2015), Paula Hawkins' first crime story, became an overnight sensation, claimed to be the fastest-selling adult hardcover novel in history. The highly readable story, a cocktail of Woolrich and Flynn with a dash of Christie's *4.50 from Paddington*, unfolds through three female viewpoints. Rachel takes the lead, fantasising about a couple she observes while commuting by rail.

Readers loved travelling with *The Girl on the Train*, although the journey twisted too often for some critics. For the novelist Declan Hughes,[22] the book 'marked the spectacular revival of had-I-but-known'. He warned of 'the law of diminishing plot returns that besets domestic suspense, whereby the more compelling the set-up, the more convoluted and implausible the resolution'.

A fellow Irish author, Declan Burke, highlighted the risk of cliché and stereotype:[23] 'The temptation, from a writer's point of view, is to lean too heavily on the readers' expectations, and eventually reveal the predatorial character – there being little else by way of convincing motive to explain such a dramatic volte-face – as a grotesque sociopath.'

Yet the tug of domestic suspense remains strong for writers and readers alike. And that is because the conundrum at the heart of the books has more than just a menacing allure. The books pose a fundamental and deeply personal question: *is there anyone I can really trust?*

Notes

The main sources are Luke Seaber's *Incognito Social Observation in British Literature: Certainties in Degradation*, Kate Jackson's article on June Wright in *CADS* 83 and *Domestic Noir: The New Face of 21st Century Crime Fiction*, edited by Laura Joyce and Henry Sutton.

1   *in 1940*: She told her friend and fellow crime writer Eileen Dewhurst that the actual publication date was the day Britain declared war on Germany, although that might have been an embellishment of her undoubted misfortune.

2   *the book won an Edgar Award*: It was also adapted for television as 'The Lonely Hours' in 1963, but: 'Louise became a Stepford housewife in a negligee . . . if ever there was a story that needed a brown layer of London smog this is it': Lucy Lethbridge, *The Oldie Review of Books*, Summer 2019.

3   *an outspoken advocate of euthanasia*: So was her friend Charlotte Hough,
    best known as a children's author, who published *The Bassington Murder*
    in 1980. Five years later Hough was sent to prison for assisting a suicide.

4   *The Blank Wall*: The novel was made into two films, more than half a
    century apart: *The Reckless Moment* in 1949 and *The Deep End* in 2001.

5   *June Wright*: Dorothy June Healy married at the age of twenty-two and
    eventually had six children. Her final series character was a sleuthing nun,
    but she stopped writing mysteries after her husband suffered a breakdown.

6   *Sudden Fear*: Joan Crawford played Myra in the film based on the novel,
    which was Sherry's first solo mystery. Before the war she had co-written
    two books with Milton Gropper.

7   *Jean Potts*: Her first novel, *Go, Lovely Rose*, won an Edgar.

8   *creating menace with a minimum of melodrama*: A similarly gifted, but less
    prolific contemporary of Potts was Nedra Tyre, a former social worker who
    excelled at short stories. The critic Sarah Weinman has suggested that Tyre's
    'Killed by Kindness' is a forerunner of Gillian Flynn's *Gone Girl*.

9   *The sisters . . . are in jeopardy*: Another suspenseful story about sisters,
    What Ever Happened to Baby Jane? is unusual in that the author was a
    man, Henry Farrell. The novel was filmed by Robert Aldrich.

10 *Evelyn Berckman*: An American who relocated to England, she was a clas-
    sical pianist and composer who turned to writing crime novels relatively
    late in life. Her storylines are varied, sometimes Gothic and always intriguing.
    Do You Know This Voice? was filmed in 1964.

11 *Charlotte Armstrong*: Armstrong's Edgar-winning *A Dram of Poison* involves
    a madcap chase for a missing vial of poison. Her early Gothic mystery *The
    Case of the Three Weird Sisters* was filmed as *The Three Weird Sisters*;
    improbably, the screenplay was co-written by Dylan Thomas, perhaps
    explaining why the scene of the crime became a decaying mansion in a
    Welsh mining village. *The Chocolate Cobweb* was filmed by Claude Chabrol
    as *Merci pour le Chocolat*, aka *Nightcap*. Marilyn Monroe played Nell in
    Don't Bother to Knock, the film version of *Mischief*, in 1952; the following
    year she starred in an excellent film noir, *Niagara*.

12 *Evelyn Piper's Bunny Lake is Missing*: Born Miriam Levant, Piper was known
    after her marriage as Merriam Modell. Otto Preminger's film of the book
    changed the ending but was atmospheric and disturbing. Piper was also
    well served by a chilling film version of *The Nanny*. See Sarah Weinman,
    'Merriam Modell, Domestic Suspense's Reluctant Pioneer', *CrimeReads*, 28
    November 2018.

13 *Mary Higgins Clark*: Clark collaborated with her daughter and fellow author,
    Carol, and late in her career she began a new partnership with Alafair
    Burke, co-writing the *Under Suspicion* series featuring an intrepid television
    journalist who investigates cold cases.

14 *the case of Alice Crimmins*: *The Investigation* by Dorothy Uhnak was also
    inspired by the case.

15 *A Helping Hand*: A television version screened in 1967 was scripted by
    Simon Gray.

16 *Margaret Yorke*: With the poignant *No Medals for the Major*, Yorke deserted
    detection for psychological suspense. Her tense studies of ordinary lives and
    fractured relationships include *Devil's Work*, which begins with a man
    pretending to his wife that he has not lost his job.

17 *misdescribed as 'cosy'*: 'Cosy' is a label that can easily be used as a slur, sometimes with sexist overtones. Yet 'cozy' is a popular label in the US for industrial quantities of books which have few counterparts elsewhere, light-hearted stories awash with pets, quilts, knitting patterns and recipes. Examples include Maya Corrigan's *The Tell-Tale Tarte*, an Edgar Allan Poe-themed culinary mystery, and Clea Simon's *When Bunnies Go Bad*, marketed as an example of Pet Noir.

18 *Gone Girl*: 'Gone Girl' was the title of a story in *The Name is Archer* by Ross Macdonald, an author Flynn admires. Her novel was filmed by David Fincher, whose other work includes *Zodiac*, *Panic Room* and *Se7en*. A dazzling essay by David Bordwell traces literary influences on the narrative approach of novel and film, ranging from *Bleak House* and Vera Caspary's *Bedelia* to Ben Ames Williams' *Leave Her to Heaven* and the parallel plotting of Bill S. Ballinger: http://www.davidbordwell.net/blog/2014/10/21/gone-grrrl/

19 *a real-life case*: The disappearance of Laci Peterson in 2002.

20 *a very, very small window on what feminism is*: However, Stephanie Merritt (who writes historical mysteries as S. J. Parris) has claimed that 'writing a woman who is off-kilter for various reasons – isolation, distress, hormonal changes – might inadvertently reinforce a stereotype of neurotic women, slaves to their biology.' Her arguments were melodramatically headlined: 'The Cult of the Unreliable Female Narrator Must be Stopped', *Guardian*, 19 February 2018.

21 *The Girl on the Train*: The film version was set in the US, for no discernible artistic reason. A stage version premiered in Leeds in 2018.

22 *Declan Hughes*: Noting that Hawkins began by writing romantic fiction, under the name Amy Silver, Hughes called her novel 'an inspired mash-up of the two genres . . . hugely influential, with many novelists who 10 years ago would have been published between pastel covers now drawn to that . . . dark central insight: that what may look like the happy marriage, the perfect life, is in all likelihood a terrible delusion'. Arguing that she was following in the footsteps of Charlotte Brontë and Daphne du Maurier, he added that the book's final line could have been: 'Reader, I was right all along.' Hughes added that Hawkins' second crime novel, *Into the Water*, shared with its predecessor 'a preoccupation with the stories we tell ourselves and how they conflict with each other and with the truth, and an alarming proliferation of reliably loathsome men'. ('Into the Water Review: The Girl on the Train gets a Dunking', *Irish Times*, 6 May 2017). Hughes is a playwright and author of crime novels about Ed Loy (named in tribute to Sam Spade; in Ireland, a loy is a spade).

23 *Declan Burke . . . highlighted the risk of cliché and stereotype:* In a review of Dennis Lehane's *Before We Fell*: 'Before We Fell review: Brilliantly Unconventional Domestic Noir', *Irish Times*, 20 May 2017.

FORTY-EIGHT

Mystery Games

East Asian detective fiction

At the age of twenty-three, Masako Togawa made her debut as a singer at a well-known Tokyo nightclub called the Gin Pari. It was 1954, and she'd worked as a typist for five years, but she was a natural performer. As the years passed and her musical career progressed, she transformed her sister's coffee shop in the Shibuya district into a club known as Aoi Heya, or Blue Room.

Aoi Heya became a haunt of celebrities as well as a gathering place for musicians. Togawa combined a busy personal life – her last child was born when she was forty-eight – with her own career as a *chansonnier* and actor in films and on television. A charismatic woman who favoured exotically coloured and styled hair, she released a couple of records, and, in a TV series called *Playgirl*, she took the lead role, as a mystery writer heading an all-female detective agency.

After years of helping LGBT musicians to advance their careers, Togawa came out as bisexual in 1999; three years later, she was one of the first Japanese television personalities to take an active role in the Tokyo Lesbian and Gay Parade. In later years, she became a successful music teacher, giving classes that were broadcast on a web channel. When she died at the age of eighty-five, her son Nero said they had sung together on stage at the 'Blue

Room Monday' club (a new club inspired by Aoi Heya) until the day before she was hospitalised.

For all her eclectic achievements, her reputation may ultimately rest on her sideline as a detective novelist. The *Times Literary Supplement* called her 'the P. D. James of Japan', although all that she and James had in common was that they were women who wrote distinctive crime fiction. Both deserve to be considered on their own merits.

Togawa got into the habit of scribbling down stories while waiting to perform on stage. The sinister setting of her first crime novel, *The Master Key*, aka *A Vast Illusion* (1962), was the K Apartments for Ladies. The block is due to be moved to allow a road to be widened. A single key unlocks the doors to one hundred and fifty apartments, which conceal many secrets. A strange religious cult moves into the building, and the plot thickens as a man dressed as a woman suffers a violent death.

The Mystery Writers of Japan awarded the book an Edogawa Rampo Prize and Togawa followed up with *The Lady Killer* (1963), an unsettling novel[1] in which Ichiro Honda, a computer specialist married to a rich wife, leads a blameless life from nine to five, but spends his evenings seducing women, only to abandon them. When a series of murders takes place, he becomes a prime suspect.

In *A Kiss of Fire* (1985), three boys see a bat-like creature running up the stairs of a house, breathing flames. Twenty-six years later, they find themselves involved in a series of arson attacks that take a bizarre turn when the wallet and ID card of one of the men is found in the stomach of a circus lion killed in one of the fires. The novel earned praise from Ruth Rendell, while Julian Symons said: 'the story's climax reveals one apparently guilty party after another. This may sound like the drawing-room gathering of the suspects in a Golden Age story, but the effect could hardly be more different.' The result, he concluded, was 'both preposterous and enthralling'.

The Edogawa Rampo Prize is named after the writer widely credited with inventing the modern Japanese detective story. He was born Taro Hirai in 1894, the grandson of a samurai. A youthful enthusiasm for western detective fiction led him to set about translating stories by Arthur Conan Doyle into Japanese. When he wrote a short story of his own, he adopted a pen-name in tribute to another author whom he greatly admired, Edgar Allan Poe. The Rampo name (now commonly romanized as Ranpo) is a variant of Poe's.

'The Two-Sen Copper Coin' was published in 1923 in *Shinseinen*, a popular magazine that had published translations of Conan Doyle and Chesterton. What was fresh about Ranpo's story was its focus on logical problem-solving, while a code based on a Buddhist incantation gave a specifically Japanese flavour to a familiar component of western mysteries.

Although 'The Two-Sen Coin' broke fresh ground, Ranpo was not the first Japanese crime writer. In the seventeenth century, Saikaku Ihara published a collection of forty-four stories,[2] which in turn reflected the influence of historical accounts of Chinese court cases of the type updated in Robert van Gulik's books about Judge Dee.

The late nineteenth century saw the translation into Japanese of major western crime writers,[3] such as Poe, Collins, Gaboriau and Conan Doyle and the pattern continued prior to the Second World War. Among home-grown writers, Kido Okamoto freely acknowledged that his stories about Inspector Hanshichi, which he began to write in 1916, were inspired by Sherlock Holmes. During the Golden Age, the books of Van Dine and Freeman Wills Crofts proved influential, and, in 1937, *Shinseinen* ranked Eden Phillpotts' *The Red Redmaynes* as the third best mystery of all time.

'The Case of the Murder on D. Hill' saw Ranpo tackling the locked-room mystery, while 'The Psychological Test', in which Fukiya, a gifted student at Waseda, seeks to commit the perfect murder, is an inverted mystery with echoes of the Leopold and Loeb case. Often, resemblances between aspects of Ranpo's work and those of western writers were coincidental, as with *The Beast in the Shadows* (1928), which boasts a femme fatale whose behaviour anticipates Brigid O'Shaughnessy's in Hammett's *The Maltese Falcon*.

Ranpo's major series character, Kogoro Akechi, who solves the puzzle in 'The Psychological Test', is a brilliant eccentric, expert at judo and, like his principal adversary, 'the Fiend with Twenty Faces', a master of disguise. Akechi, who often works alongside the Boys' Detective Club, Ranpo's version of the Baker Street Irregulars, has become an iconic figure in Japanese popular culture.[4]

Ranpo's later fiction focused increasingly on '*ero guro nansensu*' ('eroticism, the grotesque and the nonsensical'). An obsessive interest in the macabre and morbid sexuality is evident, as with Poe. In 1939, 'The Caterpillar', a weird story about a severely disabled and disfigured war veteran, was banned by government censors. Following the end of the Second World War, Ranpo threw himself into promoting detective fiction, and founded the Detective Authors' Club, later renamed the Mystery Writers of Japan.[5]

Ranpo's critical writings on the genre were also significant. 'The Classification of Tricks' examines ways in which writers seek to pull the wool over their readers' eyes. Ranpo discussed the prevalence of impersonation in the genre, and argued that a pioneering example of 'the criminal disguised as the victim' stratagem can be found in Dickens' historical novel *Barnaby Rudge*.

In his essay collection *The Phantom Castle*, Ranpo applied the term '*shin honkaku*' to the style of British writers of the 1940s, such as Michael Innes, Margery Allingham and Nicholas Blake, who continued to work in the Golden Age tradition. '*Honkaku*' (literally 'original method') refers to a highly orthodox form of detective story that plays a game with the reader in the manner of S. S. Van Dine and Ellery Queen. Novels of this type continued to be written after the Second World War by authors such as Seishi Yokomizo,[6] but interest in them faded rapidly in the second half of the 1950s as writers placed growing emphasis on 'social realism'.

Seichō Matsumoto was a leading advocate of social realism in the genre. Even so, in his early novel *Points and Lines* (1958), echoes of the railwayman Freeman Wills Crofts extend beyond the title, since the plot turns on an alibi concerning train times. Matsumoto, who succeeded Ranpo as head of the Mystery Writers of Japan, saw Dostoevsky as the model for crime writers to aim for, and his fiction earned the genre a degree of literary respectability that writers of *honkaku*[7] mysteries found elusive.

Matsumoto argued in 'The Dark Side of Japanese History and I' that, although more than half of Christie's plots turned on disguise or impersonation, it ought not to be a major element in a Japanese mystery, because 'disguise seems unnatural for homogeneous people like the Japanese.' In *A Quiet Place* (1971), a government official learns that his wife has suffered a fatal heart attack, but when he tries to find out more about the circumstances of her death, he starts to wonder if she was leading a double life. The story is not a whodunit; as his career developed, Matsumoto's concerns resembled those of specialists in psychological suspense[8] such as Georges Simenon and Patricia Highsmith.

The same was true of Shizuko Natsuki, even though she came to western crime fiction by way of Christie and *The Red Redmaynes*. *The Third Lady* (1987) begins with Kohei Daigo and a woman confiding in each other about someone they wish dead. When his enemy is murdered, he is sure the killer is the woman, with whom he is now quite obsessed. But can he bring himself to kill her enemy? Natsuki turns the Highsmithian scenario into a moral fable with a twist.

A trick familiar from the real-life Wallace case provided Natsuki with the starting point of *The Obituary Arrives at Two O'Clock* (1988). Kosuke Okita, a landscape gardener, receives a mysterious telephone call from a woman in need of help, and this prompts him to go out in an abortive attempt to meet and help her. At the same time, a man who has cheated him is bludgeoned to death with a golf club. With no alibi, Kosuke becomes the prime suspect, and goes on the run. The last sentence of the book supplies a grim explanation of the final mystery.

For all his reservations about *honkaku* mysteries, Matsumoto supervised the publication of a series of books in the traditional vein, but their impact was modest compared to that of Soji Shimada's exuberant debut, *The Tokyo Zodiac Murders*. Published in 1981, the novel recounts the investigation by the brilliant young astrologer Kiyoshi Mitarai and the freelance illustrator and detective fiction fan Kazumi Ishioka of a cold case dating back to 1936.

A plethora of classic trimmings – maps, footprints in the snow and a locked-room mystery – complement a race against time, grisly multiple murders and diagrams of body parts. Shimada even updates the genre's self-reflexive tradition, with Kazumi discussing Matsumoto's *Longitude 139 Degrees East* and Kiyoshi's playful criticism of Sherlock's failings as a detective, and the weirdness of 'The Speckled Band'.

Shimada's *Murder in the Crooked House* (1982) typifies the locked-room mystery in which the building where murder occurs is vividly characterised, and its unorthodox construction plays a part in the plot. Floor plans proliferate in books of this type, such as Takemaru Abiko's witty and convoluted *The 8 Mansion Murders* (1989), which references Allingham, Christie, Queen, Rawson and Carr.

The prologue to Yukito Ayatsuji's *The Decagon House Murders* (1987), which finds seven members of a university mystery club isolated on a small island with predictably fatal results, acknowledges a debt to *And Then There Were None* from the start: 'He has to kill them in order, one by one. Precisely like that story written by the famous British female writer — slowly, one after the other.' Rather than using their own names, the club members call themselves Ellery, Agatha, Carr, Leroux and so on. Ayatsuji calls this 'symbolic characterisation', and as Michael Dirda said,[9] 'This may seem a charming conceit, but Ayatsuji makes clever use of it.' The story is a love letter to Golden Age detective fiction.

Thirty years after Ayatsuji's inventive novel appeared, the *shin honkaku* movement was reinvigorated by Masahiro Imamura's multi-award-winning debut *Death among the Undead*, which introduced a fresh ingredient to the mix: zombies. This marks a striking shift away from the strictly rational traditions of the classic detective novel, but Soji Shimada points out, in his foreword to an English translation of the story, that 'Imamura . . . maintains the necessary rigour of the locked-room mystery by making the zombies bound by strict rules governing their behaviour and even their existence.' For Shimada, this is a sign of things to come: 'lately, I have seen country house murder mysteries which utilise artificial intelligence as a new and original element.'

*

Ranpo corresponded with Fred Dannay, and when Dannay visited Japan, he and Matsumoto held a public discussion about the genre, but the author who set out to become Japan's Ellery Queen was Arisu Arisugawa. A male writer whose enthusiasm for *Alice in Wonderland* led him to adopt the pen-name Alice Arisugawa, he had been a member of the Mystery Club of Dōshisha University in Kyoto. The emergence of *shin honkaku*, 'the new orthodoxy', owed much to novelists who, like Arisugawa, had shared their enthusiasm for Golden Age detection with fellow members of university mystery clubs.

Arisugawa's *The Moai Island Puzzle* (1989), an 'impossible crime' story set on an imaginary island with *moai* similar to those found on Easter Island, is an ingenious example of 'fair play' detection, with cunningly conceived clues and a challenge to the reader. Like Queen, Arisugawa creates a character sharing his own pen-name, but the fictional Arisugawa is a Watson figure. The role of Great Detective is taken by Jiro Egami.

Shimada describes the novel in an introduction to the English-language edition as 'meticulously constructed . . . Arisugawa considers this mathematical, proper process of logical reasoning more important than a showy performance.' Arisugawa's love of impossible crimes was further manifested in *The Illustrated Guide to the Locked Room 1891–1998*, a non-fiction book so seductively illustrated by Kazuichi Isoda that it holds allure even for those unable to read a word of Japanese.[10]

The verve of Shimada and his followers caused *shin honkaku* detective stories to enjoy a boom in popularity, especially with the younger generation of readers. This led to the foundation in 2000 of the Honkaku Mystery Writers' Club of Japan, modelled very broadly on the Detection Club, with Arisugawa as first President. In recent years, *honkaku* mystery fiction has cross-fertilised with other genres, such as horror, fantasy, science fiction and meta-fiction, giving rise to an eclectic mix of stories, ranging from realistic novels to stories dependent on narrative tricks, as well as films, television series, comics, anime and video games.

Rintaro Norizuki,[11] the Club's fourth President, has argued[12] that *honkaku* stories embrace 'even avant-garde forms that pose radical questions, such as "what is a mystery?", "what is a detective?" and "what does solving a case mean?" . . . It is not an easy task to explain what *honkaku* precisely is here, but perhaps one might say that it is exactly this diversity that holds the secret to the everlasting genre.'

The Club publishes annual anthologies, and has also established the Honkaku Mystery Awards. The fiction prize in 2006 was won by Keigo Higashino[13] for *The Devotion of Suspect X*.[14] In a sign of changing fashion in book-cover clichés, the book earned him the description 'the Japanese Stieg Larsson', despite the absence of an equivalent to Lisbeth Salander.

Tetsuya Ishigami, a reclusive teacher with a genius for mathematics, finds himself embroiled in the cover-up of a murder provoked by domestic violence. His obsessive love for his next-door neighbour leads him into a battle of wits with Manuba Yukawa, a brilliant physics professor who is nicknamed 'Detective Galileo' by Higashino's series detective, Inspector Kusanagi.

Higashino offers an intriguing blend of realism and ingenuity. The careful construction of his story is a reminder that he was once an engineer, just like John Rhode, although nobody has yet dubbed Yukawa 'the Japanese Dr Priestley'. One or two erudite commentators have described Higashino's treatment of the 'P versus NP' computer-science problem as simplistic, a quibble that hasn't prevented the book from selling by the million.

Recent years have seen a deluge of detection in the Far East.[15] In style and subject matter, the books range as broadly as the genre itself. One Chinese author even belongs to the small band of crime writers who have personal experience of committing murder.[16] In 2018, Liu Yongbiao was convicted of bludgeoning four people to death in a guest house more than twenty years earlier. His published fiction included *The Guilty Secret*. He'd also planned a story about a writer who gets away with murder, 'The Beautiful Writer Who Killed'.

Of the innumerable manhunt stories since *Caleb Williams*, perhaps none is as disturbing as a novel by a former Chinese police officer, A Yi. *A Perfect Crime* (2012) is a doom-laden account of the narrator's murder of an innocent young woman and the consequences of a crime committed 'out of boredom. A desire to play cat and mouse.'

Arthur Conan Doyle's shadow hovers over Chan Ho-Kei's *The Borrowed* (2015), which features Inspector Kwan, an incorruptible Hong Kong cop blessed with Sherlockian powers of deduction and a Watsonian sidekick, Detective Lok. The story moves back in time from the present to the late 1960s in half a dozen sections. The linked stories trace Kwan's career during a tumultuous period of Chinese history in a baroque confection of puzzles, clues and social realism.

The Taiwanese 'impossible crime' mystery *Death in the House of Rain* (2006) by philosophy scholar Szu-Yen Lin is another medley of old and new, with cell phones and laptops and an intellectual amateur detective. A triple killing at the eponymous house, which is a 'three-dimensional presentation' of the Chinese character for rain (floor plans of the crime scene are duly provided), provokes the interest of Ruoping Lin, a professor of philosophy. As he pursues his investigation, the body count rises.

In Japan, the illusionist Masao Atsukawa, who wrote as Awasaka Tsumao, took trickery in detective writing to a level far beyond anything Clayton Rawson attempted. His main characters included Soga Kajo, a female former magician turned detective, and Yogi Gandhi. In *The Book of Happiness*, Gandhi uncovers corruption associated with a religious cult, but his most remarkable case was *The Living and the Dead*, published in 1994. This is a novel containing a disappearing short story.

As the American commentator Steve Steinbock explains: 'What makes this book unique is that it's a 215-page novel (short by Japanese standards) that comes with the signatures uncut, so that – unless you take a scissors or razor blade and cut the pages – only 24 pages of text are visible. As you open the book, the first exposed page after the title page is page 16, followed by 17, followed by 32 and 33, followed by 48 and 49, and so on. The instructions with the title page say:

"HOW TO READ THIS BOOK: First of all, please read the book with the sealed binding. You'll read a short story. Next, cut each

page and enjoy a full-length novel. The short story has disappeared.
(signed) The Author. The Disappearing Short Story."

'And indeed, it's true. The short story involves a small group of
people at a bar, one of whom is a sad young man who seems to
have psychic abilities. But when the pages are cut, that character
disappears. There's at least one gender switch, the setting becomes
a magic club rather than a bar, and Yogi Gandhi (who doesn't
appear in the short story) is the hero. The magic only works
because of the nature of the Japanese language. It would be
impossible to translate while maintaining the effect. It also can
only work in a print version.'

In twenty-first-century China, meanwhile, mystery games have
become hugely popular, and the TV show *Star Detective* has
sparked delight in 'offline mystery games', with over four thousand
offline mystery game clubs and millions of players.

Fei Wu's *The Lost Winner* (2019) is an outgrowth of this vogue,
a three-dimensional crime story complete with a self-assembly
model of the crime scene offering clues to the solution of the
mystery. Not even Dennis Wheatley could have imagined how his
concept for the crime dossiers might metamorphose into an interactive treat for Chinese fans of the detective puzzle.

Notes

The main sources are Sari Kawana's *Murder Most Modern*, *Ellery Queen's
Japanese Golden Dozen*, John L. Apostolou and Martin H. Greenberg's *Murder
in Japan*, Makoto Ohno's 'Faulkner in Mystery', read at the 2010 conference of
the William Faulkner Society of Japan, Soji Shimada's introductions to *The
Decagon House Murders* and *The Moai Island Puzzle*. I have also benefited from
discussions with Steve Steinbock, John Pugmire, Soji Shimada, Alice Arisugawa,
Masaya Yamaguchi, Elliot Han, Fei Wu and Sangjun Lee. For convenience, I
have usually presented Japanese names in a western format. i.e. Soji Shimada,
rather than Shimada Soji.

1   *an unsettling novel*: In *Misogynies*, Joan Smith discusses similarities between
     the plot twist in *The Lady Killer* and that of Scott Turow's *Presumed Innocent*.
     (A comparable twist occurs in Shimada's *The Tokyo Zodiac Murders*). Smith
     sees Togawa's as a haunting story that evokes pity and horror, but makes
     the controversial claim that Turow's book is a key text in the 'anti-feminist
     fightback', its whole purpose 'to apportion blame . . . the book's real theme
     is that women's power is always achieved illegitimately and at the expense

of men, and sometimes at the expense of other women.' The first of Smith's five crime novels, *A Masculine Ending*, features a 'vanishing corpse' mystery, and was televised with Janet McTeer playing the feminist academic Loretta Lawson.

2 *Saikaku Ihara published a collection of forty-four stories*: *Records of Trials Held beneath a Cherry Tree* first appeared in 1689, and emulated the criminal casebook ascribed to Gui Wanrong, a twelfth-century Chinese official. Opinions vary about the precise origins of the genre in Japan, as in other countries. One candidate is the eighteenth-century writer Tsuruya Nanboku IV, who fused crime with horror.

3 *the translation into Japanese of major western crime writers*: China followed a similar pattern; a leading crime writer in the first half of the twentieth century was Cheng Xiaoqing, whose detective Huo Sang has a Watson, Bao Lang. An English-language collection of his stories appeared in 2007 as *Sherlock in Shanghai*; it included 'The Shoe', discussed by Michael Harris-Peyton in *Routledge*. Mao Tse-Tung's coming had the same chilling effect on detective fiction as those of Hitler and Mussolini. During the Cultural Revolution, Cheng Xiaoqing spent some time under house arrest.

4 *an iconic figure in Japanese popular culture*: Akechi has featured in numerous films, such as *Black Lizard*, and manga and anime series.

5 *the Mystery Writers of Japan*: The organisation established an awards system in 1948, and created the Edogawa Rampo Award in 1955.

6 *Seishi Yokomizo*: Yokomizo's love of both Golden Age detection and Japanese history and class structures is evident in books such as *The Honjin Murders*. War impacted on the *honjins* occupied by the nobility, as it did on British country-house estates and the families who owned them.

7 *honkaku*: The term *honkaku* was originally coined in the mid-1920s by Saburō Kōga. A leading pioneer was Keikichi Ōsaka, whose career lasted a mere five years, but yielded the hallucinatory stories recently collected and translated in *The Ginza Ghost*, and introduced by Taku Ashibe, who describes his own *Murder in the Red Chamber* (replete with 'grand map of Prospect Garden', family tree and cast of characters) as 'Western crime fiction, based on a Chinese classic, written in Japanese'. Post-war, Tetsuya Ayukawa's *honkaku* stories were overshadowed by the success of Matsumoto, but *The Red Locked Room* showcases his ingenuity.

8 *Matsumoto's concerns . . . resembled those of specialists in psychological suspense*: In his 'Postscript for the Nineties' to *Bloody Murder*, Julian Symons emphasised the gulf between Japanese and western attitudes, ethics and interpretations of social realism. The love of *shin honkaku* writers for Golden Age detection would no doubt have baffled him.

9 *As Michael Dirda says*: '"The Decagon House Murders" evokes Agatha Christie – in Japan', *Washington Post*, 15 July 2015. Dirda observes, 'If you were to take this novel as a serious social document, you would be appalled at its body count. But Ayatsuji keeps the reader from feeling any serious identification with the victims . . . The final revelations, including the modus operandi of the crimes, will surprise all but the most astute readers. An epilogue brings a further twist.'

10 *even for those unable to read a word of Japanese*: I am grateful to Steve Steinbock for sharing his translation of the preface.

11 *Rintarō Norizuki*: An alumnus of the Kyoto University Mystery Club, and

another admirer of Ellery Queen, he gave his own name to his series detective in true Queenian fashion.

12 *Rintaro Norizuki, the Club's fourth President, has argued*: On the Club's official website.

13 *Keigo Higashino*: His other books include an ingenious 'impossible crime' mystery, *Salvation of a Saint*.

14 The *Devotion of Suspect X*: The novel was shortlisted for an Edgar, and a film version was released in 2017. *Galileo* is a Japanese television series based on the books about Kusanagi and Yukawa.

15 *Recent years have seen a deluge of detection in the Far East*: In Korea, where there is a long history of enthusiasm for the genre, the main focus lately has been on crime in films and on television. At the time of the Tiananmen Square tragedy, Shanghai-born Qiu Xiaolong was studying in the US; rather than return home, he stayed in America, producing the Inspector Chen series, set in 1930s China. *The Mao Case*, published in 2009 and dedicated to 'the people that suffered under Mao', sees Chen's inquiries leading him to a secret which the Communist Party is desperate to keep.

16 *crime writers who have personal experience of committing murder*: Such as the Dutch author Richard Klinkhamer, who wrote a book about different ways to kill a spouse, and was convicted of killing his wife, who had gone missing nine years earlier.

FORTY-NINE

Early Graves

Difference and diversity

At nineteen, Chester Himes was an angry young man. At one time he'd planned on becoming a medical doctor. But he'd fallen down a lift shaft, suffering severe injuries, and although he'd made a good recovery, his academic studies faltered as his parents' marriage fell apart. He discovered drink, gambling and women, and got at least one girl pregnant. Before long he was breaking the law with reckless abandon.

Petty misdemeanours escalated into serious crime. He stole a car and then committed a cheque fraud that earned him a suspended jail sentence and supervised probation. With two friends, he stole a cache of pistols, and then broke into a furriers, but was arrested again. On 25 November 1928, he stole another car, and broke into a house owned by a wealthy couple, threatening the owner with a gun. He stole four valuable rings, only to be arrested in a pawn shop when he tried to sell the jewellery. At the police precinct, he was hung upside down and beaten about his testicles until he confessed. In court, he pleaded guilty, hoping for a light sentence. He was sent to prison for twenty years.

In a cement-floor cell block with an open latrine, he began to write. Gambling earned him enough money to buy a typewriter. In the outside world, he'd regarded homosexuality as a perversion, but he began a relationship with Prince Rico, another convicted robber, who encouraged his literary efforts. Prison overcrowding was so severe that legislation was introduced, retrospectively reducing his sentence to less than seven years. By the time he was released, on April Fools' Day 1936, he was contributing to *Esquire*.

Chester Bomar Himes was an inept criminal but an intelligent writer. Born in Jefferson City, Missouri, 'the third generation out of slavery', as he put it, he was the son of a college professor and a light-skinned woman who told her three boys: 'You mustn't think of yourself as coloured. . . . You both have white blood — fine white blood — in your veins.'

Once out of prison, Himes rekindled a previous relationship with a girl called Jean Johnson. His experiment with homosexuality was over and they married in 1937. He wrote for magazines, and published *If He Hollers Let Him Go* (1945), a fierce novel dealing with racism, politics and sex. During the eight weeks he spent at the artistic community at Yaddo he got to know Patricia Highsmith.

His anger and insecurity manifested themselves in rifts with fellow African American writers and left-wing activists, as well as in heavy drinking and a frightening readiness to resort to violence towards the women in his life. He hit one lover so hard that a doctor was needed, while another reacted to a slapping by slitting her wrists. By this time, he'd moved to France, where Marcel Duhamel,[1] translator of *If He Hollers Let Him Go* and founder of Gallimard's influential crime fiction imprint *La Série Noire*, encouraged him to write a 'Negro detective story'.

At first, Himes was reluctant, perhaps feeling that detective fiction was beneath a writer of his accomplishment and ambition. But he was short of money, telling one lover after another that he couldn't afford to divorce Jean, and he set about writing a novel that fitted the Duhamel creed: 'We don't give a damn who's thinking what – only what they're doing.' He drafted eighty pages of a crime story set in Harlem, only for Duhamel to insist that he needed to include police officers. Recalling two tough cops he'd known in Los Angeles, Himes invented Grave Digger Jones and Coffin Ed Johnson. This ruthless duo earned Himes the commercial success he craved.

Their first case, *A Rage in Harlem*, aka *The Five Cornered Square* and *For Love of Imabelle* (1957), was written with a sharp eye for the follies and foibles of human nature. The gullible Jackson, who works for an undertaker, falls victim to a gang of swindlers and loses everything. He steals from his employer, but is pursued by the police, and needs to seek help from his twin brother, a hoodlum who masquerades as a Sister of Mercy, selling tickets to Heaven.

When this fast, funny and ferocious novel won the Grand Prix de Littérature Policière,[2] critics outside France began to take notice, although Anthony Boucher had reservations about Himes' portrayal of 'the America that a European likes to believe in . . . a lurid world of squalor and oppression and hatred and meaningless violence'.

Himes' private life became messier than ever. At one point he was terrified that a woman he'd dumped was plotting revenge on his latest lover, Lesley Packard. Just as a confidence trickster had attacked Coffin Ed in the book, he feared that the woman would throw acid into Lesley's face.

By 1964 he was telling a journalist that his detective stories shouldn't be regarded separately from his ordinary novels:[3] 'I simply describe the social conditions of poor people who need to win money.' Patricia Highsmith commended *Cotton Comes to Harlem*[4] (1964) for its wit, pace and 'stiletto social comments'. Boucher showed growing appreciation of Himes' quality, saying that *The Heat's On* (1966) presented 'in its wild fun-house mirror way a powerfully contemptuous picture of a venal and vicious world'.

The final book in the series, *Blind Man with Pistol*, appeared in 1969, as Himes moved to Spain. Like Highsmith, he came to feel at home in Europe, perhaps because European readers and critics seemed to appreciate his work more than their American counterparts. He suffered a stroke, and his health deteriorated, although he finally got round to divorcing Jean and marrying Lesley Packard. He remained the outstanding black American crime writer[5] until the emergence of Walter Mosley,[6] creator of the private investigator Ezekiel 'Easy' Rawlins.

As recently as 2011, it was possible for Mosley to say:[7] 'Hardly anybody in America[8] has written about black male heroes . . . There are black male protagonists and black male supporting characters, but nobody else writes about black male heroes.' As the picture changes,[9] albeit slowly, Mosley's achievements have seen him become a Grand Master of the MWA.

Mosley is the son of an African American father and a Jewish mother. He self-identifies as both black and Jewish, although the significance of his Jewish heritage is sometimes underestimated. The commentator Harold Heft argued[10] that there is 'a profoundly Jewish dimension in his work . . . *Fearless Jones* revolves around Holocaust survivors and covert Israeli agents operating in the undercurrents of Los Angeles. Easy Rawlins . . . is assisted in several stories by the sympathetic Jewish detective Saul Lynx. Ben Dibbuk, the protagonist of . . . *Diablerie*, is every inch a classic Dibbuk out of Yiddish folklore. Jewish culture, together with black culture and the American collisions between different cultures, permeate every page of Mosley's work . . . Mosley described his books as a "confluence" of cultures.'

The stereotyping of Jewish culture and characters has long been a dismal feature of crime fiction, especially (but not exclusively) prior to the end of the Second World War. Malcolm J. Turnbull has argued[11] that, amid all the chauvinism and racism to be found in the genre, 'the most frequent butts of negative remarks, description or analysis . . . are Jews.'

The thriller writer Sydney Horler, for instance, 'made a speciality of the Jewish criminal', although Turnbull points out that in few Golden Age detective novels is a Jewish character revealed to be the murderer. Perhaps this reflects the same sort of snobbery that led S. S. Van Dine to say that: 'The culprit must be a decidedly worth-while person.' Even in Christianna Brand's wartime mystery *Heads You Lose* (1941), which presents a Jewish suspect sympathetically, the casual antisemitism of his family and friends is striking.

The customary role of Chinese characters in Anglo-American crime fiction prior to the Second World War was to personify 'the Yellow Peril', the threat posed, in the minds of many white authors and their readers, by people from East Asia. This fear of the foreign and the unfamiliar was exploited by Birmingham-born Arthur Henry Ward, who adopted the exotic pen-name Sax Rohmer for his thrillers about Dr Fu Manchu, a master criminal plotting global domination. At a time of tension in Europe in the years leading up to the First World War, Fu Manchu was confronted by the tough but utterly decent Englishman Denis Nayland Smith. Ward knew nothing about China, but his books became bestsellers and spawned dozens of films.[12]

The working-class Londoner Thomas Burke also enjoyed success with his Limehouse stories. For Burke's readers, the East End Chinatown was as mysterious as a far distant land, a dark haven of opium, degeneracy and crime. At the time, Burke attracted criticism for his daring portrayal of interracial sexual relationships; today it is the racist stereotyping in the stories and the present-ation of young, prematurely sexualised girls that seem disturbing.

The Harvard graduate Earl Derr Biggers[13] aimed for positivity in creating Charlie Chan, a benevolent Chinese American loosely based on a real-life detective, Hawaii's Chang Apana. While re-cuperating from illness on Waikiki Beach, Biggers dreamed up an idea for a perfect alibi, which formed the core of *The House without a Key* (1925), set in Honolulu. Chan was meant to be a minor character, but readers of the serial version of the story clamoured for him to take centre stage. Biggers presented him as wise and benevolent, the antithesis of Fu Manchu. Humble yet courageous, he speaks in a mangled form of English, and his homely aphor-isms[14] became as much a trademark as Poirot's references to 'the little grey cells'.

Charlie Chan films[15] poured out of Hollywood. The detective was played by various actors, notably Warner Oland – who was Swedish. In China, the films drew vast and appreciative audiences, inspiring a series of home-grown imitations in the 1930s and 40s; ironically, Xu Xinyuan, the actor cast as Chan, modelled his performance on Oland's.

'Wheel of fate has many spokes,' Chan pronounced, and in time he came to be perceived as a racist stereotype whose pidgin English and deference towards white people hallmarked an offensive cari-cature. Activists protested about the screening of Chan films and, in 1993, the Asian American writer Jessica Hagedorn declared that 'Charlie Chan is dead'. But fictional detectives are not so easy to kill off, and Yunte Huang has argued that critics of the detective's deferential pose 'have simply underestimated the real strength of his character'. For Huang, 'the Chinaman is here to stay. He is an American folk hero.'

Writing about 'difference' can offer rich rewards[16] for authors. Joseph Hansen captured[17] the value of fiction's magic: 'readers stand in the shoes of strangers and know what it's like to be someone else – someone perhaps very different from themselves, someone they may heretofore even have hated or feared.' One of the many benefits for readers of a more inclusive and diverse literary culture is that we can learn a great deal about communities, experiences and ways of life that are unfamiliar to us and gain a better understanding of opinions and worldviews that differ from our own.

Yet there may be risks.[18] What if some critics of a later generation are, in their way, as prejudiced and as devoid of compassion and understanding when judging books of the past as the attitudes they condemn? Will today's writers be told what they can and can't write about? Will new forms of censorship creep in? Might new forms of bigotry replace the old?

Anthony Horowitz, who is Jewish, mused[19] on the threat to authorial freedoms in *The Word is Murder* (2017): 'There are some people who argue that we are too sensitive these days, that because we're so afraid of causing offence, we no longer engage in any serious sort of argument at all. But that's how it is . . . There are narrow lines between which all public conversations have to take place and even a single poorly chosen word can bring all sorts of trouble down on your head . . .'

'Sexual perversions, other than sadism, are definitely taboo,' Marie F. Rodell advised in 1943. 'And sadism must be presented in its least sexual form.' Rodell was a leading editor who became a literary agent and occasional crime novelist under the name Marion Randolph, and her words of wisdom appeared in *Mystery Fiction: Theory and Technique*, a how-to (or, perhaps, how-not-to) book for would-be crime writers. Writing in an era when sex between men was a crime, she decreed that homosexuality 'may be hinted at, but never used as an overt and important factor in the story . . . All the other perversions are absolutely beyond the pale.'

Long before Rodell published her advice, crime novelists were writing stories that, with varying degrees of subtlety, broke her red lines. A year before Sherlock Holmes made his debut, a novel appeared that Julian Symons called 'the first transvestite detective story'.[20] *Sudden Death*, aka *My Lady the Wolf* (1886), by Britiffe Constable Skottowe begins with wealthy young Jack Buchanan witnessing an apparent murder on a cliff top. The culprit escapes only to cross Buchanan's path subsequently in Homburg. This uneven story, with sexual ambiguity at its heart, was written with such youthful verve that it is a shame Skottowe never returned to the genre.

In Gladys Mitchell's *Speedy Death* (1929), the discovery that the murder victim was a transvestite prompts one character to say: 'Rather bad luck to find out that the chap you are engaged to is a woman, what?' Sexual repression is key to the mystery,[21] but cross-dressing was still a sufficiently rare ingredient of detective fiction for a novel by Ruth Rendell to use it as a surprise development almost half a century after Mitchell's book was published.

A decade before Marie Rodell issued her strictures, the Australian Frank Walford produced a bizarre novel that was banned in his native country for almost thirty years. Walford claimed to have worked as a mule packer, prospector, buffalo shooter and alligator hunter prior to settling in Katoomba, New South Wales, where he became active in amateur boxing, journalism and radical politics. Having published a book of poems and a guide to bushwalks, as well as editing a newspaper for poultry farmers, Walford was ready to write something completely different, a Gothic mash-up of sex, murder and cod psychology.

Twisted Clay (1934) is narrated by Jean Deslines, a precocious and disturbed fifteen-year-old whose sexual experiments lead her to conclude that she prefers women. She murders her father, escapes from an asylum, becomes a prostitute and embarks on a career as a serial killer. This preposterous, taboo-smashing curiosity was written with an energy that attracted publishers in the UK and US,[22] and prompted delusional comparisons with Le Fanu, Wilkie Collins and Marie Belloc Lowndes.

More sophisticated was Q. Patrick's[23] *The Grindle Nightmare*, aka *Darker Grows the Valley* (1935). The mystery concerns an outbreak of maiming and killing in a New England village. A map of the Grindle Valley was supplied, in typical Golden Age fashion, together with a clever whodunit puzzle, but the dark storyline featuring sociopathic mutilation of animals and murder of children was decades ahead of its time. The plot draws on the *folie à deux* case of Leopold and Loeb.[24]

Thomas Savage's *The Power of the Dog* opens with a graphic description of the castration of a calf. Two brothers, Phil and George, own the biggest ranch in their Montana valley, and are on good terms, although their characters are very different. George unexpectedly marries Rose, the widow of a doctor who committed suicide after being humiliated by Phil, and brings Rose and her 'sissy' son Peter to the ranch. Appalled, Phil begins to persecute the newcomers.

As Annie Proulx has pointed out,[25] the story concerns 'repressed homosexuality displayed as homophobia in the masculine ranch world', and whether or not one considers it is a crime story, this masterly novel delivers a shocking final twist with the revelation of an ingenious and chilling murder.

The Power of the Dog was published in 1967, a year after the appearance of the genre's first avowedly gay detective. George Baxt's[26] Pharoah (*sic*) Love was black, flamboyant and addressed everyone as 'cat'. *A Queer Kind of Death* (originally titled 'Dead Cat') concerns the murder of a male model, and Baxt's camp humour impressed Anthony Boucher, although he said that the book 'deals with a Manhattan subculture wholly devoid of ethics or morality' and warned that 'staid readers may well find it "shocking"'. Two more books followed in quick succession before Baxt turned to other projects. He revived his detective in a couple of novels during the 1990s, but the Summer of Love had passed.

Joseph Hansen's work had more substance. His series about Dave Brandstetter, a gay insurance investigator, was influenced by the Lew Archer books, but Hansen said: 'My joke was to take the true hard-boiled character in an American fiction tradition and make him homosexual. He was going to be a nice man, a good man, and he was going to do his job well.' Hansen tackled a range of contemporary themes: *Early Graves* (1987) concerns a serial killer of gay men with AIDS, emphasising the hysterical reaction to the disease during the 1980s.

Thanks to the pioneering work of Hansen and other gay and lesbian crime writers, the treatment of same-sex relationships in the genre has become increasingly matter-of-fact, as in Ann Cleeves' traditional mysteries about Devonian police inspector Matthew Venn, who is married to another man. Val McDermid, whose first series character was the lesbian journalist Lindsay Gordon, has spoken for many writers[27] in making clear her reservations about labels. As she has said, 'being a lesbian doesn't define you. I go to the supermarket in a not particularly lesbian way.'

Racism, sexism and homophobia in crime fiction, to which critics long turned a blind eye, have become the subject of extensive debate. Less is said about ageism, or the way in which people suffering from disabilities have been stereotyped and stigmatised. Attitudes are slow to shift, but recent years have seen a greater awareness and willingness to tackle difficult issues.

A significant number of crime writers have faced mental health challenges,[28] yet the presentation of mental disturbance in crime fiction[29] has often been inadequate or misleading. As with their treatment of other disadvantaged minorities, authors have risked exacerbating commonly held negative perceptions about people suffering from such problems.

The suspense novelist Peter Swanson has said:[30] 'The homicidal madman, the split personality killer, and the unstable femme fatale have all been part and parcel of detective fiction since the very beginning. Of late, the depressed detective[31] has dominated the genre. Not that this is particularly new. Sherlock Holmes had his cocaine addiction . . . But Thomas Harris changed the game in *Red Dragon* by having FBI agent Will Graham's personal demons assist him in his search for serial killers. It was the birth of the protagonist whose mental health issues operate as a kind of superpower.'

The commentator Marco Roth dated[32] 'the rise of the neuro-novel', with a protagonist whose brain is damaged, to Ian McEwan's *Enduring Love*. In this mainstream novel with criminous aspects, published in 1997, Jed Parry's obsession with another man is ascribed to de Clérambault's syndrome. Two years later came Jonathan Lethem's *Motherless Brooklyn*, a subtle reinvention of the hardboiled novel, concerning the attempt of Lionel Essrog, a private detective with Tourette's syndrome who is nicknamed 'Freakshow', to solve the murder of his mentor.

Mark Haddon's *The Curious Incident of the Dog in the Night-Time* (2003) takes its title from a famous line in the Sherlock Holmes story 'Silver Blaze'. Fifteen-year-old Christopher John Francis Boone describes himself as 'a mathematician with some behavioural difficulties' and sets about investigating the suspicious death of a dog. Haddon avoids labelling Christopher's disorder in the text, and has said[33] that rather than being a study of Asperger's syndrome, 'if anything it's a novel about difference, about being an outsider, about seeing the world in a surprising and revealing way.'

Before I Go to Sleep (2011) by S. J. Watson deploys the familiar trope of the amnesiac protagonist[34] in an imaginative way. An accident has left Chrissie with anterograde amnesia, so that she can store memories for only twenty-four hours. Encouraged by a neuropsychologist, she keeps a journal that helps her to discover forgotten parts of her life. If her husband Ben is a saintly carer and not manipulating her perceptions, why has she written in her journal *Don't trust Ben*?

Senile, or supposedly senile, old people have long been a staple of the genre, occasionally playing a significant part in the plot. In Agatha Christie's *Dead Man's Folly* (1956), garrulous old Merdell, mocked as 'batty', is in fact aware of the truth about a crime of the past. As a result, his granddaughter, one of the few people to listen to his stories, is murdered. Merdell too is silenced, although not before giving Hercule Poirot a significant clue.

Christie's *By the Pricking of My Thumbs* (1968), published when her own powers were failing,[35] dwells on the troubles of old age. On a visit to a retirement home, Tommy and Tuppence Beresford encounter elderly Mrs Lancaster, who refers to a dead child behind a fireplace. When the Beresfords return to the home, Mrs Lancaster has mysteriously vanished. The premise is intriguing, but the handling of the culprit's insanity fails to convince.

Alzheimer's disease and similar conditions have received increasingly thoughtful treatment in crime fiction,[36] as in Henning Mankell's *The Troubled Man* (2009), which sees Kurt Wallander diagnosed with early-onset Alzheimer's. Chaotic memories are central to Julia Heaberlin's *Paper Ghosts* (2018), in which a man whose mind is fading is kidnapped by a woman who believes he murdered her sister, and to *Turn of Mind* (2011) by Alice LaPlante, the story of a retired female orthopaedic surgeon with dementia who is suspected of killing her best friend.

The young (and, at first, repellently ageist) protagonist in Helen FitzGerald's *The Exit* (2015) reluctantly takes a job in a local care home, where she encounters an eighty-two-year-old woman called Rosie, whose memory is failing. The story that unfolds is dark, witty and poignant: Rosie is convinced that something is amiss at the home, but nobody takes her seriously.

A similar dilemma confronts Maud in Emma Healey's *Elizabeth is Missing* (2014). The one thing she is sure of is that her friend Elizabeth is missing. As the past blurs with the present in her brain, questions arise about the fate of her sister Sukey, who also disappeared. But Alzheimer's disease plays tricks with her mind – she is the ultimate unreliable narrator.

Notes

The main sources are the biographies of Himes by Sallis and Jackson, Yunte Huang's study of Charlie Chan, the editorial material by Johnny Mains, Jim Smith and James Doig in the 2014 reprint of *Twisted Clay*, the essays in *Murder in the Closet*, edited by Curtis Evans, and Malcolm J. Turnbull's *Victims or Villains: Jewish Images in Classic English Detective Fiction*.

1 *Marcel Duhamel*: Duhamel wrote the screenplay for a French film version of Peter Cheyney's *This Man is Dangerous*, and also translated Jim Thompson's *Pop. 1280*, filmed by Bertrand Tavernier as *Coup de Torchon*, aka *Clean Slate* – with the action shifted to French West Africa.

2 *Grand Prix de Littérature Policière*: Himes was the eleventh American to win the prize. The sole previous British winner was Michael Gilbert, for *Death in Captivity*.

3   *his detective stories shouldn't be regarded separately from his ordinary novels*: The quotation comes from Jackson's biography. James Sallis' biography likens Himes' non-series thriller *Run Man Run*, 'a small masterpiece of sustained narrative momentum and intense psychological terror', in which the homicidal cop Walker investigates his own crime, to Kenneth Fearing's *The Big Clock*. Sallis is white, but has written a series featuring a black private eye, Lew Griffin, as well as *Drive*, a thriller about a stunt driver, filmed in 2011.

4   *Cotton Comes to Harlem*: The 1970 film of the novel is sometimes regarded as a precursor to the very different 'blaxploitation' films such as *Shaft* (based on a novel by Ernest Tidyman, a white writer who created in John Shaft an African American detective), and *Super Fly*. *The Heat's On* was filmed as *Come Back, Charleston Blue*. *A Rage in Harlem* was filmed in 1991.

5   *He remained the outstanding black American crime writer*: Other key figures include Iceberg Slim (Robert Maupin Beck) and Donald Goines (whose murder at the age of thirty-seven remains unsolved), both discussed by Justin Gifford in *Pimping Fictions: African American Crime Literature and the Untold Story of Black Pulp Publishing*.

6   *Walter Mosley*: Mosley, an admirer of Hammett, Chandler and Graham Greene, introduced Rawlins in *Devil in a Blue Dress*, set in post-war America, and filmed with Denzel Washington as Easy.

7   *it was still possible for Mosley to say*: In Johanna Neuman, 'The Curious Case of Walter Mosley', *Moment*, 30 November 2011.

8   *Hardly anybody in America*: Or in many other countries. One exception is Mike Phillips, a British writer of Guyanese descent, whose first novel about the black journalist Sam Dean, *Blood Rights*, was televised in 1990.

9   *As the picture changes*: With the emergence of authors such as Attica Locke, whose *Bluebird, Bluebird* explores racial tensions in Texas, and Shawn A. Cosby, whose books include *Blacktop Wasteland*. Barbara Neely, author of four crime novels, was made a Grand Master of the MWA in 2020.

10 *Harold Heft argued*: In 'Easy Call', *Tablet*, 14 April 2010.

11 *Malcolm J. Turnbull has argued*: He argues that, when read today, Horler's 'disturbing racist fantasies . . . are easily eclipsed by the insightful analysis of the Jewish situation in the greatly superior writing of Anthony Berkeley Cox.' Turnbull, also the author of a detailed study of Cox's work, noted glimpses of antisemitism in the Berkeley novels, in one of which the surprise twist is that a likeable Jewish character is a killer, but concluded that overall the approach was relatively sensitive.

12 *his books became bestsellers and spawned dozens of films*: Yunte Huang argues that the central concept of Richard Condon's twice-filmed *The Manchurian Candidate* has its roots in Rohmer's novel *President Fu Manchu*. Condon's storyline played on anti-Chinese sentiment in the aftermath of the Korean War just as Rohmer tapped into fear and ignorance decades earlier.

13 *Earl Derr Biggers*: Biggers' years at Harvard overlapped with T. S. Eliot's time there. In 1913 he published *Seven Keys to Baldpate*, a thriller which was adapted for the stage and film.

14 *his homely aphorisms*: Such as 'No poison more deadly than ink' and 'Tongue often hang man quicker than rope.'

15 *Charlie Chan films*: Among the screenwriters was Philip MacDonald, who worked on *Charlie Chan in London* and *Charlie Chan in Paris*. Robert

Altman's film *Gosford Park* features a fictitious American movie producer who is said to be researching for *Charlie Chan in London*, which like *Gosford Park* involves an outsider attending an English country-house party.

16 *rich rewards*: An obituarist pointed out that Joseph Hansen's first Brandstetter novel, *Fadeout*, appeared in 1970, as did Tony Hillerman's first book about Navajo detectives: 'Their joint success is a reminder that the mystery format has long been fruitful in helping minorities break into literature as acceptable characters' (Christopher Reed, *Guardian*, 9 December 2004).

17 *Joseph Hansen captured*: See Bill Mohr, 'Emotion Doesn't Change Facts: Remembering Joe Hansen', *LARB*, 5 December 2014: 'Hansen is careful not to preach, even obliquely. Instead, he is illustrative. He shows . . . that being gay is no more homogenizing than any other social category.'

18 *there may be risks*: Stephen Knight quotes, for instance, academics who regard female sleuths as 'deputy henchmen for the patriarchy' or 'Marlowe in drag'.

19 *Anthony Horowitz . . . mused*: Horowitz, patron of an anti-bullying charity, has occasionally been caught up in controversy: 'Anthony Horowitz: I Was Warned Off Including Black Character', *Guardian*, 21 May 2017; Danuta Kean, 'Anthony Horowitz: "People Used to Disagree. Now They Send Death Threats"', *Guardian*, 27 August 2017. Liza Cody expressed similar concerns in her 'foreword of warning' to *My People and Other Crime Stories* (2021): 'An unprecedented level of "hate-speak", abuse, and on-line bullying is making people afraid to voice their opinions in case what they say is turned against them . . . This is a toxic environment for those of us who think about ideas, characters, consequences and following a story where it wants to go rather than where a sensitivity expert says it *ought* to go. What saddens me most is that a lot of this bullying has begun in support of just causes – those I've supported all my life.'

20 *the first transvestite detective story*: Skottowe, one of whose ancestors was created a baron by Louis XVIII, also published a history of Parliament. In 1912, the American Samuel Hopkins Adams published *The Secret of Lonesome Cove*, and its treatment of transvestism is discussed by J. F. Norris in 'A Redemptive Masquerade' in *Murder in the Closet*. Cross-dressing features in *Enter Sir John*, the first collaboration between Helen Simpson and Clemence Dane (filmed by Hitchcock as *Murder!*) and *The Strange Case of Harriet Hall* by Moray Dalton, the pen-name of Katherine Mary Dalton Renoir. François Ozon's film *The New Girlfriend* takes a Ruth Rendell storyline about transvestism and focuses on questions about difference and prejudice, with an emphasis on suspense, intrigue and wit rather than crime.

21 *Sexual repression is key to the mystery*: As it is in Mitchell's *The Saltmarsh Murders* and Nicholas Blake's *A Question of Proof*.

22 *publishers in the UK and US*: With masterly British understatement, T. Werner Laurie described the novel as 'an unpleasant but quite unusual story'. The US publisher, Claude Kendall, was murdered in 1937; see Curtis Evans, 'The Playboy and the Publisher', *CrimeReads*, 14 November 2019.

23 *Q. Patrick*: The pen-name was used by Richard Wilson Webb, an Englishman who emigrated to the United States, for books he wrote himself and in collaboration at different times with Martha Mott Kelley, Mary Louise Aswell and another British expatriate, Hugh Callingham Wheeler. Aswell and Wheeler have both been suggested as co-authors of *The Grindle Nightmare*,

but Curtis Evans speculates that the book was written either by Webb alone or with the benefit of limited input from Wheeler. Webb and Wheeler were gay men whose partnership was personal as well as professional; they later wrote novels together as Jonathan Stagge and as Patrick Quentin before their relationship broke down. Wheeler continued to write crime as Quentin, although *The Crippled Muse*, a novel of literary detection and imposture set on Capri, appeared under his own name. As well as librettos, he wrote screenplays, including the black comedy *Something for Everyone*.

24 *The plot draws on the folie à deux case of Leopold and Loeb*: So, explicitly, does 'Death Comes Softly', an episode of the TV cop series *Taggart* from 1990.

25 *As Annie Proulx has pointed out*: In her afterword to a 2001 reprint; she explains that, shockingly, Savage took some of the characters as well as the plot twist from life.

26 *George Baxt*: Baxt wrote for television and film, scripting crime movies such as *Payroll* and *Strangler's Web* as well as the Grand Guignol film *Circus of Horrors*. His series with celebrities solving fictional mysteries culminated in *The Clark Gable and Carole Lombard Murder Case*.

27 *Val McDermid . . . has spoken for many writers*: See Jake Kerridge, 'Harrogate Crime Festival', *The Daily Telegraph*, 28 July 2009.

28 *crime writers have faced mental health challenges*: See Simon Brett, 'I Couldn't Make a Road: Writers and Depression', www.moodscope.com

29 *The presentation of mental disturbance in crime fiction*: Samantha Walton's *Guilty but Insane* discusses Golden Age treatments of insanity, including Brand's *Heads You Lose*, a village mystery complete with map and list of characters ('Among these ten very ordinary people were found two victims and a murderer').

30 *Peter Swanson has said*: 'Ten Thrillers that Explore Mental Health', *CrimeReads*, 6 March 2019. Swanson praises Josephine Tey's account of Alan Grant's mental turmoil in *The Singing Sands*, and discusses Dennis Lehane's *Shutter Island*, in which 'delusion and paranoia take center stage', and Gillian Flynn's *Sharp Objects*, where Camille Preaker deals with her demons by self-harm.

31 *the depressed detective*: Such as Lo Blacklock in Ruth Ware's *The Woman in Cabin 10*, whose clinical depression offers an easy excuse for those who wish to dismiss her supposed hallucinations.

32 *Marco Roth dated*: See 'The Rise of the Neuronovel', *n+1*, Fall Issue, 2009. Roth argues that 'the trend follows a cultural . . . shift away from environmental and relational theories of personality back to the study of brains themselves, as the source of who we are' – that is, an abandonment of Freud. He describes *Motherless Brooklyn* as 'Hamlet by way of Philip Marlowe'.

33 *Haddon . . . has said*: In his blog post, 'Asperger's and Autism', 16 July 2009.

34 *the amnesiac protagonist*: Amnesia offers storytellers a wide range of narrative options, illustrated by such diverse books as Margery Allingham's *Traitor's Purse*, Cornell Woolrich's *The Black Curtain*, Patrick Quentin's *Puzzle for Fiends*, Robert Ludlum's *The Bourne Identity*, George Baxt's *The Affair at Royalties*, Joy Fielding's *See Jane Run* and Tana French's *In the Woods*. Alan R. Clark's *The High Wall*, published in 1936, became a post-war film noir, reflecting interest in psychotherapy in the late 1940s.

35 *her own powers were failing*: Poignantly, research on the changes in her use of vocabulary in her penultimate novel *Elephants Can Remember*, suggests that she experienced some form of dementia: Jad Abumrad and Robert Krulwich, 'Agatha Christie and Nuns Tell a Tale of Alzheimer's', *NPR*, 1 June 2010.

36 *increasingly thoughtful treatment in crime fiction*: Walter Mosley's *The Last Days of Ptolemy Grey* defies simple categorisation; it concerns a ninety-one-year-old African American man with dementia whose great-nephew is killed in a drive-by shooting and who is offered an extraordinary Faustian exchange.

FIFTY

A Suitable Job for a Woman

Women writing about private investigators

'I could poison him with oleander,' she told herself.

It wasn't such a crazy idea. Oleander was easy to find; you saw it all over California. She remembered what someone had told her on seeing oleanders in the yard of her house in Santa Barbara. Oleander was so poisonous that one ounce of its powdered leaves mixed with a ton of hay was enough to kill five hundred head of cattle.

The man she wanted to kill was her second husband, an insurance man she'd met on a blind date when on the rebound from a disastrous first marriage. Her upbringing had been dysfunctional, and her mother had committed suicide. She'd persuaded herself that she wanted an ordinary life, but ten years trapped in safe suburban domesticity only made her miserable. On the strength of selling the film rights of a book called *The Lolly-Madonna War* (1969), she'd fled to Los Angeles, and had a fling with a British man whom she mistakenly believed was a fellow free spirit. Now she was writing for television and doing secretarial work on the side while locked in a long-running and bitter custody dispute.

She found herself concocting a plan for a perfect murder: 'I imagined making copies of my children's keys to their father's house – we had joint custody at the time – so that I could sneak in and put powdered oleander in his allergy capsules. The next hay fever attack – no more ex-husband.'

There was only one drawback: she'd be the prime suspect. 'Since I didn't want to spend the rest of my life in a shapeless prison dress,' she said in later years, 'I decided to turn my homicidal fantasy into a mystery novel.'

The novel offered a form of catharsis. An admirer of the Lew Archer stories, she thought it natural to write a private-eye novel in the first person. The vital difference was that her detective was a woman. Even more than Archer, this gumshoe embodied the principle of the writer as detective. She was twice divorced, and a brown-eyed brunette, like her creator, but the resemblances ran deeper: 'in some essential way, we see the world the same.'

On page one, she tells us: 'The day before yesterday, I killed someone, and the fact weighs heavily on my mind.' What sets her apart from Spade, Marlowe and Archer is captured in the fourth sentence: 'I'm a nice person and I have a lot of friends.' The narrative voice belongs to a *likeable* detective, the alter ego of a woman who, after surviving a wretched childhood and two misjudged marriages, eventually came to regret those fantasies about killing her ex, admitting it was hard to fault him for his outrage.

In the novel, Laurence Fife's wife is accused of poisoning him 'with oleander, ground to a fine powder and substituted for the medication in the capsule he took; not a masterly plot . . .' The setting is Santa Barbara masquerading as Santa Teresa, a name borrowed in tribute to Lew Archer.

The book, *A is for Alibi* (1982), marked the start of the thirty-five-year career of a private eye who solves twenty-five alphabet mysteries all the way up to *Y is for Yesterday* (2017). Her name was Kinsey Millhone, and her creator was Sue Grafton.

The dedication in *A is for Alibi* reads: 'For my father, Chip Grafton, who set me on this path'. Cornelius Warren 'Chip' Grafton died on New Year's Day 1982, four months before the novel was published; she'd wanted to surprise him with it, but never had the chance. A municipal bond attorney in Kentucky, Chip Grafton wrote crime fiction, but he and his wife were both alcoholics, and after his third mystery[1] appeared in 1950, he never wrote another.

Each morning, Sue Grafton said, 'my father downed two jiggers of whiskey and went to the office. My mother, similarly fortified, went to sleep on the couch. From the age of five onward, I was left to raise myself, which I did as well as I could, having had no formal training in parenthood.' In her parallel existence, Kinsey Millhone was orphaned at the age of five.

Grafton worked in television, and she and her third husband, Steven Humphrey, collaborated on scripts for TV versions of two Agatha Christie novels, *A Caribbean Mystery* and *Sparkling Cyanide*. But a screenwriter has minimal control over the end result; the rewards are handsome, but the price is powerlessness. Grafton hated being at the mercy of others, and resolved that the Kinsey Millhone books would never be televised or filmed.

She took care to deliver what her readers wanted while allowing herself an occasional experiment. In *S is for Silence* (2005), she utilised multiple viewpoints, and *T is for Trespass* (2007) includes sections told from the point of view of a sociopath as well as Kinsey's narrative. The detective ages at an enviably sedate pace, and the whole series is set in the 1980s. 'I don't want to idealize her or turn her into a political statement,' Grafton said. 'I want her to be flawed and inconsistent and cranky and quirky – not a walking, talking feminist polemic, but a realistic portrait of a woman trying to do her job and live her life.'

Kinsey is no revolutionary, as she makes clear in *M is for Malice* (1996): 'At heart, I'm a law-and-order type. I believe in my country, the flag, paying taxes and parking tickets, returning library books on time, and crossing the street with the light. Also, I'm inclined to get tears in my eyes every time I hear the National Anthem sung by somebody who really knows how to belt it out.'

Whereas Lew Archer remains shadowy and elusive to the end, Grafton created a well-rounded character. She told an interviewer that Kinsey was 'thinner and younger and braver than I . . . Through her, I can explore all sorts of feelings that I'm sure other women share. Questions about independence, ambivalence about parents, attitudes toward men, issues of morality . . .'

A self-proclaimed moralist, Grafton gloried in the freedom allowed her by the genre to write stories reflecting 'my rock-solid conviction of how I think the world should be, especially given the fact that in our society there's not that much justice.' The final words of her last novel were: 'I'm not saying justice is for sale, but if you have enough money, you can sometimes enjoy the benefits of a short-term lease.'

A decade before Kinsey Millhone came on to the scene, P. D. James introduced young Cordelia Gray in the ironically titled *An Unsuitable Job for a Woman* (1972). Cordelia's partner kills himself, and in trying to run their detective agency single-handed, she finds herself looking into the apparent suicide of a Cambridge University drop-out.

The story develops into an unorthodox exploration of how best to do justice when established protocols of law and order are inadequate. Cordelia colludes in a cover-up, and once James' series policeman Adam Dalgliesh becomes involved towards the end of the story, he takes it upon himself to turn a blind eye to what has happened. The official misinterpretation of events escapes challenge.

James resisted the temptation to develop their relationship. Although mentioned twice, the Scotland Yard man does not appear in Cordelia's second case, which appeared ten years after her first. In *The Skull Beneath the Skin*, an assignment to safeguard an actress from death threats takes her to a small island off the Dorset coast, a Christie-like setting for a revenge tragedy. By the end, Cordelia is ready to concentrate on inquiring into the whereabouts of missing cats and dogs: 'Animals . . . didn't burden you with their psychological problems . . . They didn't expect you to die for them. They didn't try to murder you.'

Like their male counterparts, Cordelia Gray and other British female private eyes[2] of her generation showed less staying power than their American peers. In 1980, Liza Cody's[3] Anna Lee, who works for a down-at-heel agency in Notting Hill, made a strong impression in *Dupe*. Unfortunately Anna's career extended to a mere half dozen reported cases, brought to a premature end after a disastrous television series,[4] which killed the author's enthusiasm for writing about her.

*

Sharon McCone, widely regarded as the first American female private eye of the modern era, was conceived in 1971. At that time, Marcia Muller[5] was 'hiding out . . . in San Francisco's Mission district . . . contending with a failed journalistic career, a failing long-distance marriage . . . all I did was read mysteries for escape.' She came up with the idea of writing about a woman who was associated with the poverty law movement.

Sharon took her bow in *Edwin of the Iron Shoes*, published in 1977. Muller, like Grafton, 'sensed a close kinship' with her detective right from the start: Sharon was 'an emotional, caring woman who . . . worked for . . . All Souls Legal Cooperative, a poverty law firm. And she had family, friends, love interests.'

The series has run for upwards of forty years, during which time Muller has employed various techniques to keep the books fresh. Sharon left All Souls to work for herself, and Muller occasionally writes from the point of view of Sharon's friends and associates.

With hindsight, 1982 stands out as a landmark year in the story of female crime writing. In addition to the publication of the second cases of Sharon McCone and Cordelia Gray, both Kinsey Millhone and Sara Paretsky's V. I. Warshawski arrived on the scene.

Warshawski is the Chicago-based daughter of a Polish-American cop and his Italian-Jewish wife, a former defence lawyer with a background in the women's movement. She was briefly married, but discovered that her husband 'only admired independent women from a distance. These days she's a serial monogamist . . . stubborn about her right to live her life according to her own principles.'

What British television did to Anna Lee, Hollywood did to Warshawski. The film *V. I. Warshawski* provoked her creator to say: 'I felt violated . . . It wasn't even close to my vision of the character; it was all very sexed-up Hollywood, with teen-boy locker-room dialogue . . . It was so frustrating that for a while I stopped being able to write.'[6]

Paretsky sees herself as working in the tradition of Virginia Woolf, who tried to kill the phantom of the Angel in the House so that she could find her own voice as a writer, but recognises that: 'It is a difficult phantom to overpower because it speaks in so many voices and with so much authority behind it . . . like Norman Mailer . . . saying that it isn't possible for women to write as well as men.'

As she points out in relation to *Gaudy Night*, Sayers 'created a complex character in Harriet Vane, but could not allow her – or the female dons of Shrewsbury – to solve their own problems. They fester in an environment of fear and mutual suspicion for almost a year before Peter Wimsey arrives. He is able to see through the situation at a glance and in a matter of days resolves the problem for them.' Paretsky identifies the academic and amateur sleuth Kate Fansler as taking over 'where Dorothy Sayers left Harriet Vane: she could solve her own problems.' Kate Fansler's creator, Amanda Cross,[7] had presented women readers and writers with 'the hero we'd been waiting for all our lives'.[8]

The barriers broken down by feminist writers such as Paretsky encouraged successors to write with verve about strong female lead characters.[9] A striking example is Janet Evanovich, who graduated from romantic fiction to writing tongue-in-cheek mysteries[10] (or misadventures, as she describes them) that belong to the tradition of screwball comedy. *One for the Money* (1994) introduced New Jersey's Stephanie Plum, who becomes a bounty hunter after losing her job as a lingerie buyer.

Stephanie is scarcely as driven as Warshawski, and the stories send up the conventions of the tough private eye thriller. Evanovich doesn't altogether shy away from addressing serious issues, such as the gang violence that plays a part in *Ten Big Ones* (2004), but her touch is light: 'The States has a gun culture which I don't fit into. I come at it from the other point-of-view, a satirical take on the American gun culture. In one of my books, I have women sitting in the beauty-parlour comparing guns.'[11]

There was little room for levity in Patricia Daniels Cornwell's gripping first book about the medical examiner Kay Scarpetta. *Postmortem* (1990) was a serial-killer thriller that brought the scientific crime novel up to date. Cornwell worked as a technical writer and a computer analyst in the office of the chief medical examiner of Virginia, during which time a local murderer, Timothy Wilson Spencer, became the first American serial killer to be convicted on the basis of DNA evidence; there are similarities between his crimes and those of Cornwell's fictitious culprit.

Cornwell's stock in trade is 'to show the technical side of how you can work very unusual crimes', and she has hired an array of expert advisers, as well as acquiring expensive laboratory equipment and weaponry to ensure that her stories remain up to date. Critical reaction to her later books has been mixed,[12] but they enjoy worldwide popularity. Her private life has become the stuff of newspaper headlines, but she appears to be philosophical:[13] 'I have always courted publicity and the media because it's a way of selling what you want people to read. You have to take the bumps with that . . . This whole series has been born in controversy and my life, weirdly, seems to follow that.'

Her single-mindedness has enabled her to remain formidably productive while becoming enmeshed in high-profile lawsuits. Her relationship with Margo Bennett, a hostage negotiator whom she met while researching at the FBI academy at Quantico, came under the spotlight when Bennett's estranged husband was convicted of her attempted murder.

Cornwell also courted controversy as a result of an extraordinary venture into true-crime writing that would have made Fryn Tennyson Jesse gasp. She invested millions of dollars in a crusade to prove that the Victorian artist Walter Sickert was Jack the Ripper. *Portrait of a Killer: Jack the Ripper – Case Closed* (2002) was received with incredulity by many experts. The consensus was that her theory was neither original nor sound.[14]

Undaunted, Cornwell took out full-page advertisements in the British press insisting that her ongoing investigation was 'far from an obsession but an excellent opportunity to provide a platform for applying modern science to a very old, highly visible case'. She started buying Sickert's paintings, and reports that she'd cut one of them up in order to hunt for clues to his guilt prompted howls of outrage from the art world. Fifteen years after her original book appeared, she demonstrated her tenacity in returning to the fray with *Ripper: The Secret Life of Walter Sickert* (2017). In her opinion, the artist was 'a narcissist and a sociopath . . . a baffling chameleon, changing his hair or name whenever the mood struck.'[15]

*

Kathy Reichs'[16] novels, although frequently bracketed with Cornwell's, are quite distinct. Reichs has enjoyed a distinguished scientific career and did not publish her first novel, *Déjà Dead* (1997) until she was forty-nine. She is a forensic anthropologist, as is her protagonist, Temperance 'Tempe' Brennan.

Reichs' rigour in matters of detail is reminiscent of Richard Austin Freeman's: 'Because I write about what I do, rather than researching the field, it gives my books greater authenticity. Many fiction writers who put the science in don't get it right.' She draws on extensive personal experience, having frequently given expert evidence in criminal trials. She testified at the United Nations tribunal on the Rwandan genocide, helped to identify people buried in mass graves in Guatemala and carried out forensic work at Ground Zero in New York City. Her first professional investigation concerned a leg in a lake, preserved since the 1950s by its nylon stocking.

Technical know-how also underpins the novels of Fred Vargas,[17] pen-name of Frédérique Audoin-Rouzeau, a French archaeozoologist and medievalist. Throughout her fiction, as Andrea Goulet has pointed out,[18] she 'intertwines scientific expertise with atmospherics of superstition, folk tales and legendary creatures from werewolves to Icelandic demons'.

Vargas' research subjects include the epidemiology of the Black Death, esoteric knowledge put to ingenious use in *Have Mercy on Us All* (2001), which features her principal series detective, Commissaire Adamsberg. Vargas cooks up a broth of biothriller, police story and cryptological puzzle with an entirely distinctive flavour.

Unlike many modern women writers, Vargas favours male protagonists. So does Kate Atkinson, whose occasional books about private investigator Jackson Brodie, such as the dazzling *When Will There Be Good News?* (2008), are notable for intricate if coincidence-heavy plots as well as wit, exuberance and a preoccupation with the nature of justice. The novels have been marketed rather defensively as 'literary crime novels', but Atkinson's credo is straightforward: 'I live to entertain, I don't live to teach or to preach or to be political'.[19]

Notes

The main sources are Hans Bertens and Theo D'haen's *Contemporary American Crime Fiction*, Charles L. P. Silet's interview of Grafton in Volume I of *Speaking of Murder*, edited by Ed German and Martin H. Greenberg, Ellen Hawkes' 'G is for Grafton', *LA Times*, 11 January 1998, Sharon Waxman's article 'Mystery Writer in the Mirror', *Washington Post*, 1 November 2001, material on the *Old Scrolls Blog* about C. W. Grafton, Sue Grafton's *Kinsey and Me*, Marcia Muller's introductions to *The McCone Files* and *McCone and Friends*, and Sara Paretsky's introduction to her anthology *A Woman's Eye*.

1   *his third mystery*: The first, *The Rat Began to Gnaw the Rope*, won the Mary Roberts Rinehart Mystery Contest; like *The Rope Began to Hang the Butcher*, it featured the lawyer Gilmore Henry. Henry also appeared in another story linked, Christie-style, to a nursery rhyme, 'The Butcher Began to Kill the Ox', but Grafton failed to complete the book. His daughter was deterred from finishing it because she didn't know how he planned to resolve the mystery. His third crime novel, *Beyond Reasonable Doubt*, combined suspense and courtroom drama.

2   *British female private eyes*: Among the more tenacious was Val McDermid's Kate Brannigan, based in Manchester, who appeared in six books during the 1990s; as a police-officer friend reminds her in *Blue Genes*, Kate's trouble is that she understands 'the moral ambiguity in life'. McDermid has also published a book about real-life female private eyes, *A Suitable Job for a Woman*.

3   *Liza Cody*: Cody (born Elizabeth Nassim) is adept at enabling readers to hear from unfamiliar voices: *Lady Bag* is about a bag lady, and Cody's infrequent, offbeat mysteries included three published in the 1990s about Eva Wylie, the first female wrestler to become a protagonist in a crime series.

4   *a disastrous television series*: The six episodes starred Imogen Stubbs as Anna Lee, with writers including Anthony Horowitz, but the series flopped. Cody's short story 'Day or Night', published in 2013, provides a suitably quirky coda to Anna's casebook.

5   *Marcia Muller*: In 1992, she married Bill Pronzini, author of the long-running 'Nameless Detective' series of PI novels. They have collaborated on several Carpenter and Quincannon novels in a series that began with a book written by Pronzini alone. They co-edited *1001 Midnights*, a weighty collection of retro reviews by crime buffs. Pronzini has also published two entertaining studies of the worst of the genre, *Gun in Cheek* and *Son of Gun in Cheek*.

6   *provoked her creator to say: 'I felt violated . . .'*: In Adam Jacques, 'Sara Paretsky', *Independent*, 20 July 2014. She added: 'I used to write books about an environmental concern or a healthcare concern, but I was beginning to be tiresome, so now I tend to make those issues part of the backdrop to a crime story instead.'

7   *Amanda Cross*: The pen-name of Carolyn Gold Heilbrun, an English professor. The Fansler novels were set in academe, and are fluently written, if flawed by a tendency to prioritise polemics over plotting. *Death in a Tenured Position*, aka *A Death in the Faculty*, tackles discrimination

against women at Harvard, but the mystery is anticlimactic. *No Word from Winifred* offers subtle parallels to the lives of Sayers and her friend Muriel St Clare Byrne. Heilbrun wrote about taking her own life when she reached seventy, making the lamentable claim that 'there is no joy in life past that point'. At seventy-seven, she expressed a sense of sadness about the universe to a friend before taking her life. Apparently she felt her life was 'completed'.

8   *'the hero we'd been waiting for all our lives'*: Julian Symons was less impressed, saying that 'in attitude and construction Cross's books are distinctly old-fashioned'. His admiration for Warshawski was tempered by his conclusion, based on the mass of detail in the books, that 'Paretsky often seems to be describing rather than creating . . . she fills a gap, the one waiting for an American Feminist Crime Writer.'

9   *strong female lead characters*: The innumerable examples include S. J. Rozan's private eye Lydia Chin and Laurie R. King's Mary Russell (who marries Sherlock Holmes), and in Britain Val McDermid's cop Karen Pirie, Ann Cleeves' DCI Vera Stanhope and Elly Griffiths' forensic archaeologist Ruth Galloway.

10   *Janet Evanovich, who graduated from romantic fiction to writing tongue-in-cheek mysteries*: The tone of her website captures the flavour of her writing: 'after twelve romance novels I ran out of sexual positions and decided to move into the mystery genre', although Bertens and D'haen made the bold claim that 'underneath the frolicking, Evanovich is redrawing the boundaries' of the genre. A film version released of *One for the Money* flopped, but Evanovich kept writing about Stephanie Plum as well as collaborating with fellow authors.

11   *'The States has a gun culture . . .'*: The book in question was *Two for the Dough*. The quotation comes from Jane Jakeman, 'Janet Evanovich: Plum Jobs for a Woman of Parts', *Independent*, 21 October 2000. The author describes her books as 'docu-comedy'.

12   *Critical reaction to her later books has been mixed*: Bertens and D'haen argue that the way she creates suspense and terror 'brings in by the back door the attitudes and perspectives of the self-absorbed and rigid masculinity of the cold war thriller and of now widely discredited PI writers such as Mickey Spillane . . . we travel back to the paranoid mentality of the illiberal 1950s.' They make the same criticism of Mary Willis Walker, whose four books (three featuring the journalist Molly Cates) enjoyed success during the 1990s but did not lead to a career as lengthy as Cornwell's.

13   *she appears to be philosophical*: Hannah Stephenson, 'Patricia Cornwell: I Celebrated Turning 60 by Getting Busier', *Irish News*, 21 November 2016

14   *The consensus was that her theory was neither original nor sound*: Caleb Carr, author of *The Alienist*, a Victorian history-mystery featuring the psychologist Dr Laszlo Kreizler, was scathing: 'She has cut corners and missed important points – and just how many quickly becomes apparent . . . a sloppy book, insulting to both its target and its audience' ('Dealing with the Work of a Fiend', *New York Times*, 15 December 2002).

15   *In her opinion, the artist was 'a narcissist and a sociopath . . .'*: Patricia Cornwell, 'I Spent $7 Million Solving the Jack the Ripper Case', *Daily Telegraph*, 7 February 2017.

16   *Kathy Reichs*: The Tempe Brennan books were adapted into a television

series, *Bones*. The quotation comes from Liz Hoggard, 'Face to Face with Death', *Observer*, 21 May 2006.

17 *Fred Vargas*: Vargas cites Agatha Christie as a model: 'Like her, I want to tell a story that identifies and deals with the dangers we face': 'Grave Concerns', *Guardian*, 16 February 2008. She wrote three books about 'the Three Evangelists', historians who become involved with detection.

18 *as Andrea Goulet has pointed out*: In 'Crime Fiction and Modern Science' in *Routledge*.

19 *'I live to entertain . . .'*: Lisa Allardice, 'Kate Atkinson', *Guardian*, 15 June 2019. In the interview, Atkinson said her next Brodie book would be a homage to Christie.

FIFTY-ONE

A Feeling for Snow

Scandinavian crime writing

In the late summer of 1969, a fifteen-year-old boy witnessed a shocking crime that had far-reaching consequences. The scene was a camping site not far from his home town, Umeå, in north-east Sweden. He was present when three friends raped a girl of their own age. She screamed repeatedly, but he did nothing to help. The victim lived near his home, and a few days later he contacted her to ask forgiveness for his cowardice.

'I'll never forgive you,' she replied.

The crime was never reported to the police, and the rapists got away scot free. What happened to the victim, and the effect it had on her in later life, are unknown. Over the years, the question of the violence inflicted by men on women came to haunt him. In his forties, Karl Stig-Erland Larsson set out to exorcise the ghosts of his past.

The outcome was a crime novel called *Men Who Hate Women*, the first book in a trilogy that he sold to a Swedish publisher. Shortly after his fiftieth birthday, and before the novel appeared in print, he suffered a fatal heart attack after climbing seven flights of stairs to his office because the lift was out of order.

Larsson didn't lack confidence in his own abilities, but not even he could have guessed the scale of the success that his novels would enjoy. Known in English as the *Millennium Trilogy*, they were published posthumously as by Stieg Larsson, with the English translation of the first book retitled *The Girl with the Dragon Tattoo* (2005).

The girl in question, Lisbeth Salander, is one of crime fiction's most memorable characters. Two film versions of the trilogy followed, in Swedish and English, and Larsson has the strange distinction of being the only mystery writer to become a worldwide bestseller despite the fact that he published no crime fiction during his lifetime. Even continuation novels written by another hand[1] have enjoyed huge sales and been made into films.

Larsson's failure to leave a valid will provoked a toxic dispute between those he left behind. As the early hype about his achievements has faded, debate has continued about the quality of his writing and his treatment of sex and violence. One aspect of his literary legacy remains beyond dispute. He demonstrated that Scandinavian crime fiction, or, as it is often termed, Nordic noir, has global appeal.

Larsson died in 2004, and myths swirl around his life, death and work. Conspiracy theories proliferate.[2] Was his death suspicious? Did someone ghostwrite his fiction? Did he solve the murder in 1986 of Swedish Prime Minister Olof Palme?[3] The answer to all these questions is probably no, but the air of mystery surrounding Larsson helps to keep the books selling.

Larsson joined the Communist Workers' League, changed the spelling of his name to avoid confusion with another author and devoted himself to political activism. A spell training female guerrillas in Eritrea was followed by his formation of the Swedish Expo Foundation, dedicated to combating right-wing extremism. He became editor of *Expo*, the Foundation's magazine. This was a frequent target for attack by political opponents, and Larsson received death threats.

For the last thirty years of his life, Larsson lived with a fellow activist, Eva Gabrielsson. She has said that he didn't make a will, or marry her, because he didn't want to draw her to the attention of his fascist enemies. *The Girl with the Dragon Tattoo* is a long book; had he lived, Larsson might have edited it down.[4] His enthusiasm for detective fiction[5] is evident from his references to such writers as Sara Paretsky, Val McDermid and Dorothy L. Sayers. The children's books of Astrid Lindgren, creator of the formidable Pippi Longstocking, influenced his characterisation of Salander.[6]

There are also distant similarities between Salander, a gifted but deeply troubled researcher, gadget-lover and computer hacker, and Peter O'Donnell's Modesty Blaise,[7] but Salander's personality and behaviour remain distinctive. Her specialism is rooting out evil-doers and making their punishment fit their crime.

Each novel represents a different branch of the genre: an updated version of the classic puzzle; a police investigation; a political thriller. The first book opens with Mikael Blomkvist, publisher of the political magazine *Millennium*, losing a high-profile libel claim. Henrik Vanger, a rich businessman, asks for Blomkvist's help in solving the mystery of Vanger's niece Harriet. She vanished during a family gathering on Hedeby Island more than thirty years ago. At the time, Hedeby was cut off from the mainland by a traffic accident on the connecting bridge, restricting the pool of suspects. With Salander's help, Blomkvist plays amateur detective in an inquiry conspicuous not only for high-stakes suspense but also for graphically described sexual violence.[8]

Larsson's work owed a debt to Maj Sjöwall and Per Wahlöö. Wahlöö, a Marxist newspaperman, met Sjöwall in a journalists' bar in the summer of 1962. She'd been twice divorced and had a child, while he was married with a daughter. Within a year, he moved in with her, and although they never married, they had two children together.

Their shared political views and enthusiasm for Simenon and Hammett led them to decide to write a series of ten crime novels together, one book per year. 'We realised,' Sjöwall said, 'that people read crime and through the stories we could show the reader that under the official image of welfare-state Sweden there was another layer of poverty, criminality and brutality. We wanted to show where Sweden was heading: towards a capitalistic, cold and inhuman society, where the rich got richer, the poor got poorer.'[9]

They wrote alternate chapters, three hundred in total. These in effect formed a single book, *The Story of a Crime*: the crime was society's betrayal of ordinary people. The idea for the first novel, *Roseanna* (1965), arose on a canal trip from Stockholm to Gothenburg. 'There was an American woman on the boat, beautiful, with dark hair, always standing alone. I caught Per looking at her. "Why don't we start the book by killing this woman?" I said.'

Roseanna opens with the dredging of a female corpse from Lake Vattern; the victim had been raped and strangled. The investigation is led by Martin Beck, a tired, decent introvert who suffers from various ailments and a crumbling marriage. His empathy makes him a skilled interrogator, but his work is as unglamorous as his home life, and solving a case usually leaves him feeling mournful. The well-researched police procedure, and the careful presentation of Beck's team of detectives, have prompted many commentators to presume that the books were modelled on Ed McBain's 87th Precinct mysteries, although Sjöwall has said that she did not read the McBain books until after the Beck series was under way.

Politics played little part in the first three novels. As the series progressed, the authors' agenda became clearer, but they did not allow it to ruin the quality of the stories. Nine bus passengers are gunned down by an unknown assassin in *The Laughing Policeman*[10] (1968). The crime seems motiveless, but Martin Beck discovers a link to an earlier crime in a storyline reminiscent of, but distinct from, the Lew Archer files.

In *The Locked Room* (1972), Sjöwall and Wahlöö adapt the sealed-room trope to suit their own purpose. The puzzle of how a corpse came to be shot through the heart in seemingly impossible circumstances is cleverly contrived, but the locked room is also a metaphor for Beck's trapped existence. Rhea Nielsen helps him both to solve the crime, and to escape his personal locked room, and discover a fresh way of looking at the world.

Wahlöö died at the age of forty-eight, before their final book, *The Terrorists* (1975), was published; he'd been working on it while terminally ill. The final word in the series is Marx. Sjöwall resisted attempts to persuade her to add to the Martin Beck canon, although she acted as consultant to a television series based on the novels.

The passage of time made her philosophical about society's

failure to transform in the way she and Wahlöö once hoped: 'Everything we feared happened, faster. People think of themselves not as human beings but consumers. The market rules and it was not that obvious in the 1960s, but you could see it coming . . . The problem was that the people who read our books already thought the same as us. Nothing changed – we changed our lives, that's all.'

Henning Mankell read *Roseanna* soon after it came out, when he was seventeen; he was already familiar with Wahlöö's early fiction, notably *The Lorry*, aka *A Necessary Action* (1962), set in fascist Spain. For him, Martin Beck's debut signalled the end of British detective fiction's domination of the Swedish market. *The Story of a Crime* exerted a profound influence on his own writing; it demonstrated that 'there was a huge unexplored territory in which crime novels could form the framework for stories containing social criticism'.

Mankell spent much of his early life in the northern settlement of Sveg, which features in his stand-alone novel about neo-Nazis, *The Return of the Dancing Master* (2000). The bleak climate, coupled with the remoteness of small rural communities where many of the stories are set, give a distinctive and compelling character to Nordic noir fiction.

Faceless Killers (1991) introduced Inspector Kurt Wallander[11] of Ystad, a melancholy everyman like Martin Beck, one more dedicated cop with a troubled personal life. He investigates the savage murder of an elderly couple in a farmhouse. The husband has been bludgeoned to death, while his wife is found with a noose around her neck; she supplies the police with what appears to be a 'dying message' clue before expiring. The story explores xenophobia and racism[12] in a society struggling to come to terms with the impact of immigration.

Wallander's daughter Linda took centre stage in *Before the Frost* (2002), intended as the first part of a trilogy, but the death of Johanna Sällström, who played Linda on Swedish television, so distressed Mankell that he felt unable to continue writing about her. His final book about Kurt Wallander, *The Troubled Man* (2009), concerned the disappearance of a retired naval officer, and the question of submarine incursions into Swedish waters during the Cold War.

Sjöwall and Wahlöö gave new impetus to the crime novel,[13] but the common assumption that they were the first Scandinavian detective novelists is as accurate as Philip Larkin's jokey suggestion that sexual intercourse began in 1963. Martin Beck's sidekick Gunvald Larsson is a fan of pulp fiction writers of the early twentieth century, such as Sweden's own Samuel August Duse, who wrote fourteen books about master detective Leo Carring in the early part of the twentieth century.

Maria Lang's[14] first novel, *The Murderer Does Not Lie Alone*, appeared in 1949, and introduced Puck Ekstedt, a young woman who collaborates with Inspector Christer Wijk. A lesbian relationship plays a part in a storyline that was daring for its time and Lang continued to include sexual elements in her plots. Because she was a woman who wrote detective stories, she earned the all-too-predictable sobriquet 'Sweden's Agatha Christie'. Her career lasted for forty years and in 1971 she became one of thirteen founder members of the Swedish Crime Writers' Academy.[15]

Detective fiction written in Norway during the first half of the twentieth century has also been overlooked. Sven Elvestad,[16] who used the pen-name Stein Riverton, is notable for *The Iron Chariot*, first published in 1909. An unnamed narrator tells the story of a holidaymaker's mysterious death on a small island, and the crucial plot twist anticipates that in a famous Golden Age whodunit.

Riverton's name lives on through the Riverton Prize, awarded since 1972 for the best Norwegian crime story. An early winner was Gunnar Staalesen,[17] whose long-running series about Varg Veum transfers elements familiar from the Californian private-eye novel to the chillier climate of Bergen. Although Staalesen's work is less overtly political than that of some other present-day Scandinavian crime writers, it is significant that Veum is a former social worker. His cases often find him trying to help clients to survive in a society under stress.

Jo Nesbø[18] won the Riverton Prize for *The Bat* (1997), the first novel of a successful new career after injury put paid to his prospects as a professional football player. The story introduced yet another brilliant, driven alcoholic cop. Harry Hole is sent to Sydney in order to assist the investigation of the murder of a Norwegian girl during her gap year. The case becomes a hunt for a serial killer.[19]

The world-weary, dyspeptic police officer battling deranged or fanatical murderers in the bleak Scandinavian midwinter has become a cliché, but Håkan Nesser's[20] Chief Inspector Van Veeteren so far contradicts the stereotypes that on leaving the police he becomes a bookseller. Even *Woman with Birthmark* (1996), a dark and disturbing serial-killer story, offers unorthodox clueing, in the form of a 1960s instrumental by The Shadows,[21] and no shortage of wit.

The Norwegian Hans Olav Lahlum has shown that it remains possible, decades after Sjöwall and Wahlöö's *The Locked Room*, to integrate Golden Age tropes with a story that casts light on character and social issues, notably the challenges facing people with disabilities. *The Human Flies*, a locked-room mystery set in 1968 but published in 2010, launched a series featuring a detective duo in the classic mould. A likeable detective inspector, Kolbjørn Kristiansen ('K2'), plays the part of Watson to a Sherlock in the form of the brilliant Patricia, a wheelchair user, as they investigate the murder of a famous hero of the Resistance. There are echoes of the relationship between Nero Wolfe and Archie Goodwin and numerous references to Christie.

Like Sjöwall and Wahlöö, Lahlum has acknowledged the influence of Simenon. So has the Danish writer Anders Bodelsen, who drew inspiration from *The Man Who Watched Trains Go By* for his psychological thriller *Think of a Number* (1968), in which an ordinary man opportunistically robs the bank where he works. Bodelsen's account of the impulses that drive a conventional member of society to abandon respectability became a bestseller and was filmed twice.[22]

Miss Smilla's Feeling for Snow,[23] aka *Smilla's Sense of Snow*, by another Danish author, Peter Høeg, was published in 1992. The story opens in Copenhagen, with a boy called Isaiah dead after falling from a snowy rooftop. The police regard this as an accident, since his were the only footprints leading to the edge of the roof. But Smilla Qaaviqaaq Jaspersen, the daughter of a female Inuit hunter from Greenland and a rich Danish doctor, is not satisfied. She had befriended Isaiah, a neighbour and fellow Greenlander, and suspects that he was somehow driven to his death. Høeg is a literary novelist[24] rather than a genre writer, but it was the success of his novel, more than any other, which was the catalyst for the worldwide breakthrough in popularity of Nordic noir.[25]

Notes

The main sources are Barry Forshaw's *Nordic Noir*, *Death in a Cold Climate* and biography of Larsson, Kurdo Baksi's memoir of Larsson, Jacob Stougard-Nielsen's *Scandinavian Crime Fiction*, Bo Lundin's *The Swedish Crime Story*, Louise France's article 'The Queen of Crime', *Observer*, 22 November 2009, and the various introductions and notes to the 2006 Harper Perennial editions of *The Story of a Crime*.

1   *continuation novels written by another hand*: The first was *The Girl in the Spider's Web*, and the author lucky enough to secure this lucrative commission was David Lagercrantz, whose previous work included *Fall of a Man in Wilmslow*, a crime novel fictionalising the life and death of codebreaker Alan Turing.

2   *Conspiracy theories proliferate*: Some are discussed by Christopher Hitchens in 'The Author Who Played with Fire', *Vanity Fair*, December 2009, and Charles McGrath in 'The Afterlife of Stieg Larsson', *New York Times Magazine*, 20 May 2010.

3   *Did he solve the murder in 1986 of Swedish Prime Minister Olof Palme?*: 'Dragon Tattoo Author "Solved" Sweden PM Murder' (Reuters), *Daily Telegraph*, 26 February 2014.

4   *had he lived, Larsson might have edited it down*: Joan Acocella conceded that Larsson 'is a very good storyteller' in 'Man of Mystery', *The New Yorker*, 10 January 2011, but was still scathing: 'However much the book was revised, it should have been revised more . . . there are blatant violations of logic and consistency. Loose ends dangle. There are vast dumps of unnecessary detail . . . The phrasing and the vocabulary are consistently banal . . . some critics have accused Larsson of having his feminism and eating it, too. They say that, under cover of condemning violence against women, he has supplied, for the reader's enjoyment . . . riveting scenes of violence against women.'

5   *His enthusiasm for detective fiction*: His friend Kurdo Baksi has noted his admiration for such writers as Erskine Childers, Arthur Conan Doyle, Agatha Christie, John Buchan and Frederick Forsyth.

6   *his characterisation of Salander*: Maureen Corrigan's review admits that the trilogy is engrossing but concludes: 'The real mystery here is how Lisbeth

Salander . . . has won over the world. That's a mystery that even Stieg Larsson, were he still alive, couldn't solve' ('Stieg Larsson and the Publishers Who Cashed In on His Name', *Washington Post*, 30 June 2011).

7 *Peter O'Donnell's Modesty Blaise*: Modesty began life as a comic strip character in the London *Evening Standard* in 1963. The strip was syndicated around the world, and led to a comedy thriller film in 1966. Quentin Tarantino is a Modesty fan, and she is referenced in *Pulp Fiction*. O'Donnell's other work included the stage play *Murder Most Logical*, aka *Mr Fothergill's Murder*.

8 *graphically described sexual violence*: When Erland Larsson read the first manuscript, he queried the level of violence in the story, only for his son to tell him that 'sex is selling': interview with Ali Karim, 3 October 2008, *Shots* (crime and thriller ezine). Tim Parks, in a wry review of the trilogy, concluded: 'Certainly the reader will not be invited to question his or her enjoyment in seeing sexual humiliation inflicted on evil rapists. That pleasure will not be spoiled' ('The Moralist', *New York Review of Books*, 9 June 2011).

9 *'We realised,' Sjöwall said, 'that people read crime . . .'*: The quotations come from Louise France's article.

10 *The Laughing Policeman*: Another crime-writing couple, Sean and Nicci French, compare the tantalising clues in the story to Agatha Christie's, and say: 'there is no doubt that Sjöwall and Wahlöö took pleasure in the conventions of classic crime fiction'. The novel became a Hollywood movie in 1973; watching it led a young Michael Connelly to the book: 'one of the best lessons a writer in waiting could ever have.' The series has also been televised.

11 *Kurt Wallander*: The Wallander books have been televised several times. Despite the omission of his love of opera from the British version, the press predictably dubbed the show 'Inspector Norse'.

12 *The story explores xenophobia and racism*: The Swedish academic Michael Tapper complains, however, in *Swedish Cops: From Sjöwall and Wahlöö to Stieg Larsson*, that: 'Rather than countering or even analysing the roots of paranoid and racist narrative, *Faceless Killers* confirms it in every detail . . .' Tapper also argues that, in *One Step Behind*, Mankell is guilty of 'blatant homophobia'. He is equally unsparing in his assessment of sexism in the books of Sjöwall and Wahlöö.

13 *Sjöwall and Wahlöö gave new impetus to the crime novel*: Their influence can be detected in the work of the Icelandic novelist Arnaldur Indridason, creator of Reykjavik's Erlendur Sveinsson, yet another world-weary cop. The third book in the series, *Jar City*, aka *Tainted Blood*, in which Erlendur investigates the death of an elderly man, reflects a concern about the misuse of genetics. Among Iceland's younger crime writers, Ragnar Jónasson is a translator of Agatha Christie as well as author of the Dark Iceland series of novels and the Hulda Trilogy, which makes effective use of reverse chronology.

14 *Maria Lang*: A television series of Puck's investigations was screened in 2013, starting with the first story (retitled *Death of a Loved One*), under the umbrella title *Crimes of Passion*.

15 *the Swedish Crime Writers' Academy*: The Academy was the brainchild of H.-K. Rönblom, who began to publish detective stories about the historian Paul Kennet in the 1950s; in Bo Lundin's view, he produced 'the first Swedish crime stories that can be enjoyed for their literary qualities'. The Academy

gives literary prizes, including the Martin Beck Award for the best crime novel in translation; the first went to Julian Symons, for *The Thirty-First of February*, and other early winners included Francis Iles, Cornell Woolrich, Sébastien Japrisot and Margaret Yorke.

16 *Sven Elvestad*: A colourful character with a taste for showmanship, he once spent a day inside the cage of a circus lion. He changed his name from Kristoffer Elvestad Svendsen after being caught embezzling from his employer and is also said to have been the first foreign journalist to interview Adolf Hitler.

17 *Gunnar Staalesen*: Staalesen was born in Bergen, where a statue of Varg Veum now stands. His extensive work in the theatre is reflected in the effective use of dialogue in his novels.

18 *Jo Nesbø*: Nesbø's stand-alone novel *Headhunters* was filmed, and became the highest-grossing Norwegian movie in history. This story of a recruitment specialist who finances his lifestyle by moonlighting as an art thief is characteristically dark and convoluted.

19 *The case becomes a hunt for a serial killer*: Gruesome serial killings also feature in Nesbø's bestsellers *The Snowman* and *The Leopard*.

20 *Håkan Nesser*: Nesser set the Van Veeteren books in Maardam, a city in an unnamed country in northern Europe. His other work includes a series featuring Swedish DI Gunnar Barbarotti.

21 *a 1960s instrumental by The Shadows*: 'The Rise and Fall of Flingel Bunt', which reached number five in the British pop charts. So did The Shadows' version of 'Man of Mystery', written to accompany the titles of the *Edgar Wallace Mysteries* TV series.

22 *was filmed twice*: Including an excellent Canadian movie, *The Silent Partner*, starring Elliott Gould.

23 *Miss Smilla's Feeling for Snow*: The US and UK translations are markedly different, and with this novel, as with *The Girl with the Dragon Tattoo*, creative differences arose between the British publisher, Christopher MacLehose, and the translators, Tiina Nunnally and Steven T. Murray respectively (who by coincidence are married): see Anthony Gardner's interview with MacLehose, www.anthonygardner.co.uk, and the interview with Murray and Nunnally on www.commonwealthclub.org. The complexities of translation inevitably complicate attempts to compare books originally written in different languages.

24 *Høeg is a literary novelist*: The antipodean science fiction writer Simon Petrie, in a review on his website, summarised Høeg's book as 'unsettlingly kaleidoscopic. In a plot that references (among many other things) jazz, ice-fishing, tropical parasitology, accounting practices, industrial espionage, navigation, the extinction of the dinosaurs and the correct form of artificial lighting for the photography of snow, Høeg also finds space for a steady undercurrent of black humour.'

25 *the worldwide breakthrough in popularity of Nordic noir*: This has been matched by the success of original television series such as *The Killing* and *The Bridge*. The commercial spin-offs include a trilogy by British crime writer David Hewson, which is based on *The Killing*, and Emma Kennedy's jokey *The Killing Handbook*, with tips on how to emulate the detective Sarah Lund, e.g. 'Smiling is your mortal enemy.'

FIFTY-TWO

Fatal Inversions

Ruth Rendell and modern psychological suspense

In 1942, when she was twelve years old, Ruth Barbara Grasemann was evacuated from suburban east London, target of Hitler's Luftwaffe, to the tranquil Cotswolds. An only child, she'd learned to live mostly in her imagination, a means of escape from the tensions of her home life. Her mother and father were both teachers, but they had little else in common, and spent much of their time at each other's throats.

Arthur Grasemann's parents had objected to his marriage to Ebba Kruse, a woman born in Sweden and raised in Denmark; his mother refused to attend the wedding. He'd been besotted with Ebba, but the reservations proved justified. The couple regularly indulged in blazing arguments, each row succeeded by angry, sulking silence. Their unhappiness was plain to their daughter.

Ruth was struck by the discovery that both her first names meant 'a stranger in a strange land': in the Bible, Ruth was exiled in an alien country, while Barbara signifies 'a foreigner'. Although she didn't think her parents had intended this coincidence, it reinforced her sense of isolation. She also thought that the two names reflected different aspects of her personality. Ruth, she felt, was 'tougher, colder, more analytical, possibly more aggressive'.

Barbara's personality was more intuitive, more feminine, more sensitive. Solitary by nature, she reacted to her parents' behaviour by hiding her emotions. Secrets fascinated her, but she felt 'imbued from a very early age with a sense of doom'.

When Ebba and Ruth were evacuated together, they were billeted in the same village, but not in the same house; Ebba stayed in the vicarage, where she could keep an eye on her pupils. Ruth was horrified when the vicar's maid, sixteen years old, drowned herself in the village pool. She was pregnant, and the secret shame was too much for her. More than forty years later, Ruth reworked the tragedy into fiction.

After leaving school, Ruth got a job as a reporter on the *Chigwell Times*, and married a fellow journalist, Don Rendell. Her career came to an ignominious end when she failed to attend a tennis club dinner, but reported it as if she'd been there. Unfortunately, the guest speaker had dropped dead while giving his speech, and her failure to land the scoop spelled the end for her in journalism.

As her son was growing up, she experimented by writing a variety of novels, but did nothing with them. Eventually, she submitted a drawing-room comedy to a publisher who, after a long delay, suggested she rewrite it. When she was unwilling to do so, they asked if she'd written anything else. She revealed that she'd concocted a detective story for her own entertainment, concerning the seemingly motiveless murder of a respectable married woman called Margaret Parsons.

This book was set in a fictional Sussex town, based on Midhurst, which she called Kingsmarkham. The police officers who led the investigation formed an updated version of the Holmes–Watson partnership. The senior member of the duo, Reginald Wexford, was strong, likeable and intelligent. His literary ancestors were Maigret and Hillary Waugh's Fred Fellows, while his sidekick, Mike Burden, was prissily conventional. When the publishers read the manuscript, they offered her £75 for the rights; the outcome was that 1964 saw the appearance of *From Doon with Death*, which introduced one of Britain's most popular fictional policemen, and launched Ruth Rendell on a career lasting more than half a century.

*

Rendell's distinctive talent was spotted at once by Julian Symons, who praised the 'intelligent, realistic writing [which] lifts the book out of the simple puzzle class'. Among crime writers whose approach to the genre influenced her fiction, Symons was second only to Patricia Highsmith. Rendell admired his work for 'the English suburban environment and the people. I like the marriage situations . . . the family relationships and the horrible tensions . . . I am very fond of houses in London and the streets and the suburbs[1] and he is very good on that.'

She once told an interviewer:[2] 'Julian Symons has said that all my novels are about sex.' Sexual taboos (for instance incest, a recurrent plot element) and secrets are at the heart of many of her mysteries. A reader coming afresh in the twenty-first century to novels such as A Sleeping Life[3] (1978), in which Wexford investigates the stabbing of an enigmatic middle-aged woman, will be struck by the scale of social transformation in Britain since the book was published. The sexual mores now seem quaint.

The same is true of From Doon with Death, as Rendell acknowledged in an afterword to a new edition fifty years after the original publication: 'A book of this kind could not be written today. Manners, speech, social life and the pace of it, have changed beyond belief.' The story had become, she recognised, a historical novel, as distantly in the past as the Victorian poetry Margaret Parsons loved, quotations from which head each chapter.

Wexford's literary birth came at the age of fifty-two, and since his popularity meant that she continued to write about him for almost half a century, Rendell modified his character, to equip him to cope with the changing face of Britain. He began as rather a tough cop, and she 'wanted him to be more literate, more liberal, kindlier, more sensitive. I was determined not to let him become one of those detectives who have failed marriages, live in a tiny, run-down flat, drink too much and are bitter and morose. Wexford had to have a happy domestic life . . .'

Literary allusions are woven into the texture of the stories. Wexford solves one case by reading a book of literary criticism.[4] Rendell's passion for literacy is also reflected in her repeated deployment of linguistic clues,[5] as in Put on by Cunning, aka Death Notes (1981), where the key to the mystery is to be found in a character's surname. Her early novels are as cleverly constructed as Christie's, but she resented the comparison. For Rendell, an ingenious puzzle was simply a pleasing component in novels about lives and communities damaged by crime rather than their *raison d'être*.

Rendell's confidence grew as the series progressed. She had no interest in police procedure or forensic science, relying on her acute perceptions about human behaviour under extreme stress to make the extraordinary events in her fiction seem believable. Family dysfunction is central to her work, but so too is the nature of love.

In *Put on by Cunning*, the troubled relationship between the flautist Manuel Camargue and his daughter Natalie, suspected of murdering him, is counterpointed by Wexford's musings about Freud,[6] and his relations with his own two daughters. Jungian analysis is an explicit ingredient of *The Veiled One* (1988), in which Burden's interrogation of Clifford Sanders, suspected of strangling his mother, has disastrous consequences.

The class divide in Britain is a recurrent theme, although Rendell presents working-class life from an outsider's perspective. Her police stories lacked the gritty texture of the work of Maurice Procter and John Wainwright. Wexford didn't age in real time[7] and his later cases addressed social, political and cultural concerns, ranging from feminist militancy to racism.[8] This reflected Rendell's social conscience, but the results were mixed. A high-profile donor to Tony Blair's Labour Party, she was elevated to the House of Lords in 1997.

A dedicated campaigner against female genital mutilation, Rendell used the popularity of the Wexford series to bring the issue to the attention of a vast readership in *Not in the Flesh* (2007). The presentation of Wexford's nightmarish imaginings about the prospect that a five-year-old girl will be mutilated and left permanently disfigured is poignant. The murder plot is, however, perfunctory, reworking an idea that Ira Levin had handled with greater panache.[9] The novel's impact was also diluted by a lack of rigorous editing, typified by repetitious references to political correctness.

From the start of her career, Rendell switched back and forth between the Kingsmarkham Chronicles and non-series novels. Her early forays into psychological crime fiction varied in merit. *Vanity Dies Hard*, aka *In Sickness and in Health* (1965), ventures into woman-in-jeopardy territory before slipping to an anticlimax, while she acknowledged that *One Across, Two Down* (1971), with its crossword-fanatic protagonist, 'could have been done in the thirties'. Even these apprentice works benefited from lucid and intense writing.

She hit her stride in *A Demon in My View*[10] (1976). Her marriage had broken down, and she and her cousin were sharing a flat with a garden. In the garden shed, she came across the torso of a shop mannequin. This discovery, and the confusion that arose because someone else living in the building had the same name as her cousin, leading to their mail becoming mixed up, gave her the impetus for a chilling mystery about a disturbed protagonist. The solitary Arthur Johnson from time to time finds satisfaction in strangling a mannequin hidden in his cellar. When the mannequin disappears, he seeks another outlet for his urges.

Arthur's fellow tenant, Anthony Johnson, is planning a thesis called 'Some Aspects of the Psychopathic Personality', while conducting a passionate affair with a married woman, whom he is giving time to choose between her husband and himself. Whether this was an oblique reference to his creator's personal life is unclear; Rendell never spoke in public about her private life, and, after divorcing Don Rendell in 1975, she remarried him[11] two years later. Her fiction reflected her view that 'if people do have very fraught, intense, passionate relationships, they do lead to a lot of grief'.

Her next stand-alone was remarkable for her audacious decision to dispense with mystery about whodunit and whydunit, with one of the genre's most stunning opening sentences. *A Judgement in Stone*[12] (1977) begins: 'Eunice Parchman killed the Coverdale family because she could not read or write.' Rendell had honed her skill to perfection: despite her abandonment of surprise, the crime novelist's stock-in-trade, the story of the Coverdales' tragedy grips the reader's attention all the way to the shocking finale.

Like Highsmith, Rendell was an only child who often wrote about only children. Psychologically damaged young men prowl through her fiction.[13] On the surface, many have the charm of a Tom Ripley, but this cannot be said of Finn, a 'lost soul' who brings doom to the unsuspecting in *The Lake of Darkness* (1980). His mother cleans for Martin Urban, a naive accountant who decides to use money won on the football pools to help people in need. Housing shortages in London provided inspiration for aspects of the plot, but here Rendell integrates social issues seamlessly into a tense plot. She toyed with the idea of bringing back Finn, Ripley-style, in a later book, but wisely decided against it.

The nightmarish quality of Rendell's stand-alones reflects the author's intense fear 'that disaster is imminent . . . It happens a lot in my novels. I feel it, I have known people who feel it . . . We dread the postman's knock, the ring of the telephone . . . It is a neurotic state. I wish I didn't have it. I have it. Many of my characters have this sense of disaster: if he had not answered the phone, gone out at this point, got up at this moment, things would have been different.'

In 1986, Rendell published *A Dark-Adapted Eye* under a pseudonym. 'Barbara Vine' paired her own second name with her grandmother's maiden name. Her publishers made no secret of her real identity, but, for the author, the objective was not so much creating a fresh commercial brand as establishing a fresh literary persona.

This time she wrote in the first person, and the book opens as the narrator's aunt Vera Hillyard is due to be hanged. Rendell includes vignettes from her own life, such as a father who likes to solve the crossword puzzle in the *Daily Telegraph*, and the focus is on family secrets. The story fictionalises the wartime death of the pregnant maid[14] that had haunted her for so long.

A Fatal Inversion (1987) was set in the long, hot English summer of 1976. Five young people, two men and three women, camp in the grounds of Wyvis Hall; ten years later, the bodies of a woman and child are found in the Hall's pet cemetery. The story is a whowasdunin, the finest example of this form of mystery. Symons described the first two Vine books as 'among the most memorable and original crime stories of the century', with crucial secrets concealed 'with a cunning Wilkie Collins might have envied and Dickens would have admired . . . *A Fatal Inversion* has the most brilliantly ironic ending of any crime story known to me.'

Symons also eulogised two suspense novels that appeared under

Rendell's own name, *The Killing Doll* (1984) and *The Bridesmaid* (1989). His only reservation concerned Rendell's habitual use of coincidence. Her achievements were all the more impressive given that, as he pointed out,[15] even Collins only wrote two masterpieces.

At her peak, Rendell matched quantity of output with quality of writing in a manner unique in the genre's history. She proved equally adept at the short story and novella. Yet even a writer blessed with rare gifts may fall into the trap of writing too much. Symons pointed out this risk in the late 1980s; she agreed with him, but a fierce work ethic drove her on.

Inevitably, some of the novels she wrote in her last twenty years disappointed in comparison to her best books. The prose remained enticing, but character types, settings and situations began to recur. The Vine novel *The Minotaur* (2005) is among those lacking her characteristic sharpness. Like the Virginia creeper which meanders over Lydstep Old Hall, this long book would have benefited from pruning.

Television and film versions[16] of Rendell's work made her a household name. Her curiosity about people burned to the end. She liked to travel on the Underground – a fascinating backdrop in the Vine novel *King Solomon's Carpet* (1991) – so as to watch and eavesdrop upon her fellow passengers; 'I want to know their secrets', she admitted, despite refusing to divulge her own. She was occasionally criticised for lack of research,[17] but her inquisitiveness extended to sex games, which play a part in another Vine novel, *The Birthday Present* (2008), written as she approached her eighties. 'Somebody I met at a party told me about adventure sex,' she said. 'He found it shocking, and I thought, "Well, I rather like that . . ."'

Several talented British novelists who promised to emulate Rendell's success have faded from view or turned elsewhere.[18] Among them was a young police officer's wife. She published five short, snappy suspense novels in the 1970s, culminating in *Making Hate* (1977), an ambitious if flawed story about a serial rapist, told from two male viewpoints. A glittering future beckoned – but it was as a children's writer that Jacqueline Wilson[19] achieved celebrity.

Minette Walters[20] and Frances Fyfield[21] have published outstanding examples of the 'psychothriller',[22] while the husband and wife partnership of Nicci Gerrard and Sean French,[23] who write as Nicci French, has produced powerful novels such as *Killing Me Softly* (1999), in which a young woman's infatuation with a charismatic mountain climber leads to appalling consequences.

French's *Complicit*, aka *The Other Side of the Door* (2009), is a whowasdunin entwining past and present narratives, each told by a young music teacher, Bonnie Graham. The story, set in the present, recounts the bizarre events that unfold once Bonnie finds the corpse of a man to whom she was close (but whose identity is not revealed); the other narrative describes the chaotic summer preceding the man's murder. Accomplished storytelling facilitates the suspension of disbelief.

Belinda Bauer made an immediate impression with *Blacklands* (2009), in which a twelve-year-old boy corresponds with a man jailed as a serial killer. In the highly original *Rubbernecker* (2013), Patrick Fort is a medical student with Asperger's syndrome and a morbid interest in the dead; the other key characters include a neglectful nurse called Tracy and Sam Galen, who is in a coma. *Snap* (2018), longlisted for the Man Booker Prize, draws on the real-life murder of pregnant Marie Wilks on the M50 in 1988.

Psychological suspense continues to attract writers capable of using the crime novel as a tool of recognition, a means of solving the puzzles of human nature, of understanding who we are. How many of them can sustain a career of sustained artistic excellence of similar length to Rendell's, or show equal command of the more conventional detective novel, is another question. Rendell wrote so well for so long that she remains the hardest of acts to follow.

Notes

The main sources are interviews with Rendell in *The Sunday Times* of 9 April 1989, in John C. Carr's *The Craft of Crime*, in Diana Cooper_Clark's *Designs of Darkness* and in the *Guardian* (Libby Brooks, 'Dark Lady of Whodunnits', 3 August 2002), and her obituaries in *The Times*, the *Guardian* and the *Daily Telegraph*.

1   *I am very fond of houses in London and the streets and the suburbs*: Even the late novel *Portobello*, with its thin characterisation of a lynch-pin character, Ella Cotswold, and the clumsy reworking of ingredients handled with finesse in *The Lake of Darkness*, is redeemed by the evocative portrayal of

the locale. The novel shares a plot device with Highsmith's *Found in the Street*, but neither book shows its author close to her best.

2   *She once told an interviewer*: John C. Carr, author of *The Craft of Crime*, in 1983.

3   *A Sleeping Life*: The key plot twist resembles that in *To Love and Be Wise* by Josephine Tey, whom Rendell admired. The love affair in *Antony and Cleopatra* sets a template for relationships in novels such as *Shake Hands for Ever* and *Make Death Love Me*, which takes its title from the play, and Rendell noted that the nature of Enobarbus, 'noble yet capable of treachery', is paralleled by a character in *A Sleeping Life*.

4   *Wexford solves one case by reading a book of literary criticism*: In *A Guilty Thing Surprised*, where a study of Wordsworth helps him to understand a relationship that holds the key to the crime.

5   *linguistic clues*:   *A Sleeping Life* and *The Secret House of Death* supply other examples.

6   *Wexford's musings about Freud*: Barbara Fass Leavy's *The Fiction of Ruth Rendell: Ancient Tragedy and the Modern Family* discusses her approach to psychology in the context of ancient Greek narratives as well as the theories of Freud and Jung.

7   *Wexford didn't age in real time*: In 2009, Rendell intimated that *The Monster in the Box*, which reaches back into Wexford's past, would be his final appearance. He returned as a consultant in *The Vault*, which amounted to a sequel to the non-series novel *A Sight for Sore Eyes*, and also in *No Man's Nightingale*, helping Mike Burden to investigate the strangling of a female vicar. Rendell contemplated a book to be published posthumously in which Wexford died, but it seems that she never wrote it.

8   *concerns, ranging from feminist militancy to racism*: The former subject is tackled in *An Unkindness of Ravens*, the latter in *Simisola*, which contains a thought-provoking variation on the 'last line' twist; in this case, the final revelation reflects the story's overarching theme.

9   *an idea that Ira Levin had handled with greater panache*: In *Deathtrap*.

10 *A Demon in my View*: The novel won a CWA Gold Dagger, the first of many awards to come Rendell's way.

11 *she remarried him*: They owned a farmhouse in the Suffolk village of Polstead. In 1827, Polstead was the location of the 'Red Barn Murder' of Maria Marten by her lover William Corder, which in 1991 provided material for a play by Christopher Bond. In Nicola Upson's *The Death of Lucy Kyte*, Josephine Tey moves to Red Barn Cottage, Polstead, and is confronted by a mystery.

12 *A Judgement in Stone*: Edmund Crispin said in *The Sunday Times* of 22 May 1977 that the book established Rendell as 'the best woman crime writer we have had since Sayers, Christie, Allingham, and Marsh'. The challenge of adapting such an unorthodox novel has not deterred several attempts. Neil Bartlett (who also adapted *Lady Audley's Secret* for the theatre) was bold enough to turn it into a musical in 1992, with music by Nicolas Bloomfield, but the result was unfortunate. Claude Chabrol filmed the book as *La Cérémonie* in 1995, and more than twenty years later, Simon Brett and Anthony Lampard adapted the story for the stage.

13 *Psychologically damaged young men prowl through her fiction*: Stephen Knight chastises her, harshly, for using 'the facile mechanism of a deranged person, like Finn in *The Lake of Darkness* or Anthony Jones [*sic*] in *A Demon*

in My View . . . without giving the character the central and powerful explanations that [Margaret] Millar could manage.' Knight prefers her work as Barbara Vine.

14 *The story fictionalises the wartime death of the pregnant maid*: Her short story 'The Orchard Walls' also made poignant use of this episode.

15 *he pointed out*: In a review for the *Sunday Times* on 25 October 1964.

16 *Television and film versions*: British TV adaptations of the Wexford stories began in 1987. *The Ruth Rendell Mysteries*, some adapted from short stories and stand-alone novels, ran to eighty-four episodes. In addition to filming *A Judgement in Stone*, Chabrol filmed *The Bridesmaid* as *La Demoiselle d'Honneur*. Another Frenchman, Claude Miller, filmed *The Tree of Hands* as *Alias Betty*, while Spain's Pedro Almodóvar adapted *Live Flesh*.

17 *She was occasionally criticised for lack of research*: Libby Brooks quotes a scathing review of *A Sight for Sore Eyes*: 'Rendell . . . knows nothing of youth culture: neither of the 90s nor, even, of the 60s. And her invented youth culture is far more peculiar than the mundane reality.' The reviewer was Nicholas Blincoe, whose own early crime novels such as *Manchester Slingback* explored a world foreign to Rendell; her characters seldom venture far from the south of England and East Anglia.

18 *talented British novelists . . . faded from view or turned elsewhere*: J. Wallis Martin's *A Likeness in Stone* marked her out as a possible heir to Rendell's mantle, but she published only four more novels in the next twenty years. Morag Joss, whose doom-drenched *Half Broken Things* updated the country-house mystery, has also proved less than prolific. The strange events of her *The Night Following* are triggered by the narrator's discovery of her husband's affair. In a state of shock, she drives off and kills an elderly female cyclist. Rather than giving herself up, she becomes obsessed by her victim's husband, who deludes himself that his wife has returned from the grave.

19 *Jacqueline Wilson*: Wilson's empathy with young people is evident in *Let's Pretend*, with events seen through the eyes of thirteen-year-old Emily Barrett. When Emily's mother goes missing, Emily suspects her stepfather of murder, but no one believes her. The key plot twist is perhaps inadequately foreshadowed, but Wilson's crime novels demonstrate her gifts as a storyteller.

20 *Minette Walters*: *The Ice House* begins with extracts from three newspaper reports about David Maybury's disappearance. Mixing conventional prose narrative with newspaper reports, police memoranda, witness statements, maps and even pictures (in *The Shape of Snakes*) became a hallmark of Walters' work. This technique of using documents to add texture to a crime story dates back to *The Notting Hill Mystery*, but Walters deployed it with particular flair.

21 *Frances Fyfield*: Her stand-alone *Blood from Stone* concerns a female barrister's mystifying suicide and won a Gold Dagger.

22 *the 'psychothriller'*: This term is used by Stephen Knight, who argues that Walters' *The Breaker* 'reads – almost deliberately – like modernised version of Sayers' *Have His Carcase*' and that Fyfield's *The Playroom*, published under her real name, Frances Hegarty, exposes 'the horror and frailty behind respectable lives'.

23 *Sean French*: French is a biographer whose eclectic subjects include Patrick Hamilton, Brigitte Bardot and Jane Fonda.

FIFTY-THREE

Dark Places

American police fiction

The body of twenty-two-year-old Elizabeth Short[1] was discovered on a vacant lot in Los Angeles on the morning of 15 January 1947. Her corpse had been severed at the waist, mutilated, drained of blood and posed with hands covering the face. The woman who found Elizabeth's remains thought at first she'd come across a shop mannequin. Elizabeth became known as 'the Black Dahlia', but despite nationwide publicity, and no shortage of confessions, the police never found her killer.

Eleven years later, another woman was brutally murdered in El Monte in Los Angeles County. Geneva Odelia Hilliker, known as Jean, had met Armand Ellroy in 1939; she was a nurse, he was an accountant. Both were natural storytellers whose imaginations often ran away with them. She claimed to have seen the Feds gun down John Dillinger; he boasted of having had an affair with Rita Hayworth. They married and had a son, Lee Earle, who later called himself James. He recalled their divorce in 1954: 'Their "irreconcilable differences" amounted to a love of the flesh. She majored in booze and minored in men. He guzzled Alka-Seltzer for his ulcer and chased women with an equal lack of discernment.'

The ten-year-old boy began his summer vacation by spending

the weekend with his father. On returning to Jean's house, he saw three black-and-white police cars outside, and a group of plain-clothes detectives. She had been strangled and her body dumped in some bushes. Her killer had taken off one of her stockings, and wrapped it around her neck after she was dead.

Like Elizabeth's murder, Jean's was never solved. The year after his mother's death, Jean's son was given Jack Webb's book *The Badge*[2] (1958) as a birthday present, and he read about the Black Dahlia case. He became fixated with it, recalling later[3] that his 'Dahlia obsession was explicitly pornographic. My imagination supplied the details that Jack Webb omitted.' The killings of Elizabeth and Jean cast a shadow over his whole life, and defined his career as a crime writer.

The trauma of James Ellroy's early years was compounded by his father's death in 1965. He took refuge from depression in drink and drugs. Expelled from school for fighting and truancy, he joined the army, only to fake a nervous breakdown in order to obtain a discharge. Homeless and rough-sleeping, he resorted to sexual voyeurism and petty crime, and was sent to prison. After a serious bout of pneumonia led to a lung abscess, he pulled himself together and joined Alcoholics Anonymous. A job as a golf caddy earned him money and time to write.

During his darkest days, he discovered *The Onion Field* (1973) by Joseph Wambaugh, a searing account of the kidnapping of two LAPD cops, one of whom was murdered. Ellroy admired the 'terrible compassion' of Wambaugh's writing, and shoplifted the book, later saving enough to buy a copy of his own. As for his own survival, he has said: 'I'll credit God with the overall save. I'll cite Joseph Wambaugh and Sex as secondary forces.'

Ellroy's first novel, *Brown's Requiem* (1981), is narrated by cop-turned-repossession agent Fritz Brown. Brown describes Philip Marlowe as his 'fictional predecessor', but Ellroy promptly renounced the private-eye story. In *Clandestine*, he employed a rookie LAPD cop as the protagonist of a complex, Freudian novel set in the 1950s that fictionalises Jean's murder. As he said later: 'The mother and the son were vividly etched. They failed only by real-life comparisons.'

Ellroy bristled with self-belief and had a flair for extravagant publicity. Styling himself as 'the Demon Dog' of crime fiction, he was never at a loss for an outrageous remark. Over the years, he has displayed an unrelenting determination to tease and shock, but his public statements have often been contradictory. On outward appearances, Ellroy has nothing in common with Dorothy L. Sayers, but in different ways, both writers hid their insecurities and real feelings about personal tragedies beneath a carefully constructed carapace.

After a few years Ellroy's career stalled. His publisher and his agent dropped him, and his luck only turned as a result of meeting the owner of the Mysterious Bookshop in New York, Otto Penzler, who also happened to be an influential editor and publisher. Three books followed featuring the maverick LA cop Lloyd Hopkins, as Ellroy completed his literary apprenticeship, and was ready to embark on a more daring project.

In *The Black Dahlia* (1987),[4] two friends and fellow cops who are rivals for the same woman become obsessed by the murder of Elizabeth Short. Ellroy had contemplated writing his first novel about the crime, but was deterred by the success of *True Confessions*,[5] John Gregory Dunne's novel about the case, which Ellroy described as 'wonderful, if fanciful'. The power of Ellroy's prose and the richness of his evocation of urban panoramas made *The Black Dahlia* a bestseller, launching the *L.A. Quartet*.

The third book, *L.A. Confidential*[6] (1990), explored police corruption and Tinseltown celebrity. In Penzler's words,[7] the manuscript was 'delivered way too long – too many pages, too many words. Most authors, when asked to cut a book, remove a sub-plot. Mr Ellroy cut 200 pages by removing words he regarded as extraneous, and his telegraphic style was born.'

Ellroy's technique of interweaving fictional characters and people taken from real life[8] is a hallmark of novels such as *The Cold Six Thousand* (2001), the second book in his Underworld USA Trilogy. So is staccato prose. As Penzler says, 'Too many writers have emulated the truncated sentence structure, but just because you mumble doesn't mean you're Marlon Brando.' Ellroy's influence can be seen, however, in the work of writers as diverse and acclaimed as Megan Abbott, who described her first two novels as 'lovesongs' to him, and Britain's David Peace.[9]

Ellroy's absorption in real-life crime is also reflected in his non-fiction. *My Dark Places*[10] (1996) fuses autobiography and crime investigation as he explains how his second wife encouraged him[11] to find out 'who his mother was and why she died'. With the help of a retired cop, Sergeant Bill Stoner, he attempted to solve a thirty-eight-year-old cold case, the murder of Jean Ellroy. His account is searing, above all in the passage in which he describes the harrowing experience of studying scene of crime and autopsy photographs. The material is graphic, the prose and emotions as stripped and raw as the corpse.

According to Anthony Boucher, the first American novel to present police procedure in a more or less realistic manner[12] was *V as in Victim* by Lawrence Treat,[13] which appeared in 1945. Treat took pains to research police work, although the storyline is unremarkable, a conventional mystery with a twist.

The semi-documentary nature of post-war American cop films and shows[14] sought to emphasise authenticity. In pulp fiction, cops tended to be stupid, thuggish or corrupt – sometimes all three. Now they were typically presented as ordinary people doing their best in a difficult job. Hillary Waugh's[15] crime writing debut was *Madam Will Not Dine Tonight* (1947), a less than cutting-edge country-house mystery solved by a private detective, but he shifted to the police procedural after reading a casebook on true crime.

A real-life puzzle, the unsolved disappearance of Paula Welden in Vermont in 1946, lay behind *Last Seen Wearing* (1952), a novel about police attempts to find out why an eighteen-year-old college student has vanished. The book benefited from a well-evoked small town setting in New England, a strong mystery plot and accuracy in technical detail. Waugh subsequently created a popular series cop, Chief Fred Fellows, and enjoyed a long career without surpassing the excellence of his first police procedural.

Unlike Treat and Waugh, Ed McBain[16] was a mainstream novelist with no previous track record in the crime genre prior to publishing *Cop Hater* in 1956. This paperback original set in a fictionalised New York City[17] began with a disclaimer: 'The City in these pages is imaginary. The people, the places, are all fictions. Only the police routine is based on established investigatory techniques.'

McBain created an ensemble cast of detectives, led by a rugged all-American boy, Steve Carella. The ethnic diversity – white, black, Hispanic and Jewish – of the cops in the 87th Precinct was striking for the 1950s. His use of official documents lent a touch of realism: Carella's worksheet, and ballistics and autopsy reports, are among the documents reproduced in *Cop Hater*. His books were short, his dialogue snappy, his credo for writing vivid stories deceptively simple: 'You just touch on things. You don't go round the room describing the furniture.'

The 87th Precinct soap opera ran for half a century, as McBain's versatility and willingness to experiment kept the books fresh. *Hail, Hail, the Gang's All Here!* (1971) juggles no fewer than fourteen different plots, while the series even boasts its own Professor Moriarty. A menacing master criminal, the Deaf Man, appears in six novels.

In *He Who Hesitates* (1964), McBain emphasises character rather than policing; for once, the cops are bit-part players in a story about a perfect crime and an interracial romance. *Candyland* (2000), presented as a collaboration between Ed McBain and Evan Hunter, is a book of two halves, each written in a different style and together forming a study of crime and punishment.

McBain's work proved highly influential.[18] He became the leader of a pack of highly professional writers of police procedurals, including Elizabeth Linington,[19] one of the first female specialists[20] in the form. Her extensive research into the workings of the LAPD strengthened a long series, published under the pen-name Dell Shannon, about the Mexican-American cop Luis Mendoza.

Joseph Wambaugh had first-hand knowledge of policing in Los Angeles. The son of a cop, he spent three years in the Marines before joining the LAPD in 1960, the year of Mendoza's first appearance in *Case Pending*. *The New Centurions*, his non-genre novel about police life[21] in the period leading up to the Watts riots of 1965, was published eleven years later; he was still a serving officer.

His portrayal of the world he knew bore scant resemblance to the sanitised pictures presented in the TV show *Dragnet* and the Mendoza chronicles. Whereas the *Dragnet* scripts were vetted by the LAPD, Wambaugh chose not to seek official approval for his work, aware that his unflinching accounts of the corrosive realities of law enforcement would dismay his superiors. Soon he became a full-time writer. As Ellroy put it,[22] 'His celebrity sandbagged him . . . Suspects recognized him and begged autographs. Agent calls and producer calls swamped the Hollenbeck squadroom.'

The Choirboys (1975) isn't a novel for the faint-hearted; an early review[23] characterised it as 'a brutal, brutalizing book – an obscenity in a toilet stall'. The story follows ten patrolmen with no illusions about either the LAPD or the people they are paid to protect. They work the night shift in pairs, and cope with stress by indulging in 'choir practice', a euphemism for drinking, having casual sex and regaling each other with grotesque tales of their encounters with desperate specimens of humanity. The humour is ferocious, but ultimately the black comedy segues into tragedy.

Wambaugh's writing drew on the way that, in *Catch-22*, Joseph Heller sought 'to dramatize the insanity of war and the stresses that drove people to madness by writing his very serious story using all of the tools of absurdist comedy . . . I thought, from now on I'll write stories that are the opposite of police procedurals which tell how the cop acts on the job. I'll flip it and dramatize how the job acts on the cop, and gallows humor will be my most potent weapon.'[24]

Truman Capote encouraged Wambaugh to write *The Onion Field* (1973), and his *In Cold Blood* was an inspiration for Wambaugh's non-fiction. In *The Blooding*[25] (1989), Wambaugh studied the Narborough murder inquiry in England. This landmark case resulted in the arrest of a sociopath called Colin Pitchfork for raping and murdering two young girls. Pitchfork became the first person to be caught as a result of mass DNA screening, and the first to be convicted of murder on the strength of genetic fingerprinting evidence. In his dry, understated way, Wambaugh makes clear his opinion of the press coverage of the case: 'There were many references to [Pitchfork's] "sickly grin" or "dead eyes", and endless allusions to "evil". Almost everyone, it seemed, preferred original sin to clinical definition.'

As a crime reporter with the *L.A. Times*, Michael Connelly gained insight into the dark side of policing the mean streets which informed his debut novel. *The Black Echo* (1992) introduced Hieronymus Bosch, known as Harry,[26] a Vietnam veteran and an exemplar of the detective as lone maverick. Having been demoted for shooting a suspected serial killer, he investigates the death of a heroin addict, who had served alongside Harry as a 'Tunnel Rat', seeking out the Vietcong in their underground strongholds.

Connelly is a skilled entertainer, but his writing does not lack ambition. He sees his books as 'contemporary reflections of life in Los Angeles, or life in our world. And so if there is a riot in Los Angeles, or if there is an OJ Simpson trial, an earthquake, it ends up in my book.' Harry has, like James Ellroy, a tormented past; his mother was also murdered when he was a child, and Connelly sought permission from Ellroy[27] before drawing on his fellow writer's past for *The Reversal* (2010).

As Connelly's confidence has grown, he has deployed a range of techniques to keep his books fresh. Harry becomes a private investigator, and although most of his cases are related in the third person, Connelly nods to the classic Californian gumshoe novel[28] by allowing him a turn as a narrator. Harry discovers that he is a half-brother of one of Connelly's other protagonists, the attorney Mickey Haller,[29] and also collaborates with another, the FBI criminal profiler Terrell 'Terry' McCaleb.[30] Harry is central to Connelly's work, but it remains the case, as it was in *The Black Echo*, that 'Harry Bosch was an outsider, always would be.'

Notes

The main sources are Le Roy Lad Panek's *The American Police Novel*, George N. Dove's *The Police Procedural*, Bargainnier and Dove's *Cops and Constables*, Steven Powell's *James Ellroy: Demon Dog of Crime Fiction* and *The Big Somewhere*, and Bertens and D'haen's *Contemporary American Crime Fiction*.

1   *Elizabeth Short*: Among many discussions of the murder are John Gilmore's
     Severed: The True Story of the Black Dahlia Murder and Piu Eatwell's *Black
     Dahlia, Red Rose*. The authors come up with different explanations of the
     crime, and identify different suspects.

2   *Jack Webb's book The Badge*: Jack Webb became famous as a result of
     producing and starring in *Dragnet*, a radio, television and film series
     recording the cases of Sergeant Joe Friday of the LAPD. The series aimed
     for realism, opening with the solemn words: 'Ladies and gentlemen: the
     story you are about to hear is true. Only the names have changed to
     protect the innocent.' *The Badge* collected true-crime stories considered too
     graphic for television at the time; Ellroy contributed an introduction to a
     2005 edition. Another author called Jack Webb started publishing paper-
     back-original mysteries in the 1950s.

3   *recalling later*: In *My Dark Places*.

4   *The Black Dahlia*: Brian De Palma filmed the novel in 2006.

5   *True Confessions*: The novel was filmed with a screenplay co-written by
     Dunne and his wife Joan Didion. Dunne's brother Dominick wrote *The Two
     Mrs Grenvilles*, a novel fictionalizing the Woodward murder of 1955.

6   *L.A. Confidential*: Curtis Hanson's film of the book earned two Academy
     Awards and seven nominations.

7   *In Penzler's words*: In 'A Master and a Masterpiece', *New York Sun*, 30
     August 2006. Penzler says that: 'In the evolution of the modern police story,
     there is a straight line from Ed McBain, the greatest of all procedural writers,
     to Joseph Wambaugh, who showed the real life of police officers, on and
     off the job, to James Ellroy, whose ambitious novels involve cops as they
     are integrated into a greater political and sociological universe.'

8   *Ellroy's technique . . . real life*: *White Jazz* takes its epigraph from Ross
     Macdonald, a man and a writer very different from Ellroy, but also a novelist
     whose career involved an attempt to come to terms with his relationship
     with a parent.

9   *Ellroy's influence can be seen . . . in the work of writers as diverse and
     acclaimed as Megan Abbott . . . and Britain's David Peace*: Essays in Steven
     Powell's *The Big Somewhere*, by Diana Powell and by David Bishop and
     Steven Powell, trace that influence in detail. Borrowing a phrase from John
     Dos Passos, Peace has said that Ellroy is, in his best work, 'the architect of
     history' ('David Peace and James Ellroy in Conversation', *Guardian*, 9
     January 2010).

10   *My Dark Places*: True-crime specialist Ann Rule described the book as an
     'often agonizing voyage . . . both compelling and disturbing' ('Little Boy
     Lost', *Washington Post*, 24 November 1996).

11   *his second wife encouraged him*: This was film critic Helen Knode, who
     wrote a crime novel of her own, *The Ticket Out*.

12   *the first American novel to present police procedure in a more or less
     realistic manner*: Between the world wars, however, Richard Edward Enright,
     who resigned as NYPD Police Commissioner after a scandal-laden tenure
     during the early years of Prohibition, wrote a detective novel followed by
     two books about the police. He was the closest equivalent in the United
     States to Sir Basil Thomson, but after publishing a police manual, he aban-
     doned writing and became director of the United Service Detective Bureau.

13   *Lawrence Treat*: Treat was a former lawyer and a co-founder of the MWA.

LeRoy Lad Panek has identified as many as fifteen conventions of police fiction in *V as in Victim*. Treat also created a psychologist, Carl Wayward, who finds clues in dreams.

14 *The semi-documentary nature of post-war American cop films and shows*: Jules Dassin's *The Naked City*, set in New York and released in 1948, is a striking example. The following year Sidney Kingsley had a hit with the stage play *Detective Story*, while *Dragnet* began on the radio, the television series beginning a couple of years later.

15 *Hillary Waugh*: Waugh's *Sleep Long, My Love*, became *Jigsaw*, a film surprisingly set in Brighton, England, with Jack Warner as a jolly good Fred Fellows. Waugh published more than fifty novels under various names and was married to a fellow crime novelist, Shannon O'Cork; both of them wrote books about the craft of mystery writing.

16 *Ed McBain*: His birth name was Salvatore Albert Lombino, but concern about prejudice towards writers with foreign names led him to change it to Evan Hunter. He used several pen-names and dabbled in different types of fiction; he also wrote stage plays and worked on a stage musical version of the film *The Night They Raided Minsky's*. As Hunter, he wrote the mainstream bestseller *The Blackboard Jungle*, as well as a fictionalization of the Borden case, *Lizzie*. He wrote the screenplay for Hitchcock's film of a Daphne du Maurier story, *The Birds*, but quarrelled with the director about the adaptation of Winston Graham's *Marnie*, and was fired. *Goldilocks*, published in 1978, launched a series featuring Florida attorney Matthew Hope; twenty years later, *The Last Best Hope* brought Hope and the 87th Precinct together. In *There Was a Little Girl*, Hope lies in a coma after being shot, and his associates try to discover who wants him dead. Two of the 87th Precinct novels, *So Long as You Both Shall Live* and *Jigsaw*, were transformed into episodes of the *Columbo* television series.

17 *a fictionalised New York City*: In geographical terms, McBain rotated the map of NYC ninety degrees clockwise. Manhattan became Isola, the Bronx Riverhead, Staten Island Bethtown, and so on.

18 *McBain's work proved highly influential*: A television series, *87th Precinct*, ran for a single season in 1961–2. McBain believed that Steven Bochco's much more successful 1980s series *Hill Street Blues* owed much to his own work; Bochco followed up in the 1990s with *NYPD Blue*. The genre developed further in the twenty-first century, notably with *The Wire*, set in Baltimore. Its creator was David Simon, husband of the leading crime novelist Laura Lippman; a book of his had previously formed the basis of the successful series *Homicide: Life on the Street*.

19 *Elizabeth Linington*: She presents Mendoza, an independently wealthy cop married to a black woman, sympathetically, although her conservatism surfaces in her portrayal of gay characters and relationships. She also wrote as Lesley Egan, Egan O'Neill and Anne Blaisdell. The Blaisdell novel *Nightmare* was a thriller filmed as *Fanatic*, aka *Die! Die! My Darling!*, with a screenplay by Richard Matheson, who adapted several of Poe's stories for the screen.

20 *one of the first female specialists*: Others included Dorothy Uhnak, an ex-cop whose white detective Christie Opara experienced a change of both name and race in the 1970s TV series *Get Christie Love!*, and Katherine V. Forrest, creator of Kate Delafield, a lesbian detective in the LAPD, who first appeared in *Amateur City* in 1984.

21 *his non-genre novel about police life*: LeRoy Lad Panek argues that: 'Wambaugh wrote about things that no earlier writer dared to touch, he broke the connection of the cop story with the mystery novel, and focused on issues that would drive the police novel for the remainder of the century,'

22 *As Ellroy put it*: When introducing a reprint of *The Choirboys*.

23 *an early review*: Kirkus Reviews, 29 October 1975.

24 *'to dramatize . . .'*: See *Mystery Scene*'s 'At the Scene' newsletter, November 2010.

25 *The Blooding*: Wambaugh's approach, and his extensive experience of lawsuits arising from his non-fiction, are discussed by Sean Mitchell, 'The Crimes of Joseph Wambaugh', *LA Times*, 26 February 1989. Mitchell somehow gained the impression that Britain is 'a country where . . . true crime stories are considered unseemly'.

26 *Hieronymus Bosch, known as Harry*: A television series, *Bosch*, first aired in 2015.

27 *Connelly sought permission from Ellroy*: Apparently, the Demon Dog replied: 'Unfortunately, I don't have a franchise on murdered mothers.' (Larry Orenstein, 'The Reversal', *The Globe and Mail*, 8 October 2020).

28 *Connelly nods to the classic Californian gumshoe novel*: He cites Robert Altman's film of *The Long Goodbye* as a major influence on his desire to become a crime writer, and even lived in the Hollywood apartment occupied in the film by Elliott Gould as Philip Marlowe (Bruce Tierney, 'Michael Connelly', *Book Page*, June 2009).

29 *Mickey Haller*: Haller made his debut in *The Lincoln Lawyer*, a novel filmed in 2011 with Matthew McConaughey in the lead role.

30 *collaborates with another, the FBI criminal profiler Terrell 'Terry' McCaleb*: The collaboration occurs in *A Darkness More than Night*, which also features the newspaperman Jack McEvoy, who is the lead character in Connelly's early serial killer novel *The Poet*. In McCaleb's first appearance, *Blood Work* (filmed in 2002 by Clint Eastwood), he is recovering from a heart transplant.

FIFTY-FOUR

Long Shadows

Historical crime

On 28 April 1954, Pauline Parker decided to murder her mother. On that day she recorded in her diary: 'Anger against mother boiled up inside. Suddenly, a means of ridding myself of this obstacle occurred to me. If she were to die . . .'

Pauline lived with her family in Christchurch, New Zealand. She was afraid that her mother was determined to destroy her friendship with a girl called Juliet Hulme. Pauline was sixteen, Juliet fifteen, and Honorah Parker, Pauline's mother, thought the relationship was unhealthy. She consulted a doctor, who diagnosed a juvenile lesbian 'pash', nothing too serious, something the girls would grow out of.

The two girls came from different social backgrounds. Juliet was British-born, the daughter of a university rector. Pauline's mother ran their home as a boarding house, and her father managed a fish shop. The pair had been inseparable except for a three-month spell the previous year; after suffering years of poor health, Juliet had contracted TB, and been confined to a sanatorium.

The girls called themselves Gina and Deborah, and lived a rich life of fantasy, creating make-believe worlds, Volumnia and Borovnia, and writing books, plays, poetry, even an opera. They slept together, took nude photographs of each other, and dreamed of travelling to New York to sign a publishing deal, before heading for Hollywood, where their stories could be made into movies. They also shoplifted slippers and socks.

The crisis was precipitated by the collapse of Juliet's parents' marriage. Her father discovered that his wife was having an affair with their lodger, and announced he was leaving for South Africa, and taking Juliet with him. Pauline wanted to go with them, and persuaded herself that Honorah was the real threat to their chances of remaining together. When Pauline told Juliet that she wanted to kill Honorah, she noted in her diary that her friend was 'rather worried but does not disagree violently'.

Pauline's diary entry for 21 June read: 'Deborah rang and we decided to use a rock in a stocking rather than a sandbag. We discussed the moider fully. I feel very keyed up, as if I were planning a Surprise party . . . So next time I write in this diary Mother will be dead. How odd, yet how pleasing.'

Her excitement shone through the final words in her diary, which she headed *The Day of the Happy Event*: 'I am writing a little of this up on the morning before the death. I felt very excited and "the night before Christmas-ish" last night. I did not have pleasant dreams, though. I am about to rise.'

That afternoon, Honorah took the girls for tea in Victoria Park. Juliet placed a small pink stone on a secluded path, and Pauline pointed it out to her mother. Honorah bent down to pick it up, as the conspirators intended.

Murder isn't easy. The girls found it necessary to rain blows down upon the defenceless woman, making it impossible for them to maintain the pretence that her death was accidental. Once they confessed to the police, their lawyers were forced to argue that they were not guilty by reason of insanity, and that their homosexuality had caused them to suffer paranoid delusions. The prosecution case was that this was a case of 'coldly, callously planned murder committed by two highly intelligent and sane but precocious and dirty-minded little girls'. They were found guilty and sent to prison, since they were too young to be hanged.

Forty years later, an author of historical mysteries living in a remote seaside village in Scotland took a telephone call from her agent. Anne Perry had recently signed a million-dollar, eight-book contract with an American publisher. She was to tour twenty-three cities in the US to promote her next book, *Traitor's Gate* (1995), about the Victorian Scotland Yard man, Inspector Thomas Pitt. Perry's success hadn't come overnight. She'd spent years in a wide range of jobs, in the clerical, retail, fashion and insurance underwriting businesses, along with a spell as an airline flight attendant, while trying in vain to establish herself as an author.

A suggestion from her stepfather about the possible identity of Jack the Ripper caused her to become 'totally absorbed by what happens to people under pressure of investigation, how old relationships and trusts are eroded, and new ones formed'. The result was *The Cater Street Hangman*, which introduced Pitt in 1979. Eleven years later, she began a series about another Victorian detective, William Monk. He suffers from amnesia, and Perry's aim was 'to explore a different, darker character, and to raise questions about responsibility, particularly that of a person for acts he cannot remember'.

Her agent was puzzled. A journalist from New Zealand had been in touch regarding a new film starring Kate Winslet. Peter Jackson's *Heavenly Creatures* was based on an old case of matricide involving two teenage girls, and the reporter believed that one of them was Anne Perry. The agent wanted to squash the story before things got out of hand.

'I'm sorry, but you can't,' Perry said. 'Because it's true.'

After leaving prison, Juliet Hulme had changed her identity, and become Anne Perry. She'd succeeded in keeping her secret while building a new life and reputation. Now, at the height of her fame as a writer of murder mysteries set in the past, the truth about her own background had finally spilled out.

The two girls were released from prison after five and a half years, and given the chance of a fresh start under new names provided they never made contact with each other again. Pauline became Hilary Nathan, and moved to England. She found redemption in the Catholic faith, and ran a riding school in rural Kent. Anne Perry also turned to religion, and became a member of the Church of Latter-Day Saints. Both of them denied that their relationship had been sexual. Hilary Nathan has never spoken publicly about the crime.

Anne Perry had no choice. The case was sensational, and the movie well made and popular. She was a public figure, an author who needed to market her crime novels, but the media frenzy left her distraught: 'It's like having some disfigurement and being stripped naked and set up in the High Street for everybody to walk by and pay their penny and have a look. I would like to put my clothes on and go home, please, be like anybody else.'

Refusing to say a word about her involvement in the murder of Honorah Parker would not protect her from merciless public scrutiny. Yet, over the years, her comments about the case have attracted criticism, much of it glib, some of it cruel. Having guarded her privacy with such zeal for decades, she cannot sensibly be accused of seeking to cash in on her notoriety.

Perry has, it seems, coped by blocking details of the murder out of her mind. On her account, she feared that Pauline would kill herself if she didn't go along with the plan. Perry has also suggested that medication taken because of her poor health may have affected her mental outlook. But she has never denied that she deserved to be punished for her part in a horrific and senseless crime. Interviewed by Ian Rankin, she said: 'The redemption comes when you no longer wish to be that kind of person . . . until you feel that you have settled the debt, you cannot move on.'

The temptation to comb through Perry's novels in search of clues to her psychological make-up is hard to resist, but reading between the lines in this way is fraught with difficulty. There's no denying the anguish of a passage in *Bluegate Fields* (1984): 'everyone should have the right to a certain degree of privacy, a chance to forget or overcome. Crime must be paid for, but not all sins or mistakes need be made public and explained for everyone to examine or remember. And sometimes victims were punished doubly, once by the offence itself, and then a second and more enduring time when others heard of it, pored over it, and imagined every intimate detail.'

The popularity of Perry's stories reflects the remarkable popularity of historical crime fiction during the past half-century, but authors were mixing mystery with history long ago. Ann Radcliffe set *The*

Mysteries of Udolpho more than two centuries before her Gothic novel was published. Distance of time, just as much as the setting in southern France and northern Italy, heightened the story's exoticism.

The most notable early historical detective was introduced by Melville Davisson Post in 1911.[1] A God-fearing student of human nature, Uncle Abner set about doing justice in the backwoods of West Virginia in the years before the American Civil War, when there was no police force to maintain law and order. His casebook includes an 'impossible crime' story, 'The Doomdorf Mystery', and 'A Twilight Adventure', in which Abner prevents a lynching. In 'The Tenth Commandment' he articulates a key theme of crime fiction: 'The law is not always justice . . .'

During the Second World War, Agatha Christie transplanted a challenge-the-reader puzzle in the Golden Age manner to ancient Egypt in *Death Comes as the End* (1944). The experiment was characteristically daring, although the body count rises so rapidly that the least-likely-person solution emerges almost by process of elimination.[2]

John Dickson Carr believed that writing 'good history is the noblest work of man'. Early in his career, he published two books set in the seventeenth century. *Devil Kinsmere* (1934), which appeared under the pen-name of Roger Fairbairn, made little impression, but *The Murder of Sir Edmund Godfrey*[3] (1936) was a credible attempt to apply detective techniques to the examination of a real-life crime. In the post-war era, when out of humour with the contemporary world, Carr began to concentrate on the historical mystery.

In 1943, Lillian de la Torre[4] hit on the idea of creating a Holmes–Watson partnership out of Dr Samuel Johnson and James Boswell. Their first case, 'The Great Seal of England', was based on a puzzle concerning the loss of the Lord Chancellor's seal in 1784, and she continued to imagine 'episodes which recall old crimes and frauds, real personalities, places and situations for the nucleus of the plot' with *élan*.

The most widely acclaimed history-mystery of the 1950s[5] was Josephine Tey's *The Daughter of Time* (1951). Her detective, Alan Grant, confined to hospital, occupies himself by researching the fate of the Princes in the Tower. Tey had tackled the question of whether Richard III was guilty of murdering the boys in a play,

Dickon, which was neither published nor performed. Her novel influenced popular attitudes towards the king known as Crookback; Grant's theory gave the oxygen of publicity to the case made by Richard III's defenders, the Ricardians, who believe that his reputation deserves to be rehabilitated.

Not until the 1970s did a major series of historical detective novels appear. Peter Lovesey[6] led the charge, winning a prize of £1,000 for his first foray into the genre. *Wobble to Death* (1970) introduced Sergeant Cribb and Constable Thackeray, who appeared in seven further books, each featuring an aspect of Victorian entertainment, from long-distance races to music halls and spiritualism.

Like Lovesey, Ellis Peters[7] did not set out to write a series when she created her historical detective. She hoped to tease out 'a plot for a murder mystery from the true history of Shrewsbury Abbey in the twelfth century'. She decided that one of the monks should solve the crime, but that he must be 'a man of wide worldly experience and an inexhaustible fund of resigned tolerance for the human condition'. Thus was born Brother Cadfael, a Welsh-born former crusader who looks after the abbey's herb garden.

Peters was sixty-three when Cadfael made his first appearance, in *A Morbid Taste for Bones* (1977). She had been toiling away in the genre under assorted pen-names since the late 1930s, as well as writing mainstream fiction under her own name. One of her books about the amiably nondescript Inspector George Felse, *Death and the Joyful Woman* (1961), won an Edgar, but didn't lead to large sales. Under her real name, Edith Pargeter, she'd already published historical novels, but the first Cadfael novel made such a modest impression that her publishers didn't bother with a paperback edition. Despite limited encouragement, Peters enjoyed writing about Cadfael. The monk returned in *One Corpse Too Many* (1979), and the series built a loyal readership.

The novels benefited from a well-evoked setting on the border between England and Wales, and a strong sense of the community within the abbey. Cadfael's knowledge of poisonous herbs proved an asset in books such as *Monk's-Hood* (1980). Yet Peters' public profile remained stubbornly low until her fortunes were transformed by an Italian scholar of semiotics.

When her publisher jumped on Umberto Eco's bandwagon, gleefully proclaiming her books as being 'in the tradition of *The Name of the Rose*', Peters was infuriated. Seven of the Cadfael Chronicles[8] had appeared, she pointed out, before Eco's novel (set two centuries later) was translated into English. But Eco's success was the catalyst for her own belated breakthrough. *The Name of the Rose*[9] (1980) made monk-detectives sexy. Eco wasn't interested in writing conventional detective fiction, but he'd created a demand for mysteries set in and around medieval monasteries. Brother Cadfael's casebook satisfied the appetite of hungry readers.

The Name of the Rose pairs a naive Benedictine novice with a learned Franciscan, Brother William of Baskerville, whose name is a hat tip to Sherlock Holmes. Young Adso of Melk acts as William's Watson, and tells the story of his master's inquiries into a series of bizarre murders in a Benedictine community in 1327. The puzzle is cooked up with ingredients familiar from Golden Age mysteries, including a plan of the library, while the ironic, downbeat finale is reminiscent of Anthony Berkeley's accounts of Roger Sheringham's less glorious detective work.

Eco's concerns encompassed medieval history, philosophy, theology and the nature of literature. A mock-apologetic preface recounting the discovery of Adso's manuscript in 1968 seeks to explain the decision to publish an 'Italian version of an obscure, neo-Gothic French version of a seventeenth-century Latin edition of a work written in Latin by a German monk toward the end of the fourteenth century . . . Let us say it is an act of love.'

A long novel of this kind teeters on a precipice, constantly at risk of plunging into the abyss of pretentiousness. Ellis Peters thought it 'unkind and unfair to market a book from the full understanding and enjoyment of which a substantial part of the readership is excluded'. *The Name of the Rose* could hardly be more different from Dan Brown's popular blockbuster *The Da Vinci Code*[10] (2003), despite shared elements such as religion, history and conspiracy, but it became a publishing phenomenon,[11] with global sales exceeding fifty million.

*

The past is a foreign country; detectives do things differently there. They are denied the marvels of genetic fingerprinting, mobile-phone tracking, surveillance of social media, internet search engines, CCTV and ANPR. Yet, although contemporary investigators have all the devices they could possibly desire to pursue criminals, the key challenge for writers is how to sustain mystery and suspense for the length of a novel.

The disfigured and unrecognisable corpse, once a staple of Golden Age puzzles, can now be identified through DNA testing. A person's life story may be traced online. Imaginative novelists conjure up workarounds, although the cell phone that fails to work in the climactic scene and the all-too-easily-deduced security password have already become clichés. As technology becomes more elaborate, it's tempting to set one's stories in simpler times.

Ever since Ellis Peters and Umberto Eco excavated the Middle Ages, crime writers have mined the past; few periods in history now lack their own series detective. Among the most popular are Lindsey Davis's books set in the Roman Empire[12] during the reign of Vespasian. Marcus Didius Falco is a toga-clad forebear of Spade and Marlowe; a spin-off series features his adopted daughter Flavia Alba, a prototype of the female private eye.

History-mysteries take an infinite variety of forms. Charles Palliser's[13] *The Quincunx* (1989) is as formidable in bulk as it is in scale of ambition. On the surface a homage to Dickens, this is a novel with many secrets. Some were so well hidden that Palliser appended a lengthy afterword to later editions, explaining why, among other things, he felt that criticisms of 'coincidences' in the plot were unfair.

The circumstances surrounding the death of Robert Grove, fellow of New College, Oxford, at the time of the 'Enlightenment', are unreliably reported in Iain Pears'[14] seventeenth-century casebook mystery *An Instance of the Fingerpost* (1997). There are four contrasting viewpoints, with several characters, including Grove, the cryptographer John Wallis and the antiquary Anthony Wood taken from real life. Although the story follows a long and winding road, a sensational revelation awaits the patient traveller.

In-depth portrayal of historical detectives broadens our understanding of past lives. Charles Todd's[15] Ian Rutledge is a Scotland Yard man whose post-First World War investigations are complicated by his own experience of PTSD. The lawyer Matthew Shardlake in C. J. Sansom's series[16] struggles with kyphosis (curvature of the spine) as well as a melancholy temperament and loneliness in a series of novels set in Tudor England. Shardlake attracts mockery (from Henry VIII among others) and distaste in an age of superstition, making him a quintessential outsider with sympathy for the weak and vulnerable. Disability shapes not only his back, but his character.

Boris Akunin's[17] Erast Fandorin is a swashbuckling Holmes–Bond hybrid who romps around nineteenth-century imperial Russia. *Murder on the Leviathan* (1998), a shipboard mystery, nods to Christie as well as *The Moonstone*, but Akunin is more than merely a playful writer. He confronts Fandorin with moral ambiguities suggestive of those present in contemporary Russian society.

Authors of historical mysteries tend to specialise in books set in a favourite period of time. The outstanding exception is Andrew Taylor, whose diverse output includes the post-Second World War Lydmouth series, about a fictional town on the England–Wales border, and books set around the aftermath of the Great Fire of London and at the time of the American War of Independence.

The Roth Trilogy[18] comprises three interlocking yet self-contained novels, each employing the conventions of different types of crime fiction, each subtly modifying the others, showing characters and events from divergent perspectives. Taylor's starting points were a real-life case, Fred West's serial killing of young girls, and the belief that such crimes have a secret history that may stretch back for generations. This led him to tell the story through reverse chronology.[19]

The Four Last Things (1997) is a psychological thriller set in north London during the 1990s and concerns the abduction of the four-year-old daughter of a trainee woman priest. *The Judgement of Strangers* (1998), a village mystery narrated by a widowed and sexually frustrated parish priest, is in the Golden Age vein; the main characters are the family at the big house and those living at the vicarage. The book boasts a map, a fete, a teashop and a cat named Lord Peter, as well as a would-be Miss Marple. *The Office of the Dead* (2000), set in a cathedral close in 1958, is a spin on the 'woman in jeopardy' mystery.

The trilogy is constructed with conspicuous care, but all writers slip up from time to time. Taylor demonstrated how a thoughtful writer can turn a minor error to advantage. While planning the third book, he re-read the second, in which 'I had invented a slim volume of Victorian verse by a minor poet. It was called *The Tongues of Angels*. The title was mentioned four times in the text. To my horror I found that on two occasions it was referred to as *The Voice of Angels*, not *The Tongues*. I hadn't noticed the mistake . . . nor the proofreaders – nor the reviewers. In fact this gave me a major subplot for *The Office of the Dead*; the Victorian poet became much more important than I had planned. There are now two slim volumes . . . Almost identical in contents, but not quite . . .' Nor was that the end of his ingenuity: the trilogy was later supplemented by a self-contained story, 'The Long Sonata of the Dead', which offers a glimpse of the poet's continuing legacy.

History-mysteries offer readers entertaining education. Julian Rathbone argued[20] that they 'invariably betray and portray the time they were written in as much as or more than they accurately present the time in which they are set'. Gifted writers ensure that this represents not a shortcoming but added value. The best examples, like Taylor's *The Royal Secret*, set in Restoration England, are 'not mere pageants performed by puppets.[21] [The] characters feel like living people who face real problems in a strange yet instantly recognisable vanished world.' Literary innovators and stylists discover as many possibilities in historical crime fiction as in stories about the street-smart twenty-first century.

Notes

The main sources are Joanne Drayton's biography of Anne Perry, Ray B. Browne and Lawrence A. Kreiser Jr's *The Detective as Historian*, Michael Burgess and Jill H. Vassilakos's *Murder in Retrospect*, Barry Forshaw's *Historical Noir*, Margaret Lewis's biography of Ellis Peters, and Andrew Taylor's website. Ian Rankin's interview of Anne Perry was published on Youtube.

1 *The most notable early historical detective was introduced . . . in 1911*: In a story called 'The Broken Stirrup Leather', later retitled 'The Angel of the Lord'. As with subsequent Abner stories, it was narrated by Abner's nephew, Martin.

2 *process of elimination*: In *A Talent to Deceive*, Robert Barnard suggests that the novel illustrates 'how much the average Christie depends on trappings: clothes, furniture, the paraphernalia of bourgeois living'. In *Agatha Christie's Secret Notebooks*, John Curran explains that in addition to contemplating alternative culprits, she also toyed with the interesting idea of writing a present-day storyline to run in parallel to the events in Thebes in 2000 BC.

3 *The Murder of Sir Edmund Godfrey*: Carr's biographer, Douglas G. Greene, argued in an afterword to a 1989 reprint that nobody had suggested a more credible candidate for the murderer.

4 *Lillian de la Torre*: Her full name was Lillian de la Torre Bueno McCue. Her *Villainy Detected* was a collection of British crimes and criminals from 1660 to 1800.

5 *The most widely acclaimed history-mystery of the 1950s*: Colin Dexter's Gold Dagger-winning *The Wench is Dead* employs a similar premise; Inspector Morse, recovering in hospital from a bleeding ulcer, looks into a Victorian mystery based on the murder in 1839 of Christina Collins on the Trent and Mersey Canal at Rugeley.

6 *Peter Lovesey*: The Cribb novels were adapted for television. Lovesey wrote three light-hearted mysteries featuring a real-life character, Bertie, Prince of Wales, as an unlikely detective: *Bertie and the Seven Bodies* is an amusing riff on *And Then There Were None*. *The False Inspector Dew* reworks elements of the Crippen case with brio, and won a Gold Dagger.

7 *Ellis Peters*: Her early ventures into the genre included a thriller set in Cornwall, *The Victim Needs a Nurse*, as by John Redfern, and four books written under the pseudonym Julyon Carr. A novella, *The Assize of the Dying*, originally published under her real name, was filmed as *The Spaniard's Curse*.

8 *The Cadfael Chronicles*: The series was adapted for television with Derek Jacobi as Cadfael. Peters was awarded the Diamond Dagger, although Julian Symons complained: 'The medieval background seems to me cardboard . . . the dialogue no more than humdrum, the characters ploddingly dull.'

9 *The Name of the Rose*: Symons wasn't Eco-friendly: 'There is a touch of condescension in his approach which makes an addict bristle.' The book was filmed with Sean Connery as William. As Eco said, 'A book like this is a club sandwich . . . the movie is obliged to choose only the lettuce or the cheese, eliminating everything else – the theological side, the political side' (Stephen Moss, 'Umberto Eco: "People are Tired of Simple Things. They Want to be Challenged."', *Guardian*, 27 November 2011).

10 *Dan Brown's popular blockbuster The Da Vinci Code*: Eco joked in an interview with the *Paris Review* that Dan Brown was really a character from his novel *Foucault's Pendulum*: 'I invented him.' *The Da Vinci Code* earned massive sales worldwide, while sparking controversy about its accuracy in matters of history, geography, religion, art and architecture. Brown's stories have provoked jealousy, harsh criticism and a flurry of lawsuits alleging plagiarism. Dismissing one copyright infringement claim in the High Court, Sir Peter Smith embedded within his judgment a polyalphabetic cipher ('How

Judge's Secret Da Vinci Code was Cracked', Dan Trench, *Guardian*, 28 April 2006).

11 *a publishing phenomenon*: The success or failure of translated fiction is highly dependent on the skill of the translator, and Eco was expertly served by William Weaver, who used his earnings to build an extension on to his villa in Tuscany, which he called 'the Eco chamber'.

12 *Lindsey Davis's books set in the Roman Empire*: America's equivalent is Steven Saylor's series featuring Gordianus the Finder.

13 *Charles Palliser*: Palliser's infrequent but inventive books include *Betrayals*, a Russian doll of a narrative in which connections emerge between apparently distinct stories. The targets of his satire included Jeffrey Archer, while the TV cop show *Taggart* became *Biggert*.

14 *Iain Pears*: Since his early series featuring art historian Jonathan Argyll, Pears' writing has become ever more adventurous; *Arcadia* is a 'natively digital novel' designed to be read as an app.

15 *Charles Todd*: The Todd name conceals the mother and son partnership of Caroline and Charles Todd, Americans whose novels are set in England. Hamish MacLeod, a soldier whom Rutledge executed for cowardice, is a constant presence throughout the series.

16 *C. J. Sansom's series*: Sansom's *Winter in Madrid* is a spy story set in the aftermath of the Spanish Civil War. *Dominion* is a slice of alternative history in a Britain conquered by the Nazis.

17 *Boris Akunin*: This pen-name of Grigory Chkhartishvili (who was born in Georgia and spent most of his life in Russia) is itself a joke: B Akunin spells the surname of the Russian anarchist Mikhail Bakunin. In the twenty-first century, British Golden Age fiction has found devotees among students in Russia, although far fewer than in China.

18 *The Roth Trilogy*: Also known as *Requiem for an Angel* and televised as *Fallen Angel*.

19 *reverse chronology*: This method of storytelling can dazzle, but only if the writers' craftsmanship matches their courage. The possibilities are shown by Iain Pears' novel *Stone's Fall,* Jeffery Deaver's *The October List* and Ragnar Jónasson's Hulda Trilogy as well as by Simon Brett's play *Silhouette*, Christopher Nolan's film *Memento*, Harry and Jack Williams' TV series *Rellik*, and Steve Pemberton and Reece Shearsmith's 'Once Removed', a witty and brilliantly economical episode of *Inside No. 9*.

20 *Julian Rathbone argued*: In an introduction to Maxim Jakubowski's *Past Poisons: An Ellis Peters Memorial Anthology of Historic Crime*. Recurring characters in Rathbone's fiction include Jan Argand, a cop in fictional (but Holland-like) Brabt, and Chris Shovelin, probably the genre's only private eye from Bournemouth.

21 *not mere pageants performed by puppets*: The quotation comes from Mark Sanderson's *Times Crime Club* newsletter of 11 May 2021.

FIFTY-FIVE

A Taste for Death

P. D. James and the truth about human character and experience

Phyllis Dorothy White started her first novel in the mid-1950s. She planned the story on the Central Line while travelling to her job as an administrator at a hospital board, and wrote it up by hand early each morning before catching the Tube. This was a form of escapism, given that her husband was in and out of psychiatric hospital.

All her life, she had wanted to become a published author, but life had got in the way. Her parents' marriage was unhappy and her mother suffered from mental illness. Phyllis had 'a childhood of some apprehension,[1] living in a sense with fear, that things might erupt, that things might go wrong'. The eldest of three siblings, she was forced to grow up prematurely. She left school at sixteen and spent eighteen miserable months working in a tax office before meeting her future husband, Connor. They married in 1941, five days after she came of age, and had two children.

Connor White became a doctor, but when he returned after serving in the war with the Royal Army Medical Corps, his mental health was irreparably damaged and Phyllis became the breadwinner. Reluctant to talk about her marriage in detail, she once said: 'One suffers with the patient and for oneself. Another human being who was once a beloved companion can become not only a stranger, but occasionally a malevolent stranger.'

Eventually, her book was finished and typed. She met the actor Miles Malleson, and he recommended his agent, Elaine Greene, who happened to commiserate with a director of Faber about the death of their premier detective writer, Cyril Hare. He said they would need to find a successor to Hare, prompting Greene to send him Phyllis's manuscript. He promptly accepted it.

Phyllis said, nearly forty years later, that receiving the news 'was one of the most exciting moments of my life'. Connor was in hospital, and her daughters were away, so there was nobody to share her excitement, but 'I knew that evening, as I pranced up and down the hall, that people do literally jump for joy.'

It never occurred to her to write other than under her maiden name, and so she chose to publish *Cover Her Face* as P. D. James, which she thought 'was enigmatic and would look best on the book spine'. Faber did not publish the novel until 1962, by which time she was forty-two. Francis Iles described her debut as 'one of those extraordinary first novels which seem to step straight into the sophisticated preserves of the experienced writer, yet retain the newcomer's freshness of approach'.

Connor died at home two years later. His widow, a private person, never discussed the circumstances of his death. She told one journalist:[2] 'He died as a result of his mental illness . . . I'm sure clinical depression is a physical illness. A descent into hell.' She also said: 'I have never found, or indeed looked for, anyone else with whom I have wanted to spend the rest of my life. I think of Connor with love and grief for all he has missed.'

And he missed a great deal. Having experienced more than her share of personal torment as a result of the illnesses of her mother and husband, she proceeded to enjoy a life of extraordinary achievement. In an obituary,[3] the Bishop of Worcester wrote: 'The term "national treasure" is over-used, but, if anyone deserved it, it was surely the novelist P. D. James, Baroness James of Holland Park, who died on Thursday of last week, aged 94, after a long and creative life. She was much loved and admired.'

*

Cover Her Face (1962), an English village mystery, introduced DCI Adam Dalgliesh of Scotland Yard.[4] Handsome, cerebral and a published poet, he is a widower who lost his wife in childbirth. He rose to the rank of Commander, a man trusted to deal with cases of the utmost sensitivity. He finds it impossible to commit to another long-term relationship, and even his relationship with James' second-string detective, Cordelia Gray, does not last. There is much of his creator in Dalgliesh, not least in his blend of personal charm, distaste for sentimentality and natural reserve. Like her, he has 'carefully insulated himself against pain' since the death of his spouse.

James continued to write detective novels in the classic vein, favouring closed communities of suspects riven by tension. Her books explore a rich variety of skilfully anatomized settings: a village, a psychiatric hospital, a forensic-science laboratory, a barristers' chambers, an inaccessible island, a cosmetic-surgery clinic, and so on. The novels usually 'had their beginnings in a part of England and in a moment of intense response to its spirit and atmosphere . . . It was one evening on Dunwich beach that . . . gave me the idea for my third book. I pictured a small dinghy drifting oarless on the tide and bearing one hapless voyager, a neatly dressed corpse with his hands severed at the wrists.'[5] The result was *Unnatural Causes* (1967).

The genesis of *Devices and Desires* (1989) was another visit to the Suffolk coast. Closing her eyes, she heard 'nothing but the tinny rattle of the shingle drawn back by the waves and the low hissing of the wind . . . I could have been standing on the self-same spot a thousand years ago, hearing the same sounds, looking out over the same sea. And then I opened my eyes and, looking south, saw the silent and stark outline of Sizewell nuclear power station . . . immediately I knew with an almost physical surge of excitement that I had a novel.'

For all her love of the traditional, James strove to ensure that her writing remained in touch with contemporary life. The bleakness of her work is profoundly different in mood and style from typical Golden Age fiction. Her memory of attending a lecture as a young Red Cross nurse during the war, in which a volunteer was fed solution through a tube in her nose, inspired the horrific murder in *Shroud for a Nightingale* (1971). Milk in a drip fed into a nurse's mouth is replaced by carbolic acid, burning away the victim's stomach.

James worked as a civil servant until she was almost sixty. Her life peerage was awarded for public service rather than her fiction; among other distinctions, she was a governor of the BBC, a magistrate, a member of the Arts Council and a lay patron of the Prayer Book Society.

A devout and thoughtful Anglican, she once said in a sermon:[6] 'there is no forbidden knowledge. We do not find things out behind God's back.' Her abiding interest in religion surfaced in a variety of ways in her novels. The title of *Devices and Desires* comes from the Book of Common Prayer, while two corpses are discovered in a welter of blood in a dingy church vestry in *A Taste for Death* (1986). *Death in Holy Orders* (2001) is set in an Anglo-Catholic theological college in East Anglia.

James didn't believe in writing too much or too fast, and was much less prolific than her friend Ruth Rendell.[7] Dalgliesh appears in a mere sixteen novels, including the two books where Cordelia Gray takes centre stage, over the course of almost half a century. His last outing came in *The Private Patient* (2008). Given the circumstances of her recruitment by Faber, with whom she remained throughout her career, it seemed fitting that James should borrow, with due acknowledgement, a plot device from Cyril Hare's elegiac final novel, *He Should Have Died Hereafter*, aka *Untimely Death* (1958).

James' published work ranged widely. Not content with updating the classic detective novel and creating one of the first female private investigators, she wrote a dystopian science fiction novel,[8] a crime fiction sequel to *Pride and Prejudice*[9] and a novel of psychological suspense. In *Innocent Blood* (1980), Philippa Palfrey, who is adopted, sets out to discover the truth about her birth parents, but after setting up home with her mother discovers that both their lives are in jeopardy.

James's fascination with real-life murder cases surfaced in *The Murder Room* (2003), in which a present-day killer mimics famous crimes, such as the 'Blazing Car' murder committed by A. A.

Rouse, which are the subjects of exhibits in the Dupayne Museum. While working in the Police Department of the Home Office, she co-wrote with a colleague, Tom Critchley, *The Maul and the Pear Tree* (1971), an account of the Ratcliffe Highway Murders of 1811. She was inspired by the atmospheric scene of the crimes in Wapping and the sheer incompetence of the investigation, which resulted in the savage treatment of the corpse of the presumed culprit, 'an act of public vengeance unique in the history of English criminal law'.

Towards the end of her life, she reinvestigated the Wallace murder case, which had previously intrigued Sayers and Raymond Chandler: 'Suddenly . . . a solution to the murder came into my mind with the strength of an absolute conviction.' In a magazine article, she claimed that Wallace did kill his wife.[10] James presented her arguments with the skill one might expect from a woman who regretted having been denied the chance to practise as a barrister. But one person's absolute conviction is another's speculation, and the case against Wallace remains threadbare. James' conclusion was all the more surprising given that she had pronounced, fourteen years earlier, that 'Wallace was innocent'.

She expressed that view in *Time to Be in Earnest: A Fragment of Autobiography* (1999), a discursive memoir focusing on twelve months in her life and published partly in self-defence, to fend off would-be biographers. The troubles she'd experienced, coupled with the strength of her personal convictions, gave her a formidable resilience. One 'malicious and scathing' reviewer was dismissed as 'not someone I would worry about'.

The critical acclaim she'd received enabled her to be forthright about the motives that sometimes lurk behind critical negativity:[11] 'There are, of course, some reviewers who use reviewing to compensate for professional, creative or sexual failure and others who criticise the author not for the book written, but for the one they think he should have written. There are also those who are reviewing not the book but the writer, and who strongly dislike what they think he stands for, his class, his sex, or, most frequently of all, his politics . . . it is stupid for any writer to take the slightest notice of them.'

*

Shortly before her ninetieth birthday, James elaborated on her views about the genre in *Talking about Detective Fiction* (2009). Like Sayers, she was a woman of strong opinions, and not afraid to express them. She believed that crime writers could and should aim high. Although she acknowledged the historical importance of *Caleb Williams*, she was unimpressed by Godwin's 'propaganda on behalf of the poor and exploited', because it was unsubtle and didactic.

Chesterton, she argued, was right to see that the detective story 'could be a vehicle for exploring and exposing the condition of society, and for saying something true about human nature' and she shared his view that 'the only thrill, even of a common thriller, is concerned somehow with the conscience and the soul.'

She praised Chandler's mastery of first-person narrative, but was sceptical about his proclaimed desire 'to give murder back to the people who committed it . . . Chandler's lone romantic hero striding down the mean streets . . . is in his way as much a figure of fantasy as is Lord Peter Wimsey, Roderick Alleyn or Albert Campion. Women too, in the American hard-boiled novel seem often devoid of reality.'

The way a privileged generation of contemporary male writers portrayed a nihilistic and bloody world that they had never personally experienced impressed her even less: 'Perhaps it is to the women we must look for psychological subtlety and the exploration of moral choice, which for me are at the heart of even the most grittily realistic of crime fiction.'

Like every commentator, however, she had blind spots, and these included Agatha Christie. Her claim that Christie 'wasn't an innovative writer and had no interest in exploring the possibilities of the genre' is uncharacteristically superficial. She wasn't alone in being deceived by Christie's accessible storytelling and straightforward prose. As Alex Michaelides[12] put it, Christie makes readers think that they are 'more intelligent than she is. It's a game she plays with you all the time.'

Sayers was a major influence on James' writing. Although she recognised her predecessor's faults, she argued that Sayers had a potent influence on later generations of crime novelists who aimed for greater authenticity, highlighting the passage in *Have His*

Carcase (1932) where Harriet Vane encounters an all-but-decapitated corpse.

'Murder, the contaminating and unique crime, is messy, horrifying and tragic,' James said, 'and the modern reader of crime fiction is not spared these realities.' She made two predictions. First, that the detective story will become ever more firmly 'rooted in the reality and the uncertainties of the twenty-first century'. Second, that crime stories will continue to supply readers with 'that central certainty that even the most intractable problems will in the end be subject to reason'.

James said she'd been 'born with this sense of the extraordinary fragility of life'. Although she cherished her privacy, she acknowledged that, while mystery writers may strive to conceal their essential natures in their work, ultimately the more deeply felt books reveal the 'topography of the writer's mind'.

'More wisdom is contained in the best crime fiction than in philosophy', said Ludwig Wittgenstein, while Cyril Connolly once predicted that 'in a hundred years our thrillers will have become text-books . . . the most authentic chronicles of how we lived.'

Thoughtful critics[13] have nevertheless wondered whether crime novelists might one day run out of fresh ideas. More than ninety years ago, Sayers said: 'There certainly does seem a possibility that the detective-story will some time come to an end, simply because the public will have learnt all the tricks.' Inevitably themes, character types and storylines recur. Often, this is because readers and publishers know what they like and demand more of the same.

But the multiplicity of voices now being heard ensures that the life of crime continues to flourish. Recent years have seen fresh and thought-provoking developments as well as the refashioning of familiar tropes for the benefit of a twenty-first century readership. Advances in technology offer opportunities for fresh narrative forms, but what endures is the eternal appeal of telling a story. Around the world, imaginative writers continue to confound expectations, to stretch their talents and to experiment. The long-term future of this branch of literature is as unpredictable and exciting as the finest crime stories.

The American poet, feminist activist and commentator Nadya

Aisenberg[14] argued that 'the crime novel . . . describes the land-scape of our darkest fears' and that 'identity is the central theme of the detective novel'. These are significant and serious subjects, and although crime fiction offers plentiful entertainment, the defeatist view that this is incompatible with literature of the highest quality seems not only unattractive but inherently flawed.

Different writers express their central preoccupations in diverse ways, but Sayers spoke for many of them: 'I believe the future to be with those writers who can contrive to strike the note of sincerity and to persuade us that violence really hurts.'

For Ian Rankin, 'crime fiction provides both a salutary warning and the catharsis common to all good drama . . . in the end, haven't we sentient creatures always been obsessed by death? . . . Crime fiction gives us a way of exploring some of the implications, while still managing to have fun in the process.'

Writers in the genre are equally concerned with the mysteries of life. Sometimes their work tells us about their own characters and experiences. Phyllis James believed that, over the years, a mystery writer's 'private emotional landscape' is revealed by their body of work – their personal life of crime.

Ken Millar developed this point in *Self-Portrait*: 'We writers, as we work our way deeper into our craft, learn to drop more and more personal clues. Like burglars who wish secretly to be caught, we leave our fingerprints on the broken locks, our voiceprints in the bugged rooms, our footprints in the wet concrete and the blowing sand.'

Today, Frances Fyfield aims to 'write about good people as well as bad . . . and always allow for the possibility of redemption . . . There are no rules. The only moral compass is honesty, writing to the best of your ability.' James Runcie[15] suggests that 'we write, and we read, not just to be entertained, but in order to work out who we are and how we might live a better and more meaningful existence on this frail earth.'

The last word goes to Reginald Hill. His prime concern wasn't simply the question of whodunit or howdunit, but 'that still greater and more complicated puzzle of what makes men and women tick'. He said the quest for the detective, the reader and the author was to reveal the truth: 'truth about human character and experience. That's the ultimate goal, isn't it?'

Notes

The main sources are P. D. James' *Time to Be in Earnest* and *Talking about Detective Fiction*, Rosemary Herbert's interviews with James and Hill in *The Fatal Art of Entertainment*, Nadya Aisenberg's *A Common Spring: Crime Novel and Classic*, and my *Howdunit* and *Taking Detective Stories Seriously*.

1   *a childhood of some apprehension*: Emma Brockes, 'Murder, She Wrote', *Guardian*, 3 March 2001. Brockes quotes Frances Fyfield on James: 'She is like the Dickens or the Trollope of the genre . . . She is the weight, the ballast, and she has dragged detective fiction kicking and screaming into the 21st century.'

2   *She told one journalist*: Nigel Farndale, in 2010, reprinted in *Daily Telegraph*, 27 November 2014.

3   *In an obituary*: *Church Times*, 5 December 2014.

4   *Adam Dalgliesh of Scotland Yard*: Dalgliesh was played on television by Roy Marsden and later Martin Shaw and Bertie Carvel.

5   *'had their beginnings . . .'*: 'Is There Arsenic Still for Tea?' in *Anglian Blood*, ed. Robert Church and Martin Edwards.

6   *she once said in sermon*: Preached at Temple Church on 1 October 2006. I am grateful to Frances Fyfield for supplying me with the text.

7   *her friend Ruth Rendell*: Rendell said: 'We were both utterly opposed to each other politically: she was . . . very much a committed Conservative, whereas I'm a socialist . . . Once we were in for a vote and crossed paths going to the two division lobbies, she to the 'content' lobby and I to the 'not content' – and we kissed in the chamber, which caused some concern and amazement' (*Guardian*, 27 November 2014). A few weeks after paying tribute to James' kindness and literary gifts, Rendell herself suffered a debilitating stroke that led to her own death.

8   *a dystopian science fiction novel*: *The Children of Men*, filmed in 2006, concerned the consequences of mass male infertility.

9   *a crime fiction sequel to Pride and Prejudice*: *Death Comes to Pemberley*, James's last book, was televised in 2013.

10 *she claimed that Wallace did kill his wife*: David Harrison, 'P. D. James Unmasks the Perfect Killer', *The Sunday Times*, 27 October 2013, discussed her views to coincide with her article appearing in *The Sunday Times Magazine*.

11 *critical negativity*: Doubtless she was unimpressed by a review of *A Certain Justice* by Geoffrey Robertson (a QC), which blustered: 'Its psychopaths are more sympathetic than its barristers, consumed by mean-minded rivalry and obsessive selfishness. These characters are too unbelievably horrid . . .' (*Guardian*, 5 October 1997).

12 *Alex Michaelides*: The quotation comes from an interview on the Goodreads website. Michaelides, whose screenplays include *The Devil You Know*, has said that his psychological thriller *The Silent Patient* was inspired by Christie's *Five Little Pigs*.

13 *Thoughtful critics*: The Sayers quotation comes from her introduction to her first omnibus of detective stories. In the *TLS* on 2 May 1942, Maurice Willson Disher fretted that: 'In three weeks three Judges of the High Court have had murder to upset their private lives in the detective stories of Mr. Cyril Hare, Mr. Phillips Oppenheim and now Mr. Dickson Carr. If these resemblances, which keep recurring in fiction, cannot be dismissed as the sport of chance, then some ominous rumblings against law and order may be signified by this disrespectful spirit.' Comparable concerns persist to this day. Mark Sanderson, himself an occasional crime novelist, said in *The Times Crime Club* newsletter on 6 April 2021: 'After pointing out the co-incidence of two new novels set in ballet land – *Watch Her Fall* by Erin Kelly and *The Turnout* by Megan Abbott – I've noticed two people have written a novel called *The Therapist*: BA Paris (April 15) and Helene Flood (July 8). Last month, Maxine Mei-Fung Chung (*The Eighth Girl*) and Catriona Ward (*The Last House on Needless Street*) explored dissociative identity disorder. Both Fiona Cummins's *When I Was Ten* and Carole Johnstone's *Mirrorland* feature twin sisters with dark secrets and are published on the same day: April 15. *Facets of Death* by Michael Stanley and *The Wild Girls* by Phoebe Morgan are both set in Botswana and published this month. Finally, in June, *Falling* by TJ Newman and *Hostage* by Clare Mackintosh take place on board flights to New York and Sydney. But what does such synchronicity say about our favourite genre? Too many books and too little originality? Or are the authors merely giving us what they think we want?'

14 *Nadya Aisenberg*: Aisenberg's thought-provoking book explores, among other things, the connections between detective fiction and myths and fairy tales.

15 *James Runcie*: the son of a former Archbishop of Canterbury, Runcie created the sleuthing vicar Sidney Chambers whose exploits are recorded in *The Grantchester Mysterie*s and adapted for television as *Grantchester*.

Select Bibliography

Thousands of books and essays, as well as magazines and journals, such as *The Armchair Detective*, *Clues*, *Mystery Scene* and *CADS* (and its supplements), discuss crime fiction and its exponents. A wealth of information swirls on the internet, for instance on the CrimeReads site, and innumerable blogs, websites and social media pages. Readers interested in exploring further may be best advised simply to see where their surfing takes them. For those preferring a more traditional approach, this list of titles – lengthy yet still inevitably selective – offers a starting point, a collection of clues (and possibly one or two red herrings) to encourage further detective work.

Ackroyd, Peter, *Wilkie Collins* (2012)
Adams, Donald, *The Mystery & Detection Annual 1972* (1973)
Adams, Donald, *The Mystery & Detection Annual 1973* (1974)
Adey, Robert, *Locked Room Murders* (1979, rev. ed. 1991, rev. ed. and supplement by Skupin, Brian, 2018, 2019)
Aisenberg, Nadya, *A Common Spring: Crime Novel and Classic* (1979)
Albert, Walter, *Detective and Mystery Fiction: An International Bibliography of Secondary Sources* (1985)
Alder, Bill, *Maigret, Simenon, and France* (2013)
Aldridge, Mark, *Agatha Christie on Screen* (2016)
Aldridge, Mark, *Agatha Christie's Poirot* (2020)

Allan, Janice, Gulddal, Jesper, King, Stewart; and Pepper, Andrew, eds., *The Routledge Companion to Crime Fiction* (2020)

Allen, Dick, and David Chatto, eds, *Detective Fiction: Crime and Compromise* (1974)

Ashley, Bob, *The Study of Popular Fiction: A Source Book* (1989)

Ashley, Mike, *The Mammoth Encyclopedia of Crime Fiction* (2002)

Atkins, John, *The British Spy Novel* (1984)

Auden, W. H., *The Dyer's Hand and Other Essays* (1962)

Bailey, Frankie Y., *Out of the Woodpile: Black Characters in Crime and Detective Fiction* (1991)

Baird, Newton, *A Key to Fredric Brown's Wonderland* (1981)

Baker, Robert A., and Nietzel, Michael T., *Private Eyes: 101 Knights* (1985)

Bakerman, Jane S., ed., *And Then There Were Nine . . .: More Women of Mystery* (1985)

Baldick, Chris, ed., *The Oxford Book of Gothic Tales* (1992)

Ball, John, ed., *The Mystery Story* (1976)

Bargainnier, Earl, ed., *Comic Crime* (1987)

Bargainnier, Earl. F., ed., *10 Women of Mystery* (1981)

Bargainnier, Earl. F., ed., *Twelve Englishmen of Mystery* (1984)

Bargainnier, Earl F., and Dove, George N., *Cops and Constables: American and British Fictional Policemen* (1986)

Barnard, Robert, *A Talent to Deceive: An Appreciation of Agatha Christie* (1980)

Barnes, Melvyn, *Francis Durbridge: A Centenary Appreciation* (2015)

Barnes, Melvyn, *Francis Durbridge: The Complete Guide* (2018)

Barnes, Melvyn, *Murder in Print: A Guide to Two Centuries of Crime Fiction* (1986)

Barzun, Jacques, and Taylor, Wendell Hertig, *A Book of Prefaces* (1978)

Barzun, Jacques, and Taylor, Wendell Hertig, *A Catalogue of Crime* (1971, rev. ed. 1989)

Bayard, Pierre, *Who Killed Roger Ackroyd? The Murderer Who Eluded Hercule Poirot and Deceived Agatha Christie* (1998)

Bell, Ian, and Graham, Daldry, eds., *Watching the Detectives: Essays on Crime Fiction* (1990)

Benstock, Bernard, ed., *Art in Crime Writing* (1983)

Benstock, Bernard, and Staley, Thomas F., eds., *British Mystery Writers* (3 volumes, 1988, 1989)

Bentley, E. C., *Those Days* (1940)

Bentley, Nicolas, *A Version of the Truth* (1960)

Bernthal, J. C., *Queering Agatha Christie* (2016)

Bertens, Hans, and D'haen, Theo, *Contemporary American Crime Fiction* (2001)

Binyon, T. J., *Murder Will Out* (1991)

Bleiler, Richard J., *Reference and Research Guide to Mystery and Detective Fiction* (1999, rev. ed. 2004)

Bloom, Clive, ed., *Twentieth-Century Suspense: The Thriller Comes of Age* (1990)

Boileau-Narcejac, *Le Roman Policier* (1975)

Bordwell, David, *Reinventing Hollywood: How 1940s Filmmakers Changed Movie Storytelling* (2017)

Borowitz, Albert, *Blood and Ink: An International Guide to Fact-Based Crime Literature* (2002)

Boström, Mattias, *From Holmes to Sherlock* (2013)

Boucher, Anthony, *Multiplying Villainies: Selected Mystery Criticism, 1942–1968* (1973)

Bourgeau, Art, *The Mystery Lover's Companion* (1986)

Brabazon, James, *Dorothy L. Sayers: A Biography* (1981)

Bradley, Geoff, *CADS*

Breen, Ian, and Greenberg, Martin Harry, eds., *Murder Off the Rack: Critical Studies of Ten Paperback Masters* (1989)

Breen, Jon L., *Novel Verdicts: A Guide to Courtroom Fiction* (1984)

Breen, Jon L., *A Shot Rang Out: Selected Mystery Criticism* (2008)

Breen, Jon L., *What about Murder? A Guide to Books about Mystery and Detective Fiction* (1981; supplementary edition 1995; subsequently supplemented by reviews in *Mystery Scene* magazine)

Browne, Ray B., *Murder on the Reservation* (2004)

Browne, Ray B., *The Spirit of Australia: The Crime Fiction of Arthur W. Upfield* (1988)

Browne, Ray B., and Kreiser, Lawrence A., Jr, *The Detective as Historian* (2000)

Bruccoli, Matthew J., and Layman, Richard, eds., *Hardboiled Mystery Writers: A Literary Reference* (1989)

Burgess, Michael, and Vassilakos, Jill H., *Murder in Retrospect: A Selective Guide to Historical Mystery Fiction* (2005)

Butler, William Vivian, *The Durable Desperadoes: A Critical Study of Some Enduring Heroes* (1973)

Cade, Jared, *Agatha Christie and the Eleven Missing Days* (1998)

Carlson, Marvin, *Deathtraps: The Postmodern Comedy Thriller* (1993)

Carnell, Jennifer, *The Literary Lives of M. E. Braddon* (2000)

Carr, John C., *The Craft of Crime: Conversations with Crime Writers* (1983)

Carr, John Dickson, *The Life of Sir Arthur Conan Doyle* (1949)

Caspary, Vera, *The Secrets of Grown-Ups: An Autobiography* (1979)

Cassiday, Bruce, ed., *Roots of Detection: The Art of Deduction before Sherlock Holmes* (1983)

Cassuto, Leonard, *Hard-Boiled Sentimentality: The Secret History of American Crime Stories* (2009)

Cawelti, John G., *Adventure, Mystery, and Romance: Formula Stories as Art and Popular Culture* (1976)

Chapman, David Ian, *If You Can Walk with Kings: A View of William Le Queux* (2016)

Chapman, David Ian, *R. Austin Freeman: A Bibliography* (2000)

Christie, Agatha, *An Autobiography* (1977)

Clark, Neil, *Stranger than Fiction: The Life of Edgar Wallace, the Man Who Created King Kong* (2014)

Clarke, Clare, *Late Victorian Crime Fiction in the Shadows of Sherlock* (2014)

Clarke, William M., *The Secret Life of Wilkie Collins* (1988)

Cole, Dame Margaret, *The Life of G. D. H. Cole* (1971)

Colenbrander, Joanna, *A Portrait of Fryn: A Biography of F. Tennyson Jesse* (1984)

Collis, Rose, *A Trouser-Wearing Character: The Life and Times of Nancy Spain* (1997)

Conan Doyle, Sir Arthur, *Memories and Adventures* (1924)

Conquest, John, *Trouble is My Business: Private Eyes in Fiction, Film and Television, 1927–1988* (1990)

Connolly, John, and Burke, Declan, eds., *Books to Die For* (2012)

Contento, William G., and Greenberg, Martin H., *Index to Crime and Mystery Anthologies* (1991; updated by CD-ROM and online)

Cooper, John, and Pike, B. A., *Artists in Crime* (1995)

Cooper, John, and Pike, B. A., *Detective Fiction: The Collector's Guide* (1988, rev. ed. 1994)

Cooper-Clark, Diana, *Designs of Darkness: Interviews with Detective Novelists* (1983)

Craig, Patricia, ed., *Julian Symons at 80: A Tribute* (1992)

Craig, Patricia, and Cadogan, Mary, *The Lady Investigates: Women Detectives and Spies in Fiction* (1981)

Curran, John, *Agatha Christie's Murder in the Making: Stories and Secrets from Her Archive* (2011)

Curran, John, *Agatha Christie's Secret Notebooks: Fifty Years of Mysteries in the Making* (2009)

Curran, John, *The Hooded Gunman: An Illustrated History of Collins Crime Club* (2019)

Dale, Alzina Stone, ed., *Dorothy L. Sayers: The Centenary Celebration* (1993)

Day-Lewis, Sean, *C. Day-Lewis: An English Literary Life* (1980)

Dean, Christopher, ed., *Encounters with Lord Peter* (1991)

DeAndrea, William L, *Encyclopedia Mysteriosa* (1994)

Delamater, Jerome H., and Prigozy, Ruth, eds., *Theory and Practice of Classic Detective Fiction* (1997)

Dibdin, Michael, ed., *The Picador Book of Crime Writing* (1993)

Dirda, Michael, *On Conan Doyle* (2012)

Docherty, Brian, ed., *American Crime Fiction: Studies in the Genre* (1988)

Donaldson, Norman, *In Search of Dr Thorndyke* (1971, rev. ed. 1998)

Dove, George N., *The Police Procedural* (1982)

Dove, George N., *The Reader and the Detective Story* (1997)

Drayton, Joanne, *Ngaio Marsh: Her Life in Crime* (2008)

Drayton, Joanne, *The Search for Anne Perry* (2012)

Drummond, Maldwin, *The Riddle* (1985)

Duncan, Paul, ed., *The Third Degree: Crime Writers in Conversation* (1997)

Earwaker, Julian, and Becker, Kathleen, *Scene of the Crime: A Guide to the Landscapes of British Detective Fiction* (2002)

Eco, Umberto, *The Role of the Reader: Explorations in the Semiotics of Texts* (1979)

Edwards, Martin, *The Golden Age of Murder* (2015)

Edwards, Martin, ed., *Howdunit: A Masterclass in Crime Writing by Members of the Detection Club* (2020)

Edwards, Martin, *The Story of Classic Crime in 100 Books* (2017)

Edwards, Martin, ed., *Taking Detective Stories Seriously: The Detective Fiction Reviews of Dorothy L. Sayers* (2016)

Emrys, A. B., *Wilkie Collins, Vera Caspary and the Evolution of the Casebook Novel* (2011)

Erzinçlioğlu, Zakaria, *Maggots, Murder, and Men: Memories and Reflections of a Forensic Entomologist* (2002)

Evans, Curtis, ed., *Clues and Corpses: The Detective Fiction and Mystery Criticism of Todd Downing* (2013)

Evans, Curtis, ed., *Murder in the Closet* (2017)

Evans, Curtis, *Masters of the 'Humdrum' Mystery: Cecil John Charles Street, Freeman Wills Crofts, Alfred Walter Stewart and the British Detective Novel, 1921–1961* (2012)

Evans, Curtis, ed., *Mysteries Unlocked: Essays in Honor of Douglas G. Greene* (2014)

Evans, Curtis, *The Spectrum of English Murder: The Detective Fiction of Henry Lancelot Aubrey-Fletcher and G. D. H. and Margaret Cole* (2015)

Ffinch, Michael, *G. K. Chesterton: A Biography* (1986)

Flügge, Anna Maria, *James Ellroy and the Novel of Obsession* (2010)

Forshaw, Barry, *Brit Noir* (2016)

Forshaw, Barry, *British Crime Film* (2012)

Forshaw, Barry, *British Crime Writing: An Encyclopaedia* (2 volumes, 2009)

Forshaw, Barry, *Crime Fiction: A Reader's Guide* (2019)

Forshaw, Barry, *Death in a Cold Climate* (2012)

Forshaw, Barry, *Euro Noir* (2014)

Forshaw, Barry, *Historical Noir* (2018)

Forshaw, Barry, *The Man Who Left Too Soon: The Biography of Stieg Larsson* (2010)

Forshaw, Barry, *Nordic Noir* (2013)

Fowler, Christopher, *The Book of Forgotten Authors* (2017)

Freeling, Nicolas, *Criminal Convictions* (1994)

French, Jack, *Private Eyelashes: Radio's Lady Detectives* (2004)

French, Sean, *Patrick Hamilton: A Life* (1993)

Gardiner, Dorothy, and Sorley Walker, Kathrine, eds., *Raymond Chandler Speaking* (1962)

Gasson, Andrew, *Wilkie Collins: An Illustrated Guide* (1998)

Geherin, David, *The American Private Eye: The Image in Fiction* (1985)

Geherin, David, *John D. MacDonald* (1982)

Geherin, David, *Scene of the Crime: The Importance of Place in Crime and Mystery Fiction* (2008)

Geherin, David, *Small Towns in Recent American Crime Fiction* (2015)

Gertzman, Jay A., *Pulp according to David Goodis* (2018)

Gielgud, Val, *Years in a Mirror* (1965)

Gielgud, Val, *Years of the Locust* (1947)

Gilbert, Michael, ed., *Crime in Good Company* (1959)

Gilbert, Sandra M., and Gubar, Susan, *The Madwoman in the Attic: The Woman Writer and the Nineteenth-Century Literary Imagination* (1979, rev. ed. 2000)

Glassman, Steve, and O'Sullivan, Maurice, eds., *Crime Fiction and Film in the Sunshine State: Florida Noir* (1997)

Goddard, John, *Agatha Christie's Golden Age: An Analysis of Poirot's Golden Age Puzzles* (2018)

Goodrich, Joseph, *Blood Relations: The Selected Letters of Ellery Queen, 1947–1950* (2012)

Goodrich, Joseph, *Unusual Suspects: Selected Non-Fiction* (2020)

Gorman, Ed, Server, Lee, and Greenberg, Martin H., eds., *The Big Book of Noir* (1998)

Gorman, Ed, and Greenberg, Martin H, eds., *Speaking of Murder* (1998) and *Speaking of Murder*, Volume II (1999)

Gorrara, Claire, ed., *French Crime Fiction* (2009)

Gorrara, Claire, *French Crime Fiction and the Second World War* (2012)

Gosselin, Adrienne Johnson, ed., *Multicultural Detective Fiction: Murder from the 'Other' Side* (1999)

Goulart, Ron, *Cheap Thrills: An Informal History of the Pulp Magazines* (1972)

Goulart, Ron, *The Dime Detectives* (1988)

Grape, Jan, James, Dean, and Nehr, Ellen, eds., *Deadly Women* (1998)

Green, Julius, *Agatha Christie: A Life in Theatre* (2015, rev. ed. 2018)

Green, Roger Lancelyn, *A. E. W. Mason* (1952)

Greene, Douglas G., *John Dickson Carr: The Man Who Explained Miracles* (1993)

Greene, Graham and Greene, Hugh, *The Spy's Bedside Book* (1957)

Greene, Graham, Greene, Hugh, and Glover, Dorothy, *Victorian Detective Fiction* (1966)

Grossvogel, David I., *Mystery and Its Fictions: From Oedipus to Agatha Christie* (1979)

Gulddal, Jesper, King, Stewart, and Rolls, Alistair, *Criminal Moves: Modes of Mobility in Crime Fiction* (2019)

Guptill Manning, Molly, *The Myth of Ephraim Tutt: Arthur Train and His Great Literary Hoax* (2012)

Hale, T. J., ed., *Great French Detective Stories* (1983)

Hall, Katharina, ed., *Crime Fiction in German* (2016)

Hall, Trevor H., *Dorothy L. Sayers: Nine Literary Studies* (1980)

Hamilton, Bruce, *The Light Went Out: A Biography of Patrick Hamilton* (1972)

Hanson, Gillian Mary, *City and Shore: The Function of Setting in the British Mystery* (2004)

Hardwick, Michael and Mollie, *The Sherlock Holmes Companion* (1962)

Hardy, Phil, *The BFI Companion in Crime* (1997)

Hart-Davis, Rupert, *Hugh Walpole* (1952)

Haste, Steve, *Criminal Sentences: True Crime in Fiction and Drama* (1997)

Hausladen, Gary J., *Places for Dead Bodies* (2000)

Haut, Woody, *Heartbreak and Vine: The Fate of Hardboiled Writers in Hollywood* (2002)

Haut, Woody, *Neon Noir: Contemporary American Crime Fiction* (1999)

Haut, Woody, *Pulp Culture and the Cold War* (1995)

Haycraft, Howard, ed., *The Art of the Mystery Story: A Collection of Critical Essays* (1946)

Haycraft, Howard, *Murder for Pleasure: The Life and Times of the Detective Story*, (1942)

Heising, Willetta L., *Detecting Men* (1998)

Heising, Willetta L., *Detecting Women* (1995, rev. eds. 1996, 1999)

Henderson, Jennifer Morag, *Josephine Tey: A Life* (2015)

Henderson, Lesley, ed., *Twentieth-Century Crime and Mystery Writers* (3rd ed., 1991)

Herbert, Rosemary, *The Fatal Art of Entertainment: Interviews with Mystery Writers* (1994)

Herbert, Rosemary, ed., *The Oxford Companion to Crime and Mystery Writing* (1999)

Herbert, Rosemary, *Whodunit? A Who's Who in Crime & Mystery Writing* (2003)

Hesse, Beatrix, *The English Crime Play in the Twentieth Century* (2015)

Hilfer, Tony, *The Crime Novel: A Deviant Genre* (1990)

Hiney, Tom, *Raymond Chandler: A Biography* (1997)

Hoffman, Megan, *Gender and Representation in British 'Golden Age' Crime Fiction* (2016)

Hoffmann, Josef, *Philosophies of Crime Fiction* (2013)

Holgate, Mike, *Stranger than Fiction: Agatha Christie's True Crime Inspirations* (2010)

Hone, Ralph E., *Dorothy L. Sayers: A Literary Biography* (1979)

Hoopes, Roy, *Cain: The Biography of James M. Cain* (1982)

Horsley, Lee, *The Noir Thriller* (2001)

Huang, Yunte, *Charlie Chan* (2010)

Hubin, Allen J., *Crime Fiction 1749–1980: A Comprehensive Bibliography* (1979, rev. ed., 1984; subsequently updated by CD-ROM and then online: crimefictioniv.com)

Hughes, Dorothy B., *Erle Stanley Gardner: The Case of the Real Perry Mason* (1978)

Jackson, Christine A., *Myth and Ritual in Women's Detective Fiction* (2002)

Jackson, Lawrence P., *Chester B. Himes* (2017)

Jago, Michael, *The Man Who Was George Smiley: The Life of John Bingham* (2013)

Jakubowski, Maxim, ed., *100 Great Detectives* (1991)

Jakubowski, Maxim, ed., *Following the Detectives: Real Locations in Crime Fiction* (2010)

James, P. D., *Talking about Detective Fiction* (2009)

James, P. D., *Time to Be in Earnest: A Fragment of Autobiography* (1999)

Jones, Julia, *The Adventures of Margery Allingham* (2009)

Jones, Nigel, *Through a Glass Darkly: The Life of Patrick Hamilton* (1991)

Joyce, Laura, and Sutton, Henry, eds., *Domestic Noir: The New Face of 21st Century Crime Fiction* (2018)

Kabatchnik, Amnon, *Blood on the Stage* (8 volumes, 2007–17)

Kawani, Sari, *Murder Most Modern: Detective Fiction & Japanese Culture* (2008)

Keating, H. R. F., ed., *Agatha Christie: First Lady of Crime* (1977)

Keating, H. R. F., *Crime & Mystery: The 100 Best Books* (1987)

Keating, H. R. F., *The Bedside Companion to Crime* (1989)

Keating, H. R. F., *Murder Must Appetize* (1975, rev. ed. 1981)

Keating, H. R. F., ed., *Whodunit? A Guide to Crime, Suspense & Spy Fiction* (1982)

Keirans, James E., *The John Dickson Carr Companion* (2015)

Kelleghan, Fiona, ed., *100 Masters of Mystery and Detective Fiction* (2 volumes, 2001)

Kenny, Catherine, *The Remarkable Case of Dorothy L. Sayers* (1990)

Kestner, Joseph A., *The Edwardian Detective, 1901–1915* (2000)

Kestner, Joseph A., *Sherlock's Sisters: The British Female Detective 1864–1913* (2003)

King, Nina, ed., *Crimes of the Scene: A Mystery Novel Guide for the International Traveler* (1997)

Klein, Kathleen Gregory, *Diversity and Detective Fiction* (1999)

Klinger, Leslie S., *The New Annotated Sherlock Holmes* (3 volumes, 2004, 2005)

Knight, Stephen, *Continent of Mystery: A Thematic History of Australian Crime Fiction* (1997)

Knight, Stephen, *Crime Fiction 1800–2000: Detection, Death, Diversity* (2004)

Knight, Stephen, *Dead Witness: Best Australian Mystery Stories* (1990)

Knight, Stephen, *Form and Ideology in Crime Fiction* (1980)

Knox, Francesca Bugliani, ed., *Ronald Knox: A Man for All Seasons* (2016)

Kramer, John E., *Academe in Mystery and Detective Fiction: An Annotated Bibliography* (2000)

La Cour, Tage, and Mogensen, Harald, *The Murder Book* (1971)

Lachman, Marvin, *The American Regional Mystery* (2000)

Lachman, Marvin, *The Heirs of Anthony Boucher: A History of Mystery Fandom* (2005, rev. ed. 2019)

Lachman, Marvin, *The Villainous Stage: Crime Plays on Broadway and in the West End* (2014)

Lambert, Gavin, *The Dangerous Edge* (1975)

Landrum, Larry, *American Mystery and Detective Novels: A Reference Guide* (1999)

Landrum, Larry N., Browne, Pat, and Browne, Ray B., eds., *Dimensions of Detective Fiction* (1976)

Lane, Christina, *Phantom Lady: Hollywood Producer Joan Harrison, the Forgotten Woman Behind Hitchcock* (2020)

Lane, Margaret, *Edgar Wallace: The Biography of a Phenomenon* (1938)

Lehman, David, *The Perfect Murder: A Study in Detection* (1989)

Leonardi, Susan J., *Dangerous by Degrees: Women at Oxford and the Somerville College Novelists* (1989)

Lewis, Margaret, *Edith Pargeter: Ellis Peters* (1984)

Lewis, Margaret, *Ngaio Marsh: A Life* (1991)

Lewis, Peter, *Eric Ambler: A Literary Biography* (1990, rev. ed. 2014)

Lewis, Peter, *John le Carré* (1985)

Light, Alison, *Forever England: Femininity, Literature and Conservatism Between the Wars* (1991)

Lobdell, Jared, *The Detective Fiction Reviews of Charles Williams, 1930–1935* (2003)

Locke, John, ed., *From Ghouls to Gangsters: The career of Arthur B. Reeve* (2007)

Lockhart, Darrell B., ed., *Latin American Mystery Writers: An A-to-Z Guide* (2004)

Loder, John, *Australian Crime Fiction* (1994)

Lofts, W. O. G., and Adley, Derek, *The Saint and Leslie Charteris: A Biography* (1972)

Lord, Graham, *Dick Francis: A Racing Life* (1999)

Loughrey, John, *Alias S. S. Van Dine: The Man Who Created Philo Vance* (1992)

Lowndes, Susan, ed., *Diaries and Letters of Marie Belloc Lowndes 1911–1947* (1971)

Luhr, William, *Film Noir* (2012)

Lundin, Bo, *The Swedish Crime Story* (1981)

Lycett, Andrew, *Conan Doyle: The Man Who Created Sherlock Holmes* (2007)

Lycett, Andrew, *Ian Fleming* (1995)

Lycett, Andrew, *Wilkie Collins: A Life of Sensation* (2013)

Macdonald, Ross, *A Collection of Reviews* (1979)

Macdonald, Ross, *Self-Portrait: Ceaselessly into the Past* (1981)

MacGowan, Kenneth, ed., *Sleuths* (1931)

MacLeod, Charlotte, *Had She but Known: A Biography of Mary Roberts Rinehart* (1994)

McAleer, John, *Rex Stout: A Majesty's Life* (1977, rev. ed. 2002)

McCormick, Donald, *Who's Who in Spy Fiction* (1997), rev. ed. McCormick, Donald, and Fletcher, Katy, *Spy Fiction: A Connoisseur's Guide* (1990)

McCormick, W. J., *Sheridan Le Fanu* (1980)

McLeish, Kenneth and Valerie, *Bloomsbury Good Reading Guide to Murder, Crime Fiction & Thrillers* (1990)

Madden, David, ed., *Tough Guy Writers of the Thirties* (1968)

Magill, Frank N., ed., *Critical Survey of Mystery and Detective Fiction* (4 volumes, 1988)

Maida, Patricia D., *Mother of Detective Fiction: The Life and Works of Anna Katharine Green* (2006)

Makinen, Merja, *Feminist Popular Fiction* (2001)

Malmgren, Carl D., *Anatomy of Murder: Mystery, Detective, and Crime Fiction* (2001)

Mandel, Ernest, *Delightful Murder: A Social History of the Crime Story* (1984)

Mangham, Andrew, *The Cambridge Companion to Sensation Fiction* (2013)

Mann, Jessica, *Deadlier than the Male* (1981)

Mannion, Elizabeth, ed., *The Contemporary Irish Detective Novel* (2016)

Marks, Jeffrey, *Anthony Boucher: A Biobibliography* (2008)

Marks, Jeffrey, *Atomic Renaissance: Women Mystery Writers of the 1940s and 1950s* (2003)

Marks, Jeffrey, *Who Was that Lady? Craig Rice: The Queen of Screwball Mystery* (2001)

Marnham, Patrick, *The Man Who Wasn't Maigret: Portrait of Georges Simenon* (1992)

Marrs, Suzanne, and Nolan, Tom, *Meanwhile, There Are Letters* (2015)

Marsh, Ngaio, *Black Beech and Honeydew: An Autobiography* (1966, rev. ed. 1981)

Marshall, Peter, *William Godwin: Philosopher, Novelist, Revolutionary* (2017)

Martin, Andy, *Reacher Said Nothing* (2015)

Martin, John, *Crime Scene Britain and Ireland: A Reader's Guide* (2014)

Martin, Richard, *Ink in Her Blood: The Life & Crime Fiction of Margery Allingham* (1988)

Masters, Anthony, *Literary Agents: The Novelist as Spy* (1987)

Mayo, Oliver, *R. Austin Freeman: The Anthropologist at Large* (1980)

Meaker, Marijane, *Highsmith: A Romance of the 1950s* (2003)

Melling, John Kennedy, *Murder Done to Death: Parody and Pastiche in Detective Fiction* (1996)

Meredith, Anne, *Three-a-Penny* (1940)

Merrill, Hugh, *The Red Hot Typewriter: The Life and Times of John D. MacDonald* (2000)

Messent, Peter, ed., *Criminal Proceedings: The Contemporary American Crime Novel* (1997)

Meyers, Richard, *TV Detectives* (1981)

Milne, A. A., *It's Too Late Now: The Autobiography of a Writer* (1939)

Mintz, Susannah B., *The Disabled Detective: Sleuthing Disability in Contemporary Crime Fiction* (2020)

Mitchell, Sheila, *H. R. F. Keating: A Life of Crime* (2020)

Moody, Susan, *The Hatchards Crime Companion* (1990)

Morgan, Janet, *Agatha Christie: A Biography* (1984)

Morrell, David, and Wagner, Hank, *Thrillers: 100 Must-Reads* (2010)

Morton, James, *The First Detective: The Life and Revolutionary Times of Vidocq* (2004)

Most, Glenn W., and Stowe, William W., eds., *The Poetics of Murder: Detective Fiction and Literary Theory* (1983)

Mottram, James, *Public Enemies: The Gangster Movie A–Z* (1998)

Mulhallen, Karen, *Descant 51: The Detection Issue* (1985)

Munt, Sally R., *Murder by the Book? Feminism and the Crime Novel* (1994)

Murch, A. E., *The Development of the Detective Novel* (1958)

Murphy, Bruce F., *The Encyclopedia of Murder and Mystery* (2001)

Murray, Stephen M., *Their Word is Law* (2002)

Narcejac, Thomas, *The Art of Simenon* (1952)

Nehr, Ellen, *Doubleday Crime Companion, 1928–91* (1992)

Nelson, Paul, and Avery, Kevin, *It's All One Case: The Illustrated Ross Macdonald Archives* (2016)

Nevins, Francis M., ed., *The Anthony Boucher Chronicles* (3 volumes, 2002)

Nevins, Francis M., *Cornell Woolrich: First You Dream, Then You Die* (1988)

Nevins, Francis M., *Cornucopia of Crime* (2010)

Nevins, Francis M., ed., *The Mystery Writer's Art* (1970)

Nevins, Francis M., Grams, Martin, Jr., *The Sound of Detection: Ellery Queen's Adventures in Radio* (2002)

Newens, Stan, *Arthur Morrison* (2008)

Nicholls, Victoria, and Thompson, Susan, *Silk Stalkings* (1998)

Nickerson, Catherine Ross, ed., *American Crime Fiction* (2010)

Nickerson, Catherine Ross, *The Web of Iniquity: Early Detective Fiction by American Women* (1998)

Nilsson, Louise, Damrosch, David, and D'haen, Theo, eds., *Crime Fiction as World Literature* (2017)

Nolan, Tom, *Ross Macdonald: A Biography* (1999)

Nolan, William F., *Hammett: A Life at the Edge* (1983)

Norton, Charles A., *Melville Davisson Post: Man of Many Mysteries* (1973)

O'Brien, Geoffrey, *Hard-Boiled America: Lurid Paperbacks and the Masters of Noir* (1981, rev. ed. 1997)

Oleksiw, Susan, *A Reader's Guide to the Classic British Mystery* (1989)

Ollerman, Rick, *Hardboiled, Noir and Gold Medals* (2017)

Oppenheim, E. Phillips, *The Pool of Memory* (1941)

Osborne, Charles, *The Life and Crimes of Agatha Christie* (1982)

Ousby, Ian, *Bloodhounds of Heaven: The Detective in English Fiction from Godwin to Conan Doyle* (1976)

Ousby, Ian, *The Crime and Mystery Book* (1997)

Palmer, Jerry, *Thrillers: Genesis and Structure of a Popular Genre* (1978)

Panek, LeRoy, *Watteau's Shepherds: The Detective Novel in Britain, 1914-1940* (1979)

Panek, LeRoy L., *The Special Branch: The British Spy Novel, 1890–1980* (1981)

Panek, LeRoy Lad, *The American Police Novel: A History* (2003)

Panek, LeRoy Lad, *Before Sherlock Holmes* (2011)

Panek, LeRoy Lad, *The Origins of the American Detective Story* (2006)

Panek, LeRoy Lad, and Bendel-Simso, Mary M., *The Essential Elements of the Detective Story, 1820–1891* (2017)

Parente, Audrey, *Once a Pulp Man: The Secret Life of Judson P. Philips as Hugh Pentecost* (2016)

Patrick, Chris, and Baister, Stephen, *William Le Queux: Master of Mystery* (2007)

Pedersen, Jay P., ed., *The St James Guide to Crime and Mystery Writers* (1991)

Penzler, Otto, *Bibliomysteries* (2014)

Penzler, Otto, ed., *The Great Detectives* (1978)

Penzler, Otto, *Mysterious Obsessions: Memoirs of a Compulsive Collector* (2019)

Penzler, Otto, and Friedman, Mickey, eds., *The Crown Crime Companion: The Top 100 Mystery Novels of All Time* (1995)

Penzler, Otto, Steinbrunner, Chris, and Lachmann, Marvin, *Detectionary* (1997)

Pepper, Andrew, *The Contemporary American Crime Novel: Race, Ethnicity, Gender, Class* (2000)

Peters, Catherine, *The King of Inventors* (1991)

Peters, Barbara, and Malling, Susan, eds., *AZ Murder Goes . . . Artful* (1998)

Peters, Barbara, and Malling, Susan, eds., *AZ Murder Goes . . . Classic* (1997)

Peterson, John, *G. K. Chesterton on Detective Fiction* (2010)

Pike, B. A., *Campion's Career* (1987)

Plain, Gill, *Ian Rankin's Black and Blue: A Reader's Guide* (2002)

Polito, Robert, *Savage Art: A Biography of Jim Thompson* (1995)

Porter, Dennis, *The Pursuit of Crime: Art and Ideology in Detective Fiction* (1981)

Powell, Steven, ed., *100 American Crime Writers* (2012)

Powell, Steven, ed., *The Big Somewhere: Essays on James Ellroy's Noir World* (2018)

Powell, Steven, *James Ellroy: Demon Dog of Crime Fiction* (2016)

Priestman, Martin, ed., *The Cambridge Companion to Crime Fiction* (2003)

Priestman, Martin, *Detective Fiction and Literature: The Figure on the Carpet* (1990)

Pronzini, Bill, *Gun in Cheek* (1982)

Pronzini, Bill, *Son of Gun in Cheek* (1987)

Pronzini, Bill, and Adrian, Jack, eds., *Hard-Boiled: An Anthology of American Crime Stories* (1995)

Pronzini, Bill, and Muller, Marcia, *1001 Midnights* (1986)

Pugh, Brian, and Spiring, Paul R., *Bertram Fletcher Robinson: A Footnote to The Hound of the Baskervilles* (2008)

Pykett, Lyn, *Wilkie Collins* (2005)

Quayle, Eric, *The Collector's Book of Detective Fiction* (1978)

Queen, Ellery, *In the Queen's Parlour* (1957)

Queen, Ellery, *Queen's Quorum* (1951, rev. ed. 1969)

Rabinowitz, Paula, *American Pulp: How Paperbacks Brought Modernism to Main Street* (2014)

Rahn, B. J., ed., *Ngaio Marsh: The Woman and Her Work* (1995)

Raymond, John, *Simenon in Court* (1968)

Read, Herbert, *Pursuits and Verdicts* (1983)

Reddy, Maureen T., *Traces, Codes and Clues: Reading Race in Crime Fiction* (2003)

Reilly, John M., ed. *Twentieth-Century Crime and Mystery Writers* (1980, rev. ed. 1985)

Rennison, Nick, *Sherlock Holmes: The Unauthorized Biography* (2005)

Reynolds, Barbara, *Dorothy L. Sayers: Her Life and Soul* (1993)

Reynolds, Barbara, *The Letters of Dorothy L. Sayers* (five volumes, 1995–2002)

Ripley, Mike, *Kiss Kiss, Bang Bang* (2017)

Ritt, Brian, *Paperback Confidential: Crime Writers of the Paperback Era*, ed. Rick Otterman (2013)

Robinson, Kenneth, *Wilkie Collins* (1974)

Robyns, Gwen, *The Mystery of Agatha Christie* (1978)

Rodriguez, Ralph E., *Brown Gumshoes: Detective Fiction and the Search for Chicana/o Identity* (2005)

Rooney, David, *The Wine of Certitude: A Literary Biography of Ronald Knox* (2009)

Roth, Laurence, *Inspecting Jews: American Jewish Detective Stories* (2004)

Roth, Marty, *Foul & Fair Play: Reading Genre in Classic Detective Fiction* (1995)

Routley, Erik, *The Puritan Pleasures of the Detective Story* (1972)

Rowland, Peter, *E. W. Hornung: The Emergence of a Popular Author, 1866–1898* (2020)

Rowland, Peter, *Raffles and His Creator* (1999)

Rowland, Susan, *From Agatha Christie to Ruth Rendell* (2001)

Rzepka, Charles J., *Detective Fiction* (2005)

Rzepka, Charles J., and Horsley, Lee, *A Companion to Crime Fiction* (2010)

Sallis, James, *Chester Himes: A Life* (2000)

Sallis, James, *Difficult Lives: Jim Thompson – David Goodis – Chester Himes* (1993)

Sauerberg, Lars Ole, *The Legal Thriller from Gardner to Grisham* (2016)

Scaggs, John, *Crime Fiction* (2005)

Schaub, Melissa, *Middlebrow Feminism in Classic British Detective Fiction: The Female Gentleman* (2013)

Schenkar, Joan, *The Talented Miss Highsmith* (2009)

Schildcrout, Jordan, *Murder Most Queer: The Homicidal Homosexual in the American Theater* (2014)

Schleh, Eugene, ed., *Mysteries of Africa* (1991)

Schwartz, Richard B., *Nice and Noir: Contemporary American Crime Fiction* (2002)

Scott, Art, and Maynard, Dr Wallace, *The Paperback Covers of Robert McGinnis* (2001)

Scott, Sutherland, *Blood in Their Ink* (1953)

Seaber, Luke, *Incognito Social Observation in British Literature: Certainties in Degradation* (2017)

Seabrook, Jack, *Martians and Misplaced Clues: The Life and Work of Fredric Brown* (1993)

Sennett, Ted, *Murder on Tape* (1997)

Server, Lee, *Encyclopedia of Pulp Fiction Writers* (2002)

Server, Lee, *Over My Dead Body: The Sensational Age of the American Paperback: 1945–1955* (1994)

Shaffer, Anthony, *So What Did You Expect?* (2001)

Shanks, Edward, *Edgar Allan Poe* (1937)

Shaw, Bruce, *Jolly Good Detecting: Humor in English Crime Fiction of the Golden Age* (2014)

Showalter, Elaine, *The Female Malady: Women, Madness, and English Culture, 1830–1980* (1985)

Shpayer-Makov, Haia, *The Ascent of the Detective* (2011)

Silver, Alain, and Ward, Elizabeth, eds., *Film Noir* (1979, rev. ed. 1992)

Simon, Reeva S., *The Middle East in Crime Fiction* (1989)

Simpson, Amelia S., *Detective Fiction from Latin America* (1990)

Sipper, Ralph B., ed., *Inward Journey: Ross Macdonald* (1984)

Sisman, Adam, *John le Carré: The Biography* (2015)

Sisterson, Craig, *Southern Cross Crime* (2020)

Skene-Melvin, David, *Canadian Crime Fiction* (1996)

Sloniowski, Jeannette, and Rose, Marilyn, eds., *Detecting Canada* (2014)

Spencer, William David, *Mysterium and Mystery: The Clerical Crime Novel* (1989)

Standish, Robert, *The Prince of Story-Tellers: The Life of E. Phillips Oppenheim* (1957)

Stanford, Peter, *C. Day-Lewis: A Life* (2007)

Stashower, Daniel, *The Beautiful Cigar Girl* (2006)

Stashower, Daniel, *Teller of Tales: The Life of Sir Arthur Conan Doyle* (1999)

Steinbrunner, Chris, and Penzler, Otto, *Encyclopedia of Mystery and Detection* (1976)

Stewart, A. W., *Alias J. J. Connington* (1947)

Stewart, J. I. M., *Myself and Michael Innes* (1987)

Stewart, Richard F., *End Game* (1999)

Stewart, R. F., . . . *And Always a Detective: Chapters on the History of Detective Fiction* (1980)

Stewart, Victoria, *Crime Writing in Interwar Britain: Fact and Fiction in the Golden Age* (2017)

Stine, Kate, *The Armchair Detective Book of Lists* (1995)

Stougaard-Nielsen, Jakob, *Scandinavian Crime Fiction* (2017)

Sullivan, Eleanor, *Whodunit: A Biblio-Bio-Anecdotal Memoir of Fredric Dannay* (1984)

Sussex, Lucy, *Blockbuster! Fergus Hume and the Mystery of a Hansom Cab* (2016)

Symons, Julian, *The 100 Best Crime Stories* (1958)

Symons, Julian, *Bloody Murder: From the Detective Story to the Crime Novel* (1972, rev. eds. 1985, 1992)

Symons, Julian, *Criminal Practices* (1994)

Symons, Julian, *Critical Occasions* (1966)

Symons, Julian, *Dashiell Hammett* (1985)

Symons, Julian, *The Detective Story in Britain* (1962, rev. ed. 1969)

Symons, Julian, *The Modern Crime Story* (1980)

Symons, Julian, *The Mystique of the Detective Story* (1981)

Symons, Julian, *The Tell-Tale Heart: The Life and Works of Edgar Allan Poe* (1978)

Tani, Stefano, *The Doomed Detective* (1984)

Tannert, Mary W., and Kratz, Henry, eds., *Early German and Austrian Detective Fiction: An Anthology* (1999)

Taylor, Thomas F., *The Golf Murders* (1997)

Thomas, Ronald, *Detective Fiction and the Rise of Forensic Science* (1999)

Thompson, Laura, *Agatha Christie: An English Mystery* (2007)

Thoms, Peter, *Detection & Its Designs: Narrative & Power in 19th-Century Detective Fiction* (1998)

Thomson, Sir Basil, *My Experiences at Scotland Yard* (1923)

Thomson, H. Douglas, *Masters of Mystery: A Study of the Detective Story* (1931)

Thomson, June, *Holmes and Watson* (1995)

Thwaite, Ann, *A. A. Milne: His Life* (1990)

Truffaut, François, *Truffaut/Hitchcock* (1993)

Tucker, Fender, ed., *A to Izzard: A Harry Stephen Keeler Companion* (2002)

Turnbull, Malcolm J., *Elusion Aforethought: the Life and Writing of Anthony Berkeley Cox* (1996)

Turnbull, Malcolm J., *Victims or Villains: Jewish Images in Classic English Detective Fiction* (1998)

Usborne, Richard, *Clubland Heroes* (1953; rev. ed. 1974)

Van Dover, J. K., *You Know My Method: The Science of the Detective* (1994)

Van Hoeven, Marianne, ed., *Margery Allingham: 100 Years of a Great Mystery Writer* (2003)

Van de Wetering, Janwillem, *The Empty Mirror: Experiences in a Japanese Zen Monastery* (1971)

Van de Wetering, Janwillem, *Robert van Gulik: His Life His Work* (1987)

Various authors, *Meet the Detective* (1935)

Vernon, Betty D., *Margaret Cole* (1986)

Wade, Francesca, *Square Haunting* (2020)

Wainwright, John, *Wainwright's Beat: Twenty Years With the West Yorkshire Police Force* (1987)

Walsdorf, Jack, and Symons, Kathleen, *Julian Symons Remembered* (1996)

Walsdorf, John J., with Allen, Bonnie J., *Julian Symons: A Bibliography* (1996)

Walsh, John Evangelist, *Midnight Dreary: The Mysterious Death of Edgar Allan Poe* (2000)

Walton, Samantha, *Guilty but Insane: Mind and Law in Golden Age Detective Fiction* (2015)

Ward, Maisie, *Gilbert Keith Chesterton* (1943)

Ward, Nathan, *The Lost Detective: Becoming Dashiell Hammett* (2015)

Watson, Colin, *Snobbery with Violence: English Crime Stories and Their Audience* (1971, rev. ed. 1979)

Waugh, Evelyn, *Ronald Knox* (1959)

Webster, Jack, *Alistair MacLean* (1991)

Weinkauf, Mary S., *Murder Most Poetic: The Mystery Novels of Ngaio Marsh* (1996)

Whiteman, Robin, *The Cadfael Companion* (1991, rev. ed. 1995)

Whittle, David, *Bruce Montgomery/Edmund Crispin: A Life in Music and Books* (2007)

Williams, John, *Into the Badlands: A Journey Through the American Dream* (1991)

Williams, Tom, *Raymond Chandler: A Life* (2012)

Williams, Valentine, *The World of Action* (1938)

Wilson, Andrew, *Beautiful Shadow: A Life of Patricia Highsmith* (2009)

Winks, Robin W., ed., *Colloquium on Crime* (1986)

Winks, Robin W., ed., *Detective Fiction: A Collection of Critical Essays* (1980)

Winks, Robin W., ed., *The Historian as Detective: Essays on Evidence* (1968)

Winks, Robin W., *Modus Operandi: An Excursion into Detective Fiction* (1982)

Winn, Dilys, ed., *Murder Ink: The Mystery Reader's Companion* (1977)

Winn, Dilys, ed., *Murderess Ink: The Better Half of the Mystery Reader* (1979)

Wolfe, Peter, *Dreamers Who Live Their Dreams: The World of Ross Macdonald's Novels* (1976)

York, R. A., *Agatha Christie: Power and Illusion* (2007)

Acknowledgements

I once wrote a short mystery satirising those lengthy and tedious acknowledgements in books that are of interest only to those who want to see if their name has been mentioned or overlooked. The story must have struck a chord, because it won a CWA prize, but the truth is that this book could be written only with the help of many people, and I do want to express my profound gratitude to them. The trouble is that I've been thinking about a book of this kind for more than half my life, and even if my memory were not imperfect, it would be impossible to mention every single person who has given me information, advice, encouragement and support over that time.

I can, however, vividly recall a conversation with Andrew Taylor more than twenty years ago when he urged me to write a 'modern version of *Bloody Murder*'. To Andrew, and my other friends in the crime-writing world, I express heartfelt gratitude for the kindnesses they have shown me over the years, as well as for the pleasure their books have given me.

Several people read drafts of the manuscript and made insightful comments. The help and support given by Nigel Moss, Steven Powell, Victoria Stewart, Helena Edwards, David Bordwell, Joseph Goodrich, Rick Ollerman, John Pugmire, Art Scott, Doug Greene and Mauro Boncampagni have been invaluable.

Over the years, I've picked the brains of innumerable students and fans of the genre and experts on particular topics, including authors of books listed in the bibliography and fellow members of panels at festivals. Particular thanks go to Geoff Bradley, John Cooper, Jamie Sturgeon, Michael Dirda, Otto Penzler, Barbara Peters, Catherine Aird, Peter Lovesey, Len Deighton, Sheila Mitchell, Arthur Robinson, Margaret Yorke, the members of Murder Squad, Dea Parkin and colleagues at the Crime Writers' Association, the Detection Club, the Mystery Writers of America, Seona Ford and fellow members of the Dorothy L. Sayers Society, David Ian Chapman, Elaine Showalter, John Norris, Eileen Dewhurst, Peter Rowland, Andrew Lycett, David Whittle, Mike Wilson, Jennifer Henderson, Steve Steinbock, Brian Skupin, Kate Stine, Janet Hutchings, Fei Wu, Elliot Han, Yangbo Zhu, Elinor Shaffer, Denis Kendal, Tony Medawar, John Curran, Melvyn Barnes, Barry Pike, Clint Stacey, Tom Schantz, Sean Sexton, Shawn Reilly Simmons, Robert Banks Stewart, Richard McCarthy, Maxim Jakubowski, Christopher Chan, Clark Sheldon, Veronica Maughan, Jim Noy, Brad Verter, Paul Harding, James Pickard, James Hallgate, Mark Sutcliffe, Jonathan Frost, Liz Gilbey, Christine Vickers, John Herrrington, Richard O'Brien, Simon King, David Stuart Davies, Philip Harbottle, Kate Jackson, Les Blatt, Christine Poulson, Jennifer Carnell, Ira Matetsky, Henrique Valle, Cally Phillips, Muireann Maguire, Catherine McAteer, Xavier Lechard, John Higgins, Philip Eastwood, Andrew Gulli, Jose Ignacio Escribano, Art McTighe, Francesca Knox, Marcia Talley, Jonathan Hopson, Nick Jones, Joe Linzalone, Robert Garni, Steve Lewis, Rod Collins, Curtis Evans, Francesca Wade, Paul Thornett, Lucy Thornett, Ian Hamilton, Fytton Rowland, Margaret Lewis, Peter Lewis, Almuth Heuner, Elizabeth Foxwell, Pietro de Palma, Rob Davies and the publications team at the British Library, Louisa Yates and colleagues at Gladstone's Library, contributors to the GA Detection Facebook page, and the bloggers listed on the blogroll at the 'Do You Write Under Your Own Name?' blog.

And finally, my thanks also go to my editor, David Brawn, and the team at HarperCollins, my agent James Wills – and above all to Helena, Jonathan and Catherine Edwards for all the support they have given throughout my own life of crime.

Index of Titles

Index of Names

Subject Index

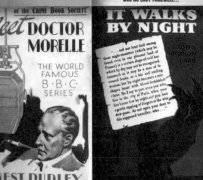

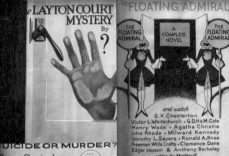

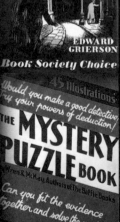
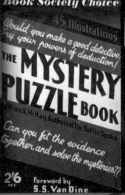

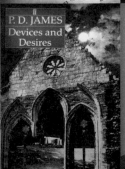